Endless Summer
NIGHTS

Endless Summer
NIGHTS

Essence Bestselling Author
DONNA HILL
GRACE OCTAVIA
DELANEY DIAMOND

HARLEQUIN® KIMANI ARABESQUE®

ENDLESS SUMMER NIGHTS
ISBN-13: 978-0-373-09154-6

Copyright © 2014 by Harlequin Books S.A.

The publisher acknowledges the copyright holders of the individual works as follows:

RISKY BUSINESS
Copyright © 2014 by Donna Hill

BEATS OF MY HEART
Copyright © 2014 by Calaya Reid

HEARTBREAK IN RIO
Copyright © 2014 by Delaney Diamond

Recycling programs for this product may not exist in your area.

HARLEQUIN®
www.Harlequin.com

Printed in U.S.A.

CONTENTS

RISKY BUSINESS

Donna Hill

Dedication

To my daddy, "Cal," who was probably a singer in another life
and made me sit front row on the couch
to watch his many performances.

Acknowledgments

I am so excited to participate in this project, seeing my name
on the cover of a book alongside authors Donna Hill and
Delaney Diamond. Also, it's quite humbling to join the ranks of
writers published on the Harlequin publishing list.
As this is my first attempt at writing "romance," I also want to
acknowledge the honor of being amongst writers and readers
who have upheld, developed and supported this often overlooked
genre that has much creativity, power and influence.

There are many people who have made this project possible.
These people were both directly involved in the writing of my
novella and indirectly connected by assisting me in continuing
my goal of offering readers compelling and edifying fiction aimed
at women embarking upon private revolution.
I thank all of you for years of support, guidance and love.

Most directly, I must thank the entire family at Harlequin,
especially my kind, gracious and patient editor Glenda Howard.
I would also like to thank those working behind the scenes at the
publishing house—those in marketing, publicity, business, art, and
management. Thank you for your hard work that I may not see,
but I am quite clear about how this affects the positive experience
I have had at Harlequin.

I would also like to thank my dear friend Tracy Sherrod and
my agent Regina Brooks of the Serendipity Literary Agency.

As always, thank you to my readers.
None of this could be possible without your support.

All Best,

Grace Octavia

graceoctavia@gmail.com

Chapter 1

"I can't wait to go on this trip. Even though it's business, I plan to get my share of pleasure out of the deal," Sydni said, as she reviewed the multiple pages outlining the details of the presentation.

"I know what you mean. You've earned it. When was the last time you were away and actually got some playtime in?" her assistant and best friend, Lynn Covington, asked. "And what better place than Brazil in February."

Sydni relaxed against her high-back leather chair and crossed her long legs. At thirty-four, Sydni Lawson was one of the highest paid and most sought after brand marketers in the country. Her day consisted of shaping the images of mega pop stars and superstar athletes, to household products and worldwide corporations. She was the one who was called when brand redefining was needed. She resuscitated fallen careers by recreating her clients and molded the up-and-coming into works of art like a master sculptor. Sydni Lawson was executive vice president of Epic International, the multimillion-dollar corporation that specialized in global branding and was owned by her father, Paul Lawson. She took the executive title to appease her father, but she never allowed herself to be dragged into the machinations of corporate volleyball—until now.

Sydni twirled a Cross pen thoughtfully between her slender fingers. "I think the last time I had a semi-vacation was more than a year ago when Blake and I traveled to London on business. We got to squeeze in a day and a half as tourists." She laughed without humor. The breakup still stung even after all this time. She pushed out a breath and memories of the past along with it. She turned to Lynn. "I'm going to want those meetings with Mr. St. James to take place as soon as possible when we hit Rio."

Lynn nodded. "I'm coordinating with his assistant this week to make that happen. It seems nearly every waking hour of his day is occupied. I didn't think it was possible for anyone to be busier than you," she said with affection.

"Hmm. Well, hopefully, if he's that busy we can work this deal quickly and then have some fun. We couldn't have picked a better time, either."

"Once I found out that he had a home in Rio, you know I worked my magic to pull this together during Carnival." They both giggled at that bit of smoke and mirrors. "Of course, the fact that it was the only time in St. James's schedule where he was in one place long enough for us to meet definitely worked into the plan."

The two women had been friends for years, dating back to their years at Spellman and then as part of the Delta Sigma Theta sorority. Sydni had reached out to her friend when she'd stepped into the VP role, offering her very talented soror the coveted position of being her right hand. Lynn was not only incredibly smart, but she understood Sydni in a way that many of her other friends never had. They'd built a bond over the years that was now unbreakable.

Sydni studied the newspaper image of Gabriel St. James with a caption below that touted the confirmed bachelor was seen at the Cannes Film Festival with supermodel Naomi Dupont.

Since she'd been assigned the project by her father, Sydni had done her homework investigating their potential new client. Everything she'd read about him screamed "playboy, eternal bachelor, mogul, rogue." Yet there was something missing in the articles and headlines, something that had not been captured about Gabriel St. James. She wasn't sure what it was, but she knew that once she discovered it, *that* would be the key to his new image.

Lynn flipped a folder closed. "I still don't understand why St. James is going through this process. He's an international figure already."

Sydni nodded her head slowly. "I thought the very same thing. Apparently, since he wants to take his privately owned company public, he wants to recast his image before launching his first public project—his chain of resorts.

"This should be one of our easiest assignments. He already has name recognition, albeit not always a great one."

Sydni held up a news article in front of her. The headline read REAL ESTATE MOGUL GABRIEL ST. JAMES AT CENTER OF DIVORCE SCANDAL. She turned the paper around to show Lynn. "It's this kind of stuff that makes him vulnerable. It was a movie director's wife that he was allegedly involved with this time."

"You'll work your mojo as you always do, and all will be well." She pushed back from her seat and stood. "You have a one o'clock with your father in his office." She checked her watch. "Ten minutes."

Sydni frowned slightly. "Yes, he's been overly involved putting this whole thing together with St. James and his people. Very uncharacteristic of him."

Lynn murmured her agreement. "Want me to order lunch or are you going out?"

"I'm pretty sure I'm going to need some air after this meeting. I'll grab something when I go out."

She grinned. "I think I'll do some vacation shopping," she teased in a very bad Portuguese accent. "Have fun at your meeting. See you when you get back."

"You are so wrong for that," Sydni called out.

Lynn gave her a quick finger wave and darted out the door.

Paul Lawson ended his call with his nephew Branford. He was always amazed at how far Branford had come from the pain-in-the-ass kid he'd been to one of the most powerful senators in the House. With Paul being the youngest of the four Lawson brothers, he and Branford were more like brothers and good friends than uncle and nephew. They shared confidences, successes and failures, had taken vacations together and even had similar tastes in women—which had caused an interesting share of friendly competition. He was looking forward to seeing him in the coming weeks. It was Branford who'd encouraged him to pursue the deal with Gabriel St. James, and after much consideration, he agreed that his nephew was right. And he would send his very capable daughter to make the deal happen.

As if on cue, Sydni gave a light knock on the partially opened door and poked her head in.

No matter how many times Paul looked at his daughter, it never ceased to amaze him how much she resembled her mother, Marie; from the slope of her amber eyes that gave her an almost exotic look, to the sculpted cheekbones, heart-shaped face and killer dimples. He only hoped that his beautiful and brilliant daughter would be able to find the happiness in her life that he and her mother had found together.

"Come in, come in."

Sydni walked in, came around the desk and gave her father a big kiss on the cheek. As much as he protested that it was totally inappropriate in the workplace, he relished her bursts of affection that he had to admit she only demonstrated when they were out of eyesight of the staff.

"How are you today?" she asked, taking a seat next to his desk.

He rocked back in his chair just a bit and linked his fingers across his stomach. "So far, no complaints. The new contract with MTV is in the works and I heard from Jamal Hendricks's agent from the NFL. He's ready to come on board."

Sydni grinned. "All in a day's work." She crossed her legs.

"Your turn."

"We've taken care of everything for the Brazil trip. I don't think there's much of anything that I don't know about Mr. St. James. I'm confident that we can map out a strategy that he will be comfortable with and move forward. I'll have him signed on the dotted line by the time I get back."

Paul nodded thoughtfully, then he leaned forward, locking eyes with his daughter. "There's more."

"Oh. What kind of more?" she asked, a bit taken aback.

"Why don't we discuss it over lunch." It wasn't a question. "I've had Hannah order in."

Sydni knew instantly that this trip was going to be a lot more labor-intensive than she'd planned for.

When Sydni left her father's office more than an hour later, she didn't know if she was furious or disappointed by her father's very calculated moving of the chess pieces with her as the pawn. She didn't like being set up—or worse, setting up a potential client. It wasn't that what her father was asking her to pull off was illegal or unethical, but simply put, it didn't feel right.

She returned to her corner office, shut the door, sat down behind her desk and began reviewing the prospectus that her father had given her.

As usual, her father and his team had done their homework. The deal was sweet, and if she could convince Gabriel St. James of its merits it would become one of the biggest corporate mergers ever, not to mention the enormous power that it would wield. What bothered her, however, was that it was in no way that cut-and-dried. If so, her father would not have been so cloak-and-dagger about it, springing it on her at the eleventh hour.

She had a lot to absorb over the next few days. She put down the thick sheaf of papers and picked up the *Forbes* magazine with a silhouetted profile of Gabriel St. James on the cover: "The Man, The Mystique." It would be up to her to peel back the layers, discover his vulnerabilities and then plant the seeds.

Sydni exhaled heavily. She was confident in her abilities. What she wasn't certain of was Gabriel St. James's reaction to them.

Chapter 2

Gabriel glanced over his shoulder and above the rim of his dark sunglasses at the sound of the sliding glass door opening behind him. His brother, Max, stepped out onto the back deck with two bottles of imported beer.

"Here, looks like you could use one," Max said, handing his younger brother a beer.

Gabriel took the proffered bottle that was so cold, beads of condensation dripped down the sides. He reached for the bottle opener on the circular glass table that sat between the two striped lounge chairs and popped the top. He took several long swallows, nearly finishing the bottle before taking it from his mouth. "Thanks," he muttered.

Max stretched out in the chair next to his brother. "You can still back out if you don't want to go through with taking the company public," he said, reading his brother's thoughts. "It's your piece of the business. Do what you want." His dark eyes flashed with humor.

Maximillian was forty, five years Gabriel's senior, but more than being his older brother, Max had been father figure, mentor and best friend. He'd had to be in the absence of any real parenting. Javier Santiago was a philanderer, a ladies' man. Their mother, Angela St. James, had left Javier long ago, as well as her two young sons, who were raised by a series of nannies and revolving-door girlfriends.

Unfortunately, the love of beautiful women did not fall far from the tree. According to the tabloids, the brothers were notorious playboys and brilliant businessmen. They managed their love lives the way they managed their businesses. They saw something they wanted, weighed the risks and went after it for as long as their conquest amused them. With striking South American looks that they'd inherited from their mother—dark wavy hair, honey-dipped complexions, haunting onyx eyes silhouetted by long black lashes—combined with their six-foot-three-inch frames, they cut impossible figures to turn away from when they entered a room.

"Ha, you make it sound so easy. Forget the months—years—of planning." He snapped his fingers. "Just like that, eh?"

Max shrugged his brows. "Where there is one plan there is always another. If something gives you trouble and doesn't make your life easier or better...get rid of it."

Gabriel shook his head in mild amusement. His brother was notorious for his flings, as well as his dismissal of anything undesirable in his life, from business to pleasure.

"I've made a commitment. I intend to grit my teeth and go through with it. If it takes a shining-up of my 'tarnished' image to secure the success of the resorts—" he lifted his hand in dismissal "—it's a small price to pay."

"Don't say I didn't warn you," Max intoned from his reclined position.

"Duly noted."

"How much do you know about this *Sydney* Lawson, anyway?"

"I had one of my assistants look him up, only to discover that he is a she—a quite beautiful she, from the picture that I've seen."

Max grinned. "Then it might not be as awful as it could be."

"Hmm. She's apparently very talented, well traveled and well respected by her clients. She's related to that senator from Louisiana. His niece, I believe."

"Ahh, a Southern…how do you say…belle." Max chuckled.

Gabriel leaned back in the reclining lounge chair and closed his eyes against the waning Rio sun. An image of Sydni Lawson slowly bloomed behind his lids, coming vividly alive in his mind. Something inside shifted, his eyes flew open and he inexplicably expected to find her standing in front of him, touching him. He quickly pushed up from the chair and went into the cool recesses of the house for another beer.

He opened the fridge and was met with a welcoming blast of cold air that helped to clear his head. He reached for a beer and another for his brother. That momentary flash was surreal. He could have sworn that he *felt* her. But of course that was nonsense.

He pushed the door closed and headed back outside only to be met halfway by Max.

"I've got to run. Plans." Max gave him a quizzical look. "Everything all right? You look…"

"I'm fine." He focused on his brother and forced a cavalier smile. "I'm going to turn in early. I want to be mildly alert and interested when I meet with Ms. Lawson tomorrow. Enjoy your evening for the both of us."

Max lifted a brow. "I will do my best. We'll talk tomorrow after your meeting." He clapped his brother on the shoulder and strode out.

Gabriel drew in a long breath and slowly gazed around the sprawling space of his four-bedroom home. He climbed the metal spiral staircase to the upper level and walked down the wide corridor toward his room at the end of the hallway. His bedroom looked out over the water and the mountains beyond.

So many stories had been written about his alleged conquests, his liaisons and salacious affairs. The truth was, this endless stream of women was more for show than anything based in reality. Unknown to anyone other than his brother, Gabriel picked and chose the women that he bedded with a meticulousness that rivaled the proverbial search for a needle in a haystack, which resulted in the women who shared his bed being very few and far between. The end result was the countless women who'd been on his arm, on his yacht, on his plane, in his home, but never in his bed; and his being unwilling to admit that he had no interest in them beyond the moment. The women often went on to tell anyone who would listen what an incredible lover he was. So rumors abounded. With his brother, Max, on the fast track to bedding every beautiful woman in the Western hemisphere, it was taken for granted that he was the same way. Like father, like sons.

Gabriel stepped out onto the balcony of his bedroom

suite and leaned casually against the railing. The view beyond was magnificent. The sun hung mere inches above the ocean in a brilliant hot orange that poured out over the water in slow ripples. The mountains were cast in a dusky relief as pinpoints of light began to ping like warning signals across the city until everything beyond twinkled like diamonds embedded in a deep blue velvet blanket, just beyond reach.

From where he stood, all looked calm and postcard-perfect. But in a matter of days the pulsing sounds of endless samba music, laughter, skies lit with brilliantly colored lights and dancers in every available space dressed in barely there or garish costumes would flood the streets for Carnival.

No matter where he was in the world, he would always make it a point to come home for Carnival. The celebrations in Rio were like none anywhere in the world, and of course, he hosted one of the many elaborate parties for his exclusive guests. He would have to make it a point to invite Ms. Lawson to his gathering so that she could witness him in his element.

His pulse quickened at the idea of Sydni Lawson, and for the first time in quite a while he was actually looking forward to meeting a new woman.

Chapter 3

The twelve-hour flight from Louisiana with a connection in Miami and then on to Rio was blissfully pleasant. The first-class accommodations, full meals, drinks, reclining seats and several movies made the long flight bearable. When Sydni and Lynn landed it was already 10:30 p.m. local time and the only thing they wanted to do was shower and hit the sack.

On the cab ride to their hotel, the Copacabana Plaza Hotel, the magnificence of Rio spread out before them; from the pinpoints of light that winked along the sprawling city teasing passersby of the nightlife just beyond, to the majestic *Pão de Açúcar,* otherwise known as Sugar Loaf Mountain, for its resemblance to the traditional shape of a concentrated loaf of refined sugar, to the rainforests in the distance.

"Amazing." Lynn sighed in awe as the landscape whizzed by them.

"I'm feeling a lot less tired," Sydni stated. "If we

didn't have that early-morning meeting I would sure 'nuff put on my party shoes." She yawned into her hand.

Lynn gave her a quick look and smirked. "Right."

The cab pulled up in front of the Copacabana Plaza, reputed to be the most famous and luxurious hotel in Rio, having catered to the rich, famous and infamous for eighty years. It had been the stopping point for Fred Astaire and Ginger Rogers, Marilyn Monroe, the Rolling Stones, Madonna and Princess Diana. Even Michael Jackson had rested his head in the luxurious hotel.

The car door was opened by the waiting bellhop and it took a moment for Sydni and Lynn to absorb the magnificence of the hotel that far exceeded any pictures.

The hotel faced the Copacabana Beach and consisted of an eight-story main building with a fourteen-story annex totaling two hundred and sixteen rooms, an Olympic-sized swimming pool, tennis court, fitness center, a three-story spa, two bars, a nightclub and two restaurants. It was a small city with an ambiance of elegance.

Once checked in they were immediately escorted to the penthouse suite that boasted two master bedrooms on either end of the penthouse, access to a private pool, terrace, an incredible view of the beach, French decor and butler service.

Sydni, who'd been used to traveling and staying in high style, had to force herself not to let her mouth drop open when they stepped off the elevator and into their suite. She paid the bellhop a very handsome tip, shut the door behind him and took one look at Lynn. They simultaneously squealed in girlish delight.

"*O-M-G,* I do not believe this place," Sydni said as she walked from room to room, touching the exquisite furnishings and taking in the stunning views. She twirled around in a circle. "You hit the jackpot with this booking."

"Well, you said money was no object and I knew that we wanted to make sure that we could impress someone like Gabriel St. James, and this was the place that kept popping up."

"With good reason." She walked over to the bar to find it fully stocked with some of the finest wines, liquors and beer.

"Actually, I'm a bit hungry. How about you?"

"Suddenly, I'm not sleepy anymore. Why don't we freshen up and maybe go down to the restaurant? Or we could always get room service."

"Or have the butler take care of it," she added with a giggle.

They opted for room service and ate a light meal on the terrace overlooking the beach.

"All of your notes for the meeting tomorrow are on your iPad. Hard copies are in the red folders. The driver will be here at ten. The ride to St. James's place is about twenty minutes. That should give you plenty of time to get there, unwind for a minute before the eleven o'clock meeting."

Sydni nodded while she listened and sipped her wine. She wouldn't admit it, not even to Lynn, but she was anxious about meeting Gabriel St. James. She couldn't quite put her finger on why, but as the hour grew nearer, the tighter the knot in her stomach became.

Sydni took longer than usual to dress, organize the wild spirals of her hair and perfect her makeup. She'd opted for a simple sleeveless dress in a soothing ocean-blue with a micro thin leather belt at the waist. The simplicity of the design belied the luxurious fab-

ric and finely tailored cut that defined, yet comple-
mented, Sydni's curves, without being obvious. Her
three-inch heels brought her to a comfortable five foot
nine and elongated her shapely legs and narrow ankles.
Her jewelry was simple: a watch, small platinum studs
in her ears and a thin platinum chain with a quarter-
sized azure stone that went perfectly with her dress.
Her purse and tote were a deep navy that matched her
sling-back shoes.

"Car is downstairs," Lynn called out.

"Coming." She checked her reflection one more time,
dropped her cell phone in her bag and then headed for
the door.

On the ride over, that entailed driving along the two-
lane highway that wound its way up and around the
mountains overlooking the ocean, Sydni and Lynn once
again reviewed the particulars that Sydni would present, questions that Gabriel might ask and what the answers would be. They also verified that they were able
to get a signal on the iPad as they turned off the main
artery and began a short drive up a curvaceous roadway. The area was suffused with massive overhang-
ing trees, manicured shrubbery and brilliant blooms of
lilac laelias, the indigenous orchid that was the country's national flower. Interspersed were pink begonias
that gave the entire atmosphere a sense of the surreal.
And then suddenly the tropical paradise opened and a
magnificent house of tempered glass, steel and wood
loomed in front of them.

Sydni's breath momentarily caught.

"Wow," Lynn breathed.

"Exactly."

The car continued down the lane until it came to a
stop at the front of the house. The driver got out and

opened the passenger door. Sydni stepped onto the grav-
eled walkway. Lynn followed and stood beside her just
as the front door opened and Gabriel St. James appeared
on the threshold.

"Oh, dayum," Sydni whispered between her teeth.
He was nothing like his pictures. His pictures lied. This
man standing in front of them was beauty personified.
And not pretty beauty, but ruggedly gorgeous in every
sense of the word, from the gentle wave of his ink-black
hair, the deep set of his onyx eyes, the curve of his full
lips to the cool brown sugar of his skin set off against
an off-white linen shirt and slacks. Gabriel St. James
was movie-idol fine.

Sydni tugged in a breath and began walking toward
him as he came toward her. They stopped inches from
each other.

"Ms. Lawson." He extended his hand.

Sydni returned the gesture and a flash of something
hot shot through her when his fingers gently wrapped
around her hand. His eyes darkened and his long lashes
lowered when he smiled.

"*Bem vindo.* Welcome." He turned his attention to
Lynn. "You must be the very efficient Ms. Covington."

"I've been called worse," Lynn teased, shaking his
hand.

He chuckled lightly. "Please come in. I've set us
up on the back deck where it's much cooler. It will be
ninety before noon. Will your driver be staying? If not,
I can arrange to have you both taken back to your hotel
when we finish our meeting." His question was directed
at them both, but his focus was on Sydni.

"No need to get a car. He'll be back for us in two
hours. I'm sure that will be enough time."

The right corner of Gabriel's mouth flickered upward. He turned toward the house and Sydni and Lynn stole happy glances at each other as they followed in his wake.

From the outside, although the great majority of the two-story structure was glass, you could not see inside the house. But once inside the views were spectacular. From the front door, the incredible sight of the mountains and the spread of the ocean on the far side of the house was visible. The entire first floor was a huge open space with designated areas distinguished by the arrangement of furniture that was mostly off-white in a burlap-type fabric with mahogany and bamboo finishings. There were vibrant pillows and throws that gave the space bursts of color. Small hand-carved statues sat on tables and in little nooks and what appeared to be very expensive pieces of art hung on the stark white walls.

Gabriel slid the glass door open that led to the enclosed deck and stepped out. He extended his hand to help Sydni and Lynn over the slight step.

A single fan blew slowly overhead and a see-through screen pulled down in front of the deck afforded a perfect view but blocked the rays of the sun.

"Please, make yourselves comfortable."

There were three reclining chairs set up around a large table that held glasses, a bucket of ice and a carafe of caipirinha—a mix of sugarcane spirit (cachaça), crushed lime, white sugar and ice—one of Brazil's most popular drinks.

"I thought you might like this if you have not tried it before." Gabriel picked up the carafe and poured a glass for each and handed them over. "What is the saying… It's five o'clock somewhere."

The trio laughed and raised their glasses.

"To a productive relationship," Gabriel said, his gaze burning into Sydni.

Sydni's hand shook ever so slightly. She took a sip, allowed the sweet liquor to sit in her mouth for a moment. "Caipirinha?"

He grinned and her stomach tumbled. "Very good." He lifted his glass in salute to her.

"I can't remember where I was, but I've tasted it before. *This,* however, is very good."

He gave a slight bow before sitting down. "How long do you plan to stay in Brazil?"

"Through Carnival," Sydni said.

"There's no Carnival like the one here in Rio. You are in for an experience."

"Better than New Orleans?" she countered.

"Absolutely. I'll be happy to show you exactly what I mean."

"I may take you up on that, but business first."

He shrugged ever so slightly. "Of course."

Lynn watched in mild amusement as the sparks flew between Sydni and Gabriel. She took the narrow binders out of her tote and handed one to Gabriel and one to Sydni.

Gabriel flipped the binder open and quickly perused the opening pages. He glanced up at Sydni. "From what I can tell, you have a good grasp on my business."

Sydni felt her cheeks heat. "I took a good deal of time to study what you've done before and what you intend to do. I'm confident that Epic can build the kind of universal brand that you want in order to launch this new venture. If you'd turn to section two, it outlines some of the steps I would like to take to begin to repackage you."

His gaze rose and landed on her. The hint of a smile teased his mouth. He dropped the binder onto the table and leaned back in his seat. He rested his hands casually on the arms of the chairs and Sydni could not help but notice his long, slender fingers. She absently ran her tongue across her lips.

"So, Ms. Lawson, you understand that this has been a family business for many years. My father built it from nothing. He began in shipping, branched out to land development. Our real-estate enterprise, the most recent addition, has done very well for us. My father would prefer to keep it that way. My brother..." He shrugged. "Max is shrewd, but easy. He doesn't like complications. The idea to take the real-estate portion of St. James Enterprises public is my doing. I've seen others try and many were dismal failures. They lost millions. I won't allow that to happen. I want to ensure success. I want the new brand, the image, to be clear and strong long before I open the doors for the world to see."

"I'm curious about one thing," Sydni said.

"Yes."

"When I was doing my research I stumbled across information that said your family name is Santiago. So why St. James?"

Gabriel grinned. "St. James, *Sant Iago,* is the great patron saint. In business we felt that St. James—my mother's maiden name—was much more acceptable on a broader scale. My certificate of birth still reads Santiago."

"I see. Any other bits of folklore that I need to know about?"

"Whatever you need to know, I'd be more than happy to provide you with the answer." He lifted his glass and took a sip.

Sydni swallowed over the sudden dry knot in her throat. "Do you have any questions for me?"

Gabriel leaned back, appraised her from beneath his lashes. "Are you free for dinner?"

Sydni blinked in surprise. "I…"

"I may have some questions once I go over the material."

"Of course. I'm sure I can adjust my schedule if it's necessary."

"Good. Then let's put work aside for now and I will give you ladies a tour of the property. Yes?"

"Sounds wonderful," Sydni said. "Our driver should be back in about forty minutes."

Gabriel stood and so did Sydni.

"You two go ahead," Lynn said. "The travel is beginning to catch up with me. I think I'll sit here and take in the view of the ocean."

"Are you sure?" Sydni asked, giving her the "you bettah come on, girl" look.

Lynn smiled. "Very." She waved her off. "Go ahead. I'll be fine." She slid on her sunglasses and leaned back.

Gabriel slid open the glass door. "After you."

Sydni squeezed by him and subtly inhaled his scent. She could feel the heat of him behind her and then he was at her side. He lightly placed his hand at the small of her back to guide her through the main level. He opened the door and extended his hand to lead her out in front of him.

"This is an amazing piece of property," Sydni said once they were outside.

"My first taste of land development was about ten years ago. I was scouting around for a place to build a home and came across this place."

"From the ground up?"

He nodded as they proceeded down the walkway that

was like taking a stroll through the Garden of Eden. "Nothing was here but wild bush, trees and the ocean."

"How long did it take you to build?"

"Hmm, four years from start to finish."

On the side of the house was a little rippling pond that was filled with koi. There was a bench that was shaded by an overhang. The atmosphere at the pond was totally soothing, almost hypnotic.

"I come out here a lot when I have things on my mind."

She glanced at him as they continued to tour the grounds. "When would you have time to sit and ponder?" she teased.

Gabriel laughed. "Unfortunately, not as often as I would like. So much of the family business takes me everywhere in the world except here."

The images of him and the countless women on his arm flashed through her head. Her brow tightened.

"If I had my way I would be here full-time. All the travel, all the people, are tiresome." He gave a short snort of disgust. "The world would have you think that it's such a fabulous life. Don't get me wrong," he continued, "having money, having access, is a powerful aphrodisiac. I only wish that it could all mean something. It's very easy to get comfortable and caught up in the trappings that all this—" he waved his hand expansively "—can afford you." He slid his hands into his pockets, turned to look at her briefly and then continued to walk.

"Well, my vision for the string of resorts is to provide a getaway of superb quality for those who would never be able to afford it. But it can't be viewed as some publicity stunt, or some charity resort," Sydni stated. She studied his thoughtful profile. This wasn't a man who took what he had and what he'd accomplished lightly. A spark of an idea began to form. *This* was the man that she would build the brand around—the man who cared, the man who had a soul, who wanted to give back for all that he had received.

Suddenly he stopped walking and turned toward her. She was compelled to look up into his magnetic gaze.

"I need to be sure that you understand me…what I want…and how to accomplish it," he said.

"You hired me because I'm *very* good at what I do."

He paused for a beat, and let his gaze sweep over her. "I'm sure you are."

The world disappeared around them. It was only Sydni and Gabriel, even as they were surrounded by the sound of nature, a waterfall in the background, the pulse of their racing hearts, the heat that radiated from them and the undeniable pull that drew them within a breath of each other.

They startled at the sudden and piercing cry of a Hyacinth Macaw flying overhead. Sydni's gaze rose up to see the rare bird's majestic royal-blue-and-gold colors soar across the sky. She laughed lightly. The spell was broken.

"This path leads to the beach," Gabriel said, seamlessly moving them from an undeniable moment of sexual arousal to the safety of an innocuous stroll. "In an ideal world, I would like the resorts to sit near beaches like this. I want to begin here in Brazil and expand from there. I envision opening five different locations simultaneously."

Sydni's brows rose. "Five? A bit ambitious. You don't plan to test the viability before expanding?"

He slightly turned his head in her direction. "They will be viable. You'll see to that. It's why I hired you… or so you told me." His mouth curved ever so slightly.

* * *

"This is quite a spread," Sydni said as they drew closer to the house, the tour of the grounds complete.

"I hope that you will make time to visit again while you're here. Actually…" He put the tip of his finger to his lip. "I host an annual Carnival party for close friends. You and your associate, Lynn, are more than welcome. No. I insist that you attend. Wonderful food, drink, music, dancing…"

Sydni smiled. "You make it very hard to say no."

His voice dropped an octave. "Then don't tell me no."

The words shimmied through her like quicksilver and pulsed between her thighs. Her heart slammed in her chest.

"Come, Lynn must think we've run away by now."

Gabriel stepped ahead of her to open the door and for a split second she squeezed her eyes shut. She was in deep trouble.

Chapter 4

"I'm telling you, Lynn, if the man had said 'I want to sex you up right here, right now, in the middle of the damned tropical rainforest,' I swear I think I would have done it." She paced the floor of the living area while she sipped a glass of wine. "Oooh." She gave her entire body a shake. "I could barely concentrate on what the man was saying. Did you see those eyes? And that mouth? Oh, Lawd, I can only imagine what gems he has under those clothes." She suddenly whirled toward Lynn, who was curled up on the couch totally trying not to burst out laughing. "What am I going to do?"

Lynn covered her grin with her glass of wine. She blinked several times. "Um, can I just say—before I get to the serious part—I'm just happy to know that it's still alive down there."

"Lynn!" Sydni stomped her foot in feigned annoyance.

"Well, it's true. I mean, ever since you and Blake split up... You haven't even been on a date in over a year."

"I've been busy," she said, bordering on petulant. Lynn gave her the side eye.

Sydni crossed the room and flopped down on a club chair. She curled her legs beneath her. "Getting over Blake was hard. You know that."

"What was hard was watching you beat yourself up for breaking it off with him, and turning inside yourself as if you'd done some horrible wrong."

"I felt like I had." Sydni blew out a breath. "I thought I wanted what he wanted. We were good together… mostly. But when I looked into the future, as much as I cared about Blake, I didn't see him in it." She glanced at Lynn, hoping to see understanding in her expression.

"It happens, and you need to stop being so hard on yourself about it. Isn't it better that you came to understand that now and not *after* the wedding?"

Sydni gave a little shiver. "I know. But if I had walked down that aisle I would have found a way to make it work."

"I know you would have. There isn't a project that you don't find a way to master, but you would have been miserable in the process."

"I know, and Blake deserved better. He's such a great guy. He'll make someone really happy."

"And so will you…when you find the right guy. Speaking of which… Gabriel St. James…Santiago. Fiyah-hot! But—" she raised her finger to make a point "—he's a client. Your father would have a natural fit, not to mention that it's *soooo* unethical."

Sydni scrunched up her face. "I know," she sighed despondently. "Figures." She took a sip from her glass. Her gaze drifted off and a slow smile moved across her mouth as images of Gabriel messed with her head.

"Besides, Syd, we're only here for two weeks. Even

if…and I'm not saying that you should…but even if you did have a mini-fling with him…to, um, get rid of the cobwebs, that man is a notorious playboy."

Sydni sat up, suddenly alert and inspired. "Exactly," she declared, slapping her palm on the arm of the chair.

"Exactly what?"

"He's a playboy. Women come and go in his life like buses. Let's say…something did happen between us…. A fling… It wouldn't mean anything. He would simply move on and so would I."

"Do you hear yourself? This isn't you. Since when do you sleep with uber-gorgeous, superrich men just for the hell of it?"

"There's a first time for everything," she said with a hopeful spring in her voice.

"Syd…"

Sydni huffed and rolled her eyes. "I know. You're right. My libido has been on lockdown for so long I guess I momentarily lost my mind for a minute. That would have to be the single most crazy thing I would ever have done and I'd regret it."

"Yeah, you would. And there's no telling how that could backfire."

"I know." She finished off her glass of wine and set the glass down on the table beside her just as her cell phone rang. She picked it up from the table and her pulse jumped when she saw the name in the dial. *It's him,* she mouthed.

"Hello, Mr. St. James."

"I hope by the time dinner is over you will want to at least call me Gabriel."

"We'll see."

He chuckled. "Is seven good for you?"

"Yes, it's fine."

"There is a wonderful place that I want to take you. I know you will enjoy it."

"Looking forward."

"I'll be out front. Until then."

The call disconnected. Sydni still gripped the phone in her hand.

"Well? Why do you look like that? What did he say?"

Sydni blinked to clear her head. "Look like what?"

"Like someone slid their hand up your skirt."

Sydni's cheeks heated. Her fingers fluttered toward her glass and she realized it was empty. "You're crazy. He just wanted to tell me he'd be here at seven to pick me up for dinner."

"Hmm, okay. So what are you wearing tonight?"

Sydni's face brightened. "Guess I better figure that out." She hopped up from her seat and padded off to her bedroom.

Lynn shook her head, mystified and concerned. Generally, Sydni was the most levelheaded person in the room. She never detoured, compromised her beliefs or settled for second place. But without a doubt she'd been thunderstruck by Gabriel. And though she wouldn't admit it to Sydni, she could definitely see why. Lynn could only hope that Sydni would use her head and stick to the script because nothing but trouble could come of things otherwise.

Sydni had taken an inordinate amount of time selecting her outfit. She'd tossed aside several dresses and finally decided on a simple claret Donna Karan dress, styled as off-the-shoulder, with a pencil skirt to just above the knee in a luster jersey fabric with ruching at the bodice and waist. The dress fit her like a well-made glove, accentuating her curves with class and elegance, projecting the illusion of a perfect hourglass figure. She'd taken the wild spirals of her hair and twisted them atop her head in an intricate design that still gave a sense of disheveled chic. As usual, she kept her jewelry to a minimum, with only studs in her ears and her watch. Her makeup was light: mascara, a red gloss for her lips, a bit of color at her cheekbones and a dusting of powder to minimize a shiny nose. She dropped her compact, lip gloss, wallet, hotel key card and cell phone into her purse. She took one last look in the mirror and, finally satisfied with her appearance, went out front to give Lynn a preview.

Lynn was curled on the lounge reading a magazine and glanced up at the sound of Sydni's heels tapping their way across the floor. Her eyes widened in appreciation. "When did you get that dress?"

Sydni grinned. "Last week."

"You sneak. You went shopping without me."

"Spur of the moment. So…what do you think?"

"I think that Gabriel will have a hard time concentrating tonight." She set the magazine down and stared at her friend. "I'm concluding that's your intention."

Sydni briefly glanced away. She lifted her chin. "Maybe."

Lynn pursed her full lips. "Just be careful, girl."

Sydni ran her hands along the sides of her dress. "I will." She turned and strutted out.

The ride down the elevator from the penthouse to the lobby seemed to take forever. Sydni could feel her heart hammering in her chest. The closer she got to the ground floor, the anticipation of seeing Gabriel grew, making her skin grow hotter until she felt as if someone had lit a match in her belly.

Mercifully, the doors opened and she was envel-

oped in an embrace of cooled air. She drew in a breath
and walked toward the exit, causing heads to turn with
every footstep she took.

The doorman held the door open for her and her
heart bumped in her chest when she crossed the threshold and Gabriel was there, leaning casually against the
side of his car.

Gabriel sensed her before he saw her. Slowly he
turned his head in the direction of the front door just
as she emerged, and whatever tacit agreement he'd made
with himself about not mixing business with pleasure
was off the table. He would have her and after... Well...
they would figure it out.

Chapter 5

Gabriel eased off the side of the gleaming black-on-black Mercedes Benz S600 sedan, and rose to his full six-foot-three-inch height. A stunning specimen by any standard, that was made clear by a group of women on their way out for the evening trying to grab his attention with sultry laughter and an extra sway of hips as they passed, but his eyes were locked on Sydni's approach.

"You could have at least acknowledged them," Sydni teased upon her arrival. "They nearly broke their necks trying to get your attention."

He took her hand and slowly lifted it to his lips and placed a tingling kiss on it, never taking his eyes off her face. "You were the only woman I saw. You look devastatingly beautiful."

The air, as always, stuck in her lungs. He released her hand and then opened the passenger door of the car and helped her inside. Sydni took those few precious moments of his rounding the car to try to compose herself, remind herself to breathe. *He's just a man.*

The driver's-side door opened and Gabriel slid in behind the wheel. His gaze ran over her while his seatbelt slid into place. "So did you tell yourself the same thing that I told myself, that nothing beyond business would happen between us?"

Sydni's lips parted. Heat curled in her belly.

His smile was wickedly charming. "Please don't answer that. Our silence will heighten the mystery of the evening." He put the car in gear and zoomed out of the hotel driveway. "I hope you're in the mood for dancing after dinner," he said, smoothly shifting the conversation away from the sexual innuendos.

"I haven't been dancing in a while," she managed, thankful for a diversion from his last comment.

"Wonderful, neither have I. We'll practice on each other." He cut a sidelong glance at her.

Sydni flashed him a look of her own and charted the half smile that lurked around his mouth. "So, where will we be having dinner?" She slowly crossed her legs.

Gabriel took a quick turn that took them away from the hotel and out onto the main roadway that led through the center of town. The city had come truly alive, buzzing with energy from the long sultry days and the sizzling nights. Those that walked sparkled at their wrists and throats; their bodies shimmered, lips glistened, and soft perfumes and heady colognes floated in the charged air. Cars of every make and model revved and gleamed in the night, lining the streets.

"I thought that since this was your first time—" he shot her a look "—I would introduce you to authentic Brazilian cuisine. Ernesto has old-world tradition mixed with modern flair, and excellent food. I know you'll like it."

"I'm sure I will."

"How *are* you enjoying your visit so far?"

Sydni angled her body toward him, which caused her dress to rise slightly, revealing more of her smooth thigh, though not enough to require a tug but enough to incite.

"So far everything's been wonderful. The accommodations at the hotel are excellent, everyone is friendly... I'm sure I'll have more to tell in the days ahead."

"Hopefully, we can conclude our business quickly and I can show you around."

"I would think you'd have other things to do besides play tour guide."

"You're probably right. There are several other things I would prefer to do...but why don't we start with the tour?"

Her gaze jumped to his profile and then he turned to her with a brow cocked in challenge. The light bounced off his dark eyes.

Sydni's pulse danced in her veins. *Two could play.* "Yes, let's start...shall we? With the tour."

"Of course."

Shortly after, they pulled up in front of Ernesto on Largo da Lapa. Gabriel parked behind the restaurant and helped Sydni out of the car. He took her hand until she was on her feet, then reached around her to shut the door. His shoulder brushed hers. He placed his hand at that dip in her lower back and guided her toward the entrance. Her spine tingled.

Every time he touched her a shock ran through her body and made the fine hairs on the back of her neck stand up. It was almost more than she could take, but she wasn't ready for it to stop.

He opened the door of the restaurant and they were quickly enveloped in the intimate, cool dimness of the space.

"Bem vindos. Boa noite!" the stunning hostess greeted. She looked from one to the other and settled her gaze on Gabriel.

"Obrigado. Thank you. I have a reservation for two for Santiago," Gabriel said.

She quickly scanned her computer screen and then looked up. *"Sim.* Yes. Please follow me." She plucked two menus from beneath the podium and turned toward the main dining room.

Gabriel possessively took Sydni's hand as they followed the hostess around the circular tables to the back of the restaurant. Her heart thumped. Her hand felt good in his. It would be so easy to simply curl her fingers around his....

"Here you are," the hostess said. "Your waiter will be with you shortly." She placed the menus on the table and plucked the drink menu from the holder and set it in front of Gabriel. "Enjoy. *Bom apetite.*"

Gabriel dipped his head slightly in acknowledgment as she departed, then came around to help Sydni into her chair. He lingered for a moment behind her and she caught a whiff of his scent, felt the charges of current flow through her body when his thumbs brushed her bare shoulders. Mercifully, he took his seat and she could finally breathe.

"I think I'll have to brush up on my Portuguese," she said, and reached for her glass of water. She fully expected it to actually sizzle on her tongue.

"I'd be happy to teach you as much as you are willing to learn." He rested his forearm on the table and studied her.

She glanced at him from beneath her lashes. "You have me keeping you quite busy, Mr. St. James, or is it Santiago tonight? Between the tours and teaching me the language..."

Gabriel chuckled. "I could live with that kind of busy. Would you like a drink?" he said, smoothly shifting the conversation.

"Yes."

A waiter appeared at their table.

"Wine or something stronger?" Gabriel asked Sydni.

"I'll have a caipirinha."

"Ahhh." He smiled. "Make that two," he said to the waiter and then turned to Sydni. "I wouldn't want you getting ahead of me."

"You don't strike me as the kind of man who would let anyone get ahead of him." She took another sip of water.

"That all depends."

"On what?"

"My mood."

Her fingertips played with the stem of the glass. "I see. And what mood are you in tonight?"

He leaned forward. His eyes locked in on her. "In the mood to fix you breakfast in the morning."

She drew in a sharp breath that screeched to a stop in the center of her chest.

"But, of course, I always defer to the wishes of the lady."

The waiter arrived with their drinks and not a minute too soon. Sydni felt like she could down the entire glass in one swallow.

"Are you ready to order now?" the waiter asked.

Gabriel looked to Sydni.

She cleared her throat. "I'll have the *bobóa de camarão* over rice."

"Would you like the shrimp spicy or mild?"

"Mild." She handed over her menu.

"And you, sir?"

"I'll take the *churrasco*."

"Right away." He took the menus and walked off.

Gabriel lifted his glass toward Sydni. "To a lovely evening."

Sydni touched her glass to his.

Gabriel took a swallow and slowly returned his glass to the table. He turned his full attention to her. "So, tell me about Sydni. What does she like? What does she do when she is not being vice president of Epic?"

It took her a moment to unscramble her thoughts with him staring at her as if she was the main course. She lightly cleared her throat.

"When I'm not working, which isn't very often, I enjoy the spa, shopping with my friends, traveling." She paused. "Staying home and simply relaxing with a good book, to be perfectly honest."

She laughed at her confession.

"My job is very consuming. Although I do have a few opportunities to do something other than work, I really enjoy being home in my own space. I suppose I enjoy it so much because I get to do it so infrequently."

Gabriel rested his chin in his palm and studied her. "You strike me as a woman who is driven by her desires." His brow flicked. "Your desire for time for yourself must balance with your desire to get the job done."

"Equal parts business and pleasure?"

"Exactly."

"Is that how you conduct your life?"

"Yes."

She took a sip from her glass. "From the articles that I've read about you, it appears that pleasure tips the scales."

He shooed the comment away. "Do you always believe everything that you read?"

"No."

"Just as I thought."

She angled her head. "Just as you thought what?"

"You aren't like everyone else." He raised his glass to her.

"Hmm. And what do I need to know about you that can't be found between the pages of a magazine or your company's balance sheet?"

"First…" He reached across the table and trailed the tip of his index finger across the curves of her knuckles. She tugged on her bottom lip with her teeth. "We will have dinner. We will drink. We will dance. We will walk along the beach. We will forget about work…and in the morning you tell me what you have uncovered."

Breathing was fruitless. She'd forgotten how. And if he didn't stop stroking her hand with his finger she was going to come all over herself.

Sydni caught sight of a waitress in her peripheral vision. She reached out and stopped her. "Excuse me. Where is the restroom?"

The young woman pointed in the direction of the restroom and Sydni quickly excused herself. Once behind the safety of the doors, she took a minute to breathe. She felt like stripping. If she didn't know better she'd think she was going through the change of life with the parade of hot flashes that she'd experienced since Gabriel St. James, née Santiago, had made his presence felt in every crevice of her being.

She stepped in front of the mirrors, stared at her reflection and was taken aback by what she saw. This was the face of a woman who'd just been made love to. Her skin was flushed, dewy almost, and her eyes had a sleepy, satiated look to them. Her nipples longed to be suckled, hard and uncomfortable against her bra and the slight dampness between her thighs signaled her willing-and-readiness.

She pressed her palms against the cool surface of the marble-topped sink. If Gabriel could do this to her with no more than a look and a light touch...

She turned on the cold water, snatched up some paper towels, dampened them and pressed them against her chest, the back of her neck and behind her knees. Straightening, she drew in a deep breath, freshened her makeup and returned to the table to find that their dinner was being set out on the table.

"Perfect timing," Gabriel said, getting up to help her into her seat. "Did I mention how wonderful you smell?" he murmured into her ear as she sat. Her nipples rose to attention again.

Her gaze followed him back to his seat and he was as disaffected by what he'd said as if he'd only mentioned that it might rain. Maybe it was the difference in cultures, or maybe her overactive libido was chomping at the bit.

"I've had the *bobóa de camarão.* It's always excellent. I hope you enjoy it."

"I'm sure I will." She gathered some of her meal onto her fork. "How long do you plan to stay in Rio?"

"At least until after Carnival. My brother and I have some business to take care of here. Once that's settled, I'll be back in the States, although I may make a stop in Trinidad and visit my grandparents." He cut into his meat.

"Is it only you and your brother?"

He chuckled as he slowly chewed his food. "My father had many women in his life, some of whom have insisted that he fathered their child. It's possible that Max and I have a few siblings, but none that we know of for sure."

"I see. Where is your father now?"

"The last time we talked, he was getting on a plane to Mexico. That was three weeks ago. He usually comes home for Carnival as well. Perhaps you will get a chance to meet him."

"Yes, and see where you got all of your charm."

His eyes shifted from his food to her face. "So you *do* find me charming."

"*Charming* will have to do until I find another adjective."

He chuckled. "I'm up to the task." He lifted his chin in her direction. "How is your meal?"

"Delicious."

"Excellent. I want you to enjoy every aspect of tonight from beginning to end."

Dinner continued along a pleasant yet mentally and emotionally challenging game of verbal fencing. With each parry and riposte, they continued with their duel of words, each laden with double entendre.

With dinner finished, Gabriel escorted Sydni back out to the car and then drove them to Club Miroir on the Lagoa. The beat and pulse of samba greeted them the moment they stepped out of the car. The air surrounding the club was energized as the beautiful people floated in and out.

Gabriel took her by the hand and led her past the line of clubbers and up to the front entrance where he was quickly waved through by security with a "Good to see you again."

Mood lighting in bold colors combined with an artsy decor and an eclectic blend of partygoers filled the tri-level club. The entire interior pulsed with the beat of the music from the six-piece live band. The enormous circular dance floor was packed with gyrating bodies.

Gabriel was greeted once again by name; this time by an exotic-looking hostess.

"Welcome, Mr. Santiago. Your usual table?"

"Yes. Thank you, Maya."

"Follow me."

Gabriel looped his arm around Sydni's waist and pulled her close to his side. "Wouldn't want to lose you," he whispered in her ear.

Sydni angled her head and was drawn to him like the gravitational pull between the ocean and the moon. He was so close and devouring her with such a look of hunger in his eyes that she waited for the kiss, right then and there. Instead, a glimmer of a smile toyed around the edges of his mouth.

Soon, he mouthed, before turning away to walk behind Maya.

Sydni was shaken. Blood roared in her ears and she was actually thankful that Gabriel had a good grip around her waist.

They walked past the enormous bar, and took the glass-and-chrome dome-shaped elevator to the top level. The glass balcony held several intimate booths; each discreetly separated for maximum privacy, yet from every angle the dance floor was visible.

Gabriel helped Sydni into her seat.

Maya placed the menus on the table. "What can I get you both from the bar?"

"A bottle of champagne."

"Right away."

Sydni settled into her seat. "Champagne. What are we celebrating?"

"Our merger."

This time dawn broke over the horizon when she experienced the full benefit of his smile. Oh, she could take that comment *so* many ways. "I see."

"I hope so." His attention was diverted by a clap on his shoulder. He turned to look up to see his brother standing behind him. "This is a surprise."

"You didn't say you'd be here," he shouted above the music.

Sydni took him in. He was long and lean and movie-idol handsome. He reminded her of a younger Antonio Banderas with a hint more coffee in his cream.

"Max. Let me introduce you to the woman who is going to change me." He leveled his dark gaze on Sydni. "Sydni Lawson, my older brother, Max Santiago."

Max came around to Sydni's side of the table. She extended her hand in greeting, which he drew to his lips.

"I've heard all about you. I hope you packed some miracles in your suitcase."

She raised a brow. "Miracles?"

"That's what it will take to change my brother. How are you finding our beautiful country so far?"

"Wonderful."

Max gave a slight nod of his head, then turned to his brother. "We'll talk tomorrow."

"Good."

"My pleasure to meet you, Ms. Lawson."

"You, too."

Max turned and melded in with the crowd. Sydni turned her attention back to Gabriel.

"Let's dance," he commanded without preamble. He stood, took her hand and drew her to her feet.

Sydni followed him around the throng of bodies and down the stairs to the lower-level dance floor that vibrated beneath their feet.

"I'm really not that good at this," Sydni shouted over the rhythmic beat of the congas and the blare of the horns.

Gabriel drew her flush against the long hard lines of his frame. He stared into her eyes. "Give your body to me…and the music."

He held her with his eyes, led her with his hands on her body. It was magic. Her feet glided across the floor, following his every step as he spun, twirled, swayed, grabbed and released her. The pitch and dip of her hips matched his. They moved as one unit—as if this syncopated ritual was what they'd always done—and Sydni wondered if he'd move his pelvis the same way when held between her thighs.

Their skin grew damp, their breathing escalated, their bodies clung to each other while one dance turned to two, three and then four.

Heated, Gabriel looped his arm around Sydni's waist and pulled her up against him. "Ready?" he nearly growled.

"For?"

"To leave…with me now…and breakfast tomorrow."

Sydni's eyes widened for an instant. There was no doubt what he meant. She should say no. She should even act insulted that he would presume…

"Yes. I'm ready."

He leaned close and pressed his lips right behind her ear, then whispered, "Come."

A shiver ran through her body as she followed him out.

Chapter 6

Gabriel drove the entire way back to his home with one hand on the wheel and the other just beneath the hem of Sydni's dress. The tips of his fingers were iron-hot when they made tiny circles on the inside of her knee, or trailed just an inch between her thighs.... Not enough to slap his hand away, but enough to keep the fire stoked and her slit wet with anticipation.

Sydni tugged back the urge to clamp her thighs tight around his wandering hand and hold it in place. The subtle pleasure was maddening. Her nipples were so hard that they ached and the fine hairs at the back of her neck stood at attention. She bit down on her bottom lip to keep from moaning and when she dared to steal a glance at Gabriel, he appeared as calm and unaffected as if he were driving alone.

Gabriel's vehicle hugged the winding roads like a possessive lover. He was in total control and that realization stirred something deep and carnal in the pit of Sydni's stomach.

The gates leading to his secluded abode appeared before them. It looked even more isolated and intimate at night. The heavy arc of towering trees and bushes pushed shadows out onto the driveway and gave the house an almost surreal appearance, like something painted on a postcard. He brought the car to a halt in front of the entrance and before she had a moment to unbuckle her seatbelt he was pulling her door open and extending his hand. Sydni placed her hand in his and stepped lightly from the car. Gabriel led the way inside without a word.

When they crossed the threshold, soft lighting gradually illuminated the space, set off by unseen sensors. In the distance, she could just make out the sound of the central air kicking on. Her eyes scanned her surroundings. It was so much more intoxicating than it had been when she'd visited during the day. Maybe it was the soft lighting or the shadow of trees, the quiet that only nighttime can bring or the anticipation of what was to come.

"Something to drink?" he asked, breaking the spell.

Sydni focused on him. "Yes. Please."

"Come in. Relax. Make yourself comfortable. Would you care for wine or something stronger?"

"Wine." She wanted to feel a bit mellow, but still needed to have her head as clear as possible.

She strolled over to the couch, put her purse on the low table and sat down. Soft music began to play on cue. She smiled to herself.

Gabriel appeared with two glasses of wine. He handed one to her. When she glanced up at him she was struck once again by how incredibly handsome he was. Gabriel exuded a tightly wound sensuality that put one in mind of a preying panther—sleek, sensual, quick and potentially deadly.

"Thank you." She took the glass from his hand. He lowered himself next to her but not too close, giving her enough space.

"How did you enjoy the evening?"

Her eyes lit up. "It was wonderful. The restaurant was exquisite. The food…" She shook her head in delight. "And the club… That was fun." She laughed. "I can't remember the last time I danced so much. I'm sure I'll pay for it in the morning."

He slowly reached toward her and gently tucked a spiral of hair behind her ear. "I hope that the dancing will not be what you'll pay for in the morning. I can think of other things."

She teased her bottom lip with her tongue.

"I'd like to taste that."

"Taste what?"

"Your tongue… To discover if it's as sweet as it looks."

Her mind went blank. She couldn't respond and she didn't need to. Everything in her extended vision was blocked as Gabriel moved toward her.

And then his mouth covered hers and all reason escaped as her senses exploded from the contact that she had only imagined.

His full lips were firm and soft and sweet as they moved possessively over hers, inching her mouth apart in increments of pleasure. The tip of his tongue slid across her lips, teased the inside of her mouth, moved slowly in and out. Gabriel's moan deepened while he played with her tongue, danced with it, captured it, made her mouth one with his.

Sydni's heart banged mercilessly in her chest. His arm slid around her and pulled her close. Fire licked her insides, and like butter on a hot skillet she felt her body melt into his. Her arms wound around his neck. Their sighs became music that they moved to, that led them up the stairs to Gabriel's bedroom at the end of the hall.

He pushed the door open with his shoulder and pulled her in behind him.

"I've wanted you since I first laid eyes on you," he said before taking her mouth again. His hands roamed along the dips and curves of her body, dispensing with her dress in the process. He eased the zipper down and the straps fell from her shoulders. The dress slid silently into a soft puddle at her feet. "Beautiful," he murmured deep and hot into her ear.

Her hands splayed across his chest and the hammering of his heart vibrated beneath her fingertips. It stirred her with the knowledge that she was exciting him the same way he was exciting her. She gave in fully to his kiss, his possessive caresses. A part of her knew that this was every which way wrong. She was about to have an all-out, curl-your-toes sex romp with a man she was sent to do business with. A man she barely knew. But her heart and body didn't give a damn about any of that—at least not right now. Not when his fingers were playing with the band of her panties and pushing them over her hips, and his mouth was leaving a burning trail along her collarbone down to the swell of her breasts. All she wanted was to find out if he would be half as good as she imagined.

Gabriel smoothly guided her toward his king-size bed. She lowered herself down on the side, where he joined her.

Everything shifted around her, receded into a space beyond the room. It was only the two of them creating this incredible heat that set off a series of sparks that popped back and forth between them. Hands and fingers and mouths and tongues sought uncovered surfaces to explore and conquer.

Gabriel stretched Sydni out on the bed like fine linen being prepared for a feast to be set upon it. Hungry eyes rolled over her, eating her up without touching her. Her pulse thumped in her veins, making her feel as if she was vibrating. Gabriel eased the straps of her bra over her shoulders, peeled down the D cups of her bra to push her breasts higher to meet his eager mouth. He sucked a taut nipple into his mouth and her body spontaneously arched up off the bed, hit by a lightning bolt of pleasure.

"Sweet," he murmured, while his lips savored the succulent fruits that rose and fell and blossomed under the attention of his mouth, his tongue and the caress of his powerful fingers.

Sydni's soft moans grew deeper, ragged almost, as Gabriel's mouth and tongue seared a slow path down to her stomach, teased her navel until the muscles of her stomach quivered.

"I want you," he breathed against the length of her inner thigh. He placed hot kisses there and along her calf and behind her knees and the dip in her ankle, then back up and down again until Sydni was one electrified nerve. Her fingertips pressed into his scalp and clung to the silken hair when his mouth settled over the hot apex of her sex.

Her mouth opened, emitting a strangling cry as he laved her through the near-sheer fabric of her panties. He held her hips down on the bed, weighing her into the mattress. The tiny crotch of her thong was soaked from Gabriel's attention and her own heightened excitement. She was so ready. *So ready.*

Gabriel tugged at the delicate black strings of fabric. Sydni gasped at the sound of shredding silk. He moved slowly back up her body, anointing her with kisses along the way until he was braced above her. His dark eyes bore into hers, holding her completely captive. He reached over into the nightstand and took out a condom packet. He held it between the tips of his fingers and gave it to Sydni.

Her teeth tugged her bottom lip while he rose up onto his knees, putting on display his erection that was magnificently full and hard and pointed right at her.

Sydni swallowed, took the packet between her teeth and ripped it open. Gingerly, she took out the thin sheath and reached for him. Her fingers wrapped around him. She drew in a sharp breath as the sensation of his silken skin over the incredible stiffness of his erection set her pulse racing. He was—in a word—magnificent to behold and to touch.

She took the rim of the condom between her thumb and forefinger and placed it over the head that was already wet with the dew of his arousal. Slowly, she unrolled it, covering him inch by incremental inch.

The air crackled with electricity. Gabriel let it surge through his limbs, igniting him even more. As desperately as he wanted her he willed himself to take his time, to savor every inch of her sweet flesh, to make her remember this night long into her future. He used his mouth, his tongue, to tease, taste and explore her from her eyelids to the dip in her ankles. He cut a searing path along her body, then used his mouth again and again to put out then reignite the fire within her.

His long fingers stroked her hips, massaged her thighs until they were as weak and pliant as a newborn. Her moans excited him as he'd never been before, and the way her body opened and responded to him held him as a willing captive.

"You... I have to have you," he ground out between the swell of her breasts. "Tell me you feel the same," he demanded of her.

"Yessss," she hissed between her teeth and gripped the sheet into her fists as he slid his middle finger inside of her.

"You're so wet," he whispered. He slowly moved his finger in and out of her until her body found and matched his rhythm. He flicked his thumb across her pulsing clit and her cry pierced the sultry air. "Again," he said. "Cry out for me again." He pushed two fingers inside of her. A strangled sob escaped from her parted lips. He found the soft spot inside her tight wet walls and pressed his finger against it.

"Ohhhh!" Her hips rose up from the bed and her body shook with a pleasure so intense that it made her lightheaded. He did it again and again. Sydni pushed her pelvis against the thrill of his hand as the sensations rolled through her, taking her on a high that she never wanted to come down from. And then she felt it—the quickening in the pit of her belly, the tingling and tightening that began to spread from the soles of her feet, sliding up the inside of her parted thighs.

Gabriel felt it, too, and the realization hardened him even more. He would take her to the brink, but he would not release her. Not yet. He rose up on his knees, pushed her thighs back so that they rested against his. "Look at me."

Sydni's eyes fluttered open and the raw expression in his nearly sent her over the edge.

"I want to see you. I want to see your face, your eyes when I enter you." He pressed the head against the slit of her opening. She moaned and gripped his shoulders. He grabbed her hips in his large hands and in one long hard thrust he drove deep inside her, expelling all the air from her lungs.

Her mouth opened but no sound emerged. She was full, full, it felt, to her throat. She didn't think she could take it. Damn, he was so thick and hard and long. She couldn't. She just couldn't.

Gabriel saw the shock, the apprehension and the longing in her eyes. He remained perfectly still, allowing her body a chance to accept the weight and fullness of him. As much as he wanted to move inside her, give her the full pleasure of his loving, he held back. Instead, he tenderly kissed her lips, reawakened her tongue. He rained kisses along her neck and behind her ears, across her throat and down to the rise of her breasts. Gently he suckled her over and over until he felt her body begin to move, needing him as much as he needed her. Yet he remained still, allowing her to set the pace, determine her need.

Her gaze leapt to his. What she saw in his eyes reflected the maddening desire that she had for him. She looped her arms around his neck and spread her thighs even farther. She couldn't breathe. She felt her body resist the swell of him, then give as he pushed and widened her and filled her and she ceased to be a separate being.

His dark, hot gaze bore into her. He draped her thighs over his arms and slowly pulled out until only the head was left inside her walls. Her body trembled in response.

"Please," she begged as her fingers pressed into his rear. He moved in and out, slow and deep and steady, gritting his teeth to keep from hollering with pleasure.

They found that perfect tempo that gave as much as it took, rising and falling like the waves of the ocean rushing toward the shore.

Gabriel had held back for as long as he could. They were both on the edge. He'd felt her insides begin to tighten, saw the perspiration glisten on her face, listened to her breathing escalate, her moans lengthen, and felt her fingers dig deeper into his skin. And then her insides clutched him, sucked him in, wrapped around his cock like a vise and pumped every ounce of his essence from his body. He growled deep in his throat in a combination of agony and ecstasy. "So good," he moaned. "So good."

Their bodies locked together in unison, becoming one entity before bursting apart into a million fragments of pleasure and then reuniting on a bed of sublime release.

They cried and whispered and roared each other's names while the thrill of their union ebbed and flowed through them until they were spent.

Chapter 7

Gabriel dropped his head into the warm hollow of Sydni's neck as his body sank into hers. The rapid speed of their breaths filled the air in competition with their racing hearts.

Sydni gently stroked the tight muscles of his back and adjusted her hips to manage his weight. Every square inch of her tingled with satisfaction. She had never before felt so connected, so complete with a man. It wasn't simply afterglow that had her head and heart spinning. It was something else. Something beyond her experience. He kissed her then, so softly on her cheek that tears sprang in her eyes and her insides instinctively clutched his still hard member.

Gabriel moved slowly inside her, still aroused, still needing her. Sydni whimpered as her body heated and melted in response. Her inner walls remained swollen and slick and equally unwilling to let him go.

This time, Gabriel only rotated his hips, not sliding

in and out of her but rather keeping himself buried deep within her heat. The pressure against her tender clit was maddening. Her body shuddered from her feet to the top of her head. She wanted to move, to thrash and buck against the thrill of his cock, but he wouldn't let her. The weight of his lower body and his hands pressed against her hipbones held her in place. He was in total control. His mouth encircled one taut nipple and he lightly ran his teeth over it until she began to claw his back and her thighs parted even farther. Her breathing escalated to a pant. The sound of his name was raw and strangled. The cords in her neck grew rope-tight. Her body was on fire. She drew her knees toward her chest, wanting all of him all the way inside of her.

"Come for me," he whispered in her ear. "Come…" He pulled out until only the head was still inside her and the sudden release of that mind-altering pressure against the apex of her sex rocked through her like a megajolt of electricity. Her eyes widened. She screamed once as he drove deep inside of her, hurtling them both over the precipice of heaven.

Gabriel flipped over onto his back and tossed his arm across his eyes. His heart continued to pound as if he'd run a marathon. His thoughts ran on top of each other. He'd lost count of how many women he'd bedded for a variety of reasons. There were some that were undoubtedly noteworthy. But this… His jaw clenched. He'd only wanted to get between those amazing thighs. He'd only wanted to soften what she presented as the tough, no-nonsense exterior. He hadn't expected this—to feel this—to want her so deeply and completely. He was still hard for her. How could this be?

Sydni knew that she was lying perfectly still, yet she

could feel her body humming as if a source of electricity was coursing through her veins. She had no words for what had happened between them. The intensity of it scared yet thrilled her. The physical power that he wielded over her left her feeling vulnerable, something that she was unfamiliar with. She should have never gone to bed with him. Some crazy part of her had imagined that it would just be good sex and that would be the end of it. How could she ever think about not having him inside of her again? Yet she knew that once this deal was done, this thing between them would be over.

Gabriel eased up out of the bed and padded into the en suite bathroom and shut the door behind him. Sydni listened to the rush of water and castigated herself for being so foolish, for letting her libido do her thinking. She pulled the soft cotton sheet up to her chin. What was she going to do now?

The bathroom door opened and Gabriel emerged with a towel draped over his arm and a bowl of warm water in his hand. He sat down on the side of the bed closest to her and placed the bowl of water on the nightstand. "No need to be shy now," he softly teased and lifted the sheet from her. A small smile curved his lush mouth. "Beautiful," he murmured while his gaze took her in.

He dipped the cloth in the warm water, rung it out and tenderly began to wash her, caring for her in such a gentle way that it brought a smile to her lips. There was nothing overtly sexual about what he was doing, but it was absolutely erotic. He washed her face and neck, her breasts, her arms, down her belly, between her legs as if he were paying homage to a treasure. When he was done, he patted her dry with the towel and drew the sheet back up to cover her. He leaned over and placed a soft kiss on her lips. "Sleep."

The sound of music playing softly in the background and the aroma of something delicious seeped into Sydni's subconscious and slowly lifted her from one of the best sleeps she'd had in ages. She blinked against the light that slid in between the floor-to-ceiling drapes that covered the massive bedroom windows. She stretched and groaned against the ache in her muscles and came fully awake when the night before came crashing back to her in a wave. A little shiver ran down her spine. She tossed the sheet aside, sat up and scanned the room for her clothes. They were gone. In their place was a robe draped over the club chair. She put it on and went in search of Gabriel.

"Ah, you are awake. Wonderful. As promised, breakfast is ready. I thought you might like to eat outside on the deck."

He was at the long island counter, shirtless—which was enough of a distraction—putting food into serving bowls and the bowls onto a tray. Between seeing Gabriel half-naked first thing in the morning, and the mouthwatering aroma of crab cakes, bacon, omelets and what looked like grits, she felt light-headed.

"I prepared a carafe of mimosas. Would you bring it outside?"

"Sure." She followed him outside to find the table already set. "How long have you been up?"

"With the sun. I went for a swim while you were sleeping and then I started breakfast."

She shook her head in admiration. All she felt like doing was eating and crawling back into bed. She settled down into a chair.

"Help yourself." He poured their drinks.

"Did you really do all this by yourself?" She was expecting his housekeeper to pop her head in at any moment.

He grinned. "Believe it or not, I'm very self-sufficient." He spooned heaping portions of food onto his plate. "I learned to take care of myself at a very young age." A slight shadow passed over his countenance and then was gone just as quickly.

Sydni took a bite of her crab cake. "Oh. My. Goodness. This is delicious."

His eyes sparkled. "Aren't you glad you stayed for breakfast?"

The furnace in the center of her stomach swooshed on. Her gaze collided with his and he looked as though he'd much rather have her for breakfast.

They passed the rest of the meal making small talk, sharing tidbits of information about themselves—from places they'd been to favorite movies and childhood friends. For some unspoken reason they stayed away from talking about the night before or anything having to do with business. It was almost as if they were really a budding couple experiencing the bloom of the morning after.

"I should be getting back to my hotel. Lynn has left me a half-dozen messages wondering where I am."

Gabriel slowly rose from his seat and looked down into Sydni's upturned face. He reached out and gently stroked her cheek with the tip of his finger. For an instant her eyes fluttered closed as a shiver of delight shimmied through her.

"I was hoping we could spend the day together. I want to show you my beautiful country."

"It's tempting…."

He pulled her to her feet and flush against him. "What do I need to do to convince you?" he whispered, then kissed her behind her ear.

"Not much if you keep that up." She stepped out of his hold and pressed her hands to his chest. "I have to get back."

Even his feigned look of defeat was sexy as hell. Sydni laughed and turned away from him. "I'm going to get dressed. Where are my clothes, by the way?"

"Your dress is hanging in the closet. Your underthings are on the dresser—at least what is left of your panties."

She paused and tossed him a look from across her shoulder. "Thanks for breakfast."

"My pleasure." He watched her walk away and already began to imagine when he would lure her back to his bed.

Chapter 8

"Girl, where were you? I've been going crazy," Lynn said, launching into Sydni the instant she walked through the door of the suite. She leapt up from the couch and stomped barefoot across the wooden floor and planted herself in Sydni's path.

"Okay, okay. I should have called when we left the restaurant."

"Ya think?"

Sydni twisted her lips, stepped out of her heels, bent down to pick them up and swung them on her fingertips. Her lips twitched as she tried to hide her smile.

"Well, dammit, was it worth it?"

Sydni felt as if the top had been taken off a boiling pot. "Lynn," she screeched and started dancing in place right in the middle of the floor. She threw her head back. "Girl… I. Am. Still. On. Fire. You hear me?"

Lynn covered her mouth but it barely muffled her shriek of delight. She snatched Sydni by the hand and pulled her over to the couch. "Don't you dare leave out one hot, sweaty detail."

Sydni plopped down next to her friend and for the next half hour divulged all the juicy details—mostly all. When she finished she rested her head against the couch and closed her eyes.

"Now what?" Lynn asked, breaking into the fantasy that played behind Sydni's closed lids.

Sydni blinked back to reality. She turned to Lynn. "I don't know," she said as if all the air had been let out of her lungs and the weight of what had transpired filled them instead.

Lynn squeezed her hand. "We came here to do a job. That has to be at the top of the agenda."

"It is. I haven't forgotten. And I'm perfectly capable of separating business from pleasure."

"You're going to have to."

Sydni lifted her chin. "Let's take a look at the presentation. I think I have a better picture now of Mr. Gabriel St. James."

Lynn shot Sydni a wary look before walking off to retrieve their iPads.

Sydni shut her eyes. Images of her and Gabriel, wet and clinging to each other, bloomed like wildflowers behind her lids. She clenched her fists. As much as her body had taken over where her good sense should have, she knew she could pull this venture off. Her father was depending on her, Gabriel was depending on her and she was not one to disappoint. She knew she should never have slept with him. But it was done. They were both adults with a mutual goal—to rebrand and market Gabriel St. James and launch his line of resorts. That must be the focus going forward. Besides, what chance could they ever have? He lived half a world away. He'd scratched her itch and now it was time to get her head back in the game.

Gabriel sat across the large conference room table, facing the smug look of his brother, Max.

"I knew it," Max announced, slapping his palm on the table. He tossed his head back and laughed. "You slept with her."

"I wouldn't say we slept." He thoughtfully rubbed his chin.

Max cut him a look. "That's usually my line." He studied the serene expression on his brother's face, quite the opposite of his usual intense countenance. "What did she do to you?" His gaze narrowed.

Gabriel stood and walked toward the window. "I don't know what you mean."

"I'm sure that you do. I won't belabor the issue, but don't let this woman get under your skin. There's no room now. We have too much at stake and too much to do to be distracted."

Gabriel turned on his heel. "I'm sure I'm capable of dealing with a woman *and* business." His jaw tightened.

Max's full mouth quirked into a half grin. "She's already gotten under your skin."

Gabriel's eyes flashed a warning, then settled. He sighed and slid his hands into the pockets of his slacks. His brother knew him better than he knew himself at times and in this instance he was right. Sydni Lawson had gotten under his skin and that knowledge unsettled him.

"Temporary," he finally said. "We are simply two adults satisfying a need. No more, no less."

Max hummed. "Be sure to keep it that way." He

paused. "What progress has been made with the branding and marketing? We need to get the investors on board."

"She will bring the proposal to me later this morning."

"Hopefully, the final negotiations will take place in the boardroom and not the bedroom."

"Many great deals have been struck in the bedroom," he tossed back playfully. "At least that's what you've professed through the years."

"It's never been your style."

"And it isn't now. I like her. I want to spend time with her, but I want this deal more. Simple. Soon she'll be back in the States and life will go on."

"If you say so, but enough about beautiful women and great sex. We have a meeting to attend."

Gabriel sat through the two-hour meeting of facts, figures and investments, nodding and commenting in all the right places, but his mind was on Sydni and the hours in between until he would see her again.

Chapter 9

"I think I should sit in on this meeting and make sure you keep your feet on the floor," Lynn called out while she looked in the bathroom mirror and applied a splash of lip gloss.

Sydni posed in the doorway with her hand on her hip. "You sound like you don't trust me."

Lynn threw her a look from across her shoulder. "I don't."

Sydni huffed. "You have nothing to worry about. I can handle a business meeting, Lynn."

Lynn dropped her lip gloss into her purse and turned to Sydni with an arched brow. "So you say."

"Fine. You do the presentation and I'll seal the deal."

"I thought you did that already." She winked and sailed past her.

The offices of St. James Enterprises were located in one of the many towering buildings in downtown Rio. After clearing security on the main level, they were told to wait in the lobby and that someone would be down to escort them to the twenty-first floor. Moments later a stunning young woman who looked like she should be on the cover of *Vogue* approached them.

"Good afternoon," she greeted in a sultry accent, smiling brightly at them. "I will take you up to see Mr. Santiago. Please follow me." She turned on her stilettos and walked to the last bank of elevators.

Sydni and Lynn shared a quick look between them and dutifully followed. They took the express elevator to the top floor.

The elevator opened to a sprawling setup that boasted gleaming hardwood floors and a wide-open concept design, low-slung white leather furnishings and floor-to-ceiling windows that spanned one full wall and offered a magnificent view of the mountains in the distance. There was a large quartz reception desk in the shape of an S in the center of the space. Another stunning woman sat behind the desk with a headset that did nothing to detract from her looks.

"This way," their guide said.

They walked around two pillars that gave the space a Romanesque feel, then turned down a wide corridor that was lined with several offices. They reached the end of the hall and were met by an imposing double oak door. Their guide knocked lightly, opened the door and stepped aside to let Sydni and Lynn enter.

Gabriel spun his chair slowly toward the door and his dark gaze locked onto hers. Sydni's heart instantly raced. The heat rose from her feet and rushed through her veins. The visceral effect he had on her with just a look rocked her to her core. He rose from his seat, adjusted his jacket and came around his desk.

"Good morning." He looked from one to the other.

"Please. Come. Make yourselves comfortable." He pulled out a chair and then another and helped them to sit, lingering a bit longer behind Sydni. The tips of his fingers brushed the back of her neck, sending a shockwave down her spine. She struggled to maintain her composure.

"Impressive office," Lynn said.

Gabriel gave a smile. "It serves its purpose. Can I offer you ladies refreshments?"

"Water is fine for me," Sydni said, finally finding her voice.

"Me, too," Lynne added.

Gabriel walked back to his desk, pressed a button on his phone and asked his secretary to bring a carafe of spring water.

The door opened and Max strode in. Lynn's mouth dropped open.

"Good morning, ladies." He came to Sydni. She extended her hand. "Good to see you again, Ms. Lawson." He lowered his head and brought her hand to his lips. He then turned all of his attention and charm on Lynn. "And you…" He held her hand and gave it a gentle squeeze. "Lynn Covington." He brought her hand to his lips and held her in place with a penetrating gaze.

Thankfully, Gabriel's secretary appeared with a tray of icy cold water. Sydni was pretty sure that it would turn to steam the instant it hit Lynn's mouth. She bit back a laugh.

"Why don't we get started," Sydni began, taking the lead. She turned on her tablet and Lynn followed suit. Max took a seat closest to Lynn.

"We've detailed the preliminary rollout," Lynn said. "The concept is to position you separate and apart from St. James Enterprises."

Gabriel frowned. Max shifted in his seat.

Sydni held up her hand to ward off the impending objections. "The reason for that is that St. James Enterprises is known worldwide as a business involved in hostile takeovers of smaller businesses, and that the heads of your corporation live a life that is in the unreachable stratosphere for everyday people. Our goal is to reposition you—" she zeroed in on Gabriel "—to be accessible, real and have the best interests of your new customers at heart." She swiped her finger across her iPad screen and turned it toward Gabriel. Lynn did the same with Max. "This is the mock-up of the preliminary promo material."

Gabriel carefully studied each screen. His face remained inscrutable.

"We also strongly believe that to reposition you, you will need to form a separate company and you will be the face of that new company with a new focus and agenda."

Gabriel leaned back in his chair. He steepled his fingers beneath his chin. "This business, our business, has succeeded for decades. I have the connections and the capital to get the resorts up and off the ground. You are suggesting that I push all this away and start like some beginner?" He pushed the iPad aside.

"What I'm suggesting is that you *use* your knowledge *and* your connections, but we introduce this business under a new umbrella."

"Without the taint of the St. James name," Max cut in, his tone of antipathy undeniable. "Your answer is to have my brother disown himself from his heritage, his legacy?" He snorted his annoyance. "That's your master plan?" He stood and walked over to the window. He kept his back to the room. "I'm only here to listen.

This is my brother's venture and his decision. I will stand behind whatever his decision is." He turned to face them. "I hope, if he agrees, that it works and that it's worth it. If not, I will personally hold you responsible…Ms. Lawson," he stated in a tone so warm and engaging that it was impossible to be offended, and at the same time the underlying implications were clear.

Sydni lifted her chin. "I'm not in the business of failure. Success is always my goal."

Max's full, rich lips quirked into the shadow of a smile that came nowhere near his eyes. He walked to the table, picked up the carafe of water and poured a glass. He handed it to Sydni then did the same for Lynn. "I have another meeting. It was good to see you again, Ms. Lawson—and Ms. Covington, I hope we will meet again before your return to the States." He glanced toward his brother, gave a short nod and strode out.

Lynn felt her shoulders relax for the first time since Max walked into the room. She glanced at Sydni, whose expression was a picture of calm, but Lynn knew her friend and sensed the irritation floating off her in waves.

Sydni took a long swallow of water before setting the glass down on the table. "That's our proposal. I have the greatest confidence that it will exceed our expectations and yours. But the decision is up to you." She opened her tote and pulled out a thin, clear binder that contained the hard copy of the proposal along with a small flash drive that would allow him to review the presentation on his computer. She handed them to Gabriel. He took them and set them back down on the table.

"I will give your proposal every consideration— perhaps we can discuss this further." His focus was completely on Sydni. She knew exactly what he was implying and the little lady between her thighs nearly answered for her. She swallowed. "Feel free to call me with any questions or concerns. We—Epic International—are eager to make this work."

"I'm sure." He stood, signaling the end of the meeting. Sydni and Lynn rose in turn. He pressed the intercom button on his phone. "Our guests are ready to leave."

Moments later the same young woman appeared and held the door open. Lynn and Sydni followed her out.

"Ms. Lawson…"

Sydni stopped and turned. Gabriel closed in on her personal space. His proposal was low and intimate. "I think it would serve us best to discuss this over dinner. Tonight. I'll pick you up from your hotel at seven."

She wouldn't give in that easily and fall for his smooth South American charm. This was business. "Make it eight." She turned and sashayed out.

Chapter 10

"Syd, you're going out with him again?" Lynn asked in a harsh whisper as the driver whisked them back to their hotel.

Sydni crossed her legs. "We're going to discuss business."

"Yeah, right. Just be careful, Syd. He's gorgeous, sexy as hell, rich and fabulous. Much too easy to fall for and fall hard. I don't want you to get hurt and I don't want your kitty cat to mess with your head and this deal."

Sydni turned to Lynn and made a face. "I'll be fine and I will get this deal done. Don't forget I saw you salivating when Max walked into the room. I thought you were going to have 'a moment' when he kissed your hand."

Lynn playfully rolled her eyes. "A girl can dream—and he *was* fine. With a capital *F*."

Sydni laughed. "That I know."

"You know you have more than one agenda here, Syd. You need to get him on board with the proposal and get on board with the merger."

Sydni swept an errant curl off her face. "I know," she said without conviction.

Gabriel reviewed the proposal. Without the distraction of Sydni in the room he could pay closer attention to the information. Slowly, he looked through each part of the finely detailed plan, the steps, the rollout and the publicity. He grudgingly admitted that it was brilliantly put together. But if he went along with it, he would ostensibly be thumbing his nose at his family's legacy and the dynasty that was built by his father.

He relaxed against the high-back leather chair. For the past decade he'd worked hard to build, maintain and grow the enterprise that his father began and his brother continued. He had equal share in the mega-million-dollar corporation. Although he was solely in charge of export and oversaw a staff of hundreds with offices in several parts of the world and was endowed with a fortune, the *entire* business was not totally his. In his gut he knew that it was time to make his move. The launch of his resorts was set up to attract and cater to those who were able to enjoy and afford the extravagance that he envisioned for his locations. All of his life he and his brother had never wanted for the luxuries of life—all they'd wanted was their parents. He wanted to be able to give something back for all that he had acquired. Sydni's proposal made that possible by allowing a portion of the resort to be made available to lower-income families. The unique and daring venture would clearly set his resorts apart from his competitors'.

He expelled a long breath and flipped the folder

closed. He ran a finger across his bottom lip. She had another week in Brazil. There was only so long that he could stretch out and delay giving her his decision. But he intended to enjoy every minute of working out the details. He'd deal with her being gone when she was gone and not a moment before.

"Everything is going well, Dad," Sydni said into the phone. Her father rarely, if ever, checked up on her during negotiations but she knew he had a personal interest in this deal being struck. Yet it was still hard for her to understand why merging with St. James Enterprises was so important. "I'm sure he will sign off on the proposal." She sat down on the side of the bed. "No. I haven't broached the merger idea yet.... I will. One thing at a time." She rested her head in her palm. "Yes. I'll keep you posted. Yes." She sighed and disconnected the call, then tossed the phone on the bed.

Quickly, she pushed up from the bed, gave her head a short shake and headed for the shower. She had a bit more than an hour to get ready before Gabriel arrived to pick her up, and the only thing she wanted to have on her mind was how to blow his.

When Sydni strutted across the lobby of the hotel, heads turned. Her wild spiral hair bounced and gleamed around her face and the body-hugging black spaghetti-strap minidress with its asymmetrical hemline did amazing things for her body and long legs.

Gabriel, who was enjoying a drink while he waited, slowly rose from the club chair and the aura of possessiveness that radiated from his muscular body and dark eyes signaled to everyone: *Look but don't touch. She is mine*. He set down his glass, straightened his jacket and cut the distance between them in three long strides. He took her forearm and pulled her close, placing a hot kiss behind her ear and whispering, "You are stunning…as always." He stepped back. "Ready?"

"Yes," she whispered over the pounding of her heart. She slid her hand through the bend at his elbow and they walked out to his waiting red Audi R8 Spyder convertible that was as sleek, sexy and gorgeous as they were.

"Nice car. Great color."

"It suits my mood tonight." Gabriel helped Sydni into her seat, hastily came around and got in behind the wheel. He gave her a quick look before taking off. "I spent all day sweating over a hot stove. I hope you will enjoy your dinner."

Sydni angled her body so that she halfway faced him. "*You* sweated…"

"And slaved," he added with a wink.

She giggled. "Right. I'm sure it will be wonderful. What's on the menu?"

"Ahhh, a three-course meal on the veranda, dessert, wine—maybe something stronger—a walk along the beach, then back to the house, maybe a little music and dancing, a long night of making love and breakfast in the morning."

A shiver scuttled up her spine. "Well-thought-out menu. I didn't hear anything on the menu about business."

He gave her a quick look. "Because it isn't." He turned on the music and sped through the streets of Rio to his home, with the sultry night wind whipping around them.

Sydni was once again taken aback by the sensual opulence of Gabriel's home. It was stylish, high-end, yet ultimately inviting. She felt embraced by every room in the house. And there were so many hidden treasures, from the small pieces of sculpture tucked away on built-in shelves to an ordinary-looking stack of books on an end table that turned out to be first editions worth millions, to artwork and antique mirrors. The intermittent splashes of color throughout evoked an additional sense of surprise.

"Make yourself comfortable. Would you like some wine before we eat?"

"Yes. I would." She placed her purse on the coffee table and followed him over to the bar that held a wine cooler.

Gabriel took out a bottle of imported white wine and poured two glasses. He handed one to her and held his up for a moment in salute. "To another wonderful evening."

Sydni lightly tapped her glass to his and took a sip.

"Let's step outside." He took her by the hand and led her to the back veranda.

She put her hand to her chest when her gaze landed on the incredible display. A circular table was draped in white linen and was topped by two white tapers with tiny flames that danced in the night. White china, gleaming silverware and two glass bowls filled with a garden salad completed the table setting. Along the far side of the enclosed space was a longer table, also draped in white linen, and lined with covered silver platters. Two bottles of wine peeked out from a bucket of ice.

Gabriel pulled out a seat from the table and helped her to sit. He walked over to the buffet and began to place seared bass, saffron rice and a mix of steamed green vegetables onto her plate and brought it to the table before fixing his own. He joined her at the table.

Sydni opened her linen napkin and placed it on her lap.

"This looks and smells delicious."

"I hope you will enjoy it."

"I'm sure I will." She began with the fresh garden salad that she lightly sprinkled with olive oil and vinegar.

Gabriel leaned back in his seat, sipping his wine. He stared at her from above the rim of his glass. "Did I tell you how incredible you look tonight?"

Sydni felt her face heat. "Yes, I think you did mention that." Her mouth flicked with a smile.

"Then let me tell you again. You are stunning and I cannot wait until the meal is over and I can take you to my bed and remind you again and again."

Sydni pressed her knees together. What do you say to something like that, something so bold and enticing? She finished her salad and pulled her plate toward her. "So…what are your thoughts on the proposal?" she asked, shifting, she hoped, into safe territory.

He gave a slight shrug. "I'm still considering."

"That's a start. Did you at least like the ideas?"

He set his wineglass down on the table and leaned slightly forward. He picked up his knife and fork and cut into his bass, put a piece in his mouth and chewed slowly. Finally, he looked at her. "Not tonight. Not tonight," he repeated in a cadence that sounded like a song. "Tonight we focus on each other, on pleasing each other. The proposal will be there tomorrow and the day after." He reached across the table and covered her hand with his. "But this moment, right now, right here…" He slowly shook his head without taking his eyes from her. "We'll never have this again."

She knew she was seated on the veranda surrounded

by the pull of the ocean, warm night air, an amazing meal and a devastatingly sexy man; and she knew that she had on all of her clothes, but she would be willing to swear that Gabriel St. James née Santiago had stripped her naked and made love to her with no more than a look and his words.

Sydni reached for her wine and took a sip. "Fine."

"This weekend begins the Carnival festivities. Dancing in the streets, parties, food, parades…" He chuckled. "Quite the spectacle." He angled his head. "I hope you will let me accompany you to some of the festivities."

"I'd like that."

"Good. I want to take you to see *Cristo Redentor*."

"Christ the Redeemer…on Corcovado Hill."

Gabriel grinned. "Very good. You've done your homework."

She smiled. "I would absolutely love to go. I've only seen pictures."

"Ahhh, yes, the personal experience is one that you will always remember." He finished off his food. "There are many things that I want to show you while you are here so that you will have fond memories of my homeland." He fixed his gaze on her. "I don't want you to forget…anything." He slowly rose and came around to her side of the table, extended his hand and helped her to her feet. "Let's walk."

They stepped out of the covered veranda into the warm night that was tempered by the cool breeze blowing in off the ocean. They walked in the direction of the beach.

Sydni reached down and took off her shoes and dangled the straps from her fingertips as they neared the sand.

Gabriel possessively slid his arm around Sydni's slim

waist and eased close. They were hip to hip as they strolled along the sand.

"Did you always want to be a high-powered executive? Is that what you saw for yourself?" Gabriel asked, the question taking her a bit by surprise.

She tilted her head to look at him. Her brows flicked as she thought. "I don't think I actually put those words to what I wanted to do. I knew for a long time that I liked people. I enjoyed working with them. In my father's business we are in contact with all types of business people from start-ups to mega-corporate heads and everything in between. That part of the business I leave to my father. What I was always fascinated with was the people and what they represented and if they were getting their message across to their consumer." She drew in a breath. "Most branding companies deal with the product. I chose to deal with the person." She glanced at him. "What about you? Did you plan to walk in your father's footsteps?"

He chuckled. "I wasn't given much of a choice. A family business is handed down, ideally, to the sons who will carry it forward." His brows drew together. "I've done what was expected. Can I say it was what I've always wanted?" He paused momentarily. "It's hard to say. It's difficult to separate the power, the wealth and the notoriety from personal wants and desires."

She thought about that for a moment and considered the position that she'd been put in because of her father's wants that went against her own. "What *are* your wants and desires?"

Gabriel stopped walking and turned her into his embrace. His warm gaze heated her cheeks. "Right now... or sometime in the future?"

Her heart jumped in her chest. "Both."

"Right now…I want to spend the rest of this evening, and whatever time we have left together, getting to know you. As for the future…" He gave a slight shrug. "I'm sure it will take care of itself. It always does."

She wished she could share his cavalier approach, but she knew what she was up against—time. She didn't have much of it. But when he took her in his arms moments later and kissed her as if his life and hers depended on it, she threw caution to the warm winds.

Gabriel thoroughly seduced her that night, using every skill in his arsenal of seduction; from the walk along the beach, wading in the warm waters, gazing at the twinkling stars and sipping wine to dancing under the moonlight.

By the time they crossed the threshold of his bedroom they were hungry for each other, their appetites teased by the evening of what they imagined to be in store.

He undressed her slowly, uncovering each part of her as if she were a work of art. He planted hot kisses along her collarbone, down the swell of her breasts. He got down on his knees and sampled the essence of her until her knees wobbled and her thighs trembled and her cries of his name filled the air.

Gabriel lifted her into his arms and carried her to his bed. He stood above her, gazing at the magnificence of her body. He was completely consumed by her. All sense of reason left him when he was with her. He knew the downfall of every great man was a woman. He didn't care. The only thought in his head while he stripped out of his clothes was having her, possessing her and branding her as his.

When he entered her and the hot wet walls of her enveloped him, he was lost. He was no longer a separate being. He was one with her. The silken feel of her surrounding him made him want to weep with pleasure. He wanted her. He wanted all of her. His body took on a life of its own, plunging into her again and again and again, straining for release while at the same time never wanting this sublime pleasure to end.

She clung to him. Her arms and legs wrapped around him like vines, binding him to her, riding with him on an exquisite high. Each time that he drove into her she wanted more—deeper, harder, faster. She couldn't get enough. She would never get enough of this man if they lived ten lifetimes together. This feeling, this feeling of being treasured, of connecting on this level with another human being was what had been missing from her life. It wasn't just great sex. She knew that and she knew that soon it would end and so she wept—tears of unimaginable joy and pain and the loss that was to come as her climax rocked her to the epicenter of her being and burst into hundreds of brilliant lights behind her eyes. And beyond the pounding of their hearts and her screams of release and Gabriel's moans as he emptied into her, she swore she heard him whisper, "Please don't leave me."

Chapter 11

"I've cleared my calendar for the rest of your stay," Gabriel said to her as he turned on the jets of the shower. He took off her robe and gently suckled her still-tender nipples, enjoying the sound of her moans before guiding her under the steaming waters. "I don't intend to let you out of my sight."

Sydni stepped under the pulsing spray and turned toward him. "Is that right? What if I have other plans?" she said in a teasing voice.

"Cancel them."

Her eyes widened for an instant when she witnessed the resolve in his.

The water slid over and between them. He reached around her and took the shower gel from the shelf, poured some into his palms and began to lather every inch of her body and then rinsed her with tender loving care.

"Turn around," he ordered, his voice suddenly thick

and raw. She did as she was told. Gabriel pressed his large hand against the back of her neck, bending her forward. He looped his arm beneath her belly and pulled her rear end toward his bulging erection. "Spread your legs."

Before she had a chance to utter a response he plunged inside her with such force that it lifted her up onto her toes. "Aggggg!"

Air hissed from between his teeth. His eyes slammed shut from the intensity of pleasure that ripped through him. For a moment he couldn't move. All he could do was allow the moment to wash over him, try to memorize this instant. But then she ground against him and white lights flashed.

He growled deep in his throat and pushed up into her again. She returned the move with the same fervent drive, bracing her hands against the tiles to support them both as they dueled each other, attacking and retreating and coming back for more until the inevitable began to build, coursing through their veins like hot lava waiting to erupt. And it did, in spectacular fashion, leaving them too weak to stand, and they sank together to the shower floor letting the now cool waters temper their heat.

Gabriel was good at his word. Much to his brother's annoyance he'd canceled and rescheduled all of his meetings.

"You've really fallen for her, haven't you?" Max asked while Gabriel made arrangements to have his helicopter readied.

Gabriel gave his brother a cursory glance. "What if I have?"

"The Santiago men have never had lasting relationships with women. We aren't built that way."

"Maybe it's time for a change, brother."

"Don't be a fool. In a matter of days this woman will be gone and back to her life and probably to a man in the States and you will be left with your cock swinging in the wind. And for what?"

He threw a glance at his brother. "You don't know what you're talking about and you don't know Sydni," he said from between clenched teeth.

Max tossed his gorgeous head back and laughed. "The fateful words of a man who has been whipped. You act as if you have never been between a pair of wonderful thighs before."

Gabriel slammed his palm down on the table. "Enough! I've lived by this archaic, macho Santiago code all my life. No more!" He stormed past Max, who maintained an amused expression on his face.

"Good luck, brother," he murmured. "You are going to need it."

"A helicopter ride?" Sydni said when Gabriel came to meet her at her hotel.

"Yes. I want you to see some of our sights from the air. And pack some of your things."

She frowned in confusion. "Pack? For what, a helicopter ride?"

"No. You'll be staying at my home until…"

She planted her hand on her hip. "What if I don't want to do that?"

He stepped up to her, wrapped his arm around her waist and pulled her hard against him. There was no missing the tight knot in his pants. "Tell me you don't want to spend the nights with me and share breakfast in the mornings, and I will forget the request."

She swallowed over the lump in her throat. It was just so damned hard to think clearly when he was staring at her like that, when he smelled so good and felt so good and he made her remember what those nights and mornings were like. She wiggled out of his arms and stepped back to gain some perspective. It wasn't much better.

"I'll bring a toothbrush…and a pair of panties," she said with as much defiance as she could summon.

He grinned wickedly. "I love to watch a beautiful woman in nothing more than a toothbrush and panties."

She huffed and shook her head, biting back a smile. Turning on her heel, she went to pack a small bag. She chuckled to herself as she tossed in toiletries, a bathing suit, a sundress and something sexy for a night on the town, and, of course, her toothbrush and panties.

Sydni had never been in a helicopter before and her first experience was one that she would not soon forget. The roar of the blades, the surge in her stomach as the bird rose straight up—unlike an airplane—and the incredible sensation of flying and being able to witness the world directly below. What was the most awesome aspect of the experience was that Gabriel was flying the chopper himself. When he got behind the controls, told her to strap in and started switching levers and talking into his headset—getting and receiving instructions—it was a turn-on akin to their morning in the shower. She nearly had an orgasm.

The landscape of Brazil spread out before them as they rose and dipped across the city.

Over the rumble of the engine and the blades, Gabriel pointed out Sugarloaf Mountain and the beaches of Ipanema. What completely took her breath was seeing what is considered one of the new Seven Wonders of the world—Cristo Redentor—sitting majestically atop the Corcovado Hill.

"The original design of the statue was created by a Brazilian, by the name of Heitor da Silva Costa," Gabriel shouted over the roar. He handed Sydni a set of headphones and indicated that she should put them on. "He was also in charge of the construction and worked on the project with a French sculptor, Paul Landowski. It took five years to build and was funded mostly with donations."

"Incredible."

"One of the big tourist attractions," he added.

"I see."

From their height soaring above the statue they could see the lines of tourists climbing the stone steps to reach the base of the statue.

They continued their aerial tour for about another half hour with Gabriel continuing to point out more sights of interest.

To say that it was a thrill ride would be an understatement. Sydni was totally turned on and couldn't wait until they returned to Gabriel's place so that she could show him just how turned on she was.

Over the ensuing days Sydni and Gabriel spent every waking moment together, talking, dancing, participating in the Carnival frenzy, swimming in the ocean, visiting eclectic restaurants and nightclubs. They talked, they laughed, they shared their feelings, watched old movies, and they made love as long and as often as they could, wherever they could. If it was on the beach or in a tight room in a nightclub, in the kitchen, on the floor, the couch, the bed and even in his office, it didn't matter where as long as they could connect in the most intimate of ways.

They forgot about business and the future. The only thing that mattered to either of them was each other.

"I know it's crazy," Sydni lamented to Lynn after finally leaving Gabriel with the promise that she would return in time for dinner. "But…I don't want to be without him. Thinking about it gets my stomach in knots."

Lynn sat down next to Sydni. "I've never seen you like this, so taken in by a man."

"I've never felt like this."

"Syd, let's be realistic. How long have you known him, a couple of weeks? And he has you twisted inside out. You have a job to do and you have yet to get him to sign off on the proposal, not to mention that you *haven't* mentioned the merger. We leave in two days."

Sydni pushed up from the couch. "I know that! I know all of that. It doesn't change how I feel." She paced.

"How do you know that he's not using you for a good time and when you leave it's simply goodbye? He does have a reputation. His whole family does. Meanwhile, you can barely take a breath without him. Come on, girl. This is not you. You have to get your head back in the game."

Sydni slowed her step. One by one, all the reasons why she was hired in the first place came hurtling toward her. Her stomach seesawed. What if Lynn was right about Gabriel? She didn't want to believe it, but it could be true. She'd let his looks, his charm and his lovemaking disconnect her from reason. There was no way that anything could become of their relationship. Deep in her soul she knew that, as much as her body tried to tell her otherwise.

She expelled a long breath. "You're right," she finally said barely above a whisper.

Gabriel's driver arrived at Sydni's hotel at five. The plan was an early dinner, perhaps a drive along the mountains and then home for the night. Mentally, she'd steeled herself against any of his advances. Tonight they must get back to business. She could not delay the process any longer.

The driver dropped her off and she let herself in. She placed her purse on the table and went in search of Gabriel. He liked to spend this part of the day on the veranda, taking in the air and the view. She walked to the back of the house, sure that she would find him.

She heard the murmur of his voice before she saw him. The door to his office was open. His back was to her and he was on the phone. She started to walk away but his words reached out and held her in place.

"We'll see each other soon, sweetheart. I promise. Yes. I love you, too."

Sydni's heart nearly stopped and then began to race. Her face heated. Somehow, she managed to turn around and go back the way she had come. She went to the bar in the living room and poured herself a glass of wine. She downed it in one long swallow. Her hand shook. Lynn was right. What had she been thinking? She poured another glass. That was the problem. She hadn't been thinking, but she was now. She finished off the wine and lifted her chin and blinked back the burn in her eyes.

"You're here. I didn't hear the car pull up," Gabriel

said as he walked up behind her and placed a kiss at the base of her neck.

Her body tightened. His arm glided around her waist. His hand slid across her belly, then up to cup her breast in his palm. "I've missed you," he breathed into her ear.

As always her body responded even as her mind fought against it. She squeezed her eyes shut as the electric sensations of his touch rippled through her. She wanted to weep at her own weakness. But now was not the time for tears. She drew in a breath and stepped out of his reach. She turned to face him and his expression registered surprise and concern.

"What's wrong? Don't tell me it's nothing. It's in your eyes and in your body. I know your body."

"It's just that…I leave in two days and we still have unfinished business to settle. It's what I came here for."

His expression tightened. The corner of his mouth jerked. He stepped back, then walked around her to the bar. He took a tumbler from the counter, then selected a bottle of bourbon and poured it without ice. He gave her his back as he downed the amber liquid. "You're right. Sometimes distractions get in the way and you forget." He turned to face her. "We'll make sure not to let that happen again." His gaze bore into her and she felt a chill that stiffened her limbs. "Some of my best deals were settled during a good meal. Since we are back to more formal terms, let's eat in the dining room, discuss this proposal further and then, if I'm satisfied with the answers, I will sign your deal and you can leave. I'll have Hector take you back to your hotel. Fair enough?"

Her throat was so tight that she barely managed to say that it was perfectly fine with her.

Gabriel turned on the music to fill in the periodic gaps of their silence during dinner. The only conversation between them was Gabriel's probing questions into the viability of hosting lower-income families at his five-star resorts. "I'm not in the business of losing money," he said, his voice distant and cold.

"You won't be. The media attention, the sponsors and your base will more than compensate for any short-falls—it's a win-win situation." She took a sip of her wine. "If you don't find this proposal suitable to your needs, I know that I can sell the concept elsewhere."

Gabriel's jaw clenched. "All business with you, Ms. Lawson. I rarely make mistakes, but it's clear I have this time."

Sydni flinched. She wanted to tell him that it was more than business, but there was no point. She was going home and he was going back to his life. There was nothing she could do to change that.

As promised, once dinner was over he went into his study and retrieved the hard copies of the proposal.

Sydni didn't know how much longer she'd be able to stand there and not break down. She hadn't known until now what it would feel like not to have the heat, the tenderness and the joy of Gabriel surround her. It felt as if a part of her had been hollowed out. He'd barely looked at her all night and when he did his eyes were cold and distant. The only thing they talked about was the fine points to the proposal and how soon it would be implemented. That was what she wanted—wasn't it?

He returned to the dining table where he'd left her. The folder was in his hand. He dropped it on the table. "Your proposal. Signed and sealed, as you Americans say. Yes?" He smiled but it didn't reach his eyes.

"Thank you. I know you'll be happy with the results and so will your new clientele."

She stood and put the contract inside her pocket-book. "I guess you can ask Hector to take me back to the hotel now," she said, fighting to keep the tremor out of her voice.

"Let me make love to you one last time," he whispered. "Take off your clothes."

She blinked. "What?"

"Undress for me, as I cannot promise that I will be as kind to them as you."

The flame from his eyes lit up inside her belly and went racing through her limbs. She stepped back and nearly stumbled. Gabriel advanced. "Take them off. Please," he repeated, and she was certain that if she didn't he really would rip them off her.

She began to unbutton her blouse and slid it from her shoulders.

"The rest."

Her heart was pumping a mile a minute. She reached behind her and unhooked her bra. She let it drop. His eyes caressed her bare breasts as surely as if he'd touched her. Her breath hitched.

"Finish." His voice had grown raspy.

She unzipped her skirt and let it fall around her feet, leaving her only in her panties. His gaze flashed. His nostrils flared.

She hooked her thumbs around the band of her panties and wiggled out of them. She watched the rapid rise and fall of his chest as if he'd been running. Then, all at once he advanced on her, propelling them both across the room until she fell back on the couch.

Gabriel sank to his knees. "Open your legs for me," he commanded.

Oh, my God. She was going to come in one second.

Sydni spread her thighs. Gabriel roughly grabbed

her hips and pulled her toward him until her everything was open and spread inches away from him.

He lowered his head and paid homage to her with his mouth, his tongue, his teeth. Teasing, tasting, suckling, licking, nibbling, drinking of her until her body lifted up as if electrified and a climax so powerful slammed through her over and over and shook her like a rag doll, while Gabriel held on to her, forcing her to climb higher.

After what felt like forever, she collapsed on the couch whimpering and shaking in the aftermath, but Gabriel had no intention of giving her a respite. He quickly undid his pants and kicked them to the floor along with his shorts. He tore his T-shirt over his head and tossed it onto the pile of clothing.

His cock was so hot and so hard that he felt as if it would either explode or break if he didn't find his way into her and relieve the agony. He wanted her in his bed but he'd never last that long. Not now.

He returned to his knees and lifted her legs over his shoulders and entered her in one long, deep plunge, knocking the air out of her lungs.

Her scream of release once again jettisoned through him and ignited his own gush of sublimation.

Their pounding hearts and rapid breaths slowly quieted. Gabriel lowered her legs from around him and pulled himself upright. He turned away, gathered his clothes and went into his bedroom without a word.

Through silent tears Sydni picked up her clothes and slowly got dressed. She'd never imagined that she would feel so sad and empty inside at the thought of never being with him again. But business, ambition and distance trumped the heart. As much as she wanted to run as far away from him as possible, she couldn't leave. She was miles away from her hotel and Hector was nowhere to be found. That reality only added salt to her wounded spirit. She could call Lynn and tell her to come and get her, but she didn't want to see the "I told you so" in her eyes.

She walked out back, started toward the beach and sat down on the bench facing the water. She wasn't sure how long she sat there going over everything that had transpired since she'd arrived in Rio, the complicated feelings she had for Gabriel and the mission that she'd been sent on. Whatever her mind had thought this was between them, clearly it was something else. There was someone else that he was in love with and she was an idiot to ever think that it could be her. What she needed to do now was get her head together, pack up and go home. In a few months this would all be a distant memory, a sexy fling with a sexy South American bachelor.

Sydni glanced out toward the horizon. Who was she kidding?

Gabriel stood in front of the panoramic window of his bedroom and looked at the lone figure sitting on the bench. His insides twisted. What had he done to turn her so cold, to no longer want anything from him but his signature on a piece of paper? He'd done everything he could to show her how he felt about her, show her that he had fallen in love with her, as crazy as that may seem. And yet... He turned away. Max was right.

Sydni didn't hear him come up behind her. She turned with a start at the sound of his voice.

"Hector is out front. He'll take you back."

She glanced up at him but he wouldn't meet her eyes.

She stood. "Thank you." She walked past him and back toward the house.

"Have a great life," he said to her back.

Her body flinched but she kept walking.

Chapter 12

"What do you mean, you didn't discuss the merger with him?" Paul boomed.

Sydni sat across from her father at the conference table. "I decided against it."

"*You* decided against it? Since when do you make unilateral decisions for this company?"

She stared her father down. "You sent me there to do the job that I was hired to do. I did it. You also sent me because you trust my judgment. There is no reason for this merger other than to build a bigger Lawson empire," she said with disdain. "What St. James does as a business goes against everything that we stand for. It's not a good fit for our company. If you want a merger with St. James Enterprises, then I suggest that you handle it or find someone who will. As a matter of fact, I'm turning over the St. James project to Lynn so that I can concentrate on other things." She stood. "Now if you'll excuse me, I have a lot of work to catch up on and clients who are depending on me." With that she got up and strode out.

Paul sat back in his chair. A smile on his face. He always knew his daughter had a tough streak in her. She'd proven it. He wanted a merger with St. James even though his associates had advised against it. He knew that Sydni was shrewd and honest. It was her opinion that mattered. What he also wanted was to see if his daughter had what it took to stand up to him and she had. That was the kind of strength and the wisdom that she would need when he handed Epic over to her. It was also clear that she'd fallen hard for Gabriel St. James. He was curious to see how that would all pan out. For as smart and business-savvy as Sydni was, she was also stubborn as a mule.

It had been almost three months since Sydni had walked out of his door, his life and back to whatever or whomever she'd left behind. He'd thought that at the very least they would be in contact because of their business dealings, which, much to his annoyance, were well under way—in Lynn's very capable hands. The reviews in the international press had already begun, interviews were scheduled and his altruistic endeavors were creating the positive buzz that Sydni had promised. He had nothing to complain about. The investors and contractors for the resorts were on board, contracts had been signed and plans to break ground were scheduled. Everything was going according to plan except that he had not planned to fall in love with a woman who lived halfway around the world and who made it clear that she was only in it for business reasons.

Knowing all this and having his hands full with his new venture didn't stop him from boarding a plane from

Brazil to Louisiana and standing in front of the reception desk at Epic International and asking to see Sydni Lawson.

Since her return from Rio, Sydni had buried herself even deeper into her work than ever before. She wanted her head so clouded with other people's issues and her body so exhausted from the long hours that she wouldn't be able to think about Gabriel or long to be held and loved by him. But nothing she did could strip her of the memories or the longing. There wasn't a day that went by that she didn't think about him, remember the fun, the laughter, the days and the nights and his words of love to another woman.

She'd done what she had always rolled her eyes at other women for doing—seeing or hearing your man do wrong and walking away without a word only to be told later that "it wasn't me," or "you got it all wrong." Every time she thought about that night she could kick herself. So the last thing she would have ever expected was to hear the receptionist on her phone telling her that *the* Gabriel Santiago was in the waiting area, requesting to see her.

Sydni hung up the phone and worked on remembering how to breathe. Her heart was beating so fast that she grew lightheaded. Gabriel. Here. What… Oh… She had to call Lynn.

She hit Lynn's extension on the phone. Lynn picked up on the second ring.

"Hey, what's up?"

"He's here," she hissed into the phone.

"Who's here?"

"Gabriel. He's at the front desk waiting to see…"

Her attention was drawn to the commotion an instant before her door was opened.

"Ms. Lawson, I'm so sorry. I asked him to wait."

Sydni slowly hung up the phone and stood. *Oh. My. God.* He was more devastatingly handsome than anything she could have remembered. A flush of heat flooded her. "It's all right, Cherise. Mr. Santiago won't be staying long."

"Yes, Ms. Lawson."

"Close the door behind you, please, Cherise." She gripped the edge of her desk to keep from wobbling on her weak knees. "What are you doing here?"

Gabriel's gaze glided over her from head to toe, re-committing every inch to his memory. "I came for you."

She was definitely going to pass out. She swallowed. "Really?" Her right brow rose skeptically. "You came a long way for nothing. The days of our being together are over."

He tilted his head slightly as he processed her words. Then his mouth twitched in a grin. "Good to know that you haven't lost the spice that I enjoy so much."

She was not going to let him charm her out of her panties. Not this time. She folded her arms as if that could keep him at bay. "What do you want, Gabriel?"

He advanced toward her, slowly, like a predator setting up his prey. She held her breath and held up her hand to stop him but he kept coming until he was a heartbeat away, forcing her to either stare at the expanse of his chest or up into his eyes.

Gabriel clasped her upper arms and a jolt of electricity hit them both.

"I've missed you," he confessed, and the heat of his words melted the ice around her heart.

Her eyes filled with the tears that for months she'd refused to shed. She pressed her lips tightly together.

"I don't want to think about another day without you."

Tears slid down her cheeks. He wiped them away with the pad of his thumb only for them to return. So he kissed them away, nourishing himself on the salt of her tears. He wrapped his arms around her and pulled her tightly against his body and for the first time in months he felt alive again.

His fingers threaded through the spiral twists of her hair and pulled her head back to give him access to the tenderness of her neck and the lush sweetness of her lips.

She moaned with incomprehensible longing as he took her mouth, reclaimed what he knew to be his, what must be his. He'd come for her and he would not leave without her.

He broke the kiss and held her face in the palms of his hands. "I love you, Sydni. That's why I came all this way. I came to say that to you."

Sydni blinked back her surprise as reality settled in as the third presence in the room. She stumbled back a step. Her brows drew together in a frown of hurt and confusion. "Love me? The same way you love the woman you were talking to that last night?"

Now Gabriel was stunned. "What woman? What are you talking about?"

Sydni spun away from him and got some distance between them so that she could think and regain clarity. She turned toward him. "That night when Hector dropped me off, I heard you on the phone when I came to look for you. You were in your office. You... You said, 'I can't wait to see you. I love you, too.' And then you had sex with me." Her chest heaved. She pressed her fist to her mouth to muffle her hurt.

"And you treated me as if I were no more than a business transaction," he tossed back, and walked toward her and kept coming until he had her pressed against the wall. "You overheard me talking to a woman I love.... My sister, Isabelle."

Sydni stiffened. *That's what they all say* was her first thought. "What sister? You don't have a sister."

"I thought you were better than that. You are so thorough with everything else."

"What are you saying?"

"You should have researched both sides of the family. Isabelle is my mother's daughter from her second marriage. She's nineteen and she lives in Portugal. She was supposed to visit with me for Carnival but it didn't work out."

"Why didn't you ever say anything?"

"I'd wanted to surprise you with her arrival, have my sister meet the woman I'd fallen in love with. When the plans fell through, it wasn't necessary. Had you only asked me." His jaw clenched. He ran his hands down her arms. "Was it so easy for you to believe the things that had been written about me that you would believe that I could make love to you with all that is in me and be in love with another woman? I suppose—as you Americans say—you didn't believe your own hype."

He stepped back. "The man that you created on paper is the man that I truly am. That other man that the world thought they knew, *he* was the fabrication. But you weren't able to see the difference." He took another step back. He pressed his hand to his chest as if his heart truly hurt.

"Believing that you were in love with someone else...

made it easier to leave." She shook her head as the words tumbled out. "I could hold it against you and absolve myself—convince myself that on top of the distance and our lives being so different, that you weren't the one." Her voice broke. "And as long as you weren't the one…I couldn't get hurt and I could stop loving you. I should have…"

The rest of her confession was swallowed up in his kiss.

Lips and tongues that were long denied access to each other savored the taste, the feel and the reconnection. Before either of them knew what was happening they were on Sydni's couch. Her skirt was up over her hips. He pushed her light sweater up to her neck to expose her breasts to his eager mouth. With his free hand he freed himself, tugged her panty aside and found his way back home.

The contact was powerful enough to make them both gasp in awe while shivers of delight spiked through them. The coupling was hard, fast and raw, propelled with long overdue need. They clung to each other with Sydni burying her head in Gabriel's neck and he in her hair to muffle their cries as that first desperately needed climax ripped through them.

With great reluctance, Gabriel eased out of her. He kissed her. "Don't move," he said and stood, "you'll be a mess."

"I couldn't even if I wanted to," she murmured and closed her eyes. "Bathroom is that way."

He walked over to the closed door that he'd already surmised was the private bathroom. He found a hand towel, soaked it in warm water and quickly washed himself and straightened his clothes. He took a second hand towel and brought it to administer to Sydni.

After she'd gotten herself together and fixed her clothes, she had that weak and vulnerable feeling again. The same feeling she always had when she'd been made love to by Gabriel.

They sat next to each other on the couch.

"How long are you going to stay?" she finally had the courage to ask.

He gave her that smile that always had the power to melt her heart. "As you know, I am a man of means."

"So they say," she teased.

"And I've decided that since I have been a remade man—by the woman that I love—I should continue to live up to the image that she has created."

"What are you saying?"

"I'm saying that I should meet your father and tell him of my intentions."

Her pulse pounded in her ears. Her eyes raced over his face.

"In my country it is a sign of respect that a man goes to the father of the woman he loves and asks for the father's blessing."

She stopped breathing.

"We could live wherever you want, anywhere in the world. I could get used to Louisiana if that's what you choose."

He cupped her chin even as her tears fell onto his hand. "Spend your life with me. We can conquer the world together. Let me love you, take care of you, challenge you to do even greater things." He kissed her slow and sweet. "Be my partner, my friend, my soul, my lover, my wife."

Sydni could barely see him through the cloud of her tears. She was crying in earnest now. The days, nights and months of emptiness, loneliness and heartache were over. Theirs was not a conventional romance. It didn't follow the formula. Instead it was like finding an exotic flower in the middle of the desert. Its beauty took your breath away, and finding it in the most unlikely place made it that much more precious.

"What do you think of my proposal?" he softly asked.

"I wouldn't want to be the one to break a tradition," she said and wiped her eyes. She stood and took his hands, urging him to his feet. "My father's office is down the hall. He should be out of his meeting by now."

As they walked hand in hand down the hallway to Paul's office, Sydni knew that she was stepping into a brand-new world, filled with excitement, new experiences, challenges and the love of a man that she knew she didn't want to live without. It wouldn't be easy. Nothing worth having ever is. More than any venture she'd ever tried, love was a risky business, but it was a risk that she would willingly take over and over again with Gabriel at her side.

They stopped in front of Paul's office door. They looked at each other and smiled.

Sydni knocked and together they crossed the threshold.

* * * * *

BEATS OF MY HEART
Grace Octavia

To my family, for your constant support and encouragement in everything I choose to pursue.

Part I

"Losing Love in Manhattan"

"Oh, Sunny Bear, when will you be back? You can't go. You need to be here with me," Kimya said.

She was whining. Oozing out every syllable with so much sugar it made my back teeth ache. Her voice sounded like she'd been eating Pixy Stix all her life and she was just six years old. But she'd just downed three glasses of Perrier-Jouët…and two Percocet…and she was nearly thirty-two….

"You'll be fine, Kimya. I'll see you in the morning. I just need to hang with my girls tonight," I replied.

I knew my monotone response meant nothing to her. It was like white noise behind the track of her flimsy needs. I would've been silent, but I knew I needed to move my mouth so I at least appeared interested or she'd never release me from the ridiculous "emergency" meeting she'd called in her all-pink-everything *salle de bain* that looked less classic French than she and her MAC Lipglass-rocking interior designer Montrell planned for her Central Park West penthouse. While the goal was to compete with Mariah Carey's posh pad up the street, the result was too tacky for kindness and looked more like a gold-streaked pool of Pepto-Bismol.

"What if something happens, Sunny? What if I neeeeeed you? What if my car is late or I can't get into the studio to record tonight? You know I·gotta have this album in by the first week of June. I only have two weeks," Kimya said. More whining. But those were things I'd thought of; it was my job to think of those things. As the first assistant to the world's longest lingering R & B diva, Kimya Lee, I couldn't afford not to.

"Ron has the number to the second car and cash for a cab. I've double-checked your studio time. Everything will be fine," I stated.

She looked up at me through her hazel contacts as if I was a man who'd broken her heart and run off with her bestie and a bag of her money in the middle of some honky-tonk country song. It was her trademark pouty face that had graced the covers of so many magazines—dejected eyes, a crinkling pink lip, sunken cheeks. I was supposed to feel bad. Cancel my one night off in forever. But I couldn't. Not that night.

I looked away. Waited. It was the old standoff between me and Kimya. Nothing new. For five years I'd endured this mess of manic moods. I'd become what her therapists called Kimya's "emotional pillow." I'd originally taken the job in hopes of using the connections to birth my dream of hitting it big as a soul music producer—reimagining new classics, real music from my heart, from my soul, all about love—the music my father had introduced me to, the music he had loved. But babysitting Kimya's whims actually derailed me from both that dream and any love I could know to write about, so there I was engaging in a tantrum tussle more native to two-year-olds than two grown women.

After two accusatory minutes: "Fine, Sunny Bear. I guess we do need some time apart."

A part of me couldn't believe I was winning the standoff. That she was letting the "emotional pillow" go. I stepped back one foot at a time and looked at her insanely slender adult body sitting all helpless on the edge of the bathtub. Then I took a deep breath and headed for the door.

My friends are beautiful. Long brown arms and legs. Shiny hair, wild or coiffed. White teeth whose brace-trained neat appearance attests to a middle-class background. Neat nails polished with Ballet Slipper lacquer. Tiny pearls posted in their earlobes, or real diamonds, no smaller than pencil erasers, that chant in repetition to all ogling eyes mantras of good taste and sweet success in a city that can eat your soul.

With the vivacious lights of New York nights pulsating behind their heads in pictures from parties I couldn't attend fed copiously to my cell phone, they look so much like a teenage girl's fantasy of what life will promise once they escape home. Drinks everywhere. Men with muscles. Quirky poses. Stumbling to the last bar on a slick black street.

Because of that, most nights like this when I did make it out, I didn't feel as if I even belonged in the pictures. I know my diamond studs are fakes, the small gap between my front teeth makes it clear my soul-singing single father couldn't afford braces and I couldn't spare three hours out of any day to spend in the beauty salon. And I'm not long, or brown. I'm short and thick and so red I can hardly sit in the sun for more than ten minutes without burning. And I'll be too tired and too broke to stumble to the last bar. And Kimya will be calling.

Still, I made believe none of that would be my truth that night. It was my best friend, Leticia's, partner celebration. After just six years at one of the top entertainment law firms in New York City, she was tapped from high up to be a partner. She was crying when she'd called to tell me this. First Clayton's marriage proposal on Valentine's Day. Now this to set off the summer? It was her year! I promised three times I would be there. But walking to the back of downtown's Cipriani, where dozens of Moët-filled crystal glasses were held high midtoast in her honor, I wasn't sure anyone would've missed me if I'd stayed away.

After the glasses came down following a speech and a few tears I witnessed from the back of the crowd, I was reminded that it was ironically impossible to be invisible in a city populated by, like, eight million people.

"Oh, my God! It's Sunshine Embry! Risen from the dead like James Brown!" Candice Miller belted out when the toast was done and everyone had gone back to their sipping and schmoozing. The queen bee of my circle of friends, Candice was the stereotype of the perfect skin, the perfect body and the perfect life. She hadn't gained a pound since college. But she had three kids and a husband and her own pediatric care clinic in a rich enclave in Jersey. Dressed in a beige turtleneck dress that left little room for Spanx or any signs of underwear, Candice was the perfect centerpiece in a circle of short dresses and high heels that made top boutique mannequins of my friends. When she spoke, all eyes in the bedecked circle of women turned to me.

"Yeah, I made it. Late, of course," I said, smiling meekly and walking into a gauntlet of kisses and smiles from faces I'd known since freshman year at Howard.

"No probs, lovey! I'm sure you were doing something totally fabulous," Candice said, clueless of my pre-evening debacle in the *salle de bain.* "I swear I wish I had your life."

"Be careful what you wish for," I said, feeling my cell phone vibrating in the purple leather purse under my arm.

"Sunny!" I heard a Christmas-morning-worthy greeting and turned to Leticia running toward me effortlessly in her black patent leather stilettos with open arms and a smile so big someone just walking by on the street would know instantly that this gathering must be about her. "You made it!"

"Of course," I said, falling into her arms, and as our hearts touched I realized how long it had been since I'd seen her. I'd promised to take her out for drinks after Clayton's proposal, but our cell phone calendars couldn't sync. Then I was in Los Angeles the day of her luau-themed engagement party. "I couldn't miss this for anything."

Leticia kissed my cheek and pulled me into the crowd like the prodigal daughter who'd returned home.

Candice was standing to the side with two of our college buddies, Willow and Antha, obviously sizing up one of the white guys from Leticia's firm who was talking to an aging, long-necked, white blonde in a perfectly tailored black suit that let everyone know she was the man in charge.

"Lettie, darling," the blonde interrupted Leticia as

she tried to introduce me to some of her colleagues sitting along the sides of the wraparound mahogany bar. "You must slow down. Enjoy your moment." Her voice was fake British, but cute like one of those imported reporters on CNN.

Leticia dragged me to the woman and introduced us over a handshake, before explaining that I was Kimya Lee's personal assistant.

"One of our biggest clients," the Brit-blonde boss noted. She was holding a glass of Scotch that wafted aged, complex notes in the air.

"My *only* client," I replied. "Thanks to Let—*Lettie* for getting me the job." I had to keep reminding myself that Leticia went by *Lettie* at work. In college, she'd decided that the "icia" on her name would stop her from getting a high-paying job.

"Yes, our Lettie is something else, isn't she?" she pointed out.

Leticia had actually signed Kimya to the firm herself when Kimya was being sued for assaulting a hotel maid with a curling iron before a concert in Memphis. Leticia had a knack for connecting with big names in entertainment right when they needed her services. Because of her, the list of clients on the firm's roster included everyone from top hockey players to emerging rappers. All of whom, like Kimya, tended to need constant representation for this or that.

After pulling me around to a few more circles, where I was introduced as Kimya Lee's personal assistant so often I felt as if it was my name, Leticia and I ended up back where we'd started in the circle of mannequins.

Candice, Antha and Willow were obviously already buzzed from the champagne and taking pictures of one another holding stemmed glasses.

"Let's take a cab over to No. 8. One of my friends is having a party in the Rec Room. Cute crowd. Boys and good drinks," Antha said to the glowing phone in her hand as she posted one of the pictures online. She was one of Candice and Leticia's sorority sisters. They'd all pledged sophomore year, but I'd held out. I didn't get the point. I went to Howard because Roberta Flack went to Howard. Donny Hathaway. Meshell Ndegeocello. Angela Winbush. Eric Roberson. My father... I wanted to write my music in the same hallways where they'd sharpened their notes. Not learn sorority greetings and cook for big sisters.

"Boys? I am not looking for a boy," Candice joked in response to Antha's suggestion.

"Looking for? Whatever," Leticia said to Candice. "You're all the way married."

"I didn't say anything about 'hooking up,'" Candice pointed out. "I said 'look.' And after being married for seven years, Lord knows I need to look at something. Mr. Milton expects the fat fairies to come eat up the pork gathering around his stomach. I love that fool but his breasts are bigger than mine."

"Stop it!" Leticia ordered Candice, laughing with us. Milton had gotten extra jolly since we'd graduated. "Sunny, you coming with us if we go?" Leticia turned to me.

One by one, each of the mannequins dropped the leftover laughter from Candice's joke and looked at me. I'd already gone to the bathroom and saw five messages from Yves saying Kimya was asking for me and had managed to crawl to the wet bar in her bedroom to pour a glass of Moët she then spilled on Yves's head. Yves was the third personal maid I'd hired for Kimya in three months…and she'd lasted the longest. I really couldn't afford to lose her.

I answered Leticia uneasily. "Yes! I'm out for the night. It's all about my bestie. Right?"

Antha was right about No. 8. There was nothing but cute boys and drinks everywhere. And while the boys looked a little young for me, the more drinks we had, the more possible anything seemed. The interesting thing about being single over thirty was that older men wanted to date women who were younger than me and younger men wanted to date women older than me. I didn't have the tight body and thirsty eyes of a spring chicken and I failed to garner the deep pockets and settled stares of a cougar. I was right in the middle—still naive enough to fall for their lies, but too mature to stick around after I'd figured out the game.

We set up camp in one of the velvet-rope areas the manager cleared himself after one of the bartenders had whispered something in his ear while pointing at us. It was one of the perks of my job I seldom enjoyed. When people discovered who my boss was, I'd get the best seats, sites and service in hopes that the new relationship would lead to a connection with Kimya.

"What about you, Sunny? You're being all quiet. What's going on with you in your love life?" asked Willow, after we'd aptly drunk in the view and everyone was spilling the beans about their love lives. She was the sweetheart/pretty girl of our circle. She had a tiny blue-black afro that showed off her cherub cheeks.

"Nothing at all," I admitted. I hadn't been on a date in so long, I'd actually forgotten the last date I'd been on.

"Stop telling your filthy lies," Candice demanded

playfully over the music. "I know you have, like, a million dudes hanging around."

"My life is so crazy with Kimya, I hardly have time to meet any men," I complained, freeing one of the olives from the toothpick in my super dirty martini with my teeth and letting the salty matter settle on my tongue. Aside from not having enough time away from Kimya to actually get out there and meet people—beyond the odd mix of weirdos my online dating profile sent my way—I had realized long ago that most of the men I dated either wanted to get close to Kimya or use me as a way to get into the entertainment industry.

"Stop! You're living the dream. Rich men. Hanging out with celebs. Weren't you in Paris last month? You didn't scoop up a Parisian garçon?" Candice asked.

"Nope. Paris isn't *Paris* if you're working for a maniac 24 hours a day," I sulked.

"You couldn't find just a little 'me time'?" Candice asked.

"You're missing the point," I added.

"And that is?" Leticia pushed.

"I'm alone and I'm fine with it. I have other things to focus on."

"I'm not convinced," Antha whispered just loud enough over the music for me to hear. The crowd was thickening.

"Speaking of fine, what's up with Marlo? I saw his delicious brown ass on the cover of some crap magazine in my mailbox. Have you sampled that sausage?" Candice asked, eyeing some guy who looked as if he'd just passed the club's age restriction.

"First, you're gross. Second, I don't know what the hell 'sample that sausage' means—is that from one of those late-night Cinemax movies? Third, I wouldn't know what's up with that scoundrel," I said. Marlo was Kimya's older brother, who seemed the more arrogant and self-absorbed of the two. While Candice was correct in mentioning how delicious Marlo was, I'd had little interaction with him in my years working for Kimya. He seldom wore a shirt that didn't accentuate his muscles, and never was without a rowdy entourage of goons and groupies. Like most men in the entertainment world, he seemed to have that old "Peter Pan" problem of never wanting to grow old. He was thirty-three and had never been married and had no kids. Still, he'd managed to date every skank in the industry.

"Wait, did you just go all British 1930s on us? Scoundrel? Are you serious? Did you just call him that?" Antha giggled.

"She can call him whatever she wants. Just make sure you call him fine," Candice added, airing sentiments half of the women in the world felt for sure. "That tight body? Those eyes? That man has the most beautiful brown skin I've ever seen. Hands down! He's right of Morris Chestnut and left of Idris Elba."

"All of that's cool, but I like the fact that the man can actually sing. You know?" Antha said. "And while there are lots of R & B singers going around who look really good, most can't sing two notes without cracking."

After more chatter about Marlo's muscles and an alleged penis size Antha had discovered online, Candice managed to disappear onto the dance floor with the baby-faced dude, leaving Antha, Leticia and me to our budding bar tab and Leticia's wedding talk. Willow was hugged up with her new club boyfriend at the bar. My cell phone was vibrating so much it seemed to be syncing with the rhythm of the horrible techno music.

I finished my third martini and had just admitted to

myself that I was drunk when Antha saw one of her exes on the dance floor and left to dance with him.

"I'm happy you came out tonight, Sunny," Leticia whispered, leaning over to me.

"Of course," I said.

"I know you're stressed."

"What? I look stressed?"

"No. I mean, you're always stressed...like with Kimya."

"I'm fine," I affirmed. "And tonight isn't about all that. It's about you."

"Thanks, but it's not me I'm thinking about. It's you," Leticia said carefully.

"Why would you be thinking about me?" I asked, feeling my phone vibrating again.

"Just because...you know," Leticia said just as the DJ switched tracks to Kimya's last *Billboard* topper, "Love Monster," and the bass drowned Leticia out. She cut her eyes at the noise and comically covered my ears. We laughed and then I saw her eyes perk up at something over my shoulder.

"What? What is it?" I asked Leticia as the enthusiasm in her eyes slid down to her lips and morphed into a smile.

"What are you doing here?" Leticia's hands fell from my ears as she hollered happily in the direction of what was behind me.

I turned and there was Clayton climbing over the velvet rope behind our table.

Leticia rose daintily and kissed him. She purred "baby" a few times and then they giggled at something I couldn't make out over Kimya screaming, "Bloody mess, you're a bloody, bloody mess!" on the Megatron track coming through the speakers.

I stood to hug Clayton, too. I didn't know him very well. He and Leticia had only been dating like six months before they'd gotten engaged. He was a single, kid-free, college-educated investment banker she'd met on the same online dating website that kept sending felons, foot-fetish freaks and four-time forty-year-old fathers my way.

"Sorry to crash the party," Clayton whispered in my ear.

"It's cool," I said.

"He came to surprise me since he couldn't make it to Cipriani," Leticia whispered in my other ear while clasping my hand.

"I was working," Clayton followed up. "She sent a text saying you guys were heading over here, so I wanted to surprise her."

"No need to explain anything to me." I felt like they were talking to me so fragilely. Like I'd actually be angry or care that Clayton was there.

"Come have a seat," Leticia said, pulling Clayton in his navy blue Water Street suit to the table.

"I can't, Lettie." Clayton frowned a little. "I'm only here for a few. Gotta get back to the office. Came to see if you wanted a dance."

Leticia smiled graciously as she drank in his words with so much pride she had to be happy I was standing right there to witness it all.

"Do you mind, Sunny?" She looked at me as if I was the veritable ugly friend she was about to leave at the table holding all of the purses.

"Do your thing," I said.

As they weaved through the crowd, they stopped a few times for Antha and then Willow and then Candice to hug and smile with Clayton in pictures they took with their phones on the dance floor.

My phone was vibrating again. I pulled it out and there was a text from "Da Boss Lady"—Kimya had typed her name into the phone herself:

DA BOSS LADY: I fired Yves. Bitch was crazy. She was stealing from me.

ME: She wasn't stealing. Why did you do that? I thought we agreed that you wouldn't do that again until we found someone to replace her.

DA BOSS LADY: Calm down, pussycat. We'll find somebody. I guess you'll have to live with me again until we do. ☺ Come to the studio. We're going to do a remix for "Love Monster." Sean is up here.

ME: What? Why is Sean there? You know what happens with you two. Jesus, Kimya. Didn't he have that restraining order on you?

DA BOSS LADY: And I got one on his ass, too! You coming?

ME: Fine.

I clicked off the screen and scrolled to Yves's name in my call log. I pressed the phone to my ear. She picked up quickly and launched right into a diatribe in Creole that ended when I decided to hang up because I couldn't hear her over the club music. I needed to get her back. I had to. I couldn't move back in with Kimya. It was bad enough that she'd made me leave my father's old

Brooklyn brownstone I'd been renovating since he'd died, and rent an apartment three blocks away from her in Manhattan.

I went to the bathroom to try to get Yves on the phone again so I could explain that Kimya was just overreacting, and she should return to work in the morning.

Listening to Yves use every curse word available to her in her Haitian Creole, I hard-eyed a lesbian couple necking right on the sink in the bathroom. They rolled their eyes as if I was the problem and headed out as some girl who smelled like a burning marijuana factory entered.

"I know she's crazy...." was all I could say when Yves finally started complaining about Kimya in English. "But I can get you a raise."

Yves switched back to Creole and even in a different language I knew I was losing our debate.

"No amount of money. I can't be bought," she said in English. "How you do it? You smart. You pretty. Why you stay with her?"

"This isn't about me. Please work with me. Please, Yves. Come back."

"I no do it. I find better. You, too. God bless you, Sunshine. You good woman."

The line went dead and suddenly the loud screaming and music and even the water dripping down the drain in the sink, toilets flushing, the scent of urine on the floor and the weedy woman in the stall beside me, dim lights and fluorescent graffiti on the walls around me flooded my senses in a storm. I had to get out of there.

I found Leticia and Clayton on the dance floor moving too slowly and kissing. I stood there for a second not knowing if I should interrupt them.

And then my phone was vibrating again.

"I have to go," I said aloud, without knowing I was about to say anything.

Leticia and Clayton stopped kissing and looked at me as if I was a little sister who was bugging them.

"What?" Leticia asked.

"I have to go."

"But Clayton is about to go. We're about to have a toast," she said loudly over the music. "Can't you wait?"

"There's an emergency."

"We understand," Clayton said.

Leticia sharpened her eyes at him and looked back to me. "But I wanted to spend more time with you."

"I really have to go."

"Well, just let me walk you out. Get you a cab," Clayton offered gallantly.

"No, I'm fine," I answered quickly before turning to Leticia. "Lunch next week?"

"Sure." Leticia kissed me on the cheek and hugged me with her arms around my neck. "I love you," she whispered in my ear.

"Love you, too," I said. "Tell everyone I said goodnight."

Outside No. 8, the line was growing and showing that the people already inside the club weren't the real party people. They were the first shift. Black cars were lined up down the block. A police car sat waiting on the corner for the disorderly conduct that would come.

I stepped off the sidewalk and held out my hand for a taxi.

A last gush of winter wind blew in the air and made it a chilly late-spring night. I felt goose bumps immediately pop out up my arms. And then there was warmth. I looked down at a familiar hand on my forearm.

"Leticia, what are you doing out here?"

"I wanted to make sure you were okay," she said.

"Okay?" I kind of laughed and lowered my arm when it was clear every cab on the street had stopped to pick up other desiring passengers. "What am I, a nutcase or something? Why do you keep asking me that? Of course I'm okay."

"You weren't having a good time," Leticia claimed.

"I was fine."

"You hardly said a word."

"You left me to go dance with Clayton. What words was I supposed to use?"

"I'm sorry about that," Leticia whined and instantly I knew she'd taken my comment the wrong way. "I know I shouldn't have left you alone."

"Left me alone?" I repeated. "I didn't mean it like that. I was fine with being at the table by myself and—" I paused. "It's nothing. If I was quiet, it was because of something going on with Kimya."

"So this isn't about him?" Leticia asked.

"Clayton?" I responded, totally confused and feeling again that Leticia was handling me with kid gloves.

"No." Leticia looked into my eyes. "Your father."

"My father?" I felt everything around me threaten to flood again. As if I was back in the bathroom. "Wh-why?" I stuttered. "Why would you bring him up?"

"It's been six years…today." Leticia looked away and then back at me again. "Since he died. You know, that was why I was surprised that you came out tonight. I figured you'd, like— That it would be too much."

My heart thumped. I felt as if I was hearing something I shouldn't be listening to. I saw the date in my head. The numbers in a month, day and year and then my throat was closing up.

"I'd forgotten," I said with unexpected solemnity.

"Sorry," Leticia offered softly, apologetically.

"Six years," I said and then I felt tears coming fast to the corners of my eyes. I turned back to the street and raised my hand again for a cab.

"It's okay to be upset," Leticia said, reaching for my arm again, but I pulled away.

"I'm fine." I looked up the street through tears, away from Leticia and her eyes, her soft voice and careful words.

"No one expects you to—"

"It's been six years. Six," I said. "I should be fine."

A cab pulled up and stopped a few steps ahead of us.

"But the way you lost him—the way he died," she pushed cautiously, "we understand if you're not."

I opened the cab door and tossed my purse and vibrating phone inside.

"I'm sorry I ruined your party. I shouldn't have come. There's just too much shit with me. Too much drama. Kimya and—"

"You riding or not?" the cabbie yelled, staring at our stalling at the curb.

"One second," Leticia snarled at him in her Bronx-girl accent, and then switched fast to me. "We all have drama. That's it."

"No. This shit with Kimya is taking over my life."

"Well, quit. You're talented, Sunny. Your music is awesome. You can go somewhere else. Start your label. Wasn't that the point of working with Kimya in the first place?"

"I need the money. I don't have any connections yet," I said.

"You're going to figure it out," Leticia said. "You have to."

"I know." I let the tears slip away from my control.

"Well, isn't that lovely," the cabbie said sarcastically,

leaning out the window beside us. "Now, are you lovers going anywhere?"

I got into the backseat and after waving goodbye to Leticia standing alone in the street and giving the cabbie the address to Megatron's Brooklyn studio where Kimya was waiting, I dutifully wanted to call her and say I was on my way. But when I lifted the purse I realized I could hardly see it past all the tears in my eyes. My eyeliner and mascara and whatever else I put over my eyes to hide the bags a lack of sleep had created were making swirls and black clouds I could hardly see through in my eye contacts.

I remembered the last time I saw my father. His body so skinny and scaled, disappearing in his bed in his Brooklyn brownstone. All those years I'd begged him to take his AZT. Didn't he want to sing again? Didn't he want to see me get married? See his grandchildren? He laughed. "Sunny Baby, every act has a closing. Mine has come," he said. He'd died the next day.

The cabbie was looking at me in the rearview mirror. His asking me, "You alright?" turned into noise bouncing around the car, mutating from a question to Yves's comments: *How you do it? Why you stay with her?* I wiped more tears and then there was Kimya yelling at me: *You can't go. You need to be here with me.* And then there was Leticia: *You're going to figure it out.... You have to.*

"Stop the car," I ordered. "I have to get out."

"But we're about to get on the Brooklyn Bridge. You can't get out here," the cabbie said.

"Stop the car!" I hollered and it sounded as if every tear I'd been crying was turned into a dreadful bass in my voice that ripped through the taxi and pushed the cabbie's foot into the brake so hard we lurched forward and I heard the tires on the car behind us screech against the pavement.

I threw my money over the seat and opened the door.

"You're fucking crazy!" the cabbie said to my back as I started running.

Horns were honking and people were yelling at me, warning me to get back into the taxi and out of Brooklyn Bridge traffic, but I kept going and soon I kicked off my heels and just started running toward the sidewalk where walkers and bike riders leaned over the edge of the bridge to stare out into the night water that rippled between Manhattan and Brooklyn. I didn't know why I was running there. I just had to get away.

I dropped my purse on the concrete beside my foot and gripped the cool metal bar at the top of the railing that held people on the bridge. I looked out into the water, into the flecks of the moon skating over the blackness that went down so deep.

What was I doing there? Not on the bridge—in my life? I had no money. Didn't have the career I wanted. No love. Nothing was how it was supposed to be. I'd taken the job with Kimya to work on my music. To produce. But I was drowning in it. Losing any ability to create anything but a warm shoulder for Kimya to lean on. And nothing, nothing left for me or anyone else to love.

Was this it? Was this what I was supposed to be? Where I was supposed to be?

I looked up at the moon and a breeze came right at my face, pushing my hair back and delivering new loose tears from my eyes.

"What should I do?" I asked aloud. "Send me a sign. Send me something."

And just like that, my purse started vibrating.

I let go of the metal bar and bent down to get my phone out of the purse.

"Where are you? I'm waiting for you!" Kimya barked drunkenly. "I need you to stay with me tonight. Where are you?"

"I—"

"Hello? Sunny? Answer me!" she demanded.

"I—" I looked up at the moon.

"What? You're outside the studio?"

"No, Kimya."

"Well, where are you?"

I closed my eyes and said from inside myself somewhere, "I'm not coming."

"Yes, you are."

"No, I'm not!" I screamed from my darkness. "I'm not coming. I quit."

"What are you talking about?" Kimya said. "Look, I know you're upset about Yves, but I'll let her come back so you don't have to live with me. Okay?"

"I quit. That's it." I opened my eyes and looked at the moon again. "I quit."

I removed the phone from my ear as Kimya continued to speak and curse and even laugh.

I held the phone out over the railing, looked into the black water and let it go.

If ever I am retelling this part of the story, I'll say I was dreaming of Sunsiree Embry that night after I dropped my cell phone into the waters beneath the Brooklyn Bridge. My father. That I was six years old and playing with my holiday African American Barbie in his bedroom again. His cologne, a bottle of English Leather, is on the dresser where Black Ken and Black Barbie are kissing hard in my hands. The cologne falls and when the glass cracks against the dusty wooden floor beside the dresser, I immediately hear my father's feet coming up the stairs. In the brownstone where I grew up in Brooklyn the steps creak as if they're snapping in half with just a little step. It's like a warning. I should run away. Pretend I wasn't in the room when the bottle broke. But I can't move. My father is singing as he ascends. It's one of his songs. One he'd written that same summer I broke the cologne bottle. His voice is beautiful—even under the snapping steps. I am only six years old, but I know this is special.

When he enters the room, he is smiling. Says he was singing about me. I say, "But it was a bird. You were singing about a bird." He laughs. Sings the chorus and says as softly, "You're a bird." I think I smile. He reaches out, picks all of me up as if I'm still five. "Who broke that bottle of cologne?" he asks once I'm in his arms and we can both smell the English Leather. "A bird," I say. He laughs and puts me back on the floor. "Guess a bird needs to clean it up." He walks out laughing and singing that song again. I stand there listening.

The truth is I have no idea what I dreamed of that night. I know I took the train home. Got into my bed. Felt the silence of no phone ringing. No expectations. I thought of my father in the Brooklyn brownstone. The English Leather. I slipped into a restful blackness.

And then there was ice. Cold ice.

Very cold ice that pricked into the darkness of sleep like thorns into the tip of an index finger. Only bigger, sharper. I screamed before I even knew what it was. Before I even opened my eyes. I felt as if I was drowning or falling in my own bed. I was wet and cold and in shock.

I opened my eyes as I tried to jump up.

"That's right! Wake up, Sunny. Get up!"

"What? What the hell!" I hollered at the sight of

Kimya straddling my stomach, her knees pinning my arms to the bed. A pitcher with water trickling down the spout.

I looked from side to side and there was water and ice around my head.

"Are you crazy?" I screamed. "Get off me." I struggled and kicked my legs up at her back.

I heard yapping and looked down beside the bed at her twin white teacup Chihuahuas, Martin and Gina, trying to jump up at me. Montrell in his too-thick MAC Lipglass was sitting in the wicker chair beside the bed, filing his nails and popping his gum.

"Whoa!" Kimya laughed as if I was a skittish horse as she climbed off me with the half-empty pitcher in her hand. "Calm down, now! I had to wake you up. Montrell kept calling your name. You wouldn't answer."

"We thought you was dead to the bed, Ms. Thang," Montrell chimed in dramatically.

I sat up. Water and ice fell to my breasts, wetting my chest and stomach. A few squares hit the floor and Martin and Gina went to licking.

"I know you were out last night. Didn't know what you'd had—pills or something maybe—the way you were talking," Kimya said.

"You're nuts," I yelled, walking out of my bedroom to get a towel out of the bathroom.

"That's no way to speak to someone who just saved your life," Montrell called out.

"Right?" Kimya said, and she and Montrell went on congratulating one another for saving my life as I wiped my face before reentering the bedroom.

"No need to thank me for saving your life," Kimya was saying. She'd switched positions with Montrell, who was standing in the middle of my bedroom in red harem pants and Chuck Taylors.

He'd picked up Gina and was stroking her little skull while looking at me disapprovingly. "Where did you get that nightgown? Walmart?"

"Why are you here?" I asked, looking past Montrell to Kimya. "And why is he with you?"

"You weren't answering your phone. Didn't come to work this morning," Kimya replied.

"That's because I quit."

"And that's how I knew something was wrong with you, and I had to come here."

"You didn't have to come anywhere," I said. "How'd you get in anyway?"

"You gave me a key, silly Sunny. Remember?" Kimya smiled and held out my spare key.

"Whatever. You have to go anyway…all four of you," I said, walking to the door and expecting Kimya and her gang to follow me, but no one moved.

"Oh, no, she ain't trying to kick us out," Montrell said. "After I came over here to save her life."

Kimya laughed with Montrell. "Look, I heard what you said last night, but you can't quit on me," she said. "I'm having lunch with Mary and Kendu in Jersey today. I need you."

"I told you I quit."

"You didn't mean that," she tittered skeptically.

"Kimya, I can't work for you anymore. It's just taking over my life. I'm supposed to be making music, producing. I'm sorry…but I really do quit."

"Well, what am I supposed to do about today?" she quizzed, unaffected.

"I don't know," I said. "It's not my job anymore. Take Montrell with you."

Kimya stood and walked over to me slowly and cautiously. She looked right into my eyes and served me a serious face. "There must be something we can do," she said.

"I don't want to talk about this right now."

"Why not?"

"Well, for one, you snuck into my apartment," I said. "And second, you brought guests."

"Fine." Kimya snapped her fingers and looked at Montrell. "You. Dogs. Car," she ordered sharply.

"Oh, I've been kicked out of better places than this," Montrell said, picking up Martin with his free hand and looking around at my belongings with disdain before swishing out of the room.

When he was gone with the dogs, Kimya took my hands.

"I know I'm impossible. Right?" she said in the most earnest way I'd ever heard come from her mouth. "But I can't do this without you. You and my brother, Marlo, you're the only people who understand me. The only people who can deal with me. Who I trust. If I didn't have the two of you, I'd be nothing."

"You do realize that's not saying much about me, right?" I asked.

"You're like my sister. Like family. I can't let you go," Kimya pleaded. "The album is due soon. Everything is on the line. I'm competing with girls who are, like, half my age. I'm hot, but let's face it, I'm not the only show in town anymore. My album last year, it went double platinum, but that was only because of Megatron. If I didn't have him making my beats, I'd be done."

"And you have Megatron working on your new songs. Why do you need me?" I asked.

"I can trust you. I know you can pick me up," Kimya said and I recalled all the times I'd literally picked her up. "What do you need?" she added. "What can I give you to convince you to stay with me? Just until I finish the new album and we find someone else."

My mind immediately went to Yves on the phone last night at the club: *I can't be bought.*

"I have to follow my dreams," I said.

"Well, your dream is in music. I can help you."

I actually started laughing. "Help me? After five years, that's finally coming to mind? That you could help me?" I walked out of the bedroom.

Kimya followed closely behind me in a complete reversal of roles.

"I know how much you admire Megatron. I could hook you two up. Get you some studio time." Kimya listed the ideas as if they were just coming to her out of the clear sky and I hadn't begged her for an opportunity three years back.

"Really? Studio time with Megatron? Original. How'd you come up with that? Even if you did actually organize studio time with Megatron—which I know you wouldn't do—when would I have time to do it, Kimya? I work, like, seven days a week, 24 hours a day."

"You can have one day off a week."

"One?" I repeated sarcastically, not realizing we were officially negotiating and not speaking in hypotheticals.

But, then, after Kimya responded with "two," I realized she was actually serious about trying to get me back.

"Two *whole* days off? Are you kidding? You couldn't survive."

We sat at the kitchen table across from each other, me in my modest nightgown and Kimya in pricey D&G jeans and a thin tank top that displayed her nipples.

"I'll get a second assistant again."

"You treated the last one so badly she sold her story to *Page Six*. Want to go through that again?"

"If it makes you happy."

"Humm." I looked away, unimpressed.

"You want more?" Kimya looked horribly perplexed.

"Yes," I said, leaning into the table like a professional arriving at a poker table in Vegas. I really hadn't considered what more I could want, because I hadn't considered Kimya showing up at my place at sunup, pouring cold water on my face and begging me to stay. I figured I'd play the situation as ridiculously as it was. Again, I remembered Yves: *No amount of money. I can't be bought*.

"So?" Kimya glared at me. "What more do you want?"

"My rent," I said randomly. "Pay my rent."

"Your rent is expensive," Kimya complained.

I frowned. I watched her money better than I watched my own. She made a mint in ringtone sales each month.

"Guess we're done here, then," I said and yawned.

"I'll pay half your rent. Is that it?"

"No. A raise. I need a raise, too."

"Hell, no!"

"You know I've been trying to finally pay off my student loans, get my father's house together. I need a twenty-five percent raise."

"You're tripping!" Kimya protested.

"You give me the raise and we have a deal," I said decisively.

Kimya narrowed her eyes on me, but I didn't look away.

"Guess you'll have to hire Montrell," I joked before getting up from the table for dramatic effect. I turned my back to her and looked into my sink at nothing really. I just wanted to smile to myself. It felt good to have Kimya on her toes.

"Fine," she murmured and then I heard her stand, her heels clicking against my kitchen floor tile. "But you're coming to Kendu and Mary's with me. I'll be back in thirty minutes. Put on something nice. And burn that nightgown. I pay you better than that now."

She went to my bedroom and when I turned back to the table, she walked back into the kitchen holding her purse.

"Deal?" she asked.

"De—" I stopped myself. "Wait."

"What? You said that was it."

"Nothing big. I just need a vacation. Just a weekend."

"We just came back from Paris!"

"*You* just came back from Paris. *I* came back from being with *you* in Paris."

"So, you want to go back to Paris?" Kimya asked.

"No. Somewhere closer," I said, looking at the collection of state-shaped magnets ganged up on my clanking refrigerator. A little peninsula was hanging near the handle about to fall off. "I want to go to the Hamptons. A weekend. Alone at the beach house." I looked back up at Kimya.

"But that's my beach house," she protested.

"Exactly. So you don't have to pay for it. I'm saving you money."

"Fine," she grumbled, and it sounded as if allowing me to enjoy the benefits of the five-thousand-square-foot beach house she almost never visited hurt more than the raise and days off.

"Fine," I repeated before shaking her hand. "Guess I'll be ready in thirty minutes."

Part II

"Seeking Love on Long Island"

Hey, Ms. Lettie Special Partner of the Universe. It's me calling you on this fine Friday morning. You'll never guess where I am.... And since you didn't answer your phone, I won't pause to await a response, so I'll drop the beans. I'm in the Hamptons, girl! Standing here on Ms. Kimya Lee's pool deck right now. Just looking out at the ocean... Anyway, I was thinking about you.... Wanted to say I'm sorry for the other night.... You know?... Of course you know.... I'm, ummmm... Hey, I have this big house all to myself and since there's no special man in my life, I wanted to invite you. Maybe you could come for the weekend.... Drinks. Sun. Fun. Me. You. Call me back. Peace and fried chicken grease.

Long Island. Growing up, those two words sounded like someplace on the moon. Where white folks lived and vacationed to get away from us poor folks in Brooklyn. The first time I actually visited—I must've been, like, ten or eleven—my father packed a heavy bag with these old white towels we got at the Salvation Army and we took the train to a bus and then another bus and walked for what seemed like forever with those bags to Jones Beach.

When my legs were tired of running into the sharp shards of sand mixed in with the grayish waves, I sat on my towel beside my father and pointed up at some of the condos behind the boardwalk. I said something like, "Can we live there?" My father laughed, put out his cigarette in the sand and asked, "You don't like Brooklyn?" He waited for my answer and after a while, he looked into my eyes and started talking to me as if I was an adult. "I'm an artist. I sing. I write what I sing. I compose what I sing. I'm free. You understand?" I'm sure I nodded, looked away from the condos and out to the sun disappearing at the back of the ocean. "Now, I could get me a job and maybe someday I could afford to move you out here and buy us a little condo. But then I wouldn't be free." He looked out at the ocean with me. We never rode that train and those two buses again.

The morning my cab pulled into the circular pebble-paved drive in front of Kimya's house in the Hamptons, I jumped out like Miss Celie returning home to claim her mother's house in *The Color Purple*. After the driver pulled my father's old guitar out of the trunk, I gave a generous tip to get rid of him fast, dropped the three bags I had draped over my shoulders and ran up the drive to the door.

The plan was to write. First, I had to ink out my next ten moves in my six-month "Get the Hell Away From Kimya" plan in the composition notebook I'd purchased and on which I'd written that very title on the cover in red ink. Second, I had to start writing my songs again. It had been too long since I'd actually written any lyrics. Even the ones I hummed aloud in the shower never made it to the page. I was hoping the waves of the Atlantic, the sun shining over me without interruption from concrete skyscrapers or telephone wires, or maybe just Kimya being out of my hair for a few days would spark my creativity.

The first few hours in the house, I walked around, fingering stuff, looking at glass things Kimya had paid too much money for. I also found some men's boxers on the kitchen floor. A men's shaver in her bathroom and a blue toothbrush. Big shoes in the bedroom. I figured they were Sean's things. That one night Kimya had somehow sneaked away with him.

I changed into my favorite sarong that had puffy prawns dancing in circles at the hem and walked out to the back deck to look at the ocean. I tried to think of something smart to write in my book, but ended up just watching a few families playing in the sand and packs of twenty-somethings staggering down the strand in bikinis, probably heading to a day party. Summer was open for business and East Hampton was already getting party fever. Kimya had already gotten a call about some teenagers partying on her pool deck and claiming they lived there when police showed up after complaints from neighbors about loud music.

I went back into the house and I picked up the empty notebook. I sat on the long black ten-seater leather couch in the living room and hummed a melody that was familiar, but nothing I could place. Looked at the guitar case and thought I should open it and play. But then I decided I was too tired. I needed to rest first. Catch up on some missed sleep.

I looked back at the wet bar behind the couch. A little cognac. A nap. I'd wake up by the time the sun went down, unpack, set my alarm and wake up in the morning, ready.

On that short list, I only achieved the cognac and a nap elongated into the night by the house on the beach becoming an unexpected, insulated womb. The scent of the ocean, the breeze whipping through the air and the waves sent me adrift into my dreams in a canoe. I was away *away*. I was floating.

And then something came crashing in. Light sound at first. Just a parade of syllables floating in the flood of water around me.

Then jabbing. The utterances were coming together into a string of shouts that grabbed a hold of me.

"What?" I jumped up in a cognac-licked haze ready to fight Kimya before she dropped another jug of water on my head.

But by the time I was on my feet and holding my fists in front of me in a sloppy fighting stance, I realized there was no Kimya in the living room. The dead sun left my world in the house completely dark, but through the open French doors that led out to the pool deck, I could see some light and hear the source of the sounds that crashed into my dream.

My perpetrator was splashing in the water. Laughing. One of Marlo's old songs was playing loudly.

And then a female's voice said before giggling, "Don't throw me in the pool, Icey!"

Then there was the crash and thrash of "Icey" delivering the opposite of her request.

"Damn teenagers," I said, remembering Kimya's police call about the teenagers in her pool.

I grabbed my cell phone off the table on my way out to the deck, ready to turn the rowdy crowd over to police.

"Whoa!" I heard someone holler and then there was another loud splash.

I slid behind the open French doors off the kitchen where a landing led to the deck, and switched on a light.

"Party over! Get out and go home!" I said, stepping out onto the landing and turning off a little radio on the table. "I'm calling the police!"

I clicked my phone on and started dialing 911, but before I hit the send button I wanted to get a glimpse of the poolside squatters whom I was sure were akin to people in those advertisements on Abercrombie & Fitch shopping bags. But the dim lights tacked to the side of the house revealed a very different picture. While I couldn't make out any faces because everyone was toward the back of the pool where the side lights hardly shined, I could tell there were no teens in that pool. One black woman with huge saline-filled breasts was thrashing about in the middle of the pool where pink bulbs at the bottom of the water sent flamingo-colored dancing strobe lights up all around her.

Two shirtless black men, whose bulging stomachs and A-cup breasts covered in chest hair let me know they were in their mid-to-late thirties, were in the pool, rushing over to her, and a brown muscly guy who was shirtless, but had diamonds dripping from his neck, I could see from the other side of the pool was standing on the deck laughing at the spectacle in the water. A busty black female in Daisy Duke shorts and a too-tiny bra was beside him.

"What the hell is this?" I think I hollered, but anything I was saying was drowned out by the thrashing and cussing of the woman in the middle of the pool, and the men who were laughing and trying to console her at the same time.

"I told y'all not to throw me in the pool!" she screamed. "I just got my hair done!"

"Get out," I cut in before anyone could get another word into the exchange.

The band of bandits froze and turned to me. I squinted to try to get a look at any of their faces, but it was still too dark where they were standing.

"This house belongs to Kimya Lee. You're all trespassing."

"Who is this trick?" the woman in the water asked.

"No—who are you?" I countered. "And by you, I mean all of you." I held my cell phone out toward the squatters and realized how outnumbered I probably was. For a second, I considered running back into the house and hiding until the police got there, but then I rationalized that it would take the man-boob twins like three minutes to get out of the pool to corner me. Basically, the only thing standing between me and survival was the tall, shirtless brother in diamonds. And that was proving to be a problem because he was actually walking toward me.

I commanded, "I'm calling the police!"

"No, wait, I can explain," the muscular, diamond-decorated man said, walking to me with his hands out as if my phone was a gun and he was defusing a hostage situation.

"Explain it to the authorities," I said, pressing Send. "You don't belong here!"

"But I do."

"Yeah, educate her ass, man," one of the guys said.

"I do belong here," the man added, finally stepping into the light where I could see all of him.

"Nine-one-one. What is your emergency?" I heard coming through my phone as my eyes decided what I was looking at. "Hello? Hello? Do you have an emergency?"

"*You* do belong here," I said, stepping toward him.

"Nine-one-one. Please state your emergency. Hello?"

"I do," he said, and seemingly from the sky a light arrived and highlighted his face even more. "Kimya's my sister."

"What is your emergency?" the 911 operator repeated for the fourth time.

"No emergency. I'm sorry." I lowered the phone to my hip and ended the call. "Marlo?"

He grinned and nodded confidently, stepping so close I felt air being drawn from my lungs. "You know the name?" he asked, like a small-town jock who'd just scored a touchdown at the homecoming game.

"Oh, damn! She knows your name!" someone spouted. "Guess you 'bout to get spanked."

The crowd in the pool laughed and the leggy girl on the deck sauntered over to Marlo standing in front of me.

"She knows my name," Marlo said, "but I don't know hers. Maybe I should be the one calling the police." He reached for the phone but I stepped back.

I suddenly felt nervous, as if I was actually in the wrong. In a whiny voice, I said, "I'm Sunshine."

To this, there was more teenagelike laughter from the pool, and quickly I was feeling like the small-town nerdy girl talking to the jock who'd just scored the touchdown.

"I don't know any Sunshine," Marlo said, leaning toward me and eyeing me hard, just as the leggy woman set her hand on the small of his back.

"I'm Kimya's assistant," I said.

"You can't be," Marlo laughed. "Ain't no way Kimya's assistant is supposed to be way out here in the Hamptons while she's in the studio in New York."

"She let me use the house this weekend. But she didn't mention you being here. Does she know you're here?" I quizzed.

"Ohh! Ohh!" the pool party chanted as if I'd said fighting words.

"I don't need permission. I have blood," Marlo snapped at me.

"We'll see about that." I turned to walk back into the house.

When I stepped over the threshold and closed the French doors, I heard the crowd erupt into laughter and soon the music started playing again.

Standing in the kitchen in my red-and-yellow sarong that now looked completely middle-aged and ridiculous in the company of the women in thong bikinis, I clicked my phone on to scroll for Kimya's name. I was about to hit the call button when I heard the door behind me open.

I turned around with my hand on the button.

"Wait!" Marlo rushed to me. "Don't call Kimya."

"What?"

Marlo came just as close to me as he'd been outside. He grabbed the phone.

"Give me the phone!" I reached, but he slipped it into his front pocket.

"You want the phone?" he asked before grinning slyly.

"Look, I don't know what game you think you're playing, but give me the phone," I said.

"Say 'please.'"

"I'm not going to ask you to give me a phone that belongs to me. Stop playing." I reached for Marlo's pocket, but he stepped back. "Now we're in second grade?" I asked. "What's the point? Why not give me the phone?"

"Don't call Kimya."

"Why? You said you don't need permission to be here. What's the big deal?"

Marlo grinned again and it was fast becoming clear this play was his common route of getting his way. It reminded me of Kimya's pout.

"Oh," I added, reading him, "you *don't* want her to know you're here?"

"Look, me and the guys, we were at a party and we've been drinking. No one wants to drive back to the city. I have a key to the house and my sister is never here."

"You could've called her."

"For what? It's my sister. I'm just staying the night. She's fine with it."

"Cool. I'll let her know." I reached for the phone and Marlo stepped back again.

"Okay. Maybe she's not fine with it. You know how she is about having people up in her spot. I'm cool, but my boys—you know how she is," Marlo said.

I crossed my arms to let him know I wasn't buying into his rationale…or the cute grin. "Of course she wouldn't be happy with you and those thugs laying up in her house with some hoochies y'all probably met at a strip club."

"How you know all that?" Marlo looked at me jokingly. "You're one of those stalking assistants?"

"Fine, Marlo, you can stay, but their asses have to go," I ordered.

"The hoochies or the thugs?" A new grin.

"I'm not playing with you."

"Stop being like this. You're too cute to be evil. Look, we'll be gone tomorrow anyway. I'm sleeping in Kimya's room. They'll be down here on the couches. No one has to know." Marlo took my hand and got down on one knee. "I'll be out of your hair and you can go back to doing whatever you were doing in your—" He looked at my sarong. "What is that?"

"It's a sarong," I said.

"Okay. I like it. It's cute."

"Yeah, right."

"For real. What are those little things on it, though? Roaches?" He squinted and pointed at the smiling prawns floating in the water in the design at the bottom of the sarong.

"No, they're prawns," I corrected him.

"Prawns? You mean shrimp?" On his knee, he pondered the images carefully. I looked into his hair, how it curled from the scalp. "I don't understand why you would have shrimp on your skirt," he said just when I thought that I wondered what his hair must feel like.

"It's a nautical theme," I snapped, stepping back from his close stare. "And prawns are my favorite food, so it's perfect and I love it. And it's a sarong—not a skirt. Look, just give me the phone." I reached again and he got back up.

"Come on, Marlo. Come back outside. Let's get in the pool," a woman's voice called from outside.

"A minute," Marlo hollered toward the voice before turning back to me. "You promise not to call Kimya?" he asked.

"I won't call her," I said. "As much as I hate to have you and your posse here, I can't be held responsible for sending your drunk asses back onto the highway. Just be gone in the morning."

"Can do," Marlo said softly, and for like thirty seconds there was this uncomfortable stare where he was looking into my eyes to learn something about me.

I blinked to break it.

"The phone," I insisted. "Give me the phone."

Marlo peacefully handed me the phone and went in the direction of the pool party I wasn't invited to.

I trudged up the steps with my attitude all around me. Another day with no music and no plans. And now I was playing Mrs. Hanigan at the hip-hop orphanage.

"And turn down that damn music," I hollered, but I knew they hadn't heard me.

I watched the sun rise over Long Island on Saturday morning.

I'd hardly slept. Marlo and the motley crew kept their little pool party popping for so long I'd threatened to call the police twice, and when they finally quieted and I'd fallen asleep I thought I heard my father's music playing on a guitar. But when I opened my eyes the only guitar in the house was on the stand beside my bed.

I got up when I was still half-asleep, and in the darkness of the guest room I forced my body out of bed, my feet into sneakers and then down the steps for a morning jog I claimed would be six miles long.

As Marlo had promised, his constituents were sprawled out all over the living room.

I tiptoed past the men slumped over couches and chairs that couldn't be comfortable; still, their loud snores said they were having no trouble sleeping. The thickest one was holding the half-empty bottle of cognac in his chubby pinky-ring-clad hand. I thought to snatch it away, but then I looked to see the cap was missing and knew he'd likely been sipping it straight from the bottle.

I rolled my eyes and looked to the women who had taken up residence on the long black couch. Lying head to head, they were cloaked in the bathrobes Kimya kept in the cabana beside the pool. One woman was clutching her cell phone. Both had tattoos on their breasts.

Walking out into the capricious darkness of a new day beginning, I resolved my annoyance at my unwelcome houseguests by reminding myself that they would all be gone soon. I'd be able to get back to my big plan to save my own life. Put one word into the empty notebook.

"Save my own life." I actually repeated my thought aloud when I kicked off and started running past the sand dunes toward the heavy wet ocean dirt where the waves had risen during the night. I repeated it twice. It was a revelation. It sounded like something I'd written on a sticky note and attached to my desk only to forget it two days later. Was I doing that? Did my life need saving?

I started running faster through the fading darkness.

My father was in my ear telling me about his diagnosis. He didn't know how he'd gotten it, but in whispers I was hearing something about my mother.

Soon, HIV became our everything. Everything we talked about. Everything we argued about. For ten months. It was our fight. It made me scream. Cry. Everyday.

"You won't be crying for too long, baby," my father said one night. "I promise."

Three miles into the jog I stopped to turn around to run back to the house, but I couldn't move. The sun had made the cloudy world above pink and there it was in front of me now, waiting.

I stood there firm in the sand. All around me, there were couples and joggers and women walking with babies hanging from their backs. Everyone in motion. And I was standing still. I remembered how Marlo had looked into my eyes last night in the kitchen before we'd parted ways. How everything seemed to stop as he'd tried to peer inside, to know me. I wondered what he'd seen. What he thought he'd learned.

When I got back to the house, I crept past the still-sleeping living room loungers and envied their slumber. I sulked up the steps and stuffed the guitar into the closet. I kicked off my sneakers and crawled into bed to bury myself under the covers. Any courage I'd had when I'd arrived at that house was gone from me then. I wanted to be a turtle. To hide myself away. Or maybe get a little more sleep. I didn't promise a new start when I woke up. Maybe it was just time to go home. Maybe I was fooling myself and everyone else about my music.

"Sunny, it's time to wake up," I heard so soon I was sure it was just a whisper in my dream.

"No," I whined groggily between my sleep and reality. "I can't."

"Yes, you can. Come on."

"I want to sleep. I'm tired of everything."

"But it's after noon. And I drove all the way out here to see you."

"What?"

"Wake up!"

I twisted around in my cotton cocoon and opened

my eyes. There was nothing but the darkness of being under covers.

"Get out from under that damned cover! No one's supposed to be sleeping this time of day!"

I waded through the covers and popped my head out to a bright guest room that I'd left darkened by blinds when I'd come in from running.

Leticia was standing at the foot of the bed smiling with Starbucks coffee in her hand.

"Leticia?"

"Don't look so surprised to see me. You told me to come," she snapped. "And I didn't know you were having company. If I had, I would've brought my cute bikini."

"They're still here?" Just then I heard music coming from downstairs. "Shit!"

"Yes, they are!" Leticia sat on the bed. "And I saw Marlo and his cute self, too. Walking around in swimming trunks. I almost fainted. Thank Gawd my mother taught me better."

"They're supposed to be gone."

"Why? Nothing wrong with having a little sexy around. You know I like sexy."

"Sexy? Did you see those people?"

"Don't be an old lady, please," Leticia begged, getting up and walking over to the window to open the blinds. "And get up. I didn't come all the way here to watch you sleep."

I started to get up. "I'm glad you came."

"I told Clayton I was working on the wedding with you. I'm back to the city in the morning, though. You know he insists we go to church every Sunday at 7:30 a.m."

"With you there, I'm surprised that church doesn't

burn down!" I joked. "So, what do you want to do today?" I added devilishly, as if there was any real trouble someone our age could get into in the Hamptons besides some heavy drinking and fainting on the beach. Then I suggested, "Breakfast?"

"More like lunch." Leticia opened the blinds a little more to reveal the brightest sun that looked as though it was hanging right outside the window.

"What time is it?"

"I told you it was after noon."

I ran over to the window to see the entire beach outside alive with sandcastle construction and boogie boards.

Leticia stood beside me with a concerned look. "Get yourself in the shower and dressed. Our day in the Hamptons awaits."

After I got myself ready, Leticia and I packed two beach bags and set out for an afternoon stroll around the Hamptons. We patrolled our usual oceanside haunts, a couple of eclectic jewelry shops and clothing boutiques that sold overpriced items that always seemed to get lost or broken within months of purchase. Still, we oohed and aahed as we walked hand in hand like old buddies through the maze of beautiful things.

Beauty wasn't the only thing catching our eyes. Throughout town, there were old bars that served up the best shrimp cocktails and straight-up cocktails. We were enticed by everything and by midafternoon our hands were filled with bags of expensive clothing and jewelry, and our tummies were filled with delicious food and alcohol. We were like walking zombies in big shades and beach hats.

During the remainder of the afternoon, I kept looking at my watch and considering when Marlo would have left the beach house. Before Leticia and I set out, we looked everywhere for him so he could explain why he was still there when he'd promised to leave in the morning, only to discover he'd gone for a "store run" per the dude who'd introduced himself as Milt.

Though Leticia and I were sure we couldn't put one more thing in our mouths, we greedily decided our last stop had to be at Scoop Du Jour. Leticia admitted that she'd only made the drive to have a little ice cream followed by one of Dreesen's doughnuts.

"Guess your little escape wasn't about me after all," I said, watching Leticia stuff both the ice cream and doughnut pieces into her mouth as we sat outside the café on a wooden bench, people-watching.

"Girl, it's never really about you," Leticia said laughing. "You know I'm on this crazy wedding diet. I've been so hungry I think I'm losing my mind sometimes."

"I'm glad your greedy behind came. This has been fun."

"We need more times like this." Leticia looked at me seriously.

I agreed. Throughout that day, I'd told Leticia all about my plan and how I was going to sever ties with Kimya as soon as I got to working on my music again. I let her know that was why I was in the Hamptons, and I even thanked her for being so direct with me about my needing a change. A lesser friend would've been shy or just talked about me behind my back.

On the way back to the house, the Saturday sun was setting and cars filled with sleepy children and party-hungry singles flashed past either side of Leticia's bright yellow Beetle.

When we turned on Lily Pond Lane, I could already

see the lights on in Kimya's living room, and this sent me into a little unexpected rage.

"What the hell are they still doing here?" I protested as Leticia pulled into the driveway. She was on the phone giggling with Clayton and his promises of missing her and hadn't yet sensed my frustration.

"What are you going on about?" Leticia asked when she'd gotten off the phone and stopped the car.

"They were supposed to be gone this morning," I complained, picking up my belongings in a scattering of shopping bags in the backseat.

"You need to calm down," Leticia said. "Getting all upset and about what? So, you have a little extra company. They can't be that bad! The more the merrier. It's that simple."

With those words of encouragement, we walked into the house.

"You back already, baby girl?" Milt asked from his position on the couch. "Why don't you chill out and watch a movie with me, my man Icey and Unique. They ain't even finished making the gumbo yet."

"Gumbo?" I spat. "Ain't nobody making gumbo. Y'all are supposed to be gone! What is going on here?" I nearly kicked the door open, and there standing before two huge pots with steam hovering above were Marlo and the woman who had been vying for his attention beside the pool.

Holding the spoon up to the woman's mouth, Marlo turned to me, still smiling, and answered, "We're cooking!"

"I see that," I said, scowling, but admittedly softening to the scent of gumbo wafting from the stove.

"Don't just see, girl, come and have a taste," the

woman proposed, oozing with delight at what Marlo had served on the spoon.

"I don't want to taste!" I protested. "I want you to—"

My anger was once again muted by Leticia's friendly chatting when she entered suddenly. "Well, I want to taste! And what is that smell?" She went right to the pot and danced her nose over the steam.

"Leticia!" I called to get her attention, but she'd fallen into some conversation with Marlo and was gearing up to taste his food. They'd met a few times before when Leticia was prepping him as a witness for one of Kimya's hearings.

Leticia stopped to answer my prodding just before eating the concoction that had Marlo smiling.

"Have you forgotten that we've already had lots to eat?" I reminded her sternly in a voice that let her know I wasn't pleased with her deception.

"There's always room for—" She paused and looked at the spoon. "You made this gumbo?"

"My very own recipe," Marlo bragged. "I only break it out for important occasions."

"Oh…and what's the occasion tonight?" Leticia asked.

"Well, dinner with my new friend Sunshine," Marlo explained.

"Really?" Leticia cooed, glancing at me suggestively.

"Yeah, she was nice to me last night. Thought I'd thank her."

"Nice… And you can cook?" Leticia said.

"I didn't ask you to do that," I pointed out as Leticia grinned behind him. "I asked you to leave."

"I know, but you just seemed so mad at me last night. I wanted to make it up to you," Marlo said. "I went and got some prawns—you said you like them, right?"

"Yes, she does!" Leticia said before I could respond.

"Great. I guess that means you two will be joining us for dinner?" Marlo asked.

"Ye—" Leticia tried, but I stopped her.

"No!"

"No?" She glared at me and asked, "Why not?" with Marlo.

"Because, as I stated, we've already eaten." I pulled Leticia from behind Marlo, so she had to stand beside me in a united front. "And we're spending quality time together. And we're not hungry."

"Speak for yourself," Leticia murmured.

Marlo looked down at us, bearing the face of a confused man, and then his gaze settled on me and with brown eyes dipped in sincerity, he asked, "So, you're letting my prawns go to waste?"

Thirty minutes later, after more prodding and insisting from my best friend, I was sitting at Kimya's long oak slab dining room table with Marlo and his crew, Leticia and a bowl of gumbo that was actually quite tasty.

Seated at the end of the rectangular table farthest from Marlo, I turned what was left of my broth around in my bowl and promised I wouldn't ask for seconds. I also promised not to participate in the conversation that buoyed between these grown folks cheering for more of Marlo's gumbo and gushing random outbursts of praise and worship at whatever he'd just said.

"So, Marlo, I'm a big fan," Leticia said after helping her greedy self to a second bowl of gumbo. "I love your music."

I shot her the ultimate stare of betrayal and gave her a little kick under the table.

"Thanks. That means a lot to me." Marlo tried to

sound humble and responded to her smile with his indulgent grin.

I sharpened my eye again. Who did he think he was fooling, trying to pretend he was all nice? He was only doing all of this so I wouldn't tell Kimya about his party.

"Sunny and I used to play your songs all night in our dorm room freshman year, especially your song 'Ridda Chick.'"

"No, we didn't," I objected.

"Yes, we did! And I remember that after we listened to that song like a million times, Sunny drove to Tower Records the day the album came out. You stood in line for hours. Remember?"

I ignored her.

"Well, I'm honored you liked my work. I wasn't excited about singing that song, but my producer insisted," Marlo explained, as I rolled my eyes at his usual self-indulgence.

"That album went, like, quadruple platinum, right?" Leticia asked.

"Not quadruple, but it did well."

"What's next for you?"

Marlo looked off timorously.

Icey jumped in with "Tell shorty about the new jam."

"Spit some bars," Milt said.

"You have new work?" Leticia asked, catching on.

"Just some stuff. I'm in the studio."

"The comeback kid at it again!" Icey bragged, getting up to slap Marlo five.

"It's more than a comeback. I'm showing these young boys how it's done. R & B isn't about grinding and humping the stage. It's love music. Truth. That's what I represent."

"I can't tell," I said a little louder than I meant to.

"Excuse me?" Marlo called and everyone got quiet.

"I said I can't tell that's what you're 'about.' Everything you put out is like grinding and humping. If you call that love music, I guess it's all love music." I laughed rather wickedly. "If it's even music."

"Shots fired!" Unique with the fake breasts said, shooting finger guns in the air.

"I don't agree with you." Marlo dropped his spoon in his bowl and the handle made a loud, angry ding on the rim.

"You are so wrong," Icey snarled.

"She can speak on it. I mean, a lot of people who aren't artists don't understand the industry...what will sell."

"So, you don't like the bumping and grinding R & B but you put it out there because it would sell?" I pushed with irony in my voice.

"I had to do what I had to do," he replied. "I wanted to be heard. I had responsibilities."

"What's going to be different now?" I asked, staring right into Marlo's eyes. "The industry hasn't changed. Have you?"

"Changed how?" Marlo leaned in with slight concern on his face.

"Changed the fact that you were obviously willing to sacrifice your art. I think they call that a 'lack of integrity.'"

"Sunny!" Leticia murmured to stop me.

Marlo sat back and laughed detachedly.

"That ain't funny, man," Icey said, looking at Marlo as if he was sitting there naked.

"Yes, it is." Marlo pushed his chair back and started getting up.

"Where you going?" Milt asked.

Send For
2 FREE BOOKS
Today!

I accept your offer!

Please send me two free novels and two mystery gifts (gifts worth about $10). I understand that these books are completely free—even the shipping and handling will be paid—and I am under no obligation to purchase anything, ever, as explained on the back of this card.

168/368 XDL GEYX

Please Print

FIRST NAME

LAST NAME

ADDRESS

APT.#   CITY

STATE/PROV.   ZIP/POSTAL CODE

Visit us online at
www.ReaderService.com

© 2013 HARLEQUIN ENTERPRISES LIMITED. ® and ™ are trademarks owned and used by the trademark owner and/or its licensee. Printed in the U.S.A.

◄ Detach card and mail today. No stamp needed.

Send For
2 FREE BOOKS
Today!

I accept your offer!

Please send me two
free novels and two mystery
gifts (gifts worth about $10).
I understand that these books
are completely free—even
the shipping and handling will
be paid—and I am under no
obligation to purchase anything,
ever, as explained on the back
of this card.

168/368 XDL GEYX

Please Print

FIRST NAME

LAST NAME

ADDRESS

APT.#   CITY

STATE/PROV.   ZIP/POSTAL CODE

Visit us online at
www.ReaderService.com

"Upstairs for a bit," Marlo said, pushing his chair in and looking everywhere in the room but at me.

"Don't go," Leticia begged. "You don't need to leave. Right, Sunny?" She looked at me.

Unique tried to get up to follow behind Marlo as the others repeated sentiments to get him to stay, but I sat back and watched him just long enough to consider that maybe I'd finally pushed him to the point of deciding to leave the house altogether.

"Anyone want more gumbo?" I asked, reaching over for the pot in the middle of the table.

Leticia looked at me and grinned nervously before attempting to get up from her seat. "Sun, I'm going upstairs to find that important thing we talked about."

"I don't remember talking about anything."

"You should come with me, so I can remind you," Leticia added, focusing her eyes on me like a mother does just before she drags a screaming five-year-old out of the grocery store for a butt-whipping.

I stood as if I'd been voted off the island on *Survivor* and trudged up the stairs in front of Leticia complaining.

"What's wrong with you?" Leticia prodded once we were in the guest room. She closed the door and pressed her back against it.

"Wrong? It's those people downstairs. The fake-ass basketball team and cheerleaders." I laughed.

"Do you hear how old and crotchety you sound?"

"With good reason. I came here to clear my mind and develop a plan for my new life—and then here they come and ruin it," I pointed out.

"Granted. But that doesn't give you the right to go insulting people. Damn!" Leticia pushed away from the door and went to sit on the bed.

"Insult? If you're talking about Marlo, drop it," I said, walking to the mirror and looking at myself. "His head is too big to be insulted. That man thinks the world of himself. God only knows why."

"Sunny, you basically told him he has no talent and no career. That's a lot to hear from someone who barely knows you. Damn, that's a lot to hear from anyone."

I remembered the softened look in Marlo's eyes before he got up. How he didn't look back at me.

"He'll be fine," I said, turning away from the mirror to sit on the bed beside Leticia. The bedspread was a weaving of watery blues and greens, so it looked as though we were both floating on top of ocean waves. "Not like my opinion counts. He was just being nice so I don't tell on him."

Just then, there was a loud splash outside the window that was quickly followed by girlish giggling. Next, music from the radio on the deck started playing.

"See, everything's back to normal," I said. "He's fine."

"This isn't about him being fine. It's about your behavior. I don't think I can ever remember you talking to anyone like that."

"He's a jerk, Leticia. Don't fall for it."

"He just seemed like a guy having a good time. A guy who was actually being pretty nice to you. You were just taking everything he did so personally that you couldn't see that. Why?"

"Why what?"

"Why are you being so critical of this dude?"

I stood up again in protest. "I'm not."

Leticia looked me up and down and grinned knowingly.

"What are you grinning about?"

"You're digging him," she said.

"You must be drunk," I replied. "Because there's no way I'm tripping over that man."

Leticia fell back on the bed cracking up as if I were doing a stand-up routine.

I jumped on the bed beside her.

"Now I'm funny?" I asked, half laughing myself.

"Because," Leticia started, snapping up quickly to look into my eyes, "Sunshine Embry, I have known you since freshman year at Howard University and I know when you have a crush on a guy."

"No!"

Leticia cut her eyes on me again like a lawyer trying to break me.

"Okay…maybe there was a crush before—like a long time ago," I confessed under duress. "What's not to like? He's handsome. And I admit, I once loved his music. But he doesn't mean anything to me."

"I don't believe you," Leticia said, lying on her back and looking up at a large skylight that invited the moon and stars into the bedroom with us. "If you like him, why don't you just go for it? You know what I think? The next time he's nice to you, you should be nice to him. Invite him in."

"Invite him in?" I repeated, lying down on the bed beside her to see the stars catching her eyes. The room was pretty dim with only the bedside lamp on. "What does that mean?"

"Let him know you're open. Don't close him out. Be available. I think you've been unavailable for too long. You know?" She turned away from the stars and looked at my silhouette.

Leticia and I lay there shoulder to shoulder, looking up at the stars for a long while. I pointed up at one shining away from the rest of the figures in the constellations.

"It's pretty," I said. "All by itself."

"Bet it gets lonely sometimes," Leticia said softly.

I felt for her fingers on the bedspread and clasped her hand.

I said, "Thank you for coming."

"Thank you for inviting me."

After a while, Leticia got up and went into the bathroom to giggle on the phone with Clayton, no doubt telling him everything that was going on in the crazy house. I kept my position on the bed, looking up at the little star and reviewing its loneliness. I started thinking about what Leticia had said about Marlo being nice to me and perhaps me being so angry I couldn't recognize it. If that was true, I wondered what else I was missing.

Listening to her laughing in the bathroom, I thought about everything I'd said to Marlo since he'd been in the house and while I understood why I'd done what I'd done, she was right. I was being mean. I hadn't come all the way to the Hamptons to crush people's dreams. I'd come to find my own.

When the shower started running in the bathroom, my mind went back to my arrival in the house. How excited I'd been. Where was that now? What had happened? I searched every step I'd taken to find where I'd lost my vision, my direction. I stumbled upon the little things. The boxers on the kitchen floor. The men's things spread out on the counter in Kimya's bathroom. Those big shoes in the bedroom. It all came together like a big puzzle. Those weren't Sean's things in Kimya's house. She hadn't been sneaking to the Hamptons to spend weekends with him. Those were Marlo's things.

He was the one who smelled like the French cologne. He was the one who'd been in the house. That was why he wasn't leaving.

I padded down the hallway toward Kimya's room to confront Marlo with my discovery. I wasn't going to call him out or scream at him. I'd already done enough of that. I just wanted the truth.

Soft chords played on a guitar outside Kimya's bedroom. The door was slightly ajar and dim light hardly escaped. I stood out there listening to the music. The notes Marlo strummed, slightly melancholy and a little kind, even open, held my feet in place beneath me but took my mind somewhere else. I rode his notes from interest to memory. The dim light on the floor became the sunlight in my father's bedroom. Then there was the dresser. His bottle of English Leather sitting on top. My little hand playing with the Black Ken and Black Barbie. Everything was in its place in my past. I was happy. I was without a past. Then the cologne fell. The glass broke. The scent came up to my little pudgy nose. I was in trouble. I needed to escape. But then the sound of Daddy's feet on the cracking Brooklyn staircase. And then his melody came to me in my memory. His singing on the way upstairs. Me not moving. Standing, not in fear, but in awe. His song about the bird. The one about me.

"I know that song," I said, finding myself standing in the threshold of Kimya's bedroom.

Marlo's brown frame was on the bed, hung over a guitar like it was something precious. He looked up slowly, as if he knew I'd been standing there. "'Bird,'" he trickled. "Embry. You familiar?"

"Very."

Marlo looked back down at the guitar and strummed

a few chords from the extended cut. "Best soul singer ever. Wrote his own music. This is his best—in my opinion." He looked back up at me. "You have *Finding Love in Brooklyn?*"

"A few copies."

"Impressive," Marlo approved with a nod. "You don't meet many people who know of musicians like Embry. He was a purist. You know?" Marlo went back into the guitar and played notes from the title track on *Finding Love in Brooklyn* and I realized he wasn't even talking to me anymore. He was somewhere tackling his thoughts with the music. "No fame. A man and his music. He risked everything for it."

"I'm sorry," I offered, stepping into the room, "about how I acted downstairs. I had no right to say those things to you."

"Humpf," was all Marlo managed over the notes. He played on.

I stood and listened for a while. I wanted to sit on the bed beside him. To sing the words I knew over the melody.

Marlo played a song from an EP my father released on his own before he was diagnosed with HIV. Marlo improvised in the spontaneous joy of the head tempo and I sensed he knew my father had passed. His play was bold but melancholy. At the end of the song, there was a buildup and release that climaxed into what anyone else could hear as noise, but Marlo played it in a new way that even my father would be proud of. When it was over, he looked tired. He set the guitar down on the bed and looked up for a long exhale that seemed to relieve his mind more than his body.

Sweating, he looked at me. "You want to go for a walk?"

The house was quiet for our escape to the beach. I think Leticia had gotten out of the shower and into bed. She was driving back to New York at dawn to get to church with Clayton. And I couldn't find any traces of Marlo's crowd in the living room.

The night sky was where and what it had always been, and still spectacular.

Marlo and I walked silently for a while. We headed through bluffs toward the ocean like strangers who were frustrated at trying to figure each other out, but thought we should. He was more than two feet away from me, and save random peeks at my feet when I slid off my flip-flops, he didn't look at me. But still, I felt as though he was staring into me again.

At the shoreline, Marlo threw a shard of broken sea glass at the stars. I imagined it never fell into the ocean, but maybe turned into a bird and flew away. I knew not to tell Marlo what I was thinking. He'd think I was crazy. Probably laugh at me.

We walked on and the weather suddenly felt cold. I think Marlo, dressed only in his tank top, was feeling the chill, too. He pushed his hands into his pockets.

"I wanted to be heard," he said suddenly. "I wanted people to hear me."

I nodded.

"So many good people came before me, they never had a chance to be heard. Better than I could ever be and they couldn't get in the door. If they did, no one wanted to listen to what they wanted to play," he said. "I didn't want that to be me."

"I understand," I said.

"No, you don't. It was my choice. But I made it self-ishly."

I wanted to tell Marlo that he didn't need to explain

himself to me. That he didn't need to say anything. But I had a feeling he wasn't saying his words to me or for me.

"I don't apologize for my decisions," he added. "I had some good times. Even with that bumping and grinding." We laughed. "It made a lot of people happy. Got me and Kimya out of Detroit." Marlo held his hands up at the map of mansions and manicured lawns dotting the land behind us and it took me back to sitting on the beach that day with my father. "Some people play ball to get here. Rap their way here. Hustle their way here. I used what I had. I don't apologize. One day, I'll be able to do what I want to do—on my terms."

We walked on, the space between us dissipating. Strangers pulled in from two feet to one foot to our shoulders touching innocently to escape the freeze in the wind.

I told him about my music, my songs, how I started in the music industry. That internship I got with a label right out of college. How I thought that as soon as I got into the studio someone would hear my lyrics and buy in to my vision. But that didn't happen. And I gave up so easily. Moved from job to job, getting further away from what I wanted to do at every turn. And then there was Kimya.

"So, what's that like?" Marlo asked with a knowing tap on my elbow.

"You want the real version or the made-for-television version?" I asked boldly.

"I don't think either could be very merciful," Marlo said. "'Duck and hide'—that's usually the best laid plan when Kimya's in charge. She's always been that way. Broke or bourgeois, she knows how to push every button."

"Very true," I agreed.

"But she's delicate, too," Marlo said. "And sensitive. Sometimes I think she may be a little too weak for this industry. I can take my hits and bruises. I came out first. I know you can't stay on top forever. But that spotlight is all my sister knows. I'm afraid of what she'll do to keep it."

After walking a little while longer and telling Marlo about my reason for coming to the Hamptons, we acknowledged that we were losing control of our extremities by the second and raced back to the house. When we got into the door we were so delirious from the cold we fell into each other's arms to find immediate warmth.

Marlo thoughtfully massaged the chill from my upper arms in friendly rubs. I shuddered and clenched my arms around his waist.

"Warm yet?" he asked innocently.

"Almost!" My teeth chattered and I wondered how I'd held out in the chilly weather for so long.

"I'm sorry I let you get so cold," he said sympathetically. "I just needed to get out of here for a second." He looked into my eyes and we stayed stuck there with his hands on my shoulders and my arms wrapped around his waist. And then the friendly touch from people who were just strangers became something more unexpected and intimate.

I looked away. Stepped back. Let my hands fall to my sides.

We both cleared our thoughts rather loudly, as if we'd done something wrong and had gotten caught in the act.

"Tea," Marlo said. "We need tea."

He turned to walk toward the kitchen.

I looked around at the dark and quiet living room that had been sleeping quarters the night before.

"Where is everyone?" I asked, following behind Marlo.

"They went back to the city. I don't think they could take the heat."

"Really? Because of me?"

"Yeah." Marlo headed to the stove.

"Again, I apologize. I don't know what got into me."

"It wasn't just you. I was in a funk. I was happy they left."

"What about that girl who was always hanging on to you? You can't be happy she left," I joked, but it came out sounding as though I was fishing for information. Maybe I was.

"Monique? Are you kidding?" Marlo laughed loud enough to wake Leticia. "She has four kids and a crazy ex-husband. I think we both know nothing's happening there."

"But I'm sure the ladies still love you. Must have one in every city," I said, watching the muscles move in his back as he worked the faucet.

"Nah. Never been my thing," he said flatly.

"Umm…you forget there are pictures and epic stories documenting your…shall we say, tour of lady loves," I pointed out.

"That's all show for the cameras." Marlo put the kettle on the stove and turned on the gas. "You know that. I've had my share, but this industry is lonely. Especially for a successful man. Once you get past the gold diggers and undercover gold diggers with degrees, you realize there aren't many people you can invite in. Everybody wants something."

"So, you're telling me you're not dating anyone?" I asked, frowning suspiciously.

"I haven't been on a date in over a year. And before

that, there was nothing significant. I think the high-light of my dating was catching a woman I thought I loved buying a positive home pregnancy test online. After that, I threw in the cards. Love is too hard on a brother. Besides, any woman who gets close to me will have to get past my jealous, crazy sister." Marlo turned to the cabinet beside the stove and started mumbling something about tea. "I know there's some blueberry in here…blueberry and Ceylon chamomile."

"What are you over there talking about?" I got up on a stool at the breakfast bar.

"Making tea," Marlo said.

"I know. I mean like… You're making tea?" I laughed. "And the gumbo last night. It was great and everything, but how do you know how to make that? It's not the manliest thing you could be doing. Just say-ing, you were on the cover of *Maxim* in your boxers. Searching for blueberry tea isn't what you would expect from someone willing to show his undies to the entire world. Great picture, by the way."

"I'm a big brother. My mother worked two jobs try-ing to stay off welfare while I was at home watching Kimya. I had to learn my way around the kitchen." Marlo found the blueberry tea just as the water started boiling in the kettle on the stove.

"That's very surprising. I never would've guessed that about you."

"There's a lot you don't know about me." Marlo turned away from the stove with two cups of steaming tea in his hands. He walked to the breakfast bar and handed me one.

"Yes—there is a lot I don't know. Like why you're being so nice to me," I said randomly. "I've been nothing short of horrible the whole time we've been here. Why are you being so nice?"

"Good question. I think it may be because I don't get told 'no' often. Not from anyone in my circle. Definitely not from someone's assistant. Most people give me whatever I want. You're the first in a long time, besides my sister, to tell me 'no' to anything. And, yes, you were horrible. But, I guess I liked it." He smiled at me.

"So, being horrible is all I need to do for you to remember my name?" I asked, setting the cup down on the counter for the tea to cool. "Five years I've been working for Kimya and we've never had a conversation."

He laughed and stepped back to give me a once-over. "It's nice to meet you now. And I like what I see."

I sucked in my gut and smiled my best smile for as long as I could and after a second I realized that Marlo had already stopped looking at my body and he was looking right into my eyes again. I didn't look away that time. "Wow," Marlo said finally, averting his eyes.

"What?"

"Nothing." He turned away and I could feel his nervousness. He went back to the cabinet. "I was just thinking—you want some honey for your tea?"

"No," I said. "I like my tea raw."

He looked back at me. "Me, too."

Night outside on Long Island grew deep black. But inside that house it was daytime wherever Marlo and I went. Laughing and sipping blueberry tea, we went from the kitchen to the living room. We talked about everything. My favorite cheese. His favorite rappers. My least favorite Kimya song. His least favorite borough. My worst date. His worst nightmare. And then we talked about our dreams. How we both wanted to make great music that touched people. That explained a love we knew was out there, but that, ironically enough, neither of us had found. And for so many reasons. Then came the stories of heartbreak. Falling in love and out of love with so many things. People. Places. Family. Dreams. I wanted to tell him about my father, I felt that I should, but I wasn't ready. I kept thinking it would be too much. I didn't want to cry in front of him. Burst out in tears as if my father had just died yesterday. Still, after just hours together, I felt that I could go there with Marlo. I just wouldn't.

A little past 3:00 a.m. and we were up in his room, me sitting on the bed playing my guitar and him on the floor singing. He sang every song I knew how to play and sometimes I just played my heart and he improvised. It felt so old in an interesting way. As if we'd been going to that beach house together and singing that way for a long time. Just making music together. Holding the tune as Marlo sang so tenderly and reverently, I pretended that history in my head was ours.

Then something happened.

"That's not the right chord," Marlo said, getting up as I tried to open Al Green's "Simply Beautiful."

"Yes, it is," I said, but what I heard was in contrast with my proclamation.

"Something's wrong. I don't think you're muting the top E string."

"I'm doing it right." I started playing again as he sat on the bed behind me.

"Sunny, put your middle finger on the D string." He wrapped his arms around my body to place his hands over my hands in position on the guitar.

We began again together. And that time it was perfect.

"That's it," Marlo coached, and I played the opening again on my own. "You make me proud," he joked.

I laughed and turned to him. And just when I was about to say something to ease the magnetic tension I was feeling with his arms around me, he kissed me on the cheek.

Still in position on the guitar and in his arms, I spun my head back around so quickly to look away from Marlo and his lips. Had I just imagined that?

"What was that?" I asked.

"It was what I was feeling," Marlo answered quickly. "Sunny…what are you feeling?"

The night, the place, the time, the beautiful man sitting behind me, so many things… And what was I feeling?

My first instinct was to clench up, to move away and say we needed to stop, cease and desist and go our separate ways. Who did he think I was? Some groupie who'd sleep with him because he sounded so good singing Al Green in my ear?

But my second instinct, the one that would prove more tumultuous than the first, was open. Open like the beach at sunset, a city street after a snowstorm, a balloon slipped from some little girl's fingers. Open in so many ways. And I wanted to be encountered, touched and set free, all at the same time. And all by that man behind me. "What the hell!" I cursed.

I gave the guitar a resting spot on the floor and stood in front of Marlo with my arms at my sides, my head cocked to the side, trying to drink all of him in through a haze of sleepiness and pure lust released. Whatever was about to happen, I wanted it to be known to me that this was my decision. If it went nowhere or everywhere, it was my decision. I was making it.

I pulled my shirt off, threw it to wherever and bent down to kiss Marlo, who was still seated on the bed.

But he stopped me. "No. Wait." He gently pushed my chin up, so I'd be standing erect again. "I want to see you."

Arms back at my sides, I looked at him looking at me as though I was a new thing. All of the breasts on all of the women he'd seen all around the world, and staring at my torso, I could read the ideas of what to do next in a furious storm in his mind. I was nude and nude. Bare to his desires.

Marlo wrapped his hands around my waist; they were big and strong, and made my waist seem like something precious.

He closed his eyes and shook his head as if he couldn't believe what was happening.

I wrapped my hand around the back of his head and played with his hair and just as I was about to try to kiss him again, he pulled me to his mouth and started kissing my belly button like a man intent to worship. This spot wasn't commonly erogenous for me, but something in his lick made me yield to him, so I found my body leaning into him, leaning for him, seeking more from his lips and tongue all over me.

His hands went to my breasts and the touch was a welcome distraction from the chill in the room.

He looked up at me from my belly button, through the chasm between my breasts with eyes of contemplation. We locked into each other's eyes, his hands on my breasts, mine playing in his hair, our bodies leaning in.

"Is this what you want to feel?" Marlo asked so directly I couldn't look away or think about my answer.

"Yes."

Marlo's hands left my breasts and moved to undo my waist-tied skirt as he kept watch on my eyes. He moved with care that still managed to be spontaneous and raw.

Soon, my skirt was on the floor, my cotton panties were straddling my ankles and Marlo's tongue had moved from my navel to my thighs, to the inside of my thighs. To that, I cooed or purred loudly. And something lifted me up onto the bed and then onto my back. I opened my eyes to the ceiling, and as Marlo worked I felt as if I was drunk or high and kept reminding myself that I was in my right mind. I heard echos of Antha and Candice and Willow and Leticia talking about this man that other night at No. 8. Their anthropological rapping about his beauty from head to toe. And there he was with me.

Marlo announced that he was done but not finished and stood up on the bed to pull down his pants.

Looking at him nude, I considered that I needed to forget everything I thought I knew about sex and learn new possibilities in his body. Every rumor anyone had ever said about what was in his pants was true.

When Marlo entered me, I realized just how lonely I'd been all those years without a man's touch. Leticia was right. I'd detached myself from touch so I couldn't feel anything I didn't want to feel. I'd been the one who'd separated myself from this feeling. Not work or Kimya or my father. Me. I mourned for the loss as he stroked. I praised the gain as he grew and grew inside of me and erupted into something that made me fall in.

And when it was done, after we'd switched positions and made new ones like old lovers trying to catch up, and Marlo was falling asleep on my stomach, I looked down at his hair and knew that all those years, all that time I hadn't been having this, I'd been waiting for him, just for him. And then I drifted off to a dream of nothing I'd remember.

It didn't take long for sunlight to come in. And while I'd fallen asleep in an orgasmic blue that made me believe my 24-hour affair would turn into a lifetime of love, in the morning, as a pastor would say, there would be truth and light.

I opened my eyes one at a time, trying not to move a muscle. My right eye found that Marlo had slipped off my stomach in the night and was on the right side of the bed, facing away from me. He looked like a man who was either in bed alone or wanted to be in bed alone. My mind went to the groupies. All those women who'd chased him and likely woke up in the morning in the very position I was in, buck-naked, on the left side of the bed...alone.

"Oh, my God!" I chastised myself, remembering the night. Embarrassed and thinking I should escape and run away to hide, I dangled my left foot off the side of the bed and began to inch over to roll off without waking Marlo.

I'd gotten half of my body free when he rolled over.

"What you doing?" he asked sleepily. "I know you're not trying to escape." He pulled me back into his arms.

"No," I said.

"Good," he added, blinking his eyes to shake off sleep. "Because you know what happened?"

"What?"

"You slept with me. And if you leave right now, it's as though you used me." He looked at me jokingly.

"Stop," I laughed.

"I'm sensitive," Marlo said comically and we both

laughed. He took a deep breath. "Think I'm going to make some breakfast. You like that?"

"Sure."

"All these one-word answers," he said, easing out of the bed. "Got a brother nervous."

"Oh, you have nothing to be nervous about," I said, openly ogling his bare penis.

"Really?" He bit his lip and grinned in his way.

"Really."

Marlo kissed me on the forehead and went about the room to get some clothes on. Before walking out, he ordered me to get some more rest. "You'll need it," he said.

"Oh, so now I'm your sex thing?" I asked and I hated how insecure I sounded.

"Now, that sounds good, but I wasn't talking about making love.... I was talking about making music. We have work to do today."

I lay back in the bed and pretended to go back to sleep until I heard Marlo moving around downstairs. Then I jumped and ran out of Kimya's room to see if Leticia was still in the guest room.

I opened the door, and although she was gone, there was a note on the bed:

Sunny:
Heard you last night. Guess you invited him in.
LOL.
See you in the City,
Leticia.

I sat on the bed and fell back with the note in my hand. I looked up at the skylight. The stars were gone.

The black sky was bright baby blue. No clouds. A seagull flew by. I sighed. What was coming next?

Something wet and soft answered my question quickly. It was at my pinky toe. It felt like a man nibbling, but I hadn't heard Marlo coming up the stairs and as freaky as I knew he was from our first encounter, getting down on the floor to suck my toes was taking it a little far.

I shot up to see what was eating me.

"Gina!"

I blinked at the white teacup Chihuahua in the pink diamond-studded collar taking my toe for a toy. It couldn't be her. Gina? Kimya's dog? In the Hamptons?

Just as I was about to question my sanity or the chance that maybe Marlo had actually drugged me with his blueberry tea and this was nothing more than a hangover apparition, in pranced a second white teacup Chihuahua in a blue diamond-studded collar.

"Martin!" I jumped up before Martin could get to my other toe. "Shit!" I ran to the window. Kimya's purple Phantom was in the driveway.

"Sunny Bear! Where are you?"Kimya hollered.

Martin and Gina started barking, calling to her voice coming from somewhere in the house to me upstairs. They looked up at me as if they knew what I'd been doing. And then they went back to yapping for Kimya.

"Marlo!" Kimya shouted and I could tell she was in the kitchen then. "What are you doing here?"

Martin and Gina looked at me through their suspicious eyes and seemed to roll them at me before disappearing to go and find Marlo and Kimya downstairs.

"Shit!" I ran into Kimya's bedroom and pieced together my clothing as I overheard her conversation downstairs with Marlo.

"Sunny Bear? You upstairs? Come down!" Kimya called soon.

I slid on my sneakers and ran downstairs as though I was in trouble.

I found Kimya in the kitchen sipping new blueberry tea in my old cup.

Behind her at the stove was Marlo looking nervous.

Martin and Gina ran over to my feet and started yapping what his eyes were saying: *Guilty! Caught! Guilty! Caught!*

"What's wrong with y'all?" Kimya said to them. "Been acting crazy since we got here."

I walked over to hug Kimya and looked at Marlo over her shoulder.

"What have you been up to without me, Sunshine Embry!" Kimya gushed when I let go.

"Just relaxing," I answered with Marlo looking at me curiously.

She looked me up and down. "You look so refreshed. Maybe we need to give you a vacation more often."

"Good call," I said. "But what are you doing here?"

"It's Sunday, silly! I'm here to pick you up," Kimya said, as if she was talking to one of the dogs as she played with my hair. "And imagine my surprise when I walked in to see my big brother in here…just making breakfast."

"That's nothing—" Marlo and I said together. "It's something—" we added in another chorus under the tension of her stare.

"Is it nothing or something?" Kimya pressed warily.

"It's nothing," Marlo stated firmly. "I just told you I drove up this morning to get away for a few hours and discovered your assistant was here."

"Good," Kimya said. "Because that would be weird!"

She laughed and linked arms with me. "Come on, Sunny. Let's go chat as he finishes my breakfast."

I was like one of those dogs following Kimya around the house, listening to her babble on about nothing and new furniture and her music and her hair and her jeans. I answered and laughed and pretended I was just like one of those dogs, but inside I was growing numb. I heard Kimya, but behind her was a loop playing of Yves and Leticia and me. I had left this behind. But I was back there again. And in the worst way. Because now I knew what was possible. After that night with Marlo, I knew what I wanted.

Still, after he had finished cooking the breakfast that was supposed to be for me, I was sitting with my numbness and anger at so many things at a table with him and his sister pretending again.

"So, I have news, guys," Kimya said, stuffing her mouth with cheese and eggs.

"What's up, sis?" Marlo asked. He was so far away from me at the table. He'd hardly looked at me.

"The album is done! And I love it!" Kimya squealed.

"Wow!" Marlo cheered.

"Right!" Kimya looked at me. "Isn't that exciting, Sunny Bear?"

"Super exciting," I murmured. Martin and Gina were sitting at my feet begging for scraps.

"Megatron says he thinks it's better than anything I've ever put out!" Kimya clapped at her success. She went on about tour plans and costumes.

As she spoke, I watched Marlo and his distance from me. How he was snatched so quickly away from me with Kimya just showing up. I don't know what I expected, but his insistence in the kitchen that there was "nothing" going on in the house made me feel like one of those groupies I'd woken up thinking about. I felt so stupid. Of course, he wasn't going to tell Kimya about our one night together. Why should he? I was just her "assistant."

"I'm so happy. I can't believe this is happening to me again," Kimya went on talking to herself as Marlo and I argued in missed glances. "And what a surprise that I have both of the most important people in my life here to share it with me. Right now! I'm so lucky to have both of you." Kimya looked at Marlo. "My big brother." She looked at me. "And my best friend." She paused for approval but we were silent.

Kimya frowned. "Well, don't all jump in to cheer me on at the same time," she joked.

Silence. More glares.

Kimya looked from me to Marlo and he looked away. She dropped her fork. "What's going on? Y'all are acting funny. And I mean funny *funny.*"

"Nothing is funny *funny,*" Marlo said. "Right, Sunny?"

Kimya looked back and forth again unconvinced. "I know *funny,* and this is *funny.*" She pushed her plate away in disgust.

"There's nothing *funny,*" I said to Kimya but spat my words at Marlo. "Nothing."

"Hum…" Kimya frowned at me. "Well, if there's something *funny,* it needs to stop. Because I can't have anything *funny* going on between you two. Not right now. Not ever."

"I just said it's nothing," Marlo barked.

Kimya nodded resolutely and went on again about her plans of her big comeback and I went back to my numbness. Then something in me flipped. It was the sadness I'd felt on the bridge, the longing on the beach.

It was anger at me and my being this "emotional pillow," accommodating someone else when I was the one suffering. And worse, there was this grown man across the table from me, doing the same thing. Suddenly, everything in my mouth, my stomach and my body was sour.

"…and I'm going to have an all-girl band, too," Kimya went on. "And backup dancers. The full package. Won't that be cool?"

I pushed back from my space at the table with no plans. Just intent to move.

"Sunny, where are you going?" I heard Kimya ask, but I couldn't see her, because I was walking away. "Sunny? You hear me? Where are you going? Stay! You stay!"

The dogs were yapping at me as if I was their sister.

"Sunny? Come back here and sit down! I'm getting tired of all of this attitude from you! You hear me. I came all the way here to pick you up and you're acting like this!"

"I'm leaving," I said.

"Leaving? You stop this right now!"

Upstairs in the guest bedroom, I started stuffing my things into my bag. I went to Kimya's bedroom and got my guitar.

I could hear Kimya placing more demands on me from downstairs. Saying she wasn't going to chase me anymore and if I wanted my job I needed to chase her. I had five minutes to get down to the car or she was leaving with my job and without me. She dared me to disobey and then she was arguing with Marlo, accusing him of sleeping with me. It sounded like a messy soap opera, an episode of *Love & Hip Hop for Fools.* Well, I was cutting myself from the cast.

I slung my bag over my shoulder and tucked the

guitar under my arm and was about to leave but remembered that I'd left my sarong in the bathroom in the guest room.

After I'd returned to the bathroom and bent down to pick it up, I heard, "Don't go. Don't leave."

I shrugged at Marlo behind me in the bathroom. "You stay. I'm going." I pushed past him and into the bedroom.

"What's wrong?"

"Don't!" I shot at him.

"What was I supposed to say to her?"

"Why are you asking me questions to things you already know?" I started walking out of the room, but he grabbed my arm.

"Last night… It just happened and I—"

"It was a mistake!" I said.

"No! It was real. But that doesn't mean Kimya needs to know about it," he said. "Not yet."

I laughed. "So, this is about protecting Kimya from what happened between us? Two grown people? You can play that game. I'm done."

"You know she's crazy," Marlo said, refusing to let go of me. "And she's stressed right now."

"I'm stressed right now!"

"Sunny, I'll tell her when it's right. After we talk about what happened. I don't know about you, but something happened to me last night with you." He tried to catch my eyes with his plea, but I looked away.

"Too bad it wasn't happening this morning, too," I said. "Look, we both know how this is going to play out. Kimya's not going to just let us walk out into the sunlight. And you're obviously willing to play her game. That's not what I want right now. And, you know what, yesterday I had no idea what I wanted from you, but right now, I know. And this isn't it. I want honesty and openness. Truth."

"Truth?" Marlo finally let me go. "You want truth, Ms. *Embry?*"

I was walking out, but stopped with my back to Marlo's hidden accusation.

"I was going to tell you about my father," I said. "It's not exactly a subject I like talking about with strangers."

"I wasn't a stranger last night," he jabbed.

"Don't you dare," I said, pointing at him. "And while we're at it, how about you not being honest about why you're here? You've been living here. What are you, broke? Homeless? If you're going to start telling Kimya the truth, you start with that fact. How can I expect you to be honest about me when you can't even be honest about your situation?"

"You don't know what you're talking about. I've just been up here to clear my mind. Get away from all of that bullshit in the industry. I'm not homeless or broke," Marlo said. "I'm working on me."

"Finally we have something in common," I agreed. "Too bad my work doesn't include being someone's secret. And if you want to continue to placate Kimya's madness, you go right on ahead and do it. I'm done." I started walking out again.

"So that's it?"

He followed me to the staircase.

Halfway down, I stopped and looked up at him.

"My father once said every act has a closing," I said. "I'm closing this act of my life."

Part III

"Fighting Love in Brazil"

"Welcome to BK's Crescent Moon Café, the realest borough's only live music lounge featuring nightly entertainment by new artists. Thanks for supporting real music. First up, we have Sunshine Embry, who's been making waves behind the scenes for a bit, but now she's stepping out on her own and she wants you to hear what she's got. So, I present Sunshine!"

I carried my father's guitar to the small square stage through a wave of complimentary applause followed by deafening silence that magnified the noise of my every awkward movement. I sat on the seat in the center stage and readjusted the microphone, avoiding the audience's stares. I'd planned all of this, but still it seemed like a surprise that I was up there and everyone was watching, waiting.

"Thank you," I said, squinting at a bright spotlight in my eyes. Glasses clinked and chatter started in the background. "This is just a little something I've been working on."

It had been three months since I'd packed up my apartment in Manhattan and moved back to my father's brownstone in Brooklyn. There had been too many dark nights with tears and uncertainty. The growing pains of change and fear of what was next. But in the past few days I'd been on the upswing. Waking up before the sun went down. Eating. Answering Leticia's text messages.

I exhaled and placed my fingers in position on the guitar.

I was there to sing a song about freedom. Riches in freedom. The first thing I wrote after I left the beach house and quit my job.

The first stanza of the song was about a woman's heart ready to surrender. But she was afraid because she didn't know who she was. But everyone kept telling her she was special and that she would know it if she only just leaped.

Kimya kept her promise of not chasing me anymore. I worked to convince myself that I didn't care, but after five years of holding her on my shoulders, I had to admit that it felt odd sometimes not to have her harassing me in the middle of the night because she couldn't sleep, or crying on my shoulder over her latest bout with Sean. For a long time, leaving her felt like a breakup. As if I'd lost someone I'd been in a really long relationship with.

In the second stanza, I stood and sang about the woman with the heart standing over her surrender, that it felt so far down, and deep and scary, but she was ready to close her eyes and just fall.

After I paid to move my things to Brooklyn and got

the brownstone to a place where I could actually lay my head down at night, my funds were low.

In the last verse of the song I sang at the Crescent Moon Café, the woman with the heart jumps with her eyes wide open. She feels she's rushing to her surrender and halfway down she starts to think she's going to die, but then, from nowhere, she's lifted. She looks back to see what's carrying her. It's her own wings. She's flying. She's no woman after all. She's a bird.

"Thank you," I uttered beneath complimentary applause from tables in the first few rows before the stage. I nodded and curtsied playfully as the emcee with the red-dyed dreadlocks returned to the microphone.

"Sunshine Embry, everyone!" he said. "Thank you."

There was more applause and one woman even approached me for a hug as I left the stage.

I walked to the bar and ordered a drink. Sat the guitar against the bar and tried to take a stool, but someone slid it away.

"That's my seat," the person with the freshly manicured hands and shiny single diamond said.

"You came?" I looked up and hugged Leticia.

"Certainly."

We sat on neighboring stools on either side of the guitar.

"Was I bad?" I asked her. "You know I don't claim to be a singer," I said. "I'm a writer. Just wanted to share my words."

Leticia smiled. "It was beautiful."

"Thanks."

The bartender set my Jack and Coke down and Leticia insisted on giving her credit card to start our tab.

"How's everything going?" I asked. "Wedding planning in full swing?"

"It's like a freaking job. I feel as though I need an assistant," Leticia complained. "Clayton and I fight over everything and the wedding planner ignores both of us. Sometimes, I just want to wake up one morning and go to the courthouse. Keep it simple!"

"But that's not what you really want." I peered at her.

"Hell, no! It's my wedding. I want it big and fab and ridiculous," she laughed. "And I'm sorry that you're not the maid of honor. This stupid family tradition. My sister has no idea what to do."

"I'm okay with it. Don't burn any bridges on my account," I said. Leticia's winter wedding spectacular was far from anything I wanted to spend my time on. The closer we got to December, the more intense and outrageous her sister's emails became. It was just late August and she was already picking out decorations for the bachelorette party.

"So what's going on with you? I see we have new music to share." Leticia nudged me.

"You know, that's the one thing that's going right with me. Seems like once I set my mind to it, sat down and finally started writing something, it all came out. For once, I have more songs than blank pages in my notebooks. It's amazing."

Leticia hugged me as I tried to be cool and say it was nothing.

"So, what's going on with the gig?" she asked.

"Looking good right now. I was in the studio for the third time last week and I think Megatron's taking a liking to my work. But you know how these things go."

After I'd written my first five songs with no idea about what I was going to do with them, I realized that the error in my plan of waiting for Kimya to pass my songs along to Megatron was hidden in the equation—

waiting for Kimya. And with that option gone, I decided to take matters into my own hands. I mean, I knew where he was. He knew who I was. There was no reason for me not to try to get my stuff to him. I just showed up at the studio one night ready to give him my notebook. I felt meek when I saw him. Went into a speech about knowing he wouldn't take me seriously because I was just someone's former assistant, but he laughed and invited me into the studio with him. He put me in the booth and said he was going to play some new music he'd been working on. I should sing whichever song I thought went with the beat. If he liked it, he'd record. Well, he liked it. And he recorded me.

"This is it," Leticia squealed as if I said I was just selected for *American Idol*.

"No, this is just a small opportunity that may pan out to be nothing," I said.

"Girl, stop it! You are working for the top freaking producer in the industry. Do you know how many people would kill for that?"

"I'm not working *for* him yet—just *with* him. No checks being cut."

"Sunny, just claim it," Leticia argued. "Stop doubting yourself."

We sat in silence for a minute as I sipped my drink and listened to a woman on the stage singing "Simply Beautiful."

"Maybe you could call him," Leticia whispered.

"Just leave it alone. I fell for his bullshit and now it's over. Stop bringing it up."

I saw Leticia glaring at me, but I kept pretending to listen to the singer.

"You know he's back in the studio?" Leticia inched out.

"I don't care."

"I'm just telling you about what's going on in his career. A successful singer we both used to love," she said, picking at me. "I read it on a blog—'New Music Coming Soon From Marlo Lee.'"

"Still don't care."

"Wonder if any of the songs are about you." Leticia turned to the singer then and pretended she was listening.

"It's been three months. If he cared, he would've called me," I said. "And you know what, I don't think I would've answered anyway. I'm doing me right now. And I don't have time for the games. Inviting him back into my life would mean more Kimya, more drama and more—whatever else."

The singer went off to loud applause and up next was some poet who was reading a poem off a cell phone screen.

Someone in the audience yelled, "Tacky!" and we all laughed.

"I understand, Sunny," Leticia said. "I was just hoping, you know, after how excited you were about him, that it would work."

"I wanted it to work," I admitted. "But you know what, it didn't. Like when you and Clayton got together, you didn't have to ask questions. You didn't have to worry. He just gave himself to you and that was it. It was love. I want that. Something mature and grown-up."

Leticia started laughing so hysterically, she covered her mouth.

"What?"

"What you said about Clayton," she said. "Being mature and easy." She leaned in to me. "No such thing. I love that man, but he's been in Leticia's Training Academy since day one. His ex-girlfriend is still stalking my Facebook page and while he was the one who had the idea to get married, I had to help him with the down payment for my engagement ring." She held out the ring to my open mouth.

"You're kidding," I said.

"Not at all. That man is swimming in student loan debt from his MBA and his credit is jacked," Leticia revealed. "But I love him."

"Why didn't you tell me all of that?"

"I wanted you and everyone else, maybe even me, to think it was perfect," she said. "But the more I'm thinking about it, the more I'm realizing that it is. It's straight-up perfect. For me. And if I'm okay with it, and he's okay with it, then whatever. We're fine. The point is, nothing's what you think it's going to be. Looking for love isn't easy."

There was silence when the poet left the stage. And I guessed he didn't have any friends there either, because not one person clapped. Even the emcee looked perplexed when he reclaimed the microphone.

I asked Leticia if she was ready to go and she downed the last of her drink like it was water. Like those parties in the Hamptons, I guessed we'd outgrown bad open-mic spots, as well.

For all my fear of passing my words along to Megatron, I couldn't believe that he seemed to love, like, everything I gave him. After those first visits to the studio, we started a routine. I'd meet him at the studio after he was done working with his artists from the label. Into and through the night we'd work on new songs.

Megatron wasn't "mega" at all. He was a small man with lots of energy. Just, like, five-six and one hundred and twenty pounds, maybe. He was so frail beneath his oversized clothing that he looked as if he'd tip over at any moment and his unlaced Timberland boots were the only thing keeping him on the ground. But still he zipped around the studio all night as though he was trying to burn calories. I'd watch him buzz about and wonder where all of the energy came from and if he ever went home to sleep, or what he had waiting at home for him.

After so many nights sitting beside him in the booth, I realized that none of the answers to my quiet questions mattered. Megatron was in his zone in the studio—connecting with his only love. When he played the music he was making, just in short samples that he'd connect into longer pieces, his little body shook with excitement, as if he was in church getting the Holy Ghost. He was all passion about his work. And I came to suspect that this was why he was so successful. What kept big stars and dreamers like me just coming out tugging his coattails. He could do what he did day in and day out, because it was never about work for him. It was about love.

"I think you're ready, Sunshine," he said one early morning in the booth.

I was sitting beside him, falling asleep and wondering when he was going to announce that it was time to wrap up our session.

"Ready for what?" I asked groggily.

He turned to me, but I couldn't see his eyes through his dark shades. "I have an artist for you. Someone I want you to work with."

"Really?" I perked up quickly, nearly fell out of my seat.

Megatron laughed and nodded slowly to let me

know he was digging my excitement. "You came in here knowing enough about music and lyrics. We just had to put it all together. I like it. I think a lot of other people will, too."

I jumped on his tiny body and squeezed. Just hearing those words at that moment made tears assemble. It could've been that I was tired and hallucinating or maybe a little high from the fumes from the bong Mega kept lit in the lounge for whoever wanted to partake.

"Damn, girl, you can't go grabbing on me like that," Mega said, looking even smaller in my grasp.

I settled myself back into my seat. "So, who is it? What's the project?"

"A singer I'm backing right now. Still working some things out with the contract, so it's on the low," he said secretively. "But if everything works out, we're gonna move fast. The label is sending us to Brazil to record. Hope you have your passport ready. Some company trip shit."

"Are you serious? Are you flipping serious?" I ignored Megatron's request that I leave space between us and jumped on him again, kissing his cheeks and making him hug me.

He held out, but after a while he started laughing and hugged me back.

"Guess this means you have a passport."

"I do!" I jumped up and clapped my hands. "When do we leave? I mean, if everything works out with the contract—"

"Next week. And don't worry about a thing. Everything is covered by the label. But you know that from working with Kimya in Brazil, right?"

"Yes," I agreed. I hadn't seen Kimya in months, but still hearing her name stung a little. By then, she knew

I was working with Megatron. We'd nearly run into each other at the studio a few times and while people thought the music industry was big, it was really like a country high school cafeteria that included the cool kids' lunch table and nerdy back corner. Having left my post with Kimya, I was supposed to have been sent to the nerdy corner, but my new connection to Megatron meant I might actually get a seat at the cool kids' table. And the way things ended with me and Kimya, I knew she wasn't happy about that. My being successful meant I could do it on my own—that I never needed her and she'd always only needed me. To Kimya, that was betrayal and she wasn't above seeking and getting revenge—when she was sober. I knew she'd come for me. It was just a matter of when and how. I wondered if she'd already tried to talk Megatron out of working with me.

Still, I was able to float home on an invisible cloud. Like someone with an amazingly wonderful secret that they were just dying to let out. From people I passed on the sidewalk when I exited the studio to everyone sitting with me in the last car of the slow-moving local D train, I wanted to shake hands and give hugs and tell my story. I was doing it! Like, really doing it!

I walked into my father's old house, nearly expecting him to come running out of his room to hear my good news. Standing in the middle of the living room on newly laid wooden tile that I'd installed myself—with some help from Leticia and Clayton on weekends—I gave myself a hug from him to me. He'd be proud of any progress I was making. And happy that I was doing it my own way. I tried so hard to smell his English Leather, feel him holding me, hear him singing in my ear. Although there was nothing, I knew he was there with me in that house. I went into the basement and pulled out *Finding Love in Brooklyn*. Put the record player needle at the start of the line indicating the third song on the black wax. Stepped back and let out a deep, humble breath as the opening bars played. I waited and waited to hear his voice next, him singing about me. But that never happened. The music, the notes rolled on, but what I heard wasn't what was on the wax. In my ears were notes being sung by another man—Marlo Lee. It was his voice singing to me, singing of me. I looked up at the ceiling and saw us sitting in that bedroom in the mansion beside the Atlantic, the guitar, a feeling in my gut that this was everything I needed. How could I have fallen so fast and so stupidly? I felt so dumb for wanting him right there with me and my news at that moment. I hadn't wanted to admit that to myself for a long time, but right then, listening to him sing, I couldn't deny it.

I wrote a love song in the basement with my energy that night. Afterward, I climbed two sets of stairs up to my old bedroom and went to bed with my heart somewhere between pure joy and confusing pain. I had great news, but the one person who would understand was gone.

I picked up the phone to tell Leticia. At least she'd be happy for me.

"Hey, girl," I said somberly when she answered. "I need to talk."

"What's up…?" She sounded just as uneasy. "What's on your mind?"

"Marlo Lee."

"Wow. I told Clayton you already knew."

"Knew what?" I anxiously opened my eyes to the darkness in the room.

"Oh…never mind." Leticia slurred her words with anxiety.

"No. Tell me. Just spit it out," I insisted, sitting up. My heart started racing, edging on palpitations. Did something happen to Marlo?

"He's engaged," Leticia said. "Well, about to get engaged or something. That's what every gossip and entertainment site is saying online."

My body screamed, but I said nothing. I could feel Leticia shaking her head.

"I know how you feel. You know that."

"Whatever—it was just one night and I don't care what he—" I started, but ended with an expected, "Who is it?"

"Pilar Amber. That Vietnamese model who was Ms. Universe. She was on—"

"Dancing With The Stars," I let out like a death announcement.

"Yes. She was on there the season he was on there. I guess they've been dating for a minute."

I looked down at my feet, laughing disgustedly. "Straight-up liar."

"At least you know now."

"Some consolation."

"I guess." Leticia sucked her teeth. "So, if you didn't know that, what were you calling about?"

"Nothing, girl," I murmured, falling back into my starting position in the bed. "Absolutely nothing."

Two weeks on contract with Megatron's publishing company and I was sitting beside him on a first-class flight to Brazil. It was a small thing, but still big to me. Just the idea that he thought I should come along for the ride to write in such a beautiful place and be with him as he was in the studio with an artist he was developing was great. A few times before the trip, Candice and Antha implied that there was a romantic reason for his attention to me, but I denied any of their claims. He'd been nothing less than a gentleman in my presence. I was sure he was just grooming me, which was far more of a compliment than trying to get into my pants.

"It's always good to get away from the city to write," he said, organizing his things in his window seat beside mine in the aisle. "Don't get me wrong—I love BK, but there's something about a beautiful place that inspires. Three nights in Brazil might be just what the doctor ordered."

"Yeah, right. You know you're just going there to see women in thongs," I joked. We'd become pretty comfy from being caged up in the studio most nights.

"Ain't nothing wrong with that. I might fool around and find my wife in Brazil."

We laughed and I went to put on my seatbelt as the flight attendants started closing the cabin for departure.

While I'd promised myself I would think of nothing but my music on the trip, already Megatron's comment about a "wife" turned a knife in my stomach that reminded me of my conversation with Leticia about Marlo and Pilar. I hadn't slept at all that night after receiving the news. Then, and most days since, I was online looking for any information I could find about Marlo's engagement. It was becoming an obsession I'd deny if anyone asked. Leticia was mostly right about her news. Everyone was talking about the new couple. Although it didn't confirm their engagement, there was that seafoam-blue ring Marlo had given Pilar, and his team's admission that he'd fallen quickly for the model. Every page had pictures of Marlo and Pilar and her long legs walking in Central Park or sitting in a bar. Some were with a smiling Kimya. Others were with celeb couples on red carpets and front row at basketball games.

I hated Marlo more each time I clicked, but I couldn't stop myself. His smile. Her legs. It set ablaze some bottomless surprise at the deception I'd so easily fallen victim to.

"Mega! I thought I spotted you. They told me you were on an earlier flight!"

Megatron and I looked up toward the cheery rattle.

Behind one of the attendants was a thin yellow face with smiling, lavender-glossed lips.

"Pilar!" Megatron climbed over me to the aisle.

Pure panic surged around in my body like a typhoon. I didn't know where to go with myself. So I smiled.

They hugged and traded a short conversation I prayed wouldn't include me. But, of course, it did.

Megatron had been standing between me and Pilar, but he backed up for an introduction.

"*O-M-G!* This is her? The writer you were talking about?" Pilar said, looking down at me in my chair all smiles. She had on no makeup, but her skin looked like a fresh bed of powder in a compact. She was almost too tall to stand in the plane and her freshly blown amber hair was photo-shoot ready.

"Yes. I'm sorry. I thought you two knew each other. You know, because of Kimya—anyway, this is Sunshine Embry." Megatron pointed to me. "Sunshine, this is Pilar Amber."

Pilar bent down like a queen greeting a subject and kissed my cheek. "Thank you so much for your songs," she offered graciously. "I'm so excited to work with you."

"Work with me?" I asked.

"Yes. This is the singer—the one I told you about from the label. She's coming to Brazil to record," Megatron said, as if he'd been saving this as a surprise.

Suddenly, I felt so stupid for trying to be nonchalant about the project and not asking more questions. I felt so stupid about so many things. Like the rock on her ring finger that looked so much like the sea glass Marlo had tossed up at the lonely star on the beach that night in the Hamptons. Stupid.

"We're going to have so much fun in Brazil!" Pilar claimed so excitedly. "Can you believe it? We're recording my first album!"

"Actually, I can't believe it," I said. "Not one bit."

A flight attendant came to the rescue, rolling her eyes to clear Pilar and Megatron from the aisle.

Luckily, Pilar's seat was rows ahead of ours. She sat next to the window and flicked her hair over the headrest, but kept looking back toward Megatron and me. The seat beside her was empty. I looked to the door and waited, but no one ever came to claim it.

There's nothing worse than feeling ugly in a beautiful place. Too bad I already knew what that was like working for Kimya, and doing it again in Brazil was like a tradition. But doing it at that point in my life felt as though I was being cheated. And that made me angry.

Megatron had been asking what was wrong with me ever since we'd taken off. I kept saying I was fine, but once we got to the hotel, I went and hid in my room for a long nap I never took. I called Leticia and complained about models singing. Could Pilar even sing? This was ridiculous. So typical of the industry. Why was I even working with Megatron? We scrolled through articles online to try to piece together what was going on. Apparently, Pilar had signed a deal with Columbia. They were putting a bunch of money behind her. Calling her the next Rihanna. Vietnam's first pop princess mixing R & B with an Asian pop vibe. Even in my pain, Leticia and I managed to laugh at that like mean girls. We said it would fail. I hoped it would fail and felt bad for doing it. I didn't even know the girl. Still, Leticia said I had every right to hate her. Sometimes, that's what best friends are for.

After a few shots at the hotel bar, I got up enough nerve to take a cab to the studio that Megatron had been texting me from all afternoon.

"Thought I lost you to the beach," he said when I walked in. The "studio" was actually a converted pool house in the back of an oceanside megamansion that belonged to one of the VPs at the label. "Remember— we work now and play later."

I nodded and took a drink from one of the women who'd welcomed me into the home. There were a couple of guys I recognized from Columbia chilling in the pool and too many beautiful girls for there not to be trouble. Still, in the pool house, Megatron was at work and focused—in Hawaiian shorts and Timberland boots.

"I was tired," I said, taking a seat beside him behind the board.

"Come on, Miss. Let's try it again," he said loudly to the empty recording booth on the opposite side of the glass in front of the music board. Quickly, Pilar popped up behind the microphone.

"Sorry. I dropped my phone," she said. "Oh, hey, Sunny!" Her voice was so kind and sweet as if we were friends. "Didn't know you were here yet!"

"You ready?" Megatron asked her with his hand on the switch to start the track again.

"I'm nervous now that my wonderful writer is here," she squeaked like a shy girl.

I smiled reticently.

"I hope I don't let you down," she said, putting her headset on. "I'll do my best."

Another fake smile was earned.

Megatron ran the track and, with her eyes closed, Pilar sang the song about the girl with wings.

During the three or four times my father took me to church when I was a kid and I got to hear the women in the gospel choir belt the words to "His Eye Is on the Sparrow" or "Amazing Grace," I really got to understand the power of an innocent cry in a woman's voice. My reaction was always knots in my stomach, as if I was sitting in the front car of a roller coaster that was about to drop down wooden tracks. I'd tense up the entire time they sang and relax only when the last note was uttered.

That's what happened to me when I heard Pilar's voice on my song. Megatron had her on a clear microphone with no echo or support, but she sounded like an example of notes to sing. Like a finely tuned piano being played by a master. It was as if the song had been written just for her to sing it right then. Her voice gave my words meaning, and I knew instantly that if she recorded those words, even without Megatron's track, and it was released, the song would go down in history as a classic. And that was rare to know at that point, but I felt it all in me. I was confident that the entire world outside the pool house studio was listening hand in hand outside. And if I turned around, they'd be lined up outside the door in tears.

"Was that okay?" Pilar asked meekly, crinkling her

face when she was done. She was looking at me through the glass as if she was at an audition.

"I—I—" The knots surprisingly still in my stomach interrupted the flow between my thoughts and words.

"Oh, wait," Pilar yelped, pulling out her chirping cell phone. "One sec." She answered the call and turned her back to the booth, laughing into the phone.

Megatron was grinning. "I told you," he said to me. "She's the truth. You'd never think it, right? Thought she was all face and no talent?" He laughed, but then looked concerned. "Why you look like that, Sunny? You alright?"

"Yes. I'm fine," I managed, though most of what Megatron was saying became a cloudy commotion in my mind.

"Don't get nervous on me now," he said. "You're about to be a rich woman. And you have her to thank for it." He pointed to Pilar, who was still on the phone. "Well, her and your talent."

"Okay! So, how was it?" Pilar turned, seeking my commentary again.

"You were great," I admitted evenly and I could actually see Pilar's shoulders slump lower at my lack of hype.

"Maybe if I do it again," she said, hinting she could be better.

Megatron looked at me and put his finger on the button to start the track again. "Run it," he said.

Pilar put her headset on and lit into the track a second time.

I got up from my seat, my stomach still in knots.

"Bathroom's in the house," Megatron offered in assumption, still working the board. "Don't take too long. Think we'll try that ballad you wrote next. Okay?"

"Sure."

I exited the studio into a blaring sunlight that could not have been more unwelcoming. The very thing that was supposed to make a paradise of my surroundings felt like an interrogating spotlight.

The small mixer by the pool had grown into something akin to a hip-hop music video set. I padded past industry insiders and execs I recognized from Kimya's label on the way to the house. One of the marketing assistants I'd worked with cornered me, blabbering about how her flight had been rerouted and was late because of some storm in New York, but she was so glad to have made it to the *New Sound* show.

"New Sound?" I asked before she explained that the whole point of the trip was to bring the label's divisions together to expose and feature new talent.

Whispering that everyone was really just there to get a free vacation, she asked why I was there and seemed surprised that I was working with Megatron.

After I untangled myself from her conversation, I walked around the complex for a few minutes to clear my mind before I made my way back to the studio.

"Oh, my God, Sunny Bear!" Kimya shrieked.

I winced at the the familiar voice when I walked in.

Dressed in a black bikini, retro biker shorts and gold chains, Kimya was posted up in the booth beside Megatron and reaching for me as if I was a long-lost twin sister.

"I can't even believe it! What are you doing here?" Kimya embraced me dramatically. I could smell marijuana in her poofy red weave. She looked like every twenty-something pop star I could think of and she was even skinnier than I'd recalled.

"What are you talking about? I told you she was—"

Megatron started but Kimya stopped him, hugging me just long enough to cut him off.

"Of course I knew she'd be in Brazil. But here at the studio? With us? How—just uncommon." She winked as though I'd snuck in after the front gate was left open.

As much as I wanted to find the right words to put Kimya in her place forever, my eyes left her and zoomed in on Pilar at the microphone in the recording booth because she was standing beside a face that robbed me of all air.

There she was with Marlo, laughing and running lyrics on a sheet of paper she was holding with him. Marlo pointed to invisible notes in the air and Pilar tried to catch them. Megatron had the booth sound off so I couldn't hear them, though I knew it was my love song.

"Oh, you noticed my sister-in-law and big brother?" Kimya noted, following my stare and stepping behind me to become a narrator in surround sound. "Cute, right? They'll make divine babies. Too bad, Sunny Bear. Can't win them all."

The crazy in me snapped on. "Cute indeed," I said, smiling at Marlo and Pilar shoulder-to-shoulder in secret conversation. "Can't wait until the wedding. Where are they registered?"

"Umm... Ummmm." Kimya and her silly, high self was flabbergasted by my lack of pain.

I decided not to await a retort. I switched to Megatron. "Let's make music. I'm inspired," I said cheerily.

I darn near pranced over to the table, bent over Megatron and flicked on the sound myself. I could see Kimya watching me, confused. "Hey, y'all. Let's get back to work!" I said into the microphone broadcasting into the recording booth. I flashed my teeth in a grin and plopped down into the newly empty seat beside Megatron that Kimya had been in. "Kimya, you staying or playing? We have history to make in here!"

Kimya rolled her eyes and Megatron cheered on my enthusiasm.

Pilar went back to looking simple and oblivious to the situation, waving as Marlo looked out at me.

"Sunshine?" he said, breathily, as if I was so much farther away and not just on the other side of the glass in the studio. As much as I fought not to feel him, his tone easily vibrated through me. He was wearing a thin white T-shirt that revealed his muscles quite deliciously, low-sitting stressed jeans and a simple green plastic rosary that seemed so opposite to the chain he'd been wearing that first night in the Hamptons.

"Hey, Marlo," I said passively.

"You two know each other?" Pilar asked. "What am I talking about—" She corrected herself, flicking her forehead. "Of course you do. Sunshine worked with Kimya."

Kimya was still standing in her stun. "Why don't you two let Sunny hear your song?" she said cheekily, obviously still trying to get a sad response from me. "That *love duet*."

"Duet?" I copied.

"Yes!" Pilar pointed to Megatron, who was sitting silent and clearly trying to piece the situation together. "Can we do it again?"

Megatron started the fade-in of the track he was considering as the background for the last love song I'd written after that night in the basement.

Pilar started the first verse, then Marlo joined her.

As they fell into the chorus, gazing into each other's eyes, Megatron leaned into me whispering, "I know you meant for this to be a solo. It was Kimya's idea to split it just now. We don't have to do it—"

"I love it," I cut him off.

"What?" Kimya said behind me. "You hate it! You don't want them to sing together."

"No. It's really great. This is how it's supposed to be sung. This is what it's about. It's not just a love song," I said as Marlo began to turn away from Pilar and look at me with frustration in his eyes as he began the second verse.

"It's about love deferred. Being in love with someone and that love on hold," I bared, feeling I was somehow singing with Marlo then. "But it doesn't matter that there's nothing there to receive the love you want to give. It's about the emotion. Inviting in. Nothing else matters."

"Whatever," Kimya snarled vacantly.

Pilar started her response to Marlo's crooning, but Marlo pulled off his earphones and walked out of the booth, leaving her alone to record.

"The hell?" Megatron said, stopping the track when Marlo busted into the sound booth.

"I can't do this," Marlo said, walking past us quickly.

"But, Marlo, we need to finish the song," Kimya forced, following behind him as he walked toward the door that led out to the deck.

"No! I won't do this!" He looked at me. "Y'all want this. Y'all do it without me." He nearly kicked the door open and disappeared into a flash of dazzling sunlight.

Kimya growled theatrically and gave chase.

"What's going on?" Megatron asked.

"Wish I knew," I answered.

Pilar had stopped singing and was back on her phone giggling as if Marlo hadn't just randomly walked out.

"Um…Pilar, hate to interrupt," Megatron said into the microphone so she could hear him.

"I'm sorry. You guys want to move on to the next song?" she chirped, unfazed, holding the phone to her chest.

"Is that Marlo on the phone?" Megatron asked. "Can you get him back in here?"

"No. It's not him. You want me to try calling him?"

Megatron looked at me confused, but I could only shrug.

Pilar got through two more songs I'd written. While she seemed as though she was at her best on the first recording, she still bested her best and with little effort. She turned sermons out of songs I'd just given Megatron as examples of what I could do. She improvised and arranged so organically and in tune with the entire production of what we were doing that there was little more instruction for Megatron and me to impose other than congratulations that were always in order.

Once it was clear there was no way we could avoid the blooming poolside party any longer, Megatron called the session to a close. He asked if I wanted to join him and some of the other producers for drinks in downtown Rio, but I declined. Truth be told, my armor was fading. I wasn't bulletproof. Not even in Brazil.

When night caught us, I went back to the hotel and put on my favorite prawn sarong for a lonely walk on the beach where I could clear my head and patch my exterior for the next day in the studio.

I'd learned long ago that the real beauty in Rio's beaches wasn't in the sunlight. The moon was its most true illuminator. Every stone, pebble and grain of sand on the beach that had been warmed by the sun all day became a glittering diamond at night. Walking on the beach in the darkness that was only broken by the warmed stones afoot was like padding over a constellation.

I walked along the shoreline for a long time, watching people in love and listening to the bands playing in the clubs up on the strand. Soon the bottom of my sarong was as wet as my cheeks from tears that escaped my eyes without reason. I was about to turn back to the hotel and seek warmth, but I decided to get my entire self wet. To walk into the water—not away from it. To invite it in. I wanted to laugh. I needed to laugh. And just be free to get wet for a second. I turned and looked at the ocean and dared myself to step in. Three times, I dared, poking my big toe into the cooling tide water. I declined and dared and tried again.

Finally, "Freak it!" I ran into the water kicking and splashing like a kid.

"I did it!" I said to the water. "I did it!" At first I was talking about entering the ocean, but soon I was talking to the sea about everything else I'd done. "I did it!" I was so far into the water that the cooling waves lapped against my thighs. I started jumping and cheering myself on. "I did it!" More tears came, but with reason. In happiness. In claiming happiness that I'd invited in.

"What are you doing here?"

I turned, and there in the sand, Marlo appeared charging toward me shoeless and clearly on his own night walk over the sandy constellations.

"What?"

"Why would you leave me on Long Island and say you never want to see me again and then come here when you knew I would be here?"

"I didn't know you would be here," I said.

"It's my label."

"It's my career. I have a right to be here," I said, stamping out of the water like a misbehaving mermaid. "Why would you care about me being here anyway? You've obviously moved on with your life."

"I could say the same about you. You know? First you sleep with me. Then you don't want to speak to me. What kind of shit is that?"

"Like you give a damn," I said, trudging through the sand toward my hotel. "You didn't call. You never even tried! And now I'm supposed to listen to you?"

"Why would I try after I got your letter? You told me everything I needed to know," he said.

"Letter?" I stopped.

"You're a trip," he said dismissively. "I can't do this."

I turned to see him leaving me standing there in the sand.

"No. Wait! What letter?"

"The one you gave Kimya with your resignation." He looked at me and started speaking in a voice to imitate mine: "'I need to follow my dreams. Please don't contact me. I don't want to hear from you. I hope you understand.'" He laughed sarcastically after recalling a few lines through angry eyes and finally commented, "At first I didn't want to believe it was you, but that voice, how you bitterly just tossed me to the curb, it sounded like you."

"Marlo, I didn't write any letter. I didn't send Kimya anything—not a resignation or any letter for you." The last time I'd seen Kimya was at the house in the Hamptons. I hadn't even gone back to her penthouse to get my favorite shoes. I'd even had her manager deposit my last check.

"I saw the letter. I read it. You're saying Kimya— she wrote it?"

"I'm saying Kimya lied to you. She wrote a letter to lie to you. I didn't write that."

"No. Why would she do that?" Marlo looked so confused and maybe heartbroken, but his aversion was clearly not aimed at me. "What am I talking about? I know why she would do that. Typical Kimya." He sighed heavily. "I should've known."

He turned and started walking toward the soft sand in the water, staring out at the stars.

I crossed my arms and watched him pondering as my throat swelled with words I wanted so badly to let out, but couldn't. I remembered him in the kitchen with the blueberry tea, smiling and telling me about the little sister he had to protect.

He bent down and picked up one of the shiny diamonds and tossed it into the water like a weight pulled right out of his heart.

In most any other circumstance, a brother in this state of confliction needed to be left alone. And I probably should've walked away. I had confliction of my own. Anger of my own. Reasons to throw my own rocks. But there was still that tightness in my throat.

"I couldn't have written that letter," I said, clearing my throat. "I couldn't have, because I don't feel that way."

"Feel what way?" Marlo threw another diamond.

My throat tickled out, "About you. About us being in contact. I don't feel that way."

Marlo scanned my face.

"I waited for you," I said. "For so long. To just call me. Even in my anger, I wanted you to try."

"How could I? I thought you didn't want me. That you were moving on without me."

"I never did," I said through a clear throat that didn't

need to struggle. "That night—" I tried, but Marlo stole my words.

"*That night*—was the best gift I've ever gotten."

My emotions limbered into a past where we'd held on to each other as familiar strangers in a night of lifetimes and I'd felt the same thing.

Marlo captured these feelings in his words. "It changed my heart. Opened it. I know that sounds corny, but that's how I've been explaining it to myself. That's what it did. And I can't be the same."

"But you didn't tell me. You never came to me."

"You know, even with the letter, I did think of that a few times. That I could just show up at the studio with flowers and tell you everything I knew about you working with Megatron and I'd—I'd tell you how much I love you and ask you to be mine, but—" he looked off "—then I realized something, Sunshine. I don't think I'm enough for you. Good enough for you."

"Really? Whatever," I said in skepticism and anger for every woman who'd ever heard that bold fib before.

"I'm serious. Your father was Sunsiree Embry. Do you know what that means to me as a singer? Who he is to me?"

"He's my father. He's not me. You were with me," I said.

"Well, then there's you, Sunny. All of you. It's as though you're cut out of every lyric he ever wrote," Marlo said with marked attachment. "You're scarred but not scared. A beautiful thing."

"I am scared," I protested.

"No, you're not. You think you are, but you're not. You're still out here fighting. Trying. Not like the rest of us. We're moving still," he said. "Stuck."

"You're not. You moved on," I said. "Pilar. And this

engagement. How could I believe any of the things you said when you've moved on like that? So quickly. What am I supposed to think? I'm so wonderful, so free, but obviously forgettable."

"It's not what you think."

"I'm thinking you're engaged, Marlo. That's what everyone is saying. She's wearing that ring and you two are together. That's not it?" I asked.

"Kimya," he spat, looking back at the water before explaining the story about his situation with Pilar in a grand scheme that would only make sense to other people in the entertainment industry.

"She's a beautiful person. She has a wonderful voice and I support her. I'm her friend. I just want what's best for her," he said.

I'd uncrossed and re-crossed my arms dozens of times to keep track of the tale that left me teetering between understanding, disbelief and even contempt a few times. I thought to walk away. To hit him. And then to hug him.

"What is Kimya getting out of this?" I asked as every plot point in the ruse led back to her.

"Well, you see it all online. We're the new 'Three Musketeers' of the blogs and gossip rags—beating out even the newbies," he shrugged. "We're in the headlines. She goes on tour in a few weeks. It's all publicity. Works for everyone."

"You?"

"I'm in the studio. The label wants to accelerate the release date of my album," he said.

"So, you're pretending to be engaged to get publicity?" I laughed. "Ridiculous."

"There you go with that again. Judging everyone for

everything," he said. "Did you even hear the other stuff I said about Pilar? About her career?"

"What? She's a lesbian and the labels don't think people will like that?" I repeated what he'd revealed. "What is it, 1950? Who cares?"

"She cares. Pilar has been in a committed relationship with the same woman for ten years. She doesn't want to compromise that, but she also wants her shot—just like the rest of us. You know how this works—how this industry is."

"I do, but I also know how I want to work. How I want to be," I said.

"What does that mean?" Marlo came in closer to me than he'd been all night.

"Not like this. Not being confused and hurt. I want to be clear…and if you or anyone else can't give that to me, then I can't do it. I just can't. Not anymore in my life."

"I wasn't trying to bring this to you, Sunshine," Marlo said.

"You keep saying that. About everything. About Kimya and now this, but you keep doing it," I said. "I need more."

Marlo looked at me like a man who was down on his luck. "I can fix it."

"I don't want you to do that."

"What do you want?"

"I don't want to compromise me or you or anything. Not anymore."

"Sunny, I gave my word. It's deeper than just being a compromise. Don't you understand?"

I shook my head and turned to go in my own direction alone again. "I guess I don't have a choice. Do I?"

That night, as I began to walk away with only the

South Atlantic wind whistling in my ear, I decided that was it. Any dream I'd had of being with Marlo was over.

"Sunny, don't!" Marlo screamed to my back.

I hurried away. Kept my pace as I began to cry.

"Sunny!"

Soon I could hear him back behind me.

"Sunny!" He spun me around, grabbed my face from either side and on my mouth he cried a caress with his tongue. Our bodies hardly touching, the sadness was communicated in an overflow.

In the morning, I called Megatron to tell him I would be leaving Brazil early. I wanted to thank him for everything. I hoped I hadn't let him down.

Through a groggy voice that sounded like rounds of drinks and Brazilian cigars he'd enjoyed the night before, Megatron begged me to stay. He reminded me of how much Pilar moved my music and he wanted me to have a chance to hear her perform my songs in front of everyone from the label at the showcase that night.

"Just stay one more night," he'd said. "I promise you'll love it. Pilar is an amazing singer, but she needed your words. I didn't tell you this before because I didn't want you to be intimidated, but I'd tried matching her voice with so many writers, but none of their words really caught what she could do, what she could say."

I was still packing in my hotel room as I listened to his plea on speaker phone. I rolled up my sarong and sat on the bed.

"Is this about Marlo?" Megatron asked carefully.

"You know?"

"I put it together. The way he looked at you in the studio—"

"I didn't mean for that to happen. I had no idea he—"

"I know. It was all Kimya's work. Her idea to get them together. To pull you in. Good old Kimya," he said, laughing, before he confirmed what I'd thought about Kimya's watchful eye over my work with him. In fact, she'd been more involved than I'd originally thought. Megatron had actually been expecting me to stop by his studio at some point because Kimya told him I was looking to hook up with him and warned him that I was a horrible writer, tramp and troublemaker and that he should stay away. Megatron said he didn't believe anything she'd said and that her warning only made him believe the opposite. "I'm my own man. I don't get involved in that industry bullshit," he said. "I'm just here to make good music."

"Thank you for giving me a chance," I said.

"No, Sunny. You gave yourself a chance. And don't lose it all over this bullshit. Can't you see that's what Kimya wants? For you to walk away with your tail between your legs?" he asked. "Here's the truth— everyone at the label knows about Pilar. Shit, she brought her girl here with her."

"She did?"

"Yes. Honey was in coach right behind us. That's why Pilar kept looking back through the whole flight," Megatron revealed.

I sat shocked, remembering Pilar looking back toward us from the front row on the flight to Brazil. I thought she was looking at me and knew about what had happened with Marlo, but she was actually making eyes with someone else.

"But I don't get it. Isn't that whole lesbian thing cool right now in entertainment?"

"Not in middle America. Not if you're a former Ms. Universe. Don't get it twisted. People are still feeling some kind of way. But really, just in the industry, even the fakes don't care about Pilar's past. They just want to make money. They made up this whole engagement thing to get her name out there and get Marlo some attention. As soon as she's on top, they'll fake a breakup and both will go their separate ways," Megatron went on. "That's the bottom line. She knows that and I know you do, too. As for Marlo, dude is a legit. I've been out here longer than him or Kimya and I know he's straight." He laughed. "Now, Kimya—she's grimy. But Marlo? If anything, he's not grimy enough for this. Too good. But as crazy as Kimya is, she's still his blood. A good man ain't gonna cross that."

"But that doesn't mean he has to play along with her. He should be his own man," I replied, feeling as if Megatron had suddenly become an old friend.

"I'm not saying you need to marry dude. I just want you to know the real. You're in my family now and I believe in protecting my team," Megatron said. "Kimya set this all up to make you give up. Walk away from writing. Walk away from Marlo. And right now, you're about to do it. If you're okay with that, cool. But you needed to know the truth."

Feeling torn about making a decision, I put on my bikini top and sarong and sat out on the beach in my big shades to watch the shades of brown buttocks go by in thin thongs and men's eyes pop out like those on dead fish.

Pilar and a woman I recognized from the flight who was just as beautiful, long and glamorous as Pilar, walked past just a few recliners away, laughing and looking at each other's feet digging into the sand as they headed to the water. They weren't holding hands and anyone watching would never think they were "to-gether," but they looked happier in each other's pres-ence than two platonic friends ever could.

Interestingly, although I hadn't known Pilar long enough to champion any cause related to what I was seeing or knew about her relationship, the little bit I'd learned about how humble and kind she'd been, even behind closed doors in the studio where saving face wasn't ever easy for a diva, made me happy for her at least having love. Feeling it. I wondered if that af-fected how she sang her songs. Who she sang to when she closed her eyes and flung her head back and belted out, crying of love.

For a few seconds, I wondered if I should say hello to Pilar. Maybe share again and under less pressure-filled consciousness how I felt about her voice. She was only a few steps away with her back to me, but I decided against it.

I was about to get up from my seat to head to the bar when Pilar's friend suddenly pulled her into an embrace that left Pilar facing me.

While her eyes were closed at first, she opened them and looked right at me. The smile she'd had broke apart and her eyes began an uneasy suffering. It was hard to think she was looking at me. Hard until I realized who I was and where we were. She waved with a crinkled and nervous hand.

"Hey," I called.

The woman let her go and turned to face me, too. They stood as if they were waiting for unkind words or maybe just one of those judgmental looks.

"Great job yesterday," I said to counter their won-dering. "I really mean that."

Pilar's smile returned. "Thank you," she said, still keeping a distance about her. "I'll see you later."

I nodded a yes and they turned away before I could remember to say I would be leaving Rio before the showcase.

When I got up to head back to the bar for a drink, standing there, just steps back, was a photographer flipping through pictures he'd just taken of Pilar in her embrace on the beach.

Something beneath my skin began to itch and I walked past the bar and back to the hotel.

Part IV

"Finding Love in Brooklyn"

"Bird" wasn't my father's favorite song to sing. That was "Finding Love in Brooklyn."

After he died, I was cleaning out his boxes, donating some of his music sheets to the Schomburg in Harlem when I saw an old feature published in the *Amsterdam News*. In the article, my father was talking about "Finding Love in Brooklyn" and why it had always been his favorite.

He'd said the song was about emotional currency. About the heart and its limitless ability to love wide-open. And even at the worst of times. In the worst of places. When it seemed like it was empty or lost or forgotten, it would show up and get found and act out. Everywhere. Even in Brooklyn.

As I recalled that memory, I cursed myself the entire way back upstairs to my room where I thought about

rebooking my flight, then sat on the bed to come up
with a plan.

The thing was, I couldn't let Pilar look out into the
audience and not see me and think maybe I'd left Rio
on account of what I'd seen on the beach. Maybe she
wouldn't even think about it or notice or care, but I sat
and knew I couldn't take the risk of someone else getting hurt, of anyone else not reaching their potential for
any reason. Seeing that photographer, who I knew had
sent those pictures out everywhere just seconds after
Pilar had walked away, made the situation so real for
me. Marlo was right. It was about so much more than
what I wanted. It was about her right to find her own
love. And I had to support that. I'd be there in the audience tonight if she looked for me. Whatever else happened with Marlo or Kimya just would. And maybe I
wanted that.

Still, I got to the showcase late. It was back at the
mansion and just overnight a crew had transformed the
outdoor area into something that looked like an open-air
concert hall. An entire live band, complete with a white
baby grand that glowed brilliantly beneath the moon,
sat atop huge wooden planks jettisoned over half of the
swimming pool. Cocktail tables, low and high, dressed
in white cloth, floating candles and lemon-colored os-
trich feathers, replaced sun recliners around the deck.
Everywhere was someone beautiful and bright, shining
in the residue of leftover suntan oil. Even from my humble, hidden seat far to the back of the crowd, I could see
faces that usually looked just okay in New York made
delectable in the opulent setting of musical celebration. Some people danced with sexy new scantily-clad
friends. Some others chatted and politicked, waiting for
the next performer and waxing about the last.

There were a couple of singers and two rappers, all of whom were amazing, but none of whom could nearly compare to Pilar, who was sitting in the front of the room at a table with the label's vice president, Marlo, Kimya and two A&Rs. A few tables over from mine in the back sat Pilar's friend from the beach with Marlo's boys Icey and Milt and two women I remembered from the pool party.

While someone else had been introducing the other artists, when it was time for Pilar to perform, Megatron was called to the stage to do the honors. Through cheers of knowing applause, he went up in his normal cool, chatting about the importance of good music and how it wasn't ever easy for even a great producer to create great music unless he had the right talent around him. He talked about meeting Pilar and hearing her voice and that he knew that once he'd found the right writer, he'd be able to produce something timeless. But that search wasn't as easy as he'd thought.

"I don't think that young lady who wrote the two songs you're about to hear is here tonight," he said, looking out into the audience and squinting to maybe find my face, but I stayed in my corner. "But she's definitely a part of this effort and the magic Pilar is about to present came from her. So, thank you, Ms. Sunshine Embry, wherever you are."

He finished by getting everyone riled up to hear the label's next hot thing, the voice of the next generation, Pilar Amber.

A sparkling parade of fireworks lit up the sky and then he was gone and Pilar was center stage in a long white gown that matched perfectly the purple orchids tucked behind her right ear.

She sang my song about flying and the buzzing

crowd became so silent it seemed they were mesmerized not only with her near-perfect notes, but also by the story of the song. I could literally feel them waiting for the next lines, the next verse. The anticipation was so palpable, a few people were standing and swaying along.

When Pilar finished the song, she thanked everyone in the audience for their support and highlighted a few people who'd been on her team since the beginning.

A man in a black tux at the piano started playing the notes to the ballad and Pilar signaled for Marlo to join her onstage.

"Ladies and gentleman, Mr. Marlo Lee," Pilar said, smiling as Marlo headed to the front.

Kimya stood and squealed as though she was his mother.

Marlo waved humbly as everyone clapped and cheered in a wave of recognition that led to a standing ovation.

"Thank you all so much," he responded, looking out at everyone, but I felt as if he was staring right at me.

Pilar introduced the meaning of the song over the piano, repeating everything I'd said in the studio, though I didn't think she'd been listening to me.

At some point as they sang as though they'd been singing together forever—Rufus and Chaka, Donny and Roberta, Ashford and Simpson—I closed my eyes to really feel the words alone inside myself. I heard someone to my left say, "This is about to change the game."

When the song was over, the crowd was on its feet again, begging for an encore.

Pilar giggled and covered her reddening face shyly.

Marlo hugged her and kissed her on the cheek before backing up to look at her. When she uncovered her face, she was crying and though she was still obviously happy, a look of seriousness dulled her joy.

"You ready for this?" Marlo asked, looking into her eyes.

"Yes," Pilar answered soberly.

Marlo pulled Pilar under his shoulder and they turned to the audience.

"What's going on?" the person in my right ear at the table asked someone else.

"Well, I think some of you may already know this, but Pilar and I wanted to go ahead and give our take on it, I guess," Marlo started, looking back and forth between the audience and Pilar protected in his hold. "A few hours ago someone released pictures of my dear friend Pilar on the internet, claiming she was here in Brazil on vacation with someone who will remain unnamed."

An audible chatter of surprise at both the news and announcement of news they already knew rumbled around the audience.

"Now, don't everyone get all upset all at once," Marlo joked. "We know who the person is and how they got those pictures. And—" he looked at Pilar, who nodded him along "—we just wanted to come out—I guess, in a way—and say that no, we are not engaged. We are just good friends. And, yes, the person Pilar was photographed with is—"

"No! You stop it! Stop it right now!" Kimya charged on her feet and headed to the stage.

Megatron and one of the A&Rs caught her and stopped the interruption, though Kimya continued to shout defiantly, "No! You'll screw everything up!"

Pilar put her microphone to her mouth and started where Marlo stopped. "Umm… I'm sorry, Kimya. And

I'm sorry, everyone, but I won't hide who I am anymore. And I can't keep lying to everyone. See, I started singing because I wanted to follow my dreams, but today I realized, with the help of my good friend Marlo," she said, looking at Marlo, "that, as the person he really loves told him, we have to be honest about who we are if we'll ever get what we truly want. Who I really am is someone who is in love with a woman."

There was more rumbling and gasps.

"And I'm not ashamed of it. And I won't hide. I won't compromise that. If I'm going to really sing about love, I have to be honest about who I love and how I love," Pilar said as her voice transformed from one filled with fear to complex openness. Her face was dried of tears.

Pilar ran off the stage with the bottom of her gown tossed over her arm and met her girlfriend halfway on the floor.

At first the rumbles of chatter simply got louder, but one person started clapping as the pair united in an embrace. Next another person was clapping. Soon a few more. Then everyone was moved to clapping and cheering and on their feet. Even the vice president and the other big wigs from the label up front had dewy faces and encouraging smiles.

As the crowd began to close in around the spectacle, Kimya shouted hysterically from her holding area, "Lies! Can't you all see it? They're lying! This isn't true! It's all a lie! A joke!" She laughed wildly like a crazy woman.

Still, neither Kimya's craziness nor the kissing ladies was the most shocking thing that I was seeing. It was Marlo. He was still standing and smiling on the stage, watching everyone gather to celebrate Pilar's coming out. He looked so full. He never once looked in Kimya's direction.

I wondered what he was thinking. If he was looking for me.

Without another thought, I began to tunnel through the crowd in a burst of feverous desire.

I wanted to be near Marlo. To kiss him under the moonlight again. To hear him tell me everything I was feeling was real and I was his best gift. Because I wanted to tell him he was mine.

"What she said—what Pilar said—was she talking about me?" I asked when I'd made it to Marlo's side on the stage over the pool.

He turned to me and this time I saw in his eyes that he was the one who'd lost his breath.

"Yes," he said so naturally. "I'm in love with you, Sunshine Embry."

We hadn't realized it, but the microphone was still on and the crowd was growing quiet again as, one by one, they realized where the sound through the speakers was coming from.

"But what Kim—" I tried.

"There's nothing in my life—nothing—that's going to keep me away from loving you and being with you for another day," he said.

"How are we going to do this?" I asked. "How do we begin?"

"Like this!" Marlo pulled me into his arms and picked me up so my head hovered over his before kissing me so passionately I could hardly imagine the world of flashing camera phones and ovations that would flood around us when I opened my eyes.

"What is this?" Kimya shouted amid the merriment.

"What are you doing, Marlo? You're ruining me. Ruining everything!"

Megatron began to pull her farther back away from the stage, but I took the microphone from Marlo to tell him to stop.

"No. Let her go," I said in front of the listening audience. "Please let her go."

Megatron and the other man released Kimya and she looked at them as though they'd tried to accost her.

She then looked back up at Marlo and me with fury in her eyes.

"You'll pay for this, Sunny Bear!" she spat with her hand held up in my direction to curse me.

"Grow up, Kimya," I offered. "You tried to beat me. You lied. You schemed. You lost. It's time for you to grow the hell up."

"I won't let you take my brother!" she hollered like a toddler unprepared to share.

I was about to respond, but Marlo took the microphone from me.

"She already has," he said rebelliously.

These words hit Kimya as if a typhoon had rolled up from the beach and threatened to pull her into the ocean.

She fell back into a dramatic faint. Luckily, Megatron and the A&R were still standing behind Kimya to catch her and pull her out of the party.

Knowing the spell would be short-lived, Marlo and I turned to each other laughing a little.

"You fine with this?" Marlo asked.

"Yes," I said. "I'm fine with all of this."

"Kiss her again!" Pilar called out and everyone laughed.

Marlo pulled me back into his arms and planted his lips against mine once more.

The crowd shouted congratulations and more lights flashed. This time the fireworks bursting over the sky were for us.

Part V

"Postlogue: Did We Ever Actually Make It to BK?"

Just like love stories, love songs have happy endings. They begin with strangers and a promise. An idea of love. And somehow along the way, those strangers find they share the same promise, the same idea. Love. And then they find a way to each other. There's a climax. An epiphany. A showering of melodies all wrapped in emotions. And then they come together to be together in love, in a happy ending. Everyone claps. They walk off into forever.

There was a whole lot of seat-changing on those flights back to New York from Brazil.

Pilar sat happy with her lover.

Megatron sat happy with his new Brazilian boo he'd found on his own late-night walk on the beach.

Kimya sat angry beside Gina and Martin.

Me?

Marlo?

We sat together. Happy. Smiling and looking out of the window, coming up with our "what next?"

I felt so ridiculous for believing the plans we were making for our touchdown. But I kept reminding myself to invite it in. To let it take hold and not be scared to just feel it.

And Marlo was holding my hand the whole time.

"You have a ride from the airport?" he asked at a point when we'd stopped talking and just reclined our seats to watch the sun setting outside the window as the plane began to creep in over New York.

"No. Just getting a taxi back to Brooklyn," I said. "What about you?"

"I was supposed to ride home with Kimya," he said, looking over at his sister struggling with her nipping teacup doggies in the seat beside her. "But I don't think that's going to happen."

I laughed.

"What are you going to do, then?" I asked.

"Can I come to Brooklyn with you?"

"What's in Brooklyn?" My cheeks were perked up over a caricature of a smile.

"You."

"Me?"

"Us."

I looked out at the new night to hide my expectant grin as the pilot announced our descent into LaGuardia International Airport.

* * * * *

HEARTBREAK IN RIO
Delaney Diamond

Chapter 1

Rio de Janeiro, Brazil

Sidney Altman sighed contentedly, taking in the sparkling waters of Copacabana Beach from the terrace of her sixth-floor suite, across the street from where a promenade ran parallel to the water's edge. The luxurious art deco building where she stayed contained four restaurants, including a piano bar she had visited last night to wind down with drinks after her long flight. After she concluded her business in the next two days, she planned to take full advantage of the hotel spa and the famous beach, where she currently watched with envy as tourists and cariocas sunbathed and frolicked in the waves.

Well-rested, she was now ready to face the buying team in her first meeting with Belo Fashions, a small Brazilian retailer that sold everyday fashions for the average woman.

Hearing her cell phone ring, she went back inside. The room had ceiling-to-floor olive-green drapes that hung over the windows. In the sitting area two chairs covered in a gold-leaf pattern and the matching love seat surrounded a glass table with plastic flowers in vibrant hues of magenta, lemon-yellow and lavender.

She picked up the phone. "Hello?"

"How's it going?" The voice of her mother, Agnes Altman, came through the line.

"Mom, you can't keep calling me every five minutes," she chided.

"I'm not. I just know how important this deal is to you. You've worked so hard to get where you are."

Her mother was her biggest cheerleader. "Stop worrying or you'll make me worry."

Agnes laughed. "I'll try not to. I don't want to jinx you."

Apparently one of Belo Fashions's assistant buyers had remembered Sidney from Coterie, an international fashion exhibition in New York, but for the life of her she couldn't remember meeting any of their buyers from that event. Regardless, the company wanted to work with the Haute Moderne fashion house and had specifically requested Sidney as the sales rep to make the presentation.

Belo Fashions had been very accommodating. They had provided a suite, first-class airfare and a driver as part of the deal to entice Haute Moderne to present next season's evening wear to their buyers. This type of accommodation was highly unusual, but she took it as a sign that they were very interested.

Their interest couldn't have come at a better time. After losing a major contract last year, this deal was make-or-break for Haute Moderne, and its success or failure rested squarely on her shoulders.

"I probably won't have much to tell you even after the meeting," Sidney said. She slipped on her shoes, a pair of coal-black pumps as comfortable as tennis shoes. "This is a totally different culture from ours. They prefer to take their time and establish a rapport with anyone they do business with. I can't rush them."

"They'll fall in love with you. I'm sure of it." Agnes paused. "Are you okay?" she asked quietly.

Sidney understood her mother's concern and a rueful smile touched her features. "Mother, the chances of me running into him are almost nonexistent. We already discussed this, remember?"

"I know, but I wanted to know how you felt about being in his country, knowing he's there somewhere."

Sidney set her coffee mug on the dresser and swallowed the painful constriction in her throat. The "he" her mother mentioned was Rodrigo Serrano, the CEO of Moda. Moda was owned by the Serrano family and as a much larger retailer than Belo, it dominated the country's competitive clothing market. It had been a year since she and Rodrigo had parted ways, and still just the thought of his name made her heart ache.

They'd met in New York and their affair had been brief and intense. After an argument, Rodrigo had left in anger and she'd never heard from him again.

She unsnapped her briefcase to double-check the contents. "Mom, I'm fine. What happened between me and...him is in the past."

She couldn't even bring herself to say his name. It was still too painful. She could still see his dark eyes and hear his husky male laugh every time she closed her eyes for longer than a second. And because he often invaded her thoughts, he was still very much a part of her life.

"You know I had to ask and make sure you're fine."

Ever since Sidney's father had passed away when she was in high school, she and her mother had become even closer and were more like sisters than mother and daughter. "Stop worrying. Anything you want me to bring you back?"

"Bring me back one of those hot Brazilian men."

"Mom!" They shared a laugh. "What am I going to do with you?"

"Sweetie, I know things you know nothing about."

Sidney laughed again. "Don't have too much fun while I'm away. I can't bail you out of jail from all the way down here." She snapped the briefcase shut. "All right, I better get out of here. The driver will be waiting for me."

"Make sure you have a little bit of fun while you're down there, okay? You work too hard. Knock 'em dead, baby. Love you."

Sidney checked her appearance in the mirror one last time before she grabbed her briefcase and took the elevator downstairs. Outside, a black sedan with tinted windows waited. While it was wintertime, cold and snowing in New York, it was summer in Brazil. She lifted her face and embraced the warmth of the sun.

It would be nice to live in a place like this, where the weather didn't have such extremes, she thought.

"*Bom dia,* Javier." She greeted the driver, who'd stepped out of the vehicle and opened the door upon seeing her. She chose to say "good morning," a simple phrase to show that she'd at least made some effort to learn a few words of Portuguese.

"Bom dia, senhora." A welcoming smile creased his leathery tan face.

Javier didn't say much on the short ride to Belo headquarters, which gave Sidney a chance to run through the introductory speech in her head. This morning would be a preliminary meeting with the buying assistants and the senior buyer who oversaw all purchases for the women's department. Tomorrow would be a follow-up to address any concerns and hopefully close the deal. Her main contact was an assistant by the name of Gilberto Ribeiro, whom she'd been in constant communication with from almost the beginning.

Belo headquarters was located in Centro, the city's historic and financial center. While there were no views of beaches that tourists could flock to, there was still plenty to see and do in that part of town. Centro was an interesting mélange of churches dating back to the eighteenth century and tall, modern buildings housing banks and other businesses. Javier dropped her off in front of the Belo building and she took the elevator to the top floor. When she stepped into the reception area, a dark-skinned older woman wearing glasses greeted her.

"Senhora Altman, *bem-vinda.* Welcome. My name is Nelza Correia. I will take care of you today."

"Thank you. It's a pleasure to be here." Sidney gave the woman a warm smile and they shook hands.

"Please have a seat." Nelza motioned to a row of cushioned chairs along the wall.

Nelza spoke to a young woman behind the reception desk and then came back to Sidney. "Senhor Ribeiro is in a very important meeting with one of our business partners, and it went longer than expected. I will take you to the conference room to wait." Her expression was apologetic. "May I get you anything to drink? A *cafezinho,* perhaps?"

Brazilians were known for their potent cups of coffee. But she'd already had her morning fix, so she declined.

Nelza led her down a long hallway, past offices on both sides where employees sat hunched over computers. The conference room itself was at the end of the hall and opened up into a large, bright room with an oak table that seated eight. At the end of the table was a projector and a screen pulled down from the ceiling. In front of the windows, a trio of mannequins wore three different designs from the Haute Moderne evening wear collection in red, black and ivory.

"You should have everything you require in here," Nelza said. "If you happen to need anything else, you can use the phone over there to dial the front desk and someone will assist you."

"Thank you, Nelza."

Sidney looked around after she left. The tan-and-brown furniture designs had a soothing effect, for which she was grateful. Her stomach was currently tied up in a series of knots. She always had a bit of nerves right before a major presentation, but once she launched into her speech and hit her stride, it was smooth sailing.

She plugged her flash drive into the computer and made sure the video was ready—a two-minute presentation of models walking down the catwalk, wearing their dresses in a display of flashing colored lights. She froze the frame on the first dress, a little black sleeveless number, the symbol of their Bonne Soirée line.

She placed catalogs, line sheets and color cards in front of each of the chairs. She then set fabric swatches next to the projector within easy reach, so she could pass them down to the attendees when the time came. Now it was a waiting game.

Sidney helped herself to a glass of lukewarm water from the pitcher sitting on the credenza against the wall. She was about to take a sip when she heard two men talking, their voices coming through the slightly open door. She froze with the glass halfway to her mouth and angled her head to hear better. One of the voices was heart-wrenchingly familiar.

She couldn't understand the words, but there was no mistaking the tone; a sound she'd never be able to forget for as long as she lived.

It can't be him, she thought even as her heart hammered a rapid beat under her ribs. Surely her ears were playing tricks on her.

The men continued talking but their footsteps came to a halt somewhere down the hall. With ears perked up and heart thumping wildly, Sidney stood frozen, clutching the slender glass. It had to be some cruel trick of the mind. She simply hadn't expected to see him. Wasn't at all *prepared* to see him.

The men started moving again and they came closer, and closer, until they pushed open the door and her stomach bottomed out. Her fondest dream and worst nightmare stood only a few feet away.

Rodrigo stood by the door talking to Gilberto Ribeiro. Both men were so deeply engaged in their conversation that they didn't notice her standing by the window. Finally, Rodrigo happened to look in her direction, but still she couldn't move. Dark eyes nailed her in place and she suddenly stopped breathing.

He had the kind of look that made women swoon and men envious. His swarthy skin, naturally tanned, was even and smooth. With a symmetrical face and prominent nose passed down from his Portuguese ancestors, he looked as though he should be on the covers of magazines.

Slowly, Sidney set her glass on the credenza. "Hello, Rodrigo." Was that her voice, sounding faint and breathless?

"*Sidney...?*" His voice echoed the same shock that filled her.

Before she could respond, Gilberto rushed forward. "Ah, Senhora Altman. I apologize for keeping you waiting. But it seems you are good, yes?"

Rodrigo came toward her, his steps measured, his eyes never leaving her face. His movement was graceful, fluid. The type of movement that came not only from his affinity for sports, but from the quiet confidence that whispered of growing up with copious amounts of money at his disposal and all the privileges that came along with it.

"What are you doing here?" he demanded.

"Senhora Altman is a sales representative from Haute Moderne, a small New York fashion house," Gilberto answered, looking confused by their reaction to each other. "They have the line I mentioned we were interested in purchasing."

"You never told me the fashion house was Haute Moderne." His words were meant for Gilberto, but he continued to stare at her in disbelief.

He spoke with perfect diction, hinting at his affluent background and years in private schools where he'd learned to speak Spanish, English and French in addition to his native Portuguese. The cadence of his cultured voice sent heat feathering across her skin, and it was all Sidney could do not to close her eyes and indulge in the sound.

Her nose caught a waft of his cologne, a very mas-
culine scent that was a mixture of amber, citrus and
sandalwood. You couldn't get it in the States. You
couldn't get it anywhere, in fact, because it had been
specially created for him. That was the kind of life he
led, where manufacturers of cologne would create a signature scent for him that no one else could have. Her
heart constricted painfully at the familiarity of it. She'd
done so well since they'd said goodbye to one another,
but her hard-won composure threatened to desert her
with his unexpected appearance.

He inspected her from head to toe, the leisurely stroll
of his gaze generating heat wherever it lingered. On her
waist. On her breasts. On her throat where she swallowed nervously to maintain some level of control over
the out-of-control response of her body.

Rodrigo was not the kind of man to hide his appreciation for the female form, and he had a habit of doing
just that. It was typical of men of his culture, to offer
such a frank appreciation of women. It had always made
her feel deliciously feminine, and the same tingly sensations resurfaced in the pit of her stomach.

"You look well," he said, a grudging note to his
voice.

"Thank you. You look well, too." Her voice softened
as she tried to maintain her professionalism. "You do
business with Belo?"

"You could say that." His cryptic answer gave her
pause.

Gilberto spoke up. "In the past few weeks, Moda and
Belo have become partners. We haven't made a formal
announcement to the media yet, but we feel this is a
good marriage. Moda bought all our stores and now,
with their high-end fashions and our everyday cloth-

ing lines, we are most certainly the largest retailer in Brazil."

Gilberto's smiling face indicated that he had no idea of the devastating news he'd just delivered. "You... you've been bought by Moda?" She squeaked the words out.

"Yes." Gilberto nodded vigorously. "We were concentrated in a few key cities in the country, but now Haute Moderne's clothes have the potential to be in stores all over Latin America!"

His excitement was palpable but not contagious. A wave of panic seized Sidney as she realized what was happening. If Moda had taken over Belo Fashions, that spelled trouble for the deal she was trying to strike with them. There was no way Rodrigo would agree to the sale—not when he knew that she was involved. From the smug look on his face, she knew he'd connected the dots.

Still in disbelief, she had to ask to make sure. "*You* own Belo now?"

"That's correct," Rodrigo said.

No, no. This can't be happening.

"I will be sitting in on this presentation," he continued with deliberate slowness, "and we'll have to make sure the line is a good fit for the stores before any contracts are signed."

Sidney felt the deal she'd been so confident about only moments before quickly slip through her grasp.

Chapter 2

There was no way Rodrigo would let Haute Moderne sell their dresses in his family's stores. Normally, he wouldn't be so closely involved in the buying process. The senior buyer was more than capable of making appropriate purchases for the stores. But since he was already here for a meeting and Sidney was involved, he thought it imperative that he remain.

If she thought she could bring her luscious lips back into his life and blindside him, she had another think coming. He'd learned his lesson the first time, and this time he would stay away from her and the temptation she presented. She'd broken his heart and bruised his pride, and he'd be damned if he let her get away with profiting from his company.

"I'll get the others in here and we can get started," Gilberto said and slipped out the door.

In the silence, Rodrigo and Sidney looked at each

other, and he unwillingly remembered all the time they'd spent together in New York. Their walks arm in arm down Park Avenue, the stops at little hole-in-the-wall restaurants he would never have visited on his own.

During those four months, he'd worked hard but spent every possible moment he could with her. She had become an obsession, an addiction he couldn't kick, culminating in the desire to have a more permanent relationship. To think he'd seen a future with her—one filled with children and where they would grow old together. She, on the other hand, hadn't seen anything of the sort, and her callous dismissal had left him reeling.

Beautiful, he thought viciously, wishing he didn't notice the way her reddish-brown hair curled and framed her round face. Or the sultriness of her dark brown eyes. Or the way the simple black suit flattered her figure, reminiscent of the designs the fashion house she represented was known for: simple, tasteful pieces that were classic, not trendy.

She ran her hands down her hips, bringing attention to their roundness and reminding him of nights spent between her legs, wishing he'd never have to leave. His loins became heavy with thoughts of the pleasures they'd shared, and the sensual, uninhibited lovemaking he'd experienced with her and hadn't been able to capture with another woman since.

"Are you going to sabotage this deal?" she asked, her gaze steady.

He focused on the concern etched in her features. "Sabotage? That's harsh, don't you think? You seem to assume that I wish you ill. I don't."

"So I have a fair shot?" she asked.

He saw the uncertainty in her eyes and even though a small part of him relished it, another part of him hated that he was the cause of her imbalance. Despite his anger, he found it difficult to take pleasure in her pain.

Still, he gritted his teeth and plowed through. "I don't owe you anything, do I?"

"I'm not asking for any special favors."

"And you won't get any."

Sidney eyed him. "I know you don't want me here, but—"

"You're right, I don't." The chair squeaked when he sat. He looked across the table at her the way a disapproving parent would look at a child who still hadn't learned the error of her ways after much scolding. "Now that you know I don't, do you plan to leave?"

"Our line is perfect for Belo stores."

"That remains to be seen." He purposely spoke in a cold, detached voice.

"I'll prove it to you. All I ask is for an open mind."

He leaned back and crossed his legs. "You're the salesperson, Sidney, and you're good at selling. You sold me a bill of goods once. Let's see how well you'll do again."

Before she could reply, Gilberto returned with two other men and a woman. He introduced the woman as senior buyer Linda Alvarez. A Colombian with a flamboyant style, she wore an orange dress with an orange-and-green scarf around her neck and thick gold jewelry on her fingers. Linda greeted Sidney with an exuberant smile and a strong handshake. Sidney immediately liked her sparkling personality.

"Now that everyone's here," Sidney said, "we can begin."

She spent the first few minutes introducing herself and giving background on Haute Moderne. She pointed out that the designers were a team of two sisters who'd always had a dream of designing clothes for the average woman.

"That's part of why this line was created," she continued.

Now that she'd found her voice, having Rodrigo right up front didn't faze her in the slightest. She'd hit her stride, and she knew that the relationship between her company and the retail store was a good match. She played the video and then answered questions about the fit of the garments and the different price points. Afterward she passed out fabric samples so they could feel the texture of the material. During the entire meeting, she watched their reactions. Even Rodrigo paid attention, seemingly interested despite his earlier comments.

"We are very impressed," Linda said, nodding her head. She and her assistants spoke briefly in Portuguese and then all eyes turned to Rodrigo.

"It's too early to make a decision," he said. Sidney got the impression he was being purposely vague to torture her. "Your products would be perfect for Belo Fashions, but now that Belo has merged with Moda, we have to strike the balance in inventory between haute couture and everyday fashions. We'll have to review the order and see how it fits into our inventory."

The buyers nodded in agreement.

"I'd be happy to answer any questions you or the buyers have."

"I have no questions," he said curtly. He rose from the chair and she was forced to look up at him. At nearly six feet four inches, he easily towered over the other men in the room and made her feel almost waiflike despite her added height in heels.

The buying team stood, as well. "I will discuss the

line with my counterpart at Moda and see if they have any questions," Linda said. "You might want to visit their offices, too. This happens to be an odd time because of the merger." She appeared apologetic.

"If you'll excuse me, I have to go back to my office." Rodrigo said goodbye to everyone in the room and cast a cursory glance in her direction before walking out.

Linda came over while the other men spoke to each other, turning over the fabric samples in their hands. "We love the dresses, but Moda is a—how do you say?—um, powerhouse in the market. This merger is good for our company, and we must defer to them on many things."

"Do you think there's any chance the senior buyer over there may not like them?"

Linda shrugged. "I see no reason why not, but they know better how they want to handle the inventory, and until all of that is straightened out, this contract may be in limbo."

Sidney couldn't afford a delay. She'd been prepared to sweeten the deal with big discounts if necessary, but now it seemed that she'd have to do much more. Since Rodrigo was the head of the company, he could override the buyers' decisions. Not only did she have to convince them, but him, too. She might as well start at the top to see if she could get him to at least consider the Bonne Soirée line.

But how would she do that when it was obvious how much he despised her?

Chapter 3

Later that day Gilberto took Sidney on a tour of Belo. Their volume of business didn't compare to Moda's, but a contract with their stores had promised to be a lucrative deal for Haute Moderne nonetheless. The merger with Moda should have presented an even greater opportunity for expansion of the Bonne Soirée line, but instead now put her in a precarious position.

For Haute Moderne, getting their line into the Brazilian market had been a priority from the time Belo had made contact. Both companies had been in talks ever since, which had become more intense when she'd been assigned as the sales representative.

Sidney had never believed in putting all your eggs in one basket, but Haute Moderne hadn't subscribed to the same beliefs. They'd devoted most of their resources to accommodating one retailer who provided 80 percent of their revenue. Instead of pursuing other opportunities, the company had settled into a false security and had been unprepared when the retailer decided out of the blue to no longer carry their designs. Now this deal was make-or-break for the fashion house.

After the tour, Sidney went to lunch with Gilberto and one of the associate buyers. That's when she inquired about the location of Moda headquarters. "Linda suggested I visit Moda, and I'd like to take some catalogs and samples down there. Do you have a name of someone I could contact?"

"That's a good idea," Gilberto said. "I'll give you the name of the senior buyer and let him know you're coming."

Sidney spent the rest of the afternoon in meetings and on teleconference calls with New York, as well as answering questions about the designs for Gilberto. From whether or not the sleeves on one of the dresses could be longer to whether or not one dress came in a different color. Hours later, she had Javier drop her in front of Moda headquarters and told him he could leave and she'd catch a taxi back to the hotel.

The offices of Moda headquarters were much swankier than those of Belo's. They were not only located in a larger building, but the state-of-the-art designs on the inside indicated a different level of wealth and success. As far as she knew, almost every country in South America and Mexico had been touched by the Serrano retail empire.

While searching the directory for the buyer, she ran across Rodrigo's name and bit her lower lip, hesitating, wondering if she should visit him. She quickly dismissed second thoughts about approaching him unannounced this late in the day. After all, she was already here, and she'd already admitted to herself that she had to win him over to make sure this deal went through.

She dropped off the catalogs and samples for the senior buyer, who was tied up in a meeting. She then rode the elevator to the top floor and walked into a large reception area with a tomblike quietness. There was no one at the front desk.

"Hello?" she called.

There was no answer, so she wandered down the hallway. In one of the offices, someone's head popped up from reviewing a document when she walked past, but he went right back to work as if she didn't exist. All the way at the back, secluded from the rest of the offices, was Rodrigo's domain, his name on the wall outside of it.

Sidney walked up to the desk of the woman sitting outside his closed office door. "I'm here to see Mr. Serrano," she said, as if she had every right to be there.

The young woman looked her up and down and then referred to her computer screen. Her brow wrinkled. "Do you have an appointment?" she asked, her eyes volleying back to Sidney.

"I don't, but I think he'll want to see me. My name is Sidney Altman."

The woman gave her the once-over again and then picked up the phone. She spoke in such low tones Sidney knew she wouldn't understand a word even if she were speaking in English.

"I'm sorry, Senhor Serrano is unavailable."

"May I schedule an appointment for tomorrow?"

"I'm sorry, he will be unavailable all week." She smiled pleasantly, but Sidney recognized a dismissal when she heard one.

"That's all right," she said, pasting an equally pleasant smile on her face. "I'll wait." He had to come out of there at some point, and she was prepared to wait all night.

She sat in one of the leather chairs across the room. Her eyes scoured the magazines on the side table, all written in Portuguese, but she picked one up and began to flip through it anyway. Every now and again she could see the woman look at her from the periphery, but she continued to browse through the magazine as if unaware.

Finally the woman picked up the phone and spoke quietly into it again. When she hung up, she stood.

"Senhor Serrano will see you now."

Nervous now that she had what she wanted, Sidney marched over to the door, which was opened from the inside. Rodrigo stood looking down at her, an air of tension crackling between them.

"Couldn't wait to see me again, Sidney?"

"I wanted to talk to you, if it's not too much to ask."

"What I want is irrelevant, isn't it?" He walked back over to the desk and sat, waving for her to take a seat in front of him.

A bank of windows behind him let daylight into the office and gave a visual of the rooftops of Rio buildings. In the distance she could see the Christ the Redeemer statue with its outstretched arms atop the Corcovado Mountain.

Sidney set her briefcase on the floor beside her and lowered herself into a guest chair, crossing her legs and feeling an immediate awareness of Rodrigo but wishing she didn't. If they were to have a productive business meeting, she had to keep a cool head.

"I thought maybe we could talk a bit—get everything out in the open."

"What are we getting out in the open, Sidney? As

far as I'm concerned, everything was said in the meeting today to the buyers. Was there something else?" His thin-lipped response barely concealed the anger simmering below the surface.

Meeting the problem head-on was the best solution, she decided. "Considering what happened in New York, I understand why you're upset."

Steepling his long fingers, Rodrigo sat forward. His watchful eyes made her feel as if he were picking apart her words to find hidden meaning among them.

"What happened in New York?"

"You know what happened," Sidney said carefully.

"No, you tell me."

She took a deep breath. "I don't want to fight with you."

"Again, you mean?" he asked calmly. "You ended our relationship. Why won't you just say it?"

"We didn't have a relationship. We were two people engaged in a fling and enjoying each other's company. It was fun while it lasted."

Emotion flashed in his eyes and disappeared. He chuckled softly and the delicious sound warmed her insides. "A fling? Is that all it was to you?"

No, their affair had meant everything to her, but she couldn't tell him the truth because then he'd demand to know why she'd ended it the way she had. "Let's not talk about this. Obviously, I started the conversation off on the wrong foot."

"A *fling?* I asked you to come back with me. I asked you to be my *wife*." The brutal way he said the words made him sound wounded or angry—she couldn't be sure which. Maybe both.

Sidney's body became rigid with tension. The conversation was not going well. "I did what I thought was best. I told you why I couldn't accept your proposal."

He watched her in silence. "My feelings for you didn't matter?"

She swallowed the painful lump in her throat and averted her eyes. At that moment she wished she didn't have to lie and pretend just to protect herself.

"Of course, they mattered," she said, hating that she had to defend her decision again. It wasn't any easier now than it had been then. "Don't my feelings matter, too? I couldn't marry you, and I wasn't going to do it because you wanted me to. I can't tell you enough how sorry I am. I truly never meant to hurt you or to lead you on." She'd chosen the easiest path; one that protected her from pain and him from disappointment.

"I never wanted our relationship to end."

"Two people have to want it," she said quietly. Their last night together she'd thrown a multitude of reasons at him, but none had been the truth.

"And you did not. You made that very clear." Their gazes locked and held, but she refused to look away first. He shifted and took a breath, as if coming to a decision. "You are correct. For a relationship to work, both people have to want it. That is the same for a business relationship."

Unease filled her. "I'm not giving up. I didn't come all the way to Brazil to go back empty-handed." Sidney squared her shoulders, ready for battle. Based on his demeanor, she was in for quite a fight. "The Belo buyers liked the line, and you know those dresses would be a good fit for the stores."

Hand fisted on the desk, his eyes bored into hers. "Why are you here, Sidney?"

"Belo contacted—"

"Why are *you* here, right now?"

She took a deep breath. "To talk to you, Rodrigo, and to convince you to not interfere with this transaction. This should be about business. Nothing else."

"Nothing else? Did you really think there would be 'nothing else' but business between us?"

"I never thought you were the kind of man to allow emotion to rule his business decisions. I know that you're angry about what happened, perhaps even thinking about revenge, but—"

He stood abruptly. Before she realized his intent, he came around the desk and she jumped to her feet. He towered over her, but she refused to be intimidated.

He was standing too close; they'd never been able to be close to each other and not touch. It seemed unnatural, and she felt him in every part of her being. His eyes darkened and his gaze lowered to her mouth before returning to her eyes. She knew that look and recognized at the same time that he didn't want to feel anything for her. It angered him.

"Revenge?" He pulled her hand and attached it to the front of his pants. "This is not revenge. This is torture."

He was aroused, and it surprised her. Instinctively her fingers closed around his thickness. His face tightened, his eyes becoming shuttered. His upper lip pulsed and he let his hand fall to the side so she could stroke him at will, his hard length elongating beneath her fingers.

"You want it, don't you?" he asked.

Sidney snatched back her hand, embarrassed by how she'd been swept away by her own desires.

"No." She shook her head emphatically.

"Yes." His eyes zeroed in on her puckered nipples. With a bitter laugh, he shook his head, his breathing still labored. "Because you can't help it. Because we can't stop what we both feel."

"If you would—"

"You should go."

"If you would just—"

"Don't you understand? This isn't going to work. I can't *function* with you here. With this between us." Dismissing her, he walked to the door and swung it open. "Goodbye."

If she walked out that door, she would not only be a failure, she could lose her job, and the secret dream she'd kept to herself for months would be completely out of reach. She hadn't even shared it with her mother. The unbearable thought plunged her into an abyss of despair where she acknowledged everything she was about to lose.

Rodrigo's cold eyes looked at her with indifference as he stood there holding open the door, waiting for her to walk out and leave with nothing.

She walked across the carpet, but when she came to where he stood, she slammed the door closed. "I'm not leaving until I get you to change your mind," she said with much more boldness than she felt.

He stared at her as if she'd gone mad.

Chapter 4

Rodrigo noted the obstinate set of Sidney's mouth, which only made her lips more attractive. She stood straight-backed, with the posture of a dancer ready to perform. It only served to turn him on even more.

"What exactly do you have in mind?" he asked. His husky voice betrayed him.

Her eyes widened in alarm. "I just want to talk. I want a chance to convince you that the Bonne Soirée line is perfect for the Belo stores at least, and no matter what animosity there is between us, I hope we can work through it."

"And that's all you want?" He could still feel her hand against the front of his pants like a brand.

The air became thick with anticipation.

He noted the movement along her slender throat as she swallowed. It temporarily distracted him, reminding him of how ticklish the side of her neck could be.

He used to kiss her there, and then stroke his fingers down her soft brown skin and she'd erupt into a fit of giggles. But that part of her neck was sensitive for another reason, too. It was an erogenous zone that, when touched just so, made her body press into his with a hunger that he could never resist.

When he lifted his eyes to hers, he saw recognition. She knew what he was thinking. One hand lifted to the side of her neck, her fingers barely touching the skin. He didn't even think she realized that she'd done it. It was an unconscious movement, but one that echoed a need that pulsed through his loins.

"You really shouldn't do that," she said.

"Do what?"

"Stare."

Seconds ticked by. "I can't seem to help myself."

"This isn't what I wanted." Her voice shook. "This isn't what I meant when I said I wanted to convince you to change your mind."

She struggled to breathe and he took it as a sign to move closer. Pressing his palms flat against the door, he imprisoned her against it. "What are we going to do? With these memories between us? *You* came here to disrupt my life."

"I had no idea about the merger," she insisted, staring up at him.

"And if you had known, would you not have come?" She didn't respond, and that was his answer. "You would have come, because you wanted to see me as much as I wanted to see you." He wrapped one of her curls around his index finger, observing the cinnamon highlights striated throughout the strands. "I haven't forgotten how you would toss your head back and moan my name. And when you were about to come, you'd sink your fingernails into my arms. Do you remember that?" he asked in a ragged whisper. "Because I do. I dream about it."

For a second Sidney closed her eyes against the words. She seemed paralyzed, rooted to the spot, mesmerized by the sound of his voice and drowning in the scent of his cologne.

He twisted the lock on the door. There was no mistaking his intention. But she felt insanely as if he was locking her in instead of locking others out.

"What are you doing?" Her voice quivered.

"What I have wanted to do since the minute I saw you again." He lowered his head.

"Stop!" She made one last frantic effort to keep everything on a professional level. But the minute he withdrew, her heart thudded in a panicked gallop.

"You don't want me to."

He grabbed her hips and pushed his hardness into her stomach. He forced her into the door and she moaned, immediately loving the way he felt against her. Maybe she was insane. But right now nothing else mattered but this man, whom she'd never stopped loving—whom, because she loved him so much, she'd willingly given up.

"You want me to stop this?" he breathed into her neck, his nose nuzzling the sensitive flesh behind her ear. "Hmm?"

She stopped breathing.

"Or this?" Rodrigo's hands glided up the inside of her thigh to the front of her pelvis and the warm spot between her legs.

Sidney moaned again, dropping her head to his chest, her hands gripping his muscular arms under his suit jacket.

No longer concerned with what was appropriate and inappropriate, she angled up her head and allowed his ravenous mouth to devour hers. The kiss was fierce. She parted her lips so his tongue could enter and trembled under the ferocity of the crushing need that overtook her.

He was demanding, grabbing the edge of her skirt and impatiently yanking it up so his hands could get reacquainted with the shape of her hips and thighs. He stroked her body proprietarily as he pressed his pelvis against her. The winterlike hibernation of her body was replaced by the scorching heat of summer racing through her veins.

She locked her arms around him and he ground his hips into hers. She mimicked his motions, arching her back further. With his right hand he caressed her between her legs, while his left hand roughly massaged her breasts, his fingers plucking at the nipples until they became rock-hard.

Rodrigo didn't make a sound. She was the one moaning in desperation. She was the one writhing wantonly against his hand, her legs parted to give him better access to the most sensitive part of her body.

Only he could make her feel this way. Only he could drive her so crazy she wanted to beg.

"Even better than I remember," Rodrigo said hoarsely against her mouth.

She answered his declaration with a moan as he slipped his fingers beneath the top of her thong and slowly slid them into her wetness. Helpless to stop him, all she could do was spread her legs wider to acknowledge that she wanted him as much as he wanted her. Maybe even more.

He cursed explicitly. Finally, a reaction from him, a

sign he was not as controlled as he appeared to be. She strained against his slow, sensuous caress as he repeatedly rubbed the moist area between her thighs. She was so ready for him, his fingers were soaked.

He groaned, their bodies rubbing and straining against each other through the barrier of clothing.

"I want to taste you."

She knew what he meant, knew what he loved to do and what she couldn't possibly resist. With ease he picked her up, walked around his desk and set her on top of it. "I haven't tasted anything so good in so long." He pressed a swift, firm kiss against her lips. "I want you to come in my mouth. You know how much I love it."

He eased her back so that she lay on top of the piles of paper covering his desk. Then he quickly tossed his jacket aside and moved to slide the thong down her legs. All resistance drained from her body, Sidney allowed him to lift both her legs and throw them over his impossibly broad shoulders, her arms flung out beside her as if he'd nailed her to the desk. His head went between her legs, his hands on her hips holding her in place against the hard surface.

His tongue was slow, teasing at first. Had he not been holding her down, she would have jackknifed off the desk. It was unbearable. Her nerve endings were raw and sensitive.

She thought fleetingly that anyone could see them from one of the adjacent buildings, putting on a show for the city in full view of the windows. But she couldn't even whisper any kind of refusal and dared not to hint at it in fear he'd stop. It felt deliriously good and was such a sweet, sweet torture.

He pressed soft, tender kisses reverentially against her core, and her head tossed from side to side, her body taut, rigid, aroused. She held his head in place, her legs wide to accommodate him. Her invitation to go deeper was accepted as Rodrigo laved her with his tongue, groaning his pleasure as her hips moved sensuously in response.

Then he penetrated her, moving the moist, pink snake of his tongue around with expert precision. Stroking the most sensitive part of her body, probing the folds, licking at her moistened flesh. He brought her closer and closer to climax but never allowed her to reach it.

He could make her come at any time, but he didn't. Instead he forced a buildup, licking and stroking, pulling back and kissing the inside of her thigh, then returning to the center of her heat. He was prolonging the pleasure, so that when he did push her over the edge, it would be all the more intense.

The swollen nub at the juncture of her thighs became the center of his attention as he circled it and sucked with concentrated determination. He flicked his tongue against it until she could do nothing but cry out against the exquisite pleasure he was inflicting.

He pushed her over the edge and she bit down on her lip to keep from crying out as her body shuddered uncontrollably against the nerve-jarring ministrations of his mouth. The orgasm racked her body with such intensity that she felt she must surely be losing her mind. He knew she was a screamer, and just as the cry left her throat, he clamped a hand over her mouth. She struggled to get away from him, to relish the moment, her body too sensitive for any more contact, but he was too powerful and wouldn't release her.

She trembled and pushed at his shoulders with her high-heeled feet, but instead only ended up pressing her heels into his hard back. And still he didn't stop, pulling her legs wider, continuing unbidden as if he hadn't heard her cry out her satisfaction. As if he didn't know she couldn't take any more of the intense pleasure he was subjecting her to, an almost painful rapture of sensation.

The second orgasm overtook her body mere seconds behind the first, though her cries were still muffled against his palm. Papers fluttered to the floor as her body writhed helplessly.

Finally he lifted his mouth from her and she lay splayed across the desk, panting to catch her breath with her eyes closed. When she opened them, he was looking down at her, his eyes dark with desire and lips set in a grim line.

Without a word, he unbuckled his belt. The expression on his face was indefinable, but he moved slowly, as if to give her time to stop him. Of course she didn't, because when his pants dropped, at the sight of him long and hard, she became aroused again even though she'd just been satisfied.

After sheathing himself in a condom, he stepped between her legs and shoved folders and papers out of the way. They hit the floor with a loud thump. His expression was so intense, her heartbeat sped up. He grasped her wrists and with her hands pinned above her head, he pushed into her, their mighty moans mingling together.

"Você está tão linda, perfeita." You're so beautiful, perfect.

Sidney's brain struggled behind a fog of pleasure. She arched up as he pushed down, open to him, taking each powerful thrust. Moving faster, he tightened his hand around her wrists, his eyes focusing on her reaction.

He lowered his head to kiss her throat and she

turned her mouth to his. The sexy kisses heightened their awareness of each other and before long she was crying out again from the force of another climax. He captured her whimpering cries in his mouth, gnawing at her lip with his teeth. Her legs tightened on his hips, her feminine muscles contracted around his shaft until he came, too. He groaned into her neck, thrusting his hips hard as an orgasm ripped through him. Above her his body shuddered once, twice. Until he collapsed, sapped of energy and crushing her between him and the hard desk.

When he finally moved from on top of her, he fell back into the executive chair. Still spent herself, Sidney only managed to rise up on her elbows. The desk looked as if a tornado had blown across its surface, tossing files to the floor and strewing papers in disarray. They both breathed as if they'd just finished a ten-kilometer run.

Rodrigo's gaze skimmed her thighs. His tongue swept across his mouth and his eyes darkened as if he were imagining tasting her again. "This is why you have to leave," he said in a hoarse voice.

Chapter 5

The phone rang as they were getting dressed. Rodrigo swiftly put the receiver to his ear, and Sidney used that time to step into her thong, feeling his eyes on her as she did so. Behind her, she heard him speaking to someone in Portuguese. When the call ended, he ran his hand over his head, smoothing down the rumpled hairs she had caused by running her fingers through the strands.

"I have a meeting to attend." He sighed. "But we need to talk about us. About what just happened."

She nodded her agreement. "Business calls, though, and I understand."

He looked distracted, his gaze sweeping the room and noting, as if for the first time, the disarray around his desk. "We really need to talk about this."

"Go to your meeting. We'll talk later."

He caught her chin in his hand. "It is obvious, isn't it, that it isn't over between us?"

Responding to him was out of the question because she still wasn't entirely lucid after what had transpired between them.

"This meeting has been planned for months and, unfortunately, I do have to go, but as soon as I can break away, I will. Though it may not be until much later."

"Whenever you get finished, call me." Her voice sounded normal enough, but what she really wanted was to curl up with him and be held. Having him walk out so soon after they'd made love made her feel empty. Used. Her only consolation was that he looked uncertain and it was obvious he didn't want to leave.

"This is not the way what we just shared should end."

"I'll be fine." She smoothed her hands over her skirt in a futile attempt to rid the fabric of its crumpled appearance.

He stepped closer. "Sidney..." He seemed at a loss for what to say. He cupped her cheek, frowning. His hand was warm and gentle against her skin. She saw in his eyes the exact moment when he changed direction from his earlier thought. "Where are you staying?"

"At the Rio Hotel," she replied.

"Then I will call you there later," he said.

After a short hesitation, he turned to leave. As soon as he was gone, she picked up her case to make her exit.

She mumbled a quick goodbye to his secretary, not bothering to look at her. She was fairly certain his assistant knew what had happened in the office, no matter how quiet they'd tried to be. Fortunately his office was located at the end of the hall, which diminished the chance of anyone else having heard them.

In her shell-shocked state, her movements were stiff and robotic. She dipped into the women's bathroom and was happy no one else was in there. She rushed into one of the stalls and leaned back against the door, clutching her briefcase to her chest as if it were a lifesaver. She took a deep breath.

She was shaking. It was impossible to be in the same room as Rodrigo and not crave him. Lesson learned.

All she'd wanted was to do her job and to get out in one piece, but she feared she wouldn't be able to hide the way she felt for much longer. The passion between them had taken her—and him—by surprise. It seemed it had grown even stronger since their time apart.

She felt as though trying to close this deal was like making a deal with the devil. Not because of Rodrigo's evil nature. In fact, she understood his initial anger at her, so it wasn't that. It was because this time, she worried it wasn't just her heart at stake. She feared she would lose her soul, too.

Rodrigo hung up the phone after his second attempt to call Sidney. He had half a mind to have the driver take him over to the hotel to see her, but he thought better of it. Maybe she'd gone to bed early. Maybe she needed time to think, something he should be doing himself.

Stressed and irritated, he rubbed his temples, wishing the headache would go away. It was *her* fault for coming here. While he hadn't forgotten about her, he'd managed to tuck away the memories of what they'd shared in New York. He had compartmentalized his feelings so he didn't have to remember what a fool he'd made of himself over a woman—over her. Sidney was damn near perfect and she smelled sweet, just as he remembered. Like honeysuckle and vanilla. Now she was here, invading his business and bringing that soft brown skin, sultry eyes and tantalizing shape back into his life.

He stood and walked to the minibar on the far side of his office. He reached for a bottle and poured a small portion of whisky into a tumbler. He swallowed the liquid in one gulp, barely registering the spicy flavor as it hit the back of his throat. Then he poured a second, more generous glass.

He'd tried to quickly wrap up the meeting with the Bangladeshi businessmen, but it had been impossible because of the serious nature of the discussion. After the collapse of one of the factories in Bangladesh that had resulted in the deaths of many of its workers, retailers were looking more closely at the conditions there.

Moda and other companies in the industry had combined to establish an initiative to strong-arm the Bangladeshi government into making reasonable concessions to ensure the safety of their workers. The men who'd arrived today owned another factory and had come to woo them back to the country with promises of better oversight. They had put controls into place themselves, without waiting for government intervention. Then there had been dinner and a promise to send one of his representatives over in the next few weeks to inspect the facility.

Rodrigo sat back down again and twisted the chair to stare out at the dark night.

In between the talks with the businessmen, information he'd requested about Sidney's company had come through. They were struggling financially, and Belo seemed to be their ticket to solvency. No wonder Sidney had come, and no wonder she had been so adamant about staying and finishing the job.

Deep in thought, he leaned back in the chair, swirling the amber liquid in the glass.

He'd spent almost every free moment in New York

with some part of his body touching hers. His arms wrapped around her, his hand holding hers. He'd been like a lovesick fool.

Tall and with plenty of curves, he'd noticed her right away at the Coterie Exhibition in New York over a year ago. She'd taught a class on the dos and don'ts of doing business in the United States. But it was her dark brown eyes and the soothing quality of her voice that had kept him enthralled during the forty-five-minute presentation that morning. He hadn't approached her afterward because he'd had an appointment with an agent to look at commercial space, but he'd made sure to attend her second session that afternoon.

At the end of her workshop, he'd invited her for coffee and had been pleased when she'd agreed. In the hotel café, they'd discussed the retail industry and she'd given him advice on approaches for the U.S. market. It wasn't long before he'd convinced her to go on a date with him. He'd spent the next four months in New York searching for property and conducting business, but as much as possible, he'd spent time with her. So it was only natural that he'd tell her of his feelings. It was only natural that he'd seen a future with her and had assumed she'd seen one with him, too.

Sidney straddled Rodrigo's lap on the sofa. Their hungry kisses had become more amorous and would undoubtedly end the way they often did—with their tangled bodies in bed together. This time, however, Sidney pressed her palms against his chest and dragged away her mouth.

"I don't want you to go," she whispered, resting her head on his shoulder.

He didn't want to leave, either. As much as he loved

his home in Brazil, going back there was the least appealing thought he'd had in months. He didn't want to leave Sidney behind. She'd come to mean more to him than he'd ever expected.

"Come back with me," he said.

She laughed softly into his shoulder, as if he were kidding. She lifted her head and asked, "Are you serious?"

"Of course." He smiled at her surprised expression.

"I can't just up and leave. I have responsibilities. But I could fly down in a few weeks once I've had a chance to straighten out a few things here. I have plenty of vacation time saved up, so there's no problem with me taking a couple of weeks off."

He cupped her face in his hands. "Not for a visit. I want you to come to stay."

Her eyes clouded in confusion. "I don't understand."

"I love you. I want you to marry me."

Even though he hadn't planned to propose to her that night, it felt right. They were a perfect match and had the same disposition. He'd enjoyed her company and wanted to introduce her to his family and friends.

Her face changed from confused to saddened, and he sensed her withdrawal. This wasn't the reaction he'd expected.

"I ca— I can't do that."

"Why not?"

"I...I was married once, and I wasn't very good at it."

He laughed easily. "What does that have to do with anything? The problem is not marriage—it's the people who come together. They have to be compatible, and we're more than compatible."

"Okay, well...I don't speak the language and the culture is so different."

His hands dropped at her paltry excuses. *"That's a strange thing to say. It's not as if you couldn't learn."*

"It might be difficult. I've lived in New York all my life, and to go to another country..." She shook her head in denial. *"What would I even do there? I love my life here, and I can't imagine living anywhere else."*

He frowned. *"What are you saying?"*

Her face became guarded and he could tell she was choosing her words carefully.

"My life is here. All my friends and family are here."

"And what about us?"

She slid off his lap and walked across the room, wrapping her arms around her waist. He waited to hear what she had to say next because surely this had to be a big misunderstanding.

"I can't marry you." Her soft voice drifted to him, and his stomach tightened.

Still in denial, he went to her. She remained turned away from him, her head bowed.

"Why not? You love me, don't you?"

"We've only known each other four months. I have a career. I have a life here."

Taking her by the shoulders, he forced her to face him. *"We talked about having children. We talked about—"*

"You talked about having children. Not me." She twisted out of his hands. *"I'm sorry, but I don't want to marry you."*

He ran his fingers through his hair. He wasn't ready to give up. *"This does not make sense."*

"I knew you'd only be here for a short time, and I never expected more."

"Tell me you don't love me, and I will leave."

"I didn't expect you to feel this way."

"I want to hear you say the words." He was confident, certain she wouldn't.

With a vigorous shake of her head, her eyes pleading, she whispered, "Don't make me hurt you."

"Say it."

She looked down at the floor. Her arms tightened around her body and the heaviness in his stomach portended the words he didn't want to hear.

"I don't."

Like a physical blow, the words had knocked the wind out of him and made him feel foolish. How could he not have seen it? He hadn't meant nearly as much to her as she'd meant to him. While he'd been thinking about forever, she'd only been thinking about right then.

Afterward they'd argued, of course, both saying things they probably shouldn't have said. Mainly because he hadn't been able to accept that she'd turned him down and had continued to push until she'd lashed out. She had accused him of feeling entitled when he really had no right to feel that way.

A fling. Her words from earlier in the day came back to haunt him.

Rodrigo looked at his drink. The trip down memory lane had been a painful reminder of what had been. She'd gotten under his skin. Having her here was a monumental distraction, but right now he didn't care if she loved him or not.

He couldn't think or concentrate, knowing she was only a short distance away. What made it even harder was imagining her moving to Brazil and becoming a permanent fixture in his life, the way he'd wanted. She was the only woman he'd ever asked to marry him, and no matter how hard he tried, he couldn't forget her. He wanted to convince her to spend more time with him. He wanted to convince her to…stay.

He swallowed the last of his drink.

He suspected Sidney hadn't told him the whole truth about why she'd turned him down. He felt there was more to her reasoning than she'd let on, and it had nothing to do with him being prideful or feeling entitled, as she'd suggested. He just knew, in his gut, that she was keeping something from him.

But what?

The attraction between them was as strong as ever. Before she left Rio, he'd find out the real reason she'd turned down his proposal, surmount it, and get her to agree to marry him this time.

After she arrived at the hotel, Sidney had checked in with her mother and then gone down to the hotel restaurant for a late meal. Wearily, she'd undressed when she'd returned to her room. The tension of the day had taken its toll and all she wanted was to crawl under the sheets and forget everything that had happened since this morning. But she didn't.

Instead, she picked up her purse and pulled out a photo that reminded her of why she'd come. She walked to the window and looked down on the lit street, the moon hovering over the landscape and reflecting in the dark water of the Atlantic Ocean. Cars honked and pedestrians wandered around below. Some holding hands, others arm in arm.

With her fingertips she traced an outline of the person in the photo. A baby.

Only a few more weeks and she could adopt the perfect little girl in the picture, with her big brown eyes and chubby cheeks—Alana. Born to a teenage mother, she'd been given up at birth and, as far as Sidney was concerned, placed with the adoption agency just for her. But she had to secure this contract first and keep her job long enough to make the adoption happen. She could potentially lose her little girl if she didn't have stable employment.

Six years ago Sidney had married the man she'd thought she'd spend the rest of her life with. But it wasn't meant to be.

Her ex-husband had come from a large Southern family and had wanted a large family of his own. They'd married right out of college and tried to get pregnant immediately, but after almost a year of trying they'd gone to the doctor and learned the truth. Sidney was unable to have children; the cause was unknown. Telling them that this was typical of 20 percent of all infertility cases hadn't helped at all. Their relationship had become strained and was only worsened by the pressure applied by his family.

She'd gone through hormone treatments and acupuncture. Every time someone else became pregnant—whether planned or unplanned—it had stung. But hearing about unwanted children abandoned at hospitals or tossed in the trash had hurt even more. She'd questioned the fairness of it. Why was it that she, who wanted a child so badly, couldn't have one but others who didn't could?

She and her husband hadn't been able to afford the more expensive fertility treatments, and in the end, their marriage hadn't survived the trials of infertility.

Over the years, jealousy, anger and other emotions friends wouldn't typically associate with her personality consumed her. She had three beautiful godchildren and loved them all. She dutifully celebrated their birthdays and other milestones, but she wanted children of her own and sometimes felt as if her friends offered her the role of godmother out of pity.

Resting her head against the window glass, she closed her eyes. That's why she couldn't marry Rodrigo. When she'd fallen in love with him, she'd wanted to tell him but hadn't been able to. In his culture family meant everything. Close family ties were prevalent in all areas of his life, and he had spoken openly of his desire to have a family.

Embarrassed, ashamed and feeling less than a woman, she'd turned down his proposal and made him think their feelings weren't mutual. It had been the hardest thing she'd ever had to do. But she'd let him go and taken his anger, rather than have him look at her with pity—or even worse, disgust. She'd seen that look before, and she couldn't bear to see it from him.

Chapter 6

Just like the day before, Javier met Sidney downstairs, but when she climbed into the back of the limo, she was not alone. Rodrigo waited for her in the interior. He smelled good and looked beyond handsome in a black three-piece suit. She cautiously slid across the seat and shyly greeted him.

"You shouldn't be surprised to see me," he said. "I tried to call you last night so we could talk, but I couldn't reach you."

"Did you?" she said instead of outright fibbing. She'd seen his calls but had wanted time to herself to think.

He didn't respond to her remark, but she could tell he knew she wasn't being totally honest by the lift at the corner of his mouth.

"We do need to talk about what happened."

"No argument there, but now may not be the best time." She glanced at the glass partition between them and Javier.

"He can't hear us." He sat back and extended his arm along the back of the seat, looking relaxed while she remained a bundle of nervous energy. "Making love to you in my office was completely unexpected, but clearly we have unfinished business between us."

Sidney twisted the belt of her dress between her fingers. "What does that mean?" she asked, afraid of the answer.

"I won't beat around the bush. When you finish in the meetings today, I want you to come home with me."

Her fidgeting stopped.

"You weren't expecting that."

"No, I wasn't."

"It is the only thing that makes sense," he said in a matter-of-fact voice. "We still have chemistry. Passion." He ran a fingertip down the side of her face, the gentle movement evoking a torrent of sensation in the exact spot he touched.

She hadn't expected him to suggest she come stay with him. In fact, she hadn't been sure what to expect at all, but she'd been ready to beg him to keep the contract if that's what it took to keep her job and ensure she wouldn't lose her chance of getting her baby. Her little girl waited on her, and she couldn't let pride get in the way of completing the adoption. She'd already invested a lot of time and thousands of dollars, and nothing in the world would prevent her from bringing home her sweet little angel.

"What about the contract?"

His eyes hardened. "Winning the contract is not contingent on sleeping with me, if that's what you're asking. I promise not to interfere."

She breathed easier, but he turned away from her. She'd angered him.

"I'll come by your room to pick you up with your luggage after I leave work."

"Thank you," Sidney said quietly.

"Thank you?" he scoffed. "For what? For being weak? For being unable to resist giving you whatever you want?"

The car pulled up in front of Moda headquarters, but he didn't wait for Javier to open the door. He climbed out without a backward glance and left her alone in the car.

She'd angered him and she regretted it, but she had to be sure that he wouldn't pull the contract from under her.

Javier then took her to Belo and she didn't hear from Rodrigo for the rest of the day.

Before leaving late that afternoon, she said goodbye to Nelza and Gilberto. At the hotel she packed up her belongings to wait for Rodrigo. With fresh makeup and every hair in place, she was ready for when he arrived.

When he did, she opened the door and noted how his eyes lit up. He had a way of making her feel like the most beautiful woman he'd ever seen.

He took her hand and brought it to his lips. *"Linda. Sempre."* Beautiful. Always.

The first time she'd heard the words in New York, she'd known what he said without a translation because they were so close to Spanish, which she had studied in college. Hearing them now brought back memories of their time together. He'd said them often, usually when they were on their way somewhere and she was dressed up. It had made her take extra care with her appearance. She would style her hair into neat curls and apply her makeup carefully, making sure her clothes were perfect so she could hear the same murmured words of appreciation.

"Thank you," she said. Her cheeks flushed with warmth.

He'd mellowed since this morning and wore the relaxed clothes to match, looking more like the man she'd met and fallen in love with. Chinos covered his long legs and a shirt open at the collar revealed his strong throat.

How many times had they lain in bed together and she'd traced the line of his collarbone with the tip of her finger? With her lips, even? Laughing at her own power when he groaned and grabbed her hips to thrust into her with a helplessness that made her feel as if she were a femme fatale who held him ensnared. The memory made her heart seize for what could have been.

No wonder they hadn't been able to help themselves yesterday. Almost from the moment they'd met, there had been a fire smoldering between them and it had only increased in heat during their time apart.

He took her luggage and placed a hand at the small of her back. He escorted her to a lead-colored late-model Jaguar XJ sedan and opened the passenger-side door.

"You drive?" she asked.

"You sound surprised."

He smiled, which prompted her to smile in return. Her gaze dropped to his mouth, and she recalled their last kiss in his office.

"I am a little. I assumed you'd have a driver at all times."

"Perhaps it's the control freak in me," he said. "I use a driver on very rare occasions."

He watched her slide onto the white soft-grain-leather seat and took in every detail of her appearance.

As always, she left him breathless. On the walk to the car her hips had swayed from side to side, a hypnotizing movement that could inspire appreciation in even the most detached man. This morning she'd worn her hair pulled back, but tonight she'd set it free and styled it into large, bouncy curls that fell onto her shoulders.

The hem of the skirt she wore swirled around her calves, and his eyes traveled upward, taking in the oversize gauzy blouse in rose. She was almost completely covered from head to toe, nothing inappropriate in her manner of dress, and yet he still thought of the treasures beneath the loose-fitting articles of clothing.

She settled in and crossed her legs, and he closed the door, flexing his fingers and reminding himself to be patient.

He'd had plenty of time to think about their situation, and with the digging he'd done, he knew the dire straits her firm faced because they'd lost a major account the year before.

If she married him, she'd never have to worry about money or losing her means of employment. She would be well taken care of. The thought of how she'd turned down his proposal still left a bad taste in his mouth, but he had a new purpose now and only a short time in which to accomplish it. He'd show her just how beautiful his city was, how rich the culture and friendly the people. At the end of it all, he'd ask her to marry him again, and this time he had no doubt she'd say yes.

Chapter 7

They exited the car in front of Rodrigo's apartment complex in Leblon, a small but upscale neighborhood and home to the priciest real estate in Rio de Janeiro. In this neighborhood, the rich and famous dined at high-end restaurants and tossed back overpriced drinks at stylish bars.

The valet came over and greeted them both. Rodrigo handed him a few bills before the young man hopped in to take the car to the garage.

The interior of the apartment complex was well lit and painted in bright colors that evoked the tropics. Two security guards sat at a U-shaped desk watching video screens. When they saw Rodrigo, they greeted him, to which he responded with a nod. Their curious eyes rested on Sidney for a moment before returning to the screens. She wondered if it was a common occurrence to see him bringing a woman home.

Inside the elevator he pushed a keycard into a panel in the wall. "My apartment is on the top floor. Only my family, the property manager and the security guards can access that level."

"How's your father?" Sidney asked.

He looked at her in surprise. "You know about his heart attack?"

"It was in the news." She'd searched out news about him and his family, but she wouldn't mention that tidbit.

"He's much better. He takes his medicine and follows doctors' orders."

"Does he live nearby?"

"Not too far, in Copacabana in the house he lived in with my mother. It's the house I grew up in and way too big for him alone, but he insists on keeping it. We think he holds on to it because of the memories. My sisters and their children often go over to visit, and he loves to have my nieces and nephews spend the weekend with him."

They both came from large families. While she was the youngest of six, he was the oldest of five. Two of his siblings lived in Rio, one in Bahia and the other in Argentina, each of them involved in some aspect of the Moda retail empire.

Rodrigo opened the door to the apartment using the same keycard, and her heels clicked on the hardwood floor as she entered ahead of him.

"What do you think?" he asked, setting her luggage on the floor.

She looked around. "It's not what I expected."

She'd expected a bachelor pad, but instead she'd arrived at a dwelling that was more like a home. All the usual types of electronics and gadgets were in place, such as the expensive stereo system and television mounted on the wall. But it was the furniture that didn't conform to her expectations. She thought for sure he would have decorated in a minimalist style, but instead the apartment contained traditional furnishings. Heavy pieces covered in bold, solid colors filled the living room. The large windows with fine drapes probably allowed plenty of sunlight to come in during the day. Photos of his family neatly lined the walls in ornately designed gold frames.

"Is that a good thing or a bad thing?" he asked.

"A good thing," she replied.

Sidney followed Rodrigo down the hall where more photos lined the walls. Most depicted children whom she assumed were his nieces and nephews. They were playing on the beach or piled on top of each other in grass. One in particular of a gorgeous little girl with a toothless grin holding her tooth between two fingers like a prize caught her eye.

The gourmet kitchen was more in line with what she'd expected. He'd obviously spared no expense, including Italian glass on the cabinet doors and restaurant-grade appliances. It was sleek and modern with a six-burner range that included a grill and a microwave and second oven built into the wall. Food simmered on the stove and covered dishes filled the air with a pleasant aroma.

"This is a lot of food. Are you expecting more people?" She lifted covers on pots and peeked under covered platters. All the delicious-looking food caused an uptick in her appetite. "You did all this?"

He stood back, watching her. "I had some help. My chef prepared the meal and left everything warming for us. Not that I couldn't do it myself, of course."

"Oh, of course. I never doubted that for a minute."

They smiled at each other, a secret one of remembered times passed, such as when he'd fixed a traditional meal of *moqueca de peixe,* a delicious fish stew made with coconut milk.

"Boa noite." The greeting came from a man who'd just entered the kitchen. Even before the introduction, Sidney knew who he was.

"This is my father, Gualtiero Serrano, who was supposed to be gone already. Father, this is Sidney Altman."

Seemingly unperturbed by his son's not-so-subtle dismissal, Gualtiero came over and greeted her with two kisses on the cheek. An older version of Rodrigo, he had thick dirty-blond hair but the same dark eyes. He was a very good-looking man with few wrinkles, and she suspected he must have been quite the Casanova in his day.

"I left my phone and had to come back for it." He held it up, but Sidney could tell it had been an excuse to check her out. "So you are Sidney Altman."

"Father."

Gualtiero brushed aside Rodrigo's warning tone with a wave of his hand. "I only wish to say welcome to my country. How long will you be here?"

Sidney laced her fingers together in front of her. "Only a couple more days."

"Why do you go back after only a short time?"

"I'm here on business and can only afford to take a couple of days off before I head back home."

"Perhaps you should stay for pleasure."

Her eyes sought out Rodrigo. She didn't know what to say to that.

"Father, you're embarrassing her."

"It is only a suggestion. Maybe you will find a reason to stay." He leaned closer. "My son is in need of a wife, and I am in need of more grandchildren," he said in a stage whisper.

"Father—"

Rodrigo was surprised by his father's comment. For years he'd made no secret of the fact that he wanted Rodrigo to marry someone from Brazil who understood the culture. But as he watched his father with Sidney, he wondered if something else was amiss. His father was a romantic, and clearly he'd softened his stance on the idea of who would make an acceptable bride for his eldest son.

The older man chuckled. He continued to speak to Sidney as if they were the only ones in the kitchen. "Ignore me. I go now, but I hope to see you again very soon. Enjoy your dinner. *Bom apetite.*" He took her hand and pulled her in for a kiss on the cheek.

"Goodbye, Father," Rodrigo said dryly. His father patted him on the shoulder on the way out. "I'm sorry about that. He has no shame, as you can tell."

Sidney smiled. "It's okay."

He walked over to the wine refrigerator. "Wine?" he asked.

"Yes, please."

"Do you have a preference?"

"Whatever you decide is fine."

He poured them both a glass of Cabernet Sauvignon. "I'm glad you decided to come."

She looked at him with a faraway expression in her eyes. "I don't think either of us had a choice in the matter, do you?"

Sadness filled her eyes, taking him by surprise. He felt a moment of guilt. Did she feel coerced into coming here? He wanted her here only if she wanted to be.

Then she smiled and he wondered if he'd imagined that look. He set aside the doubts and lifted his glass. "To...the future," he said.

She hesitated but then followed suit. "To the future."

Chapter 8

Rodrigo couldn't take his eyes off Sidney, watching her here in his home. It felt right, the way he knew it would. They set the table together and placed the entrées on it, and Rodrigo helped her into her chair before sitting across from her.

"You look leaner," he commented out of the blue. "You have more muscle."

She appeared pleased that he'd noticed. "That's because I've been working out."

"Don't tell me you're on a diet."

Rodrigo refilled her glass as a smile fanned across her lips. She always smiled with her eyes, and under this lighting, her brown eyes sparkled. Her lush mouth, one of his favorite parts of her anatomy, was covered in a glossy shade of red.

"No, I'm not on a diet. I exercise more now, but you know I'm a picky eater," she reminded him.

"You can't go wrong with any of these dishes, and I know you have a hearty appetite when you enjoy your food." At her stricken look, he hastily added, "That is a compliment. Food is meant to be enjoyed, after all."

"So we're back to that again."

"What?" he asked, feigning innocence but knowing full well to what she was referring.

"I said it before, and I'll say it again. I apologize for finishing your pasta primavera, okay? But I didn't want it to go to waste." She shrugged.

One night in New York she'd taken him to a restaurant in Little Italy where they'd ordered a mountain of food that included appetizers and plenty of fresh garlic bread. It had been so refreshing to find a woman who enjoyed a good meal as much as he did.

"I could have taken it in a dog bag." He removed the lid from the container in the center of the table.

She giggled. "It's *doggie* bag, and we were going to the theater afterward. We couldn't have taken it with us. I did you a favor by not allowing the food to go to waste." She looked up at him through her lashes, and his heart stopped. Time stood still for a moment. But the moment passed when she bowed her head to straighten the napkin across her lap, a smile still floating at the corners of her lips. "And I was hungry. Very hungry," she added.

With his elbows on the table, he rested his chin on his interlocked fingers. "Being with you in New York was the best time I have ever had visiting your city."

Her eyes met his across the table, and he saw sadness there again, just as before. He wanted to find out more about what it meant and where it came from, but he sensed now wasn't the time to pry. "You made sure that I received the full New York experience," he said, "so I will do the same for you."

"Oh, really? What do you have in mind?"

He didn't answer but began to spoon soup into a bowl. "This is *caldo verde,*" he explained. "It's a popular soup from Portugal. It contains collard greens, potatoes and sausage."

"Did you hear my question?"

She looked adorable sitting there, a fine wrinkle on her brow, demanding an answer. He decided to torture her a little bit longer. "I will explain everything later. For now, eat. *Bom apetite.*"

By the end of the meal, Sidney was almost certain she'd died and gone to heaven. The rest of the dishes consisted of food equally delicious to the soup, including a steak grilled to perfection and covered in a secret rub. She tried to pry the recipe out of Rodrigo, but to no avail. The entire delicious meal was shamelessly devoured.

Across the table, he smiled at her but said nothing.

"Go ahead, talk about my appetite," she said, dabbing her mouth with the napkin.

"No, you're sensitive. I'll leave you alone," he said, but he didn't stop smiling.

By the time they made it to the living room with glasses of wine, a sense of contentment filled her, making her wish her stay would be longer.

"What do you have planned for tomorrow?" she asked.

"I'm taking you on a tour of the city."

"You can take a whole day off like that?" She lowered to the sofa. He picked up a remote and soft music filled the room.

"When you're the boss, you can do whatever you like."

A woman's voice, soft and soothing, came from the speakers.

"Who is that?"

"Elis Regina." Rodrigo sat beside her.

"She has a beautiful voice."

"She's been dead a long time, but her voice is still considered one of the most beautiful in Brazilian music."

The sound of the guitar and the singer's voice relaxed her.

Rodrigo turned to her, resting his arm along the back of the sofa. "Do you have a man in your life?"

She blinked. "Where did that come from?"

He shrugged. "Just wondering. I want to make sure."

"No, I don't."

He didn't respond. He calmly picked up his glass from the coffee table and took a sip of the wine.

"Do you have a woman in your life?" Sidney held her breath.

"No, I don't."

She let out the breath she'd been holding. "Tell me what you have planned for tomorrow."

"Let me worry about that. Just be ready to have all day tomorrow and the day after occupied."

"And you're sure no one will miss you at work?"

"You want me all to yourself. Is that it?"

"Yes, I do."

It was nice to flirt with him. Considering how their initial meeting had gone, the relaxed evening was just what she needed, what *they* needed. She was no longer tense and on guard. Spending time with him in his home had made all the difference.

"I may have to take a few calls because this will be an unplanned leave, but you'll have my undivided attention for most of the day."

"You don't have to do this," Sidney said, although she was glad he was taking this time with her. At least then when she returned home, she'd have new memories to hold on to.

"I want to, and I want you to enjoy your time here." He took her glass and set it next to his on the table. He held her hand in both of his. "Now it's time for us to go to bed." He rose with her hand in his and led her to the bedroom where he slowly undressed her, taking his time instead of the hasty manner in which they'd made love the day before.

He spoke to her in his native tongue, the way he always did when they made love, the words flowing easily from his lips and adding to her heightened state of arousal. He pulled her onto the bed and rolled on top of her, taking little nips of her skin from her neck to her shoulders and down to her breasts. He took each nipple in turn, licking and sucking the dusky peaks. Moving restlessly on the bed, her fingers ran over the muscles of his back.

She took his hand in hers and kissed the palm. She'd missed him so much.

With a gentle push she forced him onto his back so she could sit astride his thighs. She kissed his forehead, nose and mouth, lingering there. The taste of him, the smell of him, almost seemed brand new. Their kisses were slow and leisurely, their unhurried movements similar to those of a couple who knew each other well.

She nibbled on his neck as he cupped the back of her head, using sweeping motions to caress the length of her body. She touched his shoulders, caressed the bulging muscles of his arms and moved over the contours of his powerful chest. Going lower, she licked his nipples and the curve of his pecs.

When she reached the thickness between his thighs, she licked the length of him before taking him into her mouth. His fingers tightened in her hair and he thrust upward. She sucked harder, pulling him deeper. He murmured indistinct words, his voice coaxing and encouraging, and when he couldn't take it anymore, he groaned and dragged her up onto her back.

He pulled a condom from the nightstand, and soon their joined bodies moved in a slow, sensual dance together. In the quiet of the room only breathless pants and amorous kisses could be heard. Rodrigo rocked back and forth within her until her orgasm reached a crescendo that crashed over her.

Later when she lay curled against the length of him, she listened to his even breathing as he slept. Filled with regret over her decision to let him go a year ago, she wondered if she could be honest now. Maybe she'd been too hasty in denying his proposal. Sadness coiled through her, a yearning for what had been lost after a brief taste of the ultimate happiness. If he wanted to rekindle their romance, if he still wanted to marry her, would she have the courage to tell him the whole truth?

Chapter 9

The next morning Sidney dragged out of bed into the bathroom. When Rodrigo returned from a run on the beach they took a shower together, leisurely rubbing soap all over one another's bodies before they went back into the bedroom and fell across the bed for a quickie.

Afterward, they strolled to a neighborhood bakery where they sat down to potent cups of espresso and freshly baked bread smothered with jam. The rest of the morning was spent walking around the streets of Leblon. Rodrigo took the time to explain the history of the neighborhood. He mentioned that years ago, because of its location and difficulty in accessing it, runaway slaves once used it as a hiding place. A streetcar line eventually connected it with Ipanema, and Leblon—now trendy and cosmopolitan—had grown at a faster pace.

They visited several Brazilian designer stores and other retailers, something he did often to check out the competition. They ran into a few celebrities whom he knew and introduced her to, and eventually they stopped for lunch at his favorite *botequim* in the neighborhood. He ordered them beer made on-site and a number of dishes for her to sample. One was codfish balls and *bolinho de aipim*—manioc balls—stuffed with Catupiry cheese and shrimp. Her favorite phrase became *mais uma,* which meant "one more," as they sampled the different food available.

The city tour in the helicopter was perhaps her favorite part of how they spent the day. The aerial trip took them past the Christ the Redeemer statue standing thirty-eight meters tall atop Corcovado Mountain. They flew over the Atlantic, rays from the sparkling sun bouncing off the azure waves. The helicopter dipped to the right and they had a clear view of the palm trees and white shoreline stretching from Copacabana to the east side of town down to Recreio beach.

Back on land, Rodrigo took Sidney to one of the more popular museums and waited patiently while she snapped photos. By the time they returned to Leblon, they were both winding down after the long day. They took bottles of coconut water on their afternoon walk on the beach and watched a group of older women practice tai chi while a few young people jogged along the shoreline.

On the way back to the house, they stopped at a candy shop and Rodrigo bought her *Pé de Moleque.*

"It's similar to peanut brittle," she said over a mouthful of the candy.

"Yes, but this one is made with molasses. It tastes better."

"Everything is better in Rio?" she teased.

"Sim."

At a local market they picked up fresh vegetables to make a salad to accompany the leftovers from the night before and strolled hand in hand back to Rodrigo's place. When they opened the door to his apartment, two sets of scampering feet came running toward the front.

"Tio Drigo!" the children called. A young girl wrapped her arms around his waist and a boy who looked about half her age wrapped his arms around one leg.

A woman came down the hall at a much slower pace. "Oh, you have company," she said in English, doing a poor job of looking surprised.

"Sidney, this is my sister, Branca." Branca shared the same fair hair as their father.

"I hope it's okay that we're here," she said. She glanced at Sidney.

"Of course," Rodrigo responded.

He introduced the children, too, and they smiled shyly as they greeted her. Sidney recognized the little girl as the one missing the front teeth in the photo on the wall in the hallway. She looked about eight years old now and had all her teeth.

"I'll put away the groceries," Sidney said.

She walked back to the kitchen, and while putting away the food, she heard giggling behind her. The kids were standing in the doorway.

"Water, please," the little boy said.

She smiled at him and poured a small glassful for him.

"You from New York," his sister said.

"Yes. Have you ever been?"

"No. I want to go one day. Tio Drigo has many pictures from New York. If I can make it there, I make it anywhere."

"That's right." Sidney smiled and the two kids started giggling again.

Branca came to the doorway and put her hands on her hips. "Leave her alone," she said in a stern voice. "Come on, children. We go now."

"They're fine. It's okay," Sidney said as the children hurried out.

Branca paused. "You're very kind. They can be very nosy."

"They're adorable," she said, unable to keep the wistful note out of her voice.

"They are demanding, but Rodrigo knows how to manage them. He's playful but firm at the same time. He would make a good father." She said it as if trying to sell Sidney on his finer qualities. In the background, she heard his voice in the living room with the children squealing and laughing.

"Sounds like he's very busy out there."

"Always," Branca said with a laugh. They both walked out to the living room to find the children jumping all over him.

Branca clapped her hands and spoke in a strong voice. "We have to go so Tio Drigo and his friend can have dinner."

The kids preceded their mother to the door, dragging their feet and pouting. A look passed between Branca and Rodrigo, and Sidney wondered what it meant. Seconds later, Branca said goodbye and the three of them left.

The apartment became very quiet afterward, an almost eerie silence without the sound of children laughing and playing. They went to the kitchen and worked quietly together. While Sidney prepared the salad, he set the dishes in the oven to warm.

"Everything okay?" he asked into the quiet.

"Sure."

He poured them both glasses of wine.

"I have something to tell you," Sidney said. She'd been thinking about this for a while and decided it was time to come clean with Rodrigo. Watching him with the children earlier brought home the fact that he would, in fact, make a great father. If there was any chance of them moving forward after these few days together, she had to tell him the truth. He deserved to know.

"I have something to tell you first," he said. He turned to her, his eyes earnest and his expression as grave as she'd ever seen it. "I don't want you to feel any pressure, but spending time with you has made me think about how things could be. I still want to marry you, Sidney. I want you to rethink my proposal."

"Rodrigo, wait, before you—"

"Shh. Listen to me." He took her hands and looked into her eyes. "I know you came here for business, but I think fate brought us together because neither of us expected to see each other again. My father is ready to bring you into the family and my sister likes you, too. She feels you have a good spirit, a good aura, and that's a lot coming from her. She doesn't like anyone right away."

He gently squeezed her hands and continued. "I still want to marry you, and I want us to have a family together. I know you love your family, and they would be welcomed here any time they want to visit. I could find a job for you at Moda, working in sales or buying—whatever you feel comfortable with. I'll do whatever it takes, because I want you to be my wife. To be the mother of my children."

Her stomach muscles tightened painfully. Maybe if he hadn't said the last part, she would have told him what she'd started to say before he'd interrupted. Then she would tell him yes, she would be his wife, because ever since he'd asked her a year ago, she hadn't stopped thinking about it. But hearing him mention children again was crushing and she lost her nerve.

"I can't," she whispered.

Chapter 10

The hopeful expression in his eyes died. "I don't understand. I know you love me. I can see it in your eyes, and the way we make love, you cannot fake that."

She nodded and pulled her hands away, withdrawing in the same way she'd done the first time he'd proposed. "The truth is, I do love you, but I can't marry you because I want you to be happy, and I can't give you what you want."

"What you're saying doesn't make any sense." A muscle in his jaw rippled. "Does our relationship mean nothing to you?"

"Our relationship means the world to me."

"Then how could you just end it, again?" he demanded. "I have been living in a mental hell for the past year, because I can't forget your laugh. I can't forget the way we made love, the way you gave yourself to me. Whatever your reason for not wanting to marry me, you just admitted it's not because you don't love me. We can work through it."

"It's not that easy, Rodrigo."

"Yes, it is. When you love someone—"

"Love is not enough."

At a standoff, they stared at each other. The conversation was getting heated and they simultaneously took calming breaths.

"What obstacle is so large that love cannot surmount it?" he asked, lowering his voice.

Sidney took another deep breath. "You want children so desperately, but what if we don't have any?"

"Why wouldn't we? We're both young and healthy, and we talked about it before. I told you how close I am with my family, and I want the same."

She shook her head. "*You* talked about starting a family," she reminded him. "Not me."

"Are you saying you don't want children?" he asked in shock.

"I'm saying, could you be happy if we don't?"

"That's a ridiculous question." He paced away from her, running his hand through his hair.

"Answer it," Sidney insisted. She had to know.

Rodrigo faced her again, his brow wrinkled. "I want children. I always have, and you know that. I want to be a father. I do not want to be Tio Drigo forever."

Sidney swallowed and somehow managed to keep her face from crumpling. Just like her ex-husband, Rodrigo had a passionate desire to be a father. How could she rob him of that possibility when she knew what a wonderful father he would be? Her ex hadn't been interested in adoption, and with the closeness Rodrigo shared with his blood relatives, she knew he'd feel the same. A child with his DNA, who had his features, his love of sports and his business acumen.

"That's what I thought," she said. She looked down at her fingers. "This won't work."

She started out of the kitchen.

"Sidney—"

She ignored him and hurried into the bedroom before she fell apart. He followed, watching her pack up her clothes.

"What are you doing? Where are you going?" he demanded.

"You want a marriage and babies. It's better this way."

"And you don't?"

She didn't answer.

"What about your precious contract?" Rodrigo asked, bitterness in his voice.

She stopped and swung around to face him. Her heart thumped fearfully in her chest. "You wouldn't withhold that, would you?"

"It's obvious that's all you care about," he said.

"That's not true."

"No?" He laughed mirthlessly. "Fool me twice…" He walked out.

Sidney sank onto the bed, clutching the clothes she'd been stuffing into the suitcase.

"That's not all I care about," she said to the empty room.

Two days later, Sidney woke up miserable. She'd spent the day before in her room instead of going down to the beach or enjoying the hotel's amenities as she'd planned.

She'd tossed and turned all night the night before,

and just when she was on the verge of falling asleep, she was forced to acknowledge the morning when a courier knocked at the door and brought by the executed contracts. She should be pleased Rodrigo hadn't withheld the order from her, but for some reason it made her feel like crying. The finality of his decision to give her what she wanted meant there was no going back now.

She barely closed the door before tears blurred her eyes.

"You're letting her leave?" Rodrigo's father stood in front of his desk at Moda headquarters.

"I couldn't keep her, Father. She's free to go."

"But you love her and she loves you."

Rodrigo carefully laid his pen down and sat back. "You seem certain."

"That's why I brought her here."

Rodrigo sat up with a start. "You did what?"

"Don't look at me like that. You've been sulking since you returned from the States and I had to do something to boost your spirits. Having a heart attack and leaving you to run the company on your own certainly didn't help."

His father had collapsed in a board meeting, causing quite a scare. The resulting shock waves had rippled throughout the company and the business community at large. Coming so soon after his return from the States, Rodrigo had spent much of his time maintaining order in the company while helping his younger siblings tend to his father's care at the same time.

"About six months ago," Gualtiero said, "one of the Belo buyers mentioned Haute Moderne fashion house and some of the pieces in their collection. We were already in negotiations to buy their stores, so that's where the idea came from to use them as a way to lure her down here."

Rodrigo ran his hand over his face. Now he understood why his father had changed his mind about him marrying someone from their culture. Because of his romantic nature, his father had intervened again. While his planning had worked for Branca—she'd ended up marrying the man their father had connected her with—his interference in Rodrigo's love life had proven to be a waste of time.

"You made a mistake this time," Rodrigo said. "Sidney is completely uninterested in marriage or staying here. You were wrong."

"I'm never wrong," his father insisted.

"You are this time."

Gualtiero leaned on his hands on the desk. "She told you she doesn't love you?"

"She refuses to marry me. What more proof do I need? She turned me down twice."

Gualtiero frowned. "Hmm…perhaps I was wrong," he mused. "But I had this sense… I was so sure…"

"Let it go, Father. I have plenty to do before I catch my flight this afternoon, and this conversation is very distracting." *And disheartening,* Rodrigo added silently. He continued signing the documents in front of him. "You missed the mark this time. I wish you hadn't, but you have."

Chapter 11

She had to tell him. She couldn't leave him with doubts about her love for him.

Sidney gnawed on her lip as she stepped off the elevator. Today a receptionist greeted her when she stepped off.

"Is Rodrigo Serrano in? He's not expecting me, but if you tell him Sidney Altman is here, he may be willing to see me." The receptionist didn't say a word, perhaps wondering how she thought she'd be able to see the head of the company without an appointment.

The woman held up her finger. "One minute." She spoke into the mouthpiece of the phone and then hung up. "I'm sorry, madam, but Senhor Serrano is out of the office on business and won't be back until next week. Would you like to set an appointment for then?"

She was too late.

Sidney's stomach plummeted in despair. "No," she said quietly. "That won't be necessary."

Head bent and heart heavy, she took the elevator to the bottom floor. With nowhere else to go and nothing to do since she'd already checked out of the hotel, she decided to go straight to the airport.

On the way there, she made one last call to his cell phone. It went straight to voice mail. Before she lost her nerve, she let the words rush out.

"I know you're on another business trip, and the last thing you expected was to hear from me, but I wanted you to know that I came by your office to tell you the truth. I do love you, and I've never stopped. And I would love to marry you. I didn't want you to think that I didn't want that. I—" Her voice broke and grew thicker with the pain she carried. "I want to give you those beautiful babies, but I can't, and it's not fair to you. I can't have children, Rodrigo. If you get this message and you think…" No, she was being selfish. "Goodbye."

Hours later, Sidney sat at the airport with the phone to her ear, talking to her mother.

"At least you told him," Agnes said. "Honesty is always the best policy, and you have nothing to be ashamed of."

Sidney sipped her soda through a straw. "He hasn't called back," she said glumly. She'd been watching her phone screen to see if he'd called, but, nothing.

"Maybe he's tied up."

"He couldn't handle it. Just like my ex couldn't." She wiped a tear from her cheek and listened as they called her flight for boarding. "Mom, they're boarding. I have to get on the plane."

"Bye, honey. Have a safe flight, and when you get home I'll have a pint of chocolate-chip-cookie-dough ice cream waiting for you."

Sidney smiled through her teary eyes. "Sounds like a plan."

When they called her zone, she boarded with the other passengers and buckled in. She pulled the flight magazine from the seat pouch in front of her and flipped through the contents, but there was nothing in there that captured her interest. Gazing out the window, she felt an overwhelming sadness at losing Rodrigo for a second time.

Even though she hadn't wanted to tell him the truth, she didn't have any regrets now. The burden of her infertility was off her mind, and at least now she could say she'd come clean. She looked at the photo of her soon-to-be daughter, Alana, and managed a bittersweet smile. Soon, she'd be holding her in her arms, and she had Rodrigo to thank for that. He could have denied the contract, but he hadn't, and with such a large order, she was ensured a huge commission and financial stability to put the adoption agency's mind at ease. She'd even be able to take time off—a sort of maternity leave—to bond with her new baby girl.

"Excuse me, Senhora Altman?" The flight attendant looked at her with concern, leaning over the man beside her and speaking quietly. "There is a problem with your passport. They have asked me to escort you off the plane." A burly man stood behind her, as if they thought she'd resist.

"My passport? What's wrong?"

"We must discuss this off the plane. An airline representative will greet you when you disembark."

Sidney's co-passenger let her squeeze out, and the burly male took her carry-on and walked with her off the plane. She felt like a criminal and didn't even know what the charges were.

Another flight attendant greeted her at the gate. "Please wait here," the woman said. "We are waiting for an official to arrive." She then walked away to speak to the large man who'd escorted her off the plane.

Sidney sat in the almost empty area of the gate. Surely they hadn't confused her with someone on the no-fly list. She'd never been stopped before, but she'd heard horror stories about identification mix-ups, where passengers were detained because security thought they were terrorists or criminals.

She called her mother, eyes sweeping through the crowd of passengers walking down the moving sidewalk and those rushing to their gates. "Mom, I don't know what's going on, but I just wanted you to know I won't be on the flight. There's something wrong with my passport, but they haven't told me what's wrong. Everyone's speaking in Portuguese, so I don't have any idea what they're saying. I hope—"

In the crowd, a familiar dark head appeared, dark eyes and a dark suit coming across the terminal toward her. Her heart started racing, and all she could do was stare.

"Sidney, what's wrong?" Her mother's voice was sharp with alarm.

"Let me call you back, okay?" She disconnected the call and watched as Rodrigo came closer.

He stopped only a few feet away. Her heart was beating so fast she wasn't sure if she could speak. Slowly, she rose to her feet.

"How could you leave a voice message like that and then run off?" he asked. "Why didn't you tell me?"

"I didn't know how." She bit her bottom lip. "My ex-husband… He couldn't handle it. I felt so empty and useless…and ashamed."

"And you thought I'd be like your husband," he said, a grave sadness in his voice. "You didn't trust me. You didn't trust my love for you."

"It wasn't just about you. What about your family? It's so obvious how much they want you to be a father, and even if we married, I—I didn't want your family looking at me with indifference. I've experienced that before and...I hated it."

"Do you care more about what they think about you than you do about being with me?"

When he put it that way, it seemed ridiculous to forego happiness because of what others thought.

"No," she whispered.

"I still want to marry you, Sidney." His face softened. "You should have told me."

"I know, but because of what happened before..."

"With your ex."

"Yes."

He walked closer, coming within a hairbreadth but not touching her yet. "Luckily I was at the airport and have some pull." He touched her face and she leaned into his touch. "I don't care that you can't have children. I love you, and that's all that matters. If it's just you and me until the end, I'll be happy."

"Well, it might not be just you and me until the end." Tears blurred her vision. "I'm going to adopt a little girl, and she has the biggest, most beautiful smile you've ever seen." With trembling fingers, she took out the photo and showed it to him.

He took the photo and smiled at the image of Alana. "I can't wait to meet her, and I can't wait to marry you."

"Are you proposing?"

"It depends. What would be your answer this time?"

"Yes!" She flung herself into his arms, and he lifted her into a bear hug.

"Eu te amo, querida," he whispered.

"I love you, too."

Epilogue

Sidney walked out to the courtyard where her mother stood watch over the children running around under the sprinkler. They'd sold the apartment and moved into a two-story house in Leblon so the children would have space to run around and play. Her eldest, Alana, chased the two-year-old triplets around and around in a circle, the four of them giggling and without a care in the world.

It was hard to believe that at one point she hadn't been sure if the triplets would survive. After expensive fertility treatments, she'd finally become pregnant. But complications had arisen and the triplets had been born prematurely, none of them weighing more than two pounds apiece. After weeks of vigilance in the hospital where she'd barely slept or eaten, Rodrigo had finally dragged her away and insisted she get proper rest and take care of herself so she'd be at 100 percent when they did come home.

When they were finally released, she'd slept in the nursery, worried that they would stop breathing in the middle of the night or that something would happen and she wouldn't be there to save her little miracles.

It took a long time, but she was finally able to accept that they would be fine, and Rodrigo had been patient with her. The doctors confirmed with each follow-up visit that the children were hitting each development milestone.

Rodrigo came up from behind and slipped his arm around her waist, pulling her close and out of her thoughts. "I think they are afraid of her. What do you think?"

"I think you're right," Sidney agreed.

It was a warm summer day and Agnes had flown in to avoid the winter cold and spend time with her grandchildren.

"Do you think we'll ever be able to convince her to move here?" Rodrigo asked.

Right then, his father came out the back door. "There she is," he said softly. Gualtiero completely ignored his son and daughter-in-law and walked toward Agnes and the playing children. He stopped beside her, and she looked up at him in surprise. She patted her hair and laughed at something he said.

"I'm not one hundred percent certain," Sidney said, "but I have a feeling we might be able to convince her."

Rodrigo chuckled and squeezed her tighter.

* * * * *

REQUEST YOUR FREE BOOKS!

2 FREE NOVELS PLUS 2 FREE GIFTS!

KIMANI ™
ROMANCE

Love's ultimate destination!

A sizzling new miniseries set in the wide-open spaces of Montana!

*** ★★★ ***

THE BROWARDS OF MONTANA
Passionate love in the West

JACQUELIN THOMAS	DARA GIRARD	HARMONY EVANS

WRANGLING WES	**ENGAGING BROOKE**	**LOVING LANEY**
Available April 2014	*Available May 2014*	*Available June 2014*

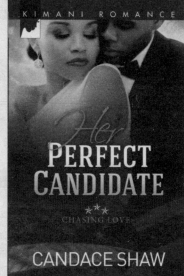

"A SHIMMERING TAPESTRY OF MAGIC AND SONG!"
—LYNN ABBEY

"Three cheers . . . for a genuinely *new* fantasy writer . . . someone special in the fantasy field."
—ANNE MCCAFFREY

"A fine poet she is!"
—KATHERINE KURTZ

"I find Nancy Springer's work to be a delightful romp in the field of what I call 'adult fairy tales.' She is in my opinion a worthy successor to the likes of Evangeline Walton and Thomas Burnett Swann . . . but, withal, possessing a literary aura distinctly all her own."
—ROBERT ADAMS

"Ms. Springer . . . knows how to tell a story and at the same time involve the reader in the emotions, fears and personal triumphs of her characters."
—ANDRE NORTON

D0681418

Nancy Springer

THE SABLE MOON

A TIMESCAPE BOOK
PUBLISHED BY POCKET BOOKS NEW YORK

Another *Original* publication of TIMESCAPE/POCKET BOOKS

A Timescape Book published by
POCKET BOOKS, a Simon & Schuster division of
GULF & WESTERN CORPORATION
1230 Avenue of the Americas, New York, N.Y. 10020

ISBN: 0-671-44378-X

First Pocket Books printing February, 1981

10   9   8   7   6   5   4   3   2

POCKET and colophon are trademarks of Simon & Schuster.

Use of the TIMESCAPE trademark is by exclusive license
from Gregory Benford, the trademark owner.

Printed in the U.S.A.

I am a crescent moon.
I am a rustle of padded paws,
I am a seed in the earth,
I am a dewdrop.
I am a hidden jewel,
I am a dream,
I am a silver harp.

I am a fruit on the Tree,
I am a beast of curving horn,
I am a swollen breast,
I am the argent moon.
I am soft rain,
I am rivers of thought,
I am sea tides,
I am a turning wheel.

I am the waning moon.
I am the mare who rides men mad,
I am the sable moon.
I am the howl of the wolf,
I am the hag,
I am the flood of destruction.
I am the ship that rides the flood,
I am the crescent moon.
I am the dark, bright, changing moon.

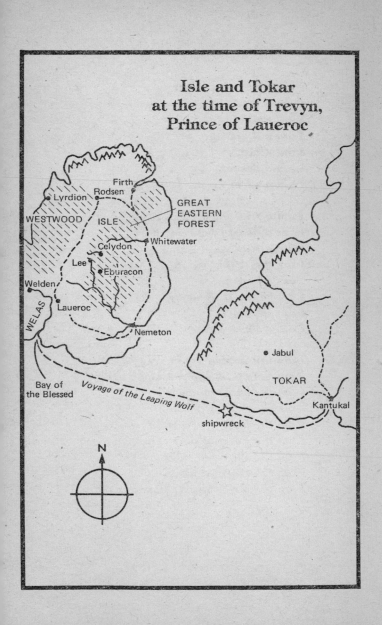

Isle and Tokar
at the time of Trevyn,
Prince of Laueroc

Firth
Rodsen
Lyrdion
GREAT
EASTERN
FOREST
WESTWOOD
ISLE
Whitewater
Celydon
Lee
Eburacon
Welden
WELAS
Laueroc
Nemeton
Jabul
TOKAR
Bay of
the Blessed
Voyage of the Leaping Wolf
Kantukal
shipwreck

N

Book One

FATE AND THE MAIDEN

Chapter One

Prince Trevyn was seventeen years old, and still struggling out of childhood like an eaglet out of the shell, when he first met Gwern. It was not a happy meeting.

Trevyn had galloped far ahead of the others, because his half-fledged falcon had led him a crazy course over the grassy downs. Muttering to himself and whistling at the bird, he topped a rise and saw a herd of yearling colts in the dingle below. Small heads, arched necks, level backs, and high-set, windswept tails—young though they were, everything about them marked them unmistakably as steeds of the royal breed. A stranger stood with them, stroking a chestnut filly on the nose.

"You, there!" Trevyn shouted hotly. "Let the horses alone!"

The fellow glanced at him without moving. Trevyn sent his mount plunging down the slope toward him.

"Let the horses alone, I say!" he called again as he approached.

The stranger, a youth of about his own age, met his angry eyes coolly. "Why so?"

Trevyn almost sputtered at the calm question. Did the dolt not know that he was Trevyn son of Alan of Laueroc, that he was Prince of Isle and Welas, sole heir of the Sun Kings? The *elwedeyn* horses had been the special pride of the Crown ever since his kindred the elves had presented them, before his birth. No uninstructed hand was permitted to touch them. Indeed, they would not lightly suffer the touch of any hand. The royal family commanded their love through the use of the Old Language that had come down to them from the Beginning. . . . Quietly, Trevyn ordered the chestnut filly away from the stranger. It unnerved him that she permitted that hand upon her at all.

The stranger looked up at him with eyes like pebbles, expressionless. "Why did you do that? Are these horses yours?"

"Ay, they are mine," replied Trevyn, trying to keep the edge out of his voice. Perhaps the yokel was a half-wit. There was something odd about his face.

"You are a fool to say so." The fellow turned away indifferently and stroked another horse, a cream-colored one. "These horses belong to no one."

Trevyn's temper flared, all the more so because the other was right, in a sense. Galled, he sprang down from his mount and jerked the stranger by the arm. "Get away, I say!"

Still expressionless, the youth pulled from his grasp and lashed back with a closed fist. In an instant, both of them were flailing at each other, then rolling in a tussle on the grass. Trevyn wore a sword, and after a bit he wished he could honorably use it. The stranger was as hard and resilient as an axe haft, and his blows hurt.

Before the fight reached a conclusion, however, the combatants found themselves hauled apart. "Now *what*," inquired a quiet voice, "is the cause of this?"

Trevyn blinked out of a blackened eye. It was his uncle, Hal, the King of the Silver Sun; and though he did not look angry, Trevyn hated to cause him sorrow. Trevyn's father, King Alan, faced him as well, and he looked angry enough for two.

"Surely," Hal remarked, "this row must have had a beginning?"

"He was bothering the horses," Trevyn accused, and pointed, childlike, at the stranger.

"The horses don't look bothered," Alan scoffed harshly.

The horses, apparently pleased by the excitement, had formed a circle of curious heads. The chestnut filly stretched her neck and nuzzled the stranger youth's hand.

Hal and Alan exchanged a surprised glance. "Fellow," Alan addressed the stranger, "what is your name?"

"Gwern." The youth spoke flatly.

"And who are your parents?"

"I have none." Gwern did not seem to find this the least bit remarkable.

"Who were you born of?" asked Alan with more patience than was his wont. "Who was your mother?"

For the first time Gwern hesitated, seeming at a loss. "Earth," he said at last.

Alan frowned and tried another tack. "Where is your home?"

"Earth," Gwern replied.

They all stared at him, not sure whether or not he was deliberately courting Alan's anger. He stared back at them with eyes like stream-washed stones, indeterminately brown. He was brown all over, his skin a curious dun, his hair like hazel tips. He was barefoot, and his clothing was of coarse unbleached wool, when most folk of these peaceful times could afford better. What was he doing in the middle of the downs, with the nearest dwelling miles away?

"Take him along home," Hal suggested mildly, "and I'll look him up in the census."

When he was king, Trevyn promised himself, he would set such nuisances in a dungeon for a week or so, to teach them some respect. Take him along home indeed!

Alan shrugged and turned back to his son, less angry at Trevyn now. "Who struck first?"

"I pulled him away from a horse, and he struck me."

"Pulled him away from a horse? And why? If an *elwedeyn* horse sees fit to bear him company, lad, you also had better learn to abide him. The horses are well able to defend themselves, and they're better judges of men than most chamberlains. Think before you fight, Trevyn." Alan was disgusted. "So now you have a black eye, and you have lost your hawk. Get on home."

They all rode silently back to the walled city of Laueroc, with Gwern behind Hal on his *elwedeyn* stallion, over rolling meadows where the larks sang through the days. For miles before they came to it they could see the castle anchored on the billowing softness of the downs like a tall ship on a shimmering, grassy sea. Atop the highest swell its ramparts vaulted skyward, and from its slender turrets floated flags of every holding in Isle. In every window, even the servants' windows, swung a circle of cut and faceted glass to catch the sun and send colors flitting about the rooms.

Centuries before, Cuin the Falconer King had raised the fortress at Laueroc with pearly, gold-veined stone brought all the way from the mountains of Welas. He had not wanted to mar his new demesne with diggings. The land at Laueroc, in Trevyn's time, was still nearly as scarless as the day it was born. The castle lay on its bosom like a crystal brooch, and two roads wound away like flat bronze chains. There were no buildings outside the walls. In the topmost chamber of the westernmost tall tower, athwart the battlements, King Hal made his study and solitary retreat.

Trevyn climbed up there after him when they had stabled the horses, and to his dismay Gwern followed. It troubled him that the dirt-colored stranger should come so familiarly to his uncle's room. Hal was more than Sunset King; he was a bard, a visionary and a seer. In all the kingdom, only three persons approached him with the love of equals: Queen Rosemary, his beloved; his brother Alan; and Lysse, the Elf-Queen, Trevyn's mother and Alan's wife. Trevyn held him in awe. When he entered the tower chamber he silently took his seat, knees loaded down with tomes of history, awaiting Hal's leisure. But Gwern poked and prowled around the circular room, disturbing Hal's scholarly clutter. And Hal stood gazing out of his high, barred window, seeming not to mind.

"What do you see?" Gwern asked suddenly. Trevyn winced at his effrontery. The King of the Silver Sun had always looked to the west, toward Welas and the reaches of the sunset stars, and Trevyn had never dared to ask him why. But Hal turned around courteously.

"I see Elwestrand, what else?" he replied, the sheen of his gray eyes going smoky dark. "And a fair sight it is."

"Where is Elwestrand?" Gwern craned his neck, peering.

"Nay, nay," Hal explained eagerly, "you must look with your inner eye. Elwestrand is beyond the western sea." His voice yearned like singing. "I have seen a tree with golden fruit, and a great white stag, and bright birds, and sleek, romping beasts. I have seen unicorns."

"Elwestrand is the grove of the dead," Trevyn told Gwern sharply, jealous that Hal would speak to him so equably.

"Grove of the dead?" Hal turned to regard his nephew with a tiny smile on his angular face. "Elwestrand is but another step on the way to the One, for all that it lies beyond the sunlit lands."

"It must be dark," Gwern said doubtfully.

"Nay, indeed!" Hal cried. "It shines like—like the fair flower of Veran used to shine, here in Isle, before the Easterners blighted it. . . . Elwestrand is lilac and celadon and pearly gray-gold and every subtle glow of the summer stars. And glow of dragons from the indigo sea, every shade of damson and quince and dusky rose. The elves remembered it all in their bright stitchery—all that this world was, and this Isle, before the Eastern invasion, before man's evil shadowed and spread." Hal turned back to his window on the west, pressing his forehead against the bars.

"My kindred the elves sailed to Elwestrand," Trevyn told Gwern more softly. "All of them except my mother."

"Now they live amidst the stuff of their dreams," Hal said from his window.

"But does no one return from Elwestrand?" Gwern asked.

"Who would wish to return?"

"Veran came from Elwestrand, did he not?" Trevyn spoke up suddenly.

"Who is Veran?" Gwern pounced on the name.

Hal turned to answer with patience Trevyn could not understand. "He from whom I derive my lineage and my crown, the first Blessed King of Welas. He sailed hither out of the west; perhaps he came from Elwestrand." Hal looked away again. "But when I go, I will not return."

"Elwestrand," Gwern sang in a rich, husky voice.

> "Elwestrand! Elwestrand!
> Be you realm but of my mind,
> Yet you've lived ten thousand lines
> Of soaring song,
> Elwestrand. Is the soul more sooth
> Than that for which it pines?
> Are there ties that closer bind
> Than call so strong?"

Hal wheeled on him sharply. "How did you know that song?" he demanded. "I made it, years ago."

"Elwestrand," Gwern chanted, and without answering he darted out of the door and skipped down the tower steps, still singing. Hal silently watched him go. Trevyn watched also, hot with jealous anger. For he, too, had felt the dream and the call, and it seemed to him as if Gwern had stolen it from him.

"Why do you abide him so tamely?" he burst out at Hal, startled by his own daring. "He is—he is uncouth!"

Hal shifted his gaze to his nephew, and as always that detached, appraising look made Trevyn shrink, inwardly cursing. Hal threatened nothing, but he saw everything, and Trevyn had dark places inside that he wanted to hide. . . . Hal frowned faintly, then turned his eyes away from the Prince to answer his question, seeming to see the answer in the air.

"He is magical," Hal said. "He is like a late shoot of those who were lost to Isle centuries ago when the star-son Bevan led his people out of the hollow hills. Magic left Isle then, and I believe nothing has been quite right since—though I have sometimes thought that Veran brought some back to Welas— and your mother's people, in their own clearheaded way—"

"Magic!" Trevyn blurted, astonished to hear longing in Hal's voice. He knew how his uncle had always avoided the touch of magic. The Easterners had made magic the horror of Isle. At Nemeton their sorcerers had performed barbaric

sacrifice to the Sacred Son and the horned god from whom
they drew their powers. Hal had been reared in the shadow of
that cult, and he and Alan had worked for years to stamp out
such black sorcery.

"I know I have taught you not to meddle with magic." Hal
sat by his nephew. "It is perilous. But all fair things are
perilous. Dragons breathe fire, and the horn of the unicorn is
sharp. Even this Gwern might be perilous, in his own rude
way." The Sunset King smiled dreamily. "But it must bode
well, I think, that he has come to us. Who or what can he be, I
wonder? I don't really expect to find him in the census."

As, in fact, he could not. So Gwern stayed on at the castle;
the Lauerocs kept him there for want of anything better to do
with him. The peculiar youth did not seem suited for any
work, but Alan claimed he was no more useless than most of
the other courtiers. He was fey, sometimes shouting and
singing with barbaric abandon, sometimes brooding. He
always went barefoot, even in the chill of late autumn, and
often he slept outdoors, beyond the city walls, on the ground.
He generally looked dirty and uncombed. He observed few
niceties. If he spoke at all, he spoke with consummate
accuracy and no tact. But he was handsome, in his earthy
way, and the castle folk seemed to find him amusing, even
attractive. Trevyn fervently disliked him. Striving as he was
for adolescent poise, he found Gwern's very existence an
affront.

Yet, with no malice that Trevyn could prove, Gwern
attached himself to the Prince, following him everywhere.
Often they would fight—only with fists, since Gwern knew
nothing of swordplay. Trevyn could hold his own, but he
never succeeded in driving Gwern away from him. The
mud-colored youth confronted him like an embodied force,
inscrutable and haphazard as wind or rainclouds, leaving only
by his own unpredictable whim.

"Father," Trevyn begged, "make him stop hounding me.
Please."

"You'll see worse troubles before you die," Alan replied.
"Find your own cure for it, Trevyn." He loved his son to the
point of heartache, but Trevyn would be King. Above all, he
must not become **soft** or spoiled. Alan had seen to his training

in statesmanship, swordsmanship, horsemanship. . . . The
discipline was no more than Alan expected of himself, his
own body trim and tough, his days given over to royal duty,
early and late. So when Trevyn saluted, soldierlike, and
silently left the room, Alan could not fault his conduct. Great
of heart that he was, it did not occur to him that Trevyn
showed too little of the heart, that he concealed too much.

Trevyn was almost able to hide his anger even from
himself, minding his manners and tending to his lessons as
Gwern dogged him through the crisp days of early winter. But
frustration swirled and seethed through his thoughts like a
buried torrent. In time Trevyn found Gwern obstinately
intruding even into his dreams at night. Gwern and a unicorn;
Gwern standing at the prow of an elf-ship, with the sea wind
in his face. . . .

"I!" Trevyn shouted in his sleep.

He felt sure that Gwern longed to go to Elwestrand, as he
did. But he swore that it was he, Prince Trevyn, who would
go, and alone, and to return, as no one had done before him.
Someday he would do that. But he could not possibly take
ship before spring. The winter stretched endlessly ahead.

Trevyn did not stay for winter. When the first snowstorm
loomed, he slipped from his bed by night and made his way to
the stable. He loaded food and blankets onto Arundel, Hal's
elwedeyn charger, the oldest and wisest of the royal steeds.
The walls and gates were lightly guarded, for it was peace-
time, and who would look for trouble in the teeth of a storm?
Warmly dressed, Trevyn rode out of a postern gate into the
dark and the freezing wind. By morning even Gwern would
not be able to follow him.

It was so. Dawn showed snow almost a foot deep, and more
still falling, blindingly thick, in the air. Folk struggled even to
cross the courtyard. It was nearly midday before Alan could
believe that Trevyn was missing, and then he could not eat for
anger and consternation. He paced the battlements for hours.
But Gwern had known as soon as he awoke what Trevyn had
done, and he had run to the walls screaming in rage.

"Alan, don't fret so." Hal came up beside his brother,
encircled his shoulders with a comforting arm. "Arundel will
see the lad through."

"Trevyn has gall," Alan fumed, "taking the old steed out in such weather. Are you not worried, Hal, or angry?"

"Why, I suppose I am," Hal admitted. "But I like Trevyn's spirit, Alan. He plans his folly with sense and subtlety. You'll have to keep a looser rein on him after this."

Alan snorted. "Worse than folly; it's lunacy! What sort of idiocy must possess the boy? I thought he was my son!" Alan paused in his pacing long enough to glare at his lovely green-eyed wife.

"He is your son, right enough." Lysse smiled. "Look at Gwern for your answers."

"Gwern!" Alan glanced down from the battlements to where the dun-faced youth stood in the courtyard pommeling the air in helpless rage. "Gwern is the nuisance that drove him away, you mean? That is no excuse."

"Nay, I mean that Gwern's passion matches Trevyn's own. The boy is no boy, Alan, but nearly a man, and he left in anger. What would Gwern do if you shackled him with lessons and books?"

"I do not understand." Alan stood scowling at his golden-haired Elf-Queen. "Are you speaking from the Sight?"

"From elf-sight and mother-sight." Her misty gray-green eyes widened in proof. "Trevyn hides his feelings from us constantly, Alan, but he cannot hide them from Gwern. Read Gwern like a weathercock for your son. Remember how surly he has been these weeks past?"

"What," Alan asked slowly, "does Gwern have to do with Trevyn?"

Lysse shrugged helplessly. "Gwern is Trevyn's wyrd," said Hal.

"Weird enough," grumbled Alan, choosing for the moment to ignore the esoteric word. Lysse was staring into nothingness, her eyes as deep as oceans. "Even now Trevyn hides his mind from me," she murmured. "I can tell that he is alive, nothing more. But Gwern knows more. All morning he has faced east."

Alan wheeled to look at the youth again; it was true. Lysse went back into her trance, her eyes like springtime pools in her delicate face.

"Lee!" she exclaimed at last with satisfaction. "He goes

toward Lee, and Arundel knows that way well. There will be a messenger from Rafe, mark my words. But do not tell Gwern."

"Lee!" Alan protested, astonished. "But how can you be so sure? Celydon also lies eastward, and Whitewater, and Nemeton. Not to speak of the whole Great Eastern Forest."

"Something awaits him at Lee," Lysse stated with quiet certainty. "Do not tell Gwern! I want to see what happens."

Chapter Two

Meg had never, not even in her silliest daydreams, fancied herself to be pretty. She knew that she had a comical, pointy face and a sharp nose like a benevolent witch. Indeed, witch was what some folk called her, all because the birds would alight on her hands. She did not mind being different, and it pleased her that the dappled deer did not fear her touch. But she minded being skinny. Some girls could make do with comeliness that bloomed below the neck, but not her, she told herself. Her skirts fell straight from her waistless middle, and she always had to sew ruffles inside the front of her blouses to give some fullness—though not fullness enough.

Still, she had never, not even in her grimmest nightmares, imagined herself looking such a fright as now. Slogging along through the snow in her old pair of men's boots, skirt torn and draggled, shawl clutched from her shoulders by the lowering Forest trees. Hatless, with her hair frazzled by the wind, eyes red and weepy, sharp nose running from cold and exertion and emotion. Flushed and panting, she struggled along, knowing it would be lunacy to stay out after dark, but too stubborn to give up.

She found her cow at last and stood frozen a moment in

astonishment that overcame her hurry. Mud! A gooshy, oozing, undulating pool of mud filled a hollow of the frost-bound Forest. From the center of the expanse, round brown eyes looked back at her. Only the cow's head showed above the surface. Wisps of steam rose around her.

"Come on, then, Molly," Meg called gently.

The cow did not budge.

Meg coaxed, pleaded, extended a bribe of oats. Molly did not even twitch an ear. The day was moving on apace. Meg rolled her eyes heavenward and went in after her.

"What is even more appealing than yer plain, everyday Meg?" she muttered viciously to herself. "Why, a Meg covered with mud, that is what! World, are ye watching?"

As she had hoped, the bottom of the mud hole was solid. She forced her way through the twenty feet of brown pudding that separated Molly from the shore and took her by the halter. Molly would not move. Meg could hardly blame her, for the mud was deliciously warm and the air increasingly cold.

"Come on, Molly, we can't stay here all night!" she cried helplessly, tugging at the cow. Then she jumped, and screamed.

Where before there had been only snow and the dark trunks of trees, now there was a rider on a beautiful silver horse—a young man, blond and very handsome. As Meg's eyes met his of stormy green, she felt an instant of utter abeyance, as if heart and soul had stopped to gaze with her. Then she came back to self with a pang, feeling how ill-prepared she was to meet him, up to her elbows in mud. Still, she saw no amusement in his face. . . . She could not know that, for his part, he had felt an odd leap of heart on seeing her. He could hardly account for it himself, and irritably shrugged off thought of it.

"I'm sorry I frightened you," he told the girl.

Meg tossed her head at that. She did not consider that she had been frightened, only—well, startled. Perhaps he had been frightened himself.

"Are you all right?" he asked. "Can you get out?"

"Ay, to be sure!" she snapped. "But I'll not leave without this cow."

Trevyn rolled his eyes at her tone. "Humor me," he urged with exaggerated courtesy, "and come out. *Please.*"

She fought her way toward the edge, retracing her steps. It was harder than she had expected. The ooze clung to her skirt as she inched along, panting. Trevyn dismounted and glanced around for a stout stick to offer her. "None strong enough," he muttered.

"Give me a hand," Meg gasped.

She meant that literally. Trevyn had not wanted to touch her. Grimacing, he grasped her by her muddy wrist and hauled her out, splattering himself with chunks of goo. She stood on the verge, breathing hard, rubbing her face and peering at him. "I've never seen anything like it," she declared.

"The mud? I've heard about these holes in the southern Forest. Some are clear water, steaming hot. Too bad your cow couldn't have chosen one of those." He unpinned his cloak as he spoke, evidently steeling himself for action.

"Ye're going to go in after her?"

"I suppose I'm going to have to," he replied ungraciously. "Arundel—" He spoke to the horse in the Old Language.

"What?" asked Meg, straining to understand the peculiar words. But then she cried out in protest as the young man took off his cloak and sliced into it with his sword. It was a thick wool cloak lined with crimson satin, more beautiful than anything she had ever owned. Trevyn stopped at her cry, looked at her quizzically.

"Is the cloak worth more than your cow?"

"That is not fair!" she answered hotly. "Molly is—is—she's family! I dare say she is not a great worth, but—" Meg fell silent and regarded Trevyn curiously. His tunic was of linen, and his sword was inlaid with gold. It was not that which gave her pause; she had seen finery before. But this youth had a proud air about him, though he had not yet reached his full growth. He was not in her lord's service; she would have noticed him if he were. Perhaps he was some lord's bard or herald, or even a lord's son? "What's yer name?" Meg asked.

Cutting strips from his cloak, he answered her without looking up. "Trevyn."

"Oh," she replied. "Are ye from Laueroc, then? I have

heard that many young men there are named after the
Prince."

"I am not named after the Prince," Trevyn stated, quite
truthfully. "But ay, I am from Laueroc."

"Are ye in the Kings' service, then? What are ye doing in
the Forest?"

"Will you ask one question at a time!" He smiled at her as
he knotted his makeshift rope. "Indeed, I am at the Kings'
service, but I am here on my own business. What is your
name?"

"Meg."

"Margaret?"

"Nay. Megan."

"Ah." Trevyn slipped off his tunic and folded it as a pad for
Arundel's neck. The girl stared at him. She had not thought
that a man could be muscular and graceful at the same time.
Trevyn laid his sword belt aside, fastened the rope around
Arundel's shoulders, took the other end, and started into the
pool of mud. Meg aroused herself. "What must I do?" she
called after him.

"Help Arundel pull."

Trevyn reached the cow and looped the rope around her
horns. Then he grasped Molly around her heavy shoulders,
braced his feet, and started to lift. As he wrestled the cow
from her mucky bed, he called to Arundel in that strange
tongue Meg had heard him use before. The horse threw his
weight against the rope, and Meg tugged with all her might.
Molly lurched forward, and Trevyn moved with her, lifting,
shoving. Within moments she was out. Meg ran to her,
kissing her broad, pink nose and feeling for injuries. Then she
turned to Trevyn, who was gingerly putting on his tunic,
scowling at the brown blobs on the fine white cloth.

"Thank ye so much."

He smiled sourly, scraping mud, and suddenly she laughed,
a sweet, healthy laugh. "Are we not pretty, though!" she
cried, so infectiously that he gave in to good humor and
grinned at her. But then he buckled on his sword and
frowned, glancing around at the trees that stood, black and
silent, on every side.

"What's to be done now?" he asked flatly. "Dark is scarcely an hour away."

Meg stopped laughing with a sigh. "I must get home, dark or no dark. My mother will be frantic with worry even now."

"There's more to think of." Trevyn leaned against a tree, judiciously. "Have you considered how Molly came to be here?"

"I have not had time to consider!" Meg bristled at his tone. "I've been hours and hours after her. She has never come this far before."

"She was chased." Trevyn pointed at the snow all around the margin of the pool. "Wolves. See their tracks?"

"Ay, those prints look fresh," Meg agreed reluctantly, "but why would wolves hunt Molly? It has been a mild autumn, and there are rabbits enough about."

"The wolves have been singing of larger game today," Trevyn said evenly. "Their voices have filled the Forest." Meg looked into his shadowy green eyes and saw foreboding there that she could not understand.

"What're ye saying?" she demanded, half frightened, half angry. "That the beasts are of a mind to attack? There is nothing in the Forest that will harm me."

"I would have said the same of myself," Trevyn muttered.

They stood eyeing each other in perplexity. Meg started to shiver as her clothes dried in the winter wind.

"Wolves or no wolves," Trevyn broke silence, "you need a fire."

"We should camp here, then," she agreed heavily. "If they come, we can get into the mud hole—"

"It's too small for all of us. Come on." Trevyn strode back the way he had come without even a glance at his horse. It followed him unled, and the cow, Molly, lowed softly and followed him as well.

Meg stared in disbelief. "The poor thing must be addled," she murmured, and trotted after.

"Gather wood," Trevyn called.

He filled his arms as he walked. After a few hundred feet he found the campsite he had noted earlier, a jumbled pile of rock protruding from a steep forest slope. Such formations were not uncommon in those parts, but this one had a jutting shelf of granite overhead. The dirt beneath was trampled clear of undergrowth, black with ashes. Many travelers had camped here—perhaps even Hal and Alan in years gone by.

Trevyn made the fire, then collected firewood feverishly until full dark stopped him. The girl tended the animals and the blaze. Arundel stamped restlessly where he stood against a wall of rock. Molly stood beside him, swaying.

"She's quite exhausted," Trevyn remarked.

"Hadn't ye better put the rope on her all the same?" Meg asked. "She'll run off if—if anything should go wrong."

Trevyn shook his head. "She will not run."

"Humor me," Meg told him pointedly. It was a phrase she had recently learned.

So he tethered the cow and came to sit by the fire. He and Meg stared silently over the flames at a wall of darkness beyond. Trevyn felt satisfied with the sizable pile of wood he had brought in, and the rock that half surrounded them retained the fire's heat almost as well as a house. Still, he had to admit that their situation lacked a certain comfort.

"Nothing to eat," Meg sighed.

"Ay." Trevyn grinned at the hint. "You're right, Meg, I've nothing."

"Drat." She shifted her position, trying to ease the contact of her bones with the hard ground. "Well, there's no use sitting here like dummies all night, waiting for shadows. Let's have a story."

"Certainly," he said agreeably. "Go ahead."

"Nay, nay, I mean a story of Laueroc! Something about courage, something to speed our blood, give us heart—a story of the Sun Kings!"

"Oh," he remarked.

"You're from Laueroc," she prodded impatiently. "Surely you know what I mean."

He did indeed. But it was not their courage that he valued most in his uncle and father.

"It's not quite what you have in mind," he said slowly, "but it's a beautiful tale. Have you ever heard about the Sun Kings and the proud lord of Caerronan?"

"Nay!" She clapped delightedly.

"Nay?" he exclaimed with mock surprise; he knew that the story was not told outside his family. "Well, it took place only a few months after King Hal and King Alan were crowned. . . ."

He felt strange, speaking of them so impersonally. As if his mind had been disjointed, bent to a new angle, he saw them differently, envisioning them as he had never actually known them, when they were nearly as young as he.

Here is the tale Trevyn told:

The young Sun Kings missed their wandering life, and they got tired of courtly ceremony. So sometimes, when they could, they would put on old clothes and slip away for a week or two. They would ride at random around Isle, camping in the open or staying at a cottage. Perhaps people humored them and were not really fooled. Hal and Alan could not bring themselves to ride any horses but their own, and the beasts were far too beautiful for ordinary wanderers. Of course, the Kings were beautiful as well.

Their wives humored them, too, but Lysse and Rosemary also got tired of staying at Laueroc. At the time of the trouble with Caerronan, Rosemary had put her foot down, with the result that she and Hal were riding court through Isle in cavalcade. Alan and Lysse were left to manage affairs at Laueroc. But after a few weeks of councils and hearings, Alan got restless and took a notion to ride by himself to Caerronan. Old Einon, the lord there, had failed to send tribute to Laueroc, give homage or take his oath of fealty. He held a small, isolated manor in the foothills of Welas, and his spurning of the Sun Kings meant practically nothing aside from insult. But Alan needed an excuse to get away.

So he rode across Welas, all alone, through the last bright days of autumn, and went to see some friends he knew from his outlaw days. They said that Einon was a hard, rough old rascal, fair within the letter of the law but entirely lacking in generosity to his tenants, his family, or anyone else. There was no hospitality to be got at his hall.

Hearing that, Alan left his horse and walked toward Caerronan. When he had reached the lord's woodlot, he found a large stone—the heaviest one he could lift—and

heaved it up and dropped it squarely on his own right foot.
He gasped, and barely kept himself from howling. Then he
took a stick and hobbled over to Einon's fortress, limping
pitifully, to request shelter and care.

Even Einon did not have the gall to turn away an injured
man. Customary law decreed that he was obliged to maintain
Alan for a reasonable length of time, as long as Alan had
need. So he had to take him in. But old Einon grudged every
bite of food that went into his guest's mouth; Alan could tell
by the way the lord eyed him over the table. Einon went
about in a velvet cap with a glittering pin, and jeweled rings,
and golden bracelets stacked halfway up his skinny arms, and
a broad gold collar that dangled jewels over his velvet jerkin.
But the old lord didn't eat much, and he seemed to think that
no one else should either.

For three days Alan lounged by Einon's warmthless hearth,
his sore foot up on a bench or soaking in a medicinal bath,
chatting with every servant who passed, winning the sympathy of every woman in the keep, and eating night and day.
Then, for another week or so, he hobbled around with a stick,
conferring with the kitchen folk and flirting with Einon's
young wife, just to gall him. Alan spoke the Welandais
tongue brokenly, with a terrible accent, but he had always
had a knack for making friends. He was not able to befriend
Einon. Still, he found out nothing untoward about the lord
except that he was stingy.

His leisure ended abruptly one night at dinnertime. Einon
had seated himself early and was watching with a sour eye as
his household arrived for the meal. As Alan entered, the old
miser went rigid, then stood up, leaning on the table and
shaking with rage, stretching out a long, trembling finger of
judgment. Alan felt as if that finger jabbed him, though he
stood half the length of the hall away.

"You cursed Islender!" Einon shrieked. "You cursed
Islendais spy! You're limping on the wrong foot!"

Fairly caught, Alan felt like a royal dolt. His foot was
healed, of course, and Einon knew it. Einon shrilled for his
guards, wanting the impostor thrown in a cell at once.
Somehow Alan didn't care to mention that he was the
Islendais King. He made some humble protestations, suitably

flattering to Einon's hospitality, and finally the two of them agreed that Alan should work off his debt of freeloading, as the old lord saw it. So Alan went to help in the kitchen, and a couple of weeks later, when Winterfest came, he was still at it.

There was not much giving of gifts in that pinched household, but there was a feast of sorts. Alan was appointed to carry the dishes to the lord's table, since he made such a fine, golden sight, and since the lord took some pleasure in seeing him kneel. And just as he presented the roast pork, a minstrel rode into the hall. He sent his horse right up to the foot of the dais, in the best old bardic tradition, and in his arms he carried a finely carved plinset, the stringed instrument esteemed by the Blessed Kings. The silver horse was so beautiful that everyone blinked, and somehow the minstrel shone, too, though he was dressed plainly enough. It was Hal, of course, back from his courtly rounds and checking on his comrade. Alan had to duck his head so that no one would see him smile.

"Greetings, Einon, son of Eread, lord of Caerronan," the minstrel proclaimed in the purest speech of the old court of Welas, without a trace of Isle in his voice or of mischief on his face. Hal was a master of sober statesmanship.

"Greetings," Einon snapped. "Are you a minstrel or a thief? Where did you get that horse?"

"It was given to me by the King of Isle, for my surpassing excellence in the tuneful arts."

"The more fool, he," the old lord growled. "I've always said those Kings of Isle must be fools, the two of them halving a throne between them, and never any gold of mine they'd see to spend on horses! You'll get no horse from me, minstrel. If you sing here, you must sing for your supper."

"Willingly," Hal replied, and dismounted, and sent Arundel to the stable, and tuned his plinset. After a while he plucked it, and sang, and the whole clattering hall quieted at the sound of his voice. He sang the great lays of Welas first, the stories of Veran and Claefe, and their twins Brand and Brenna who flew with the ravens for a season, and the story of an Islender, Alf Longshanks, who won the fair and willful Deona away from the royal court at Welden. All old songs, but he sang them into springtime newness, sending bright notes flying like birds through the hall. Servants set food before Hal, then, from the lord's own table, but he took no time to eat. He sang songs that no one had heard before, his own songs, of love and the Lady, and the white, foaming horses of the sea, and Elwestrand. Einon never moved, but Alan saw tears slide down the grooves of the old lord's face.

Finally Hal stopped singing. Lord Einon spoke a single word. "More." But Hal shook his head and reached for his wine.

"More!" Einon urged, and undid the jeweled pin from his velvet cap, tossed it to the minstrel. So Hal flexed his fingers and played again. He sang about the lost fountains of Eburacon. He sang of valiant Bevan, the star-son, who strove with Pel Blagden, the Mantled God. He sang of Ylim, the seeress, weaving prophecy in her hidden valley. He sang of Queen Gwynllian. All the food sat cooling on the tables, and no one ate. The servants had gathered in the shadows, not moving. After a while, Hal stopped again, and Einon exclaimed, "More!" and tossed him a golden ring.

All that night Hal played and sang, and no one left the hall. The servants settled to seats on the floor after a while, but no one slept. Alan had often heard Hal sing to the tune of his plinset, in manor halls or alehouses or by a lonely campfire; but he had never known him to cast such a spell as he did that night. Hearing him, or even looking at him, Alan wept. It was as if a silver magic flew on the notes of the music, moved in his face with the mood of the song, flickered in his gleaming eyes. By daybreak, old Einon's arms lay bare of gold, his jerkin stripped of jewels. He moved at last, stepped down from his dais, took off his golden collar, and fastened it around the Sunset King's neck.

"More," he begged softly.

But Hal silently held up his fingers; the tips were bleeding. Einon's face crumpled.

"Minstrel," he whispered, "I have given to you as you have given to me. But now my wealth is spent. What can I give you to sing for me?"

"For the sake of that blond-haired fellow there beside you," Hal answered quietly, "one more song."

"Him!" Einon burst out. "He is a lazy, useless, conniving Islender. What do you want with him? I'd rather give you a horse."

"I already have a horse," Hal replied, and played his last lay. It was the story of Leuin of Laueroc, who had died of torment in the Dark Tower at Nemeton, and even Einon sensed that Hal had given his all in giving that. The day brightened. Hal packed his instrument, gathered up his rewards, and rose to leave.

"Will you go with him, fellow?" Einon asked Alan roughly.

"Go with him!" Alan retorted. "I'd follow him into the sea! Good health to you, my lord." The two of them walked out into daylight with Einon blinking after.

They rode off, both of them on Arundel. "I hope you're satisfied, Alan," Hal croaked when they were a good distance away. "My throat will be sore for a week, my fingers are raw to the bone, and I never did get my supper." So Alan brought out a packet of food he had stolen from the table.

"That's how they were," Trevyn concluded. "Faithful comrades . . ." He fell silent, frowning.

"What did they do about Einon?" Meg asked after a while.

"What? Oh, nothing. They had the worth of ten years' tribute in gold and jewels, and what would have been the use of telling him so? They let him alone, and when he died at an irascible old age, they found him a more amiable heir."

"They are marvels, the Sun Kings," Meg said softly. Though she, like Trevyn, had never known the bad times before Hal's reign.

"Faithful comrades," Trevyn muttered, still scowling at the ground. It had been many months, he realized, since he had heard Hal sing. The Sunset King hardly stirred from his tower; he looked more often than ever toward the west. An uneasy ache filled Trevyn at that thought.

The moon sent prickles of light through the tangled trees, and on the north wind rose the hunting cry of the wolves.

Chapter Three

It began far off at first—eerie, almost beautiful. To the east one would yelp, and far away to north or west or south another would answer him. But Arundel snorted at the sound, and Trevyn felt his fear-sweat run, for he sensed that these were cries of blood such as no animal ought to voice. With clever ease the wolves drew closer on all sides, exulting to each other over the echoing distances of the Forest. Trevyn could no longer hope that he was not the quarry. Arundel's quivering ears bore him out. Tensely he rose, fingering his sword hilt. Meg piled wood on the fire, then stared soundlessly over the flames. In the firelight the grinning teeth of the wolves shone spectrally bright.

"You'll not fend us off with fire, Princeling," they jeered. "We are not ordinary wolves, you know."

"So you have been telling me all day," he answered them in the Ancient Tongue. He drew his sword with a flourish. "But even if you are gods, steel will separate your souls from your bodies quite effectively."

They laughed, yapping with open mouths and lolling tongues. "But there will be more, Princeling; always there will be more. We do not care if we die; blood is life to us, even

our own. And after your guts are spilled on the snow and
your brains fill our bellies, what then? What then for your
muddy cow and your skinny maid and your fine war horse
quaking against the stone?"

"Arundel is too old to fight," Trevyn excused him. But his
heart turned to water, for he knew that a steed of the elfin
blood should fight to the death, no matter what his age. And
Arundel, of all such steeds, to be so filled with terror! He who
had seen Hal through a hundred combats. . . .

"Trevyn," Meg whispered, "what is happening?"

"Just exchanging insults." He kept his eyes on the ring of
leering eyes that shone scarlet in the firelight. "They would
like to bait me out there beyond the ledge. I'll wager you
anything you like that a score of them are up there waiting to
jump me."

"Bet me a new cloak!" she demanded with comic eagerness. Trevyn grinned, and some of the sickness faded from
him.

"Keep some long sticks ready for torches," he told her.
"When it comes to fighting, light my way as best you can. But
stay back!"

"Never fear!" she retorted.

A bit farther away sat a wolf half again larger than the rest,
shining ghostly gray in a patch of moonlight. The others
yelled taunts, jumping in place as if restrained by invisible
leashes, quivering and whining with eagerness for the scuffle
and the kill and the warm human blood. But the big wolf
squatted at his ease. He barked once, and the wolves froze to
a silence that screamed like the silence of a bad dream.
Trevyn could not ignore the challenge in the leader's yellow
eyes. He met them, and his head swirled in nightmare, a
nightmare imposed on him by an alien will.

Laueroc, its green meadows overrun, its high walls
breached, the people ugly with panic. The proud *elwedeyn*
steeds fleeing, their flanks dappled with blood drawn by
tearing teeth, bursting their great hearts and falling dead with
shame and despair. His father, a giant gray form at his
throat—

"Trevyn!" Meg cried. "Beware!"

The vision vanished as Trevyn shook his head, dazed,

realizing that he had moved steps nearer to the seated leader.
"He almost had me," he murmured. "Talk to me, Meg." But
before she could say a word the big wolf barked and the
others sprang. Trevyn swung his sword like a reaper cutting a
swath, and the fight was joined.

The fine points of swordsmanship were of little use to
Trevyn against tooth and claw. But quickness and a long
reach served him well. Though the wolves lunged at him in
unison, none came nearer to him than the length of his sword.
Many fell back, yelping, and three toppled dead. At Trevyn's
back, Meg held the torch high. The wolves could not come at
him from behind without treading in the fire. Yet they pressed
the fight like things possessed. Even the wounded attacked
him. Half a dozen furry bodies now lay scattered, and the
living clawed over them in their frenzy to reach Trevyn. His
flashing sword held them off.

In his patch of moonlight, the wolf leader sat watching, but
no longer at his ease. He growled with displeasure and rose
from his haunches, padding toward the fray. Trevyn noted the
movement, and for an instant his strength ebbed from him.
That instant of hesitation nearly caused his doom. He felt
jaws close around his legs, striving to bring him down. He
beat at the wolves with his sword, but they kept their hold.
They dragged him out from the fire, and he reeled as heavy
bodies hit his back from above, teeth and claws tore at his
shoulders. He knew that if he went down he was finished. The
gray leader's face was before his, with bristly hair and long,
snarling snout but something strangely human in the jaundiced eyes. . . . What name of evil to put to this? It was over
now, they were pulling his legs from under him. . . .

A yell as fierce as any warrior's rang in Trevyn's ears, a
comet of light flew past his cheek, and unbelievably the grip
on his legs was released. Entranced, he watched a howling
wolf run madly by with the fur of its back on fire. Meg stood
before him, swinging a torch in either hand. She thrust the
leaping wolves in their gaping mouths, and they screamed and
fell aside. Two circled around and came at her from behind.
Trevyn blinked and skewered them with his sword.

"Back!" he shouted, vaulting to her side. "Get back,
Meg!" They edged back until they could feel the warmth of

the fire behind them. Still the wolves lunged to the attack like mindless things, and still the bright sword drew their life's blood. Then the leader barked, and they stopped, forming a ring just at the rim of the firelight. The big wolf sat behind them, grinning with long white teeth.

Trevyn blazed into thoughtless fury at this thing he feared and did not understand. He threw his sword to the earth at his feet. "Come out, you!" he shouted. "Fight like other things of flesh! Rend me though you will, I will wrestle you to the ground and break your foul neck with my unaided hands!"

The wolf raised his head and laughed, a high, sinister sound. "Not yet, Princeling," he cried gaily. "Let us play yet a while. The time for us to meet will come soon enough, and it will be sweet, so sweet. . . ."

Then they were gone, and the sound of weird wolfish laughter floated on the Forest air. Behind the fire, Arundel trembled and huddled against the sheltering rock.

"So!" Meg softly exclaimed. "Ye're the Prince of Laueroc."

Sunk to earth and trembling in his turn, he couldn't answer her. She tore strips from her muddy skirt, kneeled beside him, bound his hurts as best as she could before she spoke again. "I should've known it long since. But I never dreamed yer folks'd let ye go gadding about alone."

"They don't, as a rule," he muttered. "Are you all right, Meg?"

"To be sure, I'm fine!" She smiled tightly. "They didn't want *me,* those wolves."

He glanced up at her, wincing. "Is that what made you guess?"

"Everything. Yer outlandish talk, yer lovely horse, yer lovely self . . ." She teased him, not being willing to say that she had seen his eyes blaze like green fire. But he did not seem able to smile.

"You saved my life," he mumbled. "Meg, I'm sorry. . . ."

"What?" she protested. "Ye'd rather be dead?"

"Nay, nay!" He had to laugh at her, though the movement brought tears of pain to his eyes. "Sorry I didn't tell you more truth. . . . It's hard."

"I can imagine," she said wryly.

The wolves still sang, sending echoes scudding like shadows between the trees. Trevyn could not talk anymore. He sat by the fire till dawn, shivering in spite of the warmth of the flames, and Meg kept him silent company. The wolves made the whole Forest wail, but they did not return.

At daybreak, Meg and Trevyn quitted their comfortless campsite. The girl lived just beyond the Forest's edge, near Lee. They headed that way, both on Arundel, with Molly trailing along behind. Trevyn felt tense, almost too shaky to ride. He wished that they could speed out of the Forest, but they had to travel slowly because of the cow. He found himself jerking to attention at every sound or stir. But before midday he smiled and sighed with relief. A search party thundered toward them, a dozen grim, armed men, headed by Rafe, the fiery lord of Lee. The troop hurtled up to them and pulled to a jarring halt. Rafe grabbed at Trevyn and missed. He nearly fell from his horse in his excitement.

"Trevyn! Are you all right?" he shouted, and gave the youth no chance to answer. "By thunder, is that Meg?" He peered at the grimy girl. "Your father's been bellowing for you since yesterday, lass. Trev, you young rascal, what have you been up to? Rescuing fair maidens?"

Meg snorted; she had never felt less fair. Trevyn scarcely heard. "Wolves," he muttered, and felt horror ripple through him, the horror of a nightmare not his own, the horror of a shadow not understood. Wolf and stag were both in Aene, he had been taught, like hawk and hare, water and fire, and all of these part of the old order that only man sometimes leaves—so how could the wolves turn against him? They had attacked him like brigands. . . . Pale and sweating, he closed his eyes, laid his head on Arundel's neck. He felt Meg's thin arms around his shoulders, trying to steady him, but he knew he would slip away. . . . He heard a cry from Rafe, then nothing more.

He awoke hours later to find himself tucked into a monstrous sickbed. At Rafe's stronghold, he knew, because he saw that same lord seated beside him. "Have you nothing better to do?" he mumbled.

Rafe smiled. "How do you feel?"

Burns stung him, seemingly to the bone, even before he

moved. He hoisted himself painfully. "Confounded. Not long ago I hated snow. Now I could go out and roll in the stuff. I take it you've cauterized the wounds."

"Ay, we've had to brand you, lad." Rafe pulled back the sheet, reached into a bucket at his feet, and piled mounds of snow on Trevyn's legs and shoulders. "You've slept for five hours or so. Could you manage more?"

"Hardly!" Trevyn supported himself gingerly on one elbow. "I don't remember much. Did I make a fool of myself?"

"Nay, indeed! You were in a dead faint—lay like a felled tree. By my troth, I don't think I could have done it otherwise."

Startled, Trevyn glanced up to see tears sliding silently down Rafe's rugged face. He reached out to touch the older man's hand.

"Rafe, you must be spent. Get some rest. I don't need a nursemaid."

"I'm sorry, Trev," said Rafe wretchedly. "But how am I to feel? Meg told us about those wolves, and they must have been mad, rabid. What if—" Rafe gulped to a stop.

"They were not rabid."

"If you die," Rafe blurted, "it will mean more than the loss of one that I love."

"They were not rabid. You are worrying for nothing, Rafe. I am not likely to die from a few bites." Trevyn felt the touch of a shadow and lay back wearily. Still, he spoke with assurance. Rafe studied him, mindful of the visionary powers of the Lauerocs.

"You are not just saying that. You are quite certain."

"Of course." But Trevyn did not tell Rafe why he knew he would take no harm from his wounds. The big wolf, it seemed, had plans that they should meet again. Unpleasant as the thought was, it afforded some solace. Luck, in the form of Meg, had seen him through the first encounter. And the next time he would somehow be better prepared.

Chapter Four

A few days later, as soon as he felt well enough, Trevyn rode out to see Meg.

The cottage stood at the Forest's fringe. The goodman, Brock Woodsby, Meg's father, took his name from that fact. Working in the yard, he was the first to see the visitor approach, and he stumped over to the rickety gate to meet him. Watching from within the cottage, Meg put her hands to her mouth in consternation. She could not hear her father's words, but she recognized the stubborn set of his back.

"Who might it be?" Brock gruffly addressed his visitor.

Perhaps the man was a trifle dense, Trevyn thought. He introduced himself by name and title, still sitting on his horse, waiting for the gate to open. But Brock Woodsby did not move.

"I thought as much," he stated. "I thank ye for the sake of the lass, Prince. She says she'd have been lost without ye. But ye're mistaken to come gallanting hereabouts. Ye'll be the ruin of the girl. Already folk are saying ye've had yer way with her. I think not, if I know my lass, but that's the talk. And what else might ye want with her indeed?"

What indeed? But Trevyn was too young to be amused or

intrigued by the aptness of Brock's question. He bristled and fixed the goodman with an icy green glare. "What, are you denying me admittance, then?" he demanded.

"Mothers defend us!" Meg whispered. The small cry brought her own mother to her side. Glancing out the window, the goodwife fluttered like a partridge. The youth outside the gate wore a bright sword, and he looked tempted to use it on her husband.

"I deny hospitality to no one," Brock replied stiffly. "I only ask you to *think*. Think of the girl." As he spoke, the maiden in question came out of the cottage and approached him, walking serenely. He rounded on her. "Get back i' the house!"

"What? Stay out of the Forest, ye tell me, and is it stay out of the yard now? Ye'll be keeping me in the chimney corner next." Meg faced her father sunnily, and Trevyn grinned at her, all his chagrin suddenly forgotten. He slipped down from Arundel and opened the gate for himself, though a moment before he had been determined to make Brock do it. The quarrel no longer seemed worth pursuing.

"Rafe's not allowing me in the Forest, either," he remarked to Meg. "Small fear I shall disobey him in that regard."

"Nay?" she said slowly. She missed the Forest; she missed the foxes that would come and follow by her feet, the wild doves that would light on her shoulders. She felt hurt by her Forest, betrayed, that any of its creatures could turn against her as the wolves had done. But she could not explain this, and especially not to Trevyn. She didn't want him to think her queer, as so many others did.

Her mother saved her from further response. The goodwife came bustling out, having settled her hair and flung on a shawl. "Come in, young master, have some fresh, hot scones!" she beseeched Trevyn. She did not take it the least bit amiss that Meg had found a prince in the Forest. And Brock, having had his say and been ignored, led his guest to the cottage with dour courtesy.

The scones were very good. Trevyn sampled them that day and many a day to come. He stayed a month at Lee, riding out nearly every day to see Megan. His motive was only partly to gall Brock Woodsby. He would greet the goodman distantly, but he always met the girl with honest delight. Meg chatted with him like a longtime friend, and she was full of questions.

"What's yer name mean, Trevyn?"

"Beloved traveler, or some such." The youth gestured impatiently. "It's just a baby name. I shall have a sooth-name someday."

"Ay?" Meg wondered cheerfully. "How so?"

"That is as it comes," Trevyn countered. "What does your name mean, Megan?"

"Not a thing." She grinned wickedly. "We're common folk here."

Trevyn almost flushed, feeling a hint of reproach, but Meg went on unconcernedly. "What brings ye to Lee, Trevyn?"

He laughed. "Arundel! He brought me through the snow straight to the manor gates, and very surprised Rafe was to see me! I would have perished in the storm if it weren't for him. He is a marvelous horse. Twenty years ago he carried my uncle through far stranger perils in this same Great Forest and beyond."

Bemused, Meg let it pass that he had not really answered her question. "Then was yer uncle an outlaw as well?"

"He joined with the outlaws of the southern Forest after they had saved his life. Arundel brought him to them nearly dead from tortures in the Dark Tower of the evil kings."

Meg shuddered. "And he met yer father then?"

"A bit later. They did not know that they were brothers. Hal had been raised as King Iscovar's heir, but really his father was the lord of Laueroc."

"Folk say that King Iscovar killed Leuin of Laueroc and the Queen."

"Ay, and he would have liked to bend my uncle to his will. Hal roamed the land constantly to elude him, with my father as his blood brother and companion. Your lord Rafe was their friend, too, in those times; they met him and Queen Rosemary at Celydon. And they traveled to the Northern Barrens, and into Welas, the west land, and even to Veran's Mountain, where they met my kindred, the elves."

"Elves!" Megan bounced excitedly. "I thought that was just—singing, y'know."

"Nay, the elves are real. But all of them except my mother have sailed to Elwestrand, a land beyond the western sea." A faraway look filled Trevyn's eyes. "Hal sang of Elwestrand long before he knew it existed anywhere but in his mind."

Meg grappled in vain for an answer to this. Trevyn had that look sometimes that can make a woman weep, sad eyes and a smiling mouth. . . . But other times he had the look of eagles. After a moment he went on.

"When Iscovar died, Hal and his followers ousted the evil lords, and my mother gave up her immortality to marry my father. Those were strange times for him; he had never expected to be a King. But when Hal found out they were brothers, he found Father his crown. Hal had never wanted power anyway, though it was fated on him."

"How so?" Meg sat agape at this matter-of-fact talk of elves and destinies.

"It was written in *The Book of Suns*, the prophecies of the One. The Book made their kinship clear, and told them that Hal would have no heir."

"I saw him once, and Queen Rosemary, as they rode to Celydon," Meg remarked. " 'Tis a shame they've no children. But ye're lucky ye've no cousins or brothers to fight ye for the throne."

"I wish I had a dozen," Trevyn grumbled. "And they could have the throne, and welcome."

"Why?" asked Meg, not at all disconcerted.

"Never mind." Trevyn smiled in spite of himself. "Save your breath to cool your porridge, Meg."

"And let ye spend yers to swell yer wings of fancy? Ye're so bursting with portents and mysteries, how is a poor girl to know the way of it?"

He had to laugh at her. It was a relief to see his forebodings as nonsense, even for a moment. Meg's teasing was a balm on spirits too often darkened since the fight with the wolves.

Meg had long since learned that fellows liked her best if she jested with them. When she did it well, they could forget that she was a skinny, plain-faced maid and treat her simply as a friend. So she had no sweethearts, but at least she had male company at the occasional social affairs of the countryside. Her brave show fooled no one, not even herself. But she made the best of what she had: a quick mind and a droll wit. And when the Prince came, she bantered with him as was her wont.

He had known no such easy companionship from the youths and maidens of Laueroc. They had shied from his rank and his elfin strangeness. So he found it a relief and a delight to be treated with something less than royal respect. Meg's shafts of wit were never cruel, and she aimed them most often at herself. Trevyn had seen her with the wolves; he knew her courage. Her merciless honesty concerning her own short-comings was a different kind of courage, he thought, and he admired her for it.

"No doubt the bards will sing of how ye pulled the fair maiden from the mud hole," Meg mused. "They hold forth about everything ye Lauerocs do."

"No doubt," Trevyn gravely agreed.

"'Twill be known, of course, that they speak of Molly," Meg added. "As she is young, and has not yet calved."

Trevyn never tired of listening to her. He had met many kinds of women in his young life: high-scented foreign princesses, chilly court maidens, flirtatious servant girls. None of them had tempted him to more than a quick conquest. But this fine-boned, birdlike creature, bright and cheeky as a sparrow, drew him back to her again and again. He had felt for her small breast once, wondering what she kept beneath her shapeless peasant blouse, and she had pushed his hand away. "Nay, Trev," she had told him, not even angrily, only with a certainty he could not question. He did not try again, but he came to see her even more often than before. All his life he had dreamed of finding a friendship such as Hal and Alan shared, or of finding a true love. . . . But he told himself that this Megan, this homely, comical maid, was nothing more than a diversion to him. He liked to be diverted, and certainly the girl did not mind.

He was thoughtless, as Brock had feared. Otherwise he might have known how his face floated before her inward eye day and night. He should have known how he inspired her love, he who was the talk of every lass in the countryside. But it must be said that Megan hid her love well. Once she had showed fondness for a youth, and it had driven him away. Brave though he thought her to be, she would not risk showing her heart to the Prince. She fed her soul merely on the sight of him and the memory of his lighthearted words. Sometimes, lying in her bed at night, she silently wept.

"When must you be going, lad?" Rafe asked Trevyn one evening at the manor keep.

"Trying to rid yourself of me?" Trevyn retorted. Though he would talk to Meg for hours, he found little enough to say to his kindly host.

"You know that you're welcome to stay the rest of your life." Coming from Rafe, this was not hollow courtesy. "But surely you must be back to Laueroc by Winterfest."

"There will be ill cheer at my home this feast-tide," Trevyn responded sourly. "Nay. I'll stay a while longer."

Rafe gaped, for Trevyn had told him nothing about his troubles with Gwern, or about Hal's strange behavior, or even about the wolves. But the lord of Lee rose to the occasion with the enthusiasm for which he was famous. "Why, we'll make a royal festival of it, then!" He rubbed his hands in delight, for Rafe was as eager as a boy when it came to a frolic. "We'll have a regular carole, with musicians and everything, O Prince, in your honor. It will be just what this poor country place needs for some waking up."

Trevyn smiled, knowing quite well that the manor already buzzed with his presence. "I will invite Meg," he decided.

Rafe cocked a quizzical eye at him, not knowing what to make of the youth's friendship with Meg. The girl was odd, folk said, talked with animals as if they were human. . . . Of course, the Lauerocs spoke with animals, too, and possessed many stranger powers, and no one spoke ill of them.

"No harm to little Meg, lad," Rafe asked cautiously, "but why? You could have your pick of many a lass who would do you better credit as a partner."

"But Meg makes me laugh," Trevyn replied.

When he made his request of Meg she answered as

seriously as she had ever spoken to him. "I'd love to, Trev. But I have no dress, and I wouldn't know how to behave. Ye'd better ask a girl who is better prepared."

"Act like yourself, and you'll please me well enough. And as for the dress—" He frowned. Rafe was unmarried, so there was no woman to help him. "It's not quite proper, I dare say, but will you not let me take care of it?"

"What? Make it yerself? Ye'll prick yer fingers and cry. . . ."

"Nay, nay, little jester, I'll pay for it! Humor me?"

"I must ask my parents," Meg said.

They consented, though not without some argument from the goodman. It took the determined persuasion of both females to get him to agree to the plan. Rafe did not like it much better than Brock.

"Half the country will say you are betrothed!" he sputtered when Trevyn asked him the name of a dressmaker.

"I dare say worse things could happen."

"Ay! They could say she is your mistress!"

The dressmaker was a terse, tight-skinned old woman, straight and proud. The manor folk stood in awe of her, saying she had Gypsy blood. When Meg shyly presented herself in her baggy frock and heavy peasant boots, the old seamstress looked her up and down without smile or comment.

"What does the Prince like best in you?" she asked. And, although Trevyn had never told her, Meg knew the answer at once. "I make him laugh," she replied. There was a trace of bitterness in her voice, and the old woman glanced into her eyes. In an instant the Gypsy saw what Megan had so carefully hidden from everyone else.

Without a word she got her tape and carefully measured every part of Megan's slender body. Trevyn had already chosen the goods: a soft silk, dusky rose with a thread of gold, well fit to bring out the color of Meg's thin cheeks and the lights in her muted hair. The old woman held it up, and Meg stroked it speechlessly. "What sort of dress do ye want out of this, now?" the seamstress asked her.

"I know nothing of it," Meg faltered. "I have never had such a dress."

"Will ye leave it to me, then?"

"Ay, surely." It did not matter, Meg thought, what sort of dress she wore. She had never known a dress to flatter her.

"Ye will trust me in this." There was something gentle in the Gypsy's voice, and Meg looked at her and smiled.

"Ay, indeed I will. But you will have to work hard, Grandmother, to have it done in time."

"Ay, even so. But 'twill be done, little daughter."

The evening of the dance, Trevyn rode Arundel out through the frosty night to fetch Meg. The stars glowed clear as a thousand candles, and the night was full of whispering, jostling light. Over the snow the square of the cottage window shone like a beacon, near even from afar. At long last Trevyn reached it, and beams from within picked out Arundel's form, silver as a spirit of the night. Trevyn found the door and stepped inside. Then he stopped, thunderstruck. A shining sprite awaited him.

Meg's dress made no effort to conceal her thinness; quite the opposite. Tiny tucks drew the fabric snug over her small round breasts, then released it to fall in soft, clinging folds over her waist and hips. Her skirt swept the floor, and long sleeves embraced her slender arms nearly to her fingers. Only her neck was bared, and the tender curve of her collarbone below. Somewhere she had got delicate slippers to peep from under her skirt. She was lovely, and she knew it. Her eyes glowed as warm as the firelight. She met Trevyn's stare almost merrily, then turned to fetch her old brown mantle. He stopped her and took off his bright cloak of royal blue, putting it around her shoulders and fastening it with his golden brooch that bore the Sun Kings' emblem.

"Ye must be the hard one to keep in cloaks!" whispered Meg. Trevyn restrained his smile.

"I will have her back to you before midnight," he told Brock Woodsby, and they departed.

Meg moved through the evening in a happy trance. Any girl in Lee would gladly have taken her place, but their envy could not taint her with foolish triumph; it was Trevyn himself who lit the flame of her joy. He watched her, talked with her, danced only with her, guiding her through the circling patterns of the courtly carole. Megan could not hide her love

this night. It glowed in her wide eyes, misty brown as a forest
vista. Trevyn looked, and saw, and Megan felt quite certain
that something answered her gaze in his. They drifted away
from the dancers to the dim reaches of the great hall, and they
scarcely noticed at first when the stately notes of lute and viol
faltered to a stop.

"What bard is that?" Trevyn murmured.

A dark, feral voice was singing, chanting out a harsh ballad
that rang like a blast of wintry air through the warm room.

> "Out of shadowed Lyrdion
> The sword Hau Ferddas came;
> By Cuin the heir Dacaerin won
> For Bevan of Eburacon,
> To win him crown and fame.
>
> And won him fame, and won his land,
> And nearly dealt Cuin doom;
> And Bevan of the Silver Hand
> Went over sea to Elwestrand,
> Where golden apples bloom.
>
> So Cuin Dacaerin seized the cares
> To which his sword gave claim,
> High King in Laueroc, and his heirs
> Held sway for half a thousand years,
> Until the warships came.
>
> *Mighty sword of Lyrdion,*
> *Golden blade of Lyrdion,*
> *Bloody brand of Lyrdion,*
> *Long your shadow falls.*"

"What tale is that?" Meg wondered. "I have never heard
it."

"Few people have," Trevyn exclaimed under his breath.
"The magical sword of the High Kings still lies where my
uncle Hal left it; he would not use its tainted power. But only
he and my father knew of it, I thought!" The Prince moved

closer to see the singer's face, but the crowd stood in his way, held rapt by the strange song.

> "Claryon was the High King's name
> Who died without a wound;
> Culean, his son of warlike fame
> Who took Hau Ferddas, bright as flame,
> Where fortune importuned.
>
> It won him woe, it won him shame,
> And cozened him to slay him,
> By his own hand himself to maim
> To keep the sword by his own blame,
> And in a barrow lay him.
>
> And in a barrow of the Waste
> Hau Ferddas still lay gleaming,
> And Isle, her land by war disgraced,
> Lay at the feet of foes abased,
> Hope lost beyond all dreaming.
>
> *Mighty sword of Lyrdion,*
> *Golden blade of Lyrdion,*
> *Bloody brand of Lyrdion,*
> *Long your shadow falls."*

Rafe made his way to Trevyn, parting the crowd in his wake. At last Trevyn and Meg were able to see the husky-voiced singer, looking like a ruffian in his brownish wrappings. "Do you know that fellow?" Rafe asked the Prince in a low voice. "He walked straight in and started his song, and I haven't the heart to stop him, though he sounds like branches in a wind. There's an elfin look about him in a way."

"Son of a—" Trevyn groaned. It was Gwern, meeting his eyes without a hint of expression as he finished his ballad.

> "Till, half ten hundred turnings done,
> A Very King returned,
> And Alan of the Rising Sun

And Hal, the heir of Bevan, won
The crowns their mercy earned.

And scorned Hau Ferddas, spurned her calls,
And still the sword lies gleaming,
And long and fair her shadow falls,
And sweet her golden song enthralls
When warrior blood falls streaming;

And seers have said that, years to dawn,
If hand can bear to loose her,
The mighty sword of Lyrdion
Must to the western sea begone,
Or stay our fair seducer.

Mighty sword of Lyrdion,
Golden blade of Lyrdion,
Bloody brand of Lyrdion,
Still your shadow falls."

The listeners applauded, bemused, but heartened by the
names of their Kings. Gwern turned away indifferently and
headed toward the dainty foodstuffs arranged on long tables
by the walls. He started to eat ravenously, grabbing sweet-
meats with his grimy fingers. Meg stared at him in wonder.

"Yer brother?" she blurted to Trevyn. "But I know ye've
got none."

"My brother!" Trevyn cried. "I should hope not!" He
strode over to the newcomer. "Gwern, you are making a
mess."

Gwern said nothing; being Gwern, he did not care. It had
taken him days of frustration to leave Laueroc, for Alan had
doubled the guard since Trevyn's escapade. At last he had
made his break, bareback on Trevyn's golden charger
Rhyssiart, but it had been painfully slow going through the
snow. And a nameless, peculiar illness had struck him as
suddenly as a blow, sent him reeling to a shelter to lie for days
like one wounded. At last he reached Lee, starving, dirty,
ragged. Now, gazing at Meg, he forgot to eat.

Grudgingly, Trevyn made the introduction. "Meg, this is

Gwern, my—my acquaintance. Gwern, this is Megan By-the-woods."

Gwern only stared. Meg did not mind his gaze, or even think him impolite. It was like the wordless, thoughtful look a badger might have given her.

"Gwern, you're an eyesore," Trevyn said impatiently. "Get to my room, will you, and I'll have them bring you some things."

Somewhat to his surprise, Gwern did as he had said, and he sent up a servant with food and instructions for a bath. Trevyn and Meg saw no more of Gwern that night, nor did they speak of him. Megan felt Trevyn's agitation, and she was glad to feel it subside. They danced, and walked the room together, and ate fine foods that she was never able to remember to her satisfaction, and danced again. By the time the lutes and viols finished playing, she felt music moving through her even when her feet were still.

Taking her home through the frosty night, Trevyn held her before him on Arundel and felt the warmth of her slender body against his. Why should he want her, this skinny, sharp-nosed little maid? Yet something rose in him. To release it, he stopped Arundel where all the thousand stars could see, turned her to him, held her, and kissed her long and deep. He trembled, but not with cold, and felt her body quiver in answer. Then he felt tears on her face. He nestled her against his shoulder, stroking her hair and kissing her eyes until she was calm. She did not speak as he took her home. He saw her within doors and kissed her once, lightly, in the dark of the cottage; then he went without a word. Only as his hoofbeats faded away did Meg realize that she still wore his cloak and brooch.

He will come for them on the morrow, she thought, and the thought made her glad to overflowing. She undressed in the dark and lay awake on her narrow bed, feeling the touch of his kiss still on her lips. It was the first kiss she had ever known.

All the way back to the manor, Trevyn berated himself. It was mad and cruel, he scolded, to give the girl hopes. For surely he could have no serious thoughts of her! She was a commoner, without education, dower, or social grace. And she was homely, or at least so he had once thought. . . . But he was the Prince of the realm, gifted with knowledge, power, and beauty. Surely there would be a princess for him, a woman worthy of his regard—perhaps an elfin princess in fair Elwestrand across the sea! He must not see Meg again, he decided, not even for parting. He did not care to cause a scene.

When he reached his chamber, he found Gwern lounging on his bed, looking more presentable since his bath. The fey youth sat up to greet Trevyn with a perfectly unreadable face. Trevyn meant to ask him how he knew about the ancient sword of Lyrdion, why he had sung his eerie song. But Gwern spoke first.

"Meg is a beautiful girl," he said. There was no trace of mockery in his voice, and Trevyn knew by now that Gwern only spoke the most straightforward truth. Such truth sent a pang through him.

"What of it?" he retorted gruffly.

"I would like to know her better. Where does she live?"

"You!" Trevyn flared in sudden anger. "You are only fit to consort with pigs! Stay away from her!"

Gwern gravely rose from the bed. "Why, she is only a commoner, and you think she is homely," he replied without heat. "And you have decided to cast her aside. Do you grudge me your castoffs?"

"I grudge you life and breath," grated Trevyn between clenched teeth. He was white with rage; he had never felt such rage. "Stay away from her, I say!"

"Why, you need not worry," Gwern remarked reasonably. "She is the Maiden, you know. Where she would not have you, she will not have me."

Trevyn sprang at him, knocking him to the floor with one smashing fist. Blood trickled from Gwern's nose. But this time he did not punch back. Trevyn stood panting, helpless to vent his wrath, and vaguely ashamed.

Gwern got up, taking no notice of his gory nose. He went to the door. "I will tender her your parting regards," he told Trevyn levelly, "since you will not face her." There was no fight in his words, only fact. Desperately, Trevyn hit him again, hard enough to split his own knuckles. Gwern staggered and shrugged off the blow.

"If you go near her," Trevyn gasped wildly, "I will kill you!"

"You can't," Gwern stated, and ambled away down the stairs. Trevyn sensed that he was right, and in sheerest chagrin he wept.

"How was the carole?" Megan's mother asked her the next morning.

"Wonderful," her daughter answered. "There were marvelous ices. And I believe Trevyn liked my dress." She smiled in a way that made her mother's heart ache, for the goodwife hated to see the girl disappointed.

Confidently Megan waited for Trevyn to come to her. But instead came Gwern, with his bare brown feet hanging down, bareback and bridleless on Trevyn's golden stallion. The big horse obeyed him at a touch. Filled with sudden foreboding, Meg went out to the fence to meet him, and he vaulted down from his steed to speak to her.

"Prince Trevyn started back to Laueroc early this morning," he told her. "I have come to take his leave of you, since he would not."

Meg regarded him steadily, her sharp face only a little tauter than usual, for she was practiced in hiding her feelings. "And which of us has frightened him away," she asked at last, "ye or me?"

"You," Gwern said promptly. "He bears no love for me."

Her face twitched at that. "And how does it come to be," she wondered aloud, "that ye're Trevyn, and yet ye're not Trevyn?"

"I don't know," he grumbled, then looked at her with something like alarm. "Did you speak to him of that?"

"Nay! He is not ready; he is terrified." Meg was the wise woodland Maiden, as Gwern knew, but she knew herself only as a hurt and bewildered girl. Tears trickled from her eyes. "Will he ever come back to me?" she murmured.

Gwern came to her, finding his way around the rough rail fence. "Megan, I love you," he said flatly. "Let me stay with you, since Trevyn would not."

She quirked a wry smile at him, amused in spite of her misery. "I don't know much," she retorted, "but I know wild, and ye're as wild as wind. And ye cannot bear to be long away from him. How long would ye stay?"

"A few days," Gwern admitted. "But if he goes over ocean, I must learn to bear that pang. I cannot leave earth. My sustenance is in the soil beneath my feet."

"And he longs to go to Elwestrand," Meg mused. "The tides wash in his eyes. . . . Go now, Gwern. I don't need yer comfort. But if ye need mine someday, come to me."

She spoke bravely. But that night, after the fire was banked and she went to her bed, despair struck her that went too deep even for tears. She had let herself show a woman's heart, and the showing had driven Trevyn from her. For who would want to be loved by a skinny thing like her? To think it of him, and he the Prince! And yet, what of that kiss. . . .

In months to come, when she had driven from her all other hope of his regard, the memory of that kiss was still to linger in the heart of her heart, like a glowing coal in the ashes of a benighted fire.

Chapter Five

The winter holidays had nearly ended when Trevyn returned to his home—to Laueroc, fair city of meadowlarks. No birds sang now over the meadows that ringed the town, but the towers shone golden in the wintry sunlight. In the fairest tower, Trevyn knew, King Hal dreamed his visionary dreams. Below, artists of all sorts wrought their own dreams within his protecting walls. The countless concerns of the court city of Isle hummed on, and Alan saw to them all, frowning.

King Alan heard the shout go up when Trevyn rode in, and he met his son at the gates to the keep. Time was when he would have been waiting with a stick in his hand, to thrash the Prince for going out-of-bounds. Trevyn was expecting a mighty roaring at the very least. But Alan surprised him. "I am glad to see you, lad," he remarked quietly. "I ought to knock your head, but I haven't the inclination. Come get your supper."

Trevyn stood still and peered at him. "What is the matter?" he asked.

"It's Hal," Alan told him candidly. "He's been sulking in his tower for weeks now, scarcely eating, scarcely speaking. . . . I have known him for a long time, Trevyn, and borne with his moods as he bears with mine, but this—it harrows me. I don't want to speak of it. Come get your supper."

Preoccupied, Alan had not noticed Trevyn's borrowed cloak or his missing brooch, and Trevyn gave private thanks for that. He flung the cloak aside and followed his father to the huge, cobbled kitchen. None of the Lauerocs had much patience with the prerogatives of rank; they usually helped themselves rather than eating in great-hall style. Trevyn's mother and his Aunt Rosemary sat at a big plank table near the hearth, slicing bread. Rosemary smiled wanly as Trevyn entered, but Lysse jumped up to hug him, gauging his well-being with her elfin eyes.

"You have been in danger, Beloved!" she exclaimed. "What was it?"

"The snowstorm perhaps?" he hedged. He had left Rafe with the understanding that he would carry report to the Kings concerning the peculiar behavior of the wolves. But now, guiltily, he realized that he had no intention of doing so. He could not risk his newly won independence by telling his parents he had come to woe. Childishly, he felt that they would never let him out alone again, never let him sail to Elwestrand! Shaking off thoughts of duty, he turned the talk. "What is the matter with my uncle?"

"He is fey." Queen Rosemary proudly raised her lovely auburn head.

"He is Mireldeyn." Lysse spoke the name neither in agreement nor in denial. She sat down with effortless, fluid grace. "His ways are not the ways of men. He has withdrawn from men now."

Trevyn dipped himself a bowlful of stew, for he was hungry from his ride. No one else ate much; they all sat watching him. "But Uncle Hal has always been a recluse," he ventured between bites of bread and meat.

Alan distractedly shook his head. "Not like this. He was only a recluse in body, Trevyn; his mind and vision were focused on Isle and on me; I could feel his love even from afar. But now—his dreams have pulled away, like a sea pulling away from shore. He scarcely speaks to me; it is as if he is already gone. How will I rule without him? How will I live? He is Very King."

"But where—how—" Trevyn faltered. Alan looked as if he might weep, and Trevyn had never seen his father weep, even over the tiny bodies of his stillborn sisters. "I don't understand. I know you were close, but I thought—"

"You thought I ruled," Alan snapped, suddenly burying his grief in asperity. "Hal has suffered and labored for Isle, and men think I rule. He longs only for peace, and yet he was the greatest war leader this land has ever seen. Men rallied around his dreams. Likely his dreams will last longer than all my busy devices. And his wisdom in the court of law deserves to be legend. And yet, because I am the one who counts the gold, men think I rule."

"You suffered too," Trevyn protested.

"We both bear scars," Alan grumbled. "What of it? Let suffering go, Trevyn."

"Hal has never been able to let go of his pain," Rosemary whispered to her hands. "It has driven him mad."

"Nay, Ro," Lysse said gently, "the truth is cleaner and harder, I think. There will be a ship for him, at the Bay of the Blessed, to take him where the others have already gone. Aene has called him, and he goes as he has lived, in his own solitary way." Lysse shifted her gaze to include her husband. "You seem to have forgotten the days when he led and you followed."

"Why follow where there is no love?" Rosemary asked bitterly, and began to weep. Lysse turned to comfort her. Trevyn was grateful that his mother's eyes were not on him. She had said, *there will be a ship,* and his heart had leaped in his chest; it pounded still. *We will both set sail,* he thought, and strove to hide the thought. Without speaking he stumbled from the room. Then he stopped in the corridor, groping at a wall for support, blinded and dizzied by vision.

The others who had gone before, taking their magic from Isle . . . The star-son Bevan, with lustrous hands and lustrous brow, black hair parted like raven's wings, facing the sea breeze. The long line of Bevan's brethren the gods riding down to the Blessed Bay, leaving the hollow hills forever . . . Ylim, the ageless seeress, had lived and finally died in her own peaceful valley, Trevyn knew, but he envisioned her on a white ship beneath a changing moon. And the elves, his mother's people, setting sail on the swanlike boats Veran had prepared for them with his own magical hands—boats like Bevan's that went without sails. And now Hal, a Very King like Bevan of a thousand years before . . .

"All right, lad?" Alan had come out and stood before him anxiously. Trevyn blinked and nodded, shaking shreds of legend from his head.

"It's a hard thing to come home to," Alan added gruffly.

Trevyn lowered his eyes to hide a gleam of joy and wonder. Let Alan think he had been sorrowing. But he was learning the elfin Sight at last, it seemed. It had never caught him up so strongly before, except that horrible time when a wolf had given him bad dreams, false dreams. . . . But these just now had been his own dreams; he felt sure of it.

"I had better go to see my uncle," he muttered.

He climbed the long, spiraling tower stairs, his breath quickened by more than exertion. Hal did not answer the rap on his door, so the Prince pushed it open. King Hal stood staring westward through his window bars, his face haggard, his skin drawn into taut folds over the straight lines of his cheekbones. He did not stir for Trevyn's presence.

"Mireldeyn!" Trevyn called him by the sooth-name, and in a moment he trembled at his own boldness. Hal turned slowly and fixed his nephew with a silvery stare. In all the seven ages there had been no one quite like Mireldeyn, and even Trevyn, who had bounced on his lap not too many years before, could not fail to feel his greatness.

"Trevyn," Hal remarked. "I am bound for Elwestrand at last. You'll not try to sway me from my destiny, lad? You are too young for that, I think—and also, in your own foolish way, too wise."

Trevyn did not know how to react. "Elwestrand is fair, you have told me," he said at last. "But my father is saddened, my aunt angry and sad."

"I grieve that Alan must grieve." Hal turned away to his window again, his voice cold and tight. "But the ways of men are strange to me now, and I do not understand his sorrow. Nor can I see any longer what may be in store for him. But as for your aunt—she will find fulfillment that I could never give her. It was not by her fault that we have been childless,

Trevyn. Ket can better serve her, he who has loved her all these years."

"Ket!" Trevyn's astonishment left him open-mouthed, and for a moment he wondered if Hal was really mad. Ket, the former outlaw who had never learned to properly ride a horse! He had once been valiant, Trevyn knew, but now he was only the stooping, gravely courteous countryman who taught archery and served Alan as seneschal. That he should so regard the Queen!

"Do you think he has stayed in Laueroc for want of choice? He could have had any manor or town in Isle." Hal skewered Trevyn again with his icy stare. "Nay, do not mistake me, young man. Rosemary has always been faithful to me. Indeed, I believe she does not know of Ket's devotion; she is too modest to credit herself with such devotion. And Ket is a man of honor, and my friend."

"But you—has he told you?" Trevyn gasped.

"He knows there is no need to tell me. I saw his love twenty-some years ago, when he and my lady first met. But she was a lass of sixteen, my betrothed, and he was thirty, with a price on his red head. So he guarded her well, for my sake as well as her own, and he has cherished her all these years." Hal sighed, still staring into the reaches of the west. "I should have let him have her."

Trevyn could think of no answer, and left the tower room, shaken. He had thought himself adult, but in the face of adult trouble he felt very much the child. The more so because his own thoughts would cause his father pain, he knew. In days that followed he tried to give up such thoughts of sailing to Elwestrand. But vision replaced his conscious dreams, taking him at its will, day or night, flooding him like water and leaving him shaking. A silver ship, a silver harp, a winged white steed circling above the highest mountaintop. . . .

One vision came often. A woman with skin white as sea foam, hair like living gold, claret lips, and azure eyes—a woman as lovely as any elf, and yet not of elfin kind, for passion moved in her white breasts and wine mouth; Trevyn had felt it, lying limply in his bed at night. Around her hands flew ruddy robins and little gold-crested wrens; at her feet nestled leopards and deer, graceful swans—all manner of creature loveliness, even a kingly silver wolf. Hal had once said that the eagle and the serpent were friends in Elwestrand. Surely this woman was a princess in Elwestrand; could there be another place so fair? Trevyn grew certain that she awaited him there. There would be a ship for him, too, a sign to help his parents see that his destiny lay with the sea. His mother, at least, would understand if there was a sign. But Alan might never understand.

Trevyn avoided thought of Alan, let himself become lost in the dreams. He no longer worried about the wolves, or about Meg, or his uncle. And when Gwern returned from Lee, several days after himself, he scarcely minded his dogged presence. He moved through his days of lessons and training serenely, almost indifferently, with his mind's eye on the white-breasted sea.

Lysse frowned at him. "Vision is a chancy thing, Trevyn," she said to him abruptly one day. "Love or pride or sorrow—any one of them will send you astray like a strong wind. It will be years before you can read the Sight aright."

But Trevyn would not be lessoned by her, and soon her attention was demanded elsewhere. Before the winter was over, Hal left his window and took to his bed. He lay there day and night, restless at first, but later unmoving, uneating, unsleeping. Alan came to him often, to shout at him sometimes, but also to reason, and plead, and, Trevyn suspected, to weep. Rosemary came often, to sit silently by with averted eyes. Trevyn came uneasily, and as seldom as he could. But the only person to have any speech from Hal those days was Lysse. She sat by his bedside like the others who tried to care for him, but she did not lower her eyes.

"That son of yours is dreaming of glory," Hal said once. She could scarcely hear his voice, but the elves do not always need the words of the voice to hear.

"I know it," she answered. "Alan and I have expected it for years, and guarded against it, perhaps too well . . . Surely you have not forgotten the portent that attended his birth?"

On Trevyn's natal morning, great golden eagles had circled the towers of Laueroc, mighty-pinioned eagles from Veran's Mountain by the faraway western sea. Green-clad Lysse had watched them from her window as she gave her baby his first milk.

"I have forgotten nothing," Hal told her sharply.

"So he is fated to travel ways far and solitary and strange to us," she said, ignoring the tone. "He will leave the motherhood of earth, at least for a while; sea and sky will claim him. But I hope not yet. He dreams because he is young, and he shrinks from the grief that drapes his life these days. Alan is of no help to him. He is so fogged with bitterness that he scarcely sees beyond his own pain."

"I cannot help him," Hal whispered.

"I know it." Lysse spoke with mindful understanding.

"But the lad," Hal continued. "He flees from more than sorrow, I think."

"You think he flees? From Gwern?"

"Ah, the wyrd," Hal murmured. "There is a portent for you, of great weight. I tell you, Trevyn will be more important than any of us, more than King, more than Very King. Of all the Kings of Isle and Welas, I know of none that have had a wyrd."

"Why, what is a wyrd?" Lysse asked curiously.

"More than comrade, more than brother or blood brother, more than second self. Alan was all of those to me. . . ." Hal floundered. "How I wish I knew. I can only sense dimly that the wyrd is one who will be sacrificed when the time comes." Hal closed his eyes. "Suffering and sacrifice—they are required of any true king. How much more, then, of Trevyn. . . . He will blunder into the teeth of suffering soon."

"I believe he has already begun. But I don't understand." Lysse creased her fair brow. "Who will sacrifice Gwern? And why?"

"Aene. Or the goddess. For greatness." He stirred slightly, faced her again. "There are marvels to come, a quickening, new magic, or old magic made new. . . . There are things I could never do, and they will be done. That mystic sword I found will be thrown in the sea at last; I have seen that. An elfin King must hurl it away, to end the long shadow of Lyrdion on our land. I was never able to do it; 'twas all I could do to touch that weapon once, then walk away."

Lysse leaned forward with as much excitement as he had ever known her to show. "What else?"

"Something about unicorns, and the shape where two circles meet, the spindle shape. And the seeress . . . Trevyn mounted on a cat-eyed steed. Virgins and dragons . . . Do you think it might be a girl he's running from?"

"It has occurred to me," Lysse snapped. "What was Trevyn doing on such a peculiar horse?"

"Bringing the legends back to Isle, from Elwestrand. To travel to Elwestrand and return—I could never do that. It has never been done. But he shall do it. Trevyn shall, the young fool. I have seen."

"Mother of mercy," she murmured, stunned. "You haven't told him!"

"I am not a half-wit," he retorted frostily. "What is the good of a prophecy told? He must work it out himself, or make a hash of it, as the case may be. I've written it down among my things, for some scholar to grub up years hence. Then Trevyn shall have his glory, if glory is due."

"Mother of mercy," she said again. "Unicorns stand for wholeness. . . . What are the two circles that meet?"

"Gold and silver, sun and moon . . ." Hal's voice faded dreamily away. He was tired, and spoke no more, then or in the weeks that followed. He lay in deep stillness. Alan stopped trying to talk him out of his strange trance, though he was full of anger that had no vent. Sometimes he climbed the tower stairs to Hal's door and looked silently in for a while, then turned and went away. He would not sit by his brother's side.

Hal faded into brightness. Though he did not eat or move, his body remained beautiful—frail, scarred from old wounds, but glowing with spirit life. During the first days of spring, when a hint of green began to tinge the hillsides, Hal gradually, carefully ceased to breathe. Power and vision still shone from his open eyes.

Alan could not grieve anymore; how was he to grieve for one who had not truly died? But Rosemary wept, for she was a woman and she knew her loss. Trevyn clung to his dream. When the trees began to bud and Hal still did not stir, his loved ones prepared to take him to the Bay, where, Lysse's

Sight told her, an elf-ship awaited him. Alan dressed him in the bright, soft raiment of the elves and laid him in a horse litter. Beside him Rosemary placed the antique plinset that had always been his comfort. Alan brought the mighty silver crown that had come with Veran to Isle.

"Hal does not want the heavy crown," Lysse said. "He told me so. He will be no king in Elwestrand."

Alan looked at the great crown that was rayed like a silver sun. The sheen of it was the same as the tide-washed gray of Hal's eyes. Alan blinked and turned away.

"It has no place here without him," he said roughly. "He is the last of that line. I will throw it into the sea whence it came. Lysse, get him the circlet I made him, at least. . . ."

Trevyn came out, leading Rhyssiart, his golden steed, ready to ride with the others. But Alan turned on him brusquely. "Put that horse away. You are to stay here."

Trevyn's jaw dropped in astonished protest, and hot anger stirred in him; he quickly squeezed it down. He watched, motionless, as Alan and the Queens rode off with the horse litter between them. Arundel followed behind, riderless. Meadowlarks sang high overhead as the little procession moved slowly toward the Bay of the Blessed, a seven days' journey away. Trevyn stood with his disobedience already forming in his mind.

Chapter Six

"I am going, too," Gwern stated.

Trevyn sighed, gloomily accepting that Gwern knew of his plans even though he had not told him. He scarcely ever spoke to Gwern, though he had not fought with him since the row over Meg. His dislike had not abated, but he had become somewhat ashamed of it. He had decided to be dignified.

"Very well," he replied coolly, then smiled grimly to himself. He judged that Gwern would not ride with him more than a few days. Gwern would not be able to pass the haunt that guarded the Blessed Bay.

After nightfall they were off, with heavy packs of food stolen from the kitchen. Trevyn knew the sentries would be wary of him now, so they had to do some climbing with a rope. The Prince barely bothered to wonder why he trusted Gwern as his companion. Once well beyond the walls, far out on the downs, the mismatched pair called up some horses and set their course by the summer stars that hung low on the western horizon.

Trevyn had never been to the Bay of the Blessed, but he felt sure he could find the way. He would show his parents whether he was a child, to be so lightly left behind! He rode hard, to be certain of arriving before the slow horse litter. Once he had passed the haunt, the abode of bodiless spirits, he need not fear any pursuit. No mortal could withstand terror of those unresting dead except a few who still remembered the mysteries of the old order, the sound of the Old Language. Among which few, as a Laueroc, Trevyn numbered himself.

Within three days Trevyn and Gwern came to the end of the green meadows and tilled land, to the haunt, where the shades of the dead thickly clustered. Trevyn could feel their eerie presence chill the air. Smugly, he turned to watch Gwern shriek and flee. At last he would be rid of the muddy-hued upstart who hounded him! But Gwern only straightened to attention on his horse.

"Dead people!" he exclaimed, with something like delight. "But why do they not rest? Whence do they come?"

"How should I know?" Trevyn sputtered, fighting off his astonishment and the conclusions he did not wish to reach. Irrationally fleeing, he spun his mount and sent it springing into the haunt. Gwern followed without hesitation, and the wild terrain soon slowed Trevyn's pace. He and Gwern picked their way silently between looming gray rocks and dark firs. Once through the invisible barrier, Trevyn breathed easier, knowing he would not be ingloriously escorted back to Laueroc. But Gwern still rode at his side.

"I think they were gods," Gwern said with the unreasoning certainty of a child.

"Gods!" Trevyn snorted. "Only peasants talk of gods, Gwern!"

"They were little gods, such as can be killed, and they tried hard to cheat death; they still try. But the great gods cannot be killed. There is the goddess my mother; her sooth-name is Alys."

Trevyn gaped at him, staggered anew. Gwern had spoken in the Ancient Tongue, which Trevyn had never heard him use before or expected to hear from him. He hazily sensed that Gwern could not have said "Alys" in the language of Isle or any language of men. But he thought more of his earthy companion than of the goddess. There was no escaping the conclusion now: Gwern moved in the old order. He should have known it the first time he saw him touch an *elwedeyn* horse.

Gwern took no pause for his astonishment. "She answers to many names, but that is the most puissant," he continued soberly. "Call on her when you have need."

Trevyn regarded his dun-faced companion in mingled wonder and suspicion. What was this Gwern, and why should he offer aid when Trevyn had never showed him anything but hostility? "I have been taught to call only on the nameless One, and that seldom," he said at last.

Gwern shrugged. "And what is this Aene?" he asked, again in the Ancient Tongue.

"Dawn and dusk, the hawk and the hunted, sun and sable moon." Trevyn impatiently parroted the words Hal had taught him; already he had tired of riddles. "What of it? Come on, Gwern, let us be moving!"

The brown youth obeyed with a strange smile. Trevyn had just spoken the name of destiny, and in his ignorance he rushed to leave it behind.

For another three days the two rode through a wilderness of jumbled stone and giant, lowering trees. They saw no living creatures except birds and deer and the *elwedeyn* horses that also liked to explore these parts. In time they came to the Gleaming River and followed it south, down to the Bay through which Veran had entered Welas. They reached that quiet expanse without a sight of Alan and the Queens. Signaling their horses to a stop, they looked out over the shimmering water.

"There it is," Trevyn said.

Through the perpetual shadows of that dusky, brooding place moved a slim, gray elf-ship—a living thing, restless as a blooded steed between the confines of the shingle shores. Great evergreens towered overhead, the silvery water glimmered between, and the elf-boat circled like a swan, waiting. Trevyn moved closer.

"Mireldeyn is coming," he told the vessel in the Old Language. Then he gulped. "What in the name of—of my fathers is that?"

Another ship floated close to shore near the mouth of the

Bay, wallowing sullenly in the gleaming water. It was no elf-craft. It was broad, heavy, and high-headed, and it glittered all over with gold, shining like a miser's dream. The railings were riotous with gold filigree. At the bow leaped a figurehead—a golden wolf with bared teeth of mother-of-pearl. Trevyn felt sick. This could be no mere chance.

Slowly he rode along the verge of the Bay until he came to the glittering ship. There was no anchor or line holding it in place, no captain or any living being on board. The gilded wolf glared balefully, daring Trevyn to come closer. Grudgingly, he found a boarding plank, left at that sacred place from times long past, and he laid it to the polished deck.

"Don't!" Gwern whispered.

Trevyn had never seen him so frightened. Gwern's fear gave him a perverse triumph. Goaded, he stalked onto the golden boat.

The very boards of the deck were gilt. Trevyn edged across them and looked below, every muscle tense with caution. He half expected an ambush of wolves or of wolfish men. Instead, he found casks of water and provisions for a long voyage. Then he felt the ship shudder beneath him, heard the boarding plank fall away. He sprang to the deck and leaped off at once, landing over his head in icy water. He fought his way to shore, sputtering. Gwern reached out to help him, and Trevyn did not scorn to take his hand. As he stood dripping, the wolf-boat clumsily circled and came back to its place.

"In good time!" he shouted at it angrily. "I must say farewell to my father!"

All his dreams of Elwestrand had been shocked out of him by the danger he had tried too long to ignore. He would be voyaging, but not to Elwestrand, he knew now. He might have let Gwern say his farewells for him, he reflected, but he had done that once too often already. Shivering, he rode into the shelter of the trees, and Gwern helped him build a fire. There he sat and warmed himself through the rest of the day and the night. The sleek elf-ship swam impatiently about the

Bay; Trevyn could glimpse it in the moonlight. But the gaudy
wolf-ship lurked stodgily in the shadows near the shore,
flickering like marsh-lights in a darkened swamp. Already
Trevyn hated its squalid splendor. He slept little and was glad
to see the dawn.

Rosemary, Alan, and Lysse came late the next day. Gwern
and Trevyn watched from the shadow of a giant fir as the
elf-boat sped gladly to meet them and nestled close to shore
near their feet. Arundel gave a joyful whinny, the greeting of
an *elwedeyn* steed to the elfin ship that was like kindred to
him. But Alan exclaimed in consternation, "Look yonder!
What is that chunk of metal floating there?"

"Perhaps that boat does not concern us," Rosemary
murmured.

"It does not concern Hal," Lysse agreed.

So Alan put the boarding plank to the elf-boat and lifted
Hal's still body from the horse litter, cradling him like a baby.
He carried him on board his boat and settled him gently on
the open deck. Hal would lie under wheeling sun and stars on
his long voyage; his gray eyes gazed up serenely. Alan laid his
plinset beside him, in the sturdy leather case Rosemary had
made years before. Then he took the great silver crown of
Veran and flung it with all his strength far out into the Bay.
With a sigh that Trevyn felt even from afar, Alan knelt to kiss
Hal's quiet face, then left him there and stepped to shore. He
looked at Rosemary, and she nodded.

Alan slid the plank away. Instantly, the swan-ship glided
off, over the bright water, straight toward the golden light of
the setting sun. Gulls flew low, calling, and water rippled.
There was no other sound.

Trevyn watched it go. He thought he had put desire from
him, but he had not yet felt true desire. He had never felt a
force such as the mystic longing that took hold on him now.
Scarcely knowing what he did, he started from his hiding
place, running down the stony beach until his feet met the
waves. He stared after the elf-ship, yearning. The sun
reached out to him. The ship was a shape of marvel in its
embrace. It swam swiftly away, at one with the wash of waves
and the circling sea currents. Then it was gone, engulfed in

the golden horizon, and Trevyn realized that the wash of water was in his own eyes. Still he stared westward. Not until the sun slipped from view did he realize that his father stood beside him, holding him. Alan, the great of heart. Trevyn had not yet learned the depths of his love.

"You are quivering like a harp string," Alan said.

Trevyn shook his head to clear the haze of his trance. "Father," he muttered. "I have grieved you, and I must grieve you more."

"Why, Trevyn?" Lysse and Rosemary drew closer to listen. Gwern quietly emerged from the trees.

"I must go on that golden ship," he told them.

Gwern was expressionless, Rosemary too sunk in her own sorrow to care. Lysse looked at the wolf-ship with quiet eyes, seeking to pierce its secret. But Alan exploded.

"If you had not been here, you would not have seen it!" he cried. "The elf blood is strong in you. I knew that if you came to the Bay you would yearn to sail, as Hal did. . . ." Alan choked and subsided. "From the moment he saw your mother's folk taking ship to the west, he dreamed of the sea."

"I dreamed before I came to the Bay," Trevyn answered in a low voice. "But the elf-ship is gone, Father. That gaudy boat will not take me to Elwestrand."

Alan stared at his son, truly seeing him for the first time in months. There was no glory lust in Trevyn's eyes, no youthful impulsiveness. White-faced, the Prince looked as frightened as Alan had ever seen him, but still set in his resolve. "Where, then?" Alan whispered. But Trevyn had no answer to offer.

Lysse turned from her study of the strange vessel, looked at her son instead, and he did not elude her gaze. "It is true, my husband," she said to Alan. "He must go. There is a destiny on him."

Alan staggered as if he had been struck. "How can I know that?" he gasped wildly. "Suppose I defy this—this so-called destiny of yours, young man, and bid you stay. What then?"

"Then I would defy you, and I would fight you, if it came to that." Trevyn did not try to hide his misery. "Short of my killing you, nothing worse can befall us both than my biding here. No good can come to anyone who shirks a destiny, you have told me. No good can come to us if I stay."

"It will not come to that," Alan muttered. For Trevyn's sake he would yield, though in all his life he had never surrendered with good grace. "Still, I do not understand," he added bitterly, perhaps to the One. "On any other day or hour I could have borne this better."

"I can wait a few hours, or even a day," Trevyn said quietly.

"Nay, go if you must go! Are there provisions on that sickly ship?"

Trevyn only nodded.

"Confound it, let us be on with it, then!"

They put the boarding plank to the gaudy wolf-boat. Trevyn strode off and fetched a bundle of clothing from his horse. Lysse stood probing the strange, glittering craft with smoky gray-green eyes. Only when Trevyn approached did she stir from her trance.

"Your cloak," she urged, motherlike. "It will be chilly on the open sea."

Trevyn got out the garment and flung it around his shoulders. Alan watched him intently, trying to seize the moment with his mind. Trevyn fastened his cloak, not with his golden brooch, but with a simple pin.

"Your brooch," Alan said. "What has become of it?"

"I lost it somewhere along the road." But Trevyn was taken by surprise, and the lie showed plainly in his eyes. Alan stared at him, stunned. Falsehood, and at this, the last moment they had to share! Trevyn returned his father's gaze with anguish in his own. Then Alan removed the jeweled brooch from his own shoulder, the rayed emblem of the royal crown that he had worn since Hal had given it to him on the day of Trevyn's birth.

"That is yours!" Trevyn exclaimed. "Keep it. I can't take it from you!"

"Borrow it, then. Bring it back," said Alan tightly. He pinned it over his son's heart, wordlessly handed him a purse of gold.

"I will. I swear to you I will return." Trevyn's voice shook. "Father, I am sorry—"

"Hush." Alan gripped his shoulders. "There is no need for speeches. Go with all blessing. . . ." He hugged his son hard and kissed him fiercely before he released him.

"Farewell, Mother," Trevyn murmured, and embraced her hastily. Rosemary stood among the horses, her russet head bowed to Arundel's neck; Trevyn knew she was hardly aware of his departure. But Gwern stood silently by. Trevyn froze with one foot on the boarding plank, feeling suddenly, absurdly, naked and incomplete. Gwern, whom he had wanted so badly to begone—Gwern had not moved from his place.

"Nay, I cannot leave earth. You must sail alone." Gwern stolidly answered the unspoken question. A hint of pain shadowed the claylike mask of his face, and Trevyn found himself utterly taken aback, astounded by that pain, astounded by the answering pang that put its grip on him.

"I didn't know," he whispered.

"Stay, then," urged Alan.

"Nay, I must go." Hesitantly, Trevyn offered Gwern his hand, and the barefoot, brown-haired youth gripped it without comment. Trevyn turned and strode onto the gilded ship.

He kept his head low, but Alan saw the tears that streaked his face. The ship started from its place like a hound unleashed, churned away from the shore. Alan put his arm around Lysse—to give comfort or to receive? He raised his hand in salute to his son. Gwern stood like a stump.

"All good come to you, Beloved!" Lysse called.

Trevyn straightened and waved to them. They watched after him until the ship turned the headland and was lost to view, vanishing like spook lamps into the dusk.

"A wolf is an animal that roams the night and sings to the moon," Lysse said softly. "There is no great harm to it."

"East!" Alan muttered. "The wolf-boat goes east. No good lies that way."

* * *

It was not until weeks later that the goodwife found Trevyn's brooch among Meg's belongings. Fluttering, she summoned her husband. They hated to scold Megan, for she had turned silent and moody since the Prince had gone away. But the brooch was valuable, and they were frightened.

"Ye cannot keep this, Meg!" the goodman cried. "Likely 'tis solid gold!"

"'Tis mine. He gave it to me."

"He only lent it t'ye! Did he say for ye to keep it?"

"If he wanted it back, he could have come for it."

"Who are ye to say where he must come or go? He is the Prince! Why would he give ye such a thing? Folk will say ye stole it!"

Meg had looked sullenly down, but now she straightened and flared back at her father. "What was I to do? Run to his castle, peradventure, and beg an audience?"

"Ay, daughter, 'twas a hard spot, that I'll not deny." Brock's voice was softer. "Still, ye should not have hid it away. We must take it to the lord; 'twill be safer with him."

Rafe regarded Meg with compassion while Brock told the tale. He had last seen her in a dress fit for a princess, glowing with the beauty that only love gives. Now she silently stared at the floor, and Rafe could see that her cheeks were pale. The pallor of love withheld, he judged.

Goodman Brock could not be less than honest. "And there is the cloak, my lord, as well," he concluded. The girl's eyes flashed up, and Rafe quickly hid the pity in his own, for he knew she would not welcome it.

"I think there is no need to say anything of the cloak." Rafe saw, without appearing to see, Meg's relief; this remembrance at least would be left to her. "I know my liege, and I am certain he would not begrudge it to you. But this brooch"—Rafe turned it delicately in his hands—"bears the emblem of the Sun Crowns. The King must know of its whereabouts." Rafe climbed down from his audience chair and headed toward a table where lay parchment, pen and ink, sand, and sealing wax. "Come, Meg, let us write a letter to Trevyn's father."

Within a week, a messenger came to Laueroc and presented to the King the following curious missive:

On this, the ides of May, in the Nineteenth year of his reign, to Alan, Heir of Laueroc, and Rightful and Most Gracious Ruler of Isle, Greeting.

It being that a thing I hold may not be mine in truth, I hereby state my willingness to relinquish it, obedient to the word of my Liege and King.

It being that my lord the Prince graciously lent me his brooch to fasten a cloak thereby, and his returning not therefor, I have cherished the brooch on his account until this time.

It being that this brooch is of precious substance and molded in the likeness of the Royal Emblem, I have rendered it into the safe keeping of my lord Rafe of Lee until my Liege the King has seen fit to judge the ownership thereof.

With many thanks to my lord the Prince for his gracious favors on my behalf, and especially for the sake of the cow Molly.

Your humble servant, Megan By-the-woods.

By the hand of her good lord, Rafe of Lee.

Alan read this three times, then stumped off to find Lysse. "What do you make of this?"

She read it and handed it back with a wistful smile. "Poor lass. I wonder what she is like."

"Either very honest, or else commending herself to our attention. Can he have got her with child, do you think?"

"I think—I would have felt such a child."

"Perhaps." Alan sighed. "Well, Rafe can tell us if anything is amiss. I will have him send the brooch to us."

"Nay." Lysse laid her hand on his arm. "Let the girl keep it."

He looked at her in surprise. "Whatever for?"

"There will be hard times ahead for all of us." She faced him steadily. "Hard enough for you and me, my love, but we have much to sustain us. It may be that—she does not have so much."

Alan cupped her chin in his hand and regarded her closely. "Have you seen something?"

"Nay, nothing clearly. It is only feeling."

He knew that feeling. His life had been a long battle with such heavy feeling since Hal and Trevyn had left. Call it foreboding, but not yet so dark that it benighted his thoughtful curiosity. He penned a reply to Rafe, commending the girl to his watchful care, then placed Meg's letter in his files. Months later, he still remembered her name.

Book Two

MOTHER
OF MERCY

Chapter One

This gaudy craft was a dead thing, Trevyn decided, with no power of its own. Certainly it was not a living, swimming being like the elf-ship he had seen. He felt no vitality in its timbers, as often as he lay and lost himself in study of the mystery of its motion. He could discern no surge from behind or below, no gathering of heart at the bottom of the billow or of breath at the top. As the weeks went by, Trevyn became certain that the source of the power lay far ahead. He was in a bright bauble drawn by invisible wires, smacking crudely against the waves, for all the world like a child's toy being dragged across a vast watery yard. He thanked the One that the sea remained calm.

As yet, Trevyn had known nothing of the nausea that makes sea crossings a misery. To pass the time, and to keep from growing weak with the long voyage, he exercised for hours every day. Then he paced the deck as he studied the sky and sea. His course was to the south and east. Every morning at daybreak the rays of the rising sun haloed the hulking form of the wolfish figurehead. To Trevyn it seemed unfair, even treasonous, that the emblem of his father's royal greatness should bedeck the wolf, which to him had become a

symbol of lowest evil. Since he could command neither the
ship nor the sun, he learned to turn his back on this moment.

Trevyn had examined the figurehead closely on his first day
out and had found it to be nothing more than gilded wood
with glass eyes and pearly teeth. But at night it seemed to him
that the lupine form was lit with more than reflected sheen.
Amid the gleaming of the starry sea, he could not be certain.
Yet the thing gnawed him with slow fear, even colored his
dreams with its frozen leap, and he went near it no more.
Another thing troubled Trevyn: that Meg from time to time
would intrude her thin face before his inward eye. He strove
to forget her, and turned his back on her image as on the
wolf. Yet, had he noticed, where Meg's image was the dread
of the wolf was not.

By the sixth week of the voyage, Trevyn began to see birds
hunting the sea, wheeling ahead and to the left. He looked
that way eagerly, searching the horizon for land. In the
seventh week he spied it, a low, dark smudge where sky met
sea. Trevyn judged that the land was no more than a day's
voyage away, though the ship's course lay counter to the
sighting.

But the sun next day came up in a sultry, coppery glow.
The wolf loomed against it featureless and terrible, like a
faceless specter in a dream. Trevyn stared at it in spite of
himself, this thing that he could neither fight nor flee, and he
paced the deck in unrest. The sky was filled with omen, a
clamor heard with inner ears. Soon dark gray clouds blotted
out the murky sun, and the storm clamored in truth. Rain
fell, hiding the land like a molten curtain. Wind harried the
rain, and the swell grew. The glittering ship plunged on
stupidly, like a fish hauled in by a heavy hand, smashing
through the heaving water. Spray flew as constantly as the
rain; Trevyn wondered where he still found air to breathe.
The ship did not swamp, for it rode very high, but it spun and
teetered dizzily. Trevyn could not stand on the deck, and he
did not want to be trapped below. He crawled to the filigree
rail, and there he clung.

When night came, scarcely to be distinguished from the
dark day, Trevyn knew that the ship would break. He did not
care how soon. Nausea had long since purged him of any

desire and left him limp. When the shock came and timbers flew like the spray, Trevyn was torn away from the rail and hurled through a confusion of water and rubble. Feebly he fought and thrashed, clawing at illusion, gulping at water and air. His gear hampered him. He rid himself of boots, sword, purse—even his father's brooch. He seemed to be sinking into a dark and alien place. Then he was quite naked, and found that he could breathe again, and opened his eyes.

Unaccountably, the sea was calm. Not far away, the wolfish figurehead glinted, its gilded form eerily etched on the dark water by the flickering lightning of the retreating storm. Trevyn shied away from it, but it did not come at him. Straight as an arrow it made off, dragging through the water like a stick through sand, and Trevyn knew that it laid a line toward the rising sun. He wheeled a quarter turn northeastward and swam toward the remembered sight of land.

He paddled through blackness unlit even by a star. The sea was warm in these southern parts, far warmer than the day of soaking rain and chilling wind. Trevyn relaxed in its embrace, surrendered to its flow, scarcely feeling the effort of his motions. The sea was a mother, a lover for whom he yearned. He laid his face upon her bosom as on a pillow, and more than once he breathed her watery essence into his lungs. He stirred in her at random, kicking out like an infant in the womb, cushioned by warm liquid from any harm, so it seemed, for all eternity. How cruel it was, then, how unfathomably harsh, when a pounding rhythm took hold of him and forced him away from this deepest haven, rushed and battered him, tossed and shoved him through a weary stretch of time and space, abandoning him at last in a strange place from which he might never return.

Trevyn crawled up the beach, just out of reach of the grasping sea surf, and collapsed onto the cold, hard sand.

He awoke with a shock to full daylight and the sound of rough voices. Four muscular, sun-scorched men stood around him, seized him as soon as he opened his eyes. He struggled to throw them off, but he was weak and dazed; a hard cuff to the side of his head stunned him. The men bound his wrists behind him with thongs and jerked him to his feet, prodding

him to make him walk. Trevyn stumbled and fell to his knees,
then sprang up as a lash bit his shoulders. His captors roared
with laughter. "It works every time," one said.

They walked along the seaside, driving him before them.
He would bring a fine price, they said, by the goddess of many
names! Some lord would pay well to have such a handsome,
yellow-headed oddity in his household. If he had been
shipwrecked, there should be more. They would search the
beaches well.

It did not surprise Trevyn that he could understand them,
for he had studied many languages. He knew now that he was
in the country called Tokar—a villainous place. Though he
had expected nothing more, he felt desolate, like an abandoned child. Corruption flourished in Tokar; the rulers were
sunk in greed. Isle had endured such eastern rulers for seven
generations, until Hal and Alan had shed their blood to free
her. . . . And now he, a Prince of Isle, had come to the realm
of Herne's sorcery and Gwern's goddess, it seemed. Well, he
was freeborn, with a freedom dearly bought, and he would
not yield it easily, Trevyn silently vowed. Not to slavers or to
any god or goddess that bore a name.

Throughout the day the slave traders tramped the beaches,
prodding Trevyn before them or tugging him along behind.
He gave them as much trouble as he could, dragging and
blundering along. Even making allowances for his weakened
state, they soon found it necessary to discipline him with the
lash. They felt no particular desire to put welts on their
merchandise, but a balky slave would be no bargain to
anyone. By nightfall, when they had gained nothing for their
day of searching except growling stomachs, they were mightily tired of Trevyn. They hurried him through the dark,
flogging him to his feet when he fell, giving up finally and half
carrying him to the slave pen. Sick as he felt, Trevyn thrashed
when he heard the noise of bolts and bars being undone,
nearly struggled free. Cursing, the slavers quieted him with
dizzying blows. They seized him by the arms, cut his bonds,
and flung him forward. Trevyn fell through emptiness, hit the
bottom limply, and lay still. Above him he heard the bars
slide into place and the bolts clang to. He turned his face to
the dirt, letting despair take him.

From the hushed silence rose a murmur of voices; there were other people in this place. A hand touched Trevyn, feeling him over blindly. He did not stir.

"Better move aside, lad." It was an old man's voice. "They're liable to send something down on top of ye."

Trevyn moved, crawling forward, and hands guided him to a stony wall. There he huddled. The night was filled with voices and noises; he did not heed them. Dimly he sensed bodies pressed close beside him, as naked as his own. They stank, as did everything in this den, but he did not recoil. The night air was chill, and his companions, whoever they might be, were warm. Trevyn settled himself on dank earth and slept.

He awoke the next day to shouts and scramblings. Chunks of bread were falling through the high, barred trapdoor. Below it, the slaves sprang and shoved for a share. Trevyn blinked, but before he could stir his stiffened limbs the bread was all taken. He sat up slowly to watch the others eat. An old man approached him, picking his way carefully over the uneven floor. He stood before Trevyn and spoke with dignity. "I am old and have small need of this. Eat."

Trevyn took the bread and broke off a mouthful. The rest he gave back. He chewed his morsel very slowly; it was heavy stuff and sank in lumps to his stomach. When he had finished, the old man still stood before him, offering the bread. "Eat."

Trevyn shook his head, but the old man did not move. A few paces away, a big slave stirred dangerously. "If ye'll not eat it yerself, graybeard," he growled, "then give it to one who will." Yet the old man scarcely glanced at him. Turning his back contemptuously on the other, he squatted beside Trevyn and poised the bread under his nose.

"Eat!"

Trevyn ate. Bit by slow bit, the bread disappeared. The other slaves watched in silence, but no one made a move to hinder. When the bread was gone, Trevyn sank back and lay very still, afraid he might retch. But he kept it down, and toward evening he felt strength coming of it. He sat up and looked around.

"Whence d'ye come?" a slave asked him, but he only smiled and shook his head. There were about a dozen men in the pit, of all ages and sizes. Some had black hair, some brown or russet, but none were as blond as he. They stared at him curiously. "Were ye shipwrecked?" another ventured, but again Trevyn gave no spoken reply. Almost insensibly he had resolved to be a mute in this land, so that he would not betray himself. And also in silent, inward rebellion. . . . Throughout the long day on the beaches he had uttered no sound. That had been his father's stubbornness in him; they could enslave him, but, by blood, they could not make him cry out. Now Trevyn realized that his bravado might stand him in good stead. Better even to be a mute slave than a dishonored prince held for ransom, or dead, or worse.

The slavers kept Trevyn in the pit with the others for a week. The food was only bread in the morning, raw turnips or carrots at night, and dirty water that seeped down the walls into shallow stone cups. But even on this diet Trevyn gained strength, for he was allowed to rest. Indeed, he paced the stony floor with boredom and restless rage. Every once in a while some wretch was hurled down from above as he had been. Many had been slaves all their lives and picked themselves up almost as if they were used to it. Others looked as miserable as he had been. But none, Trevyn noticed, had been beaten as cruelly as he.

The morning of Trevyn's eighth day in the pit, a narrow ladder dropped through the trapdoor and a slave merchant shouted at the slaves to come up. They went docilely, almost numbly, took their places, and were roped into a line as if they were indeed nothing more than trade goods. Hatred and pride would not let Trevyn go so tamely. Let them come get him, he grimly thought. Heart pounding, he waited.

"That towheaded lout must be deaf as well as mute," he heard one slaver say.

"If he has eyes, he knows well enough what he's to do," another snapped. "If he weren't so good-looking, I'd kill him now and save someone else the trouble."

Three of them came down after him. He crouched, hands at the ready; by any god, they had better beware of him now that he had the use of his hands! They came at him from three sides. He lunged at one . . . and then they pinned him more deftly than he would have believed possible, tied his wrists with cutting force. One of them glared angrily, a bruise forming on his swarthy face.

"Give me that whip," he said, reaching for it.

"We're already late starting," the other replied testily. He turned on Trevyn. "Get up the ladder, you, or we'll leave you here to starve!"

He wanted to make them hoist him up by main force. But he sensed that the threat was not idle; the slavers seemed to have reached the last stages of exasperation. Reluctantly, slowly enough to make them lash at him from behind, he went up and took his place in line. He had never felt less willing to yield; his helplessness would not let him yield, his lost self cried out for recognition like an infant screaming in the night. But the body wished to survive.

The slavers placed him just behind the old man in the string, and Trevyn was glad of it. Even to the unspeaking, the old man provided more decent company than most. They all set out toward the distant market. The four slave traders rode shaggy ponies and led pack animals. With their whips they kept their human merchandise to a shambling trot over wild, rocky terrain. Most of the slaves went along readily enough on thickly callused feet, but Trevyn's feet, long accustomed to boots of soft leather, had not had a chance to toughen. Before the first day's journey was half over they had started to bleed. Trevyn's pace slowed, and the slavers had run out of patience with him. They kept him going with the lash.

At dusk they stopped at last, and the slaves dropped where they stood while the slavers pitched camp and built fires for themselves. After a while one moved down the line of slaves tossing each a chunk of bread and, for a wonder, a bit of cheese. But when the slave trader came to Trevyn, he only paused with a hard smile. "None for ye, bully," he said. "By the goddess, ye're too full of sauce to bear feeding. Bow when ye face me, sirrah!"

He passed on, laughing aloud, while Trevyn stared. When his back was well down the line, the old man halved his portion and passed Trevyn a share. "Pride makes a thin porridge, lad," he remarked. Trevyn was thankful that his muteness saved him the necessity of replying.

The slaves huddled their naked bodies together through the

night while their masters dozed blanket-wrapped by the fire, taking guard by turns. The next morning Trevyn's feet were oozing pus. The slaver who brought bread noticed it and came back with a bucket of brine. He grasped at his slave, but Trevyn stepped in with high head and a level look, though the pain took his breath. The man scowled and went away, bringing no bandaging for the feet.

That day was a nightmare for Trevyn. He could not keep the pace, stumbling and limping despite himself, and the slavers flogged him until his back was as raw as his feet. Pain and hunger made him reel lightheadedly. More than once he would have fallen if the old man had not caught him with the rope. Nearly hallucinating, he imagined that none of this was happening to him, that he was not himself at all, but Hal, facing the torturers in Nemeton's dark and hellish Tower. . . . Had Hal cried out? But he was Trevyn, after all. He would not cry out.

"If ye'd only yelp once in a while, or even lower yer head a bit," the old man whispered to him in honest concern, "I believe they'd treat ye less cruelly."

Trevyn answered him only with a wry smile, wishing in a way that he could take the advice, knowing that, being what he was, he could not.

Chapter Two

In a small chamber of the royal palace at Kantukal sat the king of Tokar, Rheged by name, and his counselor Wael. Rheged was a lean, long-armed man of middle age. Sparse, flabby flesh draped his loose frame; his look was hungry. He hungered insatiably, though not for food, and he could be as dangerous as a starving wolf. Wael, his advisor, was a shrunken wizard of incalculable years, a scholar of intrigue and the arts of influence as well as a sorcerer. The two men found little to like in each other and less to trust, but their mutual greed for power bound them almost as securely as love, for the time. They hunched in council over a figurehead in form of a leaping, gilded wooden wolf.

"It seemed faultless," Wael breathed in his soft old voice, hypnotic as the hissing of a serpent. "A young prince must perforce fancy a fairy boat of gold, and once he was on it, all was easy. I drew him here more surely than if I held him by a rope in my hand. Who would have thought it would ship-wreck? Never has such a storm been seen in the spring of the year. In autumn, perhaps—"

"Ay, ay," Rheged interrupted impatiently, "no one can fault your scheme, laugh though they might that we took armed men to the harbor to await a swimming wolf! They do not smile to my face, not unless they wish to die quite slowly, but I cannot stop the snickers behind my back. But that is past; the question now is, what to do about Isle? It is small use to us that the heir is dead, if his body cannot be found."

"Perhaps he is not yet dead," Wael mused. "If he got ashore, he could be anywhere by now; it has been almost two weeks. But we should hear news of him, for he would cut a strange figure in these parts. Perhaps he has been enslaved. It would be wise to check the markets."

Rheged nodded sardonically and made a note.

"If I could only have something that belonged to him, a piece of clothing or a knife or even a coin," Wael went on intensely, "I could draw him to me, dead or alive, as surely as if—"

"As if you held him by a rope in your hand," Rheged finished sourly. "What of it? Am I to send to Isle, now, for an article of his apparel?"

"Nay, nay, Majesty, send men to search the beaches! Offer rewards enough to render them honest. And send spies throughout the realm to find news of him. Offer rewards for that, also."

"You make plentifully free with my gold," muttered Rheged. "Even so, it shall be done. It will be worth much gold if I can hold that prince my hostage."

"Or even," whispered Wael, "your sacrifice at the altar of the Wolf."

"As you will," Rheged growled. "But how is that to help my invasion of Isle?"

"That upstart little country, Isle!" Wael laughed softly, a wheezing, murky sound. "King, I could have given you that victory a dozen times by now. But it is the game itself that brings more joy, and the game has just begun, do you see? Just begun!" Wael lurched forward in his intensity. "And you know wolves belong to the winter. We will strike then."

"If you say so, wizard," the monarch wearily assented. "As you say."

The slave market was nothing more than a large cobbled clearing set amid the houses and shops of a place called Jabul.

Here the traders came with their wares at the dawn of the market day, and even before the arrival of the buyers the place was crowded. Thousands of human beings filled it—an eerie gathering, Trevyn thought, for the slaves hardly moved or spoke. The silence of despair hung over them all. About half of the slaves were women, bound in their own strings apart from the men, many with babes at their breasts. Trevyn stared, gaped indeed, for they were as naked as himself. The sight did not thrill him so much as dismay him; they were as beaten, as filthy, and as bereft of dignity as he. Suddenly he thought of Meg, imagining her in such company, and his face turned hard as stone. He stood like rage immobilized while the buyers arrived and looked him over, feeling his limbs for soundness as if he were a draft animal.

"Here is a man looking for a mute!" one of the traders cried to another, leading a buyer through the lines of slaves.

"Then here is his mute!" shouted the other, striding to Trevyn and jerking him forward. "Right here, sir, a fine, strong fellow!"

"Are you quite sure he is unable to speak?" the buyer asked, addressing the slave trader with distaste he made no effort to conceal. He was a slender young man, a bit shorter than Trevyn, with a high, pale forehead over eloquent eyes. The noisy slave merchant did not seem to mind his evident distrust.

"Why, he's not made a sound these two weeks past," the slaver blustered, "not even in pain. Here, let me show ye." He grabbed Trevyn's finger and wrenched it back, but the young man gasped and struck his hand away.

"That will not be necessary," he said imperiously. "I take it, then, that he has not lost his tongue?"

"Nay," answered the slaver, crestfallen. Then he brightened. "But if ye want him, sir, I'll take the tongue out of him for ye, right enough—"

"Great goddess, nay!" The man was emphatic, and Trevyn allowed himself a sigh of relief. "Mischance enough if it was born in him." The young man turned to Trevyn, studying him, not poking at him as the others had done, but looking into his eyes. Trevyn met his gaze steadily, and the man nodded, satisfied. "How much?" he asked.

"Softly, sir, he's a handsome piece; if I put him on the block he'll bring me a pretty price."

"I cannot wait for the bidding; I have business at home. Name your price."

The slave trader named a price. It was high, but the young man doled out the gold without demur. The slaver undid Trevyn from the string, leaving his hands tied.

"He is mine now," the young man said.

"Ay."

"To do with as I like."

"Ay, to be sure!" The slave merchant laughed and cracked his whip.

"Good." The young man brought out a slender knife, such as scholars use to sharpen their pens with, and began carefully to cut Trevyn's bonds.

The slaver shouted, and his face went white. "Nay, young master! He's a wild 'un—he'll go to kill me!" But the thongs were cut, and the young man stepped back without comment. Trevyn rubbed his chafed wrists and studied the shaking slaver, who was backing cautiously away. No courage in the man without his fellows, it seemed! He would gladly have settled his score with this tormenter, and it was no cold caution that restrained him. He could not say why he stayed his hand, unless it was somehow because of the young man who stood quietly beside him. He could have leveled him with a single blow, by the looks of him, but the fellow had freed him fearlessly. . . . Trevyn turned and nodded farewell to the old man who had befriended him. Then he looked to his new master.

"Here," the young man said, handing him a sort of loincloth; hardly the raiment of a prince, but Trevyn put it on gladly. His feet were healed by now and his back mostly healed. The traders had been obliged to tend to him, not wanting to bring him to market looking like a scandal. Still, the young man winced and muttered to himself when he saw the stripes.

"This way," he said when they were both ready. They walked together through the marketplace. "My name is Emrist," he told Trevyn. "Not that it matters, I suppose," he added vaguely. "Though, of course, you can hear. . . ."

They turned out of the marketplace into a crooked alleyway that wound up terraced slopes between houses perched precariously on their foundations. At the top of the steep hill they paused for breath. If Trevyn had looked back, and if he had known, he could have seen Rheged's men entering the marketplace to search for him.

He and his new master traversed a ragged country cut by rocky ridges into patchwork gardens, vineyards, and orchards. They stopped often to rest, for Emrist was not strong. Toward noon they shared bread and cheese and a flask of weak wine. It seemed to Trevyn that Emrist was not a rich man. He went afoot, though easily tired, and his tunic and sandals looked plain and worn. Trevyn wondered how he had got the gold to buy him, and, indeed, why he had bought him at all. For his manner was gentle, and he did not seem to be the sort of person who would lightly own another.

By early afternoon they had moved into wilder country, where habitations were fewer and growth cluttered the meadows until they were really young forests. The look of the land made Trevyn wary, and he was not entirely surprised when robbers ran at them, screeching, out of the brush. There were four of the rustic brigands, each armed with a wicked-looking sword. If Trevyn had been by himself he might have run; his fray with the slavers had taught him caution. But there was Emrist to be thought of. . . . Trevyn lunged under a whistling sword, wrested the weapon from its owner, aware that Emrist had already fallen. He killed the robber with a swift stroke to the throat and turned on the other three, frantically beating them back from Emrist's prostrate form. In a moment they rallied and circled him; he took some cuts then. But he had been trained to use the sword against odds and soon felled them. Though it sickened him to do so, he made certain that each robber was dead before he turned his back on them.

Emrist was sitting in the roadway, holding his head and looking pale as a wraith. "What are you?" he whispered. "You fought like a King's man."

Trevyn laid down the bloody sword before he went near him, not wishing to alarm him. He kneeled and probed his master with careful fingers. A welt was rising on Emrist's head, but nothing else was wrong that Trevyn could find. Yet Emrist reeled and went limp under his touch. Though he hated the thought of staying any longer in these unfriendly parts, Trevyn could see nothing for it but to make camp. He slung Emrist over his shoulders and carried him into the woods, looking for shelter.

If it had not been for fear, the night would have seemed luxurious to Trevyn. He found everything he needed on the bodies of the slain robbers. In the shelter of a rocky scar he made a fire with their flint and steel. He set rabbit snares with the lacings of their sandals. Later he warmed himself against the night chill in a looted cloak while he carved his dinner with a looted knife. It was the first fresh meat he had eaten in over two months. Bits of bread, too, had been in the robbers' pockets. Trevyn saved them for the morrow.

Throughout the night he sat by the fire with naked sword in hand, starting at every shadow. Strange chance, he mused, that he, a king's son, should have become a robber of robbers. At his side lay Emrist, also wrapped in "borrowed" cloaks. From time to time the young man moaned and gazed half fearfully until Trevyn soothed him with a glance and a touch of cooling water. Strangest of chance that bound him to this slaveholding Tokarian! Not that he could ever desert a helpless man, but—was a courteous word so rare in this eastern land, a friendly glance so precious, that Emrist had sent such a flood of comfort to his heart?

Emrist awoke fully in the morning, and though he sat up painfully, the dazed look was gone from his eyes. Trevyn gave him the bread and the little wine that remained. He ate slowly, but finished it all. "Did you not sleep at all?" he asked.

Trevyn cast a wry glance at the woods all around them.

"Ay, it is an evil place," Emrist agreed. "I would rather be far away from here." He hesitated. "Good friend, it should be no more than a half-day's journey—do you think you could help me home?"

Trevyn nodded his willingness, then pointed inquiringly. Emrist laughed.

"Of course, you do not know the way! Or you would have

taken me yesterday, hah?" Trevyn grinned and nodded. "Well, it's not hard," Emrist continued. "We just follow the road. It turns to a track, then to a trail, then at last to a little path through the forest, and it ends at the house, in the clearing atop the hill. My sister will welcome us. She must be frightened by now, though she is a strong-hearted woman. There are no neighbors to comfort her. Even the robbers do not come near the haunt—" Emrist stopped short. He had spoken with dreamy happiness about his sister and his home, but now he believed that he had said too much. He stared at Trevyn in open terror.

"I beg you, do not leave me," he whispered.

Trevyn shook his head and laid a hand on his master's arm in assurance. He filled their flask at a nearby stream, and he cut Emrist a staff to lean on. Trevyn still wore his looted cloak, and he belted his captured sword to his waist, but the rest of the robbers' gear they left behind. Trevyn helped Emrist pick his way back to the road and strode beside him restively as he slowly moved away from the scene of carnage. They could not leave this place soon enough to suit him. After a while they had put it well behind them, and Trevyn's impatience quieted. But Emrist's pace grew slower yet, and soon Trevyn had to support him with a hand under his elbow. It was not yet midday when Emrist began to topple. Trevyn caught him easily and did what he had expected to have to do before then: rolled his cloak as a pillow for Emrist's head and slung the man upon his back.

Even carrying his master, Trevyn could now move far more quickly. He strode along, sharpening all his senses for any sign of danger. That his new master lived in a haunted place had been the best of good news to him. No evil would trouble him there. Only people versed in the mysteries of the Beginning could brave the haunt, and only those of good heart. But what sort of man, then, must this Emrist be that he lived among the shades?

At long last he felt the heaviness of Otherness around him and passed through the haunt to a feeling of warm welcome, even a sense of coming home. Everything was just as Emrist had said. The track had long since dwindled to a trail, and now a mere path wound up a steep hill amid tall, silent trees.

Trevyn followed it until he saw light ahead and the gables of a building. Bent under Emrist's weight, he entered the clearing. An old man looked up from his gardening, stared, and scuttled inside. A moment later a dark-clad woman came running out.

"What has happened? Oh, Em!" she was crying, but as Trevyn only stared at her she took control. "This way," she gestured, and he followed her inside, up a narrow flight of stairs. At the top, she indicated a room furnished only with a table, a cot, and a sturdy wooden chest. Trevyn laid Emrist on the shabby bed and gently turned the man's limp head to show the bruise. The woman nodded. "I shall care for him."

In the doorway stood the old man and an equally ancient woman, both shaky and gaping. Their mistress spoke to them firmly. "Dorcas, pray find our friend something to eat. Jare, prepare a room for our guest. I shall see you later." She almost shooed them all from the room. As Trevyn turned to leave, he saw Emrist's sister reach to unlock the wooden chest at the bedside.

In the kitchen old Dorcas set about heating Trevyn some dinner. She was obviously frightened of him, so he kept away from her, sitting still and looking about him. The house was simply but strongly built of stone and timbers, with a low roof and small windows—not a rich man's home, by any means. Emrist's bed had been hard enough, his chamber bare of comforts, and Trevyn saw nothing downstairs either that betokened ease. No rugs or draperies softened the floor or walls. Instead, traces of mice lay about, and cobwebs covered the windows and rafters. On the table sat some greens and a few onions. Little food for much labor, especially for the old ones. Trevyn could understand why the cleaning was neglected. And Emrist was sickly, it seemed. . . . But had he come all this way, then, just to serve such as these?

The old woman brought him a bowl of thick bean soup, setting it hastily before him and backing away as if wary of his reaction. But Trevyn was eager enough to eat it, and Dorcas watched him with less alarm; a hungry man was something she could deal with. Presently her husband, old Jare, came downstairs with a bundle of clothing, offering it to Trevyn as hesitantly as his wife had offered the soup. Trevyn took a tunic and tried to slip it over his head, but it was too small and threatened to tear. Smiling, he shook his head and handed it back. The old man retreated back up the stairs. His wife busied herself banging pots in the scullery. Suddenly, achingly, Trevyn felt the limitations of his muteness. These two would welcome no help from him for a while yet. He wandered to where a rude bench stood against the wall and draped himself over it, only for a moment, to rest. . . .

Hours later, Trevyn awoke with a start to a gentle touch. Dark had fallen, and flickering oil lamps cast a dim light. Over him stood Emrist's dark-haired sister, rendered mysterious by the night. "He wishes to speak with you," she said, and Trevyn rose swiftly to follow her.

Emrist sat propped up by pillows, with flasks and tumblers on the table near his bed. He looked much stronger, though pale. Trevyn knelt at his bedside, so that their eyes met.

"I never expected to see you here," Emrist said in tones low with wonder. "I thought perhaps you would bring me as far as the—barrier—and then drop me and bolt. If chance had favored, Maeve here might have found me. For that I would have owed you thanks enough. But this—it stuns me."

Trevyn gestured deprecation. Emrist regarded him long and thoughtfully.

"Surely you have a name, but I do not know it," he said. "I will call you Freca, if I may, for you are a brave youth."

Keen interest sprang up in Tervyn's mind. It was an *elwedeyn* name—that is to say, in the Old Language. Even as he nodded his consent, Trevyn looked on Emrist with new eyes. Emrist returned his gaze, and puzzlement creased his brown.

"I cannot believe you cannot speak!" he exclaimed. "There is song in your movements and epic in your glance. What are you, Brave One?" Trevyn stiffened in consternation; he had shown too much. But Emrist went on. "It does not matter, you know, that I have bought you. You are no slave. You are a free man. Fill your stomach with us as long as you will, or go where you will." He turned to his sister. "Is it not so, Maeve?"

"Even so," she answered.

Something let go inside Trevyn. Shackles he had not known

were gripping his spirit melted away. He forgot his muteness, but his thankfulness was too great for words; this man had just healed the deepest hurt he had ever known. He seized Emrist's hand and clung to it like a child, felt tears fall. He hid his face in the sheet. Frail fingers touched his hair.

"Ay, they were foul enough to you," Emrist said, and his voice held a sharp edge of wrath. "All because you would not hang your head and play the dog. But you stood like a caged eagle. You were free before I met you, Freca."

"He is spent, Em," said Maeve in her cool woman's voice, "and so are you. Let me show him to his room, and then I will come to fix you a draught."

Trevyn was more dazed than tired, but he followed her willingly. She led him to a room even barer than Emrist's. Still, the bed beckoned with pillows and blankets. Trevyn settled himself swiftly and lay puzzling while his tears of relief dried on his face. What was he to do? He did not know where to go. Surely he had come to this place for some reason other than to leave. . . . There was something special about Emrist. Also, the man needed him; for some secret reason, he needed a mute slave. Well, he would have a mute servant, Trevyn decided, at least for a while. There was the price of his redemption to be considered—much gold from a man who was not rich. He would like to make it up to him somehow. For the time, Trevyn wanted nothing better than to serve this Emrist in whatever way he could.

Chapter Three

For the next several days Trevyn worked feverishly, heaving rocks out of the garden for old Jare, snaring rabbits and quail for Dorcas. After a few days, Maeve gave him a plain tunic of coarse cloth, and knee breeches, and crude sandals of leather and wood. Scarcely finery, but it made him feel the more indebted. Only at mid of day, when the sun beat down, would he cease from his voluntary labors to bathe in a dark, mirrorlike pool that lay in a hollow amidst the towering forest trees.

By the time Emrist got up from his bed, a week after his injury, Trevyn had made his mark on the household. The cobwebs were gone from the rafters. Old Jare whistled tunelessly under his breath. Dorcas set more food on the table, and even the stoical Maeve moved about her tasks humming contentedly. Emrist was still weak; for a few days he came downstairs only to sit and watch. But on a rainy day, seeing Trevyn restlessly rubbing the grime from the small window panes, he spoke to him.

"It seems you will stay with us yet a while, Freca."

Trevyn was almost startled into speech, but he merely shrugged his shoulders.

"You are a very beaver for industry," remarked Emrist. "It is not necessary, you know. We won't turn you out."

Trevyn only grinned at him. Emrist sighed.

"Well, since you have decided to be of use, come help me today. It's time I was getting back to work."

With considerable curiosity as to what that work might be, Trevyn followed him up the stairs. They entered Emrist's chamber, and Trevyn waited for him to go, perhaps, to the locked chest. But instead Emrist strode to a corner and wrestled a moment with a rough wooden plank of the wall. Reluctantly, a panel slid, and another narrow staircase was revealed.

Eagerly, Trevyn followed his master up to the dusty garret. The place was close and windowless, though some light seeped in through the leaky wallboards. Emrist lit a pungent oil lamp that sent soot streaking toward the already blackened rafters. In its yellowish glow, Trevyn could see great numbers of parchments and leather-bound books ranked on splintery shelving. Fans of dried plants rustled overhead, and all kinds of formless rubble lay on the floor. Under the low peak of the roof stood a worktable cluttered with pots and urns and little jars, a brazier, and some metal caldrons. Trevyn recognized a scholarly disorder similar to Hal's, but somehow warmer and more secret. Emrist poked at some of his earthenware jugs.

"Potions for my interminable illnesses," he grumbled, "old now, and weak. And dried-up paints and dyes, and spoiled perfumes, and messes I have forgotten the meaning of." He rumaged through the containers, picking out a score or more and heaping them in Trevyn's arms. "Take them out among the trees and let the rain have them. Wash the jars and bring them back. But do not put your fingers to your mouth, hah?"

For many weeks thereafter Trevyn worked with Emrist in the cramped garret. Sometimes he ground minerals or dried plants in the mortar, taxing work that Emrist was glad to leave to him. Emrist was too easily tired to go roaming in the woods, so Trevyn would search out the plants he needed. Trevyn often wondered what to think of his master, who seemed to have knowledge of every kind of magical lore. Day after day the frail man compounded potions with long labor and greatest care. But no one came to buy his charms from him, not in this haunt, and Trevyn had found none of the strange trappings of sorcery among his things such as Hal had described from his days in Nemeton. No censers and ceremonial robes, no black-handled swords or talismans of bright metal. In fact, Trevyn doubted if high magic could be performed in the littered garret, which Emrist refused to let him clean. Spirits of ancient might would only come to surroundings suitable to their greatness.

Still, Trevyn wondered. Sometimes the two of them made candles in many subtle colors, delicately-scented tapers molded from the rare and precious beeswax no ordinary person could afford. He found traces of chalk on the floor sometimes, in strange star and circle designs. And always on the worktable a kettle of salt stood—big, stone-white crystals. Salt could never be used in any evil spell and was essential to any good one.

In time Trevyn became convinced that Emrist was not merely a dabbler in hidden lore but a master working cautiously toward some definite goal. One day, when supper was late because of a balky kitchen fire, Trevyn observed Emrist surreptitiously prodding the sodden wood into flame with a mere flick of his fingertips. Another time, Trevyn awoke in the dark of night to see his master padding down the corridor with only his raised forefinger, glowing eerily, for a light. After that, seeming to intuit that Trevyn knew his secret, Emrist showed his power more openly. He would set a streamer of nonconsuming fire in midair to read by or send objects scooting across the garret into his servant's startled hands. He could bring forth miniature whirlwinds out of stagnant air and showers of rain from clouds of arid smoke. He could make rocks split, make dirt heave and roil like bubbling broth. These were his simpler magics; to command any of them, he spoke no word, but only gestured with his graceful hands. Trevyn felt sure that Emrist was not practicing, that he did not need practice, such was the ease of his power. He had observed his master eyeing him in the light of strange, leaping flames, and he felt that Emrist must be testing his fortitude for the next step toward the hidden goal.

Apparently, Emrist was satisfied. One day he began to

summon the spirits of the elements, speaking to them in words of the Elder Tongue. Trevyn felt the ancient call and power of that language go through him like a tide of fire; all his heart must have leaped to his eyes. Emrist froze in midspell, staring at him. *"Selte a ir,"* he whispered, still in the same tongue. "Speak to me."

Trevyn only answered his stare. So long had he shackled his tongue, not speaking even to the little creatures of the forest, that his own will constrained him to silence like a brank. Even as his heart went out to Emrist, he felt that constraint stubbornly strain against the command his master had spoken. Command or plea? Hurt was in Emrist's eyes.

"Do you not yet trust me, Freca?"

Brave one, he had named him. Trevyn felt himself plentifully brave to fight, to endure, to strive, but not to love. At that moment he would far sooner have faced the fiercest of warlocks than the gentle sorcerer before him. His cowardice bound him helpless, sickened him. He lowered his eyes and sank his head in his hands. Emrist's face, had he seen, went bleak with disappointment and pity, but his voice was calm.

"Ay, they served you ill enough," he said softly, more to himself than to Trevyn. "No wonder you clench yourself against them still. Bide easy, Freca. Time will have the healing of you."

But time only locked Trevyn more into his muteness; time and Maeve, in a way. Emrist's sister was a sturdy woman who moved impassively about the never-ending work of her household. Trevyn could not guess her age; her face was unlined, but hardened with years and toil and some quality he could not name. Her body was always hidden in folds of dark cloth, even in the heat. She spoke seldom. Trevyn paid her little mind after the first few days, and he never expected to see her naked in the light of a waxing moon.

She came to him in his bedchamber, with her dark hair falling softly around her shoulders. Trevyn woke with a start and gaped, unable for a moment to think who she was. Moonlight and her nakedness had changed her; she was all sheen and surface, pearly and unfathomable, her breasts like argent globes, full and high. Her face was as blank as

Gwern's, her eyes pools of purple shadow. She sat on the bed by his side and wordlessly ran questing fingers along the smooth skin of his neck. He trembled under her touch, gulping and scarcely moving as she drew back the covers and fitted the alabaster curves of her hips onto his. Her body was thick and firm, supple from her labors. He sighed and shifted his hands to her breasts, letting her take him.

In no way could Trevyn consider Maeve his conquest. She cradled his body as a harper cradles his harp, played upon him expertly, played against him with catlike warmth and grace, and both of them as mute as the watching moon. Later she left him with catlike indifference, drifting out without a backward glance. After she was gone, Trevyn's thoughts turned unaccountably to Meg. What was she like under her baggy blouses and full peasant skirts? Fleetingly, he envisioned rosebuds and dew; he remembered the butterfly tremor of her lips when he had kissed her. Maeve's lips had been as firm as her competent hands. Suddenly, Trevyn was fiercely glad that he would not or could not speak. He wanted never to whisper endearments to Emrist's white-breasted sister.

In the days that followed, Maeve moved about the house as serenely as ever, with no change in her manner or her sober face. Trevyn found it difficult to think of her as the same woman who came to him, palely shimmering, at night. She came for the seven nights of the swelling moon; Trevyn found himself longing for Meg whenever he embraced her. When the moon had reached the full, she left him to come no more. He did not expect her or seek her out in nights that followed. She had pleasured him to satiety. He wondered guiltily how much Emrist knew, for he had sometimes suspected that the sorcerer had uncommon means of knowledge, and he had constrained himself to keep even his thoughts buried deep. But Emrist showed no sign of knowledge or displeasure.

The two of them still spent their days in the garret, invoking the disembodied essences of the elements. Trevyn practiced walking through their focus of being in the room. He found that the moistness of water did not wet him or blasts of air so much as ruffle his hair, just as he had long since learned that he would not be slain by the spirits of the dead. The invocation of fire pained him, terribly; he bore it, and found that his flesh did not shrivel. In a way, earth was more difficult to withstand. Dense, alien, crushing, an almost hostile presence choked him. Trevyn struggled for breath, but he felt Emrist's eyes upon him even through his heavy covering of insubstantial soil, and shame stiffened his spine.

After that day, Emrist sat for a week in the garret staring at nothing that Trevyn could see, waving him away when he came near. Trevyn was used to such trances. Hal had been accustomed to lose himself in visions of Elwestrand or the loveliness that had once been Isle. So Trevyn judged that Emrist was also refreshing himself in some such private retreat, gathering himself for the next drive at the hidden goal. He had seen how spell-saying sapped the magician's small physical strength.

In fact, Emrist was visiting a less pleasant place than he imagined. But Trevyn was glad enough to leave him alone, to escape the stifling garret and work in the outer air. It was the height of summer. Though cool breezes were still to be found beneath the trees, the sun beat down fiercely on the garden. Old Jare suffered from it and kept to the shade, but Trevyn gloried in the sunlight. He stripped to his loincloth as he carried water for the wilting squash and beans. His skin turned golden brown and shone with his sweat; his hair, long uncut, lay startlingly bright against his bronzed neck.

Maeve stood at the upper windows sometimes and looked on. She did not stir when one day Emrist came up and stood beside her.

"So you take your pleasure in watching these days," he remarked placidly.

"Ay," Maeve replied. "It's far enough away here that I cannot see the scars. They hurt me even to look at. Praise be, they didn't show in the moonlight."

"Have you noticed the scars of his legs and shoulders?" Emrist asked. "Not the whip welts—"

"I know the ones you mean. The vermin branded him also, it seems."

"Nay, it was not the slavers who did that. The whip stripes lie over the brands, and you know the odd, jagged shapes of them—do you think perhaps some animal attacked him and the wounds were seared for safety?''

Maeve was not listening. "Yet he moves with grace and joy in spite of it all," she murmured. As her eyes followed Trevyn, her brother was startled by the softness, almost the beauty, that transformed her time-tempered face to that of the girl he scarcely remembered. Emrist frowned in consternation.

"Do not place your contentment too much on him, Maeve," he admonished her softly. "Only the One knows what may happen in the next few days."

Her face hardened, and she turned from the window to face him. "I always knew that he came but to go," she answered. "You are ready, then?"

"Ay, but I have decided I must do that alone. Freca would stand me in good stead; he is like a lion for bravery. But his soul has been bruised, and I think he is younger than he seems—" Emrist spoke with fumbling haste. "I will not risk scarring him anew."

"But, Em," Maeve protested in exasperation, "have you forgotten why you bought him, a mute? To help you, no matter what the risk? The stakes are too high to think of one soul overmuch."

"Using him would make the stakes higher yet. Have you not sensed that he is of the old order? His eyes speak the Elder Tongue, though his mouth cannot. That is why I say he will be leaving us. He has some destiny to fulfill; I think he came here only to heal."

"Of course I know he is a special one," Maeve flared. "More special than you imagine. But what of your own special destiny? You must not spend yourself without support. Let me stand by you."

"You know Wael scorns and hates womankind," Emrist replied grimly. "Fear, perhaps, in scornful guise, for woman's love is a strong magic. . . . But most likely he would not come before you. Or if he did, your presence would only add fuel to his fire."

"Ay, the more cursed he," answered Maeve impatiently. "Well, then, send Freca on his way and get another mute! Only a few months will have been lost."

Emrist shook his head. "I must invoke Wael tonight."

"Why, in the name of the One?" She was ashen.

"Because I have seen—they have found the brooch of the Islendais Prince."

That day, when Trevyn entered the garret, he found Emrist reading from a parchment dark with age. Trevyn made shift, as he had often done before, to glance at the title, and what he saw shook him like a blow. "On the Transferring of the Living Soul." The crabbed old letters seemed to sear themselves on his eyes, for at their head leered the emblem of a leaping wolf.

"I need nothing, Freca," Emrist said without looking up, and Trevyn turned and went in a daze. He wandered out of the house and into the forest, stopping when he reached a quiet place to sit and compose his reeling thoughts. It did not occur to him to break his silence, to speak to Emrist and ask his help. His long silence had made him a spy in this household, and now his shame guarded the secret.

Trevyn's curiosity had often been piqued by his snatched moments with Emrist's lore. The properties of wingless flight. . . . The seeking of sprites. . . . The science of griffins and firedrakes. . . . Any of these things, and many more, he would gladly have studied. But he had not let Emrist know that he could read, for a mute who can read and write is a mute in tongue only. Trevyn had refrained from reading in secret; he clung at least to some shreds of his honor. But in this matter of the wolf, where life and kingdom might someday be at stake, he found his honor to be of smaller concern. He returned to the house with a calm face and a plan.

He lay awake that night until all sound in the household had long since ceased. Then he arose and made his way stealthily to Emrist's chamber. He was not too afraid of awakening Emrist; he knew that the magician took draughts to sleep, to counter the pains of his frail body. Trevyn crept into the room, heading for the garret and the ancient parchment. But surprise tingled through him. Emrist was not in his bed, nor had the coverings been disturbed. The bright moon showed that plainly. The forbidden chest stood open, nearly empty. Trevyn ran up to the garret. Emrist was not there; nor did Trevyn's hasty search find him the parchment he needed.

For all Trevyn knew, Emrist might venture out every night. Sorcerers were supposed to be partial to moonlight and stars. Yet Trevyn's very sinews sang of danger, and he descended the stairs hastily to the kitchen. Emrist was not there. Trevyn went outside and studied the night with all his senses, searching for a sign. Then he set off rapidly into the woods.

At some distance from the house, just when Trevyn was doubting the direction he had chosen, his night-sharpened eyes glimpsed a ghost of murky light somewhere ahead. He hurried on, sometimes wondering if he really saw it, so faint was the yellowish glimmer amid the white moonlight. Then he reached the brown woodland pool, which lay in the shadow of a steep rise, and his way was made clear to him. The light seeped from behind a tangle of vines and bushes halfway up the wooded scar; it streaked its pale shadow across the mirrorlike surface of the water and mingled with the reflected moon like an arrow piercing a swan. Trevyn skirted the pool and silently climbed up the rise, came to the entrance of a concealed cave that was curtained by living greenery.

Within, the air looked thick with sultry light. A malodorous smoke seeped out with the light and almost set Trevyn to coughing. Once he had caught his breath and accustomed his stinging eyes to the sulfurous gloom, he could see Emrist within. The magician wore a flowing, shimmering black robe that must have come out of his mysterious chest, for Trevyn had never seen it before. He had a rude stump of wood for a table, and on it stood black, flaring candles, smoldering saffron-colored bits of incense, an earthenware mug of water, and a tarnished metal dish of salt. Emrist held the parchment with the lupine seal, reading it, the lines of his face taut with strain. It seemed he was preparing for the summoning of some particularly difficult spirit.

As Trevyn watched, full of foreboding but uncertain what to do, Emrist began his incantation. He raised his mobile hands and half closed his eyes in concentration, chanting words in some tongue unknown to Trevyn, words even harsher than the unlovely language of Tokar: *"Zaichos kargen—Roch un hrozig—ib grocchus—"* On the parchment before him, the emblem of the leaping wolf glowed eerily bright.

Trevyn felt something coming through the air from the south and east, something of such darkness that he thought it would blot out the moon. It smote him with fear, terrible fear such as no spirit had ever caused in him, fear even beyond screaming. He silently trembled against the unfeeling earth as the focus of evil passed beside him and into the cave. Then he heard Emrist catch his breath, and, moving with leaden reluctance, he forced himself to look within. A shape of nightmare was growing in the shadows of the cave, a being of obscurest gloom that displaced the haze of Emrist's making. Trevyn felt its terror as a crushing weight that robbed him of breath or movement. It was a spectral wolf, substance only of blackness, huge, looming, floating forward, with eyes and bared teeth of flame. Emrist snatched up a handful of salt and flung it at the thing, spoke to it in the Ancient Tongue, words of exorcism: *"Este nillen, gurn olet, kenne Aene."* ["Be no more, evil thing, in the name of the One."] But his words were a trembling whisper, and had no effect. With a wrenching effort, Trevyn glanced at his master and saw him sway on his feet. The shape of shadow and fire was nearly on him, and his words stopped with a choke as he caught at the cave wall for support.

Sudden fury swept up Trevyn like a gale tearing a ship from its moorings. By the One, he would not again be unmanned by some wolfish apparition! He leaped into the inner thickness, to Emrist's side, and words long pent burst from him with a power he had not known he possessed: "Begone, vile phantom, and trouble him no more! Begone, dark thing!" In his passion, Trevyn lunged at the grinning specter to throttle it, but he blinked; his hand passed through emptiness, and his enemy vanished.

Beside him, Emrist leaned against earth with lidded eyes. Trevyn lifted him and, grasping a candle in his free hand, supported him out of the cave and down the slope to lay him by the pool. Emrist gasped painfully at the clean night air. Trevyn cradled his head in silence, dabbing water on his face and rubbing his bony chest. Presently, Emrist's breathing eased, and he opened his eyes. Wonder grew in them.

"Alberic!" he exclaimed in the Old Language. "No wonder Maeve went to you! I should have known it long ago."

Though he had never heard the name before, Trevyn understood its meaning: elf ruler, spirit ruler, eagle King and unicorn King. But he did not know why Emrist should call him by that name.

"Nay," he replied gently in the same tongue, "my name is Trevyn."

"Your sooth-name is Alberic," Emrist murmured, gazing up at him.

Trevyn could not doubt him. Though Emrist was not much older than himself, he seemed old as Isle just then, and wise as any seer. A warm ache of gratitude filled Trevyn, making him blink and tighten his arms around the frail man. Once again Emrist had given him back to himself and like a father had named him.

"Blood, what am I thinking of!" Suddenly urgent, Emrist struggled to sit up. "My lord, you are in great peril."

"Ay," Trevyn agreed regretfully, "that wolfish thing will tell its master of my whereabouts. I must leave, and quickly."

"Worse than that. They have got your brooch!"

Trevyn frowned in puzzlement, knowing he had left his brooch with Meg. "Who?"

"Rheged and that warlock Wael. They have had men hunting you these many weeks, and yesterday I saw that they had found it—" Emrist lost coherence in his earnestness. "And I, the dolt, not to realize it was you! Haven't you felt it tug, my lord? He can draw a soul to him from any such belonging, and the body of necessity with it, just as he drew the wolf-boat by a splinter of the figurehead—"

Trevyn's brow creased anew. "I have felt nothing. Can the Sight have misled you, Emrist?"

He mused. "Perhaps it was sight of future, not of present—but the peril is the same. I heard them gloating, and I saw the brooch in their hands. It was in the half-sun shape of Veran's fame, golden, with jeweled rays, a kingly thing. There was no mistaking it."

Trevyn struck his forehead with his palm. "They are mistaken even so," he exclaimed hoarsely. "It's my father's! He only lent it to me. . . . Tides and tempests, Emrist, I must get it back at once! What could happen to him?"

Emrist's eyes, full of horror, gave him answer enough. "I will come with you," he said.

Trevyn bit his lip in dismay, for he knew Emrist's traveling pace. Though he was reluctant to hurt one to whom he owed every thanks, his fear for Alan firmed his answer. "Nay. I must go with all speed."

"Then you will go with all speed into disaster!" cried an unexpected voice. "What will you do when you come to Kantukal, indeed?" Trevyn and Emrist stared as Maeve entered their little circle of light, but she ignored their discomfiture in her concern. "If your father the King is of such stuff as you, it will be many days before Wael's spell can have much effect. Perhaps it has not yet even begun. After you two come to Kantukal, there should still be time enough for Em to thwart Wael's scheming."

"Maeve," her brother interposed mildly, "how do you come to be here?"

"Did you think I would sleep through this night? I heard Freca leave and followed as soon as I could. I was loath to interrupt, loath to spy, and yet loath to steal away; so I hovered near, like a moth at the lamp."

Trevyn laughed shakily. "I know what you mean. I have been such a moth these many weeks past, afraid to singe my wings. . . . But Maeve, would you not rather have Emrist by you here and safe?"

"There was little safety for him here tonight." She met his eyes quite candidly. "And though he is frail of body, Freca, his power is a giant in him."

"His name is Trevyn," Emrist corrected her. "He who shall rule as Alberic, son of Alan, of the line of Laueroc—"

"'Freca' will do well. If we are to go a-courting to Kantukal, you cannot be my-lording me." Trevyn could not say what had changed his mind, unless it was the wisdom he had seen in Maeve's eyes. But he felt assurance at once that what he did was right for Alan as well as for Emrist.

"—of Isle," went on Emrist, unperturbed. "Heir also of Hal, of the line of Veran of Welas, King of the Setting Sun—"

"Spare me." Trevyn got to his feet. "I'll go fetch your things from the cave."

"Leave them there till they rot," Emrist replied bitterly. "I'll use them no more."

"The parchment? I would like to read it, if I may."

The magician hesitated. "It is a very evil thing," he answered slowly. "But it may yet be of use, I dare say."

Trevyn made his way up to the cave in the dark, leaving them the candle. He found the entrance mostly by the smell of pungent smoke. The other candles had drowned in their wax, and the incense had subsided to ashes, but still there was light within the cave—a small, spectral light. It had been no trick of Trevyn's mind that the emblem of the leaping wolf shone with the same warmthless shimmer as the death-lights flickering over a marsh. It almost seemed to move before his eyes, and the mouth gaped, glinting with ranked teeth. Trevyn stared at the thing awhile before he took hold of the parchment by a far corner. He rolled it so that the emblem disappeared inside, and, grateful for the darkness, made his way back to the others.

"What is her name?" Maeve asked as she and Trevyn worked in the kitchen later that night.

"Who?"

"Your sweetheart. The one you dreamed about sometimes as you lay with me." There was no bitterness in her voice, and she glanced with some surprise at his burning face. "There is no need for shame!"

"Her name is Meg," Trevyn replied slowly. "She is a little peasant who lives by the Forest near Lee. . . . I don't know why she cozens my mind so."

"There is no need for a reason." She was packing food for their journey, and Emrist was asleep; his adventure had left him exhausted. On the morrow, he and Trevyn would start toward Kantukal. But Trevyn hardly knew how to take leave of Maeve.

"It is true, I have loved you in my way," she remarked, reading his thoughts again. "But my way is only the way of the wild things that know their seasons. I am bound by nothing, and no one owns me, or is owned. . . . Go from here in all peace, Alberic."

She had made him her king, now. So, since he had nothing to say, he nodded and left her there.

Chapter Four

With first light, Trevyn and Emrist took to the road. Trevyn wore the sword he had won from the robbers, and he carried the wolfish parchment in a fold of leather, gingerly, as if it might burn. As they walked, Emrist explained to him about the cult of the Wolf.

"Wael is chief priest; he speaks for the Wolf." Trevyn nodded in understanding; Hal and Alan had banished such powerful sorcerers from Isle. "So folk raise idols in its honor in Kantukal, and the coffers of its temples grow rich. That is nothing new; there are many such gods. But this one is vile even in the reckoning of Tokarians; its rituals are unspeakable. Human sacrifice is not the worst of it. People live utterly in fear of the Wolf. I have known for months that I must try to—destroy it—"

Emrist faltered to a stop, conscious of the contrast between his slight physique and his brave talk. But Trevyn soberly waited for him to go on. He knew the power and stature of his master.

"So I went to buy a mute," Emrist said at last, "I, who have never bought a slave. I needed someone to stand by me in case my body failed me, someone who could not ever utter the spells, for they are perilous."

"And yet you did not use me?"

"Nay. . . . You had bled, Freca. . . ." Emrist grimaced, mocking himself. "Of course, Maeve offered to help. Truth is, I could not bear to risk either of you. And I wanted to face Wael myself."

"Wael? But you summoned the Wolf."

"Nay, I summoned Wael," Emrist corrected grimly. "There is no Wolf without Wael."

"But what was that black phantom—"

"A thing of smoke and fire. Your hand passed through it unharmed. Any sorcerer could make one as fine—though I confess I was not expecting it last night." Emrist glanced at Trevyn, half laughing, half angry. "Wael has made a fool of me."

"Wael was there?" Trevyn breathed.

"He was there. You felt the fear?"

"Ay, terrible fear." He shuddered at the memory.

"That was the fear of his living spirit, which I summoned. Without its mask of flesh, the evil of his soul overwhelmed us. That and the shock of something not understood." Emrist shook his head ruefully. "How stupid I was to be so taken in!"

"Well, you will have your chance for revenge," Trevyn muttered. He tripped over a twisting root and scarcely noticed the bump, thinking. "Then that was Wael, too, in the laughing wolf in Isle," he finally said.

"I thought teeth made the occasion for those brands!" Emrist exclaimed. "Ay, I do not doubt it."

"How are we to get the brooch back from him, Emrist? What do you know of Wael?"

The magician sat down on a shady bank to answer. Trevyn sat beside him, restraining his impatience at their slow progress.

"I have often watched him by the power of my inner eye," Emrist said when he was settled. "I have seen him with the king, or in court, or at his vile rites, or alone in his chamber. Rheged places much dependence on him, and his days are full of consultation."

Trevyn peered. "And where does he keep the brooch during all this consultation?"

Emrist had to smile at his eagerness. "Why, on him, of course," he answered gently. "Or else the spell would not take."

"On him?" echoed Trevyn numbly.

"Ay, even when he sleeps. It must always touch his skin, you see, to draw. He wears it pinned inside his shirt, facing his stony heart. I saw him pin it there."

"Mother of mercy!" Trevyn swore morosely. "I am likely to need this bloody hacking sword."

"Unless it is a magical sword, it will be of small avail against Wael. Nay, we can only face him with our own poor powers. . . . And what an ass he has made of me!" Emrist sighed hugely. "I might have been slain by sheer, foolish fright last night if it had not been for you. I owe you my thanks, Freca." He spoke the name with warm affection.

Trevyn reddened at the words. "You owe me nothing," he said roughly. "The debt is all mine. What about the gold you gave for me?"

Emrist smiled sheepishly. "That was only sorcerer's gold. I would not use it with honest folk. . . ."

"Why, what becomes of such gold?"

"It vanishes after a little while. . . ." Trevyn threw back his head and laughed, and Emrist joined in, a laugh from the heart that shook his small frame. "Ay, I would like to have seen those slave merchants drubbing each other for the theft of it!" he gasped.

"Is there any chance you could conjure up some horses for us?" Trevyn asked wistfully. "Or even a donkey for yourself?"

"Nay, that would be dishonor." Emrist rose to his feet with dignity. "I can do what I must without such devices. Come, let us be moving."

They traveled more east than south for the time, working their way through a maze of small valleys between wooded slopes. Eventually, following that direction, they would find the broad Way that ran due south to Kantukal. It would make traveling easier, if no less dangerous. Trevyn carried a quarterstaff of green oak as well as his sword, in case they were beset. Though he distrusted these wilds, he knew they must sleep that night, for they had scarcely rested the night before. At dusk he found them a camp within a thicket of cypress, and they watched by turns.

Nothing happened that night. But the next day Emrist's pace was slower, and pain clenched his face. Trevyn gave him the staff to lean on, but he grew weaker hour by hour. Trevyn rubbed his legs for him that evening and prepared him a draught to ease his rest. Sunk in a haze of weariness, Emrist drank what Trevyn gave him without thought or question. In a few minutes he was deeply asleep. Trevyn slung their packs onto his waist, then carefully lifted Emrist, blanket and all, to his back. The moon, nearly at the full, lit his way. Trevyn went softly, hearkening to every sound, for he would have been hard put to protect himself and Emrist if he had been taken unawares. Still, he made good speed, and by morning he found himself in a tamer country, with cottages and garden plots to be seen from time to time.

The sun was high before Emrist stiffened on his back and spoke. "By thunder, what is happening here?" Trevyn set him down and grinned at him.

"Did you rest well?"

"Like a babe in the cradle, being rocked." Emrist looked around in bewilderment. "We must be nearly to the Way! Did you not sleep at all?"

"I'll sleep tonight. Come, let us eat!" They had reached a deserted stretch, where the path wound between dirt banks topped by beech and oak; homesteads showed only in the distance. Trevyn swiftly settled himself on the ground. He was very hungry after his night's journey, already breaking the last of their bread as Emrist sat, but his hand stopped midway to his mouth as he saw the shadow on Emrist's face. "What is it?" he asked.

"Nothing." Emrist forced a smile. "Eat."

Trevyn put the bread down. "Not until you tell me what is wrong."

Emrist gestured irritably. "A foolish thing. It vexes me that once again you bear my weight for me. A fine adventurer I make, who must be carried to the fray!"

"You are man enough, Emrist," Trevyn replied quietly. "You do not need strength of the body for that. I thought you knew."

"Most of me knows." Emrist smiled, warmly this time. "But there is no such thing as a man without foolish pride. . . . Never mind me, Freca. You did what you must."

"Just as you shall, when the time comes."

Trevyn gulped his portion of food. Emrist ate more slowly, picking his way through the meager meal as if it were a puzzle he had to solve. Trevyn watched him, brooding. He couldn't really carry Emrist to Kantukal; he knew he was going to have to find him a horse somehow or they would never reach the court city in time. They were out of food now, and they had no money to buy any with. The journey seemed impossible, the quest itself impossible. He wondered if Emrist dreaded the confrontation with Wael as much as he did.

"Emrist," he asked suddenly, "can you teach me magic to face Wael with?"

Emrist looked up with thoughtful amber eyes. "You can learn magic, perhaps," he said slowly, "but I cannot teach you. Magic cannot be taught. It must always be learned anew."

"But why?" Trevyn raised his brows in bewilderment. "Are there not schools for magic, where spells are taught, and rituals, and symbols—"

"Schools!" Emrist's scorn burst from him. "Schools where the riches of the whole world and beyond are boxed into tidy charts—'a' is for *alembic*, and ten is the perfect number. Bah! Don't they know that an emerald is not just the stone of the Lady? Everything of here or Other connects, and not in neat little boxes, either—or circles, or spirals, or any design a man can understand. Not even the mighty mandorla." Emrist subsided a bit. "Really, more than two circles must join. . . . Nay, it's only Wael's kind of magic that you'll learn in such schools, Freca. Even a villain can memorize certain ancient words, the puissant words of the Elder Tongue, and if power of self-will is in him. . . ."

"So that is how a man such as Wael comes to be a

sorcerer." Trevyn glanced at Emrist mischievously, prodding him toward further asperity. "I dare say he has a black-handled sword—"

"Ay, an athane, and robes of every color, gloriously embroidered, and gongs and censers without number. All that is good for show. But I have always scorned even to make the ceremonial circle; why should I need to protect myself? And to do any magic, either good or ill, only one thing is necessary: to call upon the dusky goddess of the Sable Moon."

"The great goddess?" Trevyn yelped, shocked. He had expected Emrist to call on Aene.

"Nay, nay, only Menwy of the Sable Moon. She is only one phase of the moon, and one of the Many Names, though all are in her, nevertheless. But if one knew the true-name of the goddess, that power would encompass every pattern and power and peril."

"But someone has told me that name," Trevyn protested. "It is Alys—"

A tremendous crash and rending noise engulfed them with its vibrations, washed over them from every side. Earth moved under them and split around them; rocks slid from the slopes above and mighty trees toppled with a roar. Trevyn crouched over Emrist, shielding him with his arms, as stones and branches hailed around. A huge oak thundered to rest beside them, lifting a canopy over them with its trembling, upraised limbs. Then gradually the clamor subsided, and earth trickled to a standstill. Utter silence fell.

Trevyn and Emrist got cautiously to their feet, gazing wide-eyed at the destruction all around them. Only the little plot of land on which they sat was untouched, as if they had been at the vortex of a mighty storm.

"Where did you ever hear that name?" Emrist gasped. "Don't say it!" he added frantically.

"Gwern told me," Trevyn murmured. "But he said it without any such scene as this."

"Then he, whoever he is, must himself be of godly sort," Emrist declared.

It took them the rest of the day to fight their way out of the devastated patch of woodland. They wondered, at times, whether the wreckage stopped with the woods. But they got clear of it at last, and Trevyn was relieved to see that no households had been touched. He and Emrist went hungry that night, for they had found nothing to forage and, oddly, no animals killed by the uproar they had weathered. Trevyn's snares, set in the underbrush around their camp, netted them nothing. The situation put Emrist in a bad humor.

"You knew that name," he grumbled, "a name of incomparable power, and you let yourself by flogged half to death. . . . And played at being mute, forsooth! Who is your enemy, Prince of Isle?"

Trevyn creased his brow at him. "Why, Wael, of course!"

"Wael is just a silly old man," Emrist snapped. "He could have slain you in Isle or on shipboard, but he plays at power as some people play at dice, reluctant to consummate the game. Who is your more worthy enemy?"

"Fate, then. The goddess, if you will."

"She is friend or enemy to no man; she is above such dalliance. Guess again."

"Gwern," Trevyn hazarded.

Emrist snorted. "You want to face Wael with magic, and you do not yet even know your own enemy! Prince, what did this—Gwern—tell you about that name?"

"To use it when I had need."

"And when could you have more need than when you were enslaved? You had only to make a proper appeal, and the whips would have turned against their wielders. It is because you mentioned her so offhandedly that she threw things at us earlier. And that is but a taste of her power. We might feel more."

"So she is sending us to bed without our supper," Trevyn retorted. "I'll say 'please' to no such goddess. We Lauerocs call only on the One, and not to turn weapons at our command."

"You are your own enemy, Prince," stated Emrist softly. "Do you really think Aene is not the goddess?"

Trevyn sputtered. "Indeed, ay! Aene can have no name—"

"But all things you can name are in Aene, and Aene is in them. How can you set yourself against any of them? They are part of you as well." Emrist sighed, having vented his spleen, and lapsed into a gentler tone. "Nay, Freca, you are like a mighty castle for endurance, but you will never do true magic until you have learned the wisdom of surrender, the joy of swimming with the tides of your selfhood and your life. Women, many of them, come by that knowledge instinctively, and do not feel the need of chants and charms; they have their own spells. No wonder Wael hates and fears them so."

"Does he call on the goddess to do his kind of magic?" Trevyn asked curiously.

"Only to make her a whore for his own lusts' sake. . . . Nay, Freca, no such thing!" Emrist made startled protest against Trevyn's thought, which he had heard like speech. "You cannot use that name against him. You could bring the castle down on top of us, but, what is worse, if Wael learned that name and survived to use it, he would become invincible. Do not even think of it in his presence." Emrist quirked a wry smile. "I know you are practiced at hiding your thoughts."

"Then how are we to face him?" Trevyn demanded.

"That is as it comes. For your part, I hope that endurance is all that will be necessary, for the time."

The next morning Trevyn awoke to find himself looking into the long, mournful countenance of a horse. Its whiskery nostrils were poised within inches of his face. He reached up to grasp the halter, then scrambled to his feet and looked the beast over. It appeared to be a pack horse that had escaped from some trader's train—hardly a luxury animal, but suitable enough to carry Emrist to Kantukal. And the pack on its back contained a quantity of very barterable goods.

"I think the goddess is over her pique," Trevyn called.

Emrist sat up painfully and stared at the horse with distaste. "Don't press her," he said finally. "We're likely to find ourselves in trouble on that beast's account."

"Nay, I think the Lady has made us a gift of it. Food, Emrist, we shall have food! Come on, get up!"

He badgered Emrist onto the horse's back and traded for bread and cheese with the first cottage wife he could find, making a very bad bargain of it; he didn't care. That day, with Emrist mounted, they went along steadily, reached the Way, and turned south at last, keeping an eye out for kingsmen who might recognize Trevyn. And he was hardly inconspicuous: a golden-haired youth with sword at side leading a mouse-colored, plodding nag on which sat a companion perched atop a packsaddle! Some changes had to be made, and that evening at their campsite they attended to it.

"If you are going to ride," Trevyn decided, "you must look like a horseman."

So Emrist had to wear the sword and a cloak, for rank. He would sit on a gaily patterned blanket. Trevyn attached reins to the horse's halter, hackamore style, and brushed the animal up a bit. In these warm lands, even men of rank went bare-legged and sandal-shod during the summer. Mounted on his nag, Emrist might be able to look the part of a very minor noble.

"And, if it is not too outrageous to be endured," Emrist suggested tartly, "might we sully that crowning glory of yours?"

A more humble servitor went forth the next morning, a sun-browned fellow with flattened, grimy hair of an indeterminate muddy hue. Trevyn would not have appreciated knowing how much, except for his eyes, he looked like Gwern. There was nothing to be done about the sea-green eyes, startlingly bright in his tanned face. He cast them down, as befits a mannerly slave, and took care to lag a step or two behind his master. A horseman traveling with a slave in attendance was no rarity. Kingsmen passed them with a nod.

In a few days they came out of the jagged hill country and onto the great plain that stretched all the way to Kantukal, a flat, dusty expanse planted with famished beans and vines. They traveled it for over a week. Now and then the road crossed streams trickling deep in baked beds, each with a fringe of bright green grass. Everything else looked faded and worn, like a poor woman's dress. The occasional kingsmen on the Way seemed interested only in putting this comfortless region behind them. The sun beat down without surcease. Trevyn and Emrist moved steadily through the days, camped gratefully in the cool of evening, and sometimes talked late into the night. The journey had become an interlude for them, an entity in itself; they did not think too much about the end of it. They clung quietly to the fellowship of the road.

It must have been their tenth day on the plain, walking through the sweltering heat of southern Tokar, that Trevyn felt a breeze and smelled salt in the air. Gulls wheeled far ahead. With one accord he and Emrist stopped a moment in the road, staring at the birds and then at each other.

"We are nearing our journey's end," Trevyn said. Emrist wordlessly nodded.

By evening they could see the towers of Kantukal rising hazily out of the flat horizon. Beyond the town, more sensed than seen, lay the glimmer of the southern sea.

Trevyn and Emrist camped in a grove of acacia that night. The lamps of Kantukal colored their sky, tree trunks loomed darkly all around, and dread weighted their hearts.

Chapter Five

"We must have a plan," Trevyn insisted.

With childlike obstinacy, he desperately believed that something could be done to improve their chances of defeating Wael. Emrist sighed wearily, for they had been through this discussion before. Moreover, he had his own reasons for melancholy.

"How can we plan for such idiocy?" he grumbled. "Trust the tide, Freca."

"I'd rather depend on something I can control. This parchment, for instance."

"Control?" parried Emrist dryly. "Leave control to Wael, and perhaps he will manage to destroy himself, and perhaps not us."

Trevyn did not answer, but pulled out the parchment with silent stubbornness and unfurled it in the firelight. He could not be sure, in that orange glow, whether the emblem of the wolf was shining with its own spectral light. He took care not to touch it. He read the heading again, "On the Transferring of the Living Soul," and the text, and found that it made no more sense to him than ever. Most of it was in a harsh language that neither he nor Emrist understood. Emrist used it as Wael would use the Old Language, without comprehension.

"This is a property of Wael's cult," Trevyn said.

"Ay, to be sure. I took it—well, no matter how I come to have it. I have never been sure how to use it. I believe it is not merely a document, but a magical thing, a talisman. Note the sheen of the device."

"I've noted it," Trevyn replied sourly. "Perhaps Wael wants this parchment back. We could trade it to him for the brooch."

Emrist gravely sucked his cheeks. "Only as a last resort. It is sure to increase his power. But it saps ours; such an evil thing cannot be used for good without a dire struggle."

"Ay, I can feel it draw." Trevyn put it away and sat back with a sigh. "If only I knew Wael's sooth-name. . . ."

"Ah," the magician mocked gently. "If."

"Who was he born of, Emrist? Where is he from?"

Emrist shrugged. "Who knows? He seems to have some connection with Isle. I think he is probably Waverly, Iscovar's old sorcerer. But he could have been Marrok, who tried to win the magical sword Hau Ferddas by a spell. Or even old Pel Blagden himself, he who was vanquished in the dragon lairs of inner earth. . . . Sorcerers are like the mighty folk of legend. Gods fight and are slain, goddesses sorrow and pass away, but in a sense they never really die."

Trevyn sat up in sudden abeyance, open-mouthed and breathless, utterly forgetting Wael. Something had moved deep in Emrist's gold-flecked eyes, something that filled him with a pang of loss and longing and, nearly, recognition. "And you, Emrist," he gulped at last. "What legend from out of the past are you?"

"I am myself, young, spent, and sickly!" Indeed, Emrist looked like no legend just then. He sat huddled by the fire, hunched in pain and perhaps in despair. But after a moment he looked up, caught Trevyn with a clear glance, determined to give the Prince what he could. All he could.

"Do you know the legend of the star-son, Alberic?"

"I know what Hal has told me of Bevan," Trevyn stammered, shaken anew that Emrist had called him by his true-name. "His comrade Cuin won him Hau Ferddas from the dragons of Lyrdion. Bevan lighted it with the power of his argent hand, defeated Pel Blagden, the Mantled God. . . . Later he left the sword with Cuin and sailed to Elwestrand. That was over a thousand years ago."

"Ay, he was a star-son, and Hal, too. But the legend is older than either. Patience a moment." Emrist settled himself tenderly against a tree, watching the ebb and flow of the fire. Presently he spoke, his eyes still on the iridescent shimmer just above the restless flames.

"The story begins so long ago that the sky was still sea, the sun not yet thought of, and the moon was a pearly island on the tides. In those days the moon-mother gave birth to a star-son, for that Lady is by nature a bearer of sons and needs no help to conceive. But this was her first and best beloved son, though she has had many since. The baby grew quickly to a boy and a young man. But, except for his mother, he lived all alone on the island. So one day, when she found him sad, his mother gave him a silver harp that sang by itself to amuse him and keep him company. And the harp sang of a place where all his unborn brothers lived, the faraway dancing ground of souls, where all selves are part of one. Inconsolable longing took hold of the moon-mother's son.

"'All of life is but a decay unto death,' he exclaimed. 'Let me go to that marvelous place, Mother, quickly, before I start to wane.'

"'Death is only a journey and a change,' his mother protested. 'Stay! Look, I can give you powers to make your own marvels, and your own fair light to adorn you.' And she gave the gifts.

"'Still I must sail,' said the youth, and left the pearly land. Some say he went on a swan, or on a silver boat like a hollow crescent moon. Others say he sailed on the silver harp itself. Whatever the means, he left to wander, glowing with his own white light, across the midnight deeps like the wandering stars.

"Then the moon-mother faded and went dark. And in her despair, and not recognizing the nature of her own change, she went to the great dragon that girded the deep, the one that Sun drove down later. And she lay with the dragon and conceived. So she waxed again, great with child. But her new

babe was born as dark as the unlit lands and grew into a
serpent with coils so huge that they forced her to the fringes
of her domain.

"One day, as she was walking along the waves, she found
her first son's bones lying among the seashells, his skeletal
hand clutching the silver harp. Hungry to take him back into
herself, she ate a single finger and conceived. She hid the harp
in a cave by the sea. And her child was born as fair as the first,
and grew rapidly, and killed the serpent when he was grown.
Then heart sickness took hold of him. He cried, 'I have slain
my brother!' and lay without eating until it looked as if he
would die. Then, in despair, his mother went to the sea and
fetched the silver harp."

"Don't tell me," Trevyn interrupted. "He went—"

"He set sail, wandering like the evening star that leads in
the mother moon." Emrist stirred the fire, prodding old
embers into new flame. "There are many such tales. Sometimes the star-son weds his mother, and her love destroys
him. Or sometimes he has a dark twin with whom he quarrels.
But he always leaves, and only his seed returns.

"Bevan was one who left Isle. He was born of a goddess,
Celonwy of the Argent Moon, sister of Menwy, of whom we
have spoken, and also of the maiden Melidwen. His father
was Byve, once High King in ancient Eburacon, where
fountains flowed and golden apples grew. His hands could
command any element, bend steel, open locked doors, scale
smooth towers. . . . Sometimes they shone with pale fire.
People stood in awe of him. He never learned to be entirely at
home in the sunlit world. He would roam the night like the
chatoyant moon every night, singing across the reaches of the
dark; it was said to be good luck if one heard him. The
loveliness of his voice has become legend. When Hal sang so
beautifully at Caerronan, that was Bevan's legacy in him, that
silver voice of mystery and the moon."

Trevyn started. How could Emrist have known of that
night at Caerronan? But Emrist, eyes focused on depths of
time, seemed not to notice his discomfiture.

"Cuin left his legacy to your father. A warrior by blood, he
traced his lineage to the ancient Mothers of Lyrdion. He
loved sunlight and sport and the sweep of a good sword. He

knew a fine horse and a fine hawk. And he loved a golden maiden to whom Bevan was betrothed. Still, he followed Bevan into Pel's Pit. . . ."

"Why are you telling me this?" Trevyn whispered. The tale dismayed him, though he could hardly say why, and Emrist brooded strangely over the flames.

"I must show you the pattern," Emrist murmured, "if I can."

"What pattern?"

"The one that leads back to Veran, the seed of Bevan, and to Bevan himself and beyond. A pattern of strange binding between two distant islands, and between men. . . . Think, Alberic. Cuin could not follow his comrade across the western sea." An odd catch had taken hold of Emrist's voice.

"You are leaving," Trevyn breathed. He saw the flash of foreboding in Emrist's eyes and scrambled to his feet in alarm. "Emrist, what—"

Emrist rose quietly to face him, placed a light hand on his shoulder. "More likely it is you who will sail away from me. It seems to me that you are needed to round out the pattern, and the larger pattern, the greater tide. An age of ages may come to end and beginning if you fulfill prophecy—Ylim's prophecy—and rid Isle of the magical sword."

"I have always known I must return to Isle someday," said Trevyn shakily. "Bindings of rank on me . . . but I'd hoped to serve you yet a while. I'd follow you to world's end, if that were your pleasure. I wish we could always be together. You are my friend. . . ."

Emrist met his eyes, unsurprised, accepting. "Who is following whom, Alberic?" he asked whimsically.

"You are he," Trevyn whispered. His throat ached, as if something fluttered in it, caught. "You are the one I have yearned for . . . and now our journey's done." Bewildered, he sank to the ground, hid his face in his cupped hands. He felt Emrist's warm touch follow him. The magician settled beside him.

"Freca, I have been happy traveling with you, happier than I have been since I was a child. I know you have felt it too, good friend—and there was little enough time left to me for happiness, wherever I spent my days. I am truly grateful to have known you and to be of use to you. Can you understand?"

"Ay." Trevyn forced out the words. "You have foreseen your death. And you have journeyed to your death, and you would not tell me. . . . Why have you told me now?"

"Because I need your promise, Prince."

Emrist's tone had turned calm and faintly challenging. Steadied in spite of himself, Trevyn lifted his head to face him, puzzled. "All right. What?"

"In regard to a certain power of Wael's, the cruelest trick of the Wolf. Wael loves to drive out the soul and replace it with that of a criminal, in the same body. He has done it to the wolves in Isle, and he is likely to try to do it to us. And I am frail, as you know. . . . So if he should change me in that way, Freca, please use the sword on me, and quickly. It will not be myself that you kill. Do you understand?"

"Nay!" Trevyn swayed as if he had himself been struck; swords of fear ran through him.

"You will understand tomorrow. But you must promise me now, if I am to rest tonight."

"Is that all I can do, then?" Trevyn asked bitterly. "Endure, and be a slayer with the sword?"

"Times to come, you shall be worth ten of me. There is sky in you, and also deeps where dragons dwell; bring them to light, and you shall master us all. You shall be Sun King, Moon King, Star-Son, and Son of Earth. . . . But for now you must trust me in this. Promise."

Trevyn only nodded, for unshed tears swelled his throat. Emrist saw him bite his lip to contain them.

"Grieve later," he said gently. "I can't be sure even of doom."

"What of Maeve? She knows?"

"She knows I have need to be a man. She is strong." Emrist's face went bleak at the thought of her, and he turned away, toward his blanket. "Let us get some rest."

"Wait," cried Trevyn, clutching at hope. "We could go now, take him in his sleep—"

"With the city closed and the castle guard doubled? Nay, it must be in the morning. Courage, Prince." But Emrist faced toward the dark, not meeting his comrade's eyes. Trevyn longed to go to him and embrace him, but he could not bear to weep, or to make Emrist weep, just then. Instead, he spoke numbly.

"Let me prepare you a draught."

"Nay. I must not be slow-witted in the morning."

"Then let me rub your legs to ease you."

Emrist lay on his makeshift bed, still hiding his face, his whole body tense and aching. Trevyn rubbed until the knotted muscles relaxed, until Emrist lay quiet and deeply breathing under his hands, shoulders sagging into sleep. Then he covered him with his ragged blanket and sat beside him with all that they had said turning and turning in his mind. His father. . . . He could not have let Emrist face Wael if it were not for Alan's sake. A heart's love, newly found, to be as quickly lost. . . . Suddenly, like a stab, Meg entered his whirling thoughts. Trevyn knew that her sunny bantering would have lifted the leaden weight from his heart, but the memory afforded him no comfort—he had cut himself off from her. Anguish struck him. He longed for Meg more passionately than he had ever wanted anything, far more than he yearned for life itself. Pain twisted his face and bowed his head. By his own doing she was lost to him, even if he survived the morrow.

Chapter Six

"Did you not sleep at all?" Emrist asked in the morning.

"I'll sleep tonight," Trevyn answered. "Perhaps."

They could not eat. They took their horse and went. The city gates were just opening when they reached them, and they entered Kantukal amid a throng of farmers bringing their wares to the morning market. The towers of Rheged's court rose above the shops and temples, so they found it easily. They paused at a distance and looked in through the iron bars of the gate. Slaves scurried about the courtyard tending to early morning chores. Burly guards watched, lounging. Emrist squared his narrow shoulders, straightened his spine, and sent his nag forward at a fast walk, with Trevyn trotting at his side.

"Who goes?" inquired the gatekeeper lazily.

"Sol of Jabul, on the king's business. Open up."

"Come back after midday." The fellow began to turn away, but he was seized by Emrist's glance, held motionless like a pinned insect. Emrist's eyes flashed like jewel stones in a face turned diamond hard.

"Open up," he ordered softly, "or I will skewer your head for a present to your king, and he will thank me. . . ."

Emrist's hand went to the sword he wore and slid it in the scabbard. He had no need to show that he did not know how to use it. At the sword sound, the gatekeeper jumped to let them enter. They passed in without a word or a glance. Emrist urged his horse across the courtyard and flung himself down from him as Trevyn tethered him. Then he strode off headlong, with Trevyn trotting after. But once within doors he stopped, and Trevyn came up to him.

"Well done, my lord!" Trevyn whispered, with mischief edging at the awe in his eyes.

Emrist grimaced. But before he could speak, Trevyn's eyes narrowed in warning. A guard was studying them from the shadows at the far end of the corridor.

Emrist tightened his lips. Then, as suddenly as lightning, he smote Trevyn across the face with the back of his hand. For love of him, Trevyn did what the whips of the slavers had never made him do: yelped and flinched from the blow.

"Churl!" Emrist grated. "You shall bow when you speak to me, sirrah!" He beckoned imperiously and strode off again with Tervyn at his heels. The guard let them pass without comment.

"Again, well done, my lord!" Trevyn whispered when they came to a large open hall.

"I am sorry," Emrist murmured.

"No need; I've taken worse in sport. Which way?"

Emrist shrugged in vexation. "I can't tell. The Sight doesn't work that way; it's not a map! Just keep moving. . . . You tied the horse?"

"Only loosely. He can free himself with a jerk and go where he will. But he will wait for us yet a while."

They moved through the labyrinth of the palace purposefully but at random. The council halls stood empty, for the court officials were still in their rooms. Slaves sped by with breakfast trays, taking no notice of the strangers. Presently Emrist and Trevyn reached a rear courtyard serving the kitchen and slave quarters. They stopped, for they could not expect to find Wael there.

"We must go back," Trevyn said, "and try to find some stairs. I should think a sorcerer would be lodged in one of the towers; that is customary, is it not?"

Emrist had no chance to answer. From behind them came a startled exclamation and a clatter of pottery. Trevyn whirled. An old man sat with scrub rag in hand, his mouth agape and suds dripping unheeded down his arm. Trevyn went to him swiftly and knelt beside him.

"Peace, Grandfather," he warned softly, "for my life's sake."

"What is it, Freca?" Emrist came up beside them.

"He was a slave with me in the pit and in the string where you found me, and he was a good friend to me."

"All that flogging," the old man gasped, "and ye never spoke or squeaked—"

Trevyn pulled a wry face at the memory. "Ay, for I am a king's son, Grandfather. I could not let them master me."

"Ye're the one they seek!" the old man breathed.

"Ay, and come to beard Wael for it, if we can. Where is he to be found?"

"In the tower, as ye said. The farthest one. But ye're mad to face him. He is terrible!" The old man spoke with trembling earnestness.

"I have no choice," Trevyn told him quietly. "You'll not betray us?"

He wordlessly shook his head.

"Freca," asked Emrist worriedly, "can we trust him?"

"Ay, I think so. Anyway, what else can we do? Do you have a way to silence him?"

"I'll quiet yer fears yet a while," said the old man with dignity, rising stiffly to his feet. "I'll come with ye, to show ye the way."

"You're likely to get a drubbing, if you're missed," Emrist said.

He shrugged. "I am an old man and thick of hide; I do not mind."

"Then, many thanks. And let us go quickly."

The old slave took them up the back stairs that the servants used. They met no guards. They climbed up flight after spiraling flight, till Trevyn lost count. Their guide stopped at last at a landing leading to a corridor.

"He's within," he murmured. "I can feel it. The first door. I'll go no farther."

"Get yourself to safety," Trevyn told him. "A thousand thanks for your help."

"May yer gods defend you," the old man breathed, and hurriedly stumped down and away. Emrist and Trevyn looked at each other.

"Rest a moment, gather your strength," Trevyn whispered. He reached for the sword that hung at Emrist's side, drew it silently from its scabbard. The two steadied themselves for the count of a hundred. Then they wordlessly touched hands and walked to the fateful door. Emrist reached out, and it swung open beneath his fingertips. They entered Wael's chamber.

The room, in the properest tradition of the sorcerer's tower, surrounded and confounded them and hemmed them in with shadows and shadowy apparatus. Amid all the confusion, Trevyn's glance picked out one thing at once: the gilded form of a wooden figurehead, a wolf leaping with bared teeth of pearl. The shaggy object beside it, however, he was slower to recognize. He blinked as the grayish form turned and rose to a meager height to face them. A bent old man stood before him; yellow eyes stared at him out of a face covered with bristly gray beard. Trevyn had seen those eyes before.

"Greetings, Wael." Emrist spoke sedately.

"Little Emrist the Magician!" Wael made the name into a yelp of triumph. "Well met! And you also, Prince of Isle." His voice turned crooning. "How fortunate for you that you have come to me at last! I can make you the most powerful of Kings, King of Sun and Moon, if you let me."

Trevyn felt his heart jump at the echo of Emrist's words. But he took a tighter grip on his sword. "Is that how Rheged comes to be under your thumb? A promise of power?"

"Rheged!" Wael let out a single harsh bark of laughter. "Rheged is leaden of nature. Nay, worse than leaden; he is dross, and you could be pure gold. What, Prince, have you not yet learned the first quality of magic? I should think even Emrist might have taught you that." Wael shuffled closer, hunched and glaring with what was meant to be sincerity. "It is power, the power of perfection. Just as sorcery can raise the nature of metals, it can raise the nature of men, firing away what is base, freeing the rest to fly like the eagles, lending power like a god's. You are young and beautiful, and you could be anything your power and vision can encompass." Wael had crept to within three feet of Trevyn's staring face. "Think of it, Prince of Isle."

"He knows you well," Emrist remarked.

"Too well for honesty. He has been spying on my dreams. Picking at my thoughts with his soiled hands—" Trevyn slowly swung his sword up until it rested against Wael's gray-robed chest. "Your words sound fair, old man, but your face is the color of vomit. Get away."

Wael sprang back with surprising agility, his face ugly with rage. He abandoned his caressing tone. "That was discourtesy," he snapped, "and I will punish it as I am accustomed to punish those who cross me." A clawlike hand left his sleeve with serpent speed, and power snapped across the room. The sword fell to pieces, clattering to the floor. Pain shot up Trevyn's arm; he dropped the hilt with a gasp. "Thus," Wael added. "You see?"

Trevyn did not glance at the useless weapon. "You have a brooch of mine," he said flatly. "This causes me some discomfort. We have come to get it back."

"Indeed?" Wael mocked. "I am the master here." He fixed his jaundiced gaze on Trevyn. "I am the master here," he whispered in dreamy, hypnotic cadence. "Come to me, Trevyn of Laueroc."

Trevyn matched his stare and did not move.

"Come to me, Trevyn of Laueroc." Wael recited a spell in the same silky whisper, ill suited to the guttural language of his magic. He thinks the brooch pulls me, Trevyn thought, and ached inwardly for Alan. But Wael's efforts were ludicrous, just the same, and Trevyn felt his thoughts swerve to Meg, her teasing, her smile. He could almost hear her exclaim, "Silly old man!" Hugging memory to himself like a talisman, Trevyn threw back his head and laughed the sweet, healthy laugh she had taught him. Wael stopped his chanting abruptly, and a faint frown shadowed his eyes.

Emrist quickly pressed the advantage. "Let us see that brooch, Wael!" he cried, and power flickered through him. Wael's coarse gray garments parted like wings, and Trevyn glimpsed the sparkle of Alan's brooch within them. Excitedly he stepped forward. But in an instant Wael clapped his arms down over his robe, and Emrist was jolted as his spell was severed. Wrath crawled across Wael's face.

"Fool," he hissed, "you shall pay for that." He snapped both hands forward like spitting snakes, and Trevyn saw Emrist reel from an unseen force. "Stop that!" Trevyn shouted, and once again started toward Wael. But then the blow struck him in his turn, blinding him with the magnitude of its malice. He stopped where he was, clenching himself in helpless wonder that anything could hurt so hard and yet continue without abatement.

"Take no notice, Prince." Emrist's voice, though labored, was composed. "It's only pain."

"Very true." Trevyn forced his sluggish tongue to move, trying to match Emrist's tone.

"He drains himself of power with the making of it," Emrist went on. "When he stops, he will be the weaker."

"Still strong enough to deal with a dozen such as you!" shrieked Wael. Nevertheless, the pain stopped. Trevyn shook his head to clear the haze from his eyes. Then he stiffened. The leaping figurehead leered into his face, scarcely a foot away.

"Ay, you remember him well, do you not, Islendais Prince?" Wael gloated. "You will be his, you who have spurned me!"

Trevyn could not move or speak. Some inexplicable horror of the thing bound him immobile. Its glass eyes took on a saffron sheen from the gilded wood and held his sickened gaze. Beyond them, shielded from his reach by the wooden wolf, another pair of yellowish eyes entered his narrowed view. "Look at me, Trevyn of Laueroc," Wael whispered.

Behind Trevyn, Emrist spoke tightly, forcing words from his frail, anguished body. "Do not heed him, Prince!"

"A fine wolf, is it not?" Wael went on. "But this is only a toy. Since you will not join me, you and all yours shall be a sacrifice at the altar of the Very Wolf. Would you care to see him? Look at me!" Wael's voice rose to a hiss. "Can a Prince such as yourself not withstand the gaze of an old man?"

Trevyn looked, whether from stung pride or sheerest

compulsion he could not say. In a moment his world had
faded into nightmare. Laueroc had fallen, his father lay dead,
his mother torn and dishonored; the wolves surrounded him
in his turn, frenzied for his blood, worrying at his legs to pull
him down. The largest wolf came at him, huge, looming, dark
enough to blot out sun and day and sky. . . . Falsehood, he
knew it to be, and he pressed his mind against the vision,
struggling to see with present sight. For an instant, he thought
he had succeeded. The sorcerer's shadowy chamber was
again before him. But a giant black wolf with teeth of flame
was coming at him, leaping for his throat. . . . Trevyn could
not, or would not, scream. He closed his eyes.

"A thing of smoke and fire," said Emrist in a strong voice.
"You shall not gull us so easily again, Wael." Trevyn's eyes
snapped open. The specter had vanished. Only old Wael
faced him over a carved figurehead, his wrinkled face twisted
in fury. Emrist stood with hand raised in command, straight
as a young tree, his russet hair flying, though there was no
wind. Trevyn went swiftly to his side.

"Hold fast," Emrist murmured to him. "The worst is yet to
come." Wael was muttering a spell in the harsh language of
his cult, and Trevyn recognized some of the words; it was the
spell for the transferring of the living soul. But not until he
felt grinding misery fill his veriest being did he fully realize
what Wael was doing.

"Hold fast!" Emrist charged him again.

The new torment was not so much pain as pressure, a
straining within and a battering, hostile presence without.
Though he breathed, Trevyn felt crushed, as if he held his
breath under water, under something heavier and more alien
than water or earth, with no hope but to smother quickly. He
could see Emrist, though thick glass seemed to be between
them, and he noted that his friend's face looked white as
death. If this spell succeeded, Trevyn remembered dully, he
had promised to kill him. That would be the worst of
promises to keep. But if his own strong body felt weakened
under its magical load, how was Emrist to withstand it much
longer?

As if moving in lead, Trevyn forced a hand to his tunic,
drew from it a rolled parchment. With a wrenching effort of

will, he made his tongue move, form speech. "Wael," he asked, "do you know anything of this?" He let the scroll fall open in his fingers.

The spell left as suddenly as a weight dropping from a snapped string. In the empty moment that followed, Trevyn thought he could sense Wael's startled fear.

"Give it to me!" Wael demanded sharply.

"I will trade it for a certain brooch," Trevyn replied.

Beside him, Emrist stood breathing deeply. "Freca," he whispered between gasps, "you must by no means let him have it. It is a very evil thing."

"I will do what I must," Trevyn told him obliquely, but with a covert wink.

"Come, come," said Wael, reverting to his caressing tones. "It is a paltry thing, of no importance except that I fancy it. . . . Why struggle for it? I will take it from you either way."

"The brooch, if you please," Trevyn answered evenly.

Wael pressed his lips to a line like a scar and extended his hand. The parchment in Trevyn's grasp sent sudden pain through him like a searing iron, burning hot. He managed to keep his grip, though agony twisted his face. "False fire!" he taunted, between clenched teeth. Wael's fire did not injure him, could not consume, if he wished to keep the parchment whole.

"And water of like sort," Emrist added. Trevyn felt his hand drenched in healing coolness, though nothing was wet. Wael wheeled away from him to face Emrist in consummate fury.

"Renegade sorcerer—" Wael spat out the words with choking emphasis. "How I wish I could deal with you at my leisure! I would make you into a thing a dog would pity! But it seems that I must dispose of you here and now, if I am to have my way with this young fool. . . ." Wael swept his hand across his body like a scythe, and Emrist slid to the floor with a gasp. Trevyn stood, feeling his knees turn to water as Wael confronted him. The old warlock was grining with triumph, his gaping teeth as jagged as fangs in his ancient jaws.

"And now for you," he breathed. "See the Wolf, Princeling? You shall be His tonight." Wael turned toward the gilded wolf of wood, but froze, thunderstruck, as it burst to splinters before his eyes. From the crumpled form on the floor a movement had come; a hoarded bolt of power had dearly spent itself. Wael spun with an inarticulate screech and struck the air with his clenched fists. Emrist moaned deeply, then lay still.

"Now, I will have that scroll!" Wael advanced on Trevyn with burning eyes. Trevyn let him come without a sign. All fear for himself had left him with Emrist's moan. Rage filled him, but he did not let it show—not yet. He stilled himself until the sorcerer was within two paces, within one pace, and then he sprang with lion force, silent as Fate. Knocked to the ground, Wael gasped and flailed the air with his hands, but to no avail. Trevyn tore the brooch from his clothing. The moment he seized it, Wael slithered from his encumbered grasp and made for the door. "Guard!" he shrieked. "Guard!" The ancient warlock scuttled away down the corridor, and Trevyn let him go. With brooch and parchment in hand, he knelt by Emrist, taking his head into his arms. Emrist opened his eyes and smiled.

"You have them both?" he murmured. "That is good, very good. We wore him out at last, it seems. But you must go now, Freca, quickly."

"Let me get you on my back, then." Trevyn spoke past the lump in his throat.

"Nay, I am done." Shouts and the sound of running feet echoed through the corridor, drew nearer. "Go, make haste."

"I cannot leave you here!" Trevyn blinked back stinging tears.

"By the mighty One," Emrist begged in the Old Language, "do not let me fail in this one last thing. Alberic, as you love me, think of your kingdom and your sire and go!"

The guards reached the door. Trevyn kissed Emrist once, the kiss of death's parting, and then ran. The door opened before him; he burst through the startled guards like a stag through the bushes. The stair by which he had come was blocked. He ran the other way, the guards hard after him, found the front stair and leaped down it, careless of his neck, half crazed. He sped down another corridor, almost toppling a lean, swarthy man in a crown. The guards lagged far behind him now, but the whole palace was acry for him. Leaping, half falling, he descended some more stairs, then paused, listening. Shouts closed in from every side. He did not know which way to turn.

A hand plucked his elbow, and he whirled. The old man, his fellow slave, beckoned, led him to a servant's door behind a curtain. From there they twisted through a maze of dark, narrow passages and rooms smelling of chamber pots and unwashed bodies: the slave quarters. The shouting faded away behind them. The old man went surely, though none too quickly, with Trevyn treading restively at his heels. Slaves gaped at them from doorways, scurried out of their path.

"You'll get worse than a drubbing for this, if any of those tell," Trevyn said tightly.

"Someone will tell. But I am an old man, and quite ready for death," the slave replied placidly. They came out at last to the back courtyard where Trevyn had found him before. The old man led the way to the postern gate, gripped the iron bars, and braced himself against them. "On my back," he directed tersely.

Trevyn kicked off his sandals and climbed up, one-handed, clutching the parchment and the brooch. Wriggling, he was able to squeeze out over the pikes and drop down outside the gate. "Good speed to ye," said the old slave, and stood watching as Trevyn silently saluted him and trotted away.

He had not left the shadow of the wall before the guards sighted him. The cry went up, and as he sped away he heard the call to horse. He ran aimlessly. The town gates would be closed against him, he knew. He and Emrist had not planned for this; hopeless as their confrontation of Wael had seemed, getting Trevyn and the brooch out of Tokar had been goals as distant as the stars. Now the tumult of his mind kept him from thinking. If only because it was easier on his tiring legs, he ran downhill. Between the houses and shops he could glimpse the gleam of the southern sea. Foolishness to go that way, where he would be trapped against the endless water. Yet some deep instinct of his elfin heritage called him to the sea, the longtime deliverer of his mother's people. He ran toward the shining deep.

He ran with aching heart and burning lungs. Folk scattered before him, caught sight of his straining, tear-streaked face, his eyes blazing with a fey green brilliance, and saw that face later in their dreams. Trevyn saw nothing except the sea. He scarcely heard the shouts of his pursuers over the pounding in his ears, but as he reached the harbor the ring of hooves on cobbles cut through the clamor of his desperation. He glanced back to see Rheged's mounted warriers scarcely a stone's throw behind him. Trevyn bit his lip, darting like a deer for some escape. He reached the tip of the farthest wharf, raised his arm to hurl his treasures into the sea. Then fishermen shouted, and he followed their gaze open-mouthed. A form of dark loveliness rippled the sunlit water. A slender elf-boat skimmed toward him faster than any dead craft of men could ever sail. She sped through the crowded harbor and touched dock at his feet. Trevyn stumbled on board and sank down just as the kingsmen came up to him. The elf-boat bounded off with him the moment she felt his weight. The kingsmen scrambled aboard a merchant vessel, but Trevyn did not even trouble himself to watch the pursuit. No power of sail or slaves could match the speed of this swimming thing.

He laid his face down on her friendly deck and wept. He grieved for Emrist, and for the old slave whose name he did not know, and perhaps for himself. He hoped against reason that the elf-boat was taking him home to Isle, to his father's strength and his mother's comfort and a chance of forgiveness from Meg. He had long since forgotten to dream of Elwestrand. He wept until he could weep no more, and then he slept. The parchment lay crumpled beneath him, where his body held it. But the brooch nestled in fingers slackened by exhaustion. And presently, and quite unknown to Trevyn, a gentle wave came up and took it from him.

Chapter Seven

Alan had hardly been his ardent self since Hal had turned his face to the west. And he had struggled with the slow gnawing of despair since the springtime day that Trevyn had left on a glittering ship that sailed east. But the sharp unrest that struck him one morning in late summer was a new sensation.

"It's like something tugging under my ribs," he told Lysse.

"Indigestion," she replied in wifely tones. "You'd better stay away from the seasonings for a while."

Alan agreed and tried to think of other things. But the pang did not leave him, and in a few days he realized that its focus lay to the east. "Something is pulling at me," he explained to Lysse. "I can't tell what, or whether for good or ill."

She searched his eyes lovingly, puzzling for a clue to his malaise. "I see no good to come of it," she finally said. "You must think of your people, my lord."

"It will do no harm to journey as far as Nemeton. It has been a long time since I've seen Cory. Perhaps something in those parts needs my attention."

Lysse stared at him with worry growing in her eyes. "It sounds fair," she exclaimed, "but I feel a foreboding—must you go?"

"Ay, I must go! I'll have no rest until I know the meaning of this—this force that wrenches at me."

"Then take me with you, Alan," she said earnestly, "for, by my troth, I am afraid to let you out of my sight."

"Why, Love? Do you not trust me?"

"My heart is heavy," she said, "and I think trust has nothing to do with it."

Alan shook his head, beleaguered. "But, Love, I need you to stay here and take command for me. I cannot depend on Ket these days; he is as addle-headed as a young gallant." Lysse had to smile at that. Ket courted Rosemary with dignity and gravest courtesy, but his joy in her had made him absentminded. "Perhaps they'll soon set the date and get back to business, so you can travel with me again," Alan continued. "But this time you must stay. . . . I am sorry."

Lysse regarded him with anxious exasperation. "Give me your word, then," she demanded at last.

"To what? Say what, and it is yours."

"I hardly know. . . ." Lysse frowned. "To take no rash course. To return to me straightway, and to your throne."

"Confound it, woman, did you think I'd do less? But certainly I'll give you my word."

Once he had decided on the journey, Alan wasted no time, reaching Nemeton with a group of retainers in only ten days. This was the easternmost town in Isle, and the closest to Tokar. At Nemeton the Eastern Invaders had landed their warships, and raised their infamous Tower, and ruled. Hal had been reared there; he had broken and burned the Tower when his time came, and he and Alan had moved their government to the gentler Laueroc, their father's holding. Now the place was held in fealty by Alan's former comrade, and the horror of its memory was gradually fading from folks' minds.

"Well met, Alan! But what brings you?" Corin asked when they had embraced.

"Whim," Alan replied. "Sheerest whim. Some wind of chance blows me this way."

Corin knew better. It had been years since Alan had taken time for carefree adventuring, and now that Hal was gone . . . Cory had not seen Alan since, but he guessed from long friendship the extent of Alan's burden in spirit and in duty. And the Prince mysteriously gone as well! Corin wished he knew what to say to Alan. He watched him and wondered as they feasted that night. He wondered the more when Alan rode out the next day to the Long Beaches, for Alan had never been a lover of the sea.

Alan went alone, without even a dog for company, and watched the sun blaze on the salt water, and loped his horse along the line of the tide. But he was not all alone on the deserted beach. Before noon he reached the point that projects to the east and found Gwern sitting there. Alan had not seen him since that day at the Bay of the Blessed, though he had sometimes heard report of him. Gwern was said to be living like a wild man on the fringes of Isle, eating fish and blackberries, traveling along the sandy southeastern coast. He did not turn to the sound of Alan's horse. He sat with his bare feet buried in the sand, staring out over the water, straight at the plains of Tokar, though Alan did not know that.

Alan vaulted off his horse and let it roam, walked over to Gwern, sat beside him on the gravel and seaweed left by high tide. Gwern scarcely glanced at him before his earth-brown eyes flicked back to the east. "King," he asked with his customary lack of ceremony, "what draws you here?"

"I wish I knew." Alan was not offended by Gwern's directness. In fact, he liked it somehow, though there was no comfort of warmth to be found in Gwern. Alan was used to the fellowship of his friends, but this youth who treated him as equal was neither friend nor enemy, he sensed. Gwern was supremely himself. Nothing he did or said could reflect on Alan in any way, and nothing Alan did could much affect him. His impersonal presence refreshed Alan's raw and burning mind like a cool breeze within.

Gwern said nothing. He never said anything unless there was something of essence to say. Alan frankly stared at him, knowing he would not mind. Gwern's clothing was in tatters, his body not filthy exactly, but definitely a stranger to soap. What could this dust-colored oddity have to do with Trevyn? And yet, *watch Gwern like a weathercock for Trevyn,* Lysse had said. Well, the weathercock pointed east.

"You have been following the shoreline." Alan broke silence. "Following Trevyn?"

"As closely as I can without leaving the land." Gwern dropped the words at his leisure, like pebbles into a pond, as if they were insignificant. But Alan felt his heart jump.

"Where is he, then? What do you see?"

"I see nothing; I do not have the Sight. I do nothing. I only feel." Gwern did not look at Alan as he talked, and his face, lit by the iridescence of the sea, was utterly expressionless.

"What do you feel, then?" pursued Alan, somewhat exasperated. "For I'm pickled if I can tell."

Gwern took breath to speak, then held it. "Hot," he finally said.

"What?" Alan almost shouted.

"Hot! He is hot. I can't help it." Gwern sullenly dug himself deeper into the sand.

Alan shared his lunch with Gwern, then left to go back to Nemeton, reluctantly; the eastward pull was strong on him. The next day he returned to the beach and found Gwern no more communicative than ever. They spent the day staring out over the waves. From time to time Gwern would rise and move southward a few feet, perhaps even a furlong. Once he smiled.

"What was that?" Alan asked.

"Love," Gwern replied without hesitation. "Longing and love." Later, his face subtly changed. "What?" Alan asked again. "Despair," answered Gwern.

Alan would not leave the shore that night, sleeping fitfully on the damp gravel. The next day Corin worriedly mustered some retainers and set out in search of him. He found him pacing the verge of the waves, wet to his knees. A bit farther along the strand sat an unkempt youth who neither moved nor spoke at his approach, but glared like a madman over the featureless water. Corin stared, then dismounted and fell into step beside Alan, asking him, as an old friend will, what troubled him. The answer made little sense. Alan seemed too distraught for sense.

"I gave her my word," he blurted disjointedly, "which she had never asked of me before, never. . . . I would be a villain to betray her. But if it were not for that, days ago I would have taken ship and set sail. It must be something to do with Trevyn. If he needs me, and calls me thus . . . I may never forgive myself. But I gave her my word. . . ."

Down the beach, Gwern stirred and made a strangled sound in his throat. Alan whirled. "What was that?" he demanded.

"Dread," Gwern replied.

Alan paced through the day with scarcely a rest or a bite to eat. The tug, like an invisible hook to his heart, had grown to a racking pain that threatened to tear him asunder. Gwern edged his way down the tideline, apparently in some distress of his own; his masklike face had gone hard and tight. Corin paced beside his liege, unable to help him. That night Alan lay tossing in restless exhaustion while Cory watched beside him. With daybreak he was up and pacing as before. Gwern emerged from the woodlot where he had disappeared for the night and stood at the strand's edge, blinking into the rising sun. Once it was well up, he settled into the sand and seemed to root himself, scarcely breathing, his clay-colored face intense with subterranean anguish. Trevyn had entered Wael's chamber at Kantukal.

Alan paced frenziedly, panting in pain, scarcely seeming aware anymore of his surroundings. Suddenly, in mid-morning, he cried out, a terrible cry of tormented defeat, and hurled himself into the waves. Cory caught hold of him, and struggled with him amid the froth, and with some retainers wrestled him to the sand where he lay groaning. Alan did not attempt to rise again, and Gwern sat still as a stump. An hour passed, perhaps more, as Alan lay sweating in agony while Corin and his men stood helplessly by. Then Gwern sighed, almost sobbed, and Alan sat up, blinking in bewilderment. His pain had left him all in a moment. "What in thunder?" he murmured.

Cory knelt by him. "Are you all right?" he whispered shakily.

"Hungry and in need of a wash. . . . Do I remember sleeping on this accursed beach?" Alan got slowly to his feet. Gwern sank his head into folded arms.

"What is it?" Alan asked numbly.

"Grief," Gwern moaned. "Death and grief, death and grief, grief. . . ."

Alan stared, motionless, his mind caught on a question that would not find its way to his lips. Cory tugged at his arm.

"Alan," he begged, "come away."

In a haze of weariness, Alan followed him back to the castle. Cory got him fed and couched at once, puzzled, but very much relieved to see him better. The next day they talked, and neither of them had any explanation for the other. So, hoping for a sign of some sort, Alan lingered on at Nemeton. From time to time he rode to the Beaches, scanning earth, sea, and sky for his answer. Gwern was gone, and after a while Cory learned not to fear for Alan, letting him go alone. So no one knew what Alan found.

The answer, or so he took it to be, came to him less than a fortnight after his narrow escape. In fact, it was on Trevyn's birth day, and that awareness played through Alan's mind as he rode gently along the fingertips of the reaching sea. A glow caught his eye, a golden shine among the pebbles of the beach, and he stopped to look—he felt as if a barbed shaft had pierced him to the heart. The rayed emblem of the rising sun glinted up at him, its spokes set with gems of many hues. As slowly as a man in a nightmare, Alan got down from his mount, picked it up, and turned it over and over in his hand. There was no mistaking the brooch, Hal's gift to him on this same day eighteen years before. Alan did not weep, but desolation settled over him like a black shroud, for he felt certain now that his son was dead.

He started back to Laueroc that very day. He did not show Lysse the brooch when he arrived, proud to spare her this grief, yet blaming her in his heart. He complained of nothing. But he ceased to be the loving husband Lysse had known, and as the weeks went by she grew sad, not knowing what to do for him.

Book Three

YLIM'S LOOM

Chapter One

Trevyn was never to remember anything of the voyage except sun and stars circling, the moon twirling between—all skimming through the movements of some inscrutable dance. Vaguely puzzling, he could not discern the pattern, so intricate was its phrasing, but he could feel its voiceless rhythm. He sensed that the elf-boat also moved in the dance, and so as not to interfere he lay very still on her deck, still and staring, with no thought of food or drink, twirl the moon as it might. If rain wet him he was not to recall it, or day's heat, or night's chill. Nor did he note his coming to shore. When awareness came back to him at last, it came with pain and reluctance of body and spirit, perhaps as keen as the pain of an infant in birth. But someone held him, cradled him as if he were a child, and the warmth of the embrace eased him. Trevyn knew those strong arms, he thought.

"Father?" he faltered.

"Nay, Trev." It was a well-beloved voice he heard, but for a moment he did not recognize it. He gazed up into the sea-lit face, blinking the darkness from his eyes.

"Uncle Hal," he murmured, and sank back into oblivion.

He sensed, distantly, that he was cared for. He felt the

warmth of a bath, the taste of a strengthening drink, soft
blankets, and a bed like an embrace. But his deeper awareness labored in the misery of Tokar. Vividly envisioning the
whips of the slavers, he found that he could no longer face
them; he flinched and struggled away from them, softly
weeping. Emrist lay dying under the whips of the slavers, and
he could not help him, not even by screaming. His grief bore
him down like a weight as massive as the world. His own
frailty struck him through with pity too deep even for tears.

Somehow a white stag flitted through the scarred texture of
his dreams, leading him away, though he knew he had not
moved. It took him to a forest of huge and knotted trees,
their branches woven together into a tapestry, forming
intricate pictures of ships with wings, and myriad shining
spheres, and leopards and dragons and black flowers. In the
midst of the forest grew a slender sapling, its branches terse as
winter, reaching. A cavalcade of alabaster ladies came and
gave it their jewels for leaves, seated themselves beneath the
young and growing tree. Trevyn followed the white hart. It
sped out of the forest, plunged into the sea, and swam away,
its silver antlers shining. Trevyn stood with his feet in the
water, yearning; he could not follow it there. By the shore a
man sat playing a silver harp.

Trevyn sat and listened. The music took him up winging,
carried him out of self, let him leap with the antelope and
glide with the eagles and fight by the side of the star-son
himself in a strange little land called Isle. . . . Trevyn
blinked, and looked again, and saw that the harper was his
Uncle Hal, playing his plinset by candlelight under a shelter
of golden cloth. Trevyn propped himself up in his warm bed.

"You have ransomed me with song," he said huskily, "as
you did for Father at Caerronan."

Hal set down his instrument to come to him, and one finger
caught a string, striking a single, rich note. A form spiraled
itself out of the vibrations; a bird flew up, ensouled by that
sound, a bird of the most ardent red Trevyn had ever seen,
red so true that it enthralled the eye. The bird circled the
confines of the tent, singing a phrase that swelled Trevyn's
heart, which he was never afterward quite able to remember.

Then Hal lifted the tent flap and the bird took its leave without fright, darting skyward.

"That was my love for you," Hal explained softly, sitting by Trevyn's bedside. "Things tend to become very real here. . . . Lad, you bear scars. I am very, very sorry it has been so hard for you."

"Family tradition." Trevyn grinned with moistened eyes as joy took hold of him. "I can't deny I've felt as beaten as an old rug. . . . But one good look at you heals me. You are . . ." Trevyn did not know how to finish.

"I am content," agreed Hal.

He was more than content; he was well and whole for the first time in all his tortuous life, and Trevyn was able to sense it quite surely. Hal's eyes glowed, and his body moved with certainty and ease. Moreover, he no longer seemed aloof and appraising to Trevyn; he had greeted him with the warmth of a friend and equal. As Trevyn gazed at him, smiling but lost for words, Hal rose with feral grace and pulled back the door flap, beckoning to someone outside. A boy, perhaps twelve years old, entered with a covered tray, set it down, bowed with youthful haste, and hurried out. Could it be that all people in this place were blessed? The boy was beautiful.

"One of your cousins," Hal explained.

Cousins! Trevyn's mind reeled. He had no cousins, no relations of any sort, except perhaps in . . .

"Then this is Elwestrand," he gulped.

"Of course."

Trevyn ate his food very slowly, as Hal cautioned him. He was caught in astonishment, and his flesh sat heavily on his unaccustomed spirit. He knew now that he had not filled his stomach for the months of the voyage—that thought alone stunned him. But the simple food, porridge and honey, soothed him with its familiarity. He slept peacefully afterward, and awoke later to the soft notes of Hal's plinset, and ate again. Then he dressed in the clothing Hal gave him: a tunic of finest wool, spring green—his mother's color—and light brown hose, and cloth boots, and a short leaf-gold cloak.

"All right?" Hal asked. "Then let us go to see Adaoun. Your grandfather."

Once again Trevyn's mind was staggered. He had never had a grandfather, or expected to know one. Numbly, he followed Hal outside, to an air tremulous with sweetness. Tall, white, lilylike flowers grew wantonly as far as he could see; asphodel, he later learned they were called. Amid them clustered the rosy-purple amarinth, and amid . . . Trevyn stopped where he stood, scarcely a dozen paces from the tent. A unicorn raised its delicate, pearly-horned head from its grazing, met his gaze a moment with lilac eyes, then turned and whisked away at a floating run. Trevyn let out a long, shivering breath of delight. Hal gazed after the creature with sparkling eyes, even a smile.

"Everyone has a different notion of a unicorn," he remarked to Trevyn. "You'll see them all in time, and each one utterly beautiful, and each one true."

"You mean . . ."

"It is as I said; things become real here somehow. Thoughts. Dreams. Feelings, love and hate. All beautiful—even the darker ones, like that behind you. Look."

Trevyn whirled. A serpent confronted him, with scales like jet, a jeweled hood, blind eyes, and a crimson ribbon of tongue. Its head stood as tall, rearing, as Trevyn's waist. He took a step back.

"Is it—dangerous?" he asked edgily.

"Only if you want it to be. Sometimes men feel a need for danger."

"I feel no such need right now," Trevyn stated fervently.

"Well, come on, then." Hal turned his back on the serpent and walked away. Trevyn followed, and found that his fear ended after a few paces; he did not even look over his shoulder. Elwestrand entranced him, calling his eyes farther than he could see. He walked a curving footpath atop a gentle fold of land, watching the lush, random pattern of meadows and fragrant orchard and woven wilderness ripple away on either side. It took him a while to realize that no sun shone, that the sky, although clear, was not blue, but tender shades of peach and mauve, that the light, subtle and subdued, cast no shadows, only a kind of magenta haze. Hal seemed to read his thoughts. "We live in the afterglow here," he said.

"And is it always springtime?" The air was balmy, the land

luxurious with blossoms, many more kinds than he could name.

"Sometimes a bit hotter or colder, just for variety. Sometimes one of us dreams of snow and it falls—just for fun, I think. It quickly melts. The plants never wither, but there are seasons. I tell them by the flowers, and by the hills yonder. It is early winter in Isle."

Trevyn studied the distant, rolling hills that Hal pointed out, hills of the peculiar pinkish-gray of wintery woodland cloaked by neither leaves nor snow. "But . . ." Trevyn floundered. Hal glanced around, half laughing at him.

"The sea is wide. The voyage must have taken you three months, maybe four. It is nearly Winterfest."

"So I lay and stared all that time. All right. But if those trees are bare, there on those hills, why is it springtime here?"

Hal's smile broadened, and he sat down on a smooth-worn stone. "Now that is the marvel of all marvels here," he averred. "I believe those hills are there just for my benefit, to look at. You will never reach them by walking."

"Why not?" Trevyn sat also, glad of the rest, winded by just the small distance they had come. He wondered if Hal was teasing him on that account. But Hal seemed quite serious.

"You see that mountain—the rocky peak nearer than the hills? We call it Elundelei—Mount Sooth. Truth lives there, for those who are able to grasp it. And if you climbed to the top, you might be able to see that we are on an island far smaller than Isle, with the sea ringing it all around."

"But how can that be?" Trevyn protested. "It looks as if the land goes on forever."

"And there is room enough for everyone who comes here, and all their creations, and room to roam, and solitude for anyone who seeks it." Hal shrugged whimsically. "This is Elwestrand, Trevyn, and I dare say you will never understand it; no one does. Come, let us find Adaoun."

They walked along through wilderness interspersed with meadows, gardens, wheat fields, and occasional bright-colored canopies, graceful saillike shapes nestled into the curves of the land. Trevyn saw only a few folk, all comely even from a distance, raising hands in greeting, dressed in soft, rich-hued clothing like his own. "There is no need for crowns here," Hal declared, "and no need for settled dwellings. We move as the whim takes us. And there is no need of firewood except for cooking, praise be. You know how the elves hate to fell trees."

"Is it only elves who live here?"

"Nay, many others. Men of peace. Look, there is Adaoun."

Trevyn saw Adaoun's horse first, the splendid, blazing-white, gold-winged steed that had once flown over Welas. It grazed beside a placid stream. Beyond, on a gentle rise overlooking the meadow, a swan-white awning draped slender birch trees. On a couch beneath the awning, propped up by linen pillows, sat an old, old white-bearded man.

Trevyn approached by Hal's side, his mind clamoring. Ever since his earliest childhood, he had been told about Adaoun, father of the elves, first sung in the First Song of Aene at the beginning of time, ageless as the elements, sturdy as the mountains, visionary. . . . Surely this shrunken mortal could not be he! But the eyes that met Trevyn's plunged deep as wells, nearly drowning him in wonder. He sank to one knee beside the ancient patriarch and felt a withered hand touch his hair in the gesture of blessing.

"Alberic," said Adaoun in a voice soft and vibrant and powerful as the wind. "Welcome."

"Someone else has called me by that name," Trevyn whispered. "But I do not know why, Grandfather." He dared the old man's eyes again, and found that he could meet Adaoun's unfathomable gaze.

"Sometime you will know," Adaoun told him. "But for now I shall call you Grandson, if you like. I have grandchildren now, you know, by the hundreds, now that my children have chosen the lot of mortals and taken mortal mates. But you, whom I have never met, were the first. The years flit by like mayflies for a mortal. . . . You must be nearly of age."

"I am sev—nay, I am eighteen."

"Marvelous," Adaoun murmured. "How marvelous to be so young, and growing. . . . I remember quite well when the world was so young. But at last the One has blessed me with

ending. Day by day my body grows weaker, and it will not be
long now before I am gathered into death's embrace."

Trevyn flinched and lowered his eyes, for he was not
himself on such good terms with death. But he had no need to
respond. A young woman came toward them through the
birch grove, walking with a sway like sea wind, carrying a tray
of food. She brought it to Adaoun, her dress nearly as red as
Hal's red bird, set it before him, and wordlessly stood by his
side.

"This is Ylim." Adaoun introduced her as if her name told
all about her.

"Time's weaver beyond time, whom I met in Isle once,"
Hal added with amusement. "Alan and I blundered into her
valley where the elfin gold still flowered in spite of the blight
of the evil kings—but I did not know how to read her web
then, and I did not know her name, and certainly I did not
know her in that form."

It was the form that made Trevyn stare. How could this
lissome woman be the ancient seeress of Isle, the crone who
had given her advice to Bevan? He could believe that she was
ageless, for nothing about her suggested the tenderness of
youth. But she was also lovely, and, he sensed, dangerous, if
he so desired. Her skin, soft and lineless, glowed white as
lilies, as white as the belly of a white foal. Her hair, a ripple of
wild mane, fell almost to her knees, golden—silver. . . .
Trevyn blinked; it was of all colors, like a dream of horses, as
changeable as the moon, as shining as the sea. Indigo eyes
gazed back at him out of the full-lipped face, and something
in Ylim's level look made Trevyn lower his own eyes. They
caught on the high swell of her breasts, then closed in
confusion. Suddenly he recognized her as the "princess" he
had dreamed of in Isle.

"Well met, Alberic," said Ylim.

Her voice was husky, impersonal, not unfriendly. Trevyn
could not reply. He heard her turn and take her leave, but he
could not raise his eyes to look after her.

"You will get used to her presently," Adaoun remarked
mildly. "Come, help me eat."

He meant eat with him. There was enough food for all,
bread and mellow cheese and tangy fruits that Trevyn could

not name; perhaps they had no names. Afterward, he and
Hal followed the stream down to the seashore, where it
spread into a lagoon. Tufted grasses edged it, and tall birds
waded in the shallows, flashing blue or gray or green as they
caught the shifting light. Hal and Trevyn sat down on a
gravelly hummock to watch.

"So," blurted Trevyn, "am I dead?"

"Do you feel dead?" Hal asked dryly.

"How should I know? But Ylim is dead, I know that.
Father found her slain by lordsmen, and laid her to rest
beneath a willow tree—but she was an old woman then."

Hal puffed his lips. "Very true. But perhaps death need not
kill. Most men are born squalling, and eat and sweat and
brawl out their lives, and die, but there are some . . . Ylim is
not of mortal sort anyway. And never was. Nor is she elf. I
thing she is just—herself."

"But she has changed."

"Some are able to change—to go through the greatest of
changes—and yet not change. I knew her at once when I met
her here, though we had met only once before."

Trevyn swung his arms impatiently, batting away Hal's
words as if they were bothersome insects. "Uncle," he asked
doggedly, "am I going to be able to return to Isle? For return
I must, and quickly. There is grave peril."

"I did not want to ask before you were ready. But I can see
you have been in evil hands." Hal's eyes glinted angrily at the
thought. "What is it? The warlords again out of the north?"

"Nay. Far worse. Tokar."

"Tokar! The Eastern Invaders wish to try again! But Alan
will not let them land, Trevyn. They will be slaughtered as
they set foot on shore."

"They will not come by ship," Trevyn replied heavily. "Or
at least not at first. I think there are already invaders in Isle.
They come by magic and take for their own the bodies of
wolves." He stopped, expecting an argument, but Hal only
turned to him with a face gone intensely still.

"Do not think I disbelieve you," said Hal after a long
pause. "All things are possible. . . . But will you tell me what
has happened to make you say this?"

So Trevyn told him about the wolves, and Meg, and the

gilded ship, and Emrist, and the confrontation with Wael. He ached, thinking of Meg, and sharper pangs went through him when he spoke of Emrist. Still, those events seemed a distant and puzzling pattern to him from the far shore of Elwestrand, and he recounted them as if telling about a sorrowful dream. And with those memories still floating like lacework in his mind, he absently picked up a handful of gravel, let it trickle through his fingers, then froze, stunned. Each rough fragment had turned to a gem like a tear, silky smooth, of dusky sweet and subtle colors, shot through with winks of moth-white light. Trevyn touched them shakily.

"In another hand, or at another time," Hal marveled, "they might have become crystals, or bits of colored glass, or nothing. Expect no more, Trev. Those are the purest of gifts, as random as rain."

Trevyn picked out one that glimmered plumply, like a tiny moon, autumn pink, with a pale shape like a spindle at its heart. "For Meg, if I am ever to see her again," he stated grimly. "Which you have not yet told me, Uncle."

Hal sighed. "Not even an elf-boat can weather the winter storms on that wide sea. You must wait until spring, at least. Spring in Isle, I mean."

Trevyn jumped up, startling the wading birds, though not into flight. "While my father and my people suffer under Wael's treachery. . . . Thunder!" He turned on Hal in sudden consternation. "Do you have the brooch and the parchment safe?"

"I have the parchment, to my dismay. It is written in the court language of old Nemeton. An ugly reminder. But the brooch was not on the boat."

"Tides and tempests!" Trevyn groaned. "If Wael has it again, then all is lost."

"I dare say the sea guards it well," Hal comforted.

"She guarded it ill before. Mother of mercy, why did I not kill Wael when I had the chance!"

"Mother of mercy, why didn't you?" Hal threw the question back at him.

"Aene knows," replied Trevyn bitterly.

"Very true. "You were sent to Tokar in good time to know your enemy, but still kept from Wael's grasp. So you took it into your head to be a mute—forsooth!—which chance brought you straightway to the rare man who could help you. And that the old slave should have come to Rheged's palace—most wonderful. Ay, Aene has been at work." Hal searched Trevyn's face, and his voice softened. "I know it was a hard journey, Trev. But you must accept your scars as I have learned to accept. Everyone bears scars."

"I reproach the One for Emrist's sake," Trevyn snapped, "not my own. If only he could have been spared. . . ."

"You loved him well," Hal said gently.

"Ay. I think I could scarcely have loved him better if I had known him a lifetime, and I would gladly have befriended him that long."

"Yet you say he was not unwilling to die."

"When I left him." Trevyn turned tormented eyes to meet Hal's. "I don't know what they did to him after I had gone."

"Someone so frail would have died quickly." Hal grasped Trevyn with his gaze. "For whom, really, is it that you mourn, Alberic? Is it not, in truth, for yourself?"

Trevyn clenched his fists, but Hal went on, gentle even in his relentless understanding. "Do not think I trifle with your grief. More than one brave man has died in torment on my account."

Wild white swans sailed down between the trees, fleeting and lovely as spirits, if spirits could be seen. They skimmed past, singing softly among themselves, and disappeared over the waves before Trevyn spoke. Truth had struck him out of Hal's words like a blow to the heart, and it was with trembling voice that he brought himself to admit it. "I—I shall be so much alone, Uncle. I shall never have another such friend. And Father shall leave me before long—" He stopped, shaken by his own sureness. Hal nodded.

"Ay. The Sight is strong in you, Alberic."

Trevyn settled wearily back to his place by Hal's side, feeling weak and not understanding why. "Even if I make it back to Isle, to Megan," he murmured, "and even if she still loves me, and forgives me, and will have me, I shall be alone. Though woman's love counts for much joy."

"Much joy," agreed Hal softly, looking straight out to sea. "Nearly every night I dream of my sweet Rosemary. . . .

How I hope Ket gives her a babe, Trev. She is Isle's nurturer, the Rowan Lady of the Forest; with an heir she will be fulfilled at last. And Alan should come to me, as you have said. Far better fortune than I deserve. I was always a coward in love. . . . Bold enough in body, but a coward in my heart. Nemeton taught me early how love can be used for a torment, and I suppose I never learned better. Coming here, I thought I could not bear the pain of parting from you all. So I stilled my love, and left the pain to others."

"We understood," Trevyn protested. Hal glanced at him with a tiny smile.

"Did you? I doubt it; not Alan, anyway. . . . He is too great of heart to understand, but perhaps he will forgive. How I wish I could tell him that I love him." Hal's voice shook.

"I will tell him," said Trevyn quietly. "But will you not be able to tell him yourself, Uncle, when he comes here?"

Hal could not, or would not, answer. They sat, the two of them, side by side, and watched the sun approach, a fiery wheel out of the azure east—the edge of the west to all the rest of the world. They watched Menwy's dark dragons come up out of the sea to meet it, shaking their sinuous necks, sending up plumes of regal gold and purple spray. They circled, and the blazing disc, its gentler back turned toward Elwestrand, went down in their midst with a mighty roar of water and a bronze glow and with clouds of violet steam. Elwestrand lay beyond the sunset, as Hal had often said. The dragons plunged and vanished in a fountain of amethyst roil; twilight spread. Elwestrand went misty and charcoal gray, but still softly lit by the glow from the depths of the sea.

"He must swim all the way back by dawn," Hal said, stirring at last.

"He does so every day," Trevyn complained, annoyed by Hal's evasions. "Uncle, will you still not tell me if I am going back to Isle?"

Hal studied the darkening, pale-crested waves. "I do not know."

"You call me Alberic," cried Trevyn querulously, "and you speak of the Sight, and you say you do not know?"

"The Sight is a guide, nothing more. It is like a dream,

which deeds must make real. You must live out your own destiny, Trevyn. You must stay here, really stay, before you will be able to go."

"Say you will help me go, at least."

"I cannot say even that."

Trevyn sat staring at his uncle in perplexity. Hal would not return his gaze. Big, soft stars, like snowflakes, came out in the charcoal sky while they waited. A slender crescent moon took form atop Elundelei mountain.

"Why do you think you were brought here?" Hal broke silence at last.

"I can't tell! There is no sense to it. So that you can read me the parchment?" Trevyn laughed harshly. "That will not take until spring."

"Ay, it is for your knowledge, but in greater part, I think, it is for your healing." Hal turned to Trevyn at last, his voice soft with pity. "You have supped too full of sorrows, Trevyn. Put the cup from you a while. There is peace for you here. Taste it."

"How can I," Trevyn shouted, "when you talk riddles and will not meet my eyes? When you will give me no assurance?"

Hal sighed and wordlessly sent a flutter of plinset notes like pale green moths into the night; his instrument never lay far from his hand. A figure took form in the darkness of the beach, walking toward them. The man came and joined them, facing them, sitting cross-legged in the sand. An unaccountable trembling took hold of Trevyn.

"Emrist!" he whispered, though the stranger bore scarcely any resemblance to Emrist. He was slender, almost boyish, with dark, straight hair and coal-black eyes burning out of his fair face.

"Nay," he replied, "I am Bevan. I was in Emrist for a while before he died." His was the sweetest voice Trevyn had ever heard, manly and melodious, even lovelier than Hal's. "As I have been in others from time to time," he added, with a grave, moonlit smile at that other star-son, the Sunset King.

"I knew it!" Trevyn yelped. "Why—why would you not tell me?"

"Emrist could not know. He was himself, as he told you, and very brave. . . . I am not Emrist, Prince, though he is in me as I was in him. . . . How well I remember his love for you." Trevyn felt the touch of dark eyes. "I, myself, do not love you, not yet, but I remember. And nay, he did not suffer much at the end."

"It seems to me," Trevyn grumbled distractedly, "that everyone knows the pattern of my life except myself."

"It is always thus." Bevan wryly smiled, remembering his own entangled life. "Trust the tides, Alberic."

"That is easy for you to say, who are immortal," Trevyn retorted. "But if the tide tosses me to my death, that is the end for me."

"Why? What makes you think you are different from me? Because you are a fool? Think nothing of it, Prince. I am the one who bequeathed my kingdom a shadowed sword, who doomed my mother's people by the breaking of the caldron, who left the fairest maiden in Isle and the dearest comrade to follow a gleam." Bevan's tone was whimsical. "You are here with me, are you not, Alberic?"

Trevyn could not answer; the implications stunned him.

"Take hold of peace, Trevyn, and it will all come plain," said Hal quietly. "Lie back and watch the Wheel."

Trevyn sprang up and strode away from them both. But he paused when he reached the stream, feeling weakness overtake him. Dappled deer had come to drink; they did not tremble at his approach, but only raised their delicate heads to meet his gaze, sprinkling silvery droplets from their soft mouths. Trevyn stood, yearning, as Hal walked up beside him.

"I am afraid," Trevyn breathed. "I fear this peace. All day I have been on the edge between Elwestrand and Isle; both are like dreams to me, and I ache for both. I float, like a craft without a mooring. If I turn my thoughts away from Isle, she may be lost to me forever. I may never wish to leave this place of wonders. I may forget. And what then, if Wael has his way and sends his minions on to Elwestrand?"

"Bevan and I will take care of them." Hal sounded amused, and Trevyn snapped his head up to look at him.

"There is something you are not telling me. I don't understand."

Hal sobered. "Perhaps you will understand sometime," he

said softly. "Perhaps you will never understand. Does it matter?"

Trevyn wanted to shout that it did, and yet he vaguely sensed that it did not. The brief wisp of realization shook him, dizzied him. He lowered his head, pressed cool palms against his burning eyes, felt Hal's arms around his shoulders. He laid his head on his uncle's shoulder for a moment, feeling that touch ease him.

"Too long a day," murmured Hal. "I'm sorry. Come on; it is not far to our tent."

They trudged down the beach, side by side. The legendary Prince of Eburacon sat and watched them disappear into the dusky night, then winked out like swordlight sheathed.

Chapter Two

It took a week for Trevyn to regain normal strength. During that time he met many of his cousins and found, somewhat to his dismay, that they were all at least as handsome as he, and fleeter of foot. The girls stunned him with their beauty; he would not have dreamed of touching any of them. The people who were native to the Strand, whom the elves had wed, were as fair, but somehow unmistakably mortal, almost sensuous. Most of them had been there since the Beginning, Hal said, untouched by the shadow that had blighted Isle for a while. They were peaceful folk.

During that time also, Trevyn watched Hal populate an entire meadow with dazzling butterflies from his plinset. He experienced at least fifteen kinds of unicorn, each of them mostly white and utterly lovely. He watched Ylim's high-crested horses careering over the insubstantial distant hills. And he slept a lot, those lazy, healing days. One day, Hal came to wake him with a smile starting at the corners of his chiseled mouth.

"Have you been dreaming of trees?"

Trevyn sat up groggily. "I don't think so. Why?"

"Because they've sprung up all around the tent. Hazel,

alder, birch, rowan, kerm-oak, big and beautiful. I thought perhaps you'd been planting a grove in your sleep."

Trevyn blinked. "No, actually"—he yawned—"I think I was dreaming of Gwern."

"Of Gwern? The wyrd? Well, dream of him more often. There is always room for more trees."

Hal wandered out, singing softly. Trevyn followed, stretching and admiring his new grove. He and Hal had made a reluctant pact to begin reading the parchment he had brought from Tokar, a thing and a task that seemed supremely out of place in Elwestrand. Still, during the next few days they deciphered it, sitting beneath the dream trees. It was in the court language of the Eastern Invaders, as Hal had said, which he had been obliged to learn as a child, and he approached it with distaste. After he and Trevyn understood the spell for the transferring of the living soul, as well as they could grasp anything so vicious, they devised exorcisms in both Wael's unlovely language and in the Ancient Tongue. But Hal felt dubious.

"I have learned a bit about magic since I have been here," he expounded, "enough to know that for every spell there is a counter, and no end to it. I don't think this will settle anything, Trev—though perhaps I am not the best judge. I had some power, in Isle, but it was prophesied that I was not to use magic because the Easterners had made it shameful. A King's power must reside in rightfulness. I spurned the Sword of Lyrdion for that reason, and I still wonder if—if it is fitting for a King to do magic."

"To make birds out of air and music?" Trevyn smiled.

"Ah—but I am no King, here. And I am not the one that does it. Aene, perhaps."

"Bevan did magic, and he was the greatest of the High Kings."

"Ay, but that was in the old days." A twinge crossed Hal's face. "Before the Children of Duv went to woe, before the Easterners brought blight and shadow—"

"Magic is in us all, nevertheless. And anyway," Trevyn added, before Hal could argue, "if I can learn Wael's true-name, I'll have no need of spells. I'll need no other power to vanquish him."

"Then take care he does not learn yours." Hal's eyes narrowed. "From what you have told me, he seems like such a warlock as would have been at home in the dark keep of Nemeton. My old foe Waverly, perhaps."

"Or perhaps Bevan's old foe Pel Blagden, Emrist said. Where is Bevan? I would like to speak to him again."

Hal shook his head. "He is as hard to find as those mysterious hills of mine. I have only seen him twice, and one of those times was with you."

"You invoked him, whether you know it or not," Trevyn declared, "with your music. Well, I need some answers, Uncle. I am off to the mountain."

Hal raised his brows. "To Elundelei? Alone?"

"Of course, quite alone. Did you not tell me I could find truth there?"

"Truth and peril, ay. There might be a price to pay."

Trevyn sighed. "Well, I must risk it. And it seems to me—perhaps I have already paid."

He baked himself a supply of bread and got some cheese from the herders. Food came without great labor in Elwestrand, and people shared it cheerfully. Trevyn left on his journey the next morning, afoot, munching fruit from the wayside trees as he went. It did not occur to him, in Elwestrand, to catch a horse, subject it to his will, and ride. He would not attempt to harness any dream in this land of dreams. He walked toward the high pasturelands, the foothills of Elundelei, pausing from time to time to admire the coursers he saw.

It took him three days to top Elundelei. He met with no one after the first day, after he passed the upper meadows. The second day he wound his way up the crags—a steep path, but not perilous. Rowan and columbine grew in the cracks of the rocks, and the ledges were dense with ferns; he slept among them without a twinge. The third day, late, he reached the top and found a graceful tree with fruit that shone like Ylim's hair, silver or gold; he could hardly tell in the magenta light. He took one and ate it, for he was hungry. It filled him like bread, yet delighted him like red wine; he thought he could eat a dozen, but found he could scarcely finish the one. As he ate, he stood atop the crags and looked around him. He had heard that no one had ever been able to circle the shoreline of Elwestrand; it always stretched endlessly ahead. Yet, plainly, he stood on a tiny island, a mere speck in the vastness of the sea, which stretched into shadowy infinity on all sides. Only at the farthest reach of the east could Trevyn see a horizon, a thin, bright line. He faced it, watching for the sun. Behind him, and beside the laden tree, a seemingly bottomless cavern serpentined down between the last two upright horns of crag. The home of the moon, Trevyn knew. He would not enter there. He seated himself on the grassy plot beneath the tree and looked on from afar as the sun flamed into view, plunged and sank, boiling, into the sea. Great eagles, as golden as the sun, called and circled over Elundelei. Among them all, Trevyn saw, the largest one shone white.

"Alys," he whispered. No uproar ensued, no trembling of the mountain beneath him. "Alys!" he repeated, more loudly. Only intense stillness answered him. Even the eagles seemed stilled. The silence prickled at him, and he called no more. He sat without a fire as the purple twilight deepened into velvety night, not quite black. The strange Strand stars came out, the big, mothlike stars that formed pictures he did not quite understand: the Griffin, the Spindle, the Silver Wheel. Trevyn stared at them, and after a while, almost without conscious decision, he lay down on the grass and slept.

He was awakened by a touch of something—not a hand, something within. He looked up to see Ylim standing over him, a white gown floating around her, the half-revealed flesh of her breasts palely shining, full as the globes on the tree. With stumbling haste, he sprang up and away from her.

"Nay!" he declared. "Not again, not while Meg lives. It was shameful enough with Maeve." But she laughed at him softly.

"Have no fear; that is not my function. Come, you called, did you not?"

"Are you Alys?" he whispered.

"In a way. I can speak for her, and for Aene. But if you wish to truly meet Alys, you must come within."

"Within," he murmured weakly.

"Come," she chided, "you ate of the fruit, did you not, and still are standing? I knew you when you were a fleck on the outer rim of the Wheel. And now you fall asleep on the doorstep of the Hub."

Her tender scorn reminded him somehow of his mother. Half stung, half comforted, he followed her into the obscurity of the narrow cavern. He felt his way along the walls as the floor dropped with dizzying steepness under his feet. Ylim threaded her way swiftly before him, seeming not to need a light, through darkness so deep that he could not see even the white sheen of her dress. The passageway twisted and burrowed into the heart of the mountain. Then, just as Trevyn thought the depth and darkness would crush him, it took a gentle upward turn and leveled. Trevyn blinked in a whisper of pearly light. He could not find the source or tell the limits of the chamber. Shadows stirred all around him. In a moment his confused eye picked out the figure of a woman who sat on a glimmering curve of crescent throne, encircled by the most delicate of light: Ylim—nay, Maeve—nay, Megan! He started toward her, then stopped and swallowed at his half-formed tears as the vision flickered away.

"I can only appear to you in forms you understand, or partly understand," said a voice both distant and loving, feminine and fierce. Between the horns of the throne there appeared a blue-eyed cat, then a white swan; a silver harp; a ghostly, graceful ship. Finally there appeared the hazy form of a mandorla, shape of mystic union, floating above the crescent but still within its circular aureole. "Welcome, my well-beloved son," said the voice of the goddess.

Trevyn stood awed, but rebellion flared in him at that. "Well-beloved son! Then why do I bear scars?" he retorted curtly.

"Suffering is the mark of a Very King. Though you will be something more. . . . I demand suffering of those to whom I give my favor. Still, do not blame me for your whip weals. You could have found ways to prevent them, if you had let yourself be less than you are. If you had contented yourself to be a twittering, fluttering thing, such as most men are, instead of an eagle, you would have been spared much. The choice was yours."

"I was not aware of any choice," stated Trevyn stiffly. But the goddess of many names laughed softly at him.

"There is always a choice. . . . And now you are here. Is this what you have come for? To scold me?"

Trevyn stood strangling on his anger, vexed the more by the goddess's imperturbable good humor. It was as if, in motherly style, she did not consider his wrath worth ruffling herself. With an effort, he kept himself from stamping like a child in response. "I came to ask you about Wael," he said flatly at last. "He is my enemy; is he yours?"

"He has taken my creature, the wolf, that worships me, and turned it into a horror." For the first time Trevyn discerned an edge in the goddess's disembodied voice, and he warmed to her anger. "Wael was born as one of my children; everything is. But he has willfully dishonored me. Ay, he is my enemy. But he is not the worst enemy you face, Alberic."

Trevyn ignored that. He did not want another such lecture as Emrist had given him. "Then tell me, Goddess," he asked more politely, "how am I to defeat him?"

"Where are the dragons of Lyrdion?" she riddled in return. The mandorla twirled like a spindle, shimmering above the throne. Trevyn kept precarious hold of his temper.

"I know of a magical sword that came from Lyrdion."

"But I said nothing of magic or a sword. When you find the dragons of Lyrdion, you will know how to deal with Wael."

Trevyn shook his head at this nonsense. "I will need magic to face him."

"What is magic? The tricks Wael does? There is more magic in a stunted sour-apple tree than in all his sorcery. Be that tree, Prince, root and branch, leaf and flower, and you will know how to deal with Wael. Be whole, and you will know how to deal with Wael. Watch." The mandorla glowed brighter, and Trevyn became aware of its continuation, its beyond, the circles that formed its segments on opposing sides. Silver and gold they shone, softly at first but then with a flaming, spinning glory that stunned him beyond taking note of his surroundings. The sharp-ended curve where they met blazed with unfathomable, unsearchable candescence. Essence of sun and moon were in it, essence of earth and sky. . . .

"Aene," Trevyn whispered, hiding his eyes.

"So, there are some things you recognize readily enough." The mandorla subsided to a dusky shimmer, and Trevyn was once again able to face it. "Still, you will never be able to think of me as something other than female"—the voice changed to deeper, manly tones—"or male."

"Adaoun?" Trevyn murmured confusedly.

"Call me Wael, if you like. He is in me too." Trevyn started badly at that. But then Emrist sat for a moment on the crescent throne, smiling at him in reassurance. Adaoun; his father; Hal; a figure he did not at first recognize: it was himself, with a wolf curled at his feet. He watched himself lean down to pat it. "And in you," the voice added.

"Wael?" Trevyn protested. "If I knew his true-name, I would banish him off the earth."

"I have already told you his true-name half a dozen times. When you really know your own sooth-name, you will remember his."

The mandorla expanded, engulfed him, disappeared into the darkness on all sides. He knew it still surrounded him. Perhaps it surrounded the world. But all he could see was a simple circle before him, a halo of pale light culminating in the crescent of the throne. On impulse, Trevyn walked over to it, wondering vaguely of what metal or material it was made that it gave off such a pearly glow. He laid a hand on it and felt nothing beneath the hand—only a shock that flung him back and sent him tumbling into oblivion before he thudded against the wall.

He awoke, hours later, to find himself still confronted by the same whispering, muted light. It came from Bevan, who sat beside him on the floor, his face sober but not overly concerned.

"That was a bit bold," he remarked, "even for a Prince of Laueroc."

Trevyn sat up, rubbing a lump where his head had apparently hit something. "Have you been here long?"

"In a sense, I am always here." At Trevyn's sharp glance, Bevan smiled. "All right, no more riddles."

"Are you real?" asked Trevyn sourly.

The star-son shrugged. "Feel me, if you like. But what is 'real,' Prince?—All right, all right! Let me lead you out." He got lithely to his feet and helped Trevyn up with a warm and glowing hand.

Bevan walked with him all through the three days' journey down the mountain, though Trevyn made poor company, not talking much, only muttering to himself from time to time. "Am I to return to Isle?" he asked Bevan abruptly at one point.

"That is entirely up to you," the other coolly replied.

"Everything is up to me, and nothing is up to me!" Trevyn shouted. "I don't understand!" Bevan cupped his graceful hands, a peculiarly soothing gesture, and Trevyn subsided.

"It's all very well for you, all this mystery, Star-Son," he added tartly after a while. "The moon is your mother. But I am the son of—of a Sun King and an elf." Trevyn winced; the words rang with the wrong effect, even to his ears. "What does—what does She have to do with me? The one whose name I am not going to mention, lest I fail to utter it with proper respect and have something thrown at my sore head."

Grave Bevan almost had to laugh at his petulance. "You are also a child of the ash-maiden, and of earth," he said, restraining his mirth. "And all things are in Alys and Aene, and both are one, and both are in you; how can you separate yourself from anything? You are a star-son, as much as I. You are the child of the round-bellied mother whom we call Celonwy, the full moon, who mothers forth all things of earth. You love the maiden Melidwen, who sails her crescent boat across the sky. And Menwy of the Sable Moon—you haven't met her yet, but you will. The sea is her domain."

"I've met the others?" Trevyn asked, startled.

"Of course you've met them. Even if you've never loved a woman, there is still the goddess within."

They made their way down through the shelving, flower-studded pastureland and across the lush meadows beyond to a grove of silver beech where a man sat playing a peculiar stringed instrument to a group of wide-eyed children. A young-looking man, Trevyn thought, though gray streaked his hair. It occurred to him that Hal could not have touched a scholarly tome since he had been in Elwestrand. The former King of Welas rose to meet them, greeting Bevan with a silent touch of the hand.

"What did you find for answers?" he asked Trevyn.

"More questions. Where are the dragons of Lyrdion, and what is the magic of a rowan tree. Bah!" Trevyn flopped down amid the staring children, they who were as beautiful as he, every one of them. Hal strummed his plinset thoughtfully, picked out a jangling tune.

> "What is the stuff of magic? Clay,
>   and boughs that bleed, and roots that bind:
>
> Ardent alder brown-tipped,
>   red of hue beneath the bark;
>
> Ruddy kerm the holly-like,
>   the terebinth, the oak-twin;
>
> Mountain rowan quick-beamed,
>   high-flying, horse-taming,
>
> Royal canna arrow-swift,
>   golden ivy spiral-twining,
>
> Birch for birthing, heather, and
>   the white bloom of the bean for breath."

"What tune is that?" Trevyn asked. "Not one of yours, surely."

"Nay, it's an old, old tune I brought with me from Isle." Hal smiled ruefully. "Not a very good one, either."

"No wonder I've never heard it. Bah! Uncle, I'm done."

"Done?" asked Hal quietly.

"Done with striving, done with questioning, done with even trying to understand. There is no place for Wael in this western land, praise be. Let him go. For the time. Though I still fear . . ."

"What?" Hal sat beside him. The children shyly scattered, and Bevan saluted and wandered away between the lustrous tree trunks.

"That I will not remember to return, or wish to, come spring."

"Trust, Trevyn. Trust yourself, or trust the tide. It's all the same."

The Prince sighed shakily, like a child who has just ceased to weep, and rolled onto his stomach and went to sleep in the grass, knowing that Hal would awaken him in time for supper. Hal sat beside him without a sound. And out of Trevyn's mingling dreams formed yet another unicorn, a graceful, deerlike one with azure eyes and a spiraling golden horn. Hal glimpsed an odd curve centered in the eyes, a spindle shape—he could not be certain. The creature gravely bowed its heavy horn to him, then turned and stepped softly away on delicate lapis hooves, away toward the salt-flavored grass by the sea, as Hal looked after.

Chapter Three

Far across that sea, Tokar's treacherous attack on Isle had finally been launched. Four months of peace had passed since Trevyn had left Kantukal; it had taken Wael that long to make his preparations, so much had he been weakened by his defeat. Isle's ordeal would have been much worse if part of Wael's power had not been splintered along with a gilded figurehead. But his most essential power resided in another leaping wolf, the emblem on the parchment that set forth the Wolf's favorite spell. The talisman's potency sustained that spell even from Elwestrand, enabling Wael to run with his minions in the wilds, harrowing Isle with a horror that left folk floundering and helpless. For generations afterward, Islenders were to speak of "the Winter of Shadows," and tell its tales to their children when the mood for fear was on them.

The terror began silently, slowly. Later, no one could say exactly when or where. Some thought the first victim must have been the woodcutter who was found one day in the Forest above Nemeton with his throat torn out and coarse gray hairs stuck to his bloodied ax. Others said it was the lad from Celydon who never came back from herding the cows in the farthest meadow. Or the three guards from Whitewater who started through the Forest on horseback and never finished their journey. Robbers, folk had concluded at the time, though robbers had not troubled those parts for many years. But then rumors began of shadows, of gray, stalking forms seen amid the Forest trees at the approach of night, glimpsed by the cottage wife as she stooped for fuel or by the tenant gathering the rabbit from his snare. Fanciful talk, many said, for wolves were not likely to show themselves so boldly early in the season, when food was still plentiful. But when Rafe of Lee heard the reports of wolves, he frowned and arranged for extra patrols of the Forest purlieus.

It was the patrol, Brock Woodsby said, that saved his family and himself. Rafe's men heard the goodwife scream as they rode near the cottage and rushed in to find Brock, torn and bleeding, battling half a dozen gray brutes with the poker. The goodwife, shrieking, flung brands from the fire, and Megan wielded a table plank with a fierce abandon that had kept her thus far untouched. Meg had not screamed; this was the first time since Trevyn's departure that she had found good reason to be violent, and she was rather enjoying herself.

The wolves chose not to face swords. They scattered quickly, bursting through the windows, streaking toward the Forest. The patrollers could not follow; they were busy stamping out the flaming firewood that threatened to burn down the cottage. Moreover, their horses had bolted, and they were obliged to make their way back to barracks on foot. Brock left his family behind barred doors and went along, for doctoring and to speak to his lord.

"It was the lass they wanted," he told Rafe. "Right in at the door they came, and went for her with scarcely a glance at the wife or me. By good chance, Meg had a pot of scalding milk in her hand, and she threw it at them, kettle and all; that blinded them for a bit. But then they went at her again as bad as ever. They weren't starved wretches, my lord; they were as sleek and strong as pit dogs fed for the fight. I don't like it."

"Nor do I, no whit!" Rafe gulped. "Do you think the girl would be safe here at the manor fortress?"

"I'll send her up at once. Thank 'ee." Brock departed, and Rafe went straight to his table to write to Alan.

To my Dear Friend and Golden Protector, Alan, Liege King in Laueroc, Greeting,

the missive ran, for Rafe loved a courtly flourish.

I sorely crave your presence and advice in this matter of the wolves, of which my young lord the Prince may have told you. They have become bolder now, even entering in at the cottage door, seeking to rend the maiden Megan, which must be on the Prince's account, whom she holds dear. My mind is at pains to know the meaning of this thing, of which question the Prince could offer no answer. Now others remark it; the land is rife with talk of the daring of the beasts; my men fear them, though they will not say it; and my heart is full of unreasoning distress, though I feel the fool even to write it! Pray commend me to your lady, and pray counsel me in this matter as swiftly as you may see fit. In love and service, Rafe, from Lee, the second week of December, the twentieth year of reign.

A messenger took this swiftly to Laueroc, to the King. Alan puzzled over it for some time before he heavily climbed the stairs to Lysse's sunlit tower chamber and handed it to her. "Did he say anything to you?" he asked her.

"Trevyn?" She wondered why he would not speak their son's name.

Alan only nodded.

"Nay, he said nothing to me of wolves," Lysse replied. "Rafe seems disconcerted."

"Ay, I must go to him, I suppose. Rafe was always one to shout at a pinprick, but still . . ." Alan eyed his wife, frowning. "You told me we would have hard times. Did you see any trouble of this kind?"

"Nay. And the Sight is lost to me these days; I cannot advise you, my lord." Lysse spoke without self-pity, and kept her eyes on her hands so as not to accuse him, for she knew quite well that the cause of her loss was that he withheld his love from her. Alan knew it also, and knew she would not judge him, and found himself irked by her fineness even as he longed to comfort her. The leaden lump that was his heart had no comfort to offer. After standing awhile and finding nothing to say, he turned and left her without a word.

Within the hour he took horse toward Lee and kissed her ceremoniously from the saddle. It was the first kiss she had received from him since his return from Nemeton. She wondered if she would ever see him again; her loss was so great that she could not tell. Still, she noted that the green Elfstone she had given him shone proudly on his chest. And as he turned from her, the rayed emblem at its heart blazed back at her with sudden brilliance. Lysse thankfully accepted this sign for her sustaining, and felt it warm her as she watched her husband ride away.

When Alan came to Lee, Rafe greeted him with fervent relief. There had been more attacks: a peddler dragged from his cart, a young wife torn as she searched for her cow. The wolves struck in the evening hours, and, except in Meg's case, in the open. The patrols saw them often, grinning from twilight shadows, but then darkness and the Forest would swallow them up. Hunts had been organized to no good effect; twice Rafe's men had located wolves, but their horses shied from the attack and their quarry mocked them.

"And Meg has gone off somewhere, confound the girl," Rafe added.

Megan had responded to her father's arrangements on her behalf with silence and a tense whiteness at the tip of her pointed nose. She had obediently gone to pack her things, then slipped out of the cottage and disappeared before her parents knew she was missing. Not for any peril would she be sent to the manor town, where people would stare at her and whisper behind her back! She had not been seen since. It was hard to believe that she would have been so foolhardy as to venture into the Forest, much as she loved it. And yet . . . Still, Alan could not say where the girl might be, and he was far more concerned with the wolves then.

"How many are there, do you think?" he asked.

"I cannot tell. We know there were six at goodman Brock's. My men see them in twos and threes. . . . Travelers say that folk are in fear of them as far north as the Waste. But I hope they may not be many, only roaming far afield. They run tirelessly, as fast as a horse."

"Many or few, they will not be easily come upon," Alan grumbled. "The Forest is large."

"Vast," Rafe agreed quietly, "and few know the inwardness of it as well as you, of the place or its creatures. I have heard there are strange things deep within."

"Haunts, and hot steams, and grottos, and moss-men, and soft voices in the night." Alan eyed Rafe pensively. "All that is wild and wonderful. But no such evil as this."

"Then you know nothing of it?" Rafe was crestfallen.

"Nothing. Not even as much as you. I had heard no news of wolves before I received your letter."

"What! The lad didn't tell you—"

"Not a whisper." Alan's face darkened, but he tried to make light of Trevyn's omission. "On account of the lass, I dare say."

Rafe grinned at that, then told the tale quickly enough. Alan heard it in heavy-hearted silence, envisioning a glittering ship with a leaping wolf for figurehead and a sunburst brooch lodged in the pebbles of the Long Beaches. "I must go to Nemeton," he said abruptly when Rafe was done.

"What!" Rafe was taken aback.

"It is there that the true peril will strike. From the east; I am sure of it. I must warn Corin. And I will send for Ket, though I know he will be sorry to leave Laueroc. Perhaps his woodsmanship can help you. And I will get you men to aid you in your patrols, and I will go myself to Whitewater, to see Craig. There is one who knows the Forest, Rafe, though I expect his old bones would rather bide by the fire."

"To Nemeton!" Rafe still floundered.

"Ay!" Alan clapped him on the shoulder, as if to awaken him. "But I will return within the month, if I can. Celydon also should increase the guard. If I write some orders, will you send them for me?"

"Of course," muttered Rafe, then burst out, "There is no Forest within miles of Nemeton!"

"Those creatures are in the Forest, but not of it. Nor do I judge that we can hunt them down, though of course we must try. . . . But for now, and unless Ket advises otherwise, I think you will do well enough if you just keep them within the Forest and your folk unharmed. Waste no men in pursuing them."

Alan went off to write his letters. The hardest was the one to Lysse, appointing her his second-in-command and telling her to send Ket to await him at Lee. He knew he had treated her badly, and his warrior spirit drove him to give her what he could, if only honesty. He wrote:

I feel a foreboding beyond all measure of reason that these wolves may put an end to us, Love. So if I do not see you again, shall you still know that I love you? It is true, my heart had gone as dead as a stone within me, but that changes nothing. The sun shines even when the clouds cover it; pray trust in that, as I must. Keep Rosemary by you there, to comfort you, and do not let her come to Celydon, as I know she will long to do; it is too perilous. Tell her that I charge her to stay with you. Now I must hasten to Nemeton, to warn Cory of a danger I can scarcely describe.

He traveled to Nemeton as fast as his retainers could follow him, skirting the Forest, though the precaution galled him. After spending only one evening with Corin he pressed onward, up the Eastern Way, to take counsel with Craig, former leader of all the outlaws in the southern Forest. Even as he traveled he heard rumors of wolves. They stalked the Forest's fringes in broad daylight now, folk said, and attacked children sent to gather sticks for the hearth. People were beginning to suffer for lack of fuel, for no one dared now to go near the Forest unless in the safety of a large group. When he came to Whitewater, Alan found that Craig had already organized patrols and expeditions for the gathering of wood. The old outlaw could not explain the strange behavior of the wolves. He had never seen anything like it, not in all the years he had dwelt in the wilds.

"Surely it cannot be *all* the wolves," Craig offered in his cautious way.

"It could be a dozen, perhaps a score, and those very industrious in their perversity, hah? But there will be more, and worse trouble to come, Craig; I feel it."

"For half my life I fought brutes in men's clothing," Craig shrugged. "It will be no worse to fight brutes that wear hair and go on all fours."

"That is very true," Alan murmured. "I have never met such brutes except in human form. . . . I must make the acquaintance of these wolves."

And the next day he rode straight into the Forest, though his retainers followed him nervously and Craig creased his brow in protest. They wound their way through the wilderness in the half-light of a gray winter's day, glancing over their shoulders at the gloomy distances beneath the trees. But it was not in a shadowy assault that Alan met his adversary. While the day was still young, the company came up against a big wolf sitting on its haunches squarely in the path, as indolent as a dog on a doorstep, with its long tongue lolling from its grinning mouth. Alan motioned his men to hold.

"What game is this, little brother?" he asked in the Old Language.

The wolf laughed, a shrill, yapping sound. "The sweetest game, O Crowned Head! Likely it will give you the soundest sleep you have ever known. Your heir has learned the game, O Fading Sun; ask him about it, when you see him! Where is the Princeling, O Majesty?"

Alan flushed hotly with inarticulate rage and signaled his men to the attack. But on the instant a dozen more wolves leaped to the side of the first, facing them with gleeful snarls. The horses reared back from the sight, plunging for escape, even the *elwedeyn* horse that Alan rode. He flung himself down from his unruly steed and snatched out his sword to attack the wolves on foot, heedless of his men's frightened cries. But his enemies turned away and trotted off into the Forest, insolent in their leisure. When they were gone, Alan's fury turned all at once into sick sorrow, making him so weak that he leaned on his sword for support with the blood of his son swirling before his eyes. Shed to death by tearing teeth, Alan thought.

"If these are creatures of the One," he groaned, "then we have all been betrayed." His wrath and despair hardened within him into a cold, helpless knot of resolve.

He left the Forest, leading his retainers back to Whitewater for the night, then northward the next day onto the barren, stony expanse of the Waste. He did not tell Craig his plan. Alan did not like to speak of deeds until he had done them. And Craig would not have heard of Hau Ferddas anyway, except perhaps as the dimmest kind of legend, a children's tale of a long-ago magical sword. Even scholars who had studied the ancient Great Books hardly knew more. But Alan had seen the magnificent golden sword one day of his youth, and Hal had touched it, and renounced it, and let it lie.

"Mine by right," Alan muttered as he rode, for he traced his lineage to the ancient house of Lyrdion.

He took his men for a hard journey, pressing the pace, riding long and late, sleeping short hours on the comfortless ground. Still, Winterfest had come and gone without their notice before they reached the place Alan remembered. A copse, a scar of brittle stone, a gentle rise, and a barrow on top ringed by man-size standing stones. Alan's retainers, pallid and trembling, pulled their horses to a stop without his command. They sensed the haunt, he knew.

"Wait for me here, then," he told them, and left his horse with them, and strode, businesslike, up the hill. But halfway to the barrow the fear of the unresting shades struck him in his turn, brought him up short with astonishment that almost topped the terror: he had not felt such fear of the wakeful dead since the day, years ago, that Hal had taken his hand and led him gently through their cordon. Hal's warm touch. . . . The memory, though mixed with pain, softened the fear somewhat, and he was able to push his way through it. Bent and panting, he reached the barrow. The fear left him at the circle of standing stones, but no warm welcome awaited him. He sensed the spirits' dismay tingling through their bodiless presence all around him.

"Elwyndas," spoke a deep voice, echoing through a void of

time and Otherness. The single word, Alan's elfin name, seemed to be neither greeting nor question, but rather a reminder—of what? Prophecies and destinies? Mireldeyn had left; those days were over now.

"Culean," Alan responded coolly. The last of the High Kings had been cut off in his youth, in the ruin of his realm, and by his own hand.

"You come here with anger and hatred in your heart," the low voice of the dead King stated. "Why? You have always been full of loyalty and love." ·

"I have enemies now," Alan grimly replied, "and my loyalties have betrayed me. Aene, brother, wife, and son— they have all betrayed me." He stooped and started tugging at the barrow stones, clawing himself an entrance.

"You come for the sword? But it was not offered to you, Elwyndas, worthy as you are of all our aid. We were told that an elf-man shall take it back to the sea. Your son, perhaps."

"You will wait long for him!" Alan shouted, stung by sudden pain. He grappled furiously with the stones, then crawled into the barrow. The dim interior was much as he remembered: bones, dust, weapons, shreds of ancient finery. Centered under the dome lay a slab supporting the remains of High King Culean, his blackened crown, and his mighty sword. Stepping over skulls, Alan made his way to the skeleton's side and reached for the sword, then hesitated with his hand poised to take it, feeling an eerie reluctance seize him.

"That sword could kill one whom you love," breathed the deep, unearthly voice of the departed monarch. "It killed me." But Alan felt stubborn resentment stir in him at the dead man's interference.

"What, am I to surrender Isle to the wolves, then?" he mumbled, and grasped the golden sword by its jewel-studded hilt, wrestled it from its place. The weapon hung heavily in his hand, its massive point dragging on the ground. With an effort, Alan swung it clear and carried it outside. Strange—it had not seemed so unwieldy when Hal had lifted it, and he remembered its fair golden sheen. But now the precious metal glared coppery red in the cold daylight and the jewels crouched sullenly, unblinking, on the hilt. Alan matched their stare for a moment, frowning, then suddenly pulled off his cloak and wrapped the sword in it, scorning the winter wind. Heaving Hau Ferddas up, he hoisted it with both hands, lancelike, and trudged back to the others. The reproachful presence of the spirits followed him far down the hill.

Chapter Four

"There was no scabbard," he told Rafe crossly, a week later. He had carried Hau Ferddas to Lee wrapped in his blanket, finding himself obliged to sleep with it, when he chose to sleep. He had set course straight through the Forest and kept good guard, with fully half his men standing awake at night. Alan took turns at guard himself, swinging his heavy weapon. But no wolves were to be seen, though the Forest often rang with their mocking wails, full of darkest meaning to Alan's ears. His whole being felt dragged down into that darkness when he reached Lee. And Rafe met him with a haggard face.

"I have not succeeded in doing even what you said. The patrols cannot contain them. They stalk the land now by bright light of day, and folk huddle within doors for fear of them. Only yesterday, my men found a graybeard and his goodwife dead in their home. They froze for want of fuel."

"The wolves are to blame, even so," declared Ket. He had come from Laueroc to join Alan, bringing him Rhyssiart, Trevyn's golden charger, and a missive from Lysse. He would have need of a war horse, she said. She had put out a call for volunteers, and when companies were formed she would send them eastward. She longed to see him, even if only for a day, to talk with him. But there was no gainsaying the dread that lay over the land, a vague and shadowy fear that touched even the folk of Laueroc, who lived far from any forest. She would see him when the peril was past. Alan felt shamefully glad that he would not have to face her. For some reason he would not explain even to himself, he could not have showed her the sword.

He showed it to Ket and Rafe in private. Ket was dubious, Rafe awed and cheered by the sight of Hau Ferddas. "So that is the weapon of which Gwern sang!" he exclaimed, and Alan lifted his bent head to eye him fishily.

"Gwern sang? That must have been a treat! And how would he know of this sword?"

"What matter?" Rafe cried recklessly. "You have got yourself a magical sword to use against the wolves! Now, if only you could find a magical steed to put under it!"

Alan had ordered Rafe special troops from Laueroc, picked men mounted on horses of the elfin blood. But the news of their performance was disappointing.

"Ordinary horses flee from the wolves," Rafe reported bleakly. "The *elwedeyn* steeds flee sooner and more swiftly. They bolt at even the sound of a wolf."

"Marvelously sensible creatures," Alan grumbled. "If only we could all follow their example! But Isle is not big enough for that. Has Rhyssiart had a chance to prove himself, Ket?"

The lanky seneschal looked uncomfortable. "Ye know I'm no horseman, Alan. But the first time we spied a shadow in the Forest, he carried me clear back to the river before I could stop him."

"We must hunt the wolves afoot, then."

"That suits me," Ket drawled.

"My men have no stomach to face them afoot, not in the Forest," Rafe stated. "And I will not order them to do what I would not do myself." His fear showed frankly in his dark, ardent eyes.

"Rafe and the Forest," Alan sighed. "Will you never come to terms? Well, Ket and I are woodsmen, and we'll find some volunteers. What power will we need, do you think? How many wolves are seen these days?"

"As many as a dozen at a time!" Rafe burst out. "I've seen that many myself—and none have been slain! They will not come near a sword, though they mock a swordsman from a distance. Instead, they plague the poor folk who are helpless against them. They are clever, insolent cowards!"

"We must bait them, then, to entrap them." Alan's eyes glowed with a grim light that made Rafe stare.

"How?"

"Don't you think," Alan rejoined, "that they would like to catch themselves a King?"

Alan proposed to lure the wolves into battle, using himself as an enticement. But Ket and Rafe both opposed the plan, magical sword or no. With the Prince absent, Alan's peril also put the throne at stake. The three of them argued for hours. Rafe was so dismayed that he offered to go himself in Alan's stead. Rafe, who regarded the Forest with nightmare dread! Even in his despair, Alan was touched by such loyalty. But talk of Prince and kingdom meant nothing to him. For some reason beyond reason, he believed they were as good as lost. And he felt angrily compelled to thrust himself against his enemy. He silenced the protests at last by power of his royal command, and he and Ket laid their plans.

Alan was to venture into the Forest on horseback with a few retainers, few enough to tempt the wolves but still sufficient to provide some security. He would appear to hunt at random, but actually he would ride toward a fortified place known to him and to Ket, who had roamed these parts for years of outlawry. Ket would follow him after an hour or so with more men and with blankets and food, backpacked, in case the horses fled. Ket and Alan knew the Forest. It would take them no more than a day or two to return to Lee afoot—if they lived.

The following morning dawned gray, but clear of sky. Alan started out early with a company of half a dozen men, carrying his monstrous sword. The evening before, wolves had set upon a young tenant as he hauled water to his cottage. Alan and his men rode to the spot, then cantered into the Forest, following the tracks of their quarry. After a while they seemed to lose the trail and went on deeper into the vast woods, appearing to search aimlessly. The men glanced about them nervously, but followed their King without a murmur. Before midday the wail of the wolves arose from all sides. The men stiffened in their saddles and the horses shied, but Alan smiled grimly.

"Good," he said. "They are keeping their distance, and we will meet them as planned. Hold your pace."

They continued at the walk and heard the wolves draw gradually closer. But before long they came to the remains of what must once have been a circular tower. Twice man high at spots, it was at least waist high all around, except for the gaping doorway.

"What people could have built this, to abide here in this wilderness?" a man wondered aloud.

"A very ancient people," Alan answered him equably, "for I dare say the Forest has grown around it since. . . . Tether your horses off to one side there, and range yourselves within."

They dismounted and took positions with drawn swords. Alan himself took the door, with Hau Ferddas in hand. His eyes glinted and his nostrils pulsed at the thought of combat, a chance to vent his hatred and despair. He felt Hau Ferddas lighten in his hand, come alive. Roused, it sliced upward and poised itself, like a stooping hawk, at the level of Alan's face.

"Here they come," he told his men.

A rippling, flowing mass of gray, the wolves loped from among the trees. The horses shrieked, snapped their tethers, and bolted away. Within the moment, wolves as large as half-grown calves surrounded the ruined tower three deep, standing with trembling eagerness, jeering. Alan felt his hair prickle, for he understood their song, though he could not tell why they lusted for his blood. He recognized their leader at once: the wolf even bigger than the rest, seated apart. It was the same insolent brute he had encountered near White-water; he felt sure of it. This time Alan would not speak to it, but he studied it intently. Bristly gray snout and eyes of yellowish hue—where had he seen those bilious eyes before?

The jaundiced gaze met his, and for a moment Alan's body went as watery as tears. Hau Ferddas faltered in his hand, and he didn't notice; all he could see was Trevyn's fair form, torn and defiled by leering beasts. Then something rock-hard within him pushed the vision aside. Anger surged through him, the sword leaped in his hand, and his head snapped up, shaking off the haze of nightmare. In an instant the wolf leader yapped, and battle was joined.

Like so many arrows loosed from the same string, the wolves sprang. The sword in Alan's grasp whistled down at them of its own accord, rendered mighty by its own weight, breaking a lupine neck with its first blow. Chanting harshly, filled with a fierce, bitter joy, Alan raised a pile of dead wolves before him. But the living ones sprang again and again, gleefully, mindlessly, leaping over the bodies of their slain comrades as if they were so much grass.

Lost in the satisfaction of his own power and revenge, Alan did not notice at first that his men were tiring, flinching wide-eyed from the frenzy of the wolves. Then the man beside him gurgled and fell, borne down by the wolf that had leaped past his wearied stroke. Alan turned and smote, but the blow came too late; the beast had opened the man's throat.

"Courage!" Alan shouted to the others. "Ket should come soon." From his easy seat off to one side, the big wolf panted his pleasure. But in a moment his sneer faded, as Ket and his company burst into view.

Their horses plunged about and would not charge. So they dismounted and let the steeds bolt, forming a long line of attack on foot. Ket fought with the bow, his favorite weapon. His men used swords or cudgels. Even with swords to front and swords to back, the wolves lost none of their feverish zeal. But their numbers were lessened, and they were forced back. Hemmed in by the press, the leader rose from his place and circled, growling. "Get that one!" Alan shouted, pointing, and Ket aimed his shaft. Then he froze, stunned.

Wolves poured out of the Forest; wolves, so it seemed, by the hundred. Before Alan could stir his tongue to cry out, they engulfed Ket and his men, as sudden and deadly as a flood. Soldiers fell, screaming, and the few with Alan in the tower stood dumbfounded with shock. His own shield arm hung slack, his magical sword plummeted earthward, and before his very face loomed the grinning countenance of the yellow-eyed leader. Obstinate instinct still stirred in Alan, though hope was gone. Rallying, he cut at his bestial adversary and called on those from whom he had often received succor in the past: *"O lian elys liedendes, holme a on, il prier!"* ["Oh spirits of those who once lived, come to me, I pray!"] Then he shouted to his men, "Stand! Stand where you are, for your lives' sake!"

The presence of the spirits enveloped them instantly, and his command was lost in the uproar that resulted. Wolves and men shrieked, their screams mingling and their paths crossing as they fled into the Forest like demented things. Though the spirits came to Alan as friends in his time of need, the others felt them only as a mind-blackening terror of the unknown. The wolfish leader scuttled away from them like a kicked cur. Ket's face went as white as death, and he swayed as if he had been struck a mighty blow. "Ket! Stand!" Alan cried, dropped his sword and ran to him, leaping corpses. The spirits had already passed and gone their way. Alan held Ket until his trembling stopped and he raised his head, gasping for air like a drowning man.

"What wonder is this?" he demanded shakily. "The haunt is miles hence. Has it come to us?"

"I called the spirits, ay. Are you all right, Ket?"

"I'll live," he sighed.

"Come, help me, then." They turned their attention to the bodies that choked the place, checking them one by one. There were no survivors; the wolves had struck straight to the life's blood of each man. Alan and Ket would not meet each other's sickened eyes.

"What about the others?" Ket asked gruffly.

"We must try to round them up, I dare say. . . . But look, it is starting to snow."

Tiny, hard-edged flakes whizzed past thickly, harried by a biting wind. Already, as Alan spoke, the ground was sprinkled and the trees shrouded with white.

"The sky was clear this morning," Ket complained wearily. "Whence came this snow? And whence came those wolves, I wonder? There were none about as we rode; I would swear to that. It's as if someone conjured them up."

Alan shot him a startled glance, then shook off the thought; he did not like the notion of such a conjuror. And the present

pressed harder. He and Ket loaded themselves with blankets
and food from the dead men's packs. Alan fetched his sword.
He regarded the massive, bloody brand in sudden distaste,
cleaned it on the snowy ground, and swaddled it.

"I need a horse just to carry this thing," he grumbled,
cradling it in both arms.

He and Ket plodded off into the Forest, toward Lee, for
some of the men had run that way. They called for them as
they walked, and got no answers. Trees looked like ghosts of
trees in the snow, and an eerie silence brooded all around.
After a while Ket and Alan let their shouts trail away. Ket
peered into the wilderness, stopped, and for no reason set
arrow to his bow.

"Do we need to fear those wolves, think ye?"

"I can't say." Alan frowned, bemused. "Animals should
not fear the shades of dead men. . . . I can't even say why I
summoned the spirits, except for sheer, desperate whim. Yet
the wolves ran away with plentiful speed, Ket. I fear this snow
more right now."

In fact, the two of them were already having trouble
keeping their course toward Lee. The Forest had turned into
a directionless fog of white. Occasional sounds echoed
weirdly in the muffled silence. Ket and Alan blundered along
blindly, watching for shelter, searching for their comrades,
finding neither. The day drew on. They could not tell the hour
by the pallid light, but they felt the pressure of time. They had
to find a refuge before nightfall.

"It'll be a marvel if any of us make it back to Lee," said
Alan starkly.

Ket gasped by way of answer and raised his bow. Something gray had moved in the dizzying whiteness not far before
them. But Alan struck Ket's arrow into the air with his hand.

"There's no malice in that wolf," he exclaimed. "Look
again."

She stood facing them not ten feet away, great-bellied with
young, her gray fur fluffed softly by the wind, levelly meeting
Alan's gaze. In a moment she came up to him and tugged at
the hem of his tunic with her teeth, whining.

"*Galte faer; el rafte,*" Alan told her. ["Lead on; I'll
follow."]

"What?" Ket demanded. He could not understand the Old Language.

"She wants us to follow her." Alan strode after the wolf that bounded away through the drifting snow, swift and supple in spite of her maternal girth.

"And what if she leads us into a trap?" Ket cried, hurrying after. "If she takes us to the pack?"

"Would you rather freeze to death in the snow?" Alan shot back over his shoulder. Ket silently panted along behind him, teeth clenched against a sharp reply. "She is a brave and generous creature," Alan added more gently after a bit. "She will lead us to no harm."

They stumbled along through the darkening day, numb from cold and fatigue, straining their dazed eyes for the quick, shadowy form of the female wolf beneath the creaking trees. Sometimes she would dash back and whimper at them, impatient at their slowness. As the light grew worse, she stayed closer to them, whining anxiously. They followed her more by sound than by sight. Night had almost fallen when Ket jerked to a standstill.

"The haunt," he whispered. "We're turned clear around, and gone beyond where we started. I feel the haunt ahead."

"I know. Come on!" Alan muttered, and reached out to tug at Ket's unresponsive arm. "It's the best of good fortune that she takes us to the haunt, Ket, don't you see? Nothing evil can reach us there."

Ket plunged on a few steps, then stopped, quivering, unable to move. The Forest had gone almost black; only vaguely looming forms could be seen amid the flutter of the snow. Ahead of Alan, the wolf barked sharply.

Alan obeyed that urgent summons. He dropped his bundled sword and seized Ket as quickly as he could, lifted him bodily, and slung him over his shoulders. Taken by surprise, Ket gave a startled shout, struggling in Alan's grasp.

"Hold still!" Alan wheezed, bent nearly double under his burden, struggling after the wolf. She led him now by walking, doglike, almost at his feet. Their course lay between ancient earthworks and barrows, he dimly sensed, though not with sight. He could feel the bodiless presence of the spirits and feel Ket's fear, a taut distress that somehow augmented the man's weight on his back. If only Ket would faint, or even scream. . . . Alan wondered how much farther he had to stagger.

Then: "Look," he whispered. "A light." Ket gave no answer, though Alan could tell he turned his head to see. Not far ahead, ruddy firelight flickered. The wolf streaked toward it. The haunt lay behind them now, an encircling barrier against any harm, and Ket went limp as a rag with relief. Alan lunged forward, banging against trees, and stumbled through an open doorway. The wolf sat, panting, by the fire, under a low, vaulted roof of unhewn stone. Alan dumped Ket on the ground and straightened himself painfully to look around.

Firelight showed him a small, musty stone chamber, circular in shape, evidently long disused. Smoke stung his eyes, finding its way reluctantly from the central hearth to window slits. Wreckage of a stone stair led to rubble where an upper room had once been. Snow blew in at the doorless entry. A jumble of deadwood for burning climbed halfway up the bare walls on all sides. Beyond the fire stood a figure, very still. . . . Alan felt an unexpected leap and tumble of heart. He saw a royal-blue cloak, and he recognized the brooch that fastened it—but the person looked far too small to be his son. A mere slip of a girl confronted him, huddled in the thick cloth. A name floated effortlessly to Alan's mind.

"Meg?" he blurted.

"Ay." She frowned up at him, as bold as a trapped mouse but not, somehow, uncourteous. "And who're ye that my friend has brought me instead of dinner?"

"I—I am Trevyn's father." Alan stammered out the name, amazed to find that he could not call himself King, not to her. And why would she believe him anyway? he asked himself hotly. Covered with snow as they were, he and Ket might as well have been a pair of brigands. But Meg gazed into his face and silently nodded.

"And this is Ket the Red," Alan added, going to kneel by his companion. "Ket, this is Meg."

The poor fellow was sitting up, looking perturbed, his face nearly as pale as the snow. Alan brushed him off, grumbling softly. "Sorry to have hauled you in here like that. I should have stunned you first, but there wasn't time."

Ket rolled his eyes. "I'm as glad not to have a lump on my head."

"Can I get ye something to eat?" Meg offered doubtfully. There was not a bit of food in sight. Ket looked at her in dry amusement.

"Ay, I'm famished. What's fer supper?"

"Only a bit of cold fish," she admitted. "I was expecting Flossie to bring me a rabbit for supper, and she brought me you two instead."

Ket and Alan both eyed the wolf. She lay curled by a tangle of firewood opposite the door, her plume of a tail covering her nose, her dark eyes shining over it. Lovely eyes, Alan thought. "We're grateful," he said suddenly. "Bring the fish, Meg, and we'll put something more with it."

He and Ket started digging in their packs, scattering blankets in the process. "Such beautiful blankets!" Meg breathed, though they were mostly plain brown. Then she gazed, wide-eyed, as food began to appear.

As it turned out, no one even touched the fish. They ate fresh bread lightly toasted by the fire, and bits of cheese, and dried apple snits, and sausage that they roasted on sticks until it dripped and sizzled. Alan and Ket fixed a blanket over the gaping doorway with arrows jammed between the stones. Meg sat by the fire, flushed pink from warmth and food and excitement. She had not felt so comfortable and full in weeks, and already she adored Alan, though she stood in awe of him. Her shy smile eased the taut angles of her face. Watching the quiet way her small head rode above her borrowed finery, Alan began to understand how Trevyn might have loved her. She moved with the unschooled poise of all the wild things.

Ket had heard about Meg and Trevyn at Lee. He felt ready to be fond of her, since she, a country person like himself, had likewise found herself entangled with these mysterious Lauerocs. He also regarded her with something of wonder. "So ye're Rafe's runaway!" he exclaimed, sitting at his ease. "And in the haunt! I roamed these parts for more years than I care to remember and never met a man who could brave this haunt, except a certain pair of rogues who became Kings. And now I've had to be carried into it. How'd ye ever come here, lass?"

"I can't say," she answered, puzzled. "I just didn't care, that's all. . . . I was cold and tired and disgusted, and I wasn't going to be tracked down and taken back to Lee, not for anything. People have been snickering at me ever since . . ." She stopped.

"Since my son left you," Alan put in quietly from his side of the fire.

"Ay. They envied us when we were together, and now they are glad to see me saddened. I would rather live among the beasts; they are kinder." Meg talked to the fire, but in a moment she straightened to meet Alan's eyes. "What news of Trevyn, Liege?"

"He's dead," said Alan harshly.

"What!" shouted Ket, and for no reason scrambled to his feet, utterly startled.

"He's dead, I say. I dream of his corpse at night." Alan turned away from them both, tired tears wetting his face. He could not say what had moved him to speak the truth as he perceived it. He had hurt the girl to no purpose, he berated himself. He could have let her hope yet a while. . . . Still, it felt good, the warm release of tears on his cheeks.

"Sire." Meg came to stand before him, facing him. "Have ye seen Gwern about this?"

"Nay." Alan found that he did not mind her steady-eyed presence. "Why, lass?"

"He will know where Trevyn is, or if he is really dead. I am sure of it."

Alan grimaced in exasperation. "Gwern, this and Gwern, that! Gwern eats of my food and sings of my sword. . . . Who is this Gwern, that he knows everything and does nothing?" The King waved his arms in a grand gesture of futility. "I can't go chasing after a barefoot weathercock, lass! I am likely to have a war to fight."

"I'll go." She returned sedately to her place by the fire.

"You'll go nowhere except back to Lee," Alan stated, suddenly annoyed. "Your folk are worried about you."

She glanced up in genuine surprise at his apparent lack of common sense. "Ye can tell them ye saw me."

Ket stiffened and sputtered into his flask, apparently choking on the liquor. Alan choked, too, on nothing but air, though he had not been above running errands in his time. "You have no business traipsing about Isle, putting yourself in danger," he flared at last. "These are perilous times, Megan! Get home, where you belong!"

"I belong here as much as anywhere," Megan flared back. "Who're ye to tell me where I may or may not go?"

Caught in another paroxysm, Ket expelled a wheeze that was indeterminate as to emotional color. Alan let out a harried bark, half laugh, half roar of rage.

"Your King, girl! Just your poor, old King, that's all. You should obey me, unquestioning!"

"Drag me to Laueroc, then. Put me in chains." She glared at him.

"Halt! Truce! *Hold!*" Ket jumped to his feet with such an air of desperate command that they both gaped at him. "Ye're not going anywhere for several days, neither of ye, if I read this storm aright. So take a breath! Alan, where is that big, bloody sword ye've latched onto?"

Alan stared at him a moment, thinking, then began to laugh soundlessly. "I let it drop when I jumped you. . . . Confound it, I can only just carry so much! Why do you ask, Ket? Do you think I should use it on her?"

"I asked," Ket replied pointedly, "to take yer mind off yer spleen. Anger is comfortless in these close quarters." He turned sternly to the girl. "Meg, tread more lightly, if ye please! We have watched brave men die today."

"I am sorry," she said with no cringing, only cleanest sympathy. "I didn't know. The wolves?"

"Ay." Alan sat down, surprised to find how suddenly and intensely he liked her. "Ket is right; I am out of sorts. I beg pardon for my manner, Meg. But I am still concerned for your safety."

"I must go to Gwern," she said softly, "as the salmon must go to the sea, or the stag to the meadow, safety or no safety. Can ye understand?"

"I understand many things I don't like. But I know Trevyn cared for you, as I am beginning to care for you myself. Give him something to return to. He may wish to wed you, for all I know. The young fool."

"You just told me he was dead!" Meg cried.

Alan blinked at her. "For a moment, just now, I thought he was alive," he whispered, and bowed his head as pain washed over him.

Ket got up and kicked ashes over the embers of the fire. "Sleep," he ordered with the succinct authority of the servant. He distributed blankets, giving Meg an extra one. The night was icy cold, even within walls. They lay with their feet to the fire, and close together, for warmth.

"What place is this?" Alan wondered aloud. A place that had already changed him, he sensed.

"A sort of a—a mighty ruin." Meg's voice floated through the darkness, hushed, like a moth. "The fish live in circular pools rimmed with stone," she added, after a long pause. "They lie right under the ice. There were a few apples still hanging from the trees when I first came."

"What place could it have been!" Alan murmured. Exhausted, he could not think, and in a moment he fell asleep. The she-wolf came and settled comfortably into the bony curve of Megan's side. Sleeping warmer than she had slept for many days, Meg dreamed of a white stag. But Alan, slumbering in a sentry tower of shattered Eburacon, dreamed of his son, and saw him laughing, whole, and well.

Chapter Five

It snowed, on and off, for five days, as Ket had predicted. When it didn't snow, it blew. So the odd threesome was stuck in their lodging for a week, seldom venturing out, and then hurriedly, ducking through a blur of white. By the fourth day, they had eaten all their sausage and were already growing tired of fish. Despite that, and despite occasional sparring between Alan and Meg, they got along well. They played countless guessing games to pass the time, and drew puzzles in the dirt. In the evenings they sat talking for hours, keeping the fire going as late as they could. Flossie, the wolf, would lie in her own place by the fire, gnawing at the ends of their scorned fish. She made no doglike displays of affection, encouraged no impudence, but joined their circle companionably—as an equal, they sensed.

The wolf had befriended her quite of its own accord, Meg explained. Her first, freezing night in the open, shivering under her ragged blanket, Meg had awakened to find the big, furry body pressed against hers. By morning, the two females were on familiar terms, and Meg had named her new comrade after her favorite childhood doll. Flossie had helped her evade the patrols Rafe had sent searching for her. Flossie had held back a skulking pack of unfriendly wolves with her snarls, leading Meg through a confusion of taunting howls to safety in the haunt. Awestruck, Alan and Ket stared at the placid creature.

"Wolves are beasts!" Alan protested in bewilderment. "They go their own ways like other beasts; they hunt, and run, and mate and fight and die, and pay little attention to men if they can help it. That they should take up war against us is—it is most unnatural. And that this one should protect you, Meg, is a happier chance, but no more fitting for a wolf. What can it mean? Her eyes—I have known wolves, lass. Their eyes shine yellow in moonlight, red in firelight, spectral as a cat's. But hers are the eyes of a lovely woman. Look."

Flossie gazed steadily back at them all, seemingly unperturbed. Her eyes were of a warm brown with a purplish tinge, deepening in the firelight to the color of violets. As Alan had said, they looked as if they should have been courted with candlelight and wine. He envisioned those eyes closing under smooth human lids, then shuddered.

"Countryfolk say that certain people are marked to turn to wolves," Ket said doubtfully. "Those who're born with teeth or with brows that meet over their noses—"

"Lying tales!" Alan retorted somewhat more violently than he had expected to. "I know I have not lived forever, Ket," he added more discreetly, "but I—we—roamed the wilderness for years and learned no great harm of wolves. Most of the time they paid us no mind. But I remember one night when—Hal felt sad and played it out on the plinset, and the wolves ringed the fire to listen." Alan swallowed. "We were not afraid."

"I have never been able to think too badly of wolves," Ket said quietly, "since the time they circled the rowan grove at my lady's feet and did homage to her."

The three of them had become very close, as people sometimes will when they are confined together. Shy Ket had found ways to speak of his longstanding love for the Queen. Meg had told with wry amusement of her dealings with Trevyn and Gwern. And Alan seemed more like himself than he had been for many months, Ket thought, gentler, more open—but still not happy. Ket longed for Alan's happiness.

"Hal—" Alan pronounced the name with difficulty. "Hal never placed credence in werewolves. He said that men fear wolves because they are so much like dogs. But dogs are friendly, and wolves are not, and they are cannibals, and rend each other from time to time. . . ." Alan gulped again. "That is their own business, but men think, what if dogs should act like that? Or what if my other friends, my fellowmen, my neighbors, should go wild, betray me, turn on me to rend me, bite off my outstretched hand. . . ." He paused to steady his voice, wondering at his own emotion. "Men fear themselves most. That is why they speak of werewolves. . . ."

"Dogs are famed for their faithfulness," Ket murmured.

Meg looked down at the wolf that lay unmoved at her side. "D'ye really think Flossie would turn on me t' rend me?" she challenged.

"Nay," Alan replied gruffly, "I cannot think that, even now. Even though . . ."

"Well, what?" Ket prodded gently, after a long pause.

"Even though," Alan blurted, not understanding why, "my own most faithful comrade has betrayed me, rent me to the heart, though not with teeth or steel." Alan hid his face in his hands, though his eyes remained dry and burning as coals. "How, how, could he leave me so, without a tear?"

Meg came around the fire to kneel before him, her hands light as leaves on his shoulders. In an instant he understood why he had spoken after all the silent months: healing stirred in her lightest touch. "D'ye mean King Hal, Liege?"

"Of course, Hal." He raised his twitching face to her scrutiny and smiled slowly, distraught as he was. "Trevyn gave me a tear or two."

"Ay, well, he didn't honor me with so much as a wish-ye-well." Meg smiled bitterly in her turn. "So, Liege, though I hadn't much claim on yer son, I can feel perhaps the tithe of what ye're feeling. And I know ye're angry enough to burst."

"Angry?" He drew back from her touch. "At Trevyn? But he's dead."

"He's not!" she snapped in exasperation. "And anyhow, I meant at Hal. So ye'll give him no tears, either?"

"I—" he sputtered, found he could not speak, and

scrambled to his feet. "I'm not angry!" he shouted at last. Ket snorted quietly from his place by the fire. Alan ignored him.

"Are ye made of flesh, then?" Meg inquired politely.

"Let be, lass." Ket spoke up unexpectedly. "Alan—"

"What?" the monarch muttered, face turned away.

"If ever ye're to see Hal again, what will ye do or say?"

For an instant, the question blazed through Alan. Shouts, blows, tears, an embrace; each flashed like fire across his mind, burned, and vanished. Nothing remained but a stark conviction and a black abyss of gloom.

"I am never to see him again," he mumbled.

"Why not?" Ket sensed that Alan needed hope. "Ye're as special as he was."

But Alan would talk no more about Hal. He refused to explain what he instinctively knew—that the Sword of Lyrdion had somehow cut him off from his brother. For all time.

The weather cleared during the night; the wind stopped and the clouds wandered away. At midnight, Flossie roused Megan with her firm, cool nose, and the girl silently slipped out, clutching her pack and her ragged blanket, leaving the others slumbering by the ashes of the fire. Even struggling through waist-high snow, she would be miles away by morning, well on her way southward to seek Gwern.

"Confound it!" Ket shouted when he awoke the next morning to find her gone. "There's another one that's left without a word. . . . The girl must be daft, Alan." He sounded aggrieved, but Alan seemed amused, even relieved. He smiled whimsically.

"Nay, she's a wise lass. She knew I could not really keep her from going her way, but she spared me the facing of it. So I still have some shreds of pride and honor left. . . . Well, we had better get back to Lee as quickly as we can. Rafe will be fit for a madhouse."

"But we have to find Meg," Ket protested incredulously. "She'll freeze, or—or something."

"Mothers, nay! I pity anything that tries to harm her with Flossie near. She'll be rocking at her ease when I'm turning to dust. Find some food, Ket."

They packed what they could and crawled out of their shelter, then stood motionless, blinking. Deep snow glinted in the wintry light, but that was not what took their breath. A vast, ghostly, snow-draped vista from out of the deep past confronted them. Battlements and broken towers, turrets and court and ruined keep, silent fountains and tumbled walls—all quiet, shrouded and overgrown.

"It must have been a city!" Ket gasped. "Here, in the midst of the Forest?"

"Eburacon," Alan murmured, suddenly understanding.

"I have heard that name when men talk around the hilltop fires of magic and the way Isle used to be. . . . That is a most ancient shrine of the Lady. But what is Meg, that she was able to come here all alone?"

"My son was an ass to leave her," Alan growled in oblique reply, and abruptly stalked away. "Come on!"

He led Ket back the way they had come, as near as he could reckon, and started searching for the giant sword of Lyrdion. It was difficult to find underneath the snow. Alan burrowed busily while Ket watched, frowning. "Is it within the ring of the barrows?" he asked suddenly.

"Just at the barrows. Where you lost your—ah—strength."

"I'll venture to say, then," Ket drawled, "that no one'll come near it. Let it lie, Alan."

"And get it later, you mean? There won't be time; I'll need it." Alan glanced up impatiently. "Come on, Ket; help me!"

"Alan, let it go." A trace of desperation tinged Ket's calm voice. "It's not worth the price, at any price. It has changed you. Thanks be, you've gained some healing here. . . ."

Alan paused, snow-caked and statuesque, half stooped, glaring. "Do you want me to give Isle over to the wolves, then?" he barked.

"What matter!" Ket cried, suddenly anguished. "You were as wolfish as any of them for a while." Alan met his wide eyes, looking as white and frozen as the snow. Ket saw a pang go through him. But then something else settled, hard and heavy.

"What price I have paid is already paid," Alan answered hollowly. "And I'll keep what I have bargained for, Ket. My mistress, if you will. All I have left. Here she lies." He strode with uncanny sureness to a spot a few yards away, reached into the snow and drew forth the sword. Hau Ferddas hung sullenly in his hand. Ket stared without moving, caught up in horror and mute appeal. Alan met his gaze with a flash of rage.

"To Lee," he ordered coldly, in tones he would formerly not have used to the balkiest of servitors.

They trudged through the snow to Lee without speaking for the two days of the journey. Alan glared blackly for most of that time, and Ket kept silence as much from sorrow as from hurt pride. Late the second day they met Rafe and a patrol near the fringes of the Forest. Rafe looked frenzied. "All gods be praised!" he exclaimed thankfully when he saw Alan. He vaulted down from his mount and ran toward him to embrace him. Then he noticed Alan's glowering face and offered his horse instead. He shepherded the two strays back to his fortress, sent the servants hustling with demands for warmth and food. Only when he had seen Ket and Alan fed and settled by a crackling fire did he speak again.

"Half a dozen of my men made it back," he stated quietly. "They've given me news of what happened. The wolves use horror as their weapon now, it seems."

"Nay, the fear was my weapon." Alan spoke thickly. "A double-edged blade. . . . It also worked against me. My men fled as well as the wolves. Only Ket stayed."

Ket stirred at that. "More may yet make it home," he offered.

"I doubt it." Rafe touched his forehead distractedly, wild-eyed from sleepless nights and comfortless days. "Nearly fifty men lost! What went wrong?"

Alan seemed not to hear. "Nothing," Ket told him at last, "except that there were more wolves than we expected. We slew a few score, and left eleven men dead."

Rafe gaped. "How many wolves?" he breathed at last.

"Hundreds," Alan answered flatly. "A forest's worth." Rafe looked into his hard, set face and found nothing to say to him.

"Perhaps the rising sun will shed a brighter light on it," he floundered at last. Rafe had never known the distress that warmth and food and sound sleep could not cure, though more than once he had felt the cold finger of death on his shoulder. "Come, both of you, your beds are warmed and turned for you." For Rafe did not understand that Alan was chilled by more than mere loss of life.

Alan went numbly and slept a sleep like death, though blood colored his dreams. He did not ride out the next day, or the next. In fact, he did not stir from his chamber. He accepted food with ill grace, light not at all, and warned away all visitors. Neither Rafe nor Ket could shake him out of the gloom that had taken hold of him like a sickness.

Alan had no way of knowing that Wael, cloaked in his lupine form, lay frightened, powerless, and exhausted in his own dark den. That enemy had paid dearly for his victory. There had been no wolves seen for the week since the battle; folk thanked the deep snow for that. And yet, so peculiar is the mind of man, they blamed the wolves for the deaths of the soldiers who did not return from the Forest. In fact, Wael and his legions lay through the storm with noses on paws and no thoughts of troubling the desperate wanderers in their wilderness domain. All strength of evil had gone out of them for the time.

Merest curiosity stirred Alan from his retreat at last, as the days ranked themselves into weeks and the wolves did not strike. Ket rode forth daily with Rafe's patrols, and every evening he reported to his liege, gravely oblivious to black stares and thunderous noises. His keen woodsman's eye had seen no sign of wolves, not the faintest pawprint, and that fact pricked Alan into action at last.

"No report of them at all?" he demanded one night.

"No one has even heard a howl." Ket masked his delight as he encouraged Alan into further response. "Folk devoutly hope that they are gone for good."

"Fools!" Alan exploded. "They have only moved on. . . . Any word from Celydon?"

"Ay, and all is well there. We hear nothing from Whitewater, though. No one dares to venture through the Forest."

"Least of all myself," Alan retorted sardonically. "If we are to check on Whitewater, it will be by way of Nemeton. But I have no doubt at all that we shall find them strewing bodies to the south and east."

"Are we to ride, then?" Ket spoke diffidently.

"Certainly!" Alan glared at him. "Did you think I would stay the winter in this hole? We'll ride tomorrow, early. See to it!"

Ket bowed and left the room without a word, saving his smile until he was well down the corridor.

They departed from Lee at sunrise, with scant courtesy from Alan, though Rafe saw him off with warm affection. It was three weeks before they came to Nemeton, for they swung wide of the Forest. When they arrived at last, in murky weather, Corin looked askance at Alan, wondering when he had lost his smile. He was thankful he had no ill news to report. Messengers from Whitewater had brought word of no new attacks in the past month or more. Troops from Laueroc had arrived and been billeted, but as yet there was no work for them. Lookouts posted at the seaside reported no hostile craft on the water. Patrols roaming the southern reaches of the Forest found no sign of wolves and nothing amiss.

"Do not slack your guard. The siege will come before long," said Alan, and with ill grace he settled himself to wait. Ruddy, swelling tree buds whispered of the coming spring when the air was still icy cold, and folk began to hope that the terror might be over. Who had ever heard of wolf attacks except in the starving season of winter? But Alan had not yet been at Nemeton a fortnight when the patrollers' horses came home riderless in the dusk. Alan and Ket and Cory rode out with a retinue the next day and found the men laid out, every one, with gaping gullets and vacant, staring eyes. They were not even within the Forest ways, but well out upon the wealds, with nothing but grass around them. Bodies of three wolves lay nearby.

"These were brave men," Cory whispered, sickened. "How could they fare so badly, here where nothing concealed their enemy?"

"If their steeds were as brave, they might have done better," Alan answered bitterly.

"Failing that," Ket suggested, "they might henceforth carry larger shields, and form their own fortress when their mounts desert them."

"Ay, let them carry shields to their toes, and cupboards

stocked with siege food!" railed Alan. "No wonder the
wolves mock us."

Ket faced him steadily. "What do you propose, Sire?"

"Nothing," Alan retorted morosely. "I have no proposal."
He would not meet their eyes. He turned away to ride back to
Nemeton, and they followed him silently.

Scarcely a day followed thereafter that did not bring some
news of grisly death: a hunter found slain before his huddled
hounds, a priestess beset at her altar, a cottage family killed.
Within a week, a carefully concerned missive arrived from
Craig in Whitewater and a nearly panicky one from Rafe in
Lee. Wolves roamed their demesnes once again, and they
could not protect all who deserved their aid. Folk had been
killed. Those who lived survived as if under siege, huddled
within walls and already running low on food. Some had fled
their lands altogether, seeking a place far from the Forest.
Famine threatened, for tilling could be done only under
guard. Trade had come to a halt. The land cowered under a
shadow of terror like a chick beneath the hawk. What was to
be done?

Alan had no answer, no hope to offer. There were not
enough men in Isle, he knew, to subdue the Forest. Nor could
he yet believe or understand that its creatures had turned
against him: he, who had slept the nights of his youth
fearlessly beneath its leafy shelter! His mind stumbled in
darkness; his heart felt like a stony weight. Only obstinacy
sustained him. He moved through the days numbly, riding
out with the patrols, doing battle at times, viewing the dead,
feeling as if he already lay among them. Ket stayed constantly
beside him. After a while, Rafe and the others came and held
council, laid plans, asked his approval. Alan nodded, hardly
hearing what they were saying. One hand held to his mighty
sword. These days, he hardly ever put it down.

Chapter Six

"I must soon be going back," Trevyn said to Hal when the first trace of springtime red tinged the distant hills.

"Stay a few more days," Hal replied, "and help us send your grandfather to his rest. Death will come soon for him; don't you feel it?"

He did, indeed, sense Adaoun's gradual departure. It seemed that all of life and death lay open now to the touch of his mind. They surrounded him like an ocean, in Elwestrand. Trevyn had flown higher than the eagles on the back of the immortal white winged horse; he had tangled his hands in the mane at first, and later learned to trust. He had bathed in the sunset sea with Menwy's jewel-black dragons, and he had walked beside the shy, sinuous leopards of Elundelei. He had slept fearlessly upon earth's bosom, wherever night found him. Elwestrand was a land to mother all lands, he decided: marvelous, relentless, and yet most gently healing. He looked into her indigo lakes and saw Meg there, lovelier than any elf-maiden in all the bright valleys of this paradise. Trevyn wondered why he had not perceived her so before.

So at the first faint signs of spring, Trevyn's heart bounded like a stag, thinking he might soon be on his way back to his beloved, to Meg. If he had not lost her. . . . He would not think that. No use to think that, with three months yet to spend on the ship, even if he left in the morning. And he no longer tried to hasten the circling years of his life. He, too, moved in the cosmic dance, Trevyn knew, and made up some small part of its beauty. Its rhythm would guide and sustain him for all time, if only he could heed its soundless motion.

"You will know when it is time to go," Hal agreed, reading his thoughts.

That evening there were new faces around the cooking fires, elves and elf-kin and fair folk of other lineage, drifting in and taking their places without a word of explanation, as floating leaves come to shore. All the next morning more came, until several thousand were gathered. They sat by the sea and watched their children run along the lapping waves. Trevyn sat with them and listened to the melody of their talk. After a while, something moved in him, and he got up and went to Adaoun.

The ancient elf lay on his couch beneath his snowy canopy, as he had lain since Trevyn had known him. At no great distance, Ylim sat beneath the birch trees, weaving white lace of delicate pattern on a hand loom. With a nod to her, Trevyn settled himself by Adaoun's bedside, taking a frail, dry hand into his own.

"Alberic," Adaoun greeted him, though his eyes could no longer see him. "Do you yet know the meaning of your name, lad?"

"Partly, Grandfather." Trevyn spoke softly, knowing that the patriarch understood him not so much through sound as through some soundless meeting of spirit with spirit. "It has something to do with unicorns, and white and gold. . . . They told me on Elundelei, and they told me the sooth-name of my enemy, but I cannot remember."

"You should be able to remember when the time comes. Enmity has small meaning here."

"I should be able to remember. For it seems to me," Trevyn added, after a long pause, "that the words of the goddess were words that my mother tried to tell me long ago."

"Ah, your mother!" Adaoun smiled, the labored smile of

great age. "I can see her in my mind's eye, all green and golden, spring leaves in sunshine. What was it she told you, lad?"

"That I am—all one." The words seemed lacking, and Trevyn's lips tightened as he spoke again. "That I am all alone. I am not sure why."

"The star-son in you." There was no trace of pity in Adaoun's tones, only mindful understanding. "You will always yearn for fellowship. Hal yearned, all his life. . . . Had he turned his back on the call that brought him here, it would have been like killing his veriest self. If your father cannot understand, it is because he has always been at one with anyone he befriends—but even he will need some healing here. The price of kingship is high."

"And I," Trevyn murmured, "will I ever return?"

"I cannot say. Ask Ylim."

"Nay, I don't want to ask her. I don't want to know what—what I already know." Trevyn's voice broke. "A person cannot expect to come twice to Elwestrand."

"Perhaps you are right. I dare not say. . . . But Elwestrand is in you now, lad, and you will carry it with you wherever you go. Something of it may come to you also in other ways. Be comforted, Grandson. . . ." The old elf's voice trailed away to a whisper like that of winter leaves.

"I will remember, Grandfather, and I thank you. But I am to blame for wearying you with talking. I had better go."

"Nay, stay a bit longer. It is not the talking that drains my strength; life wearies me. But I shall rest from it before long. They will send us off together, lad." Adaoun's smile broadened. "I also go to the sea, to Menwy's domain. My ashes will flow with the circling waters and ripple with the wind, touching many shores. . . . Take me out of here, Grandson, to a place where I may lie on the earth and feel the sky. I don't want to die under a roof."

The airy canopy was hardly to be called a roof, but to Adaoun, father of all elves, it was an irksome interruption of Aene's song. So Trevyn gathered him up, light as a bundle of dried kindling, and carried him out to a wooded slope where the wind sounded in the trees and eagles sang far overhead.

"Here," Adaoun whispered.

Trevyn laid him down on the bare earth, feeling a pang as he did it.

"Now go, Grandson." Adaoun spoke in words scarcely more than a movement. "I crave no company for dying. Farewell."

"Farewell, Grandfather," Trevyn murmured, then went down to the sea to wait with the others. He told no one what had passed. But they knew it nevertheless. As the descending sun approached the sea crests, tipping them with gold, and as the sea-drakes formed their escort, the elves raised their heads and hearkened as if to unseen wings. Then Hal and some others got up and went to the place where Adaoun lay, as surely as if they had seen. They returned to the seaside in soft twilight, bearing the leaf-light body on a litter between them, shoulder high. Adaoun lay with eyes bright and open, robed in white, with a purple cloak trailing over his feet. Evergreen ivy girdled him and garlanded his head; a curled frond encircled his right hand. His kindred surrounded him in awe too deep for words. These were not people who made much of death: the leaf greened and withered and returned to earth, as was just. But Adaoun was one who had been with them since the Beginning. His passing brought the elves to the fullness of all the circling ages they had known.

Trevyn had never expected to see the elves revel with fire. Trees, like all living things, were most precious to them, and they hated to cut them even to clear land for their crops. But on this night, they spent freely of all things, fire and food and selves. The ranged great pyres along the strand, and danced around them in solemn triumph, and sang to the music of Hal's instrument and many more. Between times they feasted, roasting nuts on the glowing coals, toasting bread over the flames. Feral eyes shone from the shadows at the reaches of the firelight: unicorns, and bright birds, and many other rare creatures stood there to watch this unaccustomed feast of fires. Huddled on the sand, blanket-wrapped children gazed wide-eyed at the leaping flames and at Adaoun, whose still form sometimes seemed to stir in the flickering light. When they dozed off at last, flames still leaped before their lidded eyes. The older elves did not sleep, nor did Trevyn. They exulted through the night on Adaoun's account, and when the sun blazed up at last, sending streamers of brightness over the sea, it seemed simply the just reflection of the glory on shore.

Dawn's light showed Trevyn a boat waiting restively in the shallows. Close by it floated a far smaller vessel, a mere platform of wood, almost flush with the water. The elves waded around it, stacking on it their precious stores of fuel, cord upon cord, until a couch of wood was formed. On this they laid Adaoun, folding his cloak beneath him, settling him tenderly. Then, scarcely speaking, they turned to Trevyn. Hal embraced him in farewell.

"I'll see Father off to you when it is time," Trevyn said.

"I know it. And yet, that is entirely up to him!" Hal smiled wryly. "Do you understand now? Destinies must discover themselves. . . . So I'll watch the sea and hope. You are going to light Adaoun's pyre for us?"

"If I may." Trevyn regarded his uncle lovingly. "A fitting time for the trying of power, is it not?"

"None better, since power is not to be used lightly. . . . I have put that parchment with your things. But have a care how you handle it!"

"If all goes well against Wael, I'll gladly destroy it. Though I may have to barter it to him yet. . . . But I must go; my heart cries in me to be gone." Trevyn cast a yearning glance at the marvels that lined the shore, the white swans, the subtle cats, the unicorns. . . . "My heart cries," he amended. "Let me go swiftly. Farewell, Uncle, and—many thanks."

"All blessing go with you," Hal said, and kissed him, and released him. The sun still clung to the sea as Trevyn climbed on board the elf-boat and threw away ladder and rope. The ship swirled away from shore with the still form of the departed patriarch following in its wake. Trevyn looked beyond and saw the hundreds of his friends and kindred raise their hands to him in silent salute. He gazed until he could no longer see their faces, then blinked as he turned to front the rising sun.

When he glanced back again, they were just dark posts on the rim of the water, so swiftly did the elf-boat swim. Trevyn waited until they had almost faded into his horizon. Then he spoke a soft command. *"Luppe,"* he said, "halt," and the elf-boat eased to a stop, turning aside from Adaoun's trailing bark. Trevyn loosed the rope that bound it to his ship, letting it drop into the sea. Then he stretched out his hand.

"Alys," he whispered, "hear me. A fire for my grandfather, if you please. A bright blossom to adorn his going and seed his remnants where it will." He moved his hand, and fire burst from the bark, curving and cupping Adaoun and cradling him in its glow. Sea birds circled overhead with wondering cries, winged shapes of aching whiteness against the sky. A far larger form circled above, blazing white and gold: Wynnda, the immortal winged horse, bidding farewell to his only master. For a moment, to the watchers on shore, sun and ship, pyre and gold-pinioned steed converged. Then the sun, streaming, tore loose of the sea, the ship sailed from view, the steed wheeled away and the fire sank into the water with only a plume of white smoke to mark its place: and that, too, soon faded into oneness with the spinning wind, as Adaoun's ashes drifted with the dance of the sea.

Trevyn watched the horse and the fire until his eyes could bear no more beauty. Then he whispered, *"Switte,* go on," and the ship swirled away once more, quartering north of the rising sun. Trevyn leaned on her prow and watched the waters cleave, and would not look back. More than time and seas, he knew, would sunder him from that place of peace. Star-sons had sailed to Elwestrand, but none had ever returned. . . . He did not know how Bevan stood looking after him on that far shore, with his hands cupped to comfort Hal.

Book Four

MENWY AND MAGIC

Chapter One

Trevyn did not lie and stare through this voyage; his body pulsed too full of eager life for that. He paced and pondered and studied sea and sky. The elf-ship was plentifully stocked with everything he needed, and some baubles besides, to amuse him. He ate provisions worthy of a King's son, and slept in bright blankets, and dressed in soft clothing embroidered as beautifully as a ballad. All in all, he stood the months of the voyage well. His dealings with the goddess had taught him a kind of wry serenity. Still, his heart jolted him to his feet when, one day as the sun neared its equinox, a gray seabird flew overhead and circled to meet him.

"How near lies Isle, little brother?" he hailed it.

"No more than a skim and a flitter," it cried cheerfully, "for you fly faster than I—phew!" The bird circled away as it fell behind. Trevyn scanned the horizon that day until his eyes burned. Disorderly thoughts crowded his mind—fleeting visions of his home and people there, sometimes people he scarcely knew; but mostly he thought of Meg. He stayed on deck that evening until full dark had fallen, and saw nothing. But the next morning the rocky headlands of Welas lay so

close that he shouted and reached out as if to touch them.
Cliffs soared from seaside to mountaintops; Trevyn could see
every tree that clung to them, and he hugged the elf-boat's
prow in wet-eyed delight.

Before midday she turned the point and entered the Bay of
the Blessed. Trevyn gulped, for at the far end someone
awaited him, a still figure beside a white horse. No ordinary
person could be about; this was a forbidden place. . . . His
mother, perhaps? Nay, he could see now, it was Gwern!
Trevyn felt only faintly surprised by the warm surge of joy
that went through him. In a moment the elf-boat slid to the
shore by Gwern's bare feet, and he silently positioned the
boarding plank for Trevyn to disembark. Gwern's brown face
no longer seemed quite so unreadable; Trevyn saw him bite
his lip to still it, and grinned in unsolicited reply. He
shouldered his blanketroll and strode to shore, extended a
hand, touched fingertips the color of earth. To his chagrin, his
full eyes overflowed.

"I wasn't expecting anyone to meet me," he mumbled.

Gwern turned without comment and pulled the plank to
shore. The elf-boat wheeled away and scudded out of the
Bay. Trevyn stood watching her as one watches a departing
friend, almost dismayed that she had spoken no word of
farewell. Then he blinked and shook his head, as if to shake
off foolishness.

"Did it hurt to leave Elwestrand?" Gwern asked in his
curiously flat, husky voice.

"Ay. . . . And yet, I am so glad to be back, Gwern! This is
home, after all." He breathed deeply, looking around at the
land that somehow sang particularly to him. Then his glance
caught on the white horse, and his breath stopped in his
throat.

"For you," Gwern said stolidly. "You'll have need of a bold
horse."

The stallion wore not a thread of trapping except a lunula
of silver on its breast, held there by silklike scarlet cord. It
was light and graceful of build, swan-necked, not thewed like
a war horse but with something of unicorn fineness, Trevyn
thought, and perhaps unicorn fierceness, if fierceness were

called for. Bright azure eyes blazed down at him from the stallion's high-flung, bony head. It was these that stopped Trevyn's breath, for the pupils were spindle-shaped, like a cat's, and the strange, blue sheen was ringed with fey white. Trevyn found his voice only after a moment's sincere search.

"Where, in mercy—" he began, but Gwern interrupted him irritably.

"I don't know! I woke up one morning, and there he stood, moon mark and all. But he's yours, right enough. Find out for yourself."

"That's no *elwedeyn* horse," Trevyn protested. "That's more like one of Ylim's wild star-crossed steeds from the foothills of Elundelei."

The horse jerked down its head so that its azure gaze met his of opal green, and Trevyn felt its impatient command. "All right," he breathed, and moved to its side, vaulted onto its back, half expecting to be flung off headlong. But the horse stood taut and still for his mounting. Gwern handed up his blanketroll.

"Why does he serve me?" Trevyn demanded. "There's not a speck of love or loyalty in him."

Gwern shrugged, then whistled like a plover, calling an *elwedeyn* colt out of the woods for his own use. He had no gear, not so much as a cup to drink from, and his ragged clothing fluttered about him like brown, tattered leaves. Perhaps he smelled, also, but Trevyn either did not notice or did not mind. The two of them set off side by side at trot and canter toward Laueroc. The land was green and lovely, lush with early June rains, surpassingly beautiful even to Trevyn's elfin eyes.

"Have you seen Meg?" he asked before they had ridden very far.

"She has traveled with me all spring." Coming from Gwern, this statement sounded perfectly unremarkable, and meant not a nuance more than it said. "She left me a week ago, when I felt sure you were coming to land. She is bound eastward, to see your father."

Trevyn tried to muddle this through for a moment. "Is she—is she very angry with me?" he asked at last.

"She loves you." Gwern's tone did not even try to reassure; he spoke only simple fact. "But she has her qualms, and she is not likely to come to you. You'll have to seek her out."

"But I won't be able to, not for a while," said Trevyn painfully. "I mean . . ."

"The wolves, ay. All of Isle is under the shadow of them."

"And my father; what has he done about them? Where is he? Has battle been joined?"

Gwern grimaced uncomfortably. "I don't know. How should I know? Some things I can tell, but others . . . I know your father thinks you're dead. Meg said so."

"What!" Trevyn had never felt so alive, and he sputtered in astonishment that anyone, especially his father, could fail to feel his wellbeing. "Whatever gave him that idea?" he cried.

"I don't know. Meg's gone to tell him you're coming. But if we ride hard, we're likely to find him before she does."

They rode until deep dark, ate Trevyn's elfin viands, and were up by the following dawn. They rode rapidly and companionably through that day and the next. Trevyn could not understand why he had ever disliked Gwern. The brown youth's plainspoken presence cheered and soothed and excited him now; he felt some feeling both achingly lovely and as comfortable as old clothes. Gwern, like Trevyn, guided his unbridled steed with a touch and a word of the Elder Tongue. Gwern was someone as alone as himself, Trevyn understood now, and very much like himself. The glow he felt was more than comradeship. But for the time he would not give it any other name.

They made Laueroc on the fourth day. Trevyn noted, as they traversed the town, how still the streets seemed, how lacking in chatter and workaday bustle. Those few folk who were about gave him no salute except a stare. An air of dread and hopelessness brooded over the place, as palpable as a cloud of fog. Trevyn entered the castle grounds with foreboding. The courtyard was empty. He left Gwern there with the horses and ran into the keep, up the spiraling stairway toward the living quarters. Halfway up, he almost collided with Rosemary. She gasped at the sight of him.

"Hello, Aunt Ro." He kissed her hastily. "Wherever is everyone?"

"At the fighting, Trevyn," she answered softly, "or else fled."

He nodded, unsurprised. "Where is Mother?"

"Above." Trevyn turned to go, but Rosemary laid a hand on his arm. "Trev—she is not herself."

"How so?" He had not foreseen this.

"She is sad and troubled, even more than most of us. . . . But I hope your coming will cheer her."

"Aene be willing," he muttered, and plunged up the stairs.

Lysse was sitting at the loom in the large central chamber—only sitting, not weaving. She did not glance up as Trevyn entered, and he stopped for a moment to look at her, feeling the sight jab him like a knife. She was not so much changed; her dress was still soft green, her hair a flow of gold and her face rose-petal smooth. But her eyes were locked on pain like prison iron.

"Mother," he whispered, then went and took her by the shoulders. "Mother." She looked up at him and smiled, but the smile touched only the surface of her pain. He hugged her.

"Had you forgotten I was coming back?"

"Nay, not a bit." Her face did not change. "I am glad to see you, Trev. There is much work for you here."

"Mother," he queried very gently, "will you tell me what ails you?"

"Nay, that I will not." Her jaw hardened with the resolve. "But if you send your father back to me, perhaps we can cure it."

"Where is he?"

"In the midlands somewhere." She faced him, helpless to gauge the extent of his knowledge, now that her Sight was gone. "Have you heard about the wolves?"

"I have spoken to no one here except Gwern. But I have met those wolves already, here and in Tokar. How bad is it?"

"In loss of life, not really severe. . . . Perhaps some few hundred folk have fallen their prey. But the whole land quakes in terror of them. They roam at will, insolently bold.

Even within doors people do not feel safe from them. They have pulled an infant from a cradle at the mother's feet and torn a grandmother sitting by her fire. They spread nightmare like a pestilence. Strong men who have seen no more than a gray shadow have left cottage and land, thinking somehow to escape them. But the dread is everywhere."

"How far afield do they range?"

"I believe they have not yet ventured far into the south. . . . A few have come to Laueroc, and you have seen how the town has emptied on their account. In the east, the land is desolate."

"I must be off at once." Trevyn rose restively. "I don't have time to go hunting dragons. . . . Mother, where are the dragons of Lyrdion?"

"Long gone!" She peered at him, justly puzzled. "They have not been seen for years and years, not since Veran's time."

"Riddles," Trevyn grumbled. "There is no time for riddles. I must go, and . . . Mother, I know you must stay here; you are the governor, with Father gone. But shouldn't Aunt Rosemary be in Celydon?"

"I know she longs to go to her home. But Alan and Ket have both bid her stay by me, for her own safety and also to keep me company. Celydon is hard beset. What could she do there?"

"Do? Perhaps nothing." Trevyn gestured helplessly. "She is the gentle Lady of All Trees, Mother. The wolves worshiped her once at the Rowan grove. Her presence could—I don't know. Could stir the Forest back toward the old order."

Lysse gazed, vague and absorbed, as if a distant bell had rung. "Of course," she murmured. "A dark spell needs magic to combat it. But Isle has nearly forgotten the old magic. . . ."

"See if Aunt Ro can get to Celydon. I cannot take her there; I must go to Father. I'll send tidings when I can, Mother." He started out.

"Trevyn," she warned, "the horses will not face the wolves, not even Arundel, before he died in the winter."

"I knew old Arundel would not last long without Hal. But I

have a horse of a different sort." He paused a moment, bemused, thinking of that horse, then turned away again.

"Trevyn," Lysse called after him, "you'll need a sword."

"Indeed!" He grinned at her; she almost sounded like his mother again. "I lost mine when that gaudy ship went down. What do you suggest?"

"Take Hal's, then, and his shield and helm. And Trevyn," she called him back again, "take care."

"I will." He regarded her a moment, then said quite suddenly, "Mother, your father sends you his love and greeting. He is with the tide now."

"Ah!" Her face softened. "Then he is content. What is it like, that Elwestrand?"

"A gentle country, full of peace and enchantment and singing. I'll tell you when I return. . . . Farewell, Mother." He left her with light of Elwestrand in her eyes, and it eased his going.

Gwern had put some harness on the horses, Trevyn discovered when he clattered back to the courtyard. For his own part, he had armed himself and found Gwern a pack and some clothes. He instinctively knew better than to offer Gwern weapons. He had seen Gwern angry, even furious, but he could not envision him taking part in any ordered combat.

"I don't need those things," Gwern complained.

"Carry them for me, then. Come on." They took some food from the kitchen, then departed. It felt odd to ride out through the deserted courtyard, the nearly unmanned gates of the city. Trevyn looked about uneasily. Laueroc seemed ready to yield with scarcely a struggle to a Tokarian invasion, and much of the rest of Isle might be the same. The warships might already have landed.

It took Gwern and Trevyn a week of hard riding to reach the midlands, and another two days to locate Alan. Wolves and King and liegemen had joined battle on a grassy plain near the Black River, a plain that had seen battle before, and more than once. In evening light the fighters appeared as a dark, struggling mass, like gurgling mud. A coppery blaze shot through it, and Trevyn pulled up his fey white steed. "The sword!" he gasped, stricken, and they both stared. Even

at the distance, they could hear Alan roaring and snarling like
the wolves he smote. The sound was blood red and crushing,
like the mighty weapon in his hand.

"By my troth," Trevyn breathed, "I'd as soon beard a
dragon as handle that blade. The song you sang, Gwern . . ."

"Hal's song. I could always feel him singing, inside. . . .
He felt the shadow of Hau Ferddas, and the prophecy."

"That it must be flung into the sea—"

"By a mortal of elfin kind. Your father is not the man,
Prince."

They had come up behind the wolves, opposite Alan, and
Gwern's steed had already started to plunge and buck at the
lupine scent. Resigned, he dismounted and let the horse
pound away. "Go on," he told Trevyn. "I'll join you later."

"To do what? I have no desire to kill wolves, poor things!
And I'm not going to touch that bloody sword, either."

"Go on! Just go to your father. He needs you, and he
certainly doesn't need to see me. Go on."

Trevyn bit his lip and nodded. He unsheathed his silver
sword, a gesture only of defense, and put heels to white
flanks. Without hesitation, the cat-eyed steed cantered forward.

Alan raised a sword that flew on wings of rage. The battle
meant nothing to him except the release of rage; kingdom,
family, friends, and folk had long since ceased to matter to
him. His innermost will was locked into hatred, and he
watched in bitter triumph as his sword beat back those who
tried to slay him.

His men, and men from all the southern towns, and from
Whitewater and Lee and as far north as Firth, followed him
apprehensively. Perhaps their King was demented, but what
choice was theirs? They hoped they kept the wolves from
doing other harm, that they saved a few lives in Nemeton.
Alan wanted to drive the wolves clear away from the Forest
into the southern sea. It appeared as if he even thought he
succeeded. But his men could see that every day the creatures
made a mockery of their efforts, toyed with them gleefully,
leaving them cheerfully at sundown to return as cheerfully in
the morning. If Alan's army moved, it was because the wolves

chivied them and harried them and herded them here and there, picking off panicky men who faced them only because they had found it was worse to run, to feel the shadowy horror panting behind. Only Alan seemed oblivious to dread of the wolves. He dreaded night worse. While his men took all too brief a respite, he paced, shutting out a nightmare he refused even to name. He strode to battle almost eagerly in the mornings, for then he could lose himself in the glory of his magical sword.

So when the setting sun blinded him one evening, blazing in his eyes, he cursed; he hated it. He hated to remember that Hal and Trevyn had passed beyond the sunset, to the uttermost west, whence there was no return. . . . What figure rode toward him, emerging out of the sunset, a form armed in silver but haloed in rays of gold? It shimmered before Alan's blinking eyes like a vision of the glorious past that he had nearly forgotten in the gory present. It was Hal! But it could not be Hal. . . . Hau Ferddas thudded to the ground, and Alan stood without noticing, watching the rider draw nearer. A shout sounded in his ears, someone seized him and tugged him back from the fray, but he only stared. The approaching horse was white, its forehead blazing white, on its breast a crescent of silver. It sprang fiercely, almost joyfully, into the midst of the wolves, scattering them with its hooves. The rider laid about him with the flat of his sword. Golden hair shone under the silver helm, and gray-green eyes flashed beneath. It was not Hal, then, but someone like him, a hero of elfin stature whom Alan did not know. He had spied the enemy leader now, the big wolf that always sat and grinned; he sent his horse lunging toward it. But the wolf shied away, yapped once, and all of the wolves loped off. The men cheered, but the rider sat his horse and watched the gray beasts go without pursuing them.

Alan pulled away from the arms that held him, walked forward without realizing he had taken a step. His bloody sword hung from his limp hand and dragged in the dirt as he stumbled around bodies of men and beasts. The rider heard him coming, glanced around, and snatched off his helm as he slid to the ground. "Father!" he exclaimed, coming toward him.

"Trevyn?" Alan whispered.

"Ay, to be sure!" The young man gripped him, for Alan swayed where he stood. "What, have you forgotten me already?"

"Nay, indeed. But you have changed." Alan looked as pale as if he had seen a ghost. "And I felt quite sure that you were dead of shipwreck."

"Why? Did I not tell you I would return?" Trevyn smiled, teasing, trying to rouse Alan to some touch of joy. But Alan only fumbled at an inner pocket and brought forth a jeweled brooch, a sunburst of gold.

"I picked this up along the shore," he explained dully.

"That brooch," said Trevyn with feeling, "has taken part in more mischief than I can fathom! Guard it carefully, and keep it away from the sea. By the tides, I shall tell you a tale of that brooch! But first I must tell you a tale of these wolves. Let us go where we can talk. . . . Father, you look spent. Take my horse."

Trevyn had to help him onto the cat-eyed steed. As they prepared to leave, Ket came up and merely glanced at Trevyn in greeting.

"Liege," he addressed Alan, "shall I have the men advance their position?"

"Do what you like," Alan told him numbly, and turned away. But Trevyn shook his head, and Ket silently acknowledged.

Trevyn walked off by Alan to the cottage where he had established his post of command, a mile away. Ket ordered the men to stay where they were for the time. Then, discreetly, he also made his way toward the cottage, to watch over Alan as he had done for many weeks, and to speak with Trevyn when he could.

Inside the cottage, Alan sank onto a seat without moving even to clean the blood from his hands. His clotted sword rested between his knees, naked under its coat of gore. Trevyn quietly found wine and poured his father a tumbler full, which he handed to him with some biscuit. He did the same for himself and found himself a bench along the wall.

"You will have heard by now that I met with these wolves before I left Isle."

Alan scarcely nodded. Dazed from weariness, Trevyn thought. He went on.

"I was a fool not to tell you of them. I hope I have gained better wisdom since then, but at least I can offer knowledge."

As briefly as he could, Trevyn recounted his adventures, speaking not so much of what he had done as of what he had learned. He brought forth the parchment that was headed by a leaping wolf and explained its meaning. Silence rang hollowly in the room after he finished. It was a long moment before Alan stirred and spoke.

"You have studied in sorcery?"

"After a fashion, ay." Trevyn frowned in puzzlement. His father hardly seemed to have heard him.

"Well, you'll use no sorcery here."

Trevyn gaped in astonishment, fighting to keep his composure. "You face a wizard," he said carefully. "How will you defeat him?"

"With a bright blade." Alan's hands twitched on the jeweled hilt they grasped.

"Do you plan to slay every wolf in Isle?" Trevyn protested. "They are victims of Wael's treachery as much as we ourselves!" But Alan exploded into sudden fury.

"You think I don't know my enemy!" he shouted. "By the Wheel, I will be King in my kingdom, and those that have shed my people's blood shall feel my wrath! And you, if you cross me! There shall be no sorcery, or talk of sorcery, in my land. Heed me well!"

"That is a sword full of ancient sorcery in your hand," Trevyn told him quietly.

With an inarticulate roar, Alan lifted the weapon and rushed against the bright figure of a brash youth who had threatened his power. His son was dead; nothing remained to him except his rage and his power. . . . *"Dounamir!"* Trevyn gasped. "Father!" But even the Old Language had no power on Alan's hearing anymore.

Frozen and incredulous, Trevyn watched him come. Though his own sword hung at his belt, he could not move to draw it, not against Alan. . . . He was too stunned to flee. But as the invincible blade of Lyrdion whistled toward his head, Ket burst in and caught Alan's descending arm. "Alan, ye're as mad as a mad dog!" he cried. "Look before ye! Who is it that ye smite!"

Startled, Alan looked, and saw anguish in the eyes of—his son! Shaking, he dropped Hau Ferddas clattering to the floor and sobbed into his bloody hands. Trevyn went to his father, motioning Ket away. Ket hesitated, then seized the sword and retreated.

Alan wept tears of blood, or at least so it seemed. They ran in red streaks down his face, as if they had been torn from his heart. Trevyn clutched him tightly. "It has been hard for you, far too hard," he faltered. "The whole land in shadow, and you most of all, being King. . . . And that accursed sword—"

"There is no excuse for me," Alan choked. "I was half lunatic before I ever touched the sword. Trev, I have wronged you—"

"Hush."

"And not only you." Words burst from Alan in a feverish torrent, like his red torrent of tears. "Your mother has had nothing from me these many months but hard looks. . . . And Rafe! He who stood by me all through this hellish business, dead days ago, with no thanks for his constancy but the rough side of my tongue—"

"Hush," said Trevyn more firmly, swallowing his own sorrow. "Rafe needed no thanks from you. . . . Father, of all people in Isle you have been hardest beset, and I must badger you yet again. In very truth, our fate depends on the morrow. May we speak of it once again?"

"Nay." Alan quieted and faced his son with desperate honesty. "Nay, there is no need. It is as Ket has said; I am unfit. The command is yours. If anyone questions your authority, send them to me. But I think they will all be glad enough to obey you."

Trevyn regarded him with aching heart, finding nothing to say. "Will you sleep now?" he asked at last.

"By my troth, ay!" Alan murmured in wonder. "Ay, I shall sleep well." He started toward his bed, but turned to stand before Trevyn a moment longer. "I believe I forgot to say welcome!" he told him, and grasped his shoulders and kissed him.

Chapter Two

"It's just as well," Ket said when Trevyn told him of the change of command. But Trevyn disagreed.

"It's not a bit well," he sighed. "But he shall be well, Ket, mark my words. . . . What have you done with that great, bloody sword?"

Ket looked at the ground. "I've hidden it—and I'll reveal it to no one, Prince. Not even t' ye." His brown eyes flashed up, pleading for understanding. Trevyn smiled wearily.

"You're wise," he acknowledged. "You know I'm no more proof against its spell than Father was. But what of yourself, Ket? How long do you think it will be before thoughts of the thing eat away your reason and contentment?"

"Better me than ye," Ket snapped unhappily. "I'll call council."

"Wait!" Trevyn exclaimed. A familiar form was approaching through the dusk. Gwern trudged up to stand by his elbow, raising his straight, shaggy brows in blank inquiry at the stares he was receiving from two sides.

"Gwern," Trevyn declared, "I believe you might finally become useful in your own peculiar way."

"Ay," Ket muttered. "Ay, it can't touch him; even a fish

can feel that." He disappeared into the gathering darkness and reappeared shortly with the sword, offering it to Gwern as if he could not wait to be rid of it. The weapon lay blanket-wrapped on his outstretched hands with the covering slipping away from the blade. Gwern stared as if he were confronted with something indecent.

"Take charge of the sword, Gwern," Trevyn instructed. "Don't let anyone have it, least of all my father. A deadly magic is in it."

"I'll bury it, then," said Gwern. "Earth is good for such ills."

"Nay, some fool will dig it up again. You must keep it by you."

Gwern shrugged and grasped it, not at the hilt but by the midpoint, as if it were a stick. He lifted it with a grunt and bundled it under one arm, blade backmost. Trevyn made fast the wrappings that hid the bright metal.

"What a nuisance," Gwern remarked, hefting the bulky thing.

"Guard it at all times," Trevyn charged him. "See to it, Gwern." The son of earth sighed and wandered off with his unwieldy burden.

Later that evening, Trevyn sat around a fire with Ket, and Craig, and Robin of Firth, and lords and captains of all the southern towns—far older men than Trevyn, all of them. Yet they looked to him for guidance.

"If there is any question of my right to command," Trevyn told them, "the King has said it must come to him. I hope there will be none, for he is sleeping."

"There shall be none," growled old Craig, glancing about him with a hint of menace. No one gainsaid him.

"Good," Trevyn stated. "Now, I shall not tell you how I came by certain knowledge, for it makes far too long a tale. But be assured of this: it is not beasts we fight here. By sorcery, the souls of brigands and murderers have been spirited into the bodies of the wolves. An ancient wizard named Wael has done this, to smooth the way for an invasion by his master, Rheged of Tokar. So it does not avail us to slay the wolves: when one is killed, it is a simple matter for Wael to transfer the captive soul to another. And if he lacked wolves, I dare say he could use another scheme."

"Lack wolves!" Ket exclaimed wryly. "Why, there are more wolves in Isle than men! The Westwood is full of them, and the mountains of Welas, and the Northern Barrens—"

"Exactly." Trevyn smiled at him.

"So what is to be done?" someone asked.

"I must confront Wael and strive to reverse the spell. Failing that, I might be able to strike a bargain with him. I have something he wants."

"Wael would be the big one," Robin said. "The laughing wolf."

"Ay. So far he has no more than trifled with you, waiting for the Tokarian fleet. But he knows me, and fears me a little. I expect him to strike with all his force in the morning. So draw the lines tight."

Throughout that night the captains roused tired men and instructed them to fall back toward Alan's position, forming a compact group in preparation for the morrow. When all was ready, a few hours before dawn, Ket and Craig and the others went to snatch a bit of sleep. But Trevyn wandered, fighting to keep the calm he had brought from Elwestrand, trying to dream himself back to a certain night on Elundelei. He settled at last on the roots of an elm, near the cottage where Alan slumbered, and looked for a legend in the moon and wandering stars.

At the first light of day the men stood ranked, tensely awaiting the attack. Trevyn rode the lines on his lithe white horse to steady them. But full day dawned, and no wolves came.

Alan awoke hours after sunrise to the same eerie silence. It did not seem odd to him at first. He smiled drowsily in the bright sunlight and turned to look for Lysse. He had embraced her in a dream, and for a moment he could not understand where she was, where he was, or why. When he remembered, he could not explain his own happiness. Hastily he washed his hands and face in the cold water that awaited him. Only when he reached for his sword and found it missing did Alan recall the events of the past evening. No wonder he had slept late; he would not be leading any battles now.

Slowly, ashamed in spite of his joy, he moved to his cottage door. The mass of his men stood ranked not far away, waiting. Even closer at hand lounged the lanky, red-haired form of Ket. It was no use going weaponless, Alan decided, with a battle forming. "Do you think I might have a sword?" he hailed him.

"I have your own sword here, my lord," Ket said quietly, not quite looking at him. He brought it over. It was the one with the lion's-head hilt, the one he had worn for years, and Ket must have spent half the night polishing it, Alan judged, when he should have been getting his rest. Alan peered at his seneschal. "Why are you my-lording me?" he asked.

"For the sake of respect, I was told." Ket studied Alan's face and smiled his slow, warm smile. "Ye don't remember!"

"I seem to remember being the worst kind of an ass," Alan sighed, "but the details are lost to me, praise be. Will you forget the respect now?"

"As you say," Ket drawled. There was little need for words between these two old friends. But the greatest of debts constrained Alan to speak.

"And for what you did last evening, Ket—a thousand thanks."

Ket flushed, and helped Alan into his helm without comment. Trevyn cantered up and dismounted, facing his father with grave affection. "Are you all right?" he asked.

"I'm as likely to be a dolt as ever, Trev." Alan grinned broadly. "Since my gladness is out of all proportion with the occasion. Would you look at that tree!"

"Why, what about that tree?" Ket gasped, staring at the muscular elm as if it might conceal a wolf.

"Look at the way it spreads deep and high, joining earth and sky. It has flesh and skin, flowing blood and reaching fingertips; it's as alive as I am. And it shall remain, it or its seed, long after we are gone."

Ket's face sobered at this strange talk, but Trevyn nodded. "Ay," he said softly, "and once you have hold on such truth, nothing can utterly destroy you."

"In regard to destruction," Alan rejoined lightly, "what am I to do today?"

"Keep clear of the fighting if you can; your reflexes are not likely to be at their best. Take this oddity of a horse, and lend your presence to the lines." Trevyn handed him the reins. "The men are anxious about you; it will hearten them to see you."

"And you? Should you not be mounted?"

"Nay. . . . Can you lend me that brooch, Father, the ill-fated one? Perhaps it'll give Wael a moment's pause."

Alan brought out the jeweled pin and watched Trevyn fasten it to his cloak. "Why, what are your plans?" he asked worriedly.

"I can't really plan for Wael. . . . Though I admit, I wish I could remember a—a certain name, as it was promised I would. But I have a spell or two to try on him. We'll spar at spells, that is all."

"Are you sure—" Alan began, but even as he spoke a shout went up. The wolves had appeared, running to the charge. "Take care, Father!" Trevyn cried, and sprinted to the battle line.

On a rise, a bit apart from the other wolves, the yellow-eyed leader sat. Trevyn strode out to face him, feeling very alone and yet not entirely alone; something shielded him, kept the snarling brutes he passed from snapping at him. Alys, perhaps? He hardly dared to hope it. He walked up to the big, gray wolf with his naked sword leveled at its chest, and it sat unmoved, grinning at him.

"Are you ready, Wael?" Trevyn asked curtly.

"Ready!" Lupine laughter curdled the air. "What readiness might I need for a pup like you!"

Trevyn's mind still darted in search of the elusive name. He fiercely constrained it to focus on the task at hand. Slowly, strongly, he began to recite the words that Hal had taught him, grim words of the old Eastern tongue, that would compel these wretched spirits back to their proper bodies: *"Zaichos Karben, arb ud Grezig. . . ."* Souls moved to obey; Trevyn could feel their stifling heaviness in the air around him. Behind him, the wolves faltered in their attack, and men cheered. But Wael's will strove with Trevyn's. His yellow eyes narrowed with strain and his borrowed body tightened beyond the sword's point. Forcing himself to concentrate on the struggle, hoping somehow to breach his enemy's power, if only for an instant, Trevyn brought forth the parchment from his tunic and fingered it as he continued with his counterspell. Crushing strength opposed him, and he felt the sway of the balance; he seemed neither to win nor lose.

"If you did not have that scroll you thieved from me," Wael panted, "your strength would be no equal to mine." Though he dreaded that Trevyn might try to turn the talisman's power to his own account, Wael hoped the Prince would value the parchment and preserve it with greatest care. But Trevyn glanced at the thing with loathing so sudden and intense that it drove all spellwords and strategy from his mind.

"I will take no power from a thing so evil," he grated. "Fire of Menwy have it!" His fingers flicked, and the parchment puffed into flame. Wael shrieked in despair, lunged to save it, but even as his lupine body leaped the scroll vanished, leaving only a shower of ash. Wael's self and his spell left Isle like smoke whisked away by a strong wind. Terrified and confused, the wolves sped toward their Forest home; they were only pitiful animals now.

The largest one lay impaled on Trevyn's sword, mutely suffering, its golden eyes bewildered. Beside it lay the Prince, as still as death, though not a mark showed on him. Alan reached him first, and killed the wolf, for mercy—it had been a long time since he had killed so gently. But he could not rouse his son.

Not long afterward, Gwern appeared anxiously at Alan's cottage door. Trevyn lay on the narrow bed, stripped to the waist, and Alan held him while Ket tried to give him wine. But the crimson liquid spilled over him, and he never moved. Alan was weeping.

"He's not dead," Gwern stated, a bit too loudly. "Why do you weep?"

"Have you seen these welts?" Alan choked.

Gwern looked at the whip scars and shuddered like a horse when the fly bites. His claylike face moved, and he turned away without a word. Alan railed on.

"I'd like to know who gave him those stripes. . . . I'd hunt them down and rip them apart with my fingers! Sweet

Mothers, all things gained, and then it seems all falls to ruin again. What ails him, Gwern? We can't help him."

Gwern came closer and studied the Prince. "Shadows," he said at last. "Years ago, you would have cured him with the little yellow flower."

"Veran's gold? None has bloomed hereabouts for hundreds of years. We had some in jars, but it all turned to dust when Hal went." Alan's face twisted with the pain of the memory. Then he stiffened, noticing for the first time the bundle that Gwern carried. "Mother of mercy!" he breathed. "Get that accursed sword away from me!"

"Trevyn told me to keep hold of it," Gwern said.

"Then do so, but keep it far from me! I feel it draw. . . ." Alan shook where he sat cradling his son in his arms. Only that inert form kept him seated, Ket sensed. "It cozens me like a woman, and I thought I was past such folly! It shames me. Get it away, Gwern!"

"I'm going." Gwern retreated a few paces. "May I borrow Trevyn's horse? I'll go get Meg."

"Meg?" Alan straightened, his fear suddenly gone. "Take any horse you like. How can you find her?"

"Easily enough." Gwern slouched out of the door and was on his way within the minute.

"Meg," Alan murmured. "There is healing in her lightest touch." He felt the almost forgotten stirrings of hope.

For the five days of Gwern's absence, Trevyn lay, and ate nothing, and drank scarcely anything, and never came to himself. Sometimes he thrashed and moaned in black dreams, crying out against the wolves, or against the slavers, cursing them. Once he pleaded, "Let him be. . . ." Later he whispered, "Oh, my sorrow, what did they do to him after I had gone and left him?" Alan talked to him constantly, stroking his brow, calling to him, trying to calm him. If he succeeded, it was only to see Trevyn sink into a deeper stupor.

There had been no sign of the wolves, no messengers, no action of any kind. Alan's army camped at his feet and waited, almost breathlessly, for news of wolves, or war, or the Prince. Unmistakably, the shadow that had been on the land was gone. For the first time in months, the men really felt sunshine, felt it with a relief too deep for rejoicing, even if rejoicing had been fitting, with the Prince so ill. . . . Every man of the thousands gathered there longed to aid Alan in some way. Ket spent his time stumping in and out of the cottage, almost as sleepless as Alan. "Let me watch the lad for a while," he would say gruffly from time to time. But Alan would not yield his seat for long, not to anyone.

As Trevyn weakened for lack of food or rest, he began to call Meg. He would stare past his father, gazing at some insubstantial form of horror, and sob out her name as if he called on his god for succor. "Name of Aene, may she come soon," Alan breathed.

She came in the twilight of the fifth day, cantering through the staring soldiers without an answering glance, looking like a dark-cloaked queen of ancient legend with her pale face proudly raised over her moon-marked steed. She might have been as starved as Trevyn; her hair clung tremulously by her hollow cheek. But the sun brooch at her throat shone bright. Alan left his place at Trevyn's side to meet her, helped her from her horse with outstretched arms, and led her to his son.

The Prince tossed restlessly, moaning, "Meg—Meg— forgive—" Yet, he did not see her. The girl sank down beside him, grasping his faltering hands. "Sweet Prince, be whole!" she begged, but he looked past her without a sign.

"Call him, lass," Alan urged.

"Trev! 'Tis I, Meg!" she beseeched him, but to no avail. Trevyn flinched away from her touch, and sweat stood out on his face.

"He doesn't know you," Alan whispered.

"Trevyn!" Meg pleaded. But he turned away from her, hiding his face and cursing the slave pits of Tokar.

Alan felt as if, hope won and healing in sight, all his world had fallen to ruin yet once more. Groaning, he fell to his knees at the bedside, clenching his fists in fury and despair. If Trevyn should really die . . . The forbidden thought went through Alan with a force that laid open the deepest reaches of his soul.

He sprang to his feet, gripping the glimmering Elfstone that hung on his chest, his gift of hope from Lysse at their first parting. "Alberic!" he cried, though a moment before he had not known the name or its meaning. "By all that is beautiful, by all things that render you fealty, I charge you—govern yourself! *Pelle mir*—look at me, Alberic!"

Slowly and painfully, Trevyn focused his eyes on him. "My sire," he breathed.

"Trevyn," said Alan, quite gently, "you have a visitor. Welcome her."

Meg sat biting her lip in misery at her failure, stunned to silence by Alan's passion. But as Trevyn's eyes turned upon her, she instantly knew what she must do. Like dawn after shadows, her wan face lit with the smile she knew he loved. "Hello, Trev," she said.

He only stared at her with widening eyes and speechless mouth, and she accosted him tenderly but saucily. "What, fair Prince, d'ye not remember me? Me and my sister Molly, the one with the red hair?"

Trevyn could not quite find his voice. "Meg!" he whispered hoarsely, and reached out to her. She came and sat beside him on the bed, and he flung his arms about her. "Oh, Meg!" The cry was like a moan, and she bit her lip again, for he was weeping. "Hush, Trev; ye'll be all right," she faltered, and her hands came up to cradle his head.

Alan went out. An hour later, when he looked in again, Trevyn lay deeply asleep with his head on Megan's lap; she sat absently stroking his golden hair. Alan smiled shakily. "Meg, lass, you look spent," he whispered. "Come, let's find you some food and a place to rest." He gently placed Trevyn's head back on its pillow and took the girl out, an arm around her thin shoulders.

During the night, Gwern trudged stoically in, still toting his swaddled burden of sword. During the night also, Megan slipped out of her tent and away, to the confusion of the sentries, who had been given no orders concerning her. Alan slept until an hour or two after dawn, then heard the news with wholehearted vexation and dismay, in manner so much like his old, ardent self that Ket wept. When that was taken care of, they went to the cottage and found Gwern dozing by Trevyn, his bare, grimy feet planted on the bedframe. This time, somehow, Alan managed to ignore the sword. He and Ket sat companionably, waiting for Trevyn to awaken.

It was nearly noon before Trevyn rolled over and looked

around, confused. Alan went to him, his face still drawn and gray with strain in spite of his rest. "Go to bed," Trevyn told him promptly. "What day is it? How was I hurt?"

"It has been nearly a week." Alan smiled at him dryly. "You weren't wounded. I think Wael gave you some bad dreams."

"Thunder, ay!" Trevyn shuddered at the memory. "But something comforted me. . . ." Suddenly he sat bolt upright, nearly falling in his excitement. "Meg! Was she really here?"

"Ay, she was, Trev." Alan spoke unhappily. "But she's gone again. I can't imagine what ails the girl."

"I can." Trevyn settled back with a sigh and a frown, then caught sight of Gwern snoring beside him and smiled in spite of his disappointment. "Can't I even have a bed to myself?" he complained.

"You like him better than you used to," Alan asked, "don't you?"

"I—" Trevyn did not know how to admit that he loved Gwern like a brother. "Well, he went for Meg, did he not?" he barked at last.

"Ay."

"Let him sleep, then. What's to eat?"

But he was too weak to eat much, or even sit up for long. He dozed off again shortly, and awoke in late afternoon. Busy, clattering sounds drifted in from outside; the men were breaking camp. Alan stumped in to face his son with a worried frown.

"I've just had a messenger from Corin, Trev. Tokarian warships have been sighted off the Long Beaches; they may have landed by now. I must march my men eastward."

Trevyn gaped at him for a long moment, digesting this news, adjusting his sense of time; then he let out a shout that roused Gwern.

"Tides and tempests!" he cried. "Do you mean to tell me that all the time I've been lolling about, an army has been lolling about with me?"

"I did seem to remember something about a Tokarian invasion," Alan retorted stiffly, "and I sent Craig off with half the men. But now I must go, and quickly." Alan's tone softened. "I am sorry, Trev—we've scarcely had time to talk.

But I must go myself. I owe my people some kingship, after—after all my foolery. I'll leave a company with you—"

"Mothers, nay!" said Trevyn emphatically. "Take every man. Gwern and I will be fine by ourselves. I'll ride after you in a few days."

"You should rest for at least a week."

"I'm stronger already. Look." Trevyn slipped out of bed and stood, tottering. Alan eyed him doubtfully. But Gwern extended a hand to steady him, and unexpectedly spoke.

"I'll feed him well," he volunteered, "and he'll stay here till he's healed. He's never been able to get the best of me yet," Gwern added darkly.

"We'll see, in the morning," Alan hedged.

But in the morning Trevyn walked to the table to eat, and Alan made ready to march with all his men, muttering. He had called his son Alberic, King That Shall Be. But it was hard to let go of the little boy that once was. For his own part, Trevyn seemed as protective of his father.

"Be wary," he warned. "Rheged is full of treachery. And Wael is probably with him."

"I thought you dispatched him!" Alan exclaimed.

"Nay, I only slew his borrowed body, poor thing. . . . And I believe I did away with the transferring of living souls when I destroyed the parchment. But Wael still has plenty of tricks left."

"I don't mind any magic, now that that shadow's gone," Alan grumbled. "Trev, lad, be gentle with yourself. . . ." They embraced, and Alan strode to the golden charger Rhyssiart, took saddle. Trevyn stood on the doorstep and raised a hand in farewell as his father jingled off at the head of his army. The men saluted him as they passed, and Trevyn bit his lip, feeling his knees forsake him; he couldn't weaken now! Gwern slipped a casual hand under his elbow.

"Thanks," Trevyn hissed between clenched teeth.

They stood until the last of the troops had passed. Then Trevyn staggered inside and collapsed on his bed, groaning. "I must be out of my mind," he lamented. "Gwern, you are an execrable cook, and I know it."

"I'm no cook at all," Gwern stated in his factual way.

They ate cold food for three days, until Trevyn was well

enough to make himself some soup. Then they spent another
three days in almost constant baking and roasting, preparing
supplies for their journey. They had no way of knowing what
was happening in Nemeton, but Trevyn felt sure there must
be fighting. Peasants wandered by their windows in bewilderment, some fleeing the rumored invasion, some returning to
their homes since the threat of the wolves had passed. The
proper owners of their cottage came back to it and peeked
timidly in.

"We'll leave in the morning," Trevyn assured them.

He and Gwern spent the evening packing. Trevyn worked
silently, frowning in thought. "Meg is wandering somewhere
in all this confusion," he said suddenly, when they were done.
"How am I ever to find her, Gwern, since she won't come to
me? How did you find her to bring her here?"

Gwern kept uneasy silence for a moment, moving his big
hands, fumbling for words. "She is to the east, somewhere
near Nemeton," he said finally. "I can feel the focus of her
being in much the same way as I am always drawn to you,
but—it is through your love for her that I sense her. When I
see her, it is through your eyes."

"And you love her," Trevyn murmured.

"Through your heart."

Trevyn stood staring at him, afraid to put into words
something unfathomable he had felt. "But you must be
yourself, Gwern," he protested at last. "You always have
been. Everyone is."

"I—I'm not sure."

Chapter Three

They left the cottage at dawn and rode toward Nemeton, with Trevyn on his strange, cat-eyed steed and Gwern on his colt. They rode all day, steadily but not hard, since Trevyn had still not regained his full strength. His own frailty troubled him, and starting the journey brought all his concerns to the fore.

"Confound it, Gwern," he grumbled by the campfire that evening, "do you know anything about the dragons of Lyrdion?"

"Nay."

"Confound it!" Trevyn exclaimed again. "How am I ever going to defeat Wael? I can't remember—I am nothing more than I was the last time I faced him and nearly died of it."

"But it was not Wael that hurt you the last time," Gwern remarked reasonably.

"It wasn't?" Trevyn whispered. "Then—Menwy? Why, that black—" With difficulty he restrained himself from applying the epithet of female dog to the goddess.

"She had to work through your hatred." Gwern neither reproved nor explained. That toneless voice calmed Trevyn.

"Well, if I can't use her—Gwern, the problem remains the

same. I am no match for Wael. And I must face him again, soon or late, whether he awaits me at Nemeton or not."

"Perhaps you will not have to face him alone," Gwern said. Trevyn turned to him curiously, sensing—what?

"What do you have in mind, Gwern?" he asked slowly. But Gwern shrugged and would not answer, sitting blank-faced by a hulking bundle of sword.

The next morning they traveled on. To make for easier fording of the Black River, they headed slightly north. Three days later they crossed the main river and reached the point of land between its arms at the southern fringe of the Forest. Trevyn tried to stun rabbits for their supper as they rode, but his stones all missed. Muttering, he wished out loud that he had a hunting bird like the one he had lost, some time back, fighting with Gwern.

"Look!" Gwern pointed. "An eagle."

The great golden raptor, shining like the sun, skimmed just over the treetops, its wings nearly five feet in span. "It must have come all the way from Veran's Mountain!" Trevyn exclaimed. *"Laifrita thae,* little brother, you have seen far; what news?" He held up an arm for the bird, calling it to him. But the eagle swooped past his outstretched wrist and on toward Gwern, striking with a screech at the base of his neck where it met the shoulder. Curved talons drew blood, and Gwern, utterly startled, fell off his horse with a thud. The eagle flapped heavily away, and Trevyn jumped down from his own mount, hurried to Gwern. The youth was sitting up, looking browner than ever with leaf mold and rubbing his head in surprise.

"I'm sorry!" Trevyn exclaimed. "I never in a thousand years would have expected that. . . . Are you all right?" He tried to examine Gwern's cuts, but Gwern pushed his hand away, gently enough.

"Scratches. I'm just stunned. Can Wael be setting the eagles against us now?"

"I hope not!" Trevyn shuddered. Gwern looked up thoughtfully.

"The eagles are the messengers of the goddess. But I can't think how I might have offended her."

"Still, I didn't smell any stench of Wael," Trevyn mused.

They rode on a little farther and camped in a Forest glade not too far from the river. They set a snare and had a rabbit for their supper. But in the morning Gwern groaned and struggled to rise from his bed. His face looked flushed under its habitual coat of grime. Trevyn pushed him back to his blanket, feeling the heat of his forehead with alarm. The cuts the eagle had given him looked swollen and raw.

Trevyn cursed. "By blood, Gwern, that's what you get for never washing!" he shouted in conclusion, and trudged to the river, grumbling. He returned with pans of water and bathed Gwern's cuts and face. They did not ride that day. Trevyn spent the time cooking soup, but Gwern hardly ate any. He drank water from time to time. Trevyn made trip after trip to the river, bringing cool water, laying a cool cloth on the infected cuts. He didn't sleep much that night, tending Gwern almost as frequently as he had during the day. But by the following morning Gwern no longer knew him. His wounds had swollen to double size, and he cried and moaned in delirious pain.

Trevyn tried the only crude treatment he knew. Braving Gwern's struggles and screams, he sliced the scabs open, squeezed out the pus, and seared the cuts with a hot blade. To do this, he had to sit on top of Gwern and pin down his flailing arms; later, he went off in the woods, and retched, and wept. Still later, in a sort of penance, he sat for hours by Gwern, patiently washing him, peeling away the tattered clothing that seemed to have adhered to his skin. Beneath the rags he found scars. It took him a while to realize that the marks were identical, line for line, with his own scars from the slave whips and the wolves. When he could no longer deny it, he wept again. That night, every time he tried to sleep, he seemed to hear Gwern's screams under his knife-wielding hand.

The searing did not help. Contagion crept down Gwern's arm and up his neck; Trevyn thought the skin would break with swelling, and half of Gwern's face turned a vivid puce, like a bruise; he looked as if he had been beaten. Whenever he moved, he shrieked with pain. Trevyn scarcely dared to touch him, even with the wet cloth. He no longer attempted to sleep. Exhaustion would take him for a few moments from time to time, and then he would wake with a start and try to comfort Gwern, if only with clumsy words.

By the time Trevyn lost count of days, Gwern no longer had strength to scream. He lay softly moaning, but Trevyn could tell that his pain had not abated. Then one day, near evening, Gwern suddenly quieted, lying limp and still. Filled with dread, Trevyn felt for his breath. But Gwern opened his eyes and fixed them on Trevyn's haggard face.

"The pain is gone," he whispered wonderingly.

Trevyn only swallowed, and Gwern looked thoughtful. "Not good," he added after a pause.

"Nay." Trevyn had heard about the respite that sometimes came just before death.

"Tell me," Gwern said.

"Your whole arm is purple with infection, and your shoulder down to your ribs, and your neck and face. . . ." For a moment, Trevyn closed his own burning eyes. "I can't help you. I've tried to help, and I've only hurt you."

"But I can't die," Gwern murmured incredulously. "I don't understand."

"That's what I keep saying," Trevyn groaned. "I don't understand. Sometimes I think I have been accursed since the day I was born. I had only just learned to—to love you, Gwern, and then this—"

"But I can't sicken! I am not mortal; I was never born," Gwern explained laboriously. "Alys made me, somehow, to embody your deepest being, the Prince you liked the least. She ensouled me with her own breath. So I am Alys and I am you; how can I die while either of you lives? I have wept when you wept, loved when you loved, kept that feeling safe and helped it bring you back to Isle. I am wyrd; how can I just end? I don't understand. . . ."

"You are more than friend, even more than brother," Trevyn whispered, shaking. "You are second self. . . ."

"I am your inner fate. I am the child you have tried to leave behind; I am the white hart, the wild thing, and I am the wilderness within. I have loved you when you would not love yourself."

"Yet, you are also yourself, Gwern," said Trevyn tightly, "to our sorrow."

"I am selfhead and godhead. So how have I become doomed to a mortal death. . . ." Weary, Gwern closed his eyes.

Still trembling, unable to speak, Trevyn took his good left hand and held it between his own, stroking it, warming it when it began to grow cold. He did not dare a larger embrace; he would not risk jostling Gwern and causing him pain when he lay so peacefully. He could hardly tell when Gwern ceased to breathe, but he saw the purple tinge creep all the way across his still face, felt the chill in his hand. Trevyn laid it down and edged away, sensing dark waters of hatred on all sides, welling up within him, drowning deep. He staggered to his feet, turned blindly and ran.

Within a few strides he surged into rage that he thought would destroy him, destroy the world; he didn't care. He careered against trees, punishing them and himself with all the strength in his body, smashing them with head and hands and knees, shrieking, but not with pain. He cursed with curses torn up from his reddest depths, cursed every person of the goddess, cursed Aene. Sometimes he stumbled and fell, ripping at earth with his bloodied hands. Sometimes he scrambled along, crashing through thickets like a hunted deer. He came up headlong against rocks, seized them and hurled them against the unresponsive earth, then plunged aimlessly onward. But he was too weak from fatigue and from his own recent illness to run mad for long. After a while he lay feebly thrashing, too exhausted to rise, too stubborn to weep. Later, eerily, he reached a calm even deeper than his hatred, and he knew quite surely that the goddess had not stirred for all his rage and all his grief. He felt her implacable love and understood that he would always be hers, always be alone. He bowed his head in acquiescence, laid his face in the dirt and slept.

Something awakened him before dawn, some internal pang. He stared at the shadowy Forest, and remembered, and groaned. Then, unsteadily, he rose, wondering how far he had come from his campsite and how he would bury his—his companion; he could not bear to think of a more fitting title.

He did not even know which direction would take him back to
Gwern. But a faintly scornful snort sounded through the
darkness and a white blur walked up to him: his wild-eyed
horse. He crawled onto the beast, and it carried him off
without a word of instruction through the gray dusk of dawn.

He found Gwern, no more than a lump in the dim light,
and beyond him a bundle that had been impatiently pushed
out of the way. Trevyn needed the massive sword of Lyrdion
now. He pulled the weapon from its wrappings, took it and
felt his way to the top of a slight rise beyond the glade. There
he began to hack a hole in the ground for his wyrd.

He worked through bright dawn and sunrise. The hacking
and scraping soothed him somehow. But even through the
numbness of his grief he could feel the haunting tug of the
sword. Culean had killed himself with that weapon, Trevyn
grimly remembered, and with less cause than he had, he
thought. . . . No matter. He dared say he put it to more
fitting use. When he judged the grave was done, he went to
get the body.

He reached the edge of the glade, stopped and reached
shakily for a tree. Gwern lay where he had left him. But he
looked like a graceful young god, lying there, like a woman's
dream of her sleeping lover somehow caught in light and
form. His rugged face and the bare rise of his chest caught the
early sun and took on a golden glow; no trace of sickly purple
remained. Trevyn walked over to him, knelt beside him and
felt the movement of his ribs, felt the warm pulse of his neck,
felt breath, scarcely daring to believe. Gwern stirred under
his touch, blinked, then sat up and gaped at him.

"What on earth—" he exclaimed, as agitated as Trevyn had
ever seen him. "What—Trev, what has happened? You're all
blood and dirt; you're a mess! You look—like me!"

Trevyn felt for his voice; it came out a hoarse whisper.
"And you look better than I can fathom." He raised a hand,
and with the bruised fingertips he delicately traced the
smooth line of Gwern's neck and shoulder. "Not so much as a
scar on you," he marveled.

Gwern stiffened, stunned by memory. "I was dead!" he
gulped. "Was—wasn't I dead?"

"Stark and cold." Trevyn shivered with horror and growing joy.

"I was dead, and now I am alive. . . . Sweet Mothers, Trev, what have you done? What—what ransom have you paid for me?"

"I think I have sacrificed nothing but my pride. By my wounds, Gwern, I'm glad you couldn't see me! I threw a fit." Trevyn collapsed beside Gwern with a tremulous laugh. "I railed like a child—and after a while I knew—I understood—and now I don't understand! Bah!" He sat up again. "Mother of mercy, is there to be no end of riddling?"

Gwern made a small sound that Trevyn could not identify, not until he saw the tears running down the gentle brown slopes of his counterpart's face. He had never seen Gwern weep, and at first he could not react or comprehend. "My Prince—" Gwern spoke huskily.

"Gwern, what—" Trevyn awkwardly reached out toward him, touching only one cupped hand.

"Trev, I love you; I owe you everything. Will you try not to leave me again? I want only to be at one with you for as long as the riddles shall last. Without end."

"Then come here," Trevyn breathed, stirred to his soul's depths. "Come here, my second self." He embraced the son of earth, drew him in with both arms, felt Gwern's answering embrace, warm head on his shoulder, hair by his cheek, bare, smooth chest against his heart, tears—all in an instant, and for the first time, he felt that, and then it vanished with an odd twinge. He held a bundle of blossoms and leafy sticks wrapped in vines and sealed with clay. Crying out, Trevyn leaped to his feet and flung it away, breaking the clay binding. "My curse on all your devices!" he wailed at the goddess, at the entire heedless world. Then he sank to the ground again and wept. "Oh, I have destroyed him!" he choked to no listener. "He loved me, and I have destroyed him!"

He wept for hours, sometimes pacing in circles, sometimes quieting only to begin again. When the sun neared its zenith, he calmed somewhat at last and sat staring dully at white bean blossoms, ruddy tips of rowan and fragrant purple heather, all fresh and thriving. For no reason, his eyes glanced beyond the strewn sticks to where a wolf sat at the foot of a tall oak tree, gazing back at him. A wolf with lovely, violet eyes. . . .

"Alys?" he whispered.

"Nay, it is Maeve. I am only one small speck in Alys." The wolf trotted up to sit gravely beside him, laid a paw on his knee in a gesture not so much doglike as human: for his comforting, he knew. He could barely speak.

"Wael transformed you?" he faltered.

"Nay, I came of my own accord. There was need of—of some balance. But the Lady has returned to the Forest now, and my task will soon be done. . . . Freca, why do you grieve? The earth-son is not gone. He is at one with you, just as he wished."

Trevyn had sensed this truth even before she spoke. He knew where the dragons of Lyrdion were: in honeycomb depths of earth, his to loose as he had loosed his rage, for he was at one with that earth now. He could feel the song of a rowan's root. He knew Wael's sooth-name: it was the obverse of his own, encompassing his own despair and death. Gwern had given him all knowledge in making him whole. He comprehended mysteries of all realms, whether sky, sea, Isle or twilit Elwestrand—all stations of the sun, all phases of the changing moon. And all pain; he stiffened stubbornly against that knowledge.

"I don't care," he grumbled. "Gwern was himself, as well as me, and now he's dead."

"Changed, Alberic, only changed," she said gently. She nosed at the disorderly array of sticks and blossoms that had been the wyrd. "Plant these in that trail of tears you've left, and you'll have a grove that will be the glory of Isle in years to come, and better than any monument to his memory."

Even tired as he was, he obeyed her, thrusting the leafy shoots into the ground, spacing them in a sort of outward spiral. He surveyed his finished work sourly.

"A poor substitute for a warm and gentle touch," he stated.

"Come with me now," she told him, and led him to the tall oak tree at the edge of the glade. Nestled between its roots lay a wolf pup, soft, bright-eyed, still in its first fur. It gazed up at him with mingled valor and distress, wriggling. Automatically, Trevyn sat down so that his size would not frighten it, reached out to caress it. The little thing ran onto his lap and nuzzled under his chin, pressing against him, sending a spasm of longing through him.

"Your son," Maeve said.

"What?" he whispered.

"Your son, and his destiny is far stranger than yours. Being born a wolf may be the least of it." She gazed at him out of dusky damson eyes. "Take him with you, to comfort you, and to grieve you when it is time."

He stood, cradling the wolf cub against his chest, where it lay contentedly. "But Maeve," he faltered, "won't you miss him?"

"The babe is weaned," she answered, then stood grinning toothily at him. "Prince, you know I am a creature of the wilds! Get on to Nemeton; they have need of you there." She turned and trotted across the glade, between the newly planted trees. At the edge she faced around. "Look above you," she added, then disappeared into the Forest.

Trevyn looked. The eagle perched on a limb of the oak, staring down at him with hard, topaz eyes. Trevyn sighed, put out an arm, and the bird glided down to him, landing gently just above his wrist. He held it at a level with his face, and it regarded him steadily.

"So you did only what you had to do," he acceded. "What the goddess told you to do. All right. Will you get me something to eat, little brother, if you please? Or I am likely to starve before I ever reach Nemeton."

He put the golden sword of Lyrdion in Gwern's grave, pushed earth over it with his hands, planted heather and white blossoms of bean to mark the place. He knew he would have to come back for it, but he would not take it where it might cause his father pain. Later, he rode away on a fey white horse, with a belly full of half-cooked rabbit, holding a wolf cub on the saddle before him. An eagle flew close overhead. It was only a few hours until dusk, but Trevyn would not stay another night in the place where he had so painfully become whole. He rode through twilight, deep into night, noticing to his vague surprise that his horse's forehead shone with a clear, faint light, white on white, like a star. It had not done so before.

"A quaint sight I make," he muttered, "looking like a wild man, riding to face a sorcerer, all two of me, on a mad mystery of a horse, with a baby werewolf in my arms and an eagle almost bigger than I am thumping down on me from time to time. . . . Rheged may run when he sees me, but Wael is likely to laugh himself into oblivion."

Chapter Four

After three days of hard riding, not even taking time to wash, he approached Alan's encampment outside the walls of Nemeton. Alan blinked, watching him. "Gwern?" he queried, and then, as the rider drew closer, incredulously, "Trevyn?"

"I think I shall be, mostly, when I'm bathed." Trevyn dismounted, letting the wolf sit in the saddle. He had named the little one Dair, a word of strong comfort. Already Dair balanced expertly on the horse, in company with the eagle, which fed him scraps of raw meat. Alan glanced, open-mouthed, from the odd trio to his son's thin, hollow-eyed face.

"What in mercy has been going on?"

"Gwern took ill and died—or seemed to die. . . ." Trevyn sat limply on the ground beneath his horse's nose. "Father, I can't begin to tell you half of what's been happening to me. But Maeve—someone told me I was needed here."

"I'm relieved to see you; I've been expecting you for a week. But what you can do, I'm not sure." Alan sat beside his son. "We've wiped the countryside clear of the invaders at last. It's been grim work, but my men fight well now that the shadow of the wolves is gone and now—now that you are back and I am better. We've scuttled their clumsy ships. But on the day that I arrived some of the enemy took Nemeton, and they're holed up there yet. It would be no trouble to starve them out, but Corin is in there, and some others who were too stubborn to flee. . . ."

"Meg among them," Trevyn murmured. He had felt her presence long since, with all of Gwern's sureness.

"Ay." Alan's face showed his distress. "She got caught up in the confusion, it seems, and took refuge there. . . . But how did you know, lad?"

"I just know. . . . She's come to no harm so far, Father. I'd feel it if she had."

"And Cory? And the others?" Alan leaned forward eagerly.

"I can't tell about them," Trevyn admitted, hating to disappoint him. "I can only tell that Meg is all right. And I seem to catch a whiff of Wael."

"Ay, he's there, I think. Talk has it that a particularly villainous-looking, yellow-eyed old devil landed with Rheged. But you must have drawn his fangs, Trev. He's given us no trouble."

"I doubt it," Trevyn said. "He's just waiting for a time that suits his fancy. Wael is peculiar that way. And he hates me worse than poison. You'll see some fireworks yet. We must strike quickly, Father, before—"

Before Wael harmed Meg, Alan knew, though Trevyn could not say it. "As quickly as may be," he gruffly replied. "I have men at work up by the Forest constructing siege towers."

"No need. I can open the gates for you with a touch. I have the ancient powers of Bevan now, Father. Watch." Trevyn indicated his blanketroll, scarcely moving his finger, and it undid itself from his saddle, floated gently through the air, and settled at his feet. The wolf cub jumped down, pattered over, and curled up in his lap.

"What—what have you bargained away for this power?" Alan breathed, startled and dismayed. "What have you sacrificed, Trevyn?"

"Gwern is gone." Trevyn could not still the spasm of pain

that crossed his face. "But there was no bargaining done, Father, believe me. I would far rather . . ." For a moment he could not go on. "I even think it might have been Gwern's idea," he finally said.

"You don't look strong enough to break a biscuit," Alan told him roughly, to temper his concern.

"I'm as weak as a kitten," Trevyn acknowledged. "But in a way I'm stronger than I ever was before. And I won't be able to sleep until this is settled—until I see Meg safe. Tomorrow, Father. Please."

Alan hesitated, measuring his stature and his need. "Only if I am never far from your side," he said at last.

"I'll be glad of your shield."

"All right, then. . . . Where did you get the wolf?"

Trevyn lifted the creature to his face, rested his taut cheek for a moment in its warm fur. "From the All-Mother," he answered after a pause, "and he's dearer to me than life, Father. Will you guard him, too?"

"Of course. Trevyn, will I ever understand?"

"When this is over, I'll sleep for a month. Then we'll talk for a year."

In the morning a messenger arrived whose news sent Alan stamping in circles with anxiety. "A second wave of invaders has landed," he told Trevyn. "They're marching on us across deserted countryside. My men are faithful, but they have been fighting for months; those who live are worn to the bone. They can't take much more of this."

"All the more reason to regain Nemeton quickly," said Trevyn. Alan nodded and called his army into battle readiness.

He and Trevyn reached the main gate under cover provided by Craig's expert archers. Still, rocks and hot lead hailed down upon them as they stood before the iron-sheathed doors. Holding a cowhide over himself and his son, Alan waited patiently while Trevyn ran questing fingers along the timbers, spoke a soft command. Nothing happened, and the Prince frowned.

"Wael has put a locking spell on these gates," he explained. "So we can't afford to be delicate. . . ." A quiet light flickered through his sea-green eyes. He judged that he had power now to call on the dark goddess once more. He need not possess strength of body; Emrist had showed him that. He need only assent completely to her aid. "Here goes," he muttered, and struck the gates once, lightly, with clenched fist. "Break them, Menwy, break them!"

The huge portals burst inward, hurling splinters and metal shards for a hundred feet. The portcullis that stood just beyond them writhed apart and flew through the air like nightmare snakes. Even the stones of the gatehouse flew. Within an instant, Alan found himself staring through a clean, open passageway into the main street of Nemeton, where a troop of Tokarians stood at muster. Luckily, the enemy soldiers were even more startled than he, and some were already mortally wounded. Hastily, Alan pulled Trevyn aside and bellowed for the charge.

Half of the Tokarians were trapped on the walls, demoralized by the sudden change in their circumstances. Alan's army swirled in and took them from behind, quickly dispatching them. Others of the enemy were hunted through the streets and deserted houses of the town; this was slow, nerve-racking work. Ket spotted a glimpse of golden crown and was pleased to take Rheged his prisoner. Alan didn't know. As soon as he could, he set a company to barricading the blasted gates, saw Trevyn onto his weird white steed, gathered some mounted retainers, and led on to Corin's keep. There another set of barred and guarded doors awaited them.

The Tokarians within the keep saw them coming and met them with a shower of arrows and rocks. Sensing doom, they fought feverishly, hurling anything they could think of to hold vengeance at a distance. But Trevyn drew rein just beyond the range of their fire and flung up one arm. The gates toppled as if pushed by a strong wind, and he galloped over them, ducking, a wolf cub sheltered against his chest. The Tokarians scattered, and Alan's liegemen began stoically to hunt them down.

"The dungeons," Alan said.

"Meg's on the roof," Trevyn murmured, peering up. He could see nothing but his eagle, high overhead.

"There are enemies on the stairs. Let the men take care of them. The dungeons, first."

Robin of Firth, Corin's foster brother, was also intent on reaching the dungeons. He sped down the dark stairs ahead of them and greeted Cory with a shout of joyful relief. The lord of Nemeton and his followers sat fettered to their cell walls, looking somewhat starved and rather bewildered by the explosive noises they had been hearing. "No use breaking up the place," Alan remarked as Trevyn reached for a lock. "We might need it."

"You're right," Trevyn sighed. "Find the keys, Father; I'm tired." He collapsed onto a dank stone step, laid his head against the rough-cut doorjamb, and closed his eyes. Robin had already found the keys and was opening cells, unlocking fetters. Alan glanced worriedly at his son, then looked up sharply as Ket brought his royal prisoner clattering down the stairs. Cory hugged Robin and came over to speak to Alan, rubbing his sore wrists.

"The girl, Meg," he asked, "where might she be? Tokar's sinister old spellbinder came down here a short while ago and took her."

"Just like Wael," Rheged snarled, "to shelter behind a wench, saving his own ancient hide, while brave men suffer—"

"Silence!" Alan roared at him. Trevyn stood up, arrow swift, arrow straight, but pale beneath his grime. Ket put the captured king in a cell.

"Witch's whelp," Rheged sneered at Trevyn from behind the bars. "Pretty warlock, Wael will put an end to you yet. He was deathless and strong before you were born."

Trevyn gave him not even a glance for reply. "Upstairs," he ordered the others, and began toiling up the tower steps. Several times he had to stop to gather strength, cursing at his own slowness. Alan followed him closely. Corin, Robin, and some retainers puffed along behind. The way out onto the platform was by a trapdoor; Alan insisted on going first, but no one was waiting to knock off their heads. Wael stood at the opposite extreme of the circular space, very close to the edge, with Megan arranged before him like a shield, her arms twisted behind her back. Trevyn knew that Wael did not have much physical strength in his withered, clawlike hands, but he also knew his power to terrify and deceive. Meg looked frozen; she might as well have been held in a vise.

"By my troth," Alan exclaimed, "it's Waverly!"

"Hal thought as much," Trevyn remarked.

"I am flattered, Laueroc!" hissed the chamberlain of the late and evil Iscovar. "That you should remember me after all these years! Though of course I remember you well. You drove me forth from this very court, set my old bones to wandering the weary seas, you and your bastard brother, a pair of pups! So I set my course toward revenge. But all has gone against me: the bastard has escaped me, and this elf-sprout has thwarted and defied me at every turn." Wael glared venomously at Trevyn. "At last he robbed and destroyed the ancient thing that sustained me. Yet I will have my revenge at last, and you will both learn to hate the day you ever crossed me!" He twitched Megan nearer to the edge, where a smooth wall dropped hundreds of feet to the cobbled courtyard below.

"As I recall it," Alan said, courteously enough, "you were asked only to obey Hal as heir to the throne. Instead, you slipped away and took ship of your own accord."

"Do not speak to me of obedience!" shrieked Wael. "If I were in strength, you would all bow down to me and beg to know my will! Dogs! Sons of she-dogs! You would grovel before the Wolf as the jackal before the lion!"

"By thunder," Alan grated, "here is one lion that would willingly tame your wolf!" He drew his sword with the golden lion on the hilt. Wael's eyes glittered, and one hand flicked out to send the weapon flying with an invisible bolt. But at that instant, Trevyn quietly spoke a single word.

"Melidwen."

Megan came out of her pallid trance with a blaze of fury. "Filthy old man! Let go!" she cried, kicking back at Wael's knee. He yelped, and she broke lightly away from him, sped toward Trevyn. But at the last moment she seemed to remember that she was angry with him, swerved aside, and darted toward the stairs.

"Father!" Trevyn called. "Catch her!"

"Got her," Alan tersely replied.

"Don't let her go," Trevyn panted between clenched teeth. "I want to talk to her!" He tensed himself against pain. Wael was hopping about on his end of the platform, frenzied and gibbering with rage, raining invisible blows on the Prince. "Stop that!" Trevyn shouted. "Stop it! Begone, you—you Crebla!" He spoke the sooth-name.

Wael vanished. Without even a gesture or a puff of smoke, he disappeared. A tall, cloaked figure stood on the platform in his stead, very still, very silent, unfathomably black, with only the black vortex of a hood for face. All of Isle seemed to stop, simply stop. Even the distant clatter of soldiers in the courtyard ceased, and the slight, random movement of clouds in the sky.

"Pel Blagden," Trevyn breathed, and took a single step back.

"Nay," said a sweet, dusky woman's voice, "it is I." Then Trevyn noticed that tiny silver bells hung from the points of the apparition's empty sleeves. He went down on one knee, not in worship so much as in limp relief.

"Menwy," he whispered. "Dark lady, thank you. But why are you faceless, like the mantled lord?"

"Because he is in me, as Wael is in me now. I must appear to you in forms you can understand." Looming, she stalked over to Trevyn, stooped and extended to him the black cavern of her sleeve. Alan could not have aided his son, then, if both their lives had depended on it. He could not move even to retreat. But Trevyn reached up, grasped the invisible hand, and rose lightly to his feet. The lovely Black Virgin faced him now, with pearls draped over her shimmering forehead. Corin moaned and hid his eyes. He who had faced the faceless one could not withstand that beauty. But she looked up to Trevyn like a lover.

"Where are the dragons of Lyrdion, Alberic?" she asked him.

He had to clear his throat. "Within. Bound in the depths," he answered huskily. "Until now, by all that is dark and beautiful." He raised a hand, pointed eastward, and the others looked, stood rigid. Beyond the walls and turrets of

Nemeton they could plainly see, from their height, the grasslands that rolled away toward the sea—on which came the newly landed Tokarian army, marching.

But the earth of the plain moved like so much water, bubbled and burst. And the dragons arose through the rippling, parting grass, loosed by Trevyn's gesture, scores and hundreds of them, with flashing, scaly flanks of ruddy gold, red-crested, black-clawed, launching themselves against the invaders with a flick of their fluted wings, letting out brazen cries that seemed to echo across the world. Trevyn was never to forget the sound of that fierce, nasal battle chant.

Everyone on the tower stood staring, agape. Even Menwy watched as the dragons drove off the Tokarians with tail-lashing leaps and puffs of fiery breath. The scene worked itself out within that middle distance where everything looks suspended, very solid but not quite real. They could not hear the cries of the enemy soldiers, but they could see them fall. The men could not flee fast enough to evade the dragons; they were trampled, crushed, and burned. The dragons trumpeted in triumph. Only one of them had fallen, killed by a lucky arrow to the eye. The others intently pursued their human prey.

"Bloodthirsty," Trevyn blurted, sickened. "Too blood-thirsty! Why can't they just drive them back to the ships?"

"Mercy is not in the nature of dragons," Menwy replied, though Trevyn had not really expected any reply.

The dragons and the fleeing remnants of the army topped a rise and disappeared toward the Long Beaches. Nothing remained of the strange tableau except a lumpy expanse of strewn bodies. Trevyn looked away from them, faced the goddess again.

"Why does it trouble you?" she asked. "You have saved many of your father's liegemen, perhaps even saved your land."

"Because—I know those dragons are mine. They are in me."

"So you were able to loose them to good effect. And if you have gained the victory over Wael, Prince, it is because you no longer hate the shadowy deeps, the realm of the sable moon. My workings are not all for ill, Alberic. Even a villain such as Wael cannot help but do some good. In a sense, he brought you two together, Prince and Maiden."

With his eyes still on Menwy's subtle, sculpted face, Trevyn held out an arm and felt Meg move to fill it. The slender girl pressed against him, took the wolf cub from his cupped hand, and cradled it by her own small breasts.

"Without darkness, there would be no dawn," Menwy added.

"So you, who flung me into the hands of slavers, who stole my father's brooch to make mischief with, now choose to aid me." Trevyn sounded merely whimsical, not bitter, just then. "Why, ancient lady?"

"Because you are fair; no better reason."

Trevyn risked a glance at Meg, felt with a shock her fine-drawn loveliness, saw Dair, his baby son, lay a searching muzzle along her neck.

"And I will give the Tokarians fair winds home, those who live, as I have given them foul winds hither," added Menwy, with a hint of jealous edge to her voice. "Still, I am no one's servant. So, lest you lose all respect for me, Prince—feel this!"

A shock sent Trevyn staggering. Meg screamed; Menwy loomed taller and ever taller, in form of the fearsome horned god, her head a skull with the antlers of a stag.

"Farewell, Prince of Isle," she sang, before he had recovered, and engulfed him. In an instant the tower was only a fleck caught in the hem of her cloak, in a black and roaring, directionless blackness darker than a thousand nights. Trevyn clutched at Meg, hid his face in her hair; Robin moaned, and Alan flung an arm over his eyes. Then they all looked up at bright sky and blinked. Voices sounded from the courtyard; Trevyn's eagle swooped down to perch on a parapet. The day moved on apace.

"Are ye hurt!" Megan demanded. Trevyn held on to her for support with one hand, and the other held on to his head.

"I think I'm going to swoon," he said plaintively. "Be here when I wake up, Meg. Promise!"

"All right, I·promise!" She peered up at him anxiously. "Trev—"

"Is it really all over?" Alan exclaimed incredulously, gazing down at the quiet town, the empty battle plain. "Is it really done?"

"I'm done in," Trevyn murmured. "Meg, take good care of that wolf."

"Of course."

"It's my son," he explained, lucidly.

"Of course. Trevyn, will ye sit down before ye fall and hurt yerself?"

"Not until I've kissed you." But he missed his aim, lurching.

"Later," she told him, and shouted at the others, "Dolts, will ye help me with this big oaf!"

They were all still dazed, gaping like Alan. "Can it really be all over?" he marveled again. "After all these hellish months?"

"My dream has just begun," Trevyn protested softly, and folded onto the paving stones.

Chapter Five

They got him into a bed presently, and he slept for a full day, then awoke to ravenously gulp a meal, then slept again. He kept it up, not for the month he had promised, but for a week. A few times the servants roused him and ordered him into a tub, soaking grime and brown, caked blood out of his golden hair. But no one had leisure to really nurse him, in the aftermath of war, and it was plain to see that he was well and content. The servants took to leaving food on a table by the bedside, fruit and bread and cheese and cold cooked meat. Trevyn would wake at odd hours, eat, drink water, and instantly doze off again. As he slept, he dreamed—pleasant dreams, mostly. Even when not sleeping, he dreamed with open eyes. Of Isle, and Elwestrand, and love, and Maeve, and, the seventh day, of Melidwen—

Meg burst into his room that day; Dair pattered after her and jumped up on the bed. "Trevyn, what d'ye mean!" Meg cried. "What can ye be thinking of! I can't wear this!"

He gazed at her, breathless, and not only because of the furry, gray weight on top of him. She looked like a princess— nay, some being that was freer and more magical than a

princess. She looked like someone Emrist might have invoked, spirit of starlight and daisy field and white winter
lacework of birch. Soft, sparkling cloth enfolded her like an
embrace, patterned white on white, floating richly around her
bare, smooth feet. Her sparrow-brown hair flew as airily as
the gown. She tolerated his stare for a moment, then stamped
impatiently.

"It'll take washing every blessed day," she complained.
"And everyone who saw me thinks I'm putting on airs. And
how d'ye expect me to go walking that precious son of yers in
this?"

Clutching his blankets, Trevyn wriggled out from under the
wolf in question. "Take it off, if you don't like it," he gasped.

"I adore it." Her pointed face softened into a smile. "But
it's too grand, Trev. Dream me a few that are a bit more
practical."

"I don't direct my dreams," he whispered, and reached out
to touch her fingertips, drew her down to him by her warm
fingertips, nothing more. Her flower of a mouth touched his;
he parted it tenderly, probed with consummate tenderness,
felt a sweet ache grow. Rosebuds and dew. . . . His fingers
entwined her hair, found the warm nape of her neck,
followed her tresses to the startled tip of her young breast
under the magical cloth. . . . Meg placed her hands on his,
dropped her head to his bare shoulder.

"Love me," he begged.

"I do."

"I know—I should have always known. I'd have known
how I loved you, if I'd paid heed. But love me now, Meg.
That is your wedding gown."

"Then let us ride to where the wedding party awaits us,"
she told him reasonably. "At the sacred grove."

"What?"

"At the Forest's southern skirt, where the two rivers join.
Gwern's grove."

That sobered him. He let her go and sat to face her. "How
did you know?"

"I—some things I just know—like I know that Dair really is
yer son somehow—and I know that Gwern gave ye himself.
He had to, for ye to be so whole now."

"Ay. I feel like my life has just begun, Meg. As if you've just woken me to a new world. All that's happened since—since a young fool left you at Lee—hardly seems to count."

"It counts." She grinned wickedly at him. "But ye're right about the new world. Or a new Isle, anyway. Wonders are springing up all over. The whole land's taken on a new sheen; everyone notices it."

He stared at her. "The magic is coming back," he breathed.

"Ye've dreamed it back. Ye've even made me a touch on the pretty side somehow. Won't ye go back to sleep now, like a good prince, and dream me a few more dresses?"

"Great goddess, nay," he exclaimed. "I've slept long enough. Where's Father?"

"Sped to his love."

Alan had long since gone to Lysse, as fast as horse could take him. All along the path of his swift journey he saw magic springing up. Tiny yellow flowers winked from the grass, each one a radiant coronet. Veran's crown, the Elfin Gold, had come back to Isle, and all the land glowed with intangible luster by virtue of its presence.

Lysse met Alan on the road, far outside the gates. Sight and heart had returned to her together, and she sensed his coming long before he arrived. She greeted him smiling, but he wept in her embrace. "Even at my worst, I knew you would forgive me," he told her when he could speak, "and that is a fearful knowledge."

"Hal thought the same of you."

"I know. Trevyn has told me a little. . . . My brother sends me his love, from Elwestrand. He wept to speak of me. . . . Well, I am no longer so proud that I can afford to think ill of him, Lissy." He grinned wryly. "And I can somewhat account for the change in me; but what is to account for the marvels abroad in the land?"

"A turn of the great tide. Aene is claiming back what was lost for a while." Lysse smiled dreamily. "Isle might soon be as magical as Elwestrand, I believe. But Hal and my people cannot return."

"I know. When do we sail?"

"In the spring. There will be a ship at the Bay."

"Far better fortune than I deserve," Alan said softly, "if Hal awaits me. But Lysse, when I took the wrong path, when I laid hold of that great, bloody sword, I felt sure it severed me from him. For all time. How can I feel so sure now that I shall see him again?"

"Mother of mercy," she chided, "can't you tell? Isle is like a clean-washed stone, like a bright leaf after rain, and your small transgressions are gone in the tide of time, like all others. Alan, the haunts are gone from the land."

"What?" he whispered.

"The shades have gone to rest, even the stubborn shades by the Blessed Bay. All penances are done. And the dragons have left their gloomy lairs."

"Ay, Trevyn seems to be in charge of them now. I wish I understood. . . . Love, glad as I shall be to sail to Elwestrand, I am glad we need not go soon. I would like to get to know my son."

After Trevyn was up and about for a few days, he and Meg took horse toward the place she had named. Liegemen and a few maids rode with them, for decorum's sake, and Corin, out of friendly curiosity, and Ket. Craig and Robin and the other lords had long since sped back to their demesnes. There was a tremendous amount of work to be done; unguarded cottages had been robbed, repairs had been neglected, and spring planting had gone almost entirely undone in the eastern half of the realm. Already Alan had sent messengers to Tokar demanding ransom for Rheged, not in treasure, but in food, to avert famine. And the very day of the final battle he had sent patrols throughout Isle to prevent plundering and to spread news of peace. But there was little need of such reassurance. Folk sensed comfort as if it were a fragrance in the air and returned quickly to their homes. Even Trevyn's dragons, blundering northward along the eastern shore, did not seriously upset them. All along the road to their rendezvous, the Prince and his retainers were greeted by happy folk. It seemed to awe them that he carried a young wolf in his arms.

They rode gently, in easy stages, letting Trevyn regain his

strength. Late on the seventh day they neared the river crossing, and Trevyn peered ahead with a faint frown. Against the glowing sunset sky he could see the figure of an eagle, his eagle, perched atop a tall tree, or group of trees, that he felt certain had not been there before.

"What the—" he muttered.

"Gwern's grove," Megan replied from her palfrey beside him. She rode in her lovely white dress, the only one she presently owned, though she had Trevyn's promise of more from a certain Gypsy seamstress. She had found her fears mistaken; the gown did not need daily washing. In fact, dirt did not seem to touch it at all. The paradoxical fabric, floating and crisp, seemed no more prone to mundane soil than a cloud wisp or the caught light of the moon.

The company splashed through the river branch, through water well above the horses' knees. Afterward, drops sprinkled down like strings of pearls from Meg's hem, and stayed there. A few fell to the ground and lay glimmering. Trevyn looked at them in mild surprise and let them be. Meg already wore another such magical jewel, the pink moonstone he had brought her from Elwestrand, with the mandorla at its heart. But Corin and the others picked up the gems with gasps of wonder.

"Magic!" Corin breathed. Then no one said more, not even the irrepressible Meg. They had entered under the woven shade of the Wyrdwood.

They rode through sheerest stillness. No underbrush rustled against their saddles; no branches scraped. The trees towered immensely, in form like the pillars of earth, the trunks smooth and unbranched to thirty feet above their heads. Hooves fell soundlessly on the leaf loam of a hundred seasons, so it seemed. Within a moment, the riders were swallowed by soft, random spaces like the honeycomb caverns of deep earth where dragons used to dwell, like the shadowy roots of the sea where the sun swims back to the east. Birds sang somewhere in the pinpoint foliage far above. Trevyn signaled a stop, looking all about him, to depths and heights, with eager, straining face.

"We're likely never to come out of here," Corin blurted, breaking silence. He had looked behind him and seen no trace of the way he had come; now he held the reins with sweaty hands. But Trevyn scarcely heard him, lost in longing and awe.

"By the Mothers, he's here! I can feel him. . . ." Trevyn bit back a sob. Silent tears ran down his face. "Gwern . . ."

"The place suits him," Meg said softly.

"Ay, it's a god's grove. And Gwern has invited his fellows, it seems. I feel Bevan here as well." Trevyn struggled to compose himself. Memories gripped him and made him feel weak, memories of Emrist and of Elwestrand.

"Trev," Ket burst out, "please. We're frightened."

Surprised, he scanned their pale faces. Meg sat serenely, but a couple of the maids had started to whimper.

"We're not lost!" Trevyn exclaimed. "Why, we're nearer to heart's home than we've been since birth. . . . All right, follow me. There is always a pattern. This way." He led off through the motionless dance of the trees.

He took them in a sweeping spiral, gradually closing in on an unseen vortex at the center of the hushed grove. They rounded the last gentle curve and arrived. Sunlight streamed down into a clearing amid the giants. There a single sapling grew, its leaves translucent jewels that sent flakes of color skimming like dragonflies across the grass. Resting in the sun-dappled shade sat a pair of wedding guests, Alan and Lysse. Beside them, at the sunlit base of the slender tree, lay a unicorn, moon-white, with a golden horn.

"Is that beastie yours, too, lad?" Alan asked Trevyn when they had embraced.

"Mine and everyone's." He took Meg by the hand and led her to meet his mother.

They all camped there that night, feasting on plain food that tasted better than it had any right to, talking beneath the light of a swelling moon, answering innumerable questions. Trevyn heard about Megan's travels and her lupine friend. Lysse found that she liked the girl better by the moment. Alan heard at last the full history of his jeweled brooch, and he learned that he had sworn a spell upon his green Elfstone.

"Things that show the sun crest are your talisman, as the parchment with the wolf emblem was Wael's," Trevyn explained "And your gem is magical in its own right, mightily so. . . . Only a King could have managed it. But I think nothing less could have woken me."

"I'm no sorcerer," Alan protested.

"But you've always been great in power, you and Hal. You never used your magic, that's all. . . . And you called me by my sooth-name. That was prettily done."

"It should have been done far sooner," Alan grumbled. "But it was hard for me to know you as the Very King who shall succeed me. . . . What is your talisman to be, Alberic?"

By way of answer, the unicorn came and laid its head in his lap.

They all sat half drunk with wine of magic and love. By dawn they lay drowsily, but still softly talking. At first light, Trevyn regretfully left the others and went off by himself.

By closing his eyes, he quickly found Gwern's grave, hidden under a blanket of luxuriant flowers. Though he hated to do it, he upended them with his dagger and dug away industriously, muttering at the mess he was making of himself. But he found the sword of Lyrdion before too long and lifted it, intending to hide it among his gear until he had a chance to take it to the sea. . . . A flash like the blaze of the rising sun went up from the weapon, and everyone in the grove came running.

"Bevan, you nuisance," Trevyn quietly rebuked the air, "why did you do that?"

His family and friends gathered around, absorbing the scene. "I thought Gwern lay there!" Alan exclaimed, looking at the open grave.

"Nay, Gwern lies nowhere, except—everywhere, here. All powers of loveliness seem to be met here today." Obeying an impulse, Trevyn lifted the great sword skyward. Hau Ferddas shone like a fair, golden bird, effortlessly soaring, as warm in his hand as a living thing. The gems on the hilt were pools, were eyes, were magic mirrors. The metal of the blade shimmered like a silken gown.

"What, more marvels now?" Alan breathed. "Suddenly that sword has become as fair as sunshine, a token of all honor and goodness, in your grasp."

"Bevan's doing," Trevyn said. "So that we should see it as it was for him, and understand."

"And this is the weapon you must take to the sea?" Alan murmured incredulously.

"Ay, that I must. At another place or time, it could yet become a horror." He scowled at the invisible spirit of the star-son. "And this has not made it any easier!" He swaddled the sword in its fabric bonds.

They all seemed to realize at once that they were exhausted. Of one accord they trooped back to their campsite and quickly fell asleep. But they only slept for a few hours; in late morning they were awakened by the approach of more riders. Rosemary appeared, looking lovely in cloth of russet and cream. Two countryfolk followed her. Ket ran to meet her, and Megan ran to embrace the others; they were her mother and father. Goodman Brock had earned fame for his courage and tenacity in holding his land and helping his neighbors throughout the siege of wolves. But he looked uncomfortable on horseback, and stunned to see his daughter in such finery. He scrambled down from his mount and gave her a cautious kiss, then stood disconsolately while his wife went off, chattering, with the other women. Because he felt out of place, he glowered when Trevyn greeted him.

"Whew!" Trevyn whistled. "I believe you're remembering a cocky young fool—"

Brock had to smile at that. "Why, nay, I recall no foolishness," he declared. "But I have heard much talk of a certain marvelous Prince." He gulped, and lost his smile again. "Is that a unicorn?"

"It's quite peaceable," Trevyn assured him. "Come, meet my father."

As it turned out, Brock had business with Alan. "Folk have gotten together and named me a sort of steward at Lee," he explained gruffly, "to do for them until ye can name a new lord, Sire, since Rafe left no heir. So I'm to report t' ye."

"So you're the people's chosen leader!" Alan said thoughtfully. "Why don't you just stay on, then, Goodman? Be lord yourself."

"I!" Brock protested. "I'll make no velvet-clad lord, Sire. I've no manners, no learning—"

"I'll send you a scribe. The velvet's not required. But stay a steward, then, if you don't want the title. The work's the same." Alan beckoned at him. "Come and help me with these kettles." The King was hungry, and trying to hurry along breakfast.

They all ate, finally, porridge and honey and a few boiled eggs, and in the process of dealing with the sticky meal everyone became well acquainted. Brock no longer felt out of place by the time they were done. "Now, then," Alan asked, "since we're all here, will someone tell me how these weddings are to take place?"

"By the old style, I suppose, of consent," Trevyn answered. "Or you could marry us by royal decree."

"Wait a bit," Rosemary told them. "I believe there's one person yet to come." She was the Rowan Lady, and she sensed whatever moved within the Forest. So they waited.

"Here I am, dears," a voice said after a while, and with one accord they all rose, though they had seen no one. Then, walking straight and strong, a very old woman came toward them out of the grove.

"Ylim!" Trevyn exclaimed, though he had never seen her in that form. Alan stared; he had raised a cairn over that body, but he had never known her name.

"In this place, I am Alys." She stood, not smiling and yet not unkind, folding her gnarled hands on her muslin apron. "But I must come to you in a form you understand, or partly understand."

"In the valley beyond Celydon," said Rosemary softly, "you would be the ancient seeress, the weaver."

"Ay. You are wise, Lady. Ylim is only a servant of Alys. . . . But here I am all, or nearly all. This is a place of power, my own power and power of my son. . . . The best of all places for these weddings."

"And will you stay now?" Trevyn asked. "Are you truly back in Isle?"

"Ylim will stay." She smiled at that, mostly with her deep and glowing eyes. "Alys was never gone."

Without much talk or need for thought, all was made ready for the nuptials. In a few minutes, Trevyn and Meg stood paired before the goddess beneath the young and growing tree, he in the whitest tunic the elves had given him, she in her dream dress with a spray of rare white heather in her hand. Ket and Rosemary stood behind them, more soberly clad, but arm in arm. Young Dair lay quietly in Alan's arms.

"There's small need for words," Ylim said. "Symbols show more." From her apron pockets she drew yards of lace—of her own weaving, Trevyn knew, and of pattern as intricate as all creation, simple as love, white as the unicorn. With a length of this she encircled Megan's brow, crowning her like a blossom, then sent a streamer over to Trevyn, weaving her to him.

She worked quickly, scarcely moving, directing the lace-work by gesture rather than touch. When she had finished, Trevyn stood at the center of a pattern that spread to include the jeweled tree, and a stag that wandered by, and everyone present; even the unicorn held a loop of lace with its horn. For his own part, Trevyn felt once again captured and tied, even more entangled now than he had been in Tokar. But Meg stood tranquilly.

"The bonds will remain only in your mind," Ylim said. "Kiss your bride, Alberic." He felt as if he could scarcely move, but he leaned over to comply. His lips met Meg's smoothly. And as they kissed, the lace parted into bits, fell like snowflakes to the ground. Ever afterward, the most delicate of flowers grew there, flowers found nowhere else in Isle. But Trevyn could never remember what pattern the lace had made; he had forgotten to look. And those who had looked, when he asked, each gave a different answer.

"All blessings on you, Meg and Trevyn, Ket and Rosemary," said Ylim the ancient seeress, and turned, and left. Trevyn still stood kissing Meg. Moments after Ylim had gone, he raised his head with a start. "Wait!" he exclaimed, but silence answered him.

"I forgot to ask her about anything," he complained. "About Maeve, about Dair!"

"Wait and see. . . ." The voice of Alys floated back.

Epilogue

On a bright day of the following May, the twenty-first anniversary of Alan's coronation, all the lords in Isle and Welas gathered at the gentle summit near Laueroc where Adaoun had marked the beginning and ending of an Age by wedding and crowning the Sunrise and Sunset Kings. It was not so many years before, Alan mused, that he had taken Lysse to wife on that spot and Hal had wed Rosemary. But the weight of those years had slowed him, nevertheless, and made him glad of promised rest. He brought the great crown of Veran from the treasure room, the rayed crown like the sunburst emblem of the Elfstone. He took it to the appointed place and waited for his son.

In the presence of the watching multitude, Trevyn came before his father, scorning heavy robes, clad free as the wind in a soft linen tunic and deerskin boots. He dropped to one knee, and Alan placed the ceremonial burden on his head. Then he rose, and Alan girded him with his own newly forged sword, silver of hue, with a running unicorn for hilt. He presented his son to the assembled lords.

"Here is your King now," he told them, "and I am King no more."

A great, golden bird circled overhead, scattering the meadowlarks. The lords took up the omen with a shout. "Hail, Eagle King!" they cried. "Hail, Liege King of Laueroc!" They lifted clasped hands in salute.

"You're far more than that," Alan murmured to his son.

"Ay," Trevyn agreed without a trace of hesitation. "I might just as well be called Unicorn King."

"You're silver and gold, as Hal foresaw."

Four rode out the next day: Alan, Lysse, Trevyn, and Meg on a round little mare she called Bess. The weather was fine, and they went at a leisurely pace, taking four days to pass the settled land. Meg was thrilled by the wilderness beyond. Riding through a changing pattern of slope and rocky tor, thick-woven forest and silky meadow, sunlight and shade and shadow, she drew in beauty with every breath, nourishing the budding life she carried within her—for Meg was with child.

On the seventh day of their journey, the four came to the Bay of the Blessed, a place of deepest green shade and silvery water, a place meant for moonlight. A boat swam like a dusky swan in the shallows. Alan tethered it and found the plank to board it. Then he and Lysse turned to face their son and daughter-in-law.

"How do you want to manage this matter of the sword?" Alan asked quietly.

Trevyn brought the magical weapon out of the wrappings it had worn all winter. It shone as fair as the first flower of spring. Impulsively, he offered it to his father. "You've had the most sorrow from it. Will you hurl it away?"

"Trevyn," Alan chided. "All you've been through, and you still try to meddle with fate? I don't dare to touch it. Do you want to borrow my boat?"

Trevyn shook his head. He knew what a pang of longing it would send through him to stand on the deck of an elf-ship. He stood thinking for a moment, then nodded, and pointed at a precise spot on the taut surface of the Bay. "There," he said.

The lustrous water broke like a veil, fell apart in fragments. From the rent a sea-drake with scales of dark crimson raised its dripping head, glaring out of flat carnelian eyes. Meg gulped and took a step back.

"One of Menwy's people," Trevyn explained, and he flung the sword with all his strength, sent it spinning through the air like a shining wheel. Fearlessly the dragon caught the weapon in its great mouth, held it as a dog holds a bone, and dove. The watchers on shore saw ripples trail it into the western sea.

"I hope we don't encounter such creatures on the way," Alan breathed, somewhat shaken.

"You'll never know," Trevyn answered. "You'll remember nothing but peace. Go joyfully, and regret nothing." He embraced Alan and then his mother, kissing them. Alan gripped his hand.

"I regret many things in my life," he told his son, meeting his eyes, "and some of those you know, Trev. . . . But this is not one of them. Farewell, Megan; keep him in charge. Come, Love, let us go." Alan put an arm around his Elf-Queen, and together they boarded the waiting ship.

"Go with all blessing," whispered Meg.

Trevyn lifted the plank. The quickening ship swam away from the shore. Lysse and Alan settled themselves on the deck, waving in farewell. Trevyn returned the gesture with desolation in his heart. The elf-boat carried away his only kindred in Isle except for the son that stood, four-legged, at his feet. . . . Trevyn watched the lovely boat until it rounded the headland, then turned to Meg, laid his face in her hair, and wept. His love of this woman was part of the pattern; it was very good. But in spite of her love, hers and others', Trevyn knew himself to be alone at his core, a naked thing joining earth and sky. Perhaps all men were so at the core. Being so alone, he had no way of knowing.

"Even that weird white horse," he muttered.

The moon-marked steed had left him without a backward glance, once the journey was done, leaping craggy rocks and skimming the grass between, ineffably alone, like a swift spirit blown from the far, dark places between the stars. Trevyn shook his head ruefully at the memory, and Dair sprang up, placed massive forepaws on his chest. Trevyn caressed the smooth hollow between his eyes.

"Very true, you're still here," he said. "And you'll yet be yourself in human form, Dair; mark it." He had seen that truth on an ancient woman's loom in a valley above Celydon. A startling, regal face had looked back at him from Ylim's web, a face with wide-set, feral, amethyst eyes, brows that met, nostrils that faintly pulsed—yet unmistakably the face of Dair, his son. But how would that youth come to him? When?

"Trust the tides," answered Meg, sensing his thoughts.

Trevyn and his bride spent the night on the shore, clinging together for warmth of more than body. In the morning they started back toward Laueroc, where liegemen and vassals awaited their King. Glancing behind him for one last look at the Bay, Trevyn noted a shimmer of white beneath the deepest green shadows of the firs. A unicorn stood there, watching him go.

I am the son.
I am the steadfast son,
I am the son of earth.
I am hazel roots,
I am red dragons,
I am robin and wren,
I am strong magic.

I am the eagle,
I am the soaring son,
I am the son of sky.
I am wings of wind,
I am a golden wheel,
I am a warrior,
I am the circle dance,
I am the song.

I am the swan,
I am the wandering son,
I am the son of sea.
I am changing eyes,
I am green shadow,
I am between the stars,
I am the stars.
I am the star-son.
I am the son.

Glossary of Names

ADAOUN: father of all the elves, creation of the First Song of Aene.

AENE: not, strictly speaking, a name, but the elfin term translatable as "the One": a power neither good nor evil, female nor male, but all of each.

ALAN: Sunrise King, Hal's brother and longtime companion, Trevyn's father.

ALBERIC: Trevyn's true-name or elfin name, meaning "a ruler of elfin blood," but comprising many opposites.

ALYS: the most inclusive name of the Goddess of Many Names, the earth-mother, moon-mother, maiden, and hag.

ARUNDEL: Hal's horse, who harked from the Eagle Valley of the elves.

BAY OF THE BLESSED: the estuary of the Gleaming River, where Bevan set sail for Elwestrand and Veran landed; where the elves took ship, and Hal, the last of Veran's line.

BEVAN: son of Celonwy, the moon goddess, and Byve, High King in Eburacon before the sack of that city. A star-son.

CELONWY: the moon-mother or Argent Moon, one phase of the great goddess. Within the history of Isle, Bevan's mother.

CELYDON: the Forest Island of Many Trees. Rosemary's home.

CORIN: in the wandering days, Alan's comrade. Later, lord of Nemeton.

CRAIG THE GRIM: onetime outlaw, later lord of Whitewater.

CREBLA: Wael's true-name, an anagram of Trevyn's own.

CUERT: Prince of Laueroc who fled with Veran to Welas.

CUIN: Alan's distant ancestor, Bevan's comrade, first High King of Laueroc.

CULEAN: the last High King of Laueroc. Killed himself with Hau Ferddas at the time of the Eastern invasion.

DAIR: an elfin name referring to the oak, for strength. Trevyn's son.

DEONA: Alan's great-great-grandmother, reared in Welden, through whom the blood of the Cuin found its way back to Laueroc. Cuert's granddaughter.

DOL SOLDEN: elfin for *The Book of Suns*, Veran's account of the prophecies of Aene.

DUV: an ancient name of the great mother, the goddess.

EAGLE VALLEY: inaccessible valley where Hal and Alan found the elves, on Veran's Mountain.

EBURACON: the ruined city of Bevan and Byve, surrounded by Forest and haunt.

ELUNDELEI: moon mountain, mountain of eagle vision, Mount Sooth. On Elwestrand.

ELWESTRAND: the elves' strand or the western land, a magical island beyond the sunset.

ELWYNDAS: Alan's elfin name, meaning elf brother, spirit brother, Elf-Friend.

EMRIST: a Tokarian magician.

FRECA: the name Trevyn was given in Tokar, elfin for "Brave One."

GWERN: alder-son and son of earth; Trevyn's wyrd.

HAL: Sunset King, Very King, healer, bard and seer, Alan's brother and fellow ruler at Laueroc.

HAU FERDDAS: elfin for Mighty Protector, Peace-Friend. The magical sword of Lyrdion, dangerous in its own right and darkened through the ages by the deeds of the men who used it.

HERNE: first of the Eastern Kings; invader of Isle.

ISCOVAR: Hal's purported father, the last of the hated Eastern kings who ruled at Nemeton.

ISLE: a water-ringed land that stands as a rampart between Elwestrand and the shadowed east.

KET THE RED: onetime outlaw, later seneschal of Laueroc.

LAUEROC: originally, Laveroc—that is to say, City of Meadowlarks. Founded by Cuin; longtime home of the High Kings. Later, court city of the Sun Kings.

LEUIN: seventh lord of Laueroc under the Eastern kings. Alan's father; Hal's actual father.

LYRDION: an isolated ruin along the northwest coast of Isle, once home of a dragon-king and his dragon-lords.

LYSSE: Alan's wife, Trevyn's mother. An elf and a seeress.

MAEVE: Emrist's sister; also an aspect of the goddess.

MARROK: Herne's sorcerer.

MEGAN: Trevyn's beloved; also, the maidenly aspect of the goddess.

MELIDWEN: a name for the Goddess of Many Names, applied to her aspect as maiden and crescent moon.

MENWY: Goddess of the Sable Moon, better known as the Black Virgin of the Gypsies.

MIRELDEYN: Hal's elfin name, meaning "Elf-Man, Elf-Master."

NEMETON: a city near the mouth of the Black River where the Eastern Kings, the invaders, ruled.

PEL BLAGDEN: the Mantled God, Lord of the Dead, whom Bevan vanquished.

RAFE: Hal's friend and captain, later lord of Lee.

RHEGED: king of Tokar.

ROBIN: Hal's companion and Corin's foster brother, later lord of Firth.

ROSEMARY: Hal's wife, the Lady of Celydon.

TOKAR: a country to the eastward of Isle, separated from it by the southern sea.

TREVYN: Alan's son, Prince of Isle and Welas, heir of the Sun Kings.

VERAN: a scion of Bevan, called back to Isle from Elwestrand; the first of the Blessed Kings of Welas.

VERAN'S MOUNTAIN: the tallest mountain in Welas, on top of which nestles the Eagle Valley, where the elves lived.

WAEL: a sorcerer, high priest of the Wolf cult, enemy of Isle. Formerly Waverly.

WAVERLY: Iscovar's sorcerer and chamberlain.

WELAS: the western portion of Isle, beyond the Gleaming River, where a different language is spoken.

WELDEN: the Elde Castle, founded by Veran upon the Gleaming River; court city of the Blessed Kings.

WYNNDA: the immortal white winged horse that served Adaoun.

YLIM: an immortal weaving seeress.

Glossary of Terms

Amaranth: a reddish-purple flower that never dies.

Asphodel: a white, lilylike flower that grows only in magical climes.

Athane: the black-handled sword used by sorcerers for sacrifice and for tracing the mystic circle.

Elf-ship: a graceful, gray, sailless boat made of living wood, moving swiftly and of its own volition, homing to Elwestrand. Attributed to elves, but actually first created and ridden by Bevan.

Elwedeyn: an adjective describing something of the old order—loosely, elfin.

Hollow hills: the raths where the gods lived after they gave up the sunlit lands to the Mothers of men and before they followed Bevan to the Blessed Bay, where they became shades.

Laifrita thae: elfin for "sweet peace to thee"; a greeting.

Mandorla: the mystic almond, the shape where two circles overlap. An emblem of the union of opposites.

Mothers: the mortal women who succeeded the Mother Goddess Duv and her children, the gods.

Plinset: a Welandais stringed musical instrument.

Sister-son: in the old style of reckoning descent through the woman, a man's heir.

Star-son: a wanderer from Otherness; a stranger in the midst of men who later leaves them.

Veran's crown: a healing flower, very rare after the Eastern invasion. Also called Elfin Gold, Veran's Balm.

Wyrd: the fate within, the dark twin, the rival.

Festivals

Old Style—Feasts of Fires

1 November—for repose of dead
2 February—in honor of the Mothers
1 May—for purification
2 August—for harvest

New Style—Festivals of the Sun
(Eastern reckoning)

21 December—Winterfest, a gifting time in honor of the Sacred
  Son
22 March—Glainfest, a vernal observance
24 June—Bowerfest, for the Oak King
22 September—Cornfest, for threshing

Eastern Kings

Herne
Hervyn
Heinin
Hent
Iuchar
Idno
Iscovar

Iscovar's supposed son, Hervoyel,
later reigned as Hal of Laueroc

A Brief Genealogy of the Sun Kings
Based on "The Book of Suns"*

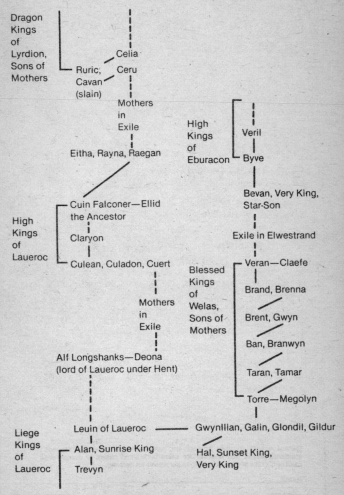

Dragon Kings of Lyrdion, Sons of Mothers

Ruric; Cavan (slain)

Celia Ceru

Mothers in Exile

Eitha, Rayna, Raegan

High Kings of Eburacon

Veril

Byve

Bevan, Very King, Star-Son

Exile in Elwestrand

Cuin Falconer—Ellid the Ancestor

High Kings of Laueroc

Claryon

Culean, Culadon, Cuert

Mothers in Exile

Veran—Claefe

Brand, Brenna

Blessed Kings of Welas, Sons of Mothers

Brent, Gwyn

Ban, Branwyn

Taran, Tamar

Torre—Megolyn

Alf Longshanks—Deona (lord of Laueroc under Hent)

Liege Kings of Laueroc

Leuin of Laueroc — Gwynllian, Galin, Glondil, Gildur

Alan, Sunrise King

Trevyn

Hal, Sunset King, Very King

*Diagonal lines signify descent through the female, in the old fashion. The mother of the king is the sister of his predecessor. The sibling relationship is indicated by a comma; wives are indicated by a dash.

Fantasy Novels *from* POCKET BOOKS

Understand Science

Jon Evans

Hodder Education

338 Euston Road, London NW1 3BH.

Hodder Education is an Hachette UK company

First published in UK 2011 by Hodder Education

First published in US 2011 by The McGraw-Hill Companies, Inc.

This edition published 2011.

10 9 8 7 6 5 4 3 2 1

The publisher has used its best endeavours to ensure that any
website addresses referred to in this book are correct and active at
the time of going to press. However, the publisher and the author
have no responsibility for the websites and can make no guarantee
that a site will remain live or that the content will remain relevant,
decent or appropriate.

The publisher has made every effort to mark as such all words
which it believes to be trademarks. The publisher should also
like to make it clear that the presence of a word in the book,
whether marked or unmarked, in no way affects its legal status as
a trademark.

Every reasonable effort has been made by the publisher to trace the
copyright holders of material in this book. Any errors or omissions
should be notified in writing to the publisher, who will endeavour
to rectify the situation for any reprints and future editions.

Hachette UK's policy is to use papers that are natural, renewable
and recyclable products and made from wood grown in sustainable
forests. The logging and manufacturing processes are expected to
conform to the environmental regulations of the country of origin.

www.hoddereducation.co.uk

Typeset by MPS Limited, a Macmillan Company.

Printed in Great Britain by CPI Cox & Wyman, Reading.

Image credits

Front cover: © Cerae – Fotolia.com

Back cover: © Jakub Semeniuk/iStockphoto.com, © Royalty-
Free/Corbis, © agencyby/iStockphoto.com, © Andy Cook/
iStockphoto.com, © Christopher Ewing/iStockphoto.com,
© zebicho – Fotolia.com, © Geoffrey Holman/iStockphoto.com,
© Photodisc/Getty Images, © James C. Pruitt/iStockphoto.com,
© Mohamed Saber – Fotolia.com

Inside: Helium (page 8) © Fabrizio Zanier. Neuron (page 72)
© sgame.

Contents

Introducing *Homo scientificus*

In certain ways, we've hardly changed at all in the 200,000 years since modern humans (*Homo sapiens*) first strode manfully onto the scene. In essence, we look, behave and think much the same now as we did then. In other ways, though, we've changed beyond all recognition.

And these changes haven't been spread evenly over the past 200,000 years; they've mainly been concentrated into the past few hundred years. We may have developed agriculture, religion, culture, warfare and cities over those 200,000 years, but up until quite recently the life of the average person hadn't really changed that much. Then we developed science and change went into overdrive.

By the simple expedient of asking questions about the universe and then conducting experiments to answer those questions, science has completely transformed our world and our lives. It has revolutionized our understanding of the universe and our place within it, and allowed us to develop previously undreamt of technologies.

We used to think that the whole universe revolved around us, both figuratively and in reality; we now know that Earth is just one of countless planets orbiting countless stars in countless galaxies. Even our universe may be just one among countless others.

Meanwhile, rather than being specifically designed, we now know that we (as every other organism on Earth) are simply the fortunate result of a blind, ratchet-like process that honed us for a specific environmental niche (which in our case was the African savannah). Still, that doesn't mean that we're not special; as far as we know, we could be the only conscious, sentient beings in the whole universe.

We have harnessed our growing scientific knowledge to develop generation upon generation of cutting-edge technologies. And these technological marvels don't just make our lives longer, easier and more enjoyable; they also confirm the accuracy of our scientific theories. We are able to build planes that fly reliably, design mobile phones that communicate reliably and produce breakfast cereals that go snap, crackle and pop reliably because our scientific theories reflect fairly accurately how the universe operates.

Science has revealed a universe that is older, larger and stranger than we could ever have imagined. It has taken us back to the very dawn of time and forward to the end of all things. It has allowed us to probe the depths of reality and explore the vast expanses of space. It has shown us how to take control of the universe: how to fly, how to communicate over vast distances, how to lace our world in light.

Science has made us who we are and given us our modern world. We are fundamentally not the same creatures that strode out onto the African savannah 200,000 years ago. We are more than human; we are practically a new species; we are *Homo scientificus*.

This book is an introduction to *Homo scientificus* and what it has achieved over the past few hundred years. In the following 30 chapters, you will learn what science has discovered about matter, space, energy, life, weather, information and the future, and how we have transformed these discoveries into our modern technologies. You will witness the birth of the solar system, follow ocean currents for thousands of miles, ride on beams of light and find out why dolphins are perhaps the most perverted creatures on the planet.

But why should you bother with science at all when you're busy cooking eggs? You appreciate that science is important and you're grateful for all the technologies it has given you, but why do you need to know how it all works? The fact that it works at all is quite enough for you.

We'll it's precisely because science is so integral to our world – that we are now *Homo scientificus* – that you really need to grasp what science has revealed about the workings of the universe. You can't ignore science, because science doesn't ignore you.

For science directly affects our lives in so many ways, both good and bad. And to make informed decisions about where the balance between the good and bad aspects should lie, we need to understand science, its theories and the technologies that arise from it. In fact, many of the most important issues currently facing mankind have a strong scientific and technological bent.

Why is global warming happening and what can we do about it; is cloning an important new medical technology or an affront to humanity; does the development of synthetic life herald a great opportunity or a great threat, or both? If you want to have a say in how we deal with these challenges and advances, then you need to understand the science behind them.

And how we deal with these challenges and advances will determine the path that *Homo scientificus* follows into the future. Will it be long and glorious or short and destructive? If science has achieved much in the past few hundred years, think how much more we could achieve over the next few hundred years, or few thousand. We could journey to the stars, live for centuries or enhance our minds and bodies in countless ways, creating a physical embodiment of *Homo scientificus*. Unless, of course, we destroy ourselves first.

But even if we manage to avoid destruction by our own hand, we are still ultimately at the mercy of the universe. Science has already revealed the many ends that we will face: the end of our solar system, the end of our galaxy, the end of our universe. Even the first of these endings – that of our solar system – is billions of years in the future, but to be forewarned is to be forearmed.

As *Homo sapiens* we would be compelled to follow the universe to its bitter end. But as *Homo scientificus*, perhaps we can find an escape route.

Acknowledgements

I would like to thank all the scientists who read chapters and provided help and assistance for this book. They were: Andrew Liddle; Max Bernstein; Alan Boss; Matt Genge; Mike Benton; Jon Strefford; Jack Cohen; Julia Potter; David Rothery; Bob Marsh; Bob Henson; Egil Lillestøl; Serge Caron; Thom LaBean; Stuart Taylor; and Mauro Ferrari. Any remaining errors are mine and mine alone.

I would also like thank everyone at Hodder Education who helped with the book. Last but not least, I would like to thank Sarah, Charlotte and Claudia for all their love and support.

Part one

How we got here

1

Bang, we're off

In this chapter you will learn:
- *about the birth of the universe and the Big Bang theory*
- *the role of quarks, leptons and other subatomic particles*
- *how the universe expanded and cooled*
- *the four fundamental forces of nature.*

Just under 14 billion years ago, there was nothing: no people, no planets, no stars, no space, no time. Nothing. Then, for reasons that are still unexplained, the entire universe suddenly and unexpectedly burst into being, in what scientists like to call 'the Big Bang'.

Initially, however, there was nothing really very big about it, because when the universe first popped into existence it did so within a volume that was much, much smaller than an atom. Almost immediately, however, the universe began to expand incredibly rapidly, in a process known as inflation, which then stopped almost as soon as it had begun. Despite lasting for just a minuscule fraction of a second, during this inflationary period the universe more than doubled in size 100 times, growing to around 30 cm.

The ending of this rapid period of expansion released a huge amount of energy, which had the handy consequence of creating all the matter that fills the universe today. But because this matter was squeezed into just 30 cm, the universe at this point was very different to the one we now inhabit.

Expanding and cooling

It consisted of an unimaginably dense soup of tiny particles at a temperature of 10^{27} degrees (which is a convenient way to write 1 followed by 27 zeros, or one thousand trillion trillion degrees). The universe didn't stay that way for long though; for although the inflationary period had ended, it kicked off a gentler period of expansion that continues to this day.

According to the latest astronomical measurements, the observable universe (meaning the universe we can see with telescopes) currently extends for around 14 billion light years (the distance that light travels in a year, or around 1 trillion kilometres) in all directions and is expanding at 74 km a second.

In fact, it was the discovery that the universe is expanding (see Box) that led to the formation of the Big Bang theory for the origin of the universe. The argument goes that if the universe is expanding now then it must have been smaller in the past, meaning that if you trace the expansion back far enough then the universe essentially disappears up its own fundament, like playing film of an explosion backwards.

By the time the universe was one ten-thousandth of a second old, this expansion had caused the temperature to drop to one trillion degrees. While still unimaginably hot, this temperature was low enough for a number of important changes to start taking place in the now slightly less dense soup of tiny particles.

Edwin Hubble, 1889–1953

If any one scientist can be said to have ushered in the modern conception of the universe, both vast and getting vaster, it is the US astronomer Edwin Hubble.

Prior to his work in the 1920s, astronomers thought our Milky Way galaxy comprised the whole universe. By studying the light released by certain types of stars, Hubble first showed that some hitherto puzzling patches of stars were not in the Milky Way at all, but were actually individual galaxies millions of light years away. He then

(Contd)

discovered that all these galaxies are moving away from us, with the furthest galaxies moving away the fastest, providing the smoking gun for the expanding universe.

Hubble was hardly a stereotypical scientist. A talented athlete in his youth, Hubble claimed that he once fought an exhibition boxing match against the French national champion. Then later, when his scientific discoveries had brought him a certain measure of renown, Hubble attended Hollywood parties with film stars of the day such as Charlie Chaplin and Greta Garbo.

His achievements are now commemorated in the form of the Hubble Space Telescope.

Quarks and leptons

By tiny particles, we mean subatomic particles: in other words, the particles that make up atoms. These particles, known collectively as fermions, can be divided into two broad groups: quarks and leptons. These two groups are further divided into three families, with the first family of each group containing the most common and familiar types of subatomic particle.

The most common quarks are known as up and down quarks, while the most common lepton is the electron. These most common subatomic particles form all the ordinary matter that we see around us – stars, planets, humans and cabbages. The less common subatomic particles (which include the muon, the tauon, neutrinos, and charm, strange, top and bottom quarks) make up more exotic forms of matter, which are generally only seen on Earth at the extremely high energies generated in particle accelerators (see Box).

Particle accelerators

Piecing together the story of the beginning of the universe has involved a combination of astronomical observations, mathematical models and particle accelerators.

These giant and hugely expensive instruments probe the intricacies of the subatomic world by slamming particles such as electrons and protons into a static target or, more recently, into each other at very high speeds. The huge amounts of energy produced by these collisions create a whole range of other subatomic particles, including exotic particles such as neutrinos.

On 10 September 2008, the largest and most powerful particle accelerator yet built was officially switched on. Housed hundreds of feet beneath the ground near Geneva in Switzerland, the Large Hadron Collider (LHC) cost $10 billion to construct and consists of a ring 17 miles in circumference.

By sending protons around this ring in opposite directions and then smashing them together at almost the speed of light, scientists hope to create subatomic particles that have never been seen before. Most famously, scientists are hoping to produce the Higgs boson, a particle that is thought to confer mass on the particles that make up normal matter.

The strong force

When the universe was younger than one ten-thousandth of a second, all these particles existed as independent entities in the extremely hot, dense soup. But as the universe expanded, the temperature dropped sufficiently for these particles to start joining together to form larger entities.

This is because temperature is a measure of the amount of energy present in a system and above a certain temperature the subatomic particles just possessed too much energy. They were colliding with such force that they simply rebounded. As the temperature dropped, however, so did the energy levels of the particles, allowing them to begin to stick together.

For quarks, this coming together was mediated by what is known as the strong force, which is one of the four fundamental forces of nature. The strong force started to operate when the temperature of the universe dropped below one trillion degrees, joining the up and down quarks together into collections of twos and threes.

As the temperature dropped further, the collections of two quarks fell apart, until all that were left were collections of two up quarks and one down quark and collections of two down quarks and one up quark. These collections now began to operate as particles in their own right, with the former collection of quarks becoming protons and the latter collection becoming neutrons. But this process ended up generating a great deal more protons than neutrons, because many of the neutrons decayed into protons.

After bringing together all the up and down quarks, the strong force then began to combine the protons and neutrons into various permutations. This included one proton and one neutron, two protons and one neutron, and two protons and two neutrons, with the latter combination being the most stable and long-lasting. Larger combinations quickly fell apart, except combinations containing three or four protons with a few neutrons thrown in, which were produced in small amounts.

All this occurred in the first three minutes of the universe's life, at which point its temperature had dropped to a balmy 1 billion degrees. Below this temperature, there was no longer enough energy around for the strong force to stick together any more protons and neutrons, but those that it had already stuck together remained together.

The universe then stayed like this for the next 380,000 years, steadily expanding and cooling. During this time, the universe consisted of various combinations of protons and neutrons, together with a load of excess single protons, and numerous electrons and other leptons all flying around ignoring each other. It also contained more unusual and less well-understood forms of matter, such as dark matter, but these need not concern us for the moment.

The electromagnetic force

The main distinction between quarks and leptons is that quarks interact via the strong force, but leptons don't. Electrons, for instance, interact solely via the electromagnetic force. This is another fundamental force of nature, which switched on about the same time as the strong force but was initially unable to have much of an influence because the temperature was too high.

The electromagnetic force acts between all particles that possess an electric charge. Such charged particles possess either a positive charge or a negative charge: particles with opposite charges attract each other, while those with identical charges repel each other. It's like holding two magnets: opposite poles snap together, while identical poles force themselves apart.

Electrons are negatively charged and so are influenced by the electromagnetic force, as are protons, which are positively charged. Neutrons, on the other hand, do not have an electric charge and so are not influenced by the electromagnetic force.

By the time the universe was 380,000 years old, its temperature had dropped to 3,000 degrees and the electromagnetic force could start bringing the oppositely charged protons and electrons together to form atoms. All atoms comprise a nucleus of protons and neutrons surrounded by a cloud of orbiting electrons. And because atoms always possess an identical number of protons and electrons, they have no overall charge.

The first atomic matter

So after 380,000 years, the first proper atomic matter finally appeared. Single electrons combined with the excess protons to form hydrogen, while pairs of electrons joined the combinations of two protons and two neutrons to form helium (see Figure 1.1). The small amount of larger combinations containing three or four protons also acquired electrons, producing lithium and beryllium respectively.

The end result of all this was the creation of a huge amount of hydrogen, accounting for around 77 per cent of the newly created matter, a smaller amount of helium (around 23 per cent) and tiny amounts of lithium and beryllium (just a fraction of a per cent). This general distribution of matter continues to this day, with the universe containing much more hydrogen and helium than anything else.

But even when atomic matter first appeared, it wasn't distributed equally over the whole universe. Instead some areas of the universe

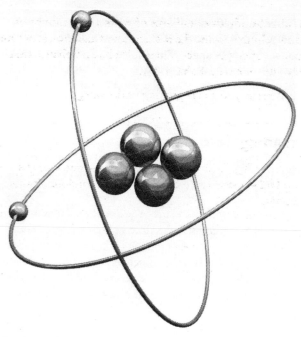

Figure 1.1 Helium atom

contained more matter than others. This was a result of random fluctuations that occurred during the inflationary period. These fluctuations introduced variations in the distribution of the newly created matter that persisted as the universe expanded, eventually leading hydrogen and helium to form slightly denser clumps in certain regions.

The force of gravity

This clumping tendency was then exacerbated by the force of gravity, which is the third of the four fundamental forces of nature (the fourth is the weak force, which is involved in some forms of radioactive decay). Gravity acts between bodies with mass, causing bodies with greater mass to attract bodies with lesser mass. As the clumps of hydrogen and helium possessed more mass than the surrounding regions, they attracted more matter to them, increasing their mass and thus attracting even more matter.

Eventually, after hundreds of millions of years, these clumps of hydrogen and helium became the first stars and galaxies, separated by vast expanses of empty space. Finally, we had a universe that was similar to the one we inhabit today.

But still, this is really just the beginning of the story.

Further reading

Singh, Simon, *The Big Bang: The most important scientific discovery of all time and why you need to know about it* (London: Harper Perennial, 2005).

2

Molecules in space

In this chapter you will learn:
- *how the 92 elements are formed*
- *about nucleosynthesis reactions*
- *about molecular clouds and the birth of new stars.*

According to the British psychedelic rock band *Hawkwind*, space is deep. It's also cold, dark and mainly empty. But even in the depths of space, lone atoms occasionally meet and react with each other, joining together to form molecules.

Cosmic rays

For despite its cold and dark reputation, space is actually suffused with ultra-violet (UV) light and streams of subatomic particles and atomic nuclei known as cosmic rays, which both come from stars. These knock electrons off hydrogen, helium and oxygen atoms, forming positively charged ions that are primed to take part in chemical reactions (see Box), even at temperatures as low as $-263°C$.

Ions

In Chapter 1, we learned that atoms normally don't posses a charge, because they contain equal numbers of negatively charged electrons and positively charged protons.

Sometimes, however, atoms can lose or gain extra electrons. If they lose one or more electrons, then they possess more protons than electrons and so become positively charged ions, known as cations.

If they gain one or more electrons, then they possess more electrons than protons and so become negatively charged ions, known as anions.

Oppositely charged ions can come together to form molecules. For example, table salt (NaCl) is a created when sodium cations (Na^+) combine with chlorine anions (Cl^-).

These reactions take place when the ions crash into each other or into atoms of carbon, iron, nitrogen and silicon, reacting to form simple molecules such as carbon monoxide, water and silicates (various combinations of oxygen and silicon, particularly SiO_4).

Silicates are essentially tiny grains of sand and provide a solid surface onto which the various other molecules can freeze, forming an icy coating. This brings a whole host of these simple molecules into close enough proximity to react together, with the energy again provided by UV light and cosmic rays. These reactions build up more complex molecules such as methanol, ammonia and formaldehyde.

If these ice-coated grains are then warmed by passing close to a star, the heat provides sufficient energy for these slightly more complex molecules to react together. This generates even larger and more complex molecules. These include: simple sugars such as glycolaldehyde; acetic acid, which is the main constituent of vinegar; and amino acetonitrile, which is related to the amino acids that are a central component of all life on Earth (see Chapter 4).

The formation of new elements

But wait a minute, where did all this oxygen, carbon, nitrogen, iron and silicon come from? In Chapter 1, we learned that the Big Bang generated loads of hydrogen, quite a lot of helium and a tiny amount of lithium and beryllium. How did the universe end up with the other 88 naturally occurring elements, producing 92 elements in total? Each of these elements has characteristic numbers of protons and electrons, and by joining together to form molecules, they produce all the matter we see around us today.

Well, the simple answer is that most of these other elements were forged in the fiery furnaces of stars under conditions of extreme violence.

The first stars lit up around 300 million years after the Big Bang, as gravity caused the vast clouds of hydrogen and helium to clump together into galaxies and then to collapse into individual stars. As a cloud collapses, its core becomes more and more compressed and therefore hotter and hotter. As a result, atoms of hydrogen and helium (we can ignore the lithium) start slamming into each other.

At around 50,000°C, the atoms slam into each other with such ferocity that the collisions strip away their electrons, forming a mixture of hydrogen and helium nuclei surrounded by a gas of electrons. But the collapse carries on regardless: the hydrogen and helium nuclei keep smacking into each other and the heat continues to rise.

At 10 million degrees, the single protons that make up hydrogen nuclei hit each other with enough force to fuse together. But this force also causes one of the protons to decay into a neutron and so the end result is the nucleus of a deuterium atom, which is an isotope of hydrogen (see Box). Thus, the process by which new elements are formed, known as nucleosynthesis, has begun, although the heat is still too low for helium nuclei to get involved.

Isotopes

In the famous periodic table, every element has its place. But in the real world things aren't quite so clear cut, because many elements exist in a number of different forms, known as isotopes.

The isotopes of an element all have the same number of electrons and protons, but different numbers of neutrons. So a standard hydrogen atom has a nucleus made up of just one proton, but there are also two other isotopes of hydrogen: deuterium, with one proton and one neutron; and tritium, with one proton and two neutrons.

Different elements have different numbers of isotopes, from one to 10 (for tin). Although an element's isotopes tend to behave in similar ways, the rate at which they take part in chemical reactions can differ, with some important consequences.

Carbon has two main isotopes, known as carbon-12 and carbon-13, which have nuclei consisting of six protons and either six or seven neutrons (hence the numbers). Life on Earth is based on carbon, but

Now deuterium nuclei are flying around along with the hydrogen and helium nuclei. Deuterium nuclei start colliding with protons and fusing together, forming an unusual type of helium nucleus comprising two protons and one neutron. When two of these nuclei collide, they fuse together to become a standard helium nucleus comprising two protons and two neutrons, ejecting the two spare protons.

The helium nucleus is the end point of this suite of nucleosynthesis reactions, which release a huge amount of energy in the form of gamma rays. During their passage through the star, these gamma rays turn into other forms of electromagnetic radiation (see Chapter 17), including visible light, and generate an outward force that counters the collapse. Nevertheless, this force is not yet sufficient to prevent the core from collapsing further.

NUCLEOSYNTHESIS AND THE FORMATION OF STARS

At 25 million degrees, however, these nucleosynthesis reactions release enough electromagnetic radiation to halt the collapse and a stable, light-emitting star is born. During the remainder of its lifetime, the star will burn the store of hydrogen in its core as fuel, transforming it into helium and releasing electromagnetic radiation in the process. Outside the core, though, hydrogen doesn't burn, because it never gets hot enough.

The extent of a star's lifetime depends on its size. The largest stars (around 60 times larger than our sun) are the shortest lived, burning through the hydrogen in their cores in just 60 million years and shining over 100,000 times brighter than our sun. In contrast, the smallest stars (just one-tenth the size of our sun) live for over 800 billion years and shine only one thousandth as brightly. Our middle-aged sun should shine for around 10 billion years.

At the end of a star's life, having used up all the hydrogen fuel, its core begins to collapse again. This causes the temperature to rise even higher, triggering successive rounds of nucleosynthesis reactions. At 100 million degrees, the helium nuclei in the core start fusing together to produce carbon nuclei. (For the pedants out there, the three elements between helium and carbon in the periodic table – lithium, beryllium and boron – are not synthesized within stars. They are instead produced by cosmic rays careering into elements such as carbon and nitrogen in the depths of space, in a process known as cosmic ray spallation.)

As the core heats up, so do the outer layers of the star, triggering nucleosynthesis reactions in those layers that were hitherto too cold. All these nucleosynthesis reactions now taking place in the core and outer regions generate an enormous amount of electromagnetic radiation. This temporarily halts the collapse of the core and inflates the outer layers of the star, causing the star to expand by a factor of 100 to form a red giant.

But the core soon starts to contract again, as the star uses up each of its nucleosynthesis fuels, turning up the heat and triggering a new round of reactions. Inexorably, the temperature in the core rises from 100 million degrees to 6 billion degrees, synthesizing in turn the 21 elements in the periodic table from oxygen to iron. At this point, the whole nucleosynthesis process grinds to a halt, because iron is too stable to take part in any further reactions.

Without any nucleosynthesis reactions to prop it up, the core collapses until it can collapse no more, squeezing the iron nuclei and electrons into one huge nucleus with a mass six times larger than our sun. The core then explodes in a shower of neutrons and subatomic particles that rip the star apart, transforming it into a roaring fireball called a supernova that for a few months shines brighter than a whole galaxy.

As they tear through the star, the neutrons and subatomic particles collide with all the elements from carbon to iron now being produced via nucleosynthesis in the outer layers. This builds up the remaining 66 naturally occurring elements, which are then all flung far out into the depths of space.

Only the largest stars – those at least 20 times larger than the sun – are able to go the full hog, synthesizing the complete set of 87 new elements. Stars ten times larger than the sun only get as far as synthesizing silicon in their cores, but do still explode as supernovae.

Stars three times larger than the sun only get as far as carbon, while the sun will only ever get as far as helium. And rather than their cores exploding violently, they gently expire by exhaling huge flows of protons and electrons known as stellar wind.

Since the first stars appeared 12 billion years ago, countless generations have been born and died. Billions of stars exploding in a huge continuous firework display that blasts the 87 elements throughout the universe, with the largest stars ejecting more matter than is found in 20 suns. Despite this, hydrogen and helium still make up the vast majority (98.1 per cent) of the detectable matter in the universe. Carbon, nitrogen and oxygen are the next most abundant, making up 1.4 per cent, with the remaining 87 elements bringing up the rear on 0.5 per cent.

Spreading through space, these elements mingle with the clouds of hydrogen and helium left over from the Big Bang to form the dense molecular clouds that are the cradles of new generations of stars.

Sir Fred Hoyle, 1915–2001

Many of the details of how elements form in stars were worked out in the 1940s and 1950s by a British astrophysicist named Fred Hoyle, based on his knowledge of nuclear physics.

Later in his career, Hoyle went slightly off the scientific rails by arguing that simple life didn't originate on Earth but was carried here by comets. Known as panspermia, this idea is a step too far for most scientists and not supported by firm evidence. He also claimed that Earth was still being bombarded by deliveries of extraterrestrial bacteria and viruses, triggering cancers and global pandemics.

His other claims to fame were coining the term 'the Big Bang', although he always thought this theory of how the universe began was incorrect, and writing several science-fiction novels.

These dense molecular clouds, which can stretch for hundreds or thousands of light years, are also where the majority of the interesting interstellar chemistry takes place. This is because, as their name suggests, these clouds contain a greater concentration of material than is found in more diffuse regions of space.

But dense is a relative term in the depths of space, because the concentration of material in a molecular cloud corresponds to the best vacuum that can be produced by scientists on Earth. Nevertheless, molecules and atoms collide or freeze onto silicate grains much more regularly in such clouds than in more diffuse regions of space.

The clouds also afford a degree of protection against the harsh environment of space, where UV light and cosmic rays can destroy molecules just as easily as they can create them. Outside of dense molecular clouds, only robust molecules such as carbon monoxide and a group of large, chicken-wire-shaped carbon-based molecules known as polycyclic aromatic hydrocarbons (PAHs) are able to survive for extended periods. On entering molecular clouds, the UV light and cosmic rays quickly lose much of their energy, allowing them to promote chemical reactions without destroying the results.

Using radio and infrared telescopes, especially orbiting telescopes such as the European Space Agency's Infrared Space Observatory and NASA's Spitzer Space Telescope, scientists are continuously discovering new molecules in these molecular clouds (see Chapter 17). At the time of writing, over 150 different molecules have been detected, including all those mentioned at the start of this chapter.

Some of the most complex molecules, such as ethyl formate, are detected in dense molecular clouds that have just given birth to a new star, such as the cloud known as Large Molecule Heimat. This supports the idea that such complex molecules are produced via the heating of ice-coated grains.

But laboratory experiments that involve heating simulated ice grains covered with molecules such as methanol, water, ammonia and carbon monoxide have generated even more complex organic molecules. These include a molecule called hexamethylenetetramine, which can spontaneously form amino acids when exposed to acid.

No amino acids have yet been conclusively detected in dense molecular clouds, perhaps because molecules as complex as amino acids are difficult to identify. But they have been found in a type of meteorite known as a carbonaceous chondrite, along with many other biologically-important molecules. Carbonaceous chondrites are thought never to have been exposed to intense heat and so probably reflect the composition of the dense molecular cloud that gave birth to our solar system.

Similar biologically important molecules have also been detected in comets. These collections of dust and ice formed at the far edge of our solar system and are also thought to retain the composition of the parent molecular cloud.

So a propensity for life may have been imprinted on our solar system right from the start.

Further reading

Chown, Marcus, *The Magic Furnace: The search for the origin of atoms* (London: Vintage, 2000).

3

Recipe for a solar system

In this chapter you will learn:
- *how our solar system formed*
- *how the Moon came into being*
- *why hot Jupiters are so called.*

To make a tasty solar system, first take a fresh dense molecular cloud. This should mainly consist of hydrogen and helium left over from the Big Bang. But it should also contain much smaller concentrations of the other naturally occurring elements spewed out by nearby supernovae, and simple molecules such as carbon monoxide, water and silicates formed by chemical reactions between these elements.

Then expose this dense molecular cloud to the shock waves produced by a nearby supernova, which will trigger the collapse of regions of the cloud under the force of gravity. Then wait a few hundred thousand years, at which point the temperature at the centres of these collapsing regions will have risen sufficiently to trigger nucleosynthesis, heralding the birth of new stars.

The collapse will also cause the new stars to rotate faster and faster. And being fairly massive, they will start to drag the rest of the collapsing regions around with them. Where once there was a molecular cloud, now there will be a whole host of new stars, each orbited by huge, flat expanses of rotating dust and gas extending for billions of kilometres. These are known as circumstellar disks.

Our solar system

Then just leave to simmer for around 100 million years, during which time these circumstellar disks will naturally turn into mouth-watering solar systems.

At least, that is the cosmic recipe that scientists think led to the formation of our solar system around 4.5 billion years ago. Our solar system now comprises the four inner rocky planets (Mercury, Venus, the Earth and Mars) and the four outer gas giants (Jupiter, Saturn, Uranus, Neptune) separated by the asteroid belt. Far out beyond the orbit of Neptune, there's also a tiny icy planet called Pluto, but whether it should actually count as a planet is a matter of some controversy (see Figure 3.1).

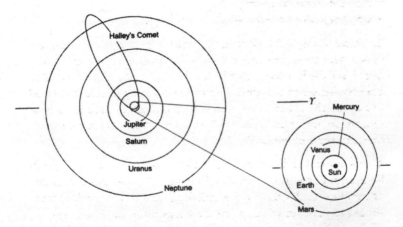

Figure 3.1 The solar system

Beyond Pluto is a large orbiting collection of icy bodies known as the Kuiper belt. Consisting mainly of comets, the Kuiper belt also contains small icy planets of a similar size to Pluto. Hence the controversy over whether Pluto should actually count as a proper planet at all. Or whether, along with the other small icy planets, it should be classified as a dwarf planet, which has been its official designation since 2006.

There is also an even larger collection of comets called the Oort cloud. Whereas the Kuiper belt probably contains millions of comets orbiting in a flat ring, the Oort cloud is thought to contain 100 billion comets orbiting as a quasi-spherical heap.

When considering distances in the solar system, kilometres are really too small a unit of measurement, but light years are too big. So astronomers tend to measure distances in terms of astronomical units (AU), which equals the distance from the Earth to the sun (around 150 million kilometres). Using this measure, Mercury orbits at a distance of 0.4AU from the sun, Jupiter orbits at 5.2AU and Neptune orbits at 30.1AU. The Kuiper belt extends from about 30AU to 55AU, while the Oort cloud extends from 2,000AU to 50,000AU or more.

THE TRANSFORMATION OF A CIRCUMSTELLAR DISK INTO OUR SOLAR SYSTEM

Astronomers also think they have a pretty good understanding of the process that transformed the circumstellar disk orbiting the young sun into our solar system. The gas in this disk would have consisted mainly of hydrogen and helium, with some oxygen, carbon and nitrogen thrown in, while the dust would mainly have consisted of silicates of iron and magnesium with some additional grains of carbon, PAHs and metallic iron.

In total, the dust and gas would have equalled at most 10 per cent of the mass of the sun, with gas accounting for 98.5 per cent and the dust accounting for the remaining 1.5 per cent. Initially, turbulence within the disk kept the gas and dust mixed together. But after the young sun had finished forming, this turbulence would have subsided and the dust begun to settle out, in the same way that sand in a glass of water will quickly settle out if you stop stirring it. This took place over a period of just a few thousand years, after which the circumstellar disk consisted of a flat disk of dust surrounding by a thicker disk of gas.

Due to a combination of the heat generated as the dust and gas were pulled into the circumstellar disk and the heat generated by the young sun itself, the temperature of the disk now began to increase, with regions of the disk close to the sun getting hotter than those further away. And it is this range of temperatures along the disk, stretching from hot at the centre to cold at the edges, that dictated what our solar system would eventually look like.

ICY COATINGS

In Chapter 2, we learned that in the depths of space simple molecules such as water and carbon dioxide readily freeze onto tiny silicate grains, forming an icy coating. This brings the simple molecules in close enough proximity to react together, forming more complex molecules such as methanol, ammonia and formaldehyde.

The dust grains present in the circumstellar disk around the young sun will have possessed such icy coatings, but the precise fate of those coatings depended on where a grain was located in the disk. Closer in to the sun than the current orbit of Jupiter (5.2AU), the temperature of the circumstellar disk would have been above freezing, which in space is around −50°C. Thus the icy coatings on the grains in the inner portion of the circumstellar disk would soon have evaporated away, leaving behind bare silicate grains. Beyond about 5.2AU, known as the snow line, the temperature of the got above freezing and so the silicate grains

...? disk orbited around the young sun, the silicate
...ck together, forming small conglomerations that
...e bigger as they swept up more and more grains,
like i... ...owball down a hill. After around a million years,
this process ... ...d formed around 30 protoplanets varying from
Moon-sized to Mars-sized within the snow line.

Beyond the snow line, however, the protoplanets built up much
faster, simply because ice-coated silicate grains are slightly more
massive than bare silicate grains. On top of this, the water and other
molecules that evaporated from silicate grains within the snow line
condensed back onto grains as soon they reached the snow line,
adding even more mass to the icy coatings.

As a result, after a million years a protoplanet with a mass greater
than ten Earths had built up at the snow line. This protoplanet was
now massive enough to start pulling all the gas and other matter in
the surrounding area towards it under the influence of gravity. Within
another million years, this process had bulked up the protoplanet to
30 times the mass of the Earth and surrounded it with an enormous
gaseous layer equivalent to almost 288 times the mass of the Earth.
Jupiter was born.

A similar process built up the three other gas giants, but it was
increasingly less effective. This was because Jupiter had already
captured a large proportion of the gas in the circumstellar disk, while
the rest of the gas was now being blown away by a strong solar wind.
So there was less gas for Saturn, Uranus and Neptune to wrap around
themselves. Whereas Jupiter is 318 times more massive than the
Earth, Saturn is just 94 times more massive, and Uranus and Neptune
are less than 20 times more massive.

In the warmer environs within the snow line, the rocky protoplanets
never grew anywhere near large enough to acquire a huge gaseous
atmosphere. Their existence was also more violent, as they were
subject to repeated collisions, which either built them up or destroyed
them. Eventually, after about one hundred million years, this

demolition derby resulted in the formation of four rocky planets, as well as a collection of debris known as the asteroid belt.

The formation of the Earth

The largest of these rocky planets was the Earth, which like the other rocky planets consisted mainly of a mixture of silicates and iron. As well as building up the Earth, the continual collisions turned its surface into a huge sea of molten lava. The intense heat at the surface caused the interior of the planet to heat up, melting both the silicates and the iron. Because iron is denser than silicates, the molten iron began to flow down through the silicates to the centre of the Earth, eventually forming a molten iron core that exists to this day (see Chapter 11).

Towards the end of this process, the Earth suffered a huge collision, in which a protoplanet slightly larger than Mars caught it a glancing blow. This collision destroyed the protoplanet and blasted a huge chunk of the Earth into space, where it formed an orbiting ring. Over a period of 10 million years, this rocky debris came together to form the Moon.

After that huge collision, things calmed down a bit for the Earth; until countless comets and asteroids started slamming into it, in a heavy bombardment that continued for the next 500 million years. Consisting of agglomerations of ice-coated grains, these comets had formed out beyond the snow line and initially travelled in circular orbits around the sun.

But the growth of the gas giants disturbed their orbits, flinging the comets all over the place. Some were flung completely out of the solar system, and some ended up forming the Oort cloud. Others were sent speeding towards the inner solar system, where they ran the risk of colliding with the four rocky planets.

For the Earth, however, the heavy bombardment had an up-side, because these comets delivered both the water that filled up the oceans and much of the carbon-based material that eventually spawned life.

Philosopher's raindrops

The idea that the sun and solar system formed from the same expanse of matter is by no means a new one, having been first postulated by the German philosopher Immanuel Kant in 1755 and then advanced by the French mathematician Pierre Simon de Laplace a decade later. Their evidence was the fact that all the planets orbit in a single plane, on nearly circular orbits, in the same direction, implying that they evolved out of single rotating disk of material.

Determining the mechanism by which this happened was a bit trickier, involving many scientists and many dead ends. For instance, in 1905 two US scientists, Forest Ray Moulton and Thomas Chamberlain, proposed that the planets had formed from gaseous filaments dragged out of the sun by the close passing of another star.

It wasn't until the late 1960s that a Russian astronomer called Victor Safronov pulled together the modern explanation for the formation of the solar system. He did this without recourse to a computer and by taking advantage of a theory developed to study the coagulation of raindrops in the Earth's atmosphere.

Further reading

Boss, Alan, *Looking for Earths: The race to find new solar systems* (New York: John Wiley & Sons, Inc., 1998).

4

Life begins

In this chapter you will learn:
- *the first signs of life on Earth*
- *a definition of life itself*
- *the importance of amino acids*
- *about the RNA World.*

Around 3.8 billion years ago, the Earth was not a particularly pleasant place.

The period of heavy bombardment had only just finished, leaving the ground and sea boiling at temperatures of over 100°C. Volcanoes were everywhere, constantly spewing out huge volumes of steam and carbon dioxide, as well as sulphur dioxide, hydrogen and nitrogen. This produced a thick, suffocating atmosphere consisting mainly of carbon dioxide, with smaller amounts of methane, carbon monoxide and nitrogen. Incessant acid rain lashed through these heavy skies, scarring the rocks on the ground. And all the while, comets and meteorites were still occasionally slamming into the Earth.

But still, in the middle of this Dantesque vision, life may well have made its first appearance. Or at least rocks of this age in Greenland, which are some of the oldest known, contain evidence that life existed when they formed. Now this evidence, consisting of a slight overabundance of carbon-12 over carbon-13 (see Chapter 2), is hotly disputed. This is because the rocks have been extensively modified by heat over the ages, making any interpretation of their chemical composition very tricky.

But if life wasn't around just at that point, it probably didn't wait much longer to show up. Rocks from Australia dating back almost 3.5 billion years contain microscopic structures that look very much like the fossilized remains of tiny bacteria, while some fossilized colonies of such bacteria, known as stromatolites, have also been dated to around the same time.

So just over 500 million years after the end of the ferocious bombardment of meteorites and comets, which would have snuffed out any life that tried to get going, the seas of the Earth were probably full of microbes. Now this is a surprisingly short amount of time to go from lifeless to teeming and suggests that given the right conditions life arises without too much trouble, perhaps within as little as 20 million years. But exactly how it arose is still very much open to question.

LUCA

The problem is that there's no way to see that far back into the mists of time. Early bacteria may have left fossilized remains, but the very first life form, termed LUCA (last universal common ancestor), didn't. So, in piecing together what actually happened, scientists have been following two lines of inquiry.

The first approach involves discovering those 'right conditions' that led to life. By working out the kind of chemical compounds that would have existed on the early Earth and the kind of reactions that could have taken place between them, scientists are trying to work out how these chemicals came together to form life. The second approach involves looking at the basic components of current life and then working backwards to determine how they may have developed.

The first can be seen as a kind of bottom-up approach, going from lifeless to life, and the second as a kind of top-down approach, going from life to lifeless. The hope is that these two approaches will eventually meet in the middle to produce a plausible route from lifeless chemicals to seas teeming with bacteria. The semblance of such a route is now just beginning to appear.

Replicating one of the likely stages in the formation of life is actually fairly easy, at least for an academic chemist. Simply fill a flask with a mixture of methane, ammonia, hydrogen and water vapour (to simulate the early atmosphere), and repeatedly apply heat and electricity (to simulate volcanoes and lightning).

When a young US chemist called Stanley Miller did this in 1953, he found that after a few days the water turned brown. Analysing this water, he detected a whole range of complex organic molecules, including several amino acids found in proteins. An analysis of stored samples from this experiment with more advanced instruments in 2008 revealed an even greater range of amino acids.

Scientists now think that the early Earth's atmosphere probably contained much more carbon dioxide than methane or ammonia, and when the same experiment is performed with this mixture of gases far fewer organic molecules are produced. Nevertheless, Miller's experiment goes down in history as the first to show that biologically-important molecules can spontaneously be produced from a simple mixture of gases.

A definition of life

But before we start tramping along this route, perhaps it would be useful to define what we actually mean by life. Now while it may seem fairly simple to distinguish life from non-life – dogs are alive, stones aren't – producing a formal definition is actually quite difficult.

Perhaps the most obvious criterion for life is being able to reproduce. If something is alive, then it must be able to produce copies of itself, which may or may not be identical. But this criterion is not sufficient on its own, because crystals are able to grow and produce identical copies of themselves if placed in salt solutions. And no one would argue that crystals are alive.

To the ability to reproduce we need to add the ability to evolve. For something to be alive, the copies it produces of itself need to be able to change gradually across the generations in response to environmental factors. Evolution will be explained more fully in Chapter 5, but it is responsible for transforming the simple bacteria that floated in the seas of the early Earth into the multitudinous variety of life forms that exist today (and have ever existed).

THE ESSENTIAL PROPERTIES OF LIFE

Now we have a basic definition of life, we can start to pick out its essential properties, which should have been possessed by the very earliest forms. The most essential of these essential properties is that all life on Earth is constructed from molecules containing carbon and hydrogen, known as organic molecules. And if there's one aspect of the early Earth that scientists are fairly certain about, it's that there was an abundant supply of organic molecules.

This supply came from a number of different sources. For a start, the meteorites and comets that pummelled the early Earth brought with them huge amounts of different organic molecules. Organic molecules were also naturally produced in the thick atmosphere, as a result of reactions powered by lightning and sunlight. Finally, organic molecules would have been produced under the sea at hydrothermal vents. These are cracks in the Earth's surface that emit large amounts of carbon dioxide and various other chemical compounds, which can react to form organic molecules.

So any body of water on the early Earth, from oceans to puddles, would have been awash with organic molecules. Heated by the sun or volcanoes, these molecules would have started reacting together. Now in many cases this would simply have resulted in an almighty mess, but occasionally a stable system of reactions would get going, in which the product of one set of reactions would feed into the next set. In this way, order would have emerged from chaos for the first time.

How were amino acids joined together?

One family of organic molecules that would have been available on the early Earth is the amino acids, which consist of various combinations of carbon, hydrogen, oxygen and nitrogen surrounding a central carbon atom. Scientists know this because they have detected a wide range of amino acids in both meteorites and comets.

Furthermore, experiments simulating the kind of reactions that would have taken place in the early Earth's atmosphere and around hydrothermal vents also produce amino acids (see Box).

This is interesting, because amino acids are the building blocks of proteins and proteins are the very cornerstone of all current life on Earth. Life is built from proteins and works due to proteins. And all the thousands and thousands of proteins utilized by all the life forms on Earth are made up of long chains of just 20 different amino acids.

The challenge then is to find a mechanism that naturally joins amino acids together into these long chains. Today, this is done within cells in a complex process that involves lots of different components, based on instructions coded in the cell's genes. How could proteins have been produced without all this cellular apparatus? Furthermore, amino acids can't simply join together randomly; they have to join together in a set order to produce a set protein with set properties. How could that have happened without any kind of biological guidance?

RNA AND ROCKS

Well one theory is that it didn't initially happen with proteins at all, but rather with a molecule known as RNA (ribonucleic acid), which is very similar to the DNA that makes up genes. Like DNA, RNA is made up of organic molecules known as nucleotides (see Chapter 6), which were also probably lying around on the early Earth (or at least their component parts were).

The advantage RNA has over proteins is that RNA theoretically contains the instructions for replicating itself (via a process that will be explained in Chapter 6), offering a way for the same molecule to be made over and over again. What is more, scientists have discovered that certain RNA molecules can perform some of the same functions as proteins, including speeding up certain chemical reactions.

So perhaps RNA came first, forming the basis for the earliest forms of life and creating what is known as the 'RNA World', before eventually synthesizing the proteins that subsequently took over. But that still leaves a big gap between the first stable reactions and the dawning of the RNA World; what could possibly have bridged that gap?

The answer may well be as simple as 'rocks'. The idea is that the ultimate products of the stable reactions, perhaps including several nucleotides, would have regularly washed up onto rocks on the shore of some sea or lake. Here, the molecules would have joined together to produce more complex molecules, with the surface of the rocks acting as a template, aligning the molecules and helping them link together in set ways. As the surface of rocks don't change very rapidly and the same organic molecules were repeatedly washed onto them, the rocks acted like an assembly line, continuously producing the same complex molecules.

With this process repeated all over the early Earth for tens or hundreds of millions of years, it's perhaps not too surprising that eventually a range of RNA molecules (or initially perhaps slightly simpler versions) were produced. Then all it would take was for some of these molecules to become incorporated within fatty bubbles in the water and, hey presto, LUCA appears.

Now, of course, this is all speculation. Although scientists have found a certain amount of laboratory evidence for their theories, including chemical routes for producing certain biologically-important molecules and RNA molecules that can replicate other RNA molecules, they are still a long way off finding a plausible route from non-life to life.

Once life got going, however, there is abundant evidence for what happened next.

Are we all Martians?

Another theory is that life didn't originate on Earth at all, but rather started on Mars and then spread to Earth. There's quite a bit of evidence that early in the history of Mars it was much warmer and wetter than it is at the moment, with a thick atmosphere of carbon dioxide. Indeed, Mars may well have developed the necessary conditions for life millions of years before the Earth did.

So if life did originate on Mars, how did it then travel to Earth? Well, microbial life could have been blasted off the surface of Mars following a meteorite or comet impact. Attached to a rock that wasn't heated too much in the blast, these microbes would have taken around 8 million years to get to Earth, during which they time they could have survived in a dormant state.

This may all sound rather far-fetched but around 40 Martian rocks have been found on Earth. And one of those rocks, known as ALH84001, contains compounds and structures that some scientists have interpreted as signs of life, but again this interpretation is hotly disputed.

Further reading

Davies, Paul, *The Origin of Life* (London: Penguin, 2006).

5

....

Evolution and extinction

In this chapter you will learn:
- *about reproduction and mutation*
- *about Charles Darwin and the theory of evolution*
- *the impact of the environment on evolution*
- *the roles of photosynthesis and sex.*

As soon as the first living, reproducing microbes began to appear in the seas of the early Earth, evolution by natural selection kicked into gear.

Now, it can be argued that a form of chemical evolution was operating even in the non-biological era, eventually leading to the development of life. But it was only once life finally appeared that evolution really had something to get its teeth into.

For as we saw in Chapter 4, one of the defining features of life is the ability to reproduce. But reproducing all the components of a living organism, even a microbe, is a lot more complicated than reproducing a simple non-biological structure such as a crystal, which merely consists of repeating a physical pattern. With this added complexity comes an increased chance of making a mistake and such mistakes (or mutations) drive evolution.

Beneficial mutations

Often the mutations will be small enough to have little or no noticeable effect on the microbial offspring. But occasionally the mutations will result in the microbial offspring being slightly different to the parent. Sometimes this difference will be detrimental to the offspring, resulting in its quick death, but occasionally it will be beneficial, providing the new microbe with an advantage over all the other microbes in the vicinity.

As a result, this new, upgraded microbe will be able to out-compete its fellows for resources, allowing it to grow faster and reproduce more. Its offspring will therefore come to dominate the microbial population, until eventually every microbe is upgraded. This process continues over and over again with each new generation, causing the microbes to change and evolve as they gradually accumulate beneficial mutations.

This is how evolution by natural selection, as first postulated by the British naturalist Charles Darwin over 150 years ago (see Box), essentially works. Reproduction is the centre-piece of the whole process. It provides both the mechanism by which organisms change and the mechanism by which any beneficial changes propagate through the population, because organisms with such changes reproduce more than those without.

Charles Darwin, 1809–82

For Charles Darwin, 2009 was a momentous year. It marked 200 years since his birth and 150 years since the publication of his ground-breaking book *On the Origin of Species*, in which he first set out his theory of evolution by natural selection.

The theory came out of Darwin's years of meticulous study of a whole range of different organisms, from dogs to worms. Perhaps most important was his trip to South America on board the HMS Beagle from 1831 to 1836. As part of this trip, he stopped at the Galapagos Islands and noticed how each individual island contained its own unique species of animals and plants.

Darwin first came up with his theory in 1838, but mindful of the likely impact he held off publicizing his ideas for almost 20 years. Only when a young naturalist called Alfred Russell Wallace wrote to him expressing similar thoughts did he go public.

As he predicted, the effects were seismic. He had come up with the first plausible mechanism for explaining the entire diversity of life on Earth that didn't require the hand of a creator.

The role of the environment

The other main player is the environment, in the form of food sources, competitors, predators and the physical habitat, because this dictates which changes are beneficial and which aren't. Beneficial changes are those that enhance an individual's ability to operate in its specific environment – allowing it to gain food, compete against its fellows, avoid predators and safely navigate its habitat – thereby giving it a better chance of reproducing.

This means that changes that are beneficial in one specific environment could well be detrimental in another. For example, the ability to withstand hot temperatures would be very useful for a microbe living near a boiling hydrothermal vent, but far less useful for one living in a frozen lake.

So as soon as the first living, reproducing microbes appeared in the seas of the early Earth, evolution began changing them. The first major evolutionary leap occurred pretty quickly, when some of the microbes evolved the ability to photosynthesize. In other words, powered by the energy in sunlight, they were able to take the abundant carbon dioxide in the atmosphere and make it react with the water in which they floated to produce organic molecules, specifically simple forms of sugar.

CYANOBACTERIA AND PHOTOSYNTHESIS

The first organisms known to be able to do this are called cyanobacteria (which are still around today) and they formed the stromatolites that provide some of the earliest indications of life (see Chapter 4). This means that photosynthesizing cyanobacteria may have first appeared around 3.5 billion years ago.

The ability to photosynthesize represents an incredibly important advance. By generating their own nutrients, microbes no longer had to rely on an external source, which lifted a lot of restrictions. The newly photosynthesizing microbes were able to grow more rapidly and travel much more widely, allowing them to colonize the whole planet.

THE RISE IN OXYGEN LEVELS

There was also a less immediate but perhaps even more important consequence. Like all photosynthesizing organisms, cyanobacteria

34

produce sugars by combining the carbon in carbon dioxide with the hydrogen in water, but this leaves a lot of unwanted oxygen, which photosynthesizing organisms simply release into the atmosphere.

Now, a single cyanobacterium releases a miniscule amount of oxygen in its lifetime, but countless cyanobacteria continuously producing oxygen over millions and millions of years gradually transformed the Earth. The released oxygen reacted with rocks, dissolved in the oceans and then built up in the atmosphere. Whereas 3.5 billion years ago oxygen accounted for just 0.1 per cent of the Earth's atmosphere, by 2 billion years ago it had risen to 3 per cent (it now accounts for around 20 per cent).

This rise in oxygen levels then kicked off the next major evolutionary leap. Oxygen may be essential for most current life on Earth, but it is an extremely reactive element that damages biological structures given half the chance. So the early microbes were forced to evolve mechanisms to deal with the higher concentrations of oxygen.

Some microbes went one step further and actually made use of the oxygen. They utilized its high level of reactivity to break down organic molecules more fully than they were previously able to, releasing more energy and inventing respiration.

Other microbes sought refuge within hardier colleagues. These microbes eventually merged to become one, creating larger and more complex microbes collectively known as eukaryotes. This process also resulted in the first major split in Earth's life forms. Those eukaryotes that housed photosynthesizing microbes became photophytes, which are the ancestors of all plants, while those that housed respiring microbes became protozoans, which are the ancestors of all animals.

This all occurred around 2 billion years ago. Life then had to wait another 500 million years for the next evolutionary leap, but it was well worth it. For around 1.5 billion years ago, the eukaryotes invented sex.

Sexual reproduction

Now, sex may have a number of benefits (see Chapter 8), but the one that concerns us here is that it super-charges evolution. By mixing the genetic traits from two individuals, sexual reproduction produces offspring that always differ from their parents. Whereas asexual organisms can only evolve at the whim of random mistakes, sexual organisms have change built into their very being.

Sex greatly expanded the range of opportunities available to evolution. In fact, it was probably essential for the next major evolutionary leap, which took life over a particularly high hurdle. Life may have first appeared on Earth 3.5 billion years ago, but 2.5 billion years later it still consisted of numerous single-celled microbes floating in the sea.

THE FIRST MULTI-CELLED ORGANISMS

Only at this point did the single-celled eukaryotes start to come together to form larger groups and colonies. At first, the eukaryotes making up these groups were all the same. Eventually, however, the eukaryotes started to specialize and differentiate, resulting in the formation of the first multi-celled organisms around 750 million years ago.

At first, these were mainly types of jellyfish and sponges, but over the next 150 million years organisms with exterior skeletons, such as trilobites, started to appear (see Figure 5.1). Just 85 million years later, the seas were full of a huge array of different organisms, including the first fish with backbones. Around 100 million years after that, plants began to migrate from the seas and onto the land, leading to a vegetation explosion.

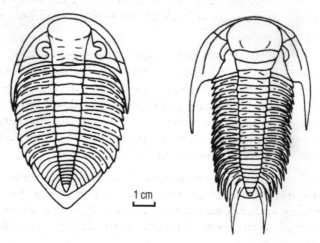

Figure 5.1 Trilobites

With the land now covered in edible plants, animals also began to leave the sea. Scorpions were first, around 390 million years ago, followed by a whole variety of other invertebrates that soon evolved into insects. Then 30 million years later, the first fish crawled on their fins up onto the land, evolving first into amphibians and then reptiles.

By 225 million years ago, some of the reptiles had become quite large, ushering in the age of the dinosaurs, which lasted for the next 160 million years. During this time, the world also witnessed the appearance of the first mammals, around 200 million years ago, and the first flowering plants, around 75 million years ago.

MASS EXTINCTIONS

Evolution has both winners and losers. So alongside the appearance of all these new types of life, others were going extinct. Now extinction is a process that runs alongside evolution: individual species go extinct all the time as a result of their habitat changing or being out-competed by more effective species. On top of this, however, large numbers of different species occasionally become extinct in a relatively short period of time, such as a few hundred thousand years.

Such events are known as mass extinctions. They can vary considerably in severity and extent, but five mass extinctions have been severe enough to affect almost all life on Earth. The exact causes of these five mass extinctions have still not really been pinned down, but probably involved one or more of the following: impact by a meteorite or comet, major volcanic activity lasting for millions of years and the ice ages.

As well as the immediate damage, major volcanic activity and meteorite or comet strikes also cause more long-lasting difficulties. Meteorites can throw huge volumes of debris into the atmosphere, blocking out the sun and killing off vegetation, while volcanoes can release massive amounts of carbon dioxide, which cause the Earth to heat up through global warming (see Chapter 23). Ice ages cause damage through falling temperatures and shrinking oceans.

The third and fifth of these mass extinctions are the best known. The third one, which occurred around 250 million years ago, is the largest ever mass extinction, killing up to 90 per cent of all living organisms. The last one, which occurred 65 million years ago, famously killed off the dinosaurs.

The emergence of man

But mass extinctions are not all bad news, because they create the conditions for a whole new round of evolution. Habitats that were until recently home to numerous species are now available for new species to colonize. Indeed, only 5–10 million years after a mass extinction takes place the diversity of life often exceeds that before the mass extinction.

To give an example close to home, the end of the dinosaurs proved to be a tremendous opportunity for the mammals, which they grasped with all paws, going on to spread over the entire Earth. And as they spread out, they evolved, until eventually, around 200,000 years ago, modern man first strode onto the scene.

Any old fossils

Scientists have pieced together the history of life on Earth from the fossil record. Fossils are essentially mineral-based imprints of organisms that lived millions of years ago. They are produced when newly dead plants and animals are covered in sediment, either silt or mud in water, or sand and volcanic ash on the land.

As more and more material is laid on top, the sediment surrounding the dead organism is compressed until it hardens into sedimentary rock like sandstone and limestone. Organic material such as flesh quickly decomposes away, leaving behind the mineral components of bones and teeth or gaps that fill with mineral deposits. In this way, the original organism is replaced by a mineral facsimile in the rock.

Although you're unlikely to find a whole dinosaur skeleton, smaller fossils can be found wherever there are sedimentary rocks. For instance, some of the first fossils were found along the Dorset coast around Lyme Regis, which remains a fossil hot spot.

Further reading

Benton, Michael, *The History of Life: A very short introduction* (Oxford: OUP, 2008).

Part two

Way of all flesh

6

Life in sequence

In this chapter you will learn:
- *the relationship between genes and proteins*
- *the components of DNA*
- *the different function of genes and RNA*
- *about the Human Genome Project and what we still don't know.*

Over the years, scientists have occasionally fallen into the trap of thinking that they're on the cusp of a complete understanding of some area of science just as that understanding is comprehensively blown out of the water.

It happened to physics in the early years of the 20th century, when scientists first discovered that the subatomic world could not be explained by classical physics, ushering in the new field of quantum physics (see Chapter 25). Now it seems to be happening to biology.

The proteins that make up life

The problem lies in the relationship between DNA and proteins. As we saw in Chapter 4, proteins are the cornerstone of all life on Earth. Life is built from proteins and works due to proteins.

Each of the tens of thousands of different proteins utilized by life is made up of just 20 different types of amino acid, which are joined together to form long molecular chains. The longest of these chains contains over 20,000 amino acid molecules, although the average protein only contains a few hundred, but the important point is that the sequence of amino acids in these chains is unique for each protein.

The amino acids are able to link together into chains because their ends are essentially sticky. This stickiness takes the form of a chemical bond, which attaches each amino acid molecule to its immediate neighbours, producing long, flat chains.

But that's not all, because some of the amino acids can also link up with colleagues in other, more distant parts of the chain via other chemical bonds. These chemical bonds pull the flat chains of amino acids into a complex three-dimensional structure, like a form of molecular origami, with the precise shape of the structure determined purely by the sequence of amino acids. And it is this precise shape that determines what a protein is able to do.

STRUCTURAL AND FUNCTIONAL PROTEINS

There are basically two types of protein: structural and functional. As their name suggests, structural proteins build up biological material such as muscle, cartilage and hair. Functional proteins, on the other hand, ensure that life stays functioning. Most importantly, they do this by greatly speeding up (otherwise known as catalyzing) the numerous chemical reactions that are essential for life, such as breaking down food. Such catalytic proteins are known as enzymes and it is their precise shape that allows them to function in this way.

Proteins are produced by, and mainly act within, cells. This is true both for single-celled microbes such as bacteria and for each of the hundred trillion cells that make up our bodies (see Chapter 7). The instructions for producing the thousands of different proteins are contained within each cell's genes. If proteins are life's workers, then genes are life's managers.

The DNA molecule

Genes are able to direct the production of all these proteins because they are made up of DNA (deoxyribonucleic acid). A single molecule of DNA consists of three components: a simple sugar known as ribose that has lost one of its oxygen atoms (hence the 'deoxy' prefix); a small phosphorus-containing molecule known as a phosphate group; and a very special molecule known as a nucleotide base.

The ribose and phosphate group act as the 'backbone' of DNA, essentially providing support for the nucleotide base and linking the numerous DNA molecules together into long strands. But the really important part of a DNA molecule is the nucleotide base, which can be one of four different molecules: adenine (A), guanine (G), cytosine (C) or thymine (T).

So, in a similar vein to proteins, a strand of DNA consists of the four different nucleotide bases joined together into a specific sequence. This similarity is no coincidence, however, because the sequence of nucleotide bases is directly related to the sequence of amino acids in a protein, acting as a kind of coded instruction for producing proteins.

And that's not the only similarity with proteins. For in the same way that chemical bonds can form between different amino acids, they can also form between the nucleotide bases. Importantly, though, adenine can only form a bond with thymine and guanine can only form a bond with cytosine.

The upshot of all this is that DNA doesn't exist in the cell as a single strand but as a double, conjoined strand, in which the sequence of nucleotide bases is always matched with a kind of 'mirror-image' sequence. So A always matches with T and G always matches with C, all along the conjoined strand (see Figure 6.1).

Not only is this set-up very chemically stable, but it also provides a simple way to produce a copy of any DNA sequence, as is required for cell division (it is mistakes in this copying process that produce the mutations that drive evolution; see Chapter 5). What's more, it gives DNA its characteristic double helix shape, with the two strands wrapping around each other, as first elucidated by the British molecular biologist Francis Crick and the American biochemist James Watson in 1953.

As such, double-stranded DNA is shaped much like a twisted ladder, with the alternating ribose and phosphate groups forming each of the two vertical struts and the sequence of matching DNA bases forming the horizontal rungs.

DNA consists of two phosphate and sugar (deoxyribose) strands held together by **bases** linked by chemical bonds. This unit is repeated along the length of the DNA molecule.

The four bases can combine only in the order:
• adenine–thymine
• guanine–cytosine.
Note: In the model only A–T or T–A and C–G or G–C combinations exist. These combinations are referred to as **base pairing**.

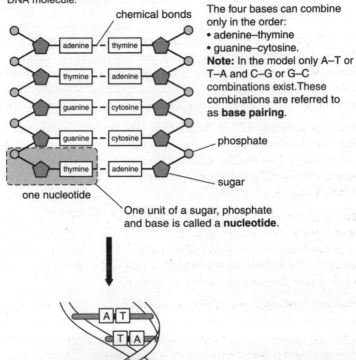

One unit of a sugar, phosphate and base is called a **nucleotide**.

The DNA is folded into a **double helix**.

Figure 6.1 DNA

DECIPHERING THE DNA CODE

So the question now is: how exactly does the sequence of nucleotide bases relate to the sequence of amino acids in a protein? Or, in other words, exactly how does this code work?

Well, first off, the long sequence of DNA bases is grouped into smaller collections known as genes. If DNA bases are letters, then genes are words: more specifically, they are effectively the names of different proteins.

To get at these genes, an enzyme splits the two DNA strands apart. Once a gene is exposed, another enzyme then creates a mirror image of that gene, but this mirror image is created from RNA (ribonucleic acid) rather than DNA.

RNA is very similar to DNA, except that its ribose section isn't missing an oxygen atom, it exists as a single strand and it contains

44

the nucleotide base uracil rather than thymine. In all other respects, however, the generated RNA strand acts as a direct mirror-image copy of the gene.

This RNA strand then travels away into the main body of the cell, where it is eventually captured by a cellular organelle known as a ribosome. This clamps round the RNA strand and then proceeds to travel along it reading the sequence of nucleotide bases.

Specifically, it reads these bases in groups of three, known as codons, because each group of three bases corresponds to a particular amino acid. So the sequence CAA corresponds to valine and the sequence UCG corresponds to serine. As it travels along the RNA strand reading each codon, the ribosome essentially brings out the corresponding amino acid from a nearby store and adds it to the growing protein (see Figure 6.2).

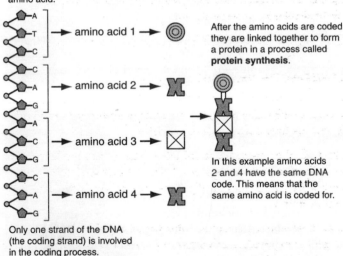

The bases are read in sequences of three. Each group of three bases is called a **codon**. Each codon codes for a particular amino acid.

amino acid 1 ➡

After the amino acids are coded they are linked together to form a protein in a process called **protein synthesis**.

amino acid 2 ➡

amino acid 3 ➡

amino acid 4 ➡

In this example amino acids 2 and 4 have the same DNA code. This means that the same amino acid is coded for.

Only one strand of the DNA (the coding strand) is involved in the coding process.

Figure 6.2 Making a protein

The Human Genome Project

So there you have it, in all its elegant glory: genes contain the instructions for producing proteins, while RNA physically carries these instructions to the cell's protein-constructing machinery. Although proteins may do all the work, it is genes that are calling the shots. It is genes that dictate who we are and what we look like; genes that encapsulate life's master plan. Understand genes and you'll understand life.

That was the thinking behind the Human Genome Project, which aimed to determine the sequence of all the 3 billion pairs of nucleotide bases making up human DNA, known as the human genome. A draft sequence of the human genome was released in 2000, with a final version published in 2003. But rather than revealing humanity's remaining genetic secrets, this completed sequence simply highlighted how much scientists still didn't understand.

The problem was that, based on the protein production process detailed in Figure 6.2, scientists had assumed that there was a one-to-one relationship between genes and proteins, with individual genes coding for individual proteins. As such, many scientists estimated that the human genome would contain around 100,000 genes. In actual fact, it contains just over 20,000.

Exons and introns

This was a major surprise, even though scientists did already know that a single gene could code for more than one protein. This is because a gene actually consists of coding regions of DNA, known as exons, and non-coding regions, known as introns. When first produced, the mirror-image RNA strand contains both exons and introns, but enzymes quickly remove the introns and then join the exons back together to form a single coding piece of RNA.

The trick is that the enzymes can join the exons together in various different orders, altering the sequence of the RNA strand and thus allowing numerous proteins to be produced from the same gene.

Using our letter and word analogy again, it's like producing several different words from the same group of letters.

Scientists knew this happened but thought it was a fairly rare occurrence. It now seems that such alternative splicing, as it is known, may occur in more than half of all human genes.

Switching genes on and off

On top of this, it appears that the genetic machinery is much more flexible than hitherto realized. Rather than being a static repository of information, a cell's DNA is continuously being chemically and structurally modified. This results in whole swathes of genes being switched on and off all the time, providing extremely fine control over protein production.

Scientists are also now discovering that unassuming RNA may be the real power behind the genetic throne. For one question that has always troubled scientists is why so much of the human genome appears to be useless. Only about 3 per cent of our genome codes for proteins; the other 97 per cent, termed junk DNA, seemed to serve no purpose.

Scientists assumed that this junk DNA had just built up over the millennia. But it now seems that some of this junk DNA is not junk at all. Instead, it codes for RNA strands that, rather than producing proteins, directly control when individual genes are turned on and off.

As far as genes are concerned, scientists are now discovering that it's not what you've got that counts, but how you use it.

Genes in sequence

Humans are just one of a large number of plants and animals that have had their genomes sequenced. Others include chimpanzees, dogs and maize. Although these organisms are all very different, their genes are made up of the same four nucleotide bases and can therefore be sequenced in exactly the same way.

(Contd)

Developed by the British chemist Fred Sanger in the 1970s, gene sequencing is an ingenious and elegant process. It involves creating numerous copies of a DNA strand, but stopping this copying process at a random point each time. Furthermore, the final nucleotide base in each copy is automatically tagged with a fluorescent compound that shines one of four different colours depending on the base.

Do this enough times and you'll be left with DNA fragments of every possible length, with each successive fragment one base longer than the previous one. Then all you need do is separate these fragments by their length, which can be done by essentially sieving them through a gel, and record the colour given off by the fluorescent tag at the end of each fragment. In this way, you can build up the sequence of the original strand (see Figure 6.3).

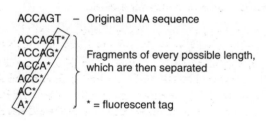

Figure 6.3 Gene sequencing

Further reading

Watson, James, *DNA: The secret of life* (London: Arrow Books, 2004).

7

From the bottom up

In this chapter you will learn:
- *how genomes differ between people*
- *how some species have more chromosomes than others*
- *the importance of Mendel's garden pea experiment*
- *the physical make-up of an average cell.*

After reading the last chapter, there is one question that should now be screaming at you. If the sole role of genes is to code for proteins, then how does that process produce us, in all our unique glory? How does it result in all our different bodily tissues and organs; how does it ensure that we are different from the other 7 billion people on the planet; how does it ensure that humans are different from the millions of other species?

The genome

In answering this question, the first point to make is that every species on Earth has a different set of genes, known as its genome. Furthermore, within each species that reproduces sexually, which includes most plants and animals, almost every individual member of that species has its own unique genome.

However, organisms that reproduce asexually, such as bacteria, produce offspring that are direct clones, possessing exactly the same genes as their lone parent (barring any genetic mutations). Species that reproduce sexually can produce offspring with identical genomes (in humans, identical twins possess exactly the same set of genes). But most organisms with two parents are genetically unique.

GENOME VARIATION

Now, genomes differ more between different species than between members of the same species. So, on average, the genomes of different humans differ by only around 0.5 per cent (the Human Genome Project sequenced an amalgamated genome derived from several different people). A large number of these differences take the form of variations in a single nucleotide base within a gene – one person may have guanine while another will have thymine. These variations are known as single nucleotide polymorphisms (SNPs).

The differences between the genomes of different species are greater, with the degree of difference generally reflecting the level of similarity between the species. Human genomes differ from chimpanzee genomes by just 1.2 per cent, but differ from mouse genomes by around 15 per cent.

Still, a 15 per cent difference is not that much considering how different men are from mice. What it indicates is that the vast majority of the genes in an individual organism's genome are concerned with keeping that individual alive, rather than differentiating it from other organisms. Perhaps unsurprisingly, mice appear to need many of the same proteins as humans. Such a small difference also supports the growing realization that what's important is not the specific genes we possess but how we use them.

The second point is that all the cells that make up an individual organism contain exactly the same set of genes. This is why we can talk about a person's genome, even though that genome is actually located in each of the hundred trillion cells that make up our bodies. Because the genome is the same in every cell, every person effectively has a single genome.

DIFFERING NUMBERS OF CHROMOSOMES

In the eukaryotic cells that form all multi-celled organisms, this genome, comprising a long sequence of paired DNA molecules, is found within a membrane-bound organelle known as a nucleus. Because the DNA sequence is very long (the human genome comprises 3 billion pairs of nucleotide bases, which if stretched out would extend for 2 metres), it is split up and wrapped tightly around proteins known as histones to form numerous chromosomes.

Different species have different numbers of chromosomes, reflecting the amount of DNA in the nuclei of their cells. In general, 'more complex' species have more chromosomes than 'simpler' species, but that is not always the case. A mouse has 20 pairs of chromosomes, while a human has 23 pairs, but a guinea pig has 32 pairs. More evidence that it's not what you've got, but how you use it.

PAIRS OF CHROMOSOMES

Note here the mention of pairs of chromosomes; each of the chromosomes in a eukaryotic cell possesses an almost identical twin. This is because the cells of organisms produced by sexual reproduction gain a chromosome from each parent.

Most of the genes on these chromosomes are identical or should be, as they code for proteins that are essential for life and are therefore the same in both parents. Indeed, having pairs of chromosomes turns out to be a pretty good defence against genetic defects. In many cases, if one copy of a gene works fine, then it doesn't matter if the other one is defective; it's only when both genes are defective that problems can arise.

This is the case with sickle cell anaemia – a genetic disorder that causes the red blood cells to become deformed, reducing their ability to carry oxygen. Sickle cell anaemia is caused by a defect in a single gene that codes for part of a protein complex known as haemoglobin; but the genes on both chromosomes need to be defective for the disorder to manifest itself fully. If only one gene is defective then the person usually remains healthy; indeed, there is even a benefit to having a single copy of this gene because it seems to confer resistance to malaria.

DOMINANT AND RECESSIVE ALLELES

Some of the genes for less essential traits can differ slightly between the pairs of chromosomes; such genes are known as alleles (with the various alleles often a result of SNPs). One allele tends to be dominant while the others are recessive, which means that the dominant allele will always be expressed over the recessive alleles (see Box).

Most human characteristics (or traits) are determined by interactions between several genes, but a few traits have been linked to a specific gene that can exist as two or more alleles. One example is whether you have free or attached ear lobes, with the free earlobe gene dominant and the attached earlobe gene recessive.

How the cell functions

But wait a minute; we still haven't explained how genes controlling protein production can lead to all the different organs, tissues and other biological traits that make up ourselves, including our appearance. To do that, we'll have to explore the cell a bit further.

The 'brain' of the eukaryotic cell is the gene-containing nucleus, but – in the same way that in addition to brains we need hearts, lungs, skin and various other organs to stay alive – the cell needs a whole host of other organelles to stay functioning. These organelles are housed outside the nucleus in a granular substance known as the cytoplasm, which makes up most of the volume of the cell.

These organelles include the endoplasmic reticulum, which forms a series of channels through which proteins and other biological molecules are transported around the cell. There are two types of endoplasmic reticulum: rough and smooth. Rough endoplasmic reticulum is covered with loads of protein-producing ribosomes, and thus produces proteins and then transports them around the cell. Smooth endoplasmic reticulum, on the other hand, produces fatty molecules known as lipids and transports those around the cell.

There is also the Golgi apparatus, which is involved in modifying, storing and transporting proteins and other biological molecules, especially if they are destined to be released from the cell. This involves passing the molecules through the cell membrane, which is the physical boundary of the cell.

The cell membrane consists of a double layer of lipid molecules embedded with proteins that act as tunnels in and out of the cell. Some cells, including bacteria and plant cells, also have an outer cell wall, providing enhanced strength and protection.

There are also various enzyme-containing sacks known as lysosomes that digest nutrients brought into the cell, producing compounds that can then be further broken down to produce energy (see below) or used as the building blocks for biological molecules. The cell is held together by the cytoskeleton, which is a scaffolding-like network of fibres.

Finally, there are important organelles called mitochondria, which use oxygen to break down simple sugars such as glucose, producing energy for the cell and generating carbon dioxide as a waste product. All the cells in our body use mitochondria to produce energy, which explains why we breathe air and exhale carbon dioxide.

OXYGEN AND CARBON DIOXIDE

Many plant cells also contain important organelles called chloroplasts, which use energy from the sun to convert carbon dioxide in the atmosphere into simple sugars like glucose, producing oxygen as a by-product. Hence, life on Earth forms a huge, mutually reinforcing cycle, in which animal cells rely on the sugars and oxygen produced by plants, and plant cells rely on the carbon dioxide produced by animals.

Different types of cells in the human body

So that is the make-up of an average cell; but then there is no such thing as an average cell. The human body consists of around 220 different types of cell, which vary widely in their size, shape and function.

Some, such as the cells in the salivary gland, produce lots of proteins and enzymes, which they secrete into their external environment, and so contain a rich system of rough endoplasmic reticulum. Some, such as the muscle cells that make up the heart, contain large numbers of mitochondria, because they need lots of energy to keep the heart pumping. Fat cells, meanwhile, mainly consist of huge sacks known as vesicles crammed full of fat molecules.

Some cells, such as red blood cells, have lost their nucleus. Others produce molecules that are not found in any other cell of the body, such as the light-responsive pigments produced by the cells that make up the retina of the eye.

But all these widely different cells contain exactly the same set of genes, meaning that theoretically a heart cell can turn into a retina cell. Their differences are explained by the fact that different genes are turned on, or expressed, in different cells, producing a unique mix of proteins that construct and operate a specific type of cell. Every cell contains the gene for producing light-responsive pigments, but it is only turned on in the cells of the retina.

There are even some cells that contain only a half set of chromosomes. It is at this point, however, that we need to pause, turn down the lights, put on some romantic music and light some scented candles, because we are about to enter the murky but exciting worlds of sex and reproduction.

▶ Fat cells, which are collectively known as adipose tissue, represent 15–20 per cent of the body weight of a normal man and 20–25 per cent of the body weight of a normal woman.

▶ The nervous system consists of a complex network of more than 100 million nerve cells, in which each nerve cell has, on average, 1,000 connections with other nerve cells.

▶ Skin cells are replaced every 15–30 days.

▶ The retina of the eye consists of 120 million rod cells, which are very sensitive to light but can't detect colour, and 6 million rod cells, which are less sensitive to light but can detect different colours. This explains why we can see in colour during the day, but mainly in black and white at night.

▶ Tooth enamel is the hardest component of the human body; it consists mainly of a form of calcium phosphate known as hydroxyapatite (96 per cent), as well as much smaller amounts of organic material (1 per cent) and water (3 per cent).

Further reading

Wolpert, Lewis, *How We Live and Why We Die: The secret life of cells* (London: Faber and Faber, 2010).

8

....

Getting it on

In this chapter you will learn:
- *how cells reproduce by mitosis and meiosis*
- *about different methods of fertilization*
- *why most organisms on Earth reproduce sexually.*

Before we get embroiled in sex, let's first deal with reproduction, because the two are by no means synonymous. Every living organism is able to reproduce – as we saw in Chapter 4, it is one of the defining features of life – but not every living organism has sex. To determine the difference between the two, we need to remain for a while at the level of the cell.

Cell reproduction and mitosis

In many cases, when a single cell wants to reproduce – whether one of the cells that makes up our body (although not all the cells in our body can reproduce) or a single-celled organism – it simply splits into two, creating a direct copy of itself. For eukaryotic cells, this process is known as mitosis. Bacteria divide by a similar process known as binary fission.

When a cell is not actively reproducing via mitosis, it is usually preparing itself for mitosis. This mainly involves the cell creating a copy of all the DNA in its nucleus, a process made fairly straightforward by the 'mirror-image' structure of DNA (see Chapter 6). In a human cell, this means a copy of each of the 46 chromosomes.

CHROMATIDS

Once this process is complete, each chromosome is accompanied by an exact copy of itself. The original chromosome and its copy are now termed chromatids and are physically joined together at a point at their centres.

As the cell starts to divide, each of the 46 chromatid twins are pulled apart and dragged towards opposite ends of the cell by long tubular structures known as spindles that traverse the cell. The cell then forms a membrane between its two halves and divides. One cell has become two, with each cell containing a full set of 46 chromosomes.

Meiosis

For the first 2 billion years of its existence, this was the only form of reproduction available to life on Earth. But around 1.5 billion years ago, a few eukaryotic cells came up with an alternative method. Instead of splitting into two, they experimented with splitting into four, in a process we now term meiosis (see Figure 8.1).

This is possible because eukaryotic cells contain pairs of chromosomes, one from each parent; so in human cells, the 46 chromosomes are actually 23 pairs of chromosomes (see Chapter 7).

As in mitosis, a cell planning to undergo meiosis first duplicates all the DNA in its nucleus, such that each chromosome is transformed into two identical chromatids. In a human cell, there are 23 pairs of chromosomes, with each chromosome now consisting of two identical chromatids, producing 92 chromatids in total ($23 \times 2 \times 2$).

At this point, however, something else happens, because each of the 23 pairs of chromosomes (with each chromosome comprising two identical chromatids) starts to exchange genes with each other. This process creates 92 totally new chromatids, each of which contains a unique mix of genes from each parent.

Then, the 23 pairs of chromosomes are separated, with one set of chromosomes pulled to each end of the cell, which then divides. Each of the daughter cells now reverts to standard mitosis, meaning that the two chromatids comprising each chromosome are pulled

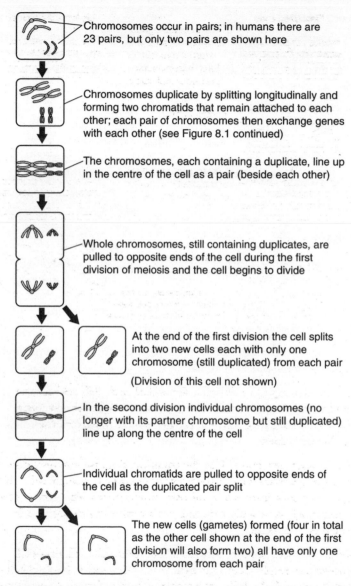

Chromosomes occur in pairs; in humans there are 23 pairs, but only two pairs are shown here

Chromosomes duplicate by splitting longitudinally and forming two chromatids that remain attached to each other; each pair of chromosomes then exchange genes with each other (see Figure 8.1 continued)

The chromosomes, each containing a duplicate, line up in the centre of the cell as a pair (beside each other)

Whole chromosomes, still containing duplicates, are pulled to opposite ends of the cell during the first division of meiosis and the cell begins to divide

At the end of the first division the cell splits into two new cells each with only one chromosome (still duplicated) from each pair

(Division of this cell not shown)

In the second division individual chromosomes (no longer with its partner chromosome but still duplicated) line up along the centre of the cell

Individual chromatids are pulled to opposite ends of the cell as the duplicated pair split

The new cells (gametes) formed (four in total as the other cell shown at the end of the first division will also form two) all have only one chromosome from each pair

Figure 8.1 Meiosis

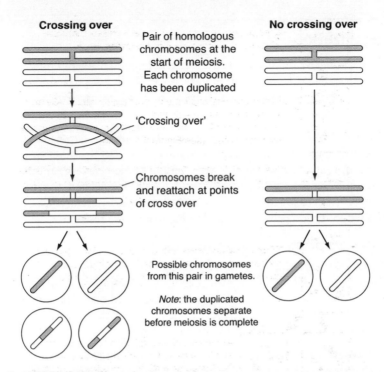

Crossing over

No crossing over

Pair of homologous chromosomes at the start of meiosis. Each chromosome has been duplicated

'Crossing over'

Chromosomes break and reattach at points of cross over

Possible chromosomes from this pair in gametes.

Note: the duplicated chromosomes separate before meiosis is complete

Figure 8.1 Meiosis (Continued)

apart and dragged to the opposite end of each cell, which then divides. In this way, one cell becomes four and, crucially, each of the four offspring contains only one copy of each of the 23 chromosomes.

Here's where sex comes into the equation, because you may now be asking yourself what is the point of meiosis. If a single cell can repeatedly split into two by mitosis, why bother with a convoluted process such as meiosis, especially as it results in just half-a-cell genetically speaking.

Well, the whole point of meiosis is that the resultant half-a-cell (known as a haploid cell) can now fuse with another haploid cell to form a cell with the full complement of paired chromosomes (known as a diploid cell). The advantage of this approach over mitosis is that it produces a genetically unique diploid cell. Rather than being a direct copy of a single parent, this diploid cell is a mixture of two parents, receiving half its genes from each.

Fertilization

So sex is merely the fusing of two different haploid cells. But how does that fusion, or fertilization, take place? Well that is the million dollar question and one to which evolution has come up with a myriad of different answers.

When the first eukaryotic cells had sex in their ancient oceans, they probably underwent meiosis after fusing rather than the other way around, as still happens today when certain single-celled organisms indulge in sexual reproduction. The advent of multi-celled organisms in the oceans changed things, however, because now meiosis was limited to certain cells and so had to happen before fusion.

THE FUSION OF MALE AND FEMALE CELLS

Furthermore, haploid cells differentiated into two types – one produced by males and one produced by females – and only male and female haploid cells, also known as gametes, could fuse. For animals, these gametes are sperm and eggs, while for plants they are pollen (male) and gametophytes or embryo sacs (female).

Initially, early marine creatures probably adopted a pretty basic sexual strategy, based around simply releasing their sperm and eggs into the water and hoping for the best. Indeed, some of today's marine creatures, such as sea urchins, still rely on this strategy.

The problem with this approach is its uncertainty; you never know whether your sperm or eggs have successfully merged with those of another member of your species. A slightly less chancy method is to make sure you only release your eggs and sperm at a propitious moment. For example, mussels and oysters, which feed by filtering nutrients from the water, only release sperm or eggs when they detect the converse gamete in the water.

Increased certainty of success can be gained if the male releases his sperm directly onto a collection of eggs already laid by a female, which is a strategy adopted by many fish and amphibians. Sometimes the male simply releases free sperm over the eggs, as is the case with fish, but other organisms such as crabs produce special packages of sperm known as spermatophores that the female rubs over the laid eggs.

INTERNAL FERTILIZATION

Alternatively, an organism can dispense with external fertilization entirely and shift to internal fertilization, where the fusing occurs inside the body of the organism, usually the female. Here success is almost guaranteed, which explains why it has been adopted by many marine creatures, including octopi and dolphins. Because animal gametes can only merge when suspended in some form of liquid, it is also the only form of fertilization open to organisms that don't live in or near large bodies of water.

Animal perverts

On the face of it, sex should come pretty far down the list of priorities for your average animal. Eating and avoiding being eaten should be much more important than getting your leg over, but that is not always the case. Some animals, such as male elephant seals, stop eating almost entirely during their mating season. Others, such as spiders and praying mantises, risk being eaten by their mate during, after and occasionally even just before sex (a male praying mantis can still have sex after losing its head to the female).

One of the ways evolution has pushed sex up the list of priorities is by making it hugely enjoyable. An offshoot of this is that many species like to indulge in some non-reproductive sexual shenanigans. For example, masturbation is regularly enjoyed by many primates, both male and female, with orang-utans rather partial to stimulating themselves with leaves and twigs.

But the most extreme sexual adventurers in the animal kingdom must be dolphins. Male bottle-nosed dolphins will have sex with practically anything that moves, including turtles, sharks and eels, while Amazon River dolphins have been observed penetrating each other's blow holes.

Many invertebrates have developed a form of internal fertilization that still utilizes spermatophores. For example, male scorpions deposit a complex spermatophore containing hooks and springs onto the ground. When a female crouches over it, the spermatophore explodes, shooting the sperm inside her.

Many spiders adopt a related strategy, in which they deposit a small blob of sperm-containing semen onto a small web. Then, using small appendages on either side of their mouth known as pedipalps, they carry this small web over to the female and manually insert the semen inside her.

Now this can be a dangerous activity because the male is usually much smaller than the female, who is prone to eating anything that comes too close to her. To avoid this fate, male spiders have developed a wide range of different strategies. A popular one is for the male to distract the female with a gift, often some form of food, while he inserts the sperm. Other organisms facing a similar danger are more imaginative: one species of fly brings the female a silk balloon to play with.

Perhaps the most fail-safe fertilization method, and the one that humans are most familiar with, is for the male to deposit sperm directly into the female. Usually, this involves the male inserting some kind of appendage, often a specialized penis, inside an opening in the female.

This is not always the case, though. Most male birds, apart from swans, ducks and ostriches, do not have penises at all; instead males and females copulate by briefly rubbing their genital openings together. The males of other organisms do have appendages for transferring sperm but don't bother inserting them into a special opening in the female. For example, small insects known as pirate bugs have a penis like a hypodermic needle and insert it straight through the female's body wall.

Some organisms seem to have developed bizarre combinations of these different fertilization methods. For example, the male of the paper nautilus, a relation of the octopus, literally fires his penis into the female, like a sort of on-heat-seeking missile.

Super-charging evolution

But why do organisms go to all this trouble to reproduce sexually when asexual reproduction is so much simpler, even for multi-celled animals. Some organisms, such as the garden snail, are hermaphrodites, able to produce both sperm and eggs, which means they are potentially able to fertilize their own eggs. But even when they have this option, many organisms only self-fertilize as a last resort; they much prefer to reproduce sexually.

The reason why most organisms on Earth reproduce sexually in one form or another is that sex super-charges evolution. Although sex can't produce new genes (only mutation can do that), it can continuously jumble those genes up to produce new combinations. These new combinations result in different patterns of genes being expressed and different traits coming to the fore, some being advantageous to the organism.

Thus sexual reproduction provides a way for a species to respond quickly to changes in the environment. This is especially important in terms of withstanding disease and parasites, as it is more difficult for a disease-causing pathogen to wipe out a population if all the members are genetically unique. This is because at least some members of the population should have a combination of genes that makes them naturally immune. In contrast, in genetically identical populations if one member succumbs to a disease then all the members will.

So there you have it, if we want to stay healthy then we need to keep having sex, at least as a species anyway.

Carl Djerassi, 1923–

Animals may enjoy a bit of non-reproductive sexual activity, but only humans have successfully managed to uncouple copulation from reproduction. In large part, this is thanks to the work of the US chemist Carl Djerassi, who is one of the founding fathers of the contraceptive pill.

Using some form of contraception to have sex while avoiding pregnancy is nothing new: condoms made from animal intestines were used from at least the Middle Ages. But Djerassi's development in 1951 of a synthetic mimic of the female sex hormone progesterone, which prevents ovulation (the release of eggs), ushered in a new age of sexual freedom, especially for women.

And that was just the first stage in Djerassi's career. As well as being a chemistry professor at Stanford University since 1959, he has also written a number of plays and novels on the subject of science and scientific research, a genre he terms science-in-fiction.

Further reading

Judson, Olivia, *Dr Tatiana's Sex Advice to All Creation: The definitive guide to the evolutionary biology of sex* (London: Vintage, 2003).

9

Man the defences

In this chapter you will learn:
- *why your body reacts so aggressively to invaders*
- *what damage viruses and bacteria do to our body's cells*
- *how invaders get through our body's defences*
- *how our immune system fights back.*

Think back to the last time you were struck down with a cold or a mild case of flu. It probably started with a just few sneezes and a cough, but before long you began to feel tired and hot, your head and muscles started to ache, and you developed a sore throat. So you went to bed and did little but sleep for a few days, after which you began to feel better. Around a week after your first symptoms, you felt right as rain.

Congratulations, you just survived infection by one of the many viruses that cause the common cold and flu, which include rhinoviruses and coronaviruses (common cold) and the eponymous influenza viruses. And the reason you managed to survive is all thanks to your immune system, which successfully tackled and defeated the viral invader.

Saying that, almost all the unpleasant symptoms of your infection were due to your immune system rather than to the invader. Unfortunately, that is the price you have to pay for remaining alive.

The main invaders

Now, in most cases, rhinoviruses, coronaviruses and influenza viruses don't cause your immune system too much trouble, which is why you just need a few days in bed to shift a cold or a mild case of flu. But your body is regularly beset by a whole range of different invaders, including other viruses, bacteria, fungi, protozoa and even parasitic worms, and your immune system has to deal with them all.

But why does your body always react so aggressively, irrespective of how troublesome these invaders are, especially as this reaction produces many of the unpleasant symptoms of infection? What would happen if our body adopted a more live-and-let-live attitude?

Well, the reason why these pathogens want to get inside us in the first place is because our body provides a nice, comfortable place to reproduce. Unfortunately, this reproduction usually ends up damaging our body's cells and tissues.

VIRUSES

Viruses, which are little more than collections of DNA or RNA housed within protein shells, can only reproduce inside cells, by hijacking the cells' own reproductive machinery. Once they've reproduced, they burst out of the host cells, killing them in the process. What's more, viruses can cause infected cells to fuse together and even turn into cancer cells. As well as cold and flu, viruses are responsible for measles, chickenpox and AIDS.

BACTERIA

Bacteria can reproduce on their own, but have a nasty habit of releasing a range of compounds that are toxic to our body's cells. These compounds, many of which are simply unwanted by-products of the bacteria's day-to-day activities, include cytotoxins, which can interfere with protein production, and lysins, which disrupt cell membranes. Bacteria are responsible for many forms of food poisoning, such as Salmonella and Listeria infections, as well as causing tuberculosis and cholera.

PROTOZOA

Protozoa, which are single-celled eukaryotic organisms, have a propensity for invading our tissues and cells, resulting in tissue damage and cell death. They are responsible for amoebic dysentery and malaria.

If left unchecked, these invaders would reproduce rapidly, eventually killing us. Indeed, if our immune system fails to defeat an invasion then that is exactly what tends to happen, unless modern drugs give it a helping hand. Hence, our immune system is ever vigilant for signs of invasion and quick to destroy any unidentified foreign organisms.

Entry through the mouth or nose

First, however, the invaders have to get inside our bodies and that is far from easy. Our first line of defence is our skin, which consists of numerous layers of flat, closely packed cells and so provides an impenetrable barrier to most invaders.

As such, invaders tend to enter our body through one of our orifices, often our mouth or nose. Either we inhale them, perhaps as a result of an already infected person coughing or sneezing, or they enter within food that we consume.

BLOOD CLOTTING

This is not a risk-free entry method, however, because the mucus that lines our nose and throat contains compounds able to kill many invaders, especially bacteria. These include lysozymes, which are enzymes that can dismantle bacterial cell walls, and transferrin, which prevents bacteria from utilizing certain nutrients required for growth. The acidic environment in the stomach helps to kill many of the invaders that come in with our food.

Invaders can also enter through any breaks in our skin barrier, such as cuts. To try to prevent this from happening, our blood quickly clots, forming a scab that acts as another physical barrier. As an added benefit, clotting also prevents us from losing too much blood.

Clotting occurs as a result of cell fragments in the blood known as platelets naturally congregating around any breaks in blood vessels. This congregation immediately acts as a plug to limit blood loss. Next, platelets promote the formation of a long, fibrous molecule known as fibrin, which forms a three-dimensional network of fibres over the break. This network, together with the platelets and other cells trapped within it, forms the scab.

The innate immune system

As we know from personal experience, however, it takes a few minutes for blood to stop flowing, even from a fairly small cut. During this time, invaders have an easy route into the body. Because of this potential danger, as soon as the body detects a break in its skin barrier, it mobilizes the first wave of our immune system, known as the innate immune system.

This mobilization is triggered by mast cells in the region of the broken skin, which release a range of chemicals as a result of damage to themselves or in response to the debris produced by damage to other cells. These chemicals all act to attract various immune system cells, including neutrophils and macrophages, to the site of the break.

Ordinarily, these immune system cells circulate in the blood, where they are collectively known as white blood cells (as opposed to the red blood cells that distribute oxygen around the body). One of the chemicals released by mast cells is histamine, which makes blood vessel walls more permeable. This allows large numbers of neutrophils and macrophages to pass out of the blood vessels and into the tissue surrounding the break, where they hunt for any invaders that may have slipped through.

PATTERN RECOGNITION RECEPTORS (PRRs)

They are able to do this because our bodies house a range of different compounds, collectively known as pattern recognition receptors (PRRs), that recognize and bind to characteristic molecules on the surface of bacteria and to viral DNA or RNA. Some of these PRRs exist independently in blood and tissue while others are found on the surface of cells, but on binding with an invader they act as beacons for neutrophils and macrophages.

On encountering a PRR-bound invader, the neutrophils and macrophages consume them. They do this by essentially absorbing them and then digesting them within special organelles called lysosomes (see Chapter 7). If you've ever seen the film *The Blob*, then you'll get the general idea. In addition, they secrete digestive enzymes into their external environment in order to break down and clear away any cellular debris.

They also stimulate the release of hormones that raise the body's temperature, which helps to suppress bacterial growth, and make us feel sleepy, in order to conserve our energy for fighting the infection.

The innate immune response is fast and effective but also fairly indiscriminate. Large numbers of neutrophils and macrophages race to the scene of any possible infection, releasing high concentrations of digestive enzymes and gobbling up any suspect looking cells. It's therefore not too surprising that a few healthy body cells tend to get caught in the crossfire. Indeed, the huge influx of immune system cells, together with the resultant build-up of fluid and dead cells, produces the characteristic inflammation that occurs around a cut or injury.

The adaptive immune system

But if the innate immune system is the heavy artillery, then the next wave – the adaptive immune system – is the tactical strike force.

The crack troops of the adaptive immune system are white blood cells known as lymphocytes, which arrive after the neutrophils and macrophages. Their tactical precision is down to the fact that every lymphocyte possesses a unique class of receptor on its surface that responds to just one specific molecule.

This receptor is generated by a clever genetic mechanism, in which the genes for constructing the receptor are randomly combined from a large collection of related genes. As a result, each lymphocyte possesses a different combination that produces a unique receptor. Biologists estimate that the lymphocytes in an average adult human are probably able to detect up to 1 billion different molecules.

Like neutrophils and macrophages, lymphocytes hunt for invaders. They do this by looking for molecules that bind to their unique surface receptors. Because our body quickly destroys any lymphocytes with receptors for molecules produced by its own cells, any molecule that binds with the receptors on a lymphocyte must come from an invader. Such foreign molecules, which are often proteins from bacterial cell walls or viral shells, are termed antigens.

When a specific lymphocyte detects an antigen, which can either be floating about in the body tissue or presented to it by other cells, it reproduces rapidly. Although all the copies possess the same receptor as the original lymphocyte, they mature to perform various different functions.

Some, known as B lymphocytes, start releasing numerous copies of their receptors, known as antibodies, which bind to the invaders. Just like PRRs, these antibodies mark the invader for consumption by neutrophils and macrophages. Others, known as cytotoxic T lymphocytes, start attacking both invaders and infected cells directly by releasing proteins that can puncture cell walls and membranes, as well as chemicals that induce cells to commit suicide.

Others become what are known as memory lymphocytes. After the original infection has been defeated, these memory lymphocytes continue circulating through the body, constantly on the look-out for a repeat attack by invaders sporting the same antigen.

Edward Jenner, 1749–1823

Memory lymphocytes are the reason why vaccines work. The idea is to inject the body with an antigen from a specific invader, such as a protein taken from a viral coat or the cell wall of a bacterium, which will stimulate an immune response but not cause an infection.

This immune response will include the production of numerous memory lymphocytes against the antigen. These will allow the immune system to respond quickly to any actual infection, defeating the invader before it can cause any problems. Vaccines are essentially a way to prime the immune system against specific diseases.

An English scientist called Edward Jenner pioneered the development of vaccines. He noticed that milkmaids who contracted cowpox did not develop the related disease smallpox, which is much more virulent and was a scourge across Europe at the time. So he injected pus from a cowpox blister into a young boy called James Phipps, who then proved immune to smallpox.

Through his development of vaccines, Jenner has been credited with saving more lives than any other person who ever lived.

SECONDARY LYMPHOID ORGANS

The same general immune response occurs when invaders enter our body via other entry points. In this case, however, it's more difficult for the body to realize there's a problem. With a cut, the body is immediately on the defensive, but that's not the case if the invader enters via the mouth. So the body has come up with a system whereby any suspected antigens are quickly taken to special points spread around the body, known as secondary lymphoid organs, that possess high concentrations of lymphocytes. These organs include the spleen, tonsils, appendix and lymph nodes.

Now we can start to piece together what happens when we are struck down with a cold or mild case of flu. The initial symptoms of high temperature, runny nose, sore throat and aching joints are all down to the quick, indiscriminate response of the innate immune system and the inflammation it causes. A few days later, the adaptive immune system kicks in and begins to rid the body of invaders, while the innate response dies down. As a result, we begin to feel better.

Furthermore, memory lymphocytes ensure that we never get exactly the same infection twice, by quickly recognizing and dealing with any invader they have met before. Fortunately for us, mercy is not a quality possessed by our immune system.

Not immune to failure

Our immune system is good but it's not infallible. For a start, people die all the time from infectious diseases, although this is more likely if their immune system isn't operating at full strength due to old age or poor diet.

In some cases, however, invaders have evolved special strategies to help them outwit the immune system. For example, certain bacteria, including those that cause tuberculosis and Legionnaires' disease, are able to survive absorption by neutrophils and macrophages. This is either because they possess a thick, enzyme-resistant outer coat, or capsule, or have ways to stop themselves from entering lysosomes.

Conversely, the immune system can become confused and decide that innocuous molecules are actually dangerous antigens. If the innocuous molecule is produced outside the body, such as pollen or food particles, the result is an allergy such as hay fever. If the innocuous molecule is produced by the body's own cells, the result is an autoimmune disease such as eczema or diabetes.

Allergies and autoimmune diseases are becoming more common in the developed world. One potential explanation is that our modern obsession with hygiene and cleanliness means that our immune systems are not being exposed to enough invaders. As a result, they are attacking the wrong targets.

Further reading

Crawford, Dorothy H., *Deadly Companions: How microbes shaped our history* (Oxford: OUP, 2009).

10

Attack of the nerves

In this chapter you will learn:
- *about different kinds of neuron and how they connect*
- *how neurons transmit action potentials to each other*
- *how we perceive the world around us.*

At a guess, reading probably comes fairly easily to you. Indeed, you may be happily reading this page while also having a cup of tea or a glass of wine, eating a biscuit and perhaps listening to music. This will all be fairly natural for you and appears to take little or no effort.

But consider all the work your brain and nervous system are actually doing at the moment. Your eyes are scanning the page, picking out the numerous contrasts between light and dark that form the letters; your hands are carefully reaching out to grab the glass, mug or biscuit and bring it to your lips; your nose and tongue are registering the complex mixture of chemicals that comprise the wine, tea or biscuit; and your ears are reacting to a continually changing stream of sound waves.

All these physical sensations are then being fed to the brain, which uses them to construct your perception of the outside world. It transforms the contrasts between light and dark into letters, and then builds those letters into comprehensible words and sentences. It transforms the chemicals detected by receptors in your tongue and nose into attractive aromas and flavours, and transforms the stream of sound waves into a pleasant melody. And it does all this simultaneously, continuously and without you really having to think about it. Quite some feat.

The neuron

Even more impressive, this feat is all down to the activity of a simple cell; or, to be more precise, to the activity of the 100 million nerve cells, or neurons, that make up our brain and nervous system. To be even more precise, it is actually the roughly 100 billion connections between these 100 million nerve cells that underlie all our rather impressive sensory and intellectual abilities, including the fact that we are conscious at all.

Nevertheless, your classic neuron is rather unprepossessing, looking like a kind of elongated tree or perhaps some bizarre alien creature (see Figure 10.1). It consists of a central cell body, which houses the nucleus and other conventional cellular apparatus. Extending out from the cell body are several protrusions known as dendrites, each of which can split into numerous branches. From the bottom of the cell body extends a single, much longer protrusion known as an axon, which forms branches only at its far end. Each of these branches culminates in a golf tee-shaped structure called an end bulb or foot.

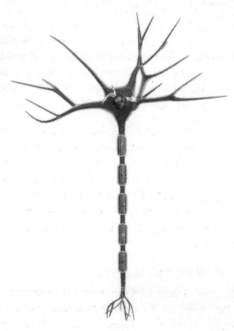

Figure 10.1 A neuron or nerve cell

Around this classic design, however, there is a great deal of variation. Human neurons range from the very small, such as many of the neurons found in the brain, to the very large, such as the single neurons that stretch around 100 cm from the bottom of the spinal cord down to the muscles of the foot.

Classic neurons, with one axon and numerous dendrites, are called multipolar and are the most common type. There are also bipolar neurons, with one axon and one dendrite and the cell body between them, and pseudounipolar neurons, with a single merged dendrite and axon and the cell body off to one side.

Furthermore, your classic neuron has an average of 1,000 connections with other nerve cells, but some neurons have many more. For instance, a type of neuron known as a Purkinje cell, which is found in a part of the brain called the cerebellum, has around 200,000 connections. The one common factor between all these different kinds of neuron is that each possesses at least one dendrite and one axon, even if they are sometimes merged.

CONNECTIONS BETWEEN NEURONS

This basic structure should give you a good idea of how different neurons connect with each other. Essentially, the bulbs found at the end of each neuron's axon connect with the dendrites on one or more other neurons. In most instances, however, there is no direct physical contact between the dendrites and axons, rather a small gap known as a synapse separates them.

So what do we actually mean when we say that two neurons connect, especially as they don't actually make contact? Well, the whole point of a neuron is that it carries a signal and it is this signal that is passed between connected neurons. What is more, a neuron carries an electrical signal, just like the wires and circuits found in electronic devices such as computers. But whereas in electronic devices the electrical signal is made up of electrons, in neurons it is made up of ions (see Chapter 2).

ANIONS AND CATIONS

Positively charged cations and negatively charged anions are found throughout the body, both inside and outside of cells. Around every neuron, however, there is an unequal balance of anions and cations, with more anions inside the neuron and more cations outside of it.

As a result, the inside of every neuron is negatively charged. Part of the reason for this is that neurons actively transport sodium cations out of the cell and prevent them returning by keeping special pores in their cell membranes closed.

When the neuron wants to generate a signal, known as an action potential, it suddenly opens these pores, causing the sodium cations to flood inside and transform the neuron from negatively charged to positively charged. This switch doesn't occur all over the neuron at the same time; rather it occurs in a specific section of the neuron. But the shift from negatively to positively charged in one section opens the pores in the next section and thus the action potential travels along the neuron, from the dendrites down to the axon.

After the action potential has passed, the pores close again and the neuron begins pumping the sodium cations back out, ready for the next action potential. This whole process is very quick, with the average neuron able to transmit around 200 action potentials per second.

NEUROTRANSMITTERS

When the action potential reaches the axon, it stimulates the end bulbs to release a special kind of chemical known as a neurotransmitter. Human nerve cells utilize over 50 different kinds of neurotransmitter, including small molecules such as dopamine and small peptides such as insulin.

These neurotransmitters diffuse across the synapse and stimulate receptors on the dendrite of a neighbouring neuron, producing one of two effects depending on the nature of the neurotransmitter and the receptor. Either the neurotransmitter excites the other neuron, promoting an action potential, or it inhibits it, stopping an action potential from occurring.

At any given time, a neuron is receiving signals from numerous other neurons, some of which are excitatory and some of which are inhibitory. Only when the excitatory signals outweigh the inhibitory signals does an action potential travel down the neuron to its axon.

Furthermore, neurons can form many different kinds of connections between each other. For instance, axon end bulbs don't just connect with dendrites, but can also connect with cell bodies, axons and other end bulbs. In this way, neurons can have a fine degree of control over each other's activity.

So the human brain and nervous system comprise an extremely complex network of interacting neurons, which scientists are still a long way from fully understanding.

SENSORY RECEPTORS

But if neurons are solely concerned with transmitting action potentials to each other, how do these action potentials begin? If you traced an action potential back to its start, where would that be? Well, you would find yourself at the sensory receptors that reveal the world to us. At the rods and cones in the eye that detect light (see Chapter 7); at the tiny hairs in the inner ear that detect sound waves; at the taste receptors in our tongue and the olfactory receptors in our nose; and at the various pain, temperature and pressure receptors that cover our skin.

All these receptors are linked to neurons and when they detect light or sound or a specific chemical they stimulate an action potential in that neuron. And via the complex network of neurons, that action potential eventually makes its way to the brain.

How vision works

Take vision. Each rod and cone is linked to a type of neuron known as a retinal ganglion cell. There are around 126 million rods and cones in the human eye, but only 1 million ganglion cells. As such, each ganglion cell receives signals from a set group of rods and cones.

Importantly, however, the rods and cones in each group are located in the same vicinity, which means that each ganglion cell integrates the responses from a very small patch of the retina, known as its receptive field. Furthermore, these receptive fields overlap and are also maximally responsive to changes in light intensity.

The axons of these retinal ganglion cells join together to form the optic nerve, which exits the back of each eye and makes its way into the brain, eventually arriving at a region known as the visual cortex, specifically an area termed V1. Here, the signals generated by the 1 million ganglion cells begin to be processed.

As we have already learnt, the receptive fields of ganglion cells are most responsive to changes in light intensity, which often correspond to edges, such as the edges between these letters and the white page. V1 of the visual cortex contains neurons that collectively respond to edges at all possible angles. Hence, in the first level of processing, the brain identifies all the edges present in the signal.

Other areas of the visual cortex respond to other aspects of the signal; for instance, V3 responds to depth, V4 responds to colour and V5 responds to motion. So the signal from the ganglion cells is passed sequentially to the numerous areas of the visual cortex, each of which responds to a different aspect.

Spotting your blind spot

In each eye, there is a hole in the retina where the optic nerve leaves the eye. Obviously, there are no rods or cones in this area of the retina, which is therefore known as the blind spot. Ordinarily, we don't notice the blind spot because it is in a different place in each eye, meaning that the visual field of one eye covers the blind spot of the other.

But you can find your blind spot in the following way. Stand with your head bent over a table and hold a pencil with a rubber on the end in your hand. Close one eye and hold the pencil horizontally just above the table and directly below your nose. While staring at the table, move the pencil in the direction of your open eye. After you have moved the pencil around 15 cm, the rubber on the end will vanish. That is your blind spot.

TRAPPED BEHIND OUR SENSES

In this way, the neurons in the brain transform the 1 million different action potentials into a coherent visual image. A similar process occurs with the signals coming in from the receptors in and on other areas of the body.

Although impressive, there is a slightly unnerving side to all this, because it means that the world we perceive around us is actually a construct of the brain. We are trapped behind our senses, unable to perceive the world directly and reliant on our brain to provide us with an accurate representation.

Determining exactly how accurate has exercized the finest philosophical minds for thousands of years. It is also a fundamental plot point in the 1999 science fiction film *The Matrix*, in which the hero discovers that his normal life is an illusion and that he is actually floating in a vat as a sort of human battery.

Learning from misfortune

Over the years, scientists have employed numerous methods to study the workings of the human brain. In the past, this has often involved directly stimulating different parts of the brain with electricity and noting the effects. Nowadays, scientists prefer to use non-invasive techniques such as positron emission tomography, which monitors blood flow to different parts of the brain as a measure of brain activity.

Another way has been to study the effect of localized forms of brain damage, as a result of accidents or strokes. This has helped to reveal that the brain processes different aspects of the same sensation, such as a visual image, in different areas and so damage to these different areas produces a different set of effects.

For instance, damage to one specific area of the visual cortex causes people to lose the ability to recognize objects, both real and drawn. Damage to another area causes people to lose the ability to detect movement, such that liquid poured from a beaker appears frozen in mid-air. Damage to yet another area causes people to lose the ability to guide their hands towards objects and pick them up.

Further reading

Gibb, Barry J., *The Rough Guide to the Brain* (London: Rough Guides, 2007).

Part three

Earth, wind and fire

11

Ground beneath our feet

In this chapter you will learn:
- *how the basic structure of the Earth has changed*
- *about plate tectonics and the movement of the continents*
- *about the magnetic field that surrounds the Earth*
- *how earthquakes are measured.*

To us puny humans, the geological Earth of rocks, mountains and continents seems pretty static, merely providing the backdrop to the constantly changing kaleidoscope of life. But viewed over a timescale of hundreds of millions of years, the geological Earth becomes a great deal more dynamic.

Continents career across the surface of the Earth like dodgems, periodically smashing into each other in giant pile-ups before flying off in the opposite direction. These giant collisions form ripples in the continents that become mountain ranges, which are then gradually eroded down to nothing at all by wind and rain. Wild swings of temperature transform the surface from parched wasteland to glacier-coated snowball; even the magnetic poles repeatedly switch positions. And this kind of breathtaking activity was taking place right from the very start of the Earth's existence.

When we left the Earth at the end of Chapter 3, or 4.5 billion years ago, it had only just reached its final mass, after agglomerating from the disk of dust and gas orbiting the sun. Towards the end, this agglomeration process was fairly violent, with the young Earth hit by a succession of rocky bodies of various sizes, including some the size of small planets. This violent bombardment generated a lot of heat, transforming the Earth into a huge molten fireball.

The basic structure of the Earth

One outcome of this was that much of the iron within the Earth separated from the surrounding silicates, because molten iron is denser than molten silicate, and collected at the centre of the Earth, forming the core. Meanwhile, the surface of the Earth was gradually cooling, turning the outer layer of molten silicates into a solid crust.

So almost as soon as it was born, the Earth adopted the basic structure that continues to this day (see Figure 11.1). At its centre is a solid iron sphere, with a diameter of 2,400 km and a temperature of around 5,500°C, known as the inner core. Surrounding this is a 2,300 km-thick layer of liquid iron, known as the outer core, with a temperature of 4,000–5,000°C.

The great pressures at the centre of the Earth keep the inner core in its solid state, despite the temperature being more than sufficient to melt iron; in actual fact, the iron exists in several crystalline forms. Also, iron may be the largest component (around 80 per cent), but the core probably also contains 5–10 per cent nickel (which travelled down with the iron), 7 per cent silicon, 4 per cent oxygen and 2 per cent sulphur.

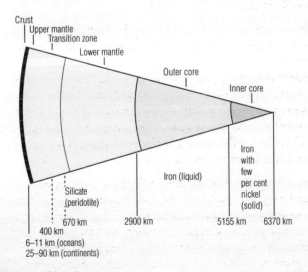

Figure 11.1 The structure of the Earth

Surrounding the core is a 2,900 km-thick layer of hot rock known as the mantle, where the temperature increases dramatically with depth, from around 500°C near the crust to around 3,700°C near the core. On top of this floats the crust, where we and everything else live, which currently ranges in thickness from 6 km to 90 km.

Originally, however, the crust was more uniform and generally thicker, ranging from 25 km to 50 km. It consisted solely of a type of rock known as basalt, produced by melting of the mantle.

Although the rocks making up the mantle are incredibly hot, the immense pressures within the Earth mean that (as with the inner core) they remain more-or-less solid, like a very thick gel. This pressure is caused by the weight of the overlying rock, meaning that it increases with depth.

Close to the surface of the Earth, however, the pressure can fall to a level where the rocks in the mantle are able to melt, producing magma. On the early Earth, when this magma cooled at the surface, it turned into basalt.

So the early Earth was quickly covered in a solid crust of basalt, but that meant that the heat travelling up from the core no longer had an outlet and began to build up underneath the crust. Eventually this build-up of heat became too much and it cracked the crust like an egg shell, allowing fresh magma to burst up through the cracks.

NEW MAGMA

This upwelling of magma forced the cracked segments of the crust apart. But, because the Earth wasn't getting any larger, the far edges of those widening segments started sliding under each other, returning to the mantle. And, once back in the furnace of the mantle, they started to melt.

This basalt crust was not the only thing to enter the mantle, however, because the presence of a solid crust meant that the water being delivered by comets had started to accumulate on the surface of the Earth. So a load of water entered the mantle along with the basalt, changing the composition of the magma being produced.

When this new magma subsequently made its way up onto the surface, either through the cracks or via proliferating volcanoes, it cooled to form rocks with a lower density than basalt, such as granite. Being less dense than basalt, this granite didn't sink as far into the underlying gel-like mantle; in the same way that a light stone doesn't sink as far into soft mud as a heavy rock. Because of this difference in buoyancy, the denser basalt became low-lying ocean floor and the lighter granite formed the higher-lying continents.

Plate tectonics

Over hundreds of millions of years, this process built up the continents that we inhabit today; it also set these continents in motion. Cracked segments of the crust are now known as plates, although these plates actually consist of the crust and the top level of the mantle, collectively known as the lithosphere. These plates continue to grow as a result of magma rising up from the mantle through the cracks, which have now become huge mountain-range-like ridges, most of which are at found the bottom of the oceans.

At the same time, the far edges of these plates continue to dive back down into the mantle, in a process known as subduction, with the denser basalt-rich ocean floor diving under the lighter continental crust. As a result, the entire plate moves, sliding over the hot mantle underneath (or, more specifically, over a layer of the mantle underneath the lithosphere called the asthenosphere). Known as plate tectonics, this process is like a conveyor belt, with the plate appearing from the mantle at one end and disappearing at the other, all driven by heat within the mantle.

DIFFERENT KINDS OF BOUNDARY

The Earth's surface is currently made up from seven major, and several minor, plates, forming a kind of irregular patchwork quilt (see Figure 11.2). These plates meet at three different kinds of boundary. The ridges where plates form are known as divergent boundaries, because two plates move off in opposite directions at each ridge. The places where two plates collide are known as convergent boundaries. At transform boundaries, two plates grind slowly past each other in opposite directions, as happens at the famous San Andreas fault in California.

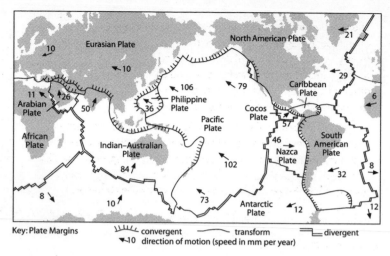

Key: Plate Margins
convergent   transform   divergent
←10 direction of motion (speed in mm per year)

Figure 11.2 Tectonic plates

Furthermore, plates don't always dive under each other when they collide, only when dense ocean floor meets lighter continental crust. If two continental crusts collide, then they simply smack straight into each other, with the force of the collision buckling the plate ends. This is currently happening in south Asia following its collision with the Indian sub-continent around 30 million years ago, resulting in the formation and continued growth of the Himalayas.

On human timescales, plate tectonics is dreadfully slow, with continents moving at the same rate at which your toenails grow. This is one of the reasons why for a long time many scientists refused to believe it was happening (see Box). On geological timescales, however, this rate of movement is sufficient to send the continents skating all over the surface of the Earth.

Alfred Wegener, 1880–1930

The idea that continents move and occasionally form giant supercontinents was first suggested by the German geophysicist Alfred Wegener in 1915. He was not the first person to notice that certain of the continents seemed to fit together like jigsaw pieces – for instance, South America and Africa – but he was the first to take this insight to its logical conclusion.

The reaction of his fellow geologists at the time was almost unanimously negative, especially in the US. Although Wegener's theory, termed continental drift, explained a number of troubling findings, including why similar rocks and animals could be found in different parts of the world, it foundered on the lack of a conceivable mechanism by which continents could move.

It took the discovery of mid-ocean ridges, detailed measurements of the distances between continents and the development of plate tectonics for the idea finally to become widely accepted in the 1950s and 1960s. By this time Wegener was long gone, having frozen to death returning from a remote scientific station in Greenland.

SUPERCONTINENTS

On at least two occasions (and probably more) during the past 4.5 billion years, the movement of plates has resulted in all the continents crashing into each other to form one enormous land mass, known as a supercontinent. The first supercontinent for which there is a reasonable amount of evidence formed around 1 billion years ago and has been termed Rodinia.

It lasted for around 200 million years, before breaking up due to the build-up of heat beneath it (as happened with the first basalt crust). Around 500 million years later, a second supercontinent formed, termed Pangea, before breaking up around 180 million years ago, eventually forming the distribution of continents we see today.

Snowball Earth

As the continents slide over the surface of the Earth, they have a major impact on our planet's climate, especially if they congregate away from the poles. If this happens, heavy rain tends to fall on the continents, eroding rocks and removing carbon dioxide from the atmosphere.

As carbon dioxide is a greenhouse gas (see Chapter 23), its removal acts to cool the Earth. This causes ice to form at the poles, which, being white, reflects heat from the sun back into space, cooling

(Contd)

the Earth even more. Usually, this ice covers up rock, slowing the erosion process and therefore the removal of carbon dioxide from the atmosphere. But without continents near the poles, there is no check on the cooling process, allowing ice to spread over the entire world.

There is ample rock-based evidence that the entire Earth was covered in ice on at least two occasions: around 750 million years ago and 600 million years ago. In each case, the Earth probably remained covered for around 10 million years, until the temperature started to rise again as a result of volcanoes pumping out carbon dioxide. The precise thickness and extent of this ice sheet is hotly debated, however, because there must have been some gaps for life to survive.

So supercontinents seem to form on a 550–700 million year cycle, which means we are on the cusp of a new one. Already, the first elements of the next supercontinent, which will probably come together in its final form in around 250 million years, are falling into place, with India crashing into Asia and Africa crashing into Europe. The Americas are still moving away from Europe, driven by the spreading caused by the mid-Atlantic ridge, and could eventually result in the Americas crashing into the far side of Asia.

THE MAGNETIC FIELD THAT SURROUNDS THE EARTH

But let's not forget the core, which despite being thousands of miles underground still has an important effect on events at the surface. For the movement of the liquid iron making up the outer core generates a magnetic field that surrounds the Earth. This field acts like a giant bar magnet, producing the north and south magnetic poles.

As well as giving us and countless magnetism-sensitive animals a way to navigate over the surface, this magnetic field provides a shield against the stream of charged particles constantly emitted by the sun, known as the solar wind. Indeed, without this shield, life probably wouldn't have been able to get a foothold on the Earth.

What is more, for reasons that scientists still do not yet fully understand, the polarity of the magnetic field repeatedly flips, with the north pole becoming the south pole and vice versa. So after the next flip a compass pointing to the magnetic north would actually be pointing towards the geographic south. Such flips happen, on average, every few hundred thousand years, although the gap between them is highly variable.

On geological timescales, therefore, the Earth is anything but static. Even on human timescales, some of the consequence of these slow geological processes can be highly dramatic.

Further reading

Fortey, Richard, *The Earth: An intimate history* (London: Harper Perennial, 2005).

12

Shake, rattle and roll

In this chapter you will learn:

- *where volcanoes and earthquakes are most common*
- *what causes earthquakes to happen and volcanoes to erupt*
- *why some volcanic eruptions are more explosive than others*
- *how earthquakes are measured.*

People in Britain are used to the quiet life, meteorologically and geologically speaking. For the most part, they don't have to put up with intense heat or cold, they don't suffer from extreme weather such as hurricanes and they don't live in fear of dangerous animals. Furthermore, the solid ground remains dependably still and they aren't required to dodge falling lava.

But even this green and pleasant land is not entirely immune from the Earth's more aggressive tendencies. Every 100 years, Britain experiences around 120 small earthquakes, with a maximum magnitude of around 5.4, usually only causing at most slight structural damage and minor injuries.

Earthquakes

CHILEAN EARTHQUAKES

Other regions of the world have it much, much worse (see Figure 12.1). On 27 February 2010, a magnitude 8.8 earthquake struck the Pacific coast of Chile, knocking out electricity, water and telephone services across much of the country and damaging over 1.5 million homes.

As the epicentre of the earthquake was out to sea, it also generated a tsunami, which travelled as far as Hawaii, California, Japan and New Zealand. By the time it reached these far off places, the tsunami had lost much of its power and the waves were fairly small. In contrast, much of the Chilean coast was battered by monster waves, which in some places were 1.8m higher than normal. At the beginning of March 2010, the death toll was over 800, with many more reported missing.

This was the fifth largest earthquake since 1900, but was just the latest in a long line of earthquakes to hit Chile. In 1960, Chile played host to the largest ever earthquake – magnitude 9.5 – and since 1973 it has experienced 13 earthquakes of magnitude 7.0 or greater. Furthermore, Chile is also littered with over 50 active volcanoes, meaning they have erupted within recorded history. Two of its volcanoes – Llaima and Chaitén – have been erupting on and off since 2008, causing nearby areas to be evacuated.

WHY CHILE?

Why should Chile be regularly beset by earthquakes and volcanic eruptions, while Britain escapes more or less scot-free? Well, it's all due to the fact that Chile lies on top of two colliding tectonic plates, while Britain lies right at the centre of a plate. If you plot the epicentres of recent earthquakes and the locations of active volcanoes, you'll find that they tend to congregate at the boundaries where plates meet or are being formed (see Figures 12.1 and 12.2 and compare them with Figure 11.2).

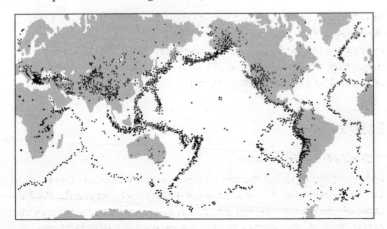

Figure 12.1 Location of major earthquakes

Chile actually lies on the so-called 'ring of fire', which borders the Pacific Ocean and is one of the most geologically active areas on Earth. On the other side of the ring lies Japan, which is even more geologically cursed than Chile, being situated close to the boundaries of three plates. As a result, Japan receives 10 per cent of the world's annual release of seismic energy (vibrations within the crust), experiencing 1,000 tremors a year. Like Chile, it is also littered with more than 50 active volcanoes.

Subduction

Chile's recent earthquake was a by-product of subduction at a convergent boundary. All along the Pacific coast of South America, the dense ocean floor of the Nazca plate is diving under the light continental rocks of the South American plate (see Figure 12.3).

In Chapter 10, we learned that this is an incredibly slow process, with the Nazca plate moving at the same speed as your growing toenails. That doesn't mean, however, that the Nazca plate smoothly slides under the South American plate at this leisurely pace, rather it proceeds in fits and starts.

As it descends, the Nazca plate keeps on sticking to the overlying South American plate. This not only results in a gradual build-up of stress as the rest of the Nazca plate bunches up behind, but it also

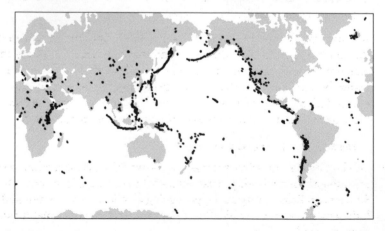

Figure 12.2 Location of major volcanoes

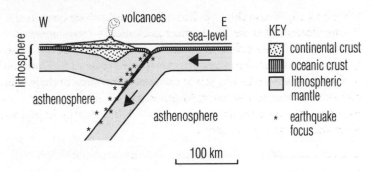

Figure 12.3 Subducting plate

pulls the edge of the South American plate downward. Eventually, the stress becomes too much and the Nazca plate breaks free, lurching down towards the mantle.

In the recent Chilean earthquake, the subducting edge of the Nazca plate would have lurched down by around 20 metres, which is some build-up of stress when you consider that the Nazca plate only moves around 50 mm a year. This lurch downwards wouldn't have happened along the entire length of the Nazca plate edge, but only along a certain section, which would still have extended for hundreds of kilometres.

As this section of the Nazca plate broke free, the South American plate would have sprung back, like a ruler twanged on the edge of a table, causing the Earth to shake violently for around 90 seconds, producing what we call an earthquake.

Because this all took place under the Pacific Ocean, the movement of the South American plate disturbed the overlying water, creating the tsunami. As with all tsunamis, there was little evidence of it in open water, because the disturbance travelled along the bottom of the ocean. Indeed, ships often sail over tsunamis completely unaware. Only once it comes close to shore does the tsunami reveal itself.

TRANSFORM BOUNDARIES

Subduction is responsible for most of the world's largest earthquakes, including the magnitude 9.3 earthquake that struck off the coast of Sumatra on Boxing Day 2004, producing an enormous tsunami and killing over 200,000 people. But it's not the only way that plates can generate earthquakes.

The well-known San Andreas fault in California also generates its fair share of earthquakes, but they are not caused by subduction. This is because the two plates that meet at the San Andreas fault form a transform boundary rather than a convergent boundary. They rub along next to each other, as the Pacific plate moves northwards and the North American plate moves southwards.

Nevertheless, the earthquakes generated at the San Andreas fault are still caused by sticking, because once again the plates don't move past each other smoothly but proceed in fits and starts. Opposing sections of the plates stick together, causing stress to build up until eventually the plates break free and lurch forward, producing an earthquake.

But the nature of the earthquake is different. Earthquakes produced by subduction shake the ground both vertically and horizontally, whereas earthquakes produced by transform boundaries just shake the ground horizontally. Because of this horizontal movement, earthquakes at transform boundaries that are under water don't produce tsunamis.

Measuring the magnitude

News reports of an earthquake will always specify its magnitude: the earthquake that struck Chile on 27 February 2010 was magnitude 8.8 and the earthquake that struck off the coast of Sumatra on 26 December 2004 was magnitude 9.3. Everyone understands that the magnitude number corresponds to the power of the earthquake: so the Sumatran earthquake was more powerful than the Chilean earthquake.

What is less well understood is that this magnitude scale, known as the Moment magnitude scale (which is a version of the better-known Richter scale), increases logarithmically rather than linearly. Each step on the scale represents an earthquake that is over 30 times more powerful (in terms of energy released) than the previous step. This means that a magnitude 9 earthquake is 1,000 times more powerful than a magnitude 7 earthquake.

An earthquake's magnitude is measured by a device known as a seismograph, which was first developed in the 1890s by a Tokyo-based British geologist called John Milne. Today, seismographs still follow Milne's basic design, consisting of three heavy weights attached to a light frame. In an earthquake, the frame moves more than the weights and this difference in movement is recorded; more powerful earthquakes produce larger differences. Each weight records movement in a different direction (two horizontal and one vertical).

Volcanoes

Transform boundaries are also not associated with volcanoes, unlike divergent and convergent boundaries (see Figure 12.2). The reason for this is that the physical conditions at divergent and convergent boundaries promote mantle melting, producing magma that is then able to rise to the surface, where it erupts as lava. At transform boundaries, however, the underlying mantle doesn't tend to melt and so volcanoes don't form.

The stereotypical image of a volcano may be a mountain-size cone with a crater at the top spraying fountains of lava all over the place, but volcanoes are very variable. Their size and shape depend on how frequently they erupt, how explosive their eruptions are and how much lava they produce.

LAVA AND PYROCLASTIC EJECTA

For as well as the characteristic lava, volcanoes also tend to produce rocky material of varying sizes, from fine ash to giant boulders weighing several tonnes, spewed over a wide area. Together, all the rocky material produced by a volcano during an eruption is known as pyroclastic ejecta.

Some volcanoes produce much more pyroclastic ejecta than lava. An example of this kind of volcano is Mount St Helens, located 200 km south of the US city of Seattle on the edge of the North American plate, which erupted spectacularly in May 1980. The force of this eruption blew away much of the volcano's side, out of which shot a lateral blast of hot gas and rocky debris that devastated 600 km² of surrounding terrain. This was followed by a vertical eruption of pyroclastic ejecta that reached a maximum height of 26 km.

In contrast, the Kilauea volcano in Hawaii mainly produces lava and has been erupting pretty much continuously for over 200 years, with the lava often merely seeping out rather than exploding. At Kilauea, scientists can safely obtain samples of lava by just picking them up with a spatula.

EXPLOSIVE ERUPTIONS

Whether a volcano erupts with a bang or a whimper depends on the constituency of the magma beneath it. For an eruption to be explosive, the magma needs to contain a lot of dissolved water and gases such as carbon dioxide. As the magma rises up from the mantle, it releases the dissolved gases and water (as steam) due to the decreasing pressure, in a process known as degassing, causing bubbles to form within the magma.

That's not a problem if the magma rises slowly to the surface, giving the bubbles sufficient time to escape. But if the bubbles aren't able to escape, then the magma will erupt explosively on reaching the surface. It's like shaking a can of fizzy drink. If you open it immediately, the outcome tends to be messy, but if you wait for the bubbles to disperse then there's no explosion.

MID-PLATE ERUPTIONS

Now, although volcanoes and earthquakes do tend to congregate around divergent and convergent boundaries, they aren't found exclusively at these locations. Even a country that is smack bang in the middle of a plate, like Britain, can experience earthquakes. And the Hawaiian Islands, which are little more than a collection of large volcanoes whose summits poke above the waves, are located right in the middle of the Pacific plate.

Scientists still have some trouble explaining these little anomalies. They think that volcanoes in the middle of plates are caused by hot, buoyant portions of the mantle, known as mantle plumes, rising from deep within the Earth. When a plume reaches the underside of the crust, it forms a hot spot that eventually burns through, allowing magma to escape.

Recent research has indicated, however, that not all mid-plate volcanoes form in this way; instead, some may be caused by magma escaping through small cracks and faults in the Earth's crust. The movement of similar small cracks and faults in the crust also probably explain mid-plate earthquakes, although this local movement may be triggered by events taking place at distant plate boundaries.

So nowhere is truly safe from the Earth's aggressive tendencies. As well as experiencing the occasional earthquake, Britain also plays host to a few volcanoes, although none have erupted for millions of years and they are all considered extinct. This is no guarantee, however: on average, one supposedly extinct volcano erupts every five years.

David Johnston, 1949–80

Most scientific disciplines are not particularly hazardous, but the study of volcanoes, known as volcanology, can be. When everyone else is fleeing from an erupting volcano, volcanologists are rushing towards it. And seeing as eruptions are inherently unpredictable, volcanologists always run the danger of being caught out, even after taking all sensible precautions.

This is what happened to David Johnston, a volcanologist with the US Geological Survey and a member of the team sent to monitor the growing activity of Mount St Helens in 1980. This activity included ground tremors and a growing bulge on the volcano's northern flank.

Johnston was stationed at a supposedly safe observation point, where he was monitoring the gases being released from the volcano. But when Mount St Helens erupted on 18 May 1980, he was swept away by the unexpected lateral blast of hot gas and rocky debris. His body was never found.

Johnston's field assistant, Harry Glicken, should have been manning the observation post, but he took the day off to attend an interview. Eleven years later, Glicken himself was killed when Mount Unzen in Japan erupted.

Further reading

Rothery, David, *Volcanoes, Earthquakes and Tsunamis: Teach Yourself* (London: Hodder Headline, 2010).

13

Earth rocks

In this chapter you will learn:
- *how peridotite transforms into other rocks*
- *how continents are formed*
- *what happens when rocks reach the surface of the Earth*
- *how to classify rocks.*

In films that involve time travel, there's almost always a bit where one of the characters travels back in time to revisit an earlier scene, allowing the viewer to watch that scene unfold from a different perspective. We are now about to do something similar, by going back to the mantle.

In Chapter 11, we learned that the mantle is a thick layer of hot rock. But it is not rock in the sense that most people know it. Scientists think that the majority of the mantle, which remember is 2,900 km thick, is made up of just one kind of rock, known as peridotite.

Now, you've probably never heard of peridotite; instead, when you think of rocks you probably think of such rocks as granite, slate and sandstone. Peridotite is the ancient ancestor of all these better-known rocks, transforming into them over the course of millions of years. But how does it do that?

Silicate groups

To answer this question, we must define what we mean by rocks. A rock is a collection of various naturally occurring crystalline structures known as minerals. Peridotite, for example, comprises a mixture of the minerals olivine and pyroxene.

The central component of both these minerals is a combination of silicon and oxygen called silica (SiO_2), arranged to form a building block known as the silicate group (SiO_4). This explains why the vast majority of the Earth outside the core, including 90 per cent of the crust, is made up of so-called silicate rocks. And this is just as it should be, seeing as silicate grains comprised a large proportion of the disk of dust and gas that gave birth to the Earth (see Chapter 3).

OLIVINE AND PYROXENE

In both olivine and pyroxene, silicate groups are joined by various metals: iron and magnesium are present in olivine, while iron, magnesium and calcium are present in pyroxene. Despite these similarities, however, olivine and pyroxene have very different structures.

In olivine, silicate groups are present as independent entities. This is because, individually, silicate groups exist as negatively charged anions, meaning they repel each other and never actually come into contact. They are held together by positively charged magnesium and iron cations, which insinuate themselves between the silicate anions to form the regular, crystal structure of olivine.

By contrast, in pyroxene the silicate groups are linked together in long chains, with each individual group sharing an oxygen atom with its two nearest neighbours. Iron, magnesium and calcium atoms then insinuate themselves between these chains. This causes the chains to fold up and bind with each other, like some kind of geometric office toy, forming the regular, crystal structure of pyroxene.

All that glitters

Minerals are not just the basis for ugly old rocks. Being crystalline, many of the minerals formed at the high pressures and temperatures found under the Earth are highly attractive, being prized as precious or semi-precious stones.

For example, silicon and oxygen don't always combine with metal ions to produce rocks. As silica, they can also keep to themselves, forming the basis for perhaps the best-known natural crystalline substance – quartz. Although quartz in itself is not terribly valuable, the presence of impurities such as iron can turn it an attractive shade of violet, in which case it becomes amethyst.

(Contd)

Rocks can also house useful deposits of metals, in which case they are known as ores. The size of these deposits varies widely for different metals, as does the economics of extracting them. Iron, which is cheap and plentiful, is not worth extracting from ores that contain less than 50 per cent iron. For aluminium, the figure is 30 per cent; for lead, 5 per cent; for copper, 1 per cent; and for silver, 0.01 per cent. For gold and platinum, the scale changes to parts per million (1 gram of gold for every 1 metric tonne of rock).

Variation within rocks

In peridotite, the crystals of olivine and pyroxene come together to form a strong, interlocked network. But in fact, all rocks, including peridotite, are highly variable, meaning that even the same rocks are not identical.

For a start, there is a flexibility in the chemical make-up of minerals that isn't found in other substances. An amino acid such as glycine will always contain the same number of carbon, oxygen, hydrogen and nitrogen atoms in the same configuration.

In olivine, however, because it doesn't matter whether the silicate anions are held together by iron cations or magnesium cations, the ratio of magnesium to iron is never fixed. Some olivine will contain more magnesium than iron and vice versa. So whereas the chemical formula of glycine is NH_2CH_2COOH, the chemical formula of olivine is written as $(Mg,Fe)_2SiO_4$, because the iron and magnesium are interchangeable. Saying that, however, due to natural differences in abundance, the olivine in the mantle usually contains more magnesium than iron.

On top of this, the proportion of olivine and pyroxene in peridotite can also vary, as can the size of the individual mineral crystals. This means that although the vast majority of the mantle consists of peridotite, the precise nature of that peridotite can differ quite a bit. This is fortunate, as it helps to explain how peridotite can transform into all the many different types of silicate rock that make up the vast majority of the crust.

PARTIAL MELTING OF THE MANTLE

As we saw in Chapter 11, the hot rock of the mantle, which we now know is mainly peridotite, is kept more or less solid by the immense pressures within the Earth, which increase with greater depth. So, at shallower depths, such as where the mantle meets the crust, the pressure isn't so great and the peridotite can begin to melt.

Because peridotite is made up of a mixture of two different minerals with varying chemical compositions, this melting doesn't happen all at once, as with ice. Instead, different portions of the peridotite melt at different temperatures and pressures, depending on their chemical composition. This is known as partial melting.

One of the outcomes of this is that the magma produced by partial melting of the mantle has a slightly different chemical composition from the original peridotite. In particular, it results in an increased silica content: peridotite contains around 45 per cent silica, whereas the magma generated from it by partial melting contains around 49 per cent silica.

Basalt and granite

On rising to the surface at ridges, this magma cools to produce rocks collectively known as basalt, which formed the basis of the Earth's early crust and now give rise to ocean floors. Because of the change in chemical composition caused by partial melting, basalt doesn't just consist of olivine and pyroxene, but also includes other minerals such as feldspar.

Eventually, this basalt returns to the mantle via subduction, where it partially melts again, producing magma with an even higher silica content (52–66 per cent). When this magma rises to the surface, it cools to produce rocks collectively known as andesites, which are less dense than basalt and consist of a different collection of minerals.

Because they're less dense, these rocks ride higher in the mantle, forming continental crust. Partial melting can also produce rocks with even higher silicate contents (above 66 per cent), which are collectively known as granite and also form continental crust.

Basalt, andesites and granite are all examples of igneous rocks, because they form from cooling magma. There are two other basic rock types – metamorphic and sedimentary – both of which are ultimately derived from these igneous rocks.

Metamorphic rocks

Metamorphic rocks are produced when existing rocks are exposed to extended periods of high pressure or high temperature. This can occur as a result of magma rising directly through faults and cracks in the crust, in which case existing rocks are exposed to heat from the magma. It can also occur when rocks at the surface are buried by subsequent deposits of lava or sediment or when they're dragged to lower depths during subduction, increasing the pressure on them.

Although not sufficient to induce partial melting, these temperatures and pressures are able to change the nature of the minerals within the rock. Such recrystallization without melting is known as metamorphism and can produce a range of new types of rock, including such well-known examples as slate and marble.

Still, as far as the rocks are concerned, it's only when they reach the surface that things get hazardous. The minerals that make up rocks are only stable at the temperatures and pressures at which they first crystallize. Below these temperatures and pressures, such as at the surface of the Earth, they are unstable and start to chemically degrade.

Water can help this process along, especially if it contains dissolved carbon dioxide. This makes the water slightly acidic, allowing it to dissolve the rock. This process tends to transform the solid rock into clay minerals such as kaolinite.

Added to this chemical degradation are the damaging physical effects of weathering. The repeated freezing and thawing of water can crack rocks and knock flakes off them, because water expands when it turns to ice. Cracks and flakes also result from the rock expanding during the heat of the day and then contracting at night. Even living organisms have a go: plants knock off bits of rock with their roots while some microbes feast on rocks.

Sedimentary rocks

The end result is that all rocks are gradually eroded away, transformed into countless tiny particles that are either washed away by rivers or blown away by the wind. At some point, the particles, which are usually either sand or clay minerals, will settle. If transported by rivers, they will form a layer of sediment on the bottom of the river, often at the point where the river meets the sea; if transported by wind, they tend to collect as sand dunes.

Over millions of years, these layers of sediment build up, squashing and heating the layers underneath. This instigates various chemical and physical changes in the layers, most importantly the forcing out of any water, which eventually transform the soft sediment into hard rock. Examples of these sedimentary rocks include the self-explanatory sandstone and claystone.

Occasionally, the remains of living organisms become incorporated in these sedimentary layers. If those organisms possess shells made of calcium carbonate, as do many species of microscopic plankton, then limestone is the result, making it the only type of rock not ultimately derived from the mantle. If the remains of plants and algae become incorporated in the layers, being buried before they have a chance to decompose, then over millions of years the heat and pressure transform them into deposits of oil, gas and coal.

The rock cycle

So the Earth's rocks are engaged in a constant process of recycling. Magma emerging from the mantle cools to form igneous rocks, which eventually become sedimentary rocks or metamorphic rocks, both of which can then repeatedly transform into each other (turning shells into limestone along the way). Eventually, some of these rocks may make their way back to the mantle via subduction, where the whole process begins again.

This is known as the rock cycle, but it could also be called a massive case of déjà vu.

What rock?

So you're walking along and you find a stone or a piece of rock; how can you tell what kind of rock it is? Well, first off, you should look at its texture, which can help cut down the possibilities.

Igneous rocks tend to be composed of interlocking mineral crystals with random orientations. In metamorphic rocks, exposure to heat and pressure often cause the minerals to re-orient themselves into layers, meaning the rock tends to facture along parallel cleavage lines. In contrast, most sedimentary rocks are composed of non-interlocking grains rather than interlocking crystals.

All these rocks can then be further grouped according to the size of the mineral crystals or grains. Igneous and metamorphic rocks can be classified as coarse-grained (average crystal size greater than 2 mm), medium-grained (0.25–2 mm) or fine-grained (less than 0.25 mm). Sedimentary rocks can be classified as boulders, cobbles, gravel, sand, silt or clay, depending on the grain size.

Nevertheless, a formal classification usually requires studying the component mineral crystals or grains with a microscope, allowing them to be identified based on their shape and colour. If all else fails, scientists turn to specialist analytical techniques to determine the specific chemical composition of the rock.

Further reading

Rothery, David, *Understand Geology: Teach Yourself* (London: Hodder Headline, 2010).

14

Wet and windy

In this chapter you will learn:
- *how the ocean transports heat around the world*
- *how winds are produced*
- *how the Coriolis force affects the winds and the currents*
- *how the ocean circulation system also circulates rubbish.*

It may be vast, comprising 320 million cubic miles of water and covering 70 per cent of the surface of the Earth, but what is the ocean for? Well, it obviously provides us with a great deal, including food, fun, transport and even artistic inspiration, but that's not what we're talking about. If the ocean can be said to have a purpose, then its purpose is to move heat around; in particular, to help move heat from the equator to the poles.

Without this movement of heat, many forms of life would be restricted to a thin band running around the middle of the Earth. Beyond this, conditions would be too cold; indeed, without the circulation of heat by the ocean, much of the Earth would probably be covered in ice.

Take London, which is as far from the equator as Calgary in Canada, where temperatures regularly fall below –10°C in the depths of winter. In contrast, average winter temperatures in London usually stay above freezing.

England's comparatively mild temperature given its position is all down to the Gulf Stream and the North Atlantic Current (NAC), ocean currents that between them bring warm water over from the Caribbean on the other side of the Atlantic. Without them, England, together with much of Western Europe, would look and feel very different.

Convection currents

The ocean is able to transport heat around the world because of convection. When water heats up it expands and becomes less dense, rising above cooler, denser water. This process sets in motion convection currents, which can be seen on a small scale when heating a glass beaker full of water. As it heats, water at the bottom of the beaker will rise to the top, displacing cooler water, which descends to the bottom to be heated. In this way, heat is circulated throughout the entire beaker.

A similar process operates in the ocean, where water is heated at the equator and cooled at the poles. In the ocean, however, the density of the water is also affected by how salty it is (or its salinity); for seawater actually differs quite a bit in salinity, depending on factors such as heat and water flow. On average, seawater contains 35 g of salt per 1,000 g of water, but this figure is lower in the Baltic Sea and Arctic Ocean, where it's cold, and higher in the Mediterranean Sea and Red Sea, where the water is confined. So the densest water is cold and salty and the least dense is warm and fresh.

THERMOHALINE CIRCULATION

In the ocean, convection is also driven by the cold rather than the heat, in a process known as the thermohaline circulation. Let's look at the northern hemisphere first. The water brought over by the Gulf Stream and the NAC is not just warm but also fairly salty and isn't just delivered to the coasts of western Europe. In the North Atlantic, the NAC splits, with some of the water going to western Europe and some travelling up to the Arctic Ocean around Iceland and Greenland.

Here, the freezing wind coursing off the arctic ice cap saps the water of its heat, transforming salty, warm water into dense, salty, cold water, which sinks to the bottom of the ocean. Imagine a vast undersea waterfall, cascading off the coast of Greenland. This constant sinking of water drives a deep-water current that extends all the way across the Earth to the southern hemisphere.

As it travels southwards, the water gradually heats up and loses its high concentration of salt by diffusion (the propensity for particles to move from a high concentration to a low concentration). And as it becomes warmer and fresher, it also becomes less dense and begins rising very slowly back to the surface. On finally reaching the surface, it puts its fate into the hands of a different kind of current.

We now need to turn our gaze upwards, from the ocean to the atmosphere. In the same way that water expands and rises when heated, so does air. The sun beating down at the equator heats the air, causing it to rise. At its summit, this tower of air splits into two, flowing towards each pole. As this flow of air cools, it drops to the Earth and splits again, travelling as a surface flow back to the equator or onward to the pole. Eventually, the poleward surface flow meets cold air coming from the pole, causing it to rise back up again and then split at high altitude, to flow either back toward the equator or towards the pole.

Circulation cells

The upshot of all this is that both the northern and southern hemispheres are embraced by three tubular air flows, known as circulation cells, extending from the equator to the poles. In each cell, the air moves in a broadly circular trajectory, but in opposite directions from its neighbours. In the cells near the equator and the poles, the air moves away from the equator at altitude (and towards the poles) and towards the equator at the surface. In each of the middle cells, however, the air moves towards the equator at altitude and away from the equator at the surface. These cells are like closely meshed atmospheric cogs, with the movement of one generating opposite movement in its neighbours.

Like the ocean, these cells transport heat from the equator to the poles, although not quite as effectively (the top 2.5 m of the ocean holds as much heat as the entire atmosphere). The surface air flows generated by these cells are also better known as wind.

The direction of prevailing winds

From this explanation, you would think that these prevailing winds should blow directly north or south, depending where you are on the surface. But that's not the case. Instead, in the northern hemisphere, the prevailing winds tend to blow from the northeast in the tropics and near the pole and from the southwest at points in-between, known as mid-latitudes. In the southern hemisphere, the situation is reversed, with the prevailing winds blowing from the southeast in the tropics and near the pole and from the northwest at mid-latitudes.

THE CORIOLIS FORCE

The reason for this is that the Earth is rotating, with the equator rotating fastest and the poles rotating slowest. So, as the winds flow north or south, they end up circling the Earth faster than the ground beneath, causing them to blow at an angle. It's like a child in the middle of a roundabout spinning clockwise who throws a ball to a child at the edge. To someone standing a little way from the roundabout, the ball will travel in a straight line; but to the child at the edge, the ball will appear to slide off to the left. This is known as the Coriolis force.

Now, wind doesn't just blow hats off and keep kites flying, it also moves surface water about, with the prevailing winds generated by circulation cells setting in motion permanent currents on the surface of the ocean. Unlike the deep currents of the thermohaline circulation, which resemble rivers in the abyss, these currents are broadly circular. Again, this is because of the Coriolis force, which acts on both the prevailing winds and the resultant surface currents.

Don't believe *The Simpsons*

There's an episode of the *The Simpsons* where Lisa tells Bart that water goes down a toilet anticlockwise in the northern hemisphere and clockwise in the southern hemisphere as a result of the Coriolis force. 'Water doesn't obey your rules,' counters Bart, before phoning a random boy in Australia and getting him to flush various toilets. As well as sparking a diplomatic incident, Bart also discovers that Lisa is correct.

Except that she isn't. That water flows down toilets or sinks in opposite directions in the northern and southern hemispheres has become a bit of an urban myth and like most urban myths it's incorrect. As we saw in the main chapter, the Coriolis force does influence the movement of water, but only noticeably on large scales, beyond around 1 km. In a toilet bowl or a sink, the Coriolis force is easily overwhelmed by small-scale factors affecting water movement, such as the shape of the bowl and how the water enters.

Circular currents in the ocean

The end result is that all over the ocean the surface water is travelling in huge circular currents known as gyres. For example, there are subtropical gyres that extend right across the middle of the Atlantic and Pacific oceans. The presence of land can interfere with these wind-driven gyres, setting in motion different current patterns. This happens at the South Pole, where a strong surface current known as the Antarctic Circumpolar Current continually circles around Antarctica.

Water pushed down from the Arctic Ocean can surface at any point along the way, depending on conditions. For instance, the Mediterranean Sea is continually sending out spinning disks of salty water that can pick up the cold water travelling down from the Arctic and carry it over to the other side of the Atlantic. If the water has an uneventful journey, however, it will travel all the way to the Antarctic before surfacing.

Here, it will either get caught up in the Antarctic Circumpolar Current and be spun round Antarctica a few times, before peeling off into the Pacific Ocean or back into the Atlantic. Or it will be cooled by frozen air coming off Antarctica and sink to the bottom of the ocean again, before being pushed towards the Atlantic, Pacific or Indian oceans, where it will gradually rise to be caught up in the various gyres found in these oceans.

Eventually, the water will make its way over to the Caribbean, where it will then be dragged back along the Gulf Stream and the NAC to the frigid waters of Greenland and Iceland to begin its journey again. In total, this circumnavigation of the Earth will probably have taken over 1,000 years.

Cold, dense water sinks to the bottom of the ocean at just two places: in the polar waters of the North Atlantic and the Weddell Sea, near Antarctica. Only here, does water become cold and dense enough to sink all the way to the bottom of the ocean, dragging warmer water away from the tropics as it does so. This simple movement of warm and cold water drives the entire, complex ocean circulation system, aided and abetted by the surface currents generated by the prevailing winds.

Only recently, by taking advantage of satellite imaging and robotic buoys that sink to the necessary depths to follow deep currents, have scientists begun to understand the full complexity of the ocean circulation system. This includes the realization that movement takes place at all scales. For example, the ocean also forms thousands of eddies – swirling water circulation systems that transport heat and salt over distances of 50–200 km – which usually only last for a few years.

POLLUTION IN THE OCEAN

Scientists have also mapped out the ocean circulation system by tracking the water-borne distribution of long-lasting pollutants such as the infamous, ozone-destroying CFCs (chlorofluorocarbons). A more obvious distribution of pollution can be found in the middle of the Pacific, where the North Pacific Gyre picks up much of the plastic rubbish thrown into the Pacific and dumps it into the relatively calm waters at its centre. This process is covering an area twice the size of Texas with increasing amounts of debris.

The ocean may be a source of food, fun, transport and artistic inspiration, as well as being the primary distributor of heat around the world, but increasingly we are also turning it into one, huge rubbish dump.

Time and tide

Tides are one of the defining features of the oceans. Twice a day, all around the world, the sea will progress a short way onto land before receding again, producing high and low tides. This is all down to the interaction between the Earth and the moon, and to a lesser extent the sun.

Tides are generated both by the gravitational force between the Earth and the moon and by the centrifugal force (which is the force that tries to eject you from a spinning roundabout) generated as the moon orbits the Earth. The gravitational force between two orbiting bodies lessens with distance, while the centrifugal force increases the further you are away from the common centre of rotation for the two bodies.

As the Earth spins, the gravitational pull of the moon is always strongest on the side of the Earth facing it, raising the ocean up on this side and generating a high tide. At the same time, on the opposite side of the Earth facing away from the moon, the centrifugal force is greatest, again pulling the oceans up and generating a high tide. At right angles to the moon, the two forces cancel each other out, producing low tides.

Occasionally, the sun also lines up with the moon, exaggerating the low and high tides to produce so-called spring tides.

Further reading

Kunzig, Robert, *Mapping the Deep: The Extraordinary Story of Ocean Science* (London: Sort of Books, 2000).

15

Stormy weather

In this chapter you will learn:
- *all about high and low pressure*
- *how clouds form and how they produce rain and snow*
- *the reason why snowflakes have different shapes*
- *the mysteries of thunderbolts and lightning, hurricanes and tornadoes.*

The interaction between the ocean and the atmosphere is not all one way. As well as prevailing winds generating surface ocean currents (see Chapter 14), the surface ocean plays a major role in our weather. The most obvious manifestation of this process is clouds.

Clouds and weather

Clouds are collections of water droplets and most of these droplets (around 80 per cent) come from the ocean (the rest come from lakes and other bodies of water). Sunlight heating the ocean causes water at the surface to evaporate, forming water vapour. As this water vapour rises into the air, it cools and condenses onto the multitudinous particles of dust, smoke and salt that fill the air, creating water droplets.

This process takes place all over the ocean, but it is intensified around the equator (where the surface waters are hottest) and in the vicinity of 'lows', which are regions of low pressure. For the atmosphere is not spread evenly over the whole Earth, rather it bunches up in some regions, forming regions of high pressure, and is more diffuse in others, forming regions of low pressure. These highs and lows are driven around the Earth by jet streams, narrow, globe-circling wind flows that operate in the upper atmosphere.

LOW PRESSURE SYSTEMS

Both highs and lows generate winds, but in opposite directions. Low pressure systems suck air in and up, while high pressure systems blow air down and out. Furthermore, the Coriolis force caused by the Earth's rotation gives the winds a bit of a sideways kick. In the northern hemisphere, winds flowing out of a high pressure system spin clockwise, while winds flowing into a low pressure system spin anti-clockwise (the situation is reversed in the southern hemisphere).

HIGH PRESSURE SYSTEMS

So when a low is over the ocean, it actively sucks up the water vapour being generated at the surface, leading to the formation of clouds. In contrast, highs are more associated with clear skies, because water vapour is blown away by the force of the downdraft. As such, highs often produce periods of either very warm or very cold weather, both on land and at sea, depending on the amount of sunlight falling on the ground and the temperature of the air brought down from above.

You say El Niño, I say La Niña

The oceans are not just restricted to producing individual storms and hurricanes; they also have a hand in many large-scale weather systems. Perhaps the most famous of these is El Niño.

Ordinarily, water and winds circulate in a dependable fashion between each side of the south Pacific. Warm water is blown by prevailing winds to the east coasts of Australia and Indonesia, causing cold water to rise to the surface along the west coast of South America.

Every 4–7 years, for reasons that are not well understood, this situation reverses: the prevailing winds weaken or even change direction, allowing warm water to spread over the whole of the Pacific Ocean and stopping the upwelling of cold water. This is known as El Niño and it usually lasts for a year or two.

El Niño tends to cause droughts in Australia and south-east Asia and heavier then normal rainfall along the west coast of North and South America. It has even been linked to unusual weather further afield, such as droughts in Africa. There is also an anti-El Niño, called La Niña, which periodically intensifies the usual flow, producing heavy rainfall in south-east Asia and drought in parts of the Americas.

If the water is fairly warm and the low extensive, then the resultant clouds can grow quite large, eventually building up into massive storm clouds, which can extend more than 16 km from top to bottom. After forming out to sea, these storm clouds can migrate with the low over land. But storm clouds can also form directly over land, especially where hot humid air (often blown in from the sea) meets cooler, drier air.

At the bottom of storm clouds, the temperature can be a comfortable 15°C, but, because it gets colder with altitude, right at the top of the largest storm clouds the temperature can be as low as −60°C. This temperature gradient not only intensifies the winds flowing through and around the cloud, but also leads to the formation of the rain and snow for which storm clouds are justifiably famous, or infamous.

The production of rain

Water vapour may get driven upwards by the wind, but once the water droplets formed by condensation become too heavy they start to fall back down. As they fall through the cloud, the droplets merge and combine to form even larger droplets, before eventually emerging from the cloud as rain. Each raindrop consists of thousands of individual water droplets.

Providing they contain a high enough concentration of water vapour, almost any size cloud can produce rain. For instance, light rain or drizzle can be produced by clouds that are just 300 m thick. Obviously, larger clouds contain more water and are thus able to produce more rain: a single storm cloud is able to release well over 500 million litres of water.

The formation of ice crystals

But rain is not the only thing produced within large storm clouds, even though it may be all that is released. As we have seen, the temperature within storm clouds quickly falls below freezing above certain heights; at this point, the water vapour will condense to form ice crystals.

However, ice crystals can only form on particles with the right structure, usually particles of dust. On other particles, the water vapour will continue to condense as liquid droplets, even though the temperature is below freezing, producing what are known as supercooled water droplets. Unlike water droplets, ice crystals don't grow by crashing into each other, but rather by picking up more and more water vapour, which freezes directly onto the ice crystal.

All clouds with regions that are below freezing produce ice crystals, but these will usually only fall as snow if the temperature both inside and outside the cloud is low enough. Otherwise, the ice crystals melt to produce rain before they hit the ground. If the melted ice crystals are still very cold when they reach the ground, they may immediately freeze again, producing freezing rain and ice storms. Or they may encounter a shallow layer of very cold air near the ground that causes them to refreeze before landing, producing sleet.

SNOWFLAKES

If snow does fall, the exact shape of the snowflakes depends on the temperature at which they form – the classic six-sided flakes form above around –18°C, below this the flakes form as hexagonal plates. And, contrary to popular opinion, each snowflake does not have a unique shape, as duplicate snowflakes have been discovered.

Ice crystals can also combine with supercooled water droplets to produce larger, more amorphous snowflakes. Alternatively, some storms produce lots of supercooled water droplets, as a result of strong winds driving water vapour high up into the cloud. When these droplets rapidly freeze onto ice crystals, this tends to result in the build-up of hail stones, some of which can grow to the size of a large grapefruit.

Thunder and lightning

Ice crystals are also responsible for perhaps the most characteristic feature of storm clouds: thunder and lightning. What happens is that as ice crystals within the cloud crash into each other they become electrically charged: one ice crystal will lose electrons to another, causing them to become positively and negatively charged respectively. The same process is responsible for the build-up of static electricity when we walk across a carpet.

For reasons that are not yet fully understood, these electrically charged ice crystals form three distinct layers within the cloud: a thick positively charged layer at the top of the cloud, an equally thick negatively charged layer in the middle and a thin positively charged layer at the bottom. When the negatively charged layer has built up enough charge, it sends a stream of electrons, known as a leader, down to the ground.

But this stream never actually reaches the ground; just before it hits, it attracts a stream of positively charged ions from the ground, which rise up to hit the cloud. It is this stream of positively charged ions, known as the return stroke, that we actually see as a lightning bolt.

Incredible forces are generated by this release of electrical charge: the average thunderstorm generates a trillion watts of lightning power, more than the combined output of all the electric power generators in the US. A single lightning bolt heats up the surrounding air to around 30,000°C, causing the air to expand rapidly and producing a thunder clap.

Cyclones, hurricanes and typhoons

A less well-known characteristic of storm clouds is that they often rotate, as a result of the Coriolis force. This is actually obvious when you think about it, because storm clouds form above lows, which generate spiralling winds. Although all storms rotate, the poster-boys for rotating storms are the tropical cyclones, which are known by different names depending on where they form. In the Atlantic and northeast Pacific oceans, they're known as hurricanes; in the northwest Pacific Ocean, as typhoons; and in the southwest Pacific and Indian oceans, as cyclones.

Tropical cyclones are the 'daddy' of all storms, being defined as storms with winds above 74 miles per hour (mph). As their name suggests, they form in tropical waters (usually where the temperature is above 26°C), just north or south of the equator (they can't form on the equator because the Coriolis force doesn't act there). They form in the same way as all storms, sucking water vapour up from the sea; in fact, they usually develop out of normal tropical storms.

The factors that cause some tropical storms to turn into cyclones are not fully understood, although it appears to involve a runaway process in which the rising hot water vapour generates strong winds that suck up even more vapour. Each year, this process produces 80–90 tropical cyclones of varying strengths, which can extend for hundreds of miles. The destructive power of these storms, especially if they reach land, is well understood: in 2005, Hurricane Katrina devastated New Orleans, causing over 1,300 deaths and tens of billions of dollars' worth of damage.

Such destruction is caused by the high winds, which can reach speeds of 200 mph, heavy rain and, more importantly, something called a storm surge, which is responsible for over 90 per cent of all hurricane deaths. At the centre of a tropical cyclone, known as its eye, the air pressure is incredibly low, sucking up seawater. In addition, the intense winds blow masses of seawater ahead of the cyclone. The end result is that as the cyclone reaches land, it brings with it a huge wall of water than can be over 10 m high.

Some hurricanes also generate wildly spinning funnels of air known as tornadoes. If anything, tornadoes can be even more destructive than hurricanes, with wind speeds inside a tornado able to top 300 mph, but over a much smaller area. Tornadoes are usually under 60 m wide and travel for less than 16 km before petering out, although some have travelled for over 100 km.

Any storm can produce tornadoes, which means they are common wherever storms are common, especially Europe, northeast India and North America. The US is particularly tornado prone, experiencing around 1,000 a year, mainly in so-called 'tornado alley', stretching over Texas, Oklahoma and Kansas.

Whereas hurricanes cause widespread destruction, tornadoes, being smaller, tend to be more particular, and more capricious. They can destroy one house, while leaving its neighbour untouched; they can toss cars and buses into the sky, but also carefully carry a jar of pickles 25 miles without breaking it.

What to do in the event of extreme weather

With a tropical cyclone, the biggest danger comes from the storm surge, and so you want to move away from the coast and towards high ground, where you should seek shelter. Don't be fooled by the eye of the storm, within which the weather may be perfectly calm, it will soon be followed by the other side of the cyclone.

(Contd)

With a tornado, you need to find the right kind of shelter, which should ideally be underground or in a windowless, internal room in a well-constructed building. Here, cover yourself with a blanket or cushions to protect from falling debris.

If thunder follows less than 30 seconds after a lightning flash, then the lightning is potentially close enough to strike you. If inside, stay away from doors and windows and don't use a corded phone. If caught outside, avoid high ground, open spaces and trees and crouch down low while keeping as little of your body touching the ground as possible.

Further reading

Henson, Robert, *The Rough Guide to Weather* (London: Rough Guides, 2007).

Part four

We have the technology

16

Full of energy

In this chapter you will learn:
- *about potential energy and kinetic energy*
- *the first and second laws of thermodynamics*
- *what happens when a vase falls off a shelf*
- *about the dark side of heat.*

All our technological marvels would not be much use without a source of energy: cars need petrol; televisions need electricity; and bikes need someone to pedal. Biological organisms are just the same: without energy in the form of food they quickly stop working.

But what is energy? Well, actually, we've already defined it, because energy is simply the ability to perform work, whether moving a car, powering a television or synthesising proteins.

Potential energy and kinetic energy

There are two basic kinds of energy: potential energy and kinetic energy. Potential energy is stored energy, poised to perform work: a vase on a high shelf has potential energy due to the effect of gravity. Kinetic energy is the energy of motion, actively performing work: if the vase is knocked off the shelf then it has kinetic energy as it plummets towards the ground.

In actual fact, what happens is that the vase's potential energy is transformed into kinetic energy as it falls, because potential energy and kinetic energy are interchangeable. Kinetic energy is used to lift the vase up to the shelf, in the form of moving arm muscles, becoming potential energy once the vase is on the shelf. This potential energy is then transformed back into kinetic energy as the vase falls.

When the vase first starts to fall, its potential energy is greater than its kinetic energy, but as it falls more and more of its potential energy turns into kinetic energy, until just before it hits the floor all its potential energy has become kinetic energy. At which point, this kinetic energy smashes the vase into pieces. Scientists may define energy as the ability to perform work, but that doesn't mean the work has to be useful.

DIFFERENT TYPES OF POTENTIAL ENERGY

There are actually various different types of potential and kinetic energy. As well as gravitational potential energy, there's elastic potential energy, which is the energy stored in a flexible object such as a spring when bent or squeezed. Chemical potential energy is the energy present in the chemical bonds that join atoms together into molecules, while nuclear potential energy is the energy possessed by the protons and neutrons in atomic nuclei. Electrical potential energy is the energy of positively or negatively charged particles in an electric field.

DIFFERENT TYPES OF KINETIC ENERGY

Kinetic energy can be split into translational kinetic energy, which is the energy of movement in straight lines, and rotational kinetic energy, which is the energy of circular movement. As with potential energy, kinetic energy applies at the smallest scales, such that both atoms and electrons possess kinetic energy.

INTERNAL ENERGY

As a consequence, the pieces of smashed vase on the floor are not devoid of energy. They may no longer possess any gravitational potential energy or kinetic energy, but they still possess both chemical and nuclear potential energy and the electrons whirling around the nuclei of their component atoms still possess kinetic energy. This is collectively known as a material's internal energy.

Energy and forces

The different forms of potential energy are each associated with the four fundamental forces of nature introduced in Chapter 1. The reason for this is that for an object to possess energy there needs to be a force pulling it back to a position of lower energy.

This is most easily understood with gravitational potential energy, where the force of gravity is pulling the vase from the shelf (high energy position) to the floor (low energy position). But it also applies to chemical and electrical potential energy, which rely on the electromagnetic force, and nuclear potential energy, which relies on the strong force. Just like vases on shelves of different heights, some chemical bonds and atomic nuclei possess more potential energy than others, meaning energy can be released by rearranging those chemical bonds or the protons and neutrons in atomic nuclei.

Because energy continually alternates between kinetic and potential, it cannot be created or destroyed. All the energy present in the universe was there right at the start and will still be there at the very end. This is known as the conservation of energy and is the first law of thermodynamics, a set of laws that govern many aspects of energy.

From energy to heat

But the switch between kinetic and potential energy also involves something else, something that has far-reaching consequences. That something is heat. When the vase breaks on the floor, after all its potential energy has turned into kinetic energy, a portion of this kinetic energy is used to break some of the chemical bonds holding the vase together and the rest is released as heat.

The kinetic energy of the falling vase becomes assimilated within the internal energy of the vase and floor, breaking the vase and causing the molecules making up the vase and floor to move more rapidly. As these molecules are held in a tight embrace within a solid material they don't actually move around faster, but vibrate more vigorously. In a gas, if the kinetic energy of the molecules increases, then these molecules do actually move around faster.

We experience this increase in molecular movement as an increase in temperature: substances with molecules that are moving fast or vibrating vigorously are hotter than substances with less active molecules. Molecules can transfer this kinetic energy to neighbouring molecules, by bumping into them or jostling them. Thus, heat passes along an iron bar when you heat one end of it.

But atoms also gradually lose their kinetic energy by releasing electromagnetic radiation (see Chapter 17), causing the host substance to cool down. What we feel as heat emanating from a hot iron bar is electromagnetic radiation.

GENERATING HEAT FROM FOSSIL FUELS

Now, this release of heat can be very useful; in fact, we rely on it to generate almost all the energy that we actually use. In 2007, over 97 per cent of our energy was generated by heat in one form or another. Of this, over 90 per cent was derived from chemical potential energy, mainly the chemical potential energy locked up in oil, coal and gas. As we saw in Chapter 13, these fossil fuels, as they are collectively known, are the remains of plants and algae that were compressed under rocks for millions of years. Now we burn them, which rearranges their chemical bonds and generates heat.

Unfortunately, because these fossil fuels are derived from living organisms, they contain lots of carbon. One of the molecules produced by the rearranging of the chemical bonds in fossil fuels is carbon dioxide, which has been blamed for global warming (see Chapter 23).

The heat produced by burning coal and gas can be used directly, such as to cook food and warm houses, but it is mainly used to generate electricity, by turning water into steam. This steam is used to drive a turbine, which, in turn, drives an electric generator.

What happens is that fast-moving jets of steam turn the blades of a rotor in a turbine. This rotational kinetic energy is then transferred to an electric generator, where magnets are rotated inside a metal coil. Because electricity and magnetism are two sides of the same coin, this movement generates electricity (see Box).

What is electricity?

Electricity is actually the collective name for a range of related phenomena produced by the presence and flow of charged particles. What we term an electric current is produced by the movement of negatively charged electrons, but this movement is not like that of a flowing stream.

In fact, electrons move comparatively slowly, at less than 1 mm a second. This slow movement is driven, however, by an electric field

(Contd)

that propagates at nearly the speed of light. So electrons don't flow from power stations to our houses, but rather power stations generate a strong electric field that induces movement in the electrons already within our electrical devices. It is this induced movement that produces an electric current and powers these devices.

Because this process involves the electromagnetic force, the movement of electrons under the influence of an electric field generates a magnetic field. The converse is also the case, which is why moving a metal coil with respect to a magnetic field generates electricity.

Oil, on the other hand, is mainly used as a transportation fuel. Heat is again central, but the heat is released explosively. In a car, this explosion drives a piston up and down, with gears transferring this translational kinetic energy into rotational kinetic energy for the wheels. In a jet plane, it is used to drive a turbine, which generates thrust by expelling hot air at high speed.

BIOFUELS

Heat can also be produced by burning plants and waste material. Like coal and gas, this heat can be used directly or to produce electricity. But like oil, this heat can also be used to power vehicles, as long as the plants and waste material are first converted into liquid biofuels such as bioethanol and biodiesel.

NUCLEAR POTENTIAL ENERGY

Finally, heat can be derived from nuclear potential energy, by splitting atoms in nuclear power stations. This is known as nuclear fission and involves hitting uranium atoms with neutrons, breaking the bonds that hold together the protons and neutrons in the uranium atom nucleus. This produces new atoms, such as barium and krypton, more neutrons, which go on to split more uranium atoms, and lots of heat. Just like coal and gas, this heat is then used to turn water into steam for producing electricity.

ENERGY NOT GENERATED BY HEAT

Less than 3 per cent of the energy we use is not ultimately generated by heat. This includes the energy generated by wind, wave, tidal and hydroelectric power, which all still use turbines to generate electricity. But they use the movement of water or wind to drive the turbine, rather than steam.

Only one energy technology does not utilize either heat or turbines and that is solar power. Here, a device known as a solar, or photovoltaic, cell takes advantage of the semiconducting properties of silicon (see Chapter 18) to convert sunlight directly into electricity.

Loss of energy

But heat also has a dark side, because it gradually reduces the amount of usable energy in the universe. This dark side manifests itself in the inefficiency of our current energy generation technologies. As can be imagined, burning coal to produce heat to turn water into steam to rotate a turbine to generate electricity is not a terribly efficient use of the chemical potential energy locked up in coal.

The electricity produced by a typical generator possesses at most 38 per cent of the energy used to produce the steam, meaning 62 per cent of the chemical potential energy is simply lost. Furthermore, another 5–10 per cent of the energy is lost as a result of transmitting this electricity through cables, which can get very hot. As a consequence, boiling water in an electrical kettle takes three or four times as much energy as boiling the same amount of water over a flame.

All our current energy generation technologies, including solar, lose large amounts of energy. This energy is lost as heat to the environment and once lost it can't be utilized again. We can make intense heat perform work, but diffuse heat can't be utilized for anything. This loss of energy as unusable heat is known by scientists as an increase in entropy and is the basis for the second law of thermodynamics.

And what is true of the Earth is true of the universe in general. Stars like the sun generate monumental amounts of energy, but most of this is simply lost into space, where it does nothing more useful than slightly warming the universe. Because of this, the amount of usable energy in the universe is steadily decreasing, with potentially alarming implications for its long-term future, as well as ours (see Chapter 30).

$E = mc^2$

It is without doubt the most famous equation in the whole of science: adorning T-shirts and posters, as well as being the title of a hit 1986 song by the rock group Big Audio Dynamite. Worked out by the great German-born physicist Albert Einstein in 1905, $E = mc^2$ says that, at heart, all matter is simply energy.

'E' stands for energy, 'm' stands for mass and 'c' stands for the speed of light, which is multiplied by itself or squared. By showing just how much energy could theoretically be liberated from matter, the equation acted as a signpost for the development of new forms of energy production.

It directly led to the idea that atomic nuclei could be split or fused with each other to produce energy, resulting in both the atomic bomb and nuclear power. It also led to increasingly powerful particle accelerators, which not only convert matter into energy but also energy into matter.

Further reading

Coopersmith, Jennifer, *Energy: The subtle concept* (Oxford: OUP, 2010).

17

Coming in waves

In this chapter you will learn:
- *about transverse and longitudinal waves*
- *what electromagnetic radiation is, from radio waves to gamma waves*
- *why a rainbow is multi-coloured and the sky is blue*
- *how to produce a radio signal.*

To transfer energy over large distances, you need waves. This can be appreciated by anyone who likes to bask in the waves of light and heat emanating from the sun, almost 150 million kilometres away.

Waves are disturbances that propagate over a distance and can be generated by the more localized movement of certain objects, from atoms to molecules to guitar strings to sections of the Earth's crust. A classic example of a wave can be seen in the ripples produced when a stone is dropped into a still pond. The ripples are known as transverse waves, because the disturbance occurs at right angles to the movement of the wave (the ripples spread out horizontally, while moving up and down vertically).

The other classic type of wave is known as a longitudinal wave, in which the disturbance moves in the same direction as the wave. Longitudinal waves can easily be produced in a spiral tube of thin wire, otherwise known as a slinky, by moving one end back and forth. This causes a region where the wires are squashed together to travel down the wire, followed by a region where the wires are more spread out. This is a longitudinal wave and is the form taken by sound waves travelling through air, where they comprise regions of high and low pressure.

Wavelength, amplitude and frequency

Both transverse and longitudinal waves possess three main characteristics: wavelength, amplitude and frequency. These characteristics can most easily be explained by considering the simplest type of transverse wave, known as a sine wave (see Figure 17.1). Now a sine wave has a formal, mathematical definition, but it is essentially what most people think of as a stereotypical wave.

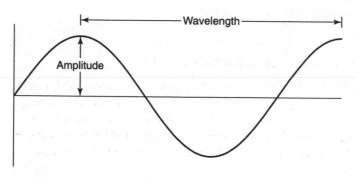

Figure 17.1 Sine wave

The wavelength is the distance covered by a single cycle of the wave, such as the distance between two consecutive peaks, measured in metres. The amplitude is the maximum disturbance from the equilibrium position: for a transverse wave, this means the height of the peak or depth of the trough in metres; for longitudinal waves, it means the maximum or minimum compression. The frequency is the number of waves passing a fixed point in a second, measured in hertz (1 hertz or Hz equals one wave, or cycle, a second).

Another important characteristic of the wave, its speed of propagation, can be calculated by simply multiplying the frequency by the wavelength. So a wave with a frequency of 5 Hz and a wavelength of 2 m is travelling at a speed of 10 m a second.

Waves and energy

As energy is required to produce movement, whether in an atom or part of the Earth's crust, the subsequent wave also possesses energy, with the amount of energy dependent on the wave's amplitude and frequency.

Now, it's obvious that waves with larger amplitudes possess a greater amount of energy. This is demonstrated by sound waves, where the amplitude is directly related to loudness, and waves on a beach, where small waves lap your feet but large waves knock you over. Frequency is also a factor because the higher the frequency the more energy-possessing waves hit a certain point over a set period of time.

It therefore takes more energy to produce waves with higher frequencies and amplitudes, as can be seen with electromagnetic radiation.

Electromagnetic radiation

Rapidly moving sections of the Earth's crust produce earthquakes, rapidly moving guitar strings produce music and rapidly moving atoms and molecules produce electromagnetic radiation. More precisely, electromagnetic radiation is produced by the movement of the charged electrons and protons that make up atoms and molecules.

Electromagnetic radiation is a transverse wave and can adopt a huge range of different wavelengths and frequencies: from radio waves at 100 Hz with wavelengths measured in thousands of kilometres to gamma waves at 10^{20} Hz with wavelengths measured in fractions of a nanometer (see Figure 17.2). The form of electromagnetic radiation that we are most familiar with, however, is visible light, which comprises a very thin band of the electromagnetic spectrum with wavelengths between 400 nanometres (nm) and 700 nm and frequencies of 400–800 trillion Hz.

All electromagnetic radiation travels at the speed of light (300,000 km a second; although see Box). As the speed of propagation of a wave is simply the wavelength multiplied by the frequency, this explains why the frequency and wavelength of electromagnetic radiation are inversely related. For all forms of electromagnetic radiation to travel at the speed of light (and nothing can travel faster than the speed of light), the frequency must increase as the wavelength falls and vice versa.

Although electromagnetic radiation is a transverse wave, it actually consists of two parts: an electrical part and a magnetic part. Indeed, electromagnetic radiation is best thought of as oscillating electric and magnetic fields travelling through space. The two parts travel in phase (meaning that the peaks of the electrical wave match up with the peaks of the magnetic wave), but at right angles to each other (so that the magnetic wave appears as a kind of shadow to the electrical wave).

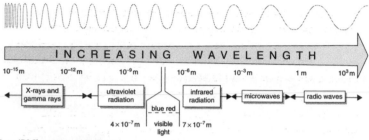

Figure 17.2 Electromagnetic spectrum

DIFFERENT FREQUENCIES

Atoms and molecules don't emit electromagnetic radiation at just a single frequency, but over a range of frequencies, with the precise range depending on how energetically they are moving. Rapidly moving or vibrating atoms and molecules (with lots of kinetic energy) emit electromagnetic radiation at higher frequencies than less rapidly vibrating atoms and molecules.

At a single frequency, electromagnetic radiation exists as a classic sine wave, but if the radiation is emitted over a range of frequencies then the individual sine waves combine to produce more complex waves. These are much less regular than the classic sine wave, with the precise shape determined by how the peaks and troughs of the individual sine waves combine. Nevertheless, because all electromagnetic radiation is simply made up of combinations of different sine waves, it can theoretically be split into its individual frequencies.

LIGHT AND COLOURS

Take visible light, which as we have seen is made up of a narrow range of frequencies. To split visible light into its component frequencies, all you need do is hold up a prism, which transforms white light into all the colours of the rainbow (see Box for an explanation of how this works). All the colours that we experience are simply different frequencies of electromagnetic radiation: from 400 trillion Hz for red light to 800 trillion Hz for violet light.

Rainbows in a blue sky

The reason a prism is able to separate white light is because electromagnetic radiation only travels at the speed of light in the vacuum of space. Passing through any kind of substance slows it down, with solid materials slowing it the most and gas slowing it the least. This explains why a straw seems to bend in a glass of water, because light is deflected by the change in speed as it goes from the water to the air.

On top of this, the degree to which electromagnetic radiation is slowed depends on its frequency. So when white light passes through a transparent prism, high frequencies slow more than low frequencies, causing the light to be split into all the colours of the rainbow. The same process also produces rainbows in the sky, with rain drops taking the place of the prism.

Light can also be scattered by molecules and other tiny particles, with the amount of scattering again dependent on the frequency of the light: higher frequencies are scattered more than lower frequencies. The reason the sky is blue is that gas molecules in the atmosphere scatter high frequency blue and violet light more than low frequency red light, causing blue light to appear to come from all points of the sky.

The colourful world that we see around us is entirely due to the fact that different materials absorb and reflect different wavelengths of light. So your T-shirt appears red because it reflects red light and absorbs all other frequencies.

INFRARED FREQUENCIES

For atoms and molecules don't just emit electromagnetic radiation, they also absorb it, with different atoms and molecules absorbing different frequencies (see Box). As a result, they move more rapidly, causing them to emit more electromagnetic radiation in a never-ending cycle.

The tendency for specific molecules to emit or absorb electromagnetic radiation at certain frequencies provides a means for identifying them. For example, our rather astonishing ability to detect molecules in molecular clouds many, many light years away (see Chapter 2) rests on the fact that molecules tend to emit and absorb electromagnetic radiation at specific radio and infrared frequencies.

Pointing a radio or infrared telescope at a dense molecular cloud illuminated by a background star produces a read-out of electromagnetic radiation at different frequencies, known as a spectrum. Without the cloud, this spectrum would contain an equal mix of the different frequencies. But because molecules in the cloud absorb and emit electromagnetic radiation at different frequencies, it actually contains peaks and troughs.

A molecule that emits light at a specific frequency will show up as a peak in the spectrum, while a molecule that absorbs light at a specific frequency will show up as a trough. By comparing these spectra with those produced in laboratories on Earth, scientists can confidently identify many of the molecules responsible for the peaks and troughs.

As we saw in Chapter 16 atoms and molecules moving more rapidly translates into a temperature increase in the host material, whether gaseous, liquid or solid. If a material absorbs electromagnetic radiation, it will heat up, which explains why almost everything gets hot on a sunny day. It will then cool down by releasing electromagnetic radiation, usually at infrared wavelenghts, which are just below the frequencies of visible light (from around 400 trillion Hz to 1 trillion Hz).

RADIO WAVES

Below the infrared frequencies are microwaves (from around 300 billion Hz to 300 million Hz) and below this are the radio waves, which form the basis for all forms of long-range communication. As we said earlier, it takes less energy to produce electromagnetic radiation at low frequencies than high frequencies. Radio waves with frequencies of a few million hertz can be produced by simply applying a varying electric current to a metal aerial. The resultant flow of electrons in the aerial generates radio waves, with the frequency of the waves depending on how rapidly the current is varied.

So to produce a radio signal all you need do is use a microphone to convert sound waves, such as speech or music, into a varying electric current. This is usually accomplished by connecting something that responds to sound waves, such as a diaphragm, to an electrode, such that the movement of the diaphragm generates an electric current. This signal is then passed straight to the aerial, producing radio waves.

Radio waves with a frequency of a few thousand hertz can travel for up to 1,000 miles before losing energy and petering out. This means that they can be picked up by a receiver some distance away, in the opposite of the transmission process, with the radio waves generating a small electric current in a receiving aerial. This current is then transferred to headphones or a speaker, which convert the electrical signal into sound waves.

CONVERTING SOUND WAVES TO RADIO WAVES

Almost all forms of long-range communication, from radio to television to mobile phones to Wi-Fi, utilize radio waves in this way. Obviously, quite a few technical hurdles have had to be overcome along the way. One of the earliest was how to convert sound waves, which have a frequency of a few hundred hertz, into radio waves with a frequency of a few million.

To do this, early radio engineers came up with a process known as modulation. The earliest form of this is known as amplitude modulation (AM), which involves altering the amplitude of a high frequency wave to match the peaks and troughs of a low frequency wave. An alternative version, know as frequency modulation (FM), does the same thing by altering the frequency of the high frequency wave and has the advantage of suffering from less interference. This is why we now have AM and FM radio.

TELEVISION

Television offered a further challenge, because now images as well as sound needed to be transmitted. To do this, engineers adopted the same basic technique, but just with a greater range of frequencies. So black and white images are sent on one set of frequencies, in the form of waves representing the brightness of hundreds of different squares, or pixels, that together form the image. Colour, sound and synchronizing pulses to match the different signals together are then all sent on separate sets of frequencies.

Increasingly, however, radio waves are no longer transmitting physical representations of sound waves or visual images, but rather just strings of ones and zeros.

Welcome to the digital age.

Further reading

Baker, Joanne, *50 Physics Ideas You Really Need to Know* (London: Quercus Publishing, 2007).

18

Information overload

In this chapter you will learn:
- *about binary digits and Boolean algebra*
- *about CDs, DVDs and the digital age*
- *about the birth of the computer.*

Think of all the books in all the libraries of the world – from the US Library of Congress to the smallest mobile library trundling around the English countryside. Think of all the information present in those books: the vast collection of knowledge, opinion and experience expressed in countless words.

Well, all those books count for just a tiny proportion of the total amount of information currently being produced by mankind; a proportion that is falling all the time. And rather than finely crafted words, this huge mass of information consists of nothing more than strings of zeros and ones – 0s and 1s.

Sounds impossible to believe? In the first few weeks of going live in 2000, the Sloan Digital Sky Survey (SDSS), an effort to map 25 per cent of the sky using a single telescope based in New Mexico, generated more data than had previously been amassed in the entire history of astronomy. Ten years later, its archive contains 140 terabytes of data (140,000 gigabytes; see Box). The Large Synoptic Survey Telescope in Chile, which will succeed the SDSS in 2016, will generate 140 terabytes every five days.

Like many large retail companies, Wal-Mart records details of its customers' purchases, amounting to more than 1 million transactions each hour. Its databases currently contain an estimated 2.5 petabytes

(2.5 million gigabytes) of data – equivalent to 167 times the books in the Library of Congress.

Think of all the emails you send and receive each day; think of all the credit card transactions you make; think of the DVDs you watch and the computer games you play; think of the internet. All of this is information that exists, ultimately, in the simple form of strings of 0s and 1s, known as binary digits. It is also growing rapidly: it has been estimated that in 2005 mankind produced 150 exabytes (150 billion gigabytes) of information; just five years later, we were probably producing something like 1,200 exabytes.

Boole and logical reasoning

But how did we get to this point? Well, in many ways, we can trace the current deluge of information back to the insight of a young US engineer called Claude Shannon, who while studying at the Massachusetts Institute of Technology in the late 1930s became very interested in electrical switches. In particular, he became interested in the possibility of using electrical switches to carry out a form of symbolic logic known as Boolean algebra.

Devised by a British mathematician called George Boole in the mid-nineteenth century, Boolean algebra allows logical reasoning to be expressed in a mathematical form. Logical reasoning involves determining whether a specific statement is true or false based on whether certain other statements are true or false, and is thus the basis for all rational argument. To give a simple example, if the statement 'All dogs are mammals' is true and the statement 'A Labrador is a dog' is true, then the statement 'All Labradors are mammals' must also be true.

Boole showed that such logical reasoning could be recast as mathematical formulae, in which the truth or falsity of specific statements are inputs to logical rules that produce outputs that can also be true or false. The above example demonstrates an AND rule in operation: if the two input statements are true then the output statement is also true; but if one or both of the input statements are false, such as if we replace 'mammal' with 'reptile', then the output statement will also be false (All Labradors are not reptiles).

Claude Shannon may have been one of the pioneers of modern computing, but there were many others as well, on both sides of the Atlantic. One of the British pioneers was the mathematician Alan Turing. In a 1936 academic article on the rather arcane mathematical subject of computational numbers, Turing first set out the theoretical design of a modern computer. This comprised a mechanical object, now known as a Turing machine, performing certain functions according to external instructions and its own internal state.

In 1950, he designed the so-called Turing test for determining whether a computer was intelligent. This involved an experimenter putting questions to an unseen human and computer; if the experimenter couldn't tell from the answers which was which then the computer could be deemed intelligent.

During the Second World War, Turing also played an important role in breaking some of the German military codes, including the notorious Enigma codes. Tragically, he died young, committing suicide after being prosecuted for homosexuality, which was then illegal.

THE DEVELOPMENT OF THE TRANSISTOR

Because the inputs and outputs in Boolean algebra can only adopt two values, true or false, Shannon realized that they could be represented by electrical switches, which can be either on or off. This means that if you join enough of these switches together they should be able to perform logical reasoning. It took another 10 years and the development of the transistor for this idea to really take off.

A transistor is essentially a tiny electrical switch made from a semiconducting material based on silicon or germanium. As its name suggests, a semiconductor sometimes conducts electricity very well and sometimes not at all, depending on certain conditions. By controlling those conditions, the transistor can be toggled between conducting and non-conducting states, thereby acting as a switch.

Once they had these tiny switches, scientists could join them together to perform specific logical functions, producing what are known as logic gates. So an AND gate has two inputs, which rather than being true or false are 1 or 0, representing either the presence or absence, respectively, of an electrical current. If both of the inputs are 1 then the output is 1, whereas if one or both of the inputs are 0 then the output is 0.

The two other basic logic gates are an OR gate and a NOT gate. In an OR gate, if one or both of the inputs are 1 then the output is 1, only if both inputs are 0 is the output 0. A NOT gate has only one input and one output, which is simply the opposite of the input: so a 1 becomes a 0, and vice versa. These patterns of inputs and outputs for each logic gate can be presented as tables, known as truth tables.

This all sounds very simple, but if several logic gates are connected together into simple circuits, such that the output of one logic gate becomes the input of another logic gate, then they can perform basic computing functions, such as arithmetic. But rather than this arithmetic being conducted in our familiar decimal system, which is based on multiples of 10, it needs to be conducted in binary, because the only numbers available are 0 and 1.

From decimals to binary

In the decimal system, numbers increase in size to the left, with each additional figure representing an increase by a factor of 10. So the number 351 is made up of one single digit, five 10s and three hundreds; if we added another figure to the left of the 3, then that would represent thousands. It is the same with binary, but here each additional figure represents an increase by a factor of two. So the number 1101 is made up of one single digit, one four and one eight (the zero in the second position means there is no two in this number). As such, 1101 is equivalent to the decimal number 13 (1+4+8).

Every decimal number has its binary equivalent, allowing suites of logic gates to perform addition, subtraction, multiplication and division. But that's just the tip of the iceberg, because it's not just decimal numbers that can be converted into binary form. Any kind of information can be converted into strings of 1s and 0s.

CONVERTING SOUND INTO 1S AND 0S

Take sound waves (see Chapter 16), which would seem pretty resistant to conversion into 1s and 0s, seeing as sound waves are continuous and 1s and 0s are individual digits (hence the term digital).

But all you need do is essentially cut the wave into lots of thin strips and then measure the amplitude of the wave in those little strips. This will produce a string of decimal numbers that change with time and, as we have seen, decimal numbers can easily be converted into binary.

If these 1s and 0s are represented by tiny pits on a flat plastic disc (where the presence of a pit represents 0 and the absence represents 1) then you have a CD. If instead of encoding just sound waves, these pits also encode brightness and colour then you have a DVD.

USING BINARY DIGITS TO STORE DATA

Rather fortuitously, it turns out that the most efficient way to encode, store and transmit any information is as binary digits, also known as bits (see Box), and it was Shannon who proved this. Say you want to display all the numbers from 1 to 999 in tokens, what is the minimum number of tokens you would need? If you were displaying the numbers as decimals then you would need 29 (two sets of 0 to 9 and one set of 1 to 9).

If, on the other hand, you were displaying the numbers as binary then you would only need 20 (10 sets of 1s and 0s), because this would allow you to represent every number up to 1,024 (2 multiplied by itself 10 times, or 2^{10}). The same is true of all information: there is no more economical way to encode it than as binary digits.

The microprocessor

Once Shannon showed that this was the case there was no turning back: the future was digital. As transistors shrunk and ever more could be fitted onto a single silicon chip, scientists were able to design more complex circuits that could process these binary digits in ever more advanced ways. The microprocessor was born, with the most advanced versions currently containing more than 1 billion transistors.

Furthermore, the results of this processing could be stored as binary digits by other transistors, producing memory. Binary digits could then travel between this memory store and the microprocessor. They could also be introduced from outside, in the form of a computer program able to control the connections between the different elements of the microprocessor. The modern computer was born.

Now computers are everywhere and they are extraordinarily powerful: there is more computing power in a modern mobile phone than was used to put a man on the moon in 1969. They have transformed every aspect of our lives: from work to entertainment to communications to relationships. They have also allowed us to process and generate unprecedented amounts of information; so much, in fact, that we are now producing more data than we have the physical capacity to store.

Bits and bytes

The term bit is a contraction of 'binary digit' and refers to each distinct digit in a stream of 1s and 0s. The bit represents the fundamental unit of digital information and, as proved by Claude Shannon, can be used to measure the information content of any message.

There are basically two components to this. First is determining the length of a message in binary notation, because a longer message can contain more information.

But this is clearly not enough, because the content of the message needs to be included, otherwise a long meaningless message could be deemed more informative than a short, meaningful message. So the length of the message needs to be multiplied by the probability of that message being true or occurring: a meaningless message has no probability of occurring and so has no information content.

The resultant formula developed by Shannon has helped guide the development of ever more efficient systems for designing and transmitting information, including the internet.

In computers, strings of bits are split into groups of eight, known as bytes, which represent the number of bits needed to encode a digital number or English letter. Bytes are now used as the unit of measurement for digital memory; so a 200 gigabyte hard disk comprises 200 billion bytes or 1.6 trillion bits. Actually, that isn't entirely true because a gigabyte is actually 2^{30} bytes (or slightly over 1 billion), because we're still working in binary. It's close enough, though.

Further reading

Von Baeyer, Hans Christian, *Information: The new language of science* (London: Phoenix, 2004).

19

Pedal to the metal

In this chapter you will learn:
- *how catalysts speed up reactions*
- *the difference between homogenous and heterogeneous catalysts*
- *why gold is like a drunk at a party*
- *how nanotechnology can help*.

The technologies discussed up to now in this section are clearly fundamental to the make-up of the modern world, which would look very different without our energy, communication and computing technologies. In this chapter, we'll consider a technology that is equally fundamental but far less well known: catalysts.

Catalysts

Without catalysts, we wouldn't have plastics, modern drugs, washing powder or petrol and we'd have far less food, clothing and dyes. Without catalysts, we also wouldn't have a hope in hell of developing the next generation of advanced energy, communication and computing technologies.

The reason for this is that molecules are inherently slovenly, preferring to laze about rather than make the effort to react with each other and create new substances. Getting these molecules off their lazy backsides requires giving them either an energetic kick, by adding heat, or a bit of friendly assistance, which is what a catalyst does. Often, it requires both.

WHAT DO CATALYSTS DO?

A catalyst is a material that instigates or speeds up a specific chemical reaction, without undergoing a chemical change itself. Almost all of the reactions required to produce the products listed above would not take place without catalysts, at least not in a reasonable period of time. Most of these reactions still require energy to be added in the form of heat, but they would require much more heat without the catalyst. Scientifically speaking, catalysts reduce the energy barrier that a reaction has to overcome before it can get going, known as the activation energy.

Another thing about catalysts is that they tend to be fairly particular about the reactions they accelerate. This means that a suite of catalysts often need to work in sequence to transform the initial chemical material, usually oil, into the wide range of chemical products used in the modern world. It's no exaggeration to say that the global oil and chemical industries would not exist without catalysts.

HOMOGENOUS AND HETEROGENEOUS CATALYSTS

Despite their many differences, catalysts can be classified into just two broad types: homogenous and heterogeneous. Homogenous catalysts exist in the same physical state, meaning gas, liquid or solid, as the reactant chemicals, while heterogeneous catalysts exist in a different state. In practice, homogenous catalysts are usually liquids and work with liquid reactants, while heterogeneous catalysts are usually solids and work with liquid or gaseous reactants.

For a catalyst to speed up a reaction, it needs to interact with the reactant chemicals. This is obviously easier for a liquid homogenous catalyst, which can simply mix with the liquid reactants, than for a heterogeneous catalyst, where the reactant chemicals need to pass over it or diffuse through it in some way.

Because of this, homogenous catalysts, which include many acids, tend to be more effective than heterogeneous catalysts. Their downside is the difficulty of separating the catalyst from the end product, especially if that too is a liquid. Also, scientists have more experience with heterogeneous catalysts than homogenous catalysts and so find it easier to develop the former. As a consequence, heterogeneous catalysts are the most commonly used type.

Nevertheless, developing a new heterogeneous catalyst is more of an art than a science, based on experience of what worked in the past rather than a detailed understanding of exactly how they speed up reactions.

INTERACTION AT THE SURFACE

What scientists do know is that it all happens at the surface of the catalyst, because this is where the reactant molecules interact with each other, perhaps after first breaking down into other, smaller molecules. The catalyst helps this process along by actively shuttling electrons between the reactant molecules, breaking and forming chemical bonds.

Scientists also know that it is usually metals (often in combination with oxygen as metal oxides) that do all the work at the surface, because metals are particularly good at shuttling electrons back and forth. Almost every heterogeneous catalyst contains one or more metals in various combinations and many metals show some form of catalytic ability, including iron, zinc, chromium, nickel, titanium and aluminium. Thus, scientists can develop catalysts for specific reactions by simply trying out different combinations of these metals.

Nature works in much the same way, because most of the reactions that take place in cells, such as protein synthesis, wouldn't happen without catalysts. In this case, the catalysts are proteins and are known as enzymes (see Chapter 6). As with industrial catalysts, metals play an important role, with many enzymes consisting of chains of amino acids surrounding a metallic core. The precise structure of the enzyme then ensures that the reactant molecules are brought together at this core.

INCREASING THE SURFACE AREA

Because everything happens at the surface of a heterogeneous catalyst, scientists want to make sure that this surface is as extensive as possible. The best way to do this is to break the catalytic material up into small particles, which will have a larger combined surface area than the original material (see Box for an explanation).

That smaller particles have a larger relative surface area can be shown with a simple box. Say you have a square box with sides 10 cm long; this box will have a volume of 1,000 cm³ (10 × 10 × 10) and a total surface area of 600 cm² (10 × 10 × 6 sides).

Now say you replace this box with two boxes exactly half the size, so that each box has a volume of 500 cm³. Each box will have sides 7.94 cm long (7.94 × 7.94 × 7.94 = 500) and a surface area of 378 cm² (7.94 × 7.94 × 6 sides), producing a combined surface area of 756 cm² for both boxes.

So simply replacing a single box with two boxes half the size increases the total surface area by more than 25 per cent. Also, the ratio of surface area to volume is larger for each of the two small boxes (0.756:1) than for the single large box (0.6:1)

As you split a set amount of material into smaller and smaller particles, the combined surface area of the particles gets larger and larger, as does the ratio of surface area to volume for each individual particle.

The tiny particles then tend to be dispersed over a solid support, often made from silica (see Chapter 13) or carbon. As well as helping to ensure the particles are spread out as widely as possible, the solid support can also enhance their catalytic effect. It can do this by chemically altering the particles and by assisting with the transfer of electrons, although in many cases the precise enhancing mechanism is unknown.

Over the past couple of decades, scientists have developed the ability to produce ever smaller particles, with ever larger combined surface areas. This has not only increased the efficiency of existing catalytic materials, but has uncovered catalytic abilities in previously non-catalytic material. It has also ushered in a whole new scientific discipline known as nanotechnology.

Nanotechnology

Nanotechnology is the manipulation of materials at the nanoscale. This means at sizes of 1–100 nanometres (nm), where 1 nm is a billionth of a metre. Using a range of newly developed technologies, scientists are now able to produce particles with defined shapes and structures at these tiny scales. And they have discovered that many of these minuscule particles, collectively known as nanoparticles, have a number of useful, and hitherto unsuspected, properties.

GOLD

Take gold. Now, the one thing that everyone knows about gold is that it's gold coloured and the one thing that every chemist knows about gold is that it's inert, meaning that it doesn't readily take part in chemical reactions. But all that changes if you transform a lump of gold into countless nanoparticles.

Then, gold will shine a range of different colours, with the precise colour (or frequency) of the emitted light depending on the size and shape of the nanoparticle. For example, rod-shaped gold nanoparticles just 20 nm wide and 60 nm long emit bright red light. This is known as fluorescence and normal gold doesn't do it.

Gold nanoparticles are also catalytic, able to instigate oxidation reactions, which in their simplest form involve adding oxygen atoms to a molecule. For example, gold nanoparticles are able to convert carbon monoxide into carbon dioxide.

This is an amazing transformation for a formerly dull, inert substance; like a shy person at a party who becomes the life and soul after a few glasses of wine. It is a result both of the great increase in surface area and the fact that certain effects become much more important at tiny scales, particularly so-called quantum effects (see Chapter 25). These effects are simply too weak to make much of an impact at large scales, but at the nanometre scale they allow gold to fluoresce and catalyse reactions.

ENHANCED CATALYTIC PROPERTIES AND HYDROGEN

Other materials show equally impressive properties at the nanoscale (see Box). But it's the enhanced catalytic properties that could prove really useful, as they could help usher in the next generation of energy technologies, which will rely on hydrogen rather than fossil fuels (see Chapter 16).

Carbon goes crazy

One of the most interesting and potentially useful of the new suite of nanomaterials are carbon nanotubes. These are tiny tubes made entirely of carbon atoms, in which each carbon atom forms a chemical bond with three of its neighbours, forming a repeated hexagon pattern.

There are two types: single-walled carbon nanotubes (SWNTs) and multi-walled carbon nanotubes (MWNTs). SWNTs can be thought of as an atom-thick layer of graphite, which also consists of carbon atoms in a hexagon pattern, rolled up into a tube 2–10 nm wide. MWNTs consist of numerous SWNTs stacked inside each other, like tree rings.

MWNTs and SWNTs are light but strong, in fact they are both much stronger than steel, and so they are already being added to products such as tennis rackets and motor vehicles to make them more robust. SWNTs can also act as either metal-like conductors or silicon-like semiconductors, depending on the orientation of the hexagon pattern, and so scientists are using them to produce a new generation of transistors and circuits.

Hydrogen can generate electricity in devices known as fuel cells. This involves breaking hydrogen atoms apart into protons and electrons at a metal conductor known as an electrode and then passing them along different paths to another electrode where they combine with oxygen to produce water. For the electrons, this path takes them around an external circuit, generating an electric current.

PLATINUM AND ITS ALTERNATIVES

As usual, the reactions at both electrodes don't take place spontaneously, only in the presence of a catalyst, and the most effective catalyst for both reactions is platinum, which is coated onto the electrodes. The problem with this set-up is that platinum is very expensive, which is preventing fuel cells from becoming a viable energy technology.

The hydrogen also has to come from somewhere and the most environmentally friendly source is water. The idea is to split water into its component hydrogen and oxygen atoms using a catalyst powered by light. Such catalysts do exist but they are also based on platinum.

Nanotechnology now offers the possibility of replacing platinum with cheaper catalysts based on nanoparticles. One option is to create nanoparticles that mix platinum with cheaper metals such as copper and cobalt. Nanoparticles consisting of a platinum-rich shell surrounding a copper-rich core have already proved to be a more effective fuel cell catalyst than pure platinum.

Another option is to get rid of the platinum entirely. For instance, nanotubes made from titanium dioxide have proved to be effective at splitting water into hydrogen and oxygen. Even more impressively, they can also produce methane (natural gas) from carbon dioxide, water vapour and sunlight.

Even with the help of nanotechnology, however, catalysts will probably remain the great unsung heroes of our modern world.

Further reading

Ball, Philip, *Molecules: A very short introduction* (Oxford: OUP, 2003).

20

....

It's alive

In this chapter you will learn:
- *how genes can be transferred between organisms*
- *how genetically modified organisms are created*
- *about Dolly the sheep and other clones*
- *about controversial research on human stem cells.*

On 20 May 2010, US scientists made scientific history by announcing the creation of the first synthetic life form. Except they didn't, not really, even if that was the headline in most of the world's newspapers.

What they actually did was to create a synthetic genome and successfully transplant it into a bacterial cell, replacing the bacterium's own genome. The genome was entirely artificial, constructed from synthetic DNA, but the rest of the bacterium was entirely natural. The synthetic genome was also an almost exact copy of a natural bacterial genome, rather than being completely novel. The bacterium was able to reproduce though, meaning that its descendants were completely controlled by the synthetic genome.

So although this bacterium was not the first synthetic life form, it still represents an important breakthrough and reflects scientists' increasing ability to control nature. We are now entering the stage where we can program and customize life in much the same way that we can program and customize computers and cars.

Although mankind has been taking advantage of biology for thousands of years, using yeast to produce bread and beer for instance, we've always been limited by what the organisms were naturally able to do. Yeast can convert sugar into alcohol and produce the carbon dioxide that makes bread rise, but it can't convert sugar into petrol.

With modern genetic techniques, scientists may soon be able to design a strain of yeast that can do just that. Or that can produce other useful chemical products such as drugs, or that can clean up pollution such as oil spills. We'll be able to tinker with organisms, customize them and bend them to our will. We'll be able to make them do whatever we want, for both good and ill.

The path to modern genetics

TRANSFERRING GENES

The work that led us to this point goes back almost 40 years to when scientists first transferred single genes between species. As we saw in Chapter 6, genes provide the instructions for making proteins, which are both the building blocks and catalysts of life. An organism's full collection of genes, known as its genome, provides the complete instruction manual for building and operating that organism.

Although most individual organisms have their own unique genome, each genome is made up of exactly the same four DNA bases, simply arranged in a different sequence. That means that a gene from one organism should work just as well in another organism, as the underlying programming language is the same. If that gene codes for a protein that provides the original organism with a useful ability, then transferring that gene to another organism should also transfer the ability.

USING PLASMID VECTORS

There are two main ways to transfer genes between organisms: plasmid vectors and viral vectors. Plasmids are circular strands of DNA found in many bacteria, existing and reproducing independently of the main bacterial chromosome. Bacteria naturally transfer plasmids to each other and this is the main mechanism by which certain genetic abilities, such as antibiotic resistance, pass quickly among bacteria.

In the early 1970s, scientists developed techniques for snipping out a gene from one organism's genome and incorporating it into a specially prepared plasmid, which is then introduced into a bacterial, fungal or eukaryotic cell. Depending on the nature of the plasmid, it either remains independent of the host cell's chromosome or becomes incorporated within it. Either way, the plasmid can be designed such that the novel gene is expressed by the cell's protein-constructing machinery, providing the cell with the novel ability.

The tricky part is getting the plasmid into the cell, but there are a number of ways this can be done. In terms of gene transfer, bacteria are fairly easy, happily picking up any plasmids added to their growth medium, but fungi and eukaryotic cells tend to be a bit pickier. Getting plasmids into these cells requires either opening up holes in the cell wall or outer membrane, which can be done by applying a short electric shock, or inserting the plasmids inside vehicles that the cells will happily take up, such as fatty bubbles known as liposomes. Alternatively, the plasmid can be attached to microscopic metal particles and literally fired into the cell.

USING VIRAL VECTORS

This whole process can be circumvented by using viral vectors. In this case, the novel gene is added to viral DNA, with viruses being little more than a strand of DNA (or RNA) surrounded by a protein shell. But viruses are very good at getting their DNA inside cells, by essentially injecting them through the cell membrane or wall. Once inside, the viral DNA either incorporates itself into the cell's genome or tricks the cell's own protein-constructing machinery into converting its genes into proteins.

Because different viruses are specialized at infecting different kinds of cells, scientists utilize several viruses as the basis for viral vectors. These viruses have been modified to enhance their ability as a gene-delivering vector and to remove their ability to cause harm, although this is not always fool-proof (see Box).

GENETICALLY MODIFIED (GM) ORGANISMS

Using plasmid and viral vectors, scientists have over the years created a whole range of organisms with foreign genes, known as genetically modified (GM) organisms. Various GM micro-organisms have been created to produce therapeutic proteins, including insulin, human growth hormones and human Factor VIII, which helps the blood to clot and is used to treat haemophilia. GM crop plants such as maize and soybeans, usually modified to be resistant to certain herbicides or to produce a natural insecticide, are now grown all over the world. GM animals are less widespread, but GM mice with human genes are now regularly used in laboratories to explore human diseases.

Gene therapy

It's not just micro-organisms, plants and animals that have been genetically modified, but also humans. Known as gene therapy, this form of genetic modification aims to cure diseases caused by faulty genes, by introducing correct versions of those genes.

Gene therapy is still very much in its infancy but has already suffered a number of major setbacks. The problem is that viral vectors are the most effective way to introduce genes into human cells and despite scientists' best efforts to ensure that these vectors are safe, they have led to some tragic incidents. In 1999, a US teenager taking part in a gene therapy trial to treat a genetic liver condition died when he reacted badly to the viral vector; in other trials, the viral vector has caused some of the participants to develop leukaemia. Still, trials are continuing.

Ideally, gene therapy would be performed on embryos, allowing any genetic faults to be fixed while we're still in the womb. But this raises the concern that parents would not be content merely to fix genetic faults, but would also want to enhance their offspring by introducing genes to make them more handsome or intelligent.

Cloning animals

Genetic technology has also continued to advance. Rather controversially, scientists are now able to clone animals, producing an exact genetic copy. Scientists are essentially creating an identical twin of an organism that has already been born.

To do this, they take an egg, meaning a female gamete (see Chapter 8), and remove its nucleus, replacing it with the nucleus of a cell from the animal being cloned, say a skin cell. Then they give the egg a short electric shock to get it to start dividing. After it has divided for four or five days, becoming a very young embryo known as a blastocyst, it is implanted into the womb of a female member of the species. Some time later, a clone is born.

The first cloned mammal was the famous Dolly the sheep, born in 1996 (see Box), but since then various other mammals have been cloned, including pigs, horses and dogs. Cloning itself has only limited practical benefits, but the same technique could also be used to produce personalized stem cells, which have great medical potential.

Dolly the sheep, 1996–2003

Produced by Ian Wilmot and his team at the Roslin Institute near Edinburgh in Scotland, Dolly was the first successfully cloned mammal. Using the technique described in the main chapter, Dolly was cloned from a mammary gland cell from a six-year-old sheep and so was named after the famously busty country singer Dolly Parton.

Dolly demonstrates the difficulties and pitfalls of cloning a mammal. For a start, she was the only lamb to make it to adulthood from 277 cloning attempts. She also died young for a sheep, which usually have a life expectancy of around 12 years, suffering from lung disease and acute arthritis.

It's still not clear, however, whether these medical conditions were exacerbated by her being a clone. It has been suggested that producing a clone from an adult cell could lead to a shorter life, simply because adult cells have already undergone some aging.

Stem cells

EMBRYONIC STEM CELLS (ESCs)

Stem cells are body cells that can reproduce indefinitely. Our bodies contain many different types of stem cell, which create new cells to replace those that have died off, but most of them can only produce a limited range of cell types. The gold standard of stem cells are embryonic stem cells (ESCs), which, as their name suggest, are only found in young embryos.

ESCs are cellular blank slates, able to produce any one of the 220 different types of cell found in the human body. They do this by repeatedly dividing, producing both more stem cells and cells that are increasingly specialized, eventually becoming a specific cell type. Because they have this ability, ESCs are described as pluripotent; less flexible stem cells that produce a smaller range of cells are described as multipotent or unipotent.

The idea is that using cloning technology you create blastocysts that are genetically identical to a patient suffering from some kind of degenerative disease. You then extract ESCs from these blastocysts and use them to produce specific cell types in the laboratory, which are then transplanted into the patient. Because these cells will be genetically identical to the patient's own cells, their immune system shouldn't attack them. If the ESCs were turned into neurons, for instance, then they could be used to treat Alzheimer's disease, which is caused by the loss of large numbers of neurons. Despite a lot of work in this area, and a false claim of success (see Chapter 21), scientists have not yet managed to produce cloned human ESCs.

INDUCED PLURIPOTENT STEM (iPS) CELLS

The controversy stems from the fact that human blastocysts are destroyed in this procedure. Even though blastocysts comprise collections of a just few hundred cells, many people find the idea of creating embryos just to destroy them morally questionable. A possible solution comes from the recent discovery that certain adult cells, including skin and fat cells, can be converted into cells with many of the same properties as ESCs by simply introducing three or four genes into them. These are known as induced pluripotent stem (iPS) cells.

This work is still at a very early stage and scientists are still investigating exactly how alike ESCs and iPS cells are, but iPS cells potentially offer a much less contentious way to obtain stem cells. Even if they do, it will still be a long time before stem cells form the basis for any treatments, because scientists are still unable to control the process by which ESCs differentiate into specific cell types. They know it's in response to specific combinations of molecules, but they haven't yet deduced the make-up of many of these combinations.

Synthetic biology

Another recent advance is that scientists can now insert suites of foreign genes into organisms rather than just single genes. They can also enhance the activity of existing genes, making them produce more protein, or reduce their activity. This 'extreme' genetic engineering is known as synthetic biology and allows scientists to provide organisms with far more advanced abilities. For instance, scientists have already developed GM organisms that can convert sugars into certain industrial chemicals and fuel-like compounds. This work is being boosted by the increasing number of organisms that have had their genomes sequenced (see Chapter 7), because it provides scientists with a bigger pool of known genes.

Scientists can also chemically synthesize all four DNA bases and join them together into strands, which means specific DNA sequences can now be produced to order. It was by combining synthetic DNA strands with synthetic biology techniques that the team of US scientists was able to produce its synthetic genome.

The moral dilemma

The aim now is to produce genomes that aren't simply replicas of natural genomes but are entirely novel constructs that provide the host organism with entirely novel abilities, such as being able to convert sugar into petrol. But as with stem cells, this new ability to program and customize life is throwing up a whole host of moral and ethical questions. We really are entering a brave new world.

Further reading

Henderson, Mark, *50 Genetics Ideas You Really Need to Know*, (London: Quercus Publishing, 2009).

Part five

When science goes bad

21

··

Fraud, fakery and fantasy

In this chapter you will learn:
- *about the stem cell scientist who illegally bought human eggs*
- *about Piltdown Man and his orang-utan jaw*
- *about the superconductor research that didn't work*
- *why scientists don't always tell the truth*.

In October 2009, the South Korean stem cell scientist Woo Suk Hwang was convicted of embezzling research funds and illegally buying human eggs. He was given a two-year suspended prison sentence.

His scientific career was already in tatters, following the retraction of two research papers that appeared in the journal *Science* in 2004 and 2005. These papers detailed Hwang's ground-breaking stem cell work. In the first paper, he claimed to have derived embryonic stem cells from a cloned human blastocyst, the holy grail of therapeutic cloning (see Chapter 20). In the second paper, he claimed to have extended this work by producing embryonic stem cells from tissue contributed by patients suffering from disorders such as diabetes and spinal cord injury, potentially offering a way to cure these and other currently intractable medical conditions.

For this work, Hwang was feted around the world, becoming a national hero in South Korea. The problem was a lot of it was fake; together with certain members of his research team at Seoul National University, Hwang had fabricated much of the data. The stem cells either did not exist or were not derived from cloned blastocysts. Hwang also paid for many of the human eggs used in the work, some of which came from his own female researchers; a major breach of medical ethics.

More cases of scientific fraud

This was perhaps the most serious and high-profile case of scientific fraud of the past few years, but it was by no means the only one. In 2006, Eric Poehlman, a former menopause and obesity researcher at the University of Vermont in Burlington, became the first US scientist to go to prison for scientific misconduct where there were no patient deaths. This followed his admission that he had falsified data in 15 grant applications and numerous journal articles, including simply making up patients.

Also in 2006, Jon Sudbø, a former researcher at the University of Oslo's Norwegian Radium Hospital specializing in cancer of the mouth, admitted to falsifying data in several important journal papers. A subsequent investigative panel found that most of Sudbø's published journal articles were bogus; like Poehlman, Sudbø was prone to inventing many of the patients in his studies.

SCIENTIFIC FRAUD IN OTHER AREAS OF SCIENCE

Scientific fraud is not just confined to biomedicine, although it has been suggested that it is more prevalent in this area of science. This may be because the stakes, in terms of financial gain and prestige, tend to be higher here than in less immediately practical scientific fields, encouraging fraudulent claims. Or simply that the strong emphasis on openness in biomedicine makes it more likely that cheats will be exposed.

But fraud has been uncovered in almost all areas of science, including chemistry, physics, environmental science, psychology and archaeology (see Box). For example, another recent major fraud occurred in organic electronics, the field of developing electronic and computing devices from carbon-based material such as plastics rather than silicon (see Chapter 27).

In the late 1990s and early 2000s, Jan Hendrik Schön, a young physicist at the prestigious Bell Laboratories in New Jersey, US, published a string of papers reporting major advances in organic electronics, including the first organic electrical laser. He also reported producing a material that was highly efficient at conducting electricity, known as a superconductor, from carbon nanoparticles called buckyballs (see Chapter 28). Most superconductors only

The missing link that wasn't

Perhaps the most famous scientific fraud of all time, so immense that it is described as a hoax rather than a fraud, is Piltdown Man. In 1912, a British solicitor and amateur archaeologist called Charles Dawson announced the discovery of fragments of an ancient skull that appeared to be that of a missing link between apes and humans. It was termed Piltdown Man after the small Sussex village where the skull was supposedly unearthed.

Almost immediately, some scientists questioned the skull's authenticity, but for the next 40 years it was generally accepted as the skull of an early human. Subsequent findings of real early human remains, however, indicated that Piltdown Man was, at the very least, an anomaly in the evolution of man.

Then in 1953 the latest analytical techniques finally proved that the skull was a forgery. It actually comprised a jawless human skull from the medieval era, attached to which was an orang-utan jaw with the teeth filed down. The perpetrator of the hoax is still unknown, although much of the evidence points to the supposed discoverer, Charles Dawson.

work at very low temperatures, but Schön claimed that his buckyball superconductor worked at much higher temperatures. In 2000 alone, Schön published eight articles in *Science* and *Nature*, the two most prestigious scientific journals.

For these breakthroughs, Schön was garlanded with awards and universally acknowledged to be on course for a Nobel Prize. Unfortunately, it was all a lie; Schön hadn't achieved any of the breakthroughs that he claimed. Suspicions were raised when other research groups couldn't replicate his work, but what finally did for him was that he used exactly the same graph to illustrate different findings in different papers. When this all came out in 2002, Schön was immediately fired by Bell Laboratories.

Data manipulation

Although such major cases of scientific fraud are fairly rare, less extreme examples of data manipulation and fabrication are probably more common. Reliable figures are hard to come by, as scientists are understandably not keen to admit their misdemeanours, but a number of anonymous surveys of such activities have been carried out over the years.

In 2009, a researcher at the University of Edinburgh in Scotland reviewed many of these surveys, finding that overall just 2 per cent of the scientists questioned admitted to fabricating, falsifying or altering data at least once.

More worryingly, however, 34 per cent of scientists admitted to other questionable research practices, including 'failing to present data that contradict one's own previous research' and 'dropping observations or data points from analyses based on a gut feeling that they were inaccurate'. Furthermore, when asked to report on the behaviour of their colleagues, 14 per cent said they knew someone who had fabricated, falsified or altered data, and over 70 per cent knew someone who had committed other questionable research practices.

So what exactly is going on? Well, part of the problem is that the world is a messy and noisy place. Scientists are often looking for a small, specific effect in the midst of numerous other variables and unavoidable fluctuations, termed noise. Coming up with definitive evidence for that effect can be difficult and often requires complex statistical analysis to separate out all the other variables and noise.

Sometimes scientists simply overstep the mark, removing or changing inconvenient data to make the world behave as they think it should and to give them the results they want. It's like a golfer surreptitiously throwing his golf ball out of the rough and on to the fairway because he knows that's where it really should have landed.

Also, scientists may like to think they're impartial searchers after truth, but in reality they are often motivated by more worldly considerations, like money, prestige, fame, awards and career advancement – as are we all. For scientists, these rewards tend to come from making important scientific findings and advances, and then publishing articles about them in prestigious journals. Hence, the incentive to come up with these findings, even if the data don't quite warrant them.

Still, it's a long way from a small bit of data manipulation, even though this is still highly undesirable, to major fraud. But most scientists don't set out to commit fraud, rather they believe that their work is genuine and just can't accept that they have not quite got the results they wanted.

The discovery of 'cold fusion'

Most scientific fraud starts out merely as wishful thinking. For example, Hwang was apparently convinced that the first stem cells he produced were derived from cloned blastocycts, even though it subsequently turned out that they weren't. In its most extreme form, however, even wishful thinking can get scientists into bother.

In 1989, the world's energy troubles seemed to be over, after two chemists at the University of Utah in the US, Stanley Pons and Martin Fleischmann, announced the discovery of 'cold fusion'. As we saw in Chapter 2, nuclear fusion takes place in the centre of stars, where atomic nuclei fuse together to form larger nuclei, releasing huge amounts of energy in the process.

Scientists have long dreamt of replicating this process on Earth, by fusing deuterium isotopes together to form helium. Deuterium is an isotope of hydrogen and is naturally found in the oceans, forming what is known as heavy water. The problem is that a sustainable fusion reaction requires immense temperatures and pressures, which are naturally generated in the centre of stars but are harder to sustain for long periods on Earth.

In 1989, however, Pons and Fleischmann announced they had produced fusion in a tank of heavy water at room temperatures, making headlines around the world. Their method involved simply passing electricity between two palladium electrodes in heavy water, in a version of a well-known technique called electrolysis. But the chemists claimed that their version produced neutrons and much more energy than could be explained by normal chemical reactions. They reasoned that deuterium nuclei absorbed by the negative electrode were being squeezed together so tightly that they fused, generating the energy and neutrons.

BYPASSING THE SCIENTIFIC JOURNALS

The problem was that not only did this breakthrough contradict the known laws of physics, but Pons and Fleischmann didn't announce it in *Science* or *Nature* but at a press conference. This was a major breach of scientific etiquette, because new scientific research is always first revealed to the world as an article in a scientific journal. This allows the research to undergo peer review, during which several experts review the article to ensure it doesn't contain any major mistakes or omissions, and it also allows the research to be described in sufficient detail for other scientists to replicate it.

Pons and Fleishmann circumvented this process and they suffered for it. Although they didn't release the full details of their cold fusion method, they gave enough information at the press conference for other scientists to form a good idea of what they had done. These scientists then started to replicate their work, but were unable to replicate their findings.

Initially, Pons and Fleischmann argued that this was because of unspecified differences between their method and the replications. But as more and more scientists were unable to find any evidence of cold fusion, and as shortcomings with Pons and Fleischmann's own experiments became apparent, it became increasingly clear that the two chemists had simply been fooling themselves.

If Pons and Fleischmann had submitted their work to a journal, then these shortcomings would probably have been identified during peer review, saving the two chemists a lot of embarrassment. But peer review can only go so far: it can't always identify work that is deliberately fraudulent, because it's only meant to identify whether the experimental method is sound, not whether the scientists have invented the data.

Fortunately, this kind of fraud tends to be uncovered by the propensity of scientists to repeat each other's work, especially work that leads to major discoveries. In many cases of scientific fraud, suspicions have first been raised by the inability of other research groups to replicate the findings.

In science, as in life in general, cheats don't tend to prosper.

Keep on going

There is one example of scientific fraud and wishful thinking that is so pervasive it refuses to go away: the perpetual motion machine. There are several different variants of this kind of machine, but they all essentially create free energy, thereby violating one or more of the laws of thermodynamics (see Chapter 16). As such, a real perpetual motion machine is impossible.

That doesn't stop people claiming to have invented one. Indeed, perpetual motion machines have a long and venerable history, going back to at least the 17th century. This is when a British physician called Robert Fludd proposed getting a waterwheel to both grind flour and pump the water driving it back up to the height it came from, providing an unlimited source of power.

Subsequent versions of the perpetual motion machine were more complex, often involving arrays of magnets, but no more successful. Even today, various companies advertize modern versions of the perpetual motion machine, which are apparently able to generate more energy than can be explained by currently accepted scientific theories. Tellingly, however, descriptions of these machines are never found in the pages of scientific journals.

Further reading

Park, Robert. *Voodoo Science: The road from foolishness to fraud* (Oxford: OUP, 2000).

22

Shocks and scares

In this chapter you will learn:
- *what we worry about*
- *why we make speedy decisions*
- *how we are influenced by stories in the news and scientific reports*.

We live in a world of fear. Despite the fact that those of us living in the developed world are generally wealthier, healthier and longer lived than ever before, there seem to be no end of things for us to worry about. And many of these things have a technological bent: GM crops, man-made chemicals, overhead power lines, mobile phones, nuclear power and vaccines. Even breast implants have been known to give us the willies.

The irony is that we owe much of our increased wealth, health and lifespan to many of the technologies that we're now so concerned about. We don't appreciate what life used to be like even just 100 years ago: the widespread poverty, hunger and disease, the high proportion of women who died in childbirth and of children who died before their fifth birthday, and the far shorter lifespans.

We forget that technologies such as water treatment, vaccination, pesticides and fertilizers successfully banished all these real terrors. Instead, we take our wealth, health and long lives for granted and focus on the small, and in many cases non-existent, dangers posed by these life-saving technologies.

System 1 and System 2

But we just can't help thinking like this. Over the past few years, scientists have discovered that we are often simply unable to assess risks in a logical and rational way, and this is especially the case when those risks involve modern technology. The reason for this is that humans appear to possess two separate systems of thought, which scientists have rather unimaginatively labelled System 1 and System 2.

System 1 is essentially intuition or gut-feeling. Its advantage is that it's quick and decisive, but it's not very deep; indeed, we are usually not aware of it at all. As such, when assessing a threat, System 1 does not dispassionately consider all the evidence before making a decision; that would take too long. Rather it uses some basic rules of thumb – what scientists call heuristics – to make a decision quickly.

In contrast, System 2 is all about dispassionately considering the evidence. It's logical and systematic, but it's also slow and takes a lot of mental effort. If we make a snap judgement about something based on a gut instinct, that's System 1. If we consider things for a long time, painstakingly weighing up the arguments for and against, that's System 2. As such, System 2 is responsible for all mankind's more impressive intellectual achievements, including science.

The problem is that the answers quickly reached by System 1 almost always colour the slower, deeper deliberations of System 2. That's if System 2 even gets involved, because in many cases it just goes with whatever System 1 has decided. Even if it does review System 1's decision, it only tends to alter or adapt it, rather than actually overrule System 1. So although System 2 represents the logical, rational aspect of our thought processes, it's the fast and loose System 1 that tends to call the shots.

In order to make its speedy judgements, System 1 operates subconsciously, because conscious thought would slow it down, which means that we often don't know how we come to our decisions. That we are able to rationalize our snap judgements stems from the fact that System 2 can usually find plausible explanations for the decisions already provided by System 1. But it was the decision that led to the explanations, rather than the other way round.

So what are the subconscious rules of thumb, or heuristics, utilized by System 1? Well, the three main ones, determined from numerous behavioural experiments (see Box), are termed the anchoring and adjustment heuristic, the representativeness heuristic and the availability heuristic. The anchoring and adjustment heuristic reflects our propensity for making an initial judgement using information we've just heard as a reference point. The representative heuristic reflects our propensity for equating typical events with likely events and the availability heuristic reflects our propensity for assuming that events that can be easily recalled are quite common.

Studying System 1

Because the heuristics and biases of System 1 operate unconsciously, scientists have had to design clever experiments to reveal their influence on our thought processes.

For example, in one study scientists asked groups of people whether the Indian political leader Mahatma Gandhi was older or younger than either nine or 140 when he died. Now, these are obviously stupid questions, but when the scientists then asked the same people to guess how old Gandhi actually was when he died these questions influenced the answers. Those who were asked whether Gandhi was older or younger than nine when he died guessed that he died at a younger age than those asked whether he was older or younger than 140. This is the anchoring and adjustment heuristic in action.

In a 1982 study, scientists asked groups of political experts meeting at a conference the likelihood that in the following year there would be either a complete suspension of diplomatic relations between the US and the Soviet Union or a Soviet invasion of Poland followed by a complete suspension of diplomatic relations. The experts rated the second scenario as more likely, even though logically the first scenario must be more likely, because the second scenario is simply a subset of the first scenario. This is the representative heuristic in action.

On top of this, System 1 also utilizes numerous 'biases' or tendencies in making its judgements. These include our tendency to be revolted by faeces and rotting material, and our tendency to seek out information that corresponds to our existing beliefs, known as the confirmation bias. Also, we tend to believe that risk and benefit are inversely related: so that risky things can't be beneficial and beneficial things can't be risky.

These heuristics and biases appear to be hard-wired in our brains, which means they are a product of evolution. And when modern man first appeared around 200,000 years ago, they were probably very valuable. At that point, if you were walking across the African savannah and saw a movement in the long grass ahead, you'd quickly need to decide whether it was being caused by a tasty antelope or a hungry lion. The heuristics and biases of System 1 could help you make that decision.

If you'd just heard someone mention a lion, if this looked like typical lion territory and if you could remember hearing about a recent lion attack, then it would probably be prudent to get the hell out of there as quickly as possible. If lion attacks weren't so high on the agenda, then it may be worth investigating further. With System 1 you wouldn't have to go through this laborious thought process, you'd just get a bad feeling and run away.

Because evolution is a slow process, System 1 is still using these heuristics and biases today, even though the world is very different. Still, System 1 can be useful when it applies its heuristics to an area where you have some expertise, allowing you to make judgements that are both quick and informed. Scientists have discovered that people working in highly stressful environments, such as fireman and air-traffic controllers, often quickly make correct decisions without being able to explain how they came to those decisions. It's when System 1 applies its heuristics to areas where people are generally less knowledgeable, such as the risks of new technology, that it can reach some highly suspect conclusions, which System 2 often doesn't correct.

WHEN SYSTEM 1 MAKES US OVERLY WORRIED

System 1 is especially thrown by the fact that we now receive information from all over the world. We may logically know that seeing a report of an abducted child on the television news doesn't make it any more likely that our child will be abducted, but System 1 doesn't know that. It simply uses the availability heuristic to deduce that hearing about an abducted child means that abduction of children is quite common, no matter where that abduction took place. Hence, we become overly worried that someone will abduct our child while they play out in the street. Scientists have discovered that people consistently overestimate the likelihood of being killed by the kind of things reported in newspapers and on the television news, such as murders, floods and fires.

The same kind of dodgy thinking lies behind many of the technological health scares of the past few years. Despite the fact that almost all of these health scares turned out to have no basis in reality, they all possess qualities that cause System 1 to sound the alarm bells.

GM crops

GM crops have been widely grown and consumed for over 10 years without any detrimental effects on the environment or people's health; in 2009, 134 million hectares of GM crops were planted in 25 countries around the world. But publicity over a few highly contentious studies that found ill effects in animals that ate certain GM produce, together with the fact that the first GM crops only benefited farmers rather than consumers, was sufficient to turn Europeans against GM crops.

Stoked by environmental groups, people are also concerned about the concentrations of man-made chemicals in the environment, whether deliberately released chemicals such as pesticides or industrial chemicals that have simply escaped into the environment. Tests on people living in the developed world have shown that their blood contains numerous man-made chemicals, some of which are toxic or potentially cancer-causing.

Now this sounds alarming, but it's not really a cause for concern. Although all our bodies are contaminated with man-made chemicals, for most people they're at such low concentrations that they won't cause us any harm. Furthermore, many of the chemical compounds produced by nature, including some that end up in our food, are toxic or potentially cancer-causing at high enough concentrations, but no one worries too much about these natural chemicals.

The American Cancer Society estimates that only around 2 per cent of all cancers are the result of exposure to man-made or naturally occurring environmental pollutants. In contrast, lifestyle factors such as smoking, drinking, diet, obesity and exercise have a much more important influence on the chances of developing cancer. But people will worry about the effects of miniscule traces of environmental pollutants in their body, while happily smoking, drinking and eating cream cakes.

Although the risks to our health from man-made chemicals tend to be fairly minimal, the risks to the environment can be much more serious.

For example, nitrogen-rich fertilizer applied to fields in the US midwest regularly wash into nearby rivers, eventually ending up in the Gulf of Mexico. Every spring and summer, this influx of fertilizer stimulates the growth of huge algal blooms that suck all the oxygen out of the water. The end result is a massive dead zone, covering 1.5 million hectares of the gulf, where nothing can live.

Safety fears have also been raised about mobile phones, where the concern is that electromagnetic fields generated by the phones may cause cancer. But, unlike with GM crops, these fears have not stopped people from happily chatting away on their phones.

All these rather irrational responses to technology can be traced back to the heuristics and biases employed by System 1. Any news reports raising doubts about the safety of a new technology, even if these doubts are later shown to be unfounded, are enough to set off the heuristics utilized by System 1, immediately giving people a bad feeling about the technology.

Furthermore, because of the risk–benefit bias, people are more willing to accept that technologies that don't seem to have a direct benefit for them, such as GM crops, are risky. Whereas they're less willing to accept that directly beneficial technologies such as mobile phones can present a danger.

Because of the confirmation bias, once someone has turned against a technology it can be very difficult to change their mind; they only pay attention to information that reinforces their belief that the technology is a risk. Often they do this by simply refusing to believe assurances that the technology is safe. Unfortunately, this sceptical stance is given credence by the few cases where assurances of safety have proven false, such as over bovine spongiform encephalopathy (also known as mad cow disease).

The MMR scare

Sometimes, however, irrational responses can have severe consequences. In 1998, a British doctor suggested a link between the three-in-one vaccine for mumps, measles and rubella, known as MMR, and the onset of the behavioural disorder known as autism. Even though the British government assured parents that the MMR jab was safe, supported by numerous studies that found no link between MMR and autism, many parents decided it was safer not to give their children the jab.

As a consequence, cases of measles and mumps in the UK soared (rubella is still thankfully rare). According to the UK Health Protection Agency, measles cases rose from 56 in 1998 to 1,144 in 2009, while mumps cases rose from 121 in 1998 to 7,628 in 2009 (with a peak of 45,000 in 2005). Not only are measles and mumps highly unpleasant diseases, but measles can also occasionally kill.

A highly speculative, and later proven to be unfounded, link between MMR and autism was sufficient to stop parents vaccinating their children against three serious diseases. Fortunately, as the scare has died down, MMR vaccination rates have returned to their former levels.

Obviously, System 2 can override the irrational responses of System 1, but even when it does System 1 can still leave us feeling uneasy. I knew that numerous studies had failed to find a link between MMR and autism, but I was still nervous when I took my children for their MMR jabs.

Usually, scientists are fighting against System 1 to assure people that a technology is safe, but occasionally they are fighting against System 1 to get people to take a threat more seriously. This is the case with global warming.

Further reading

Gardner, Dan, *Risk: The science and politics of fear* (London: Virgin Books, 2009).

23

Hot enough for you?

In this chapter you will learn:
- *what is meant by global warming and climate change*
- *how greenhouse gases affect the world*
- *about rising levels of carbon dioxide*
- *what might happen in the future.*

So far, much of this book has concentrated on areas of science that are pretty much settled. Areas where there is a reasonably good consensus among scientists about the accuracy of their current theories and understanding. They may still be a bit fuzzy on some of the specifics, but they've worked out the broad picture.

Scientists know how DNA is replicated, they know how continents move, they know how atoms are structured and they even have a fairly good idea of what happened during the first few seconds of the universe's existence. But some areas of science are far from settled; there is uncertainty, confusion and contradiction, and so arguments rage and emotions run high. This is very much the current position with climate change.

For those who have been hiding under a rock for the past few decades, climate change is the theory that rising concentrations of carbon dioxide and other gases, mainly produced by our burning of fossil fuels for energy, are causing the Earth to heat up. This theory is also known as global warming.

Climate change generates more ire and controversy than almost any other area of science. It also seems to be an area where people are forced to choose: you're either a believer in climate change or you're not – there is no middle ground. As a result, the level of antagonism between the two sides is high.

The principles of climate change

Ironically, the basic principles of climate change are, in essence, very simple and uncontroversial. Carbon dioxide is a greenhouse gas, as are methane (also known as natural gas) and nitrous oxide. As we saw in Chapter 17, different molecules absorb and emit electromagnetic radiation at different frequencies; carbon dioxide, methane and nitrous oxide all happen to absorb radiation at infrared frequencies.

Carbon dioxide, methane and nitrous oxide are all present in the atmosphere, albeit at very small concentrations (carbon dioxide currently accounts for almost 0.04 per cent of the atmosphere, while methane and nitrous oxide are present at even lower concentrations). The vast majority of the atmosphere consists of nitrogen and oxygen, accounting for 78 per cent and 21 per cent respectively, but neither of these absorbs infrared radiation.

GREENHOUSE GASES

Greenhouse gases are so-called because by absorbing infrared radiation they prevent heat escaping from the Earth, in a similar manner to a greenhouse. This infrared radiation is emitted by the surface of the Earth as it is warmed by sunlight (see Chapter 17). A good example of this kind of surface heating is provided by tarmac, which gets very hot on sunny days.

If the atmosphere consisted of nothing but nitrogen and oxygen, then this infrared radiation would simply escape back into space. Instead, much of it is absorbed by greenhouse gas molecules, causing them to move more rapidly and emit more infrared radiation back towards the ground. In this way, carbon dioxide, methane and nitrous oxide act as a kind of thermal blanket over the Earth, preventing the surface from cooling down.

Scientists have calculated that without these greenhouse gases in the atmosphere, the average temperature at the surface would be a chilly –18°C, meaning that greenhouse gases are essential for making the Earth habitable.

A quick look at Mars will confirm this point. Carbon dioxide is the main constituent of the Martian atmosphere (accounting for around 95 per cent), but this is more than offset by the fact that its atmosphere is over 100 times thinner than ours and so it traps far less heat. As a result, the average temperature at the surface of Mars is −65°C.

But you can have too much of a good thing. Take Venus: carbon dioxide is the main constituent of its atmosphere as well, but its atmosphere is 100 times thicker than the Earth's. As a result, the temperature at the surface of Venus is a furnace-like 460°C. So, broadly speaking, the more greenhouse gases you have in your atmosphere, the more heat is trapped near the surface.

INCREASED LEVELS OF CARBON DIOXIDE

And the concentration of greenhouse gases, particularly carbon dioxide, in the Earth's atmosphere is increasing. Again, this is an uncontroversial finding. Measurements of atmospheric carbon dioxide levels have been made since the 1950s and show a steady increase, from 317 parts per million (ppm) in 1959 to 387 ppm in 2009. Also uncontroversial is attributing this increase to mankind's use of carbon-rich fossil fuels such as oil, coal and gas, which produce carbon dioxide when burned.

Additional evidence is provided by studies on bubbles of air trapped in ice cores extracted from the Arctic and Antarctic. These provide an atmospheric record stretching back hundreds of thousands of years and indicate the carbon dioxide concentrations have been rising for 250 years, ever since the dawn of the industrial revolution. Although the ice cores also show that carbon dioxide concentrations naturally fluctuate, they are now the highest they've been for at least 600,000 years.

Controversy over rising air temperatures

The controversy starts heating up with the assertion that average surface air temperatures are increasing and that rising carbon dioxide levels are to blame. For although, broadly speaking, more carbon dioxide means more trapped heat, carbon dioxide is just one of the many factors that influence surface air temperature. The precise relationship between temperature and carbon dioxide is highly complex and one that scientists don't yet fully understand.

As well as providing details of historical carbon dioxide levels, ice cores can also provide information about historical temperatures, because different isotopes of oxygen are laid down in the ice at different rates depending on the temperature. Comparing this temperature record with the carbon dioxide record reveals that the two do tend to fluctuate in step. But ice cores can't reveal the precise relationship: whether the temperature fluctuates in response to fluctuating carbon dioxide levels, or vice versa; or, more likely, whether there's a complex interaction between the two.

This temperature record is also fairly coarse, which is not surprising considering that it covers hundreds of thousands of years. For more detailed records of recent history, scientists need to turn to other natural sources, such as tree rings. These not only mark a tree's age but also the temperatures it has been exposed to over its lifetime, which influence the thickness of the rings.

Using tree rings from various ancient trees, scientists have built up a record of average global temperatures over the past 1,000 years. Fluctuations are once again the name of the game, but always around a general mean.

But that changed about 150 years ago, when mankind first started taking regular measurements of the air temperature. These measurements, which are now taken at thousands of weather stations around the world and by satellites, show generally rising temperatures (although the temperature was flat from the mid-1940s to the mid-1970s). Over the past 100 years, the world's surface air temperature has warmed by close to 0.7°C.

To many critics this sounds suspiciously convenient, especially as this recent warming doesn't appear to show up in tree rings. They think this warming may have more to do with the fact that, over the years, towns and cities, which tend to be hotter than the surrounding countryside, have often built up around formerly isolated weather stations. However, climate change scientists argue that they have taken this urban warming into consideration – by, for instance, omitting readings from stations in the largest urban areas – when putting together their records of average temperature.

Even if the surface air temperature is increasing, rising carbon dioxide levels are not necessarily the sole culprit. For a start, as we have seen, carbon dioxide is not the only greenhouse gas. In fact, carbon dioxide is actually a less potent greenhouse gas than either methane or nitrous oxide, but it matters more because there is more of it in the atmosphere. Overall, it has been estimated that methane contributes about 24 per cent to global warming, while carbon dioxide contributes 70 per cent.

The effect of water vapour

But an even more important greenhouse gas than carbon dioxide, because it's much more prevalent in the atmosphere, is water vapour. Critics therefore argue that a small rise in carbon dioxide levels is relatively unimportant, because water vapour has a much larger influence on surface air temperatures. But things are not that simple.

For a start, water vapour would amplify any warming produced by rising carbon dioxide levels, because a warmer surface temperature causes more evaporation from the oceans and thus more water vapour. On the other hand, as we saw in Chapter 15, water vapour quickly condenses to form clouds, and clouds, especially white clouds, reflect incoming solar radiation, thereby helping to cool the surface. But then again, clouds can also trap some of the infrared radiation emitted by the ground.

So water vapour has conflicting effects on temperature, although scientists think that, overall, more water vapour probably leads to higher temperatures. Carbon dioxide, on the other hand, only leads to warming, at least near the Earth's surface.

Solar radiation

With similar reasoning, critics also argue that the amount of radiation the Earth receives from the sun, which varies on numerous timescales, has a much greater effect on surface air temperatures than carbon dioxide levels. If the Earth is warming, they say, then this must mainly be due to it receiving more energy from the sun.

But this argument is contradicted by observations of the sun, which indicate little change in incoming solar energy over the past few decades, and also by the findings of computer-based climate models. By chopping up the atmosphere and the Earth's surface into three-dimensional cells and then simulating various physical processes in those cells, these models attempt to replicate the workings of the climate.

Such models can only provide a very general approximation of the real climate, especially as each cell covers an area of over 100 km², but they have proved pretty accurate at replicating the warming seen over the past 100 years. They can only do this, though, by incorporating rising carbon dioxide levels. According to the models, fluctuations in solar radiation cannot on their own account for the observed warming.

Changes in the future

The models are much less certain about what will happen in the future, although they all indicate some level of warming. This lack of certainty is mainly down to the fact there is still much that we don't understand about how the climate works. We don't even know what happens to all the heat trapped at the surface by carbon dioxide.

Only a small proportion of the heat remains in the lower atmosphere and contributes directly to global warming, the vast majority is absorbed by the oceans, causing them to warm up, or goes towards melting glaciers and ice caps at the poles. But there's still a lot that's unaccounted for. A study that appeared in the journal *Science* in 2010 revealed that scientists still cannot account for roughly half the heat that is believed to have built up in recent years.

Nevertheless, despite these uncertainties, predications can still be made. In its latest report, published in 2007, the Intergovernmental Panel on Climate Change, a body set up to advise governments on climate change, predicted that average global temperatures would rise by between 1.1°C and 6.4°C by 2100. This may not sound like much, but the effects could well be dramatic.

Sea levels will start to rise, causing many coastal areas to disappear under the waves. This will be due to both warming oceans, because water expands as it warms, and melting sea ice and glaciers. Indeed, this process is already happening, with satellite measurements indicating that the seas are currently rising by over 3 mm a year.

Rising ocean temperatures and meting sea ice may also change the ocean circulation system (see Chapter 14), potentially slowing down or even switching off the thermohaline circulation (as happened in the 2004 disaster film *The Day after Tomorrow*, with dramatic but scientifically unlikely consequences). This would have the rather ironic effect of making Western Europe much colder, although there's no sign of it happening yet.

Almost everywhere will become warmer, although this warming will probably be more dramatic at night and in the winter than during the day and in the summer. The warmer temperatures will increase evaporation of water from the oceans, making it rain harder when it does rain, but they will also increase evaporation from many inland areas, making droughts more intense.

Many plants and animals will suffer, as their habitats change. It has been predicted that up to 37 per cent of plant and animal species could face extinction by 2050 if carbon dioxide levels keep on rising. It's true that more carbon dioxide in the atmosphere could cause plants to grow faster, but this will likely be offset by higher temperatures. As a result, our food supply could suffer: the yields of our most important food crops fall dramatically when temperatures are much above 30°C.

Despite the continuing controversy, virtually all the world's major scientific societies, including Britain's Royal Society and the US National Academy of Sciences, accept that global warming is a major problem and that rising levels of carbon dioxide, produced by the burning of fossil fuels, are mostly to blame. They are thus trying to move the debate away from whether global warming is happening and towards what to do about it (see Box).

What can we do about it?

Most countries now accept that they need to reduce their carbon dioxide emissions, even if global attempts to set binding targets have had mixed fortunes. Clearly, the best way for a country to reduce its carbon dioxide emissions is to burn less fossil fuels.

This generally means replacing power plants than run on coal and gas with cleaner forms of energy production. These include nuclear power, although this has its own problems, and renewable energy technologies such as solar, wind and tidal (see Chapter 16). It can also mean encouraging the use of biofuels, which are derived from plant-based material rather than oil, and the development of even cleaner transport fuels, such as hydrogen.

On a personal level, you can cut your carbon dioxide emissions by reducing the amount of energy you consume. This can be done by simple measures such as insulating your house, turning off electrical appliances and lights when they're not in use, and walking rather than driving to the local shops. When carried out by millions of people, such simple measures can add up to major reductions in emissions. As an added bonus, they can also save you money.

Further reading

Henson, Robert, *The Rough Guide to Climate Change* (London: Rough Guides, 2008).

24

Apocalypse now

In this chapter you will learn:
- *the effects of nuclear war*
- *the dangers of chemical and biological weapons*
- *what could cause long-term damage to the Earth itself.*

As global warming amply demonstrates, mankind's technological prowess has reached a stage where it can threaten the entire planet. And it's not just global warming: we can now destroy our world in whole variety of weird and wonderful ways, from nuclear war to genetically modified disease to black holes. If we're really unlucky, we may even take the rest of the universe with us.

But before exploring the various options for global annihilation, we need to make a distinction between two main types. In the first, and less catastrophic, type, it is our modern civilization that is destroyed rather than the Earth. This may involve mankind merely regressing to a less technologically advanced state following some tragedy. But it could also involve mankind being wiped off the face of the Earth, probably along with many other species.

The Earth as a whole would survive this first type of annihilation. Life in some form or other would also probably survive, thriving again after a certain period of time, as happens after mass extinctions (see Chapter 5). Mankind would no longer be around, though. The second, more catastrophic, type of annihilation involves the physical destruction of the Earth, in which case obviously nothing would survive.

Nuclear war

For many years, the most likely cause of the first type of global annihilation was nuclear war. It has been estimated that in the mid-1980s the US and the Soviet Union (now Russia) had around 65,000 nuclear warheads between them, equivalent to the explosive power of 3 tonnes of TNT for every person on the planet.

The immense destructive power of nuclear weapons is down to the fact that, per kilogram, a nuclear reaction is a million times more efficient at generating energy than a chemical explosion. In an atomic bomb, the explosion is caused by the same kind of fission reactions that take place in nuclear power stations (see Chapter 16), whereby flying neutrons split uranium atoms. The difference is that in an atomic bomb these reactions run out of control, releasing loads of heat and atomic particles in a massive explosion equivalent to over 10,000 tonnes of TNT.

THE HYDROGEN BOMB

In more advanced nuclear weapons, such as the hydrogen bomb, the explosion is caused by both fission and fusion reactions. Fusion reactions are the opposite of fission reactions, with atomic nuclei fusing together (as happens in the cores of stars; see Chapter 2), but they still release lots of energy in the form of heat and atomic particles. By combining fission and fusion reactions, with the fusion reactions involving isotopes of hydrogen, a single hydrogen bomb can produce an explosion that is equivalent to millions of tonnes of TNT (hence the term megatons).

But it is not just the size of the initial explosion that makes nuclear weapons so horrifying. The force of the explosion from a modern hydrogen bomb, together with the resultant massive fires, would send huge quantities of material up into the atmosphere, in the form of smoke and particles of rock and soil. In all likelihood, this material could stay up there for years, blocking sunlight and ushering in a nuclear winter that would make life tough for those that survive. In particular, the reduced sunlight and lower temperatures would decimate our ability to grow crops.

IONISING RADIATION

A nuclear blast also releases high levels of ionising radiation, in the form of massive numbers of highly energetic atomic nuclei and subatomic particles that can damage chemical bonds. Spreading over a large area, this ionising radiation would cause both immediate and long-term damage to survivors, including burns and genetic damage that could lead to high rates of diseases such as cancer. It would also affect future generations by greatly increasing the risk of birth defects. A global nuclear war would clearly kill off our modern civilization, if not much of humanity and many other species.

Nuclear threats

With the end of the Cold War, this nightmare scenario has become much less likely, especially as both sides have steadily been reducing their nuclear stockpiles. But although the threat of global annihilation via nuclear weapons seems to have passed, the danger that someone somewhere will use a nuclear weapon is still very much with us.

That could be unstable, erratic regimes in countries such as North Korea, which claims to have developed a nuclear bomb, and Iran, which many people think is working to develop a bomb. It could also be terrorist groups that have obtained a bomb from these unstable regimes or from old Soviet stockpiles.

Smaller versions of the Cold War are also still being played out. Both India and Pakistan have nuclear weapons and are currently engaged in a stand-off over the disputed territory of Kashmir. If Iran does develop a nuclear bomb then it will likely engage in a stand-off with Israel, which many believe already has nuclear weapons. A nuclear conflict between these countries would not result in global annihilation, but would still kill millions.

Chemical and biological attacks

Large numbers could also die from attacks with chemical and biological weapons. Such weapons are now banned under the Chemical Weapons Convention and the Biological and Toxins Weapons Convention, but that obviously doesn't stop terrorists and deranged cults from using them.

In fact, they already have. In 1995, a Japanese cult called Aum Shinrikyo released the nerve gas sarin in the Tokyo subway, killing

12 people. But nasty as chemical weapons are, biological weapons, which are based on disease-causing pathogens, pose a much greater threat. A chemical attack will only affect people in the immediate vicinity; a biological attack, on the other hand, has the potential to spread far and wide. This is both because an infectious biological pathogen can spread from person to person and because it may be several days before the authorities work out that anything is wrong.

DESIGNER PATHOGENS

Natural pathogens are deadly enough. For instance, smallpox is highly infectious and kills around a third of those infected; fortunately, widespread vaccination has all but wiped out this former scourge of humanity (see Chapter 9). But a growing danger comes from the possibility that someone will use modern genetic and synthetic biology techniques (see Chapter 20) to create a novel, designer pathogen that is more infectious and deadly than anything nature has yet conjured up.

Imagine a version of the AIDS virus that could be transmitted via the air or by touch, rather than sexual intercourse, or a version of the flu virus that kills a third or more of those infected. If released in a modern city, such an infection would quickly sweep the world, as happened with swine flu in 2009, despite all efforts to contain it. It could kill hundreds of millions.

DISASTROUS CONSEQUENCES

But a nuclear or biological attack would not need to kill millions to threaten our modern civilization; the disruption caused by a smaller attack could do that. Indeed, an attack where no one died could do it. The point is that in many ways our modern, technological civilization is quite fragile, heavily reliant on things such as energy supplies, food distribution and communication technologies.

A small nuclear or biological attack would disrupt all of these things, with potentially disastrous consequences. A cyber attack that took out large swathes of our global computer network could do much the same thing, with no immediate loss of life. In the UK, we've already had a taster of the chaos that could ensue.

In 2000, irate British truck drivers blockaded fuel refineries over the high price of fuel. Within a few days, fuel stations across the UK ran dry and the country ground to a halt. As deliveries were unable to get through, people started panic buying and shops began to run out of food. Fortunately, the blockade was lifted before things got really out of hand.

Much greater upheaval over a longer period of time would be caused by a small nuclear or biological attack, potentially including widespread electricity blackouts and serious food shortages. In an instant, modern societies would regress hundreds of years and it may take a long time to recover.

Long-term damage to the Earth

Still, none of these various apocalypses would cause any major long-term damage to the Earth. Even setting off the tens of thousands of nuclear weapons held by the US and the Soviet Union at the height of the Cold War wouldn't cause it too much trouble. The asteroid blamed for killing off the dinosaurs 65 million years ago released as much energy as one million hydrogen bombs. Apart from a bit of a dent, in the form of a 200 km-wide crater straddling the coast of Mexico, the Earth emerged pretty much unscathed.

So surely there's no way that mankind could possibly destroy the Earth. Well actually there is and the potential danger comes from a rather surprising source. As we saw in Chapter 1, in order to determine the fundamental structure and forces of the universe, physicists are slamming subatomic particles together at close to the speed of light in particle accelerators such as the Large Hadron Collider (LHC).

Assessing the apocalypse

How can you assess apocalypses dispassionately? How can you compare the severity of different apocalypses and determine what steps should be taken to prevent an apocalypse from taking place? Well, it turns out there is a simple method for assessing the severity of any threat that could result in human casualties, whether a hurricane, asteroid impact or nuclear war.

It involves multiplying the probability that the threat will happen by the magnitude of the threat, usually in terms of the number of likely casualties. Using this method, a threat that only kills a few people but is quite likely to happen is rated as severe as a threat that it is very unlikely to happen but would kill many more people.

This explains why a number of efforts are now underway to catalogue all the asteroids and comets that could cross Earth's orbit, known as near-Earth objects. The kind of asteroid impact that wiped out the dinosaurs may be very rare, occurring every 100 million years on average, but the consequences would clearly be apocalyptic.

BLACK HOLES, STRANGELETS AND OTHER CALAMITIES

For a brief moment, these collisions generate an immense amount of energy, replicating the conditions at the birth of the universe. The concern is that these high-energy collisions could potentially trigger the destruction of the Earth. There are a number of ways this could theoretically happen.

The high-energy collisions could create a microscopic black hole that proceeds to gobble up the Earth. Usually produced by the collapse of massive stars at the end of their lives, black holes are regions of space where the force of gravity is so strong that not even light can escape, meaning anything that comes too close gets pulled in.

Alternatively, they could cause the quarks that ordinarily form protons and neutrons to reassemble into a strange form of matter known as a strangelet. This could then proceed to convert all other matter, transforming the Earth into an immensely dense sphere just 100 m across. Or the collisions could convert the whole of the universe into a new stable state, known as a vacuum bubble, in which atoms could not exist. Finally, they could produce particles known as magnetic monopoles, which some theories suggest can cause protons to decay, in which case atoms would simply melt away.

Although all these possible calamities are more or less consistent with current theories, they are highly speculative and most scientists dismiss them. Also, similar high-energy collisions occur naturally all the time when cosmic rays (see Chapter 2) hit atoms in the Earth's atmosphere and these collisions haven't yet destroyed the Earth.

All the same, if you suddenly find yourself converted into a hyper-dense lump of strange matter then you'll know who to blame.

But what about zombies?

The one apocalyptic scenario that we haven't yet considered is a full-scale zombie attack, in which the dead start rising from their graves and feasting on the living. In this scenario, anyone who dies comes back as a zombie, and anyone who is bitten by a zombie dies and then comes back as a zombie.

Zombies thus represent disease made flesh; bacteria and viruses in human form. An individual zombie may not be too much of a threat; the danger comes from the fact that as their numbers grow it becomes increasingly difficult to avoid them. Indeed, most zombie films have dark endings, in which almost all the characters become zombies and mankind is assumed to be doomed.

This depressing outcome was recently confirmed by Canadian scientists, who developed a mathematical model of a likely zombie attack. This revealed that if we don't quickly eradicate every zombie (by destroying their brains) then our civilization would collapse and everyone would die or become a zombie.

Further reading

Rees, Martin, *Our Final Century: Will civilization survive the twenty-first century?* (London: Arrow Books, 2004).

25

Know your limits

In this chapter you will learn:
- *about the way scientists have worked up to now*
- *about the big questions currently facing them*
- *how computers have taken control*
- *what we cannot understand.*

The scientific method

The reason why scientists consider science to be the most accurate and reliable repository of knowledge about the universe, compared to religious revelation and philosophical musing, is all down to the scientific method. In essence, the scientific method is very simple: a scientist makes certain observations about the universe, develops a hypothesis about how the universe works based on those observations and then conducts experiments to test that hypothesis.

Simple it may be, but this method has generated some pretty fundamental insights (many of which are described in this book). Furthermore, as if to prove the accuracy of these insights, it has allowed us to develop all the technology that we enjoy today.

Now, in practice, the method is a bit more complex than just described. For a start, it's an iterative process: the results of the experiments performed to test a particular hypothesis often lead to modifications of the original hypothesis or the formation of a new hypothesis, leading to even more experiments. Furthermore, at some point all these hypotheses need to be combined into an overarching theory that accurately explains why the universe is as it is. Ideally, this theory should also make predictions that can be tested by even more experiments.

SETTING RESTRICTIONS IN EXPERIMENTS

Certain restrictions also need to be placed on the universe for the scientific method to work properly. The scientific method is essentially all about discovering cause-and-effect relationships: in an experiment, a scientist is looking for a specific effect from a specific action. To do this, he or she (only to keep things simple, we'll assume 'he' from now on) needs to make sure that nothing else can influence the outcome.

For example, if a scientist wants to study the effect of rising temperatures on a crop plant such as wheat, he'll need to keep a tight control on all the other factors that could affect the plant. These include: humidity; nutrient and water levels in the soil; sunlight intensity; and carbon dioxide levels. Otherwise the scientist won't be able to tell whether any recorded changes to the plant were due to rising temperatures or to one or more of the other factors.

But the real world isn't like this. In the real world, plants are affected by all the factors simultaneously and in combination, such that it is the interaction between these factors that truly determine the effect on the plant. Studying all of these factors individually is known as reductionism and it has allowed scientists to work out in some detail how individual parts of the universe work, such as the various organelles within a cell. But scientists know far less about how these different parts interact with each other and mesh together.

The scientific method also assumes that the scientist is independent of the process or relationship he is studying, meaning that he doesn't influence it in any way. The effects of rising temperature on a wheat plant would be just the same whether the scientist was recording them or not.

SCIENCE VERSUS RELIGION AND PHILOSOPHY

Despite these restrictions and assumptions, the scientific method has so far proved superior to any other method for accumulating knowledge about the universe. It trumps religious revelation because its theories can be tested by experiment; those that come up short are soon replaced or discarded, unlike religious tenets. It trumps philosophical musing because its theories are constructed from experimental evidence, rather than from sitting around thinking about things.

Beyond the scientific method

Recently, however, science has begun to outgrow the scientific method, at least in its classic incarnation. There are a number of reasons for this. In part, it's because all the fundamental discoveries have already been made; in part, it's because modern technology, especially computers, offers new ways to study the universe; and, in part, it's because modern science is now exploring areas where the assumptions of the classic scientific method no longer apply.

Now, it's obviously incredibly presumptuous to assert that science has already made every fundamental discovery about how the universe works. It's also plainly untrue. To mark its 125th anniversary in 2005, the scientific journal *Science* produced a list of the 25 big, unanswered questions facing science (see Box), which were picked out from an initial list of 125.

The big questions

The 25 big questions facing science were collated by the editorial staff at *Science* in 2005. The list makes interesting reading, especially as the questions relate to many of the topics already discussed in this book. Saying that, not all of the questions may make sense to a non-scientist, but they give a good indication of the breadth of issues that still need to be resolved.

1   What is the universe made of?
2   What is the biological basis of consciousness?
3   Why do humans have so few genes?
4   To what extent are genetic variation and personal health linked?
5   Can the laws of physics be unified?
6   How much can human lifespan be extended?
7   What controls organ regeneration?
8   How can a skin cell become a nerve cell?
9   How does a single somatic cell become a whole plant?
10   How does Earth's interior work?
11   Are we alone in the universe?
12   How and where did life on Earth arise?
13   What determines species diversity?

(Contd)

So there are obviously many more important discoveries to be made. But if you take a look at the list, it quickly becomes apparent that the nature of those discoveries is changing. For it includes entries such as 'What is the biological basis of human consciousness?' and 'How hot will the greenhouse world be?'. These are questions that can only be answered by studying complex systems as a whole, rather than studying different aspects of those systems in isolation.

So it's not that all the major scientific discoveries have been made, but that all the major discoveries that can be made using a reductionist approach may well have been made. We know how elements are forged in stars; we've worked out the structure of DNA and proteins; and we understand why some materials conduct electricity better than others. And this understanding came from countless experiments studying specific aspects of each phenomenon.

That approach just won't suffice, however, for determining the workings of complex systems such as human consciousness and the climate, where the interaction between different elements is more important than the elements themselves. Understanding how a single neuron works can't explain human consciousness and understanding how carbon dioxide absorbs infrared radiation can't explain the climate.

The use of computers in science

This is where computers come into their own, because one way for scientists to probe complex systems is to develop computerized models of them. As with the climate models mentioned in Chapter 23, these models represent a simplified version of the real system, replicating known physical or biological processes and the interactions between them across the system. The ability to produce such computerized models has already led to the rise of completely novel scientific disciplines. For instance: systems biology, which aims to understand the full suite of complex interactions taking place between the many biological molecules, including genes and proteins, in cells.

Indeed, computers are taking over more and more of the scientific discovery process. Many scientific experiments are now entirely automated, such as protein analysis and astronomical surveys, and generate huge amounts of data. So much, in fact, that scientists also need to use computers to analyse the data and highlight any trends.

ADAM THE ROBOT SCIENTIST

Recently, computers have started to become involved all aspects of the scientific method: from collecting data to forming a hypothesis to collecting more data. In 2009, a team of British scientists developed a robot scientist called Adam that conducted experiments on yeast, formulated hypotheses based on the results and then designed new experiments. In this way, Adam discovered new knowledge about the yeast genome.

Obviously, the potential problem with this growing reliance on computers is that scientists will understand less and less of what the computers are doing and the results they are producing. Already, computer models can be a bit of a black box, accurately replicating certain aspects of a complex system without scientists really understanding how they do it. But still, computers and computer models are probably going to be essential tools for studying complex systems, seeing as reductionism on its own is not going to cut it.

Quantum theory

If complex systems are difficult to understand, then the quantum world is completely impossible. As the late US physicist Richard Feynman famously put it: 'If anyone claims to know what the quantum theory is all about, they haven't understood it.' Quantum theory, also known as quantum mechanics, explains the behaviour of matter and energy at the level of individual atoms and below, and what it says is that at these tiny scales all the certainties of our normal world break down.

WAVE–PARTICLE DUALITY

In Chapter 17, we learned that visible light is a form of electromagnetic radiation and thus acts like a wave, which is a demonstrable, experimentally proven fact. But in some circumstances visible light also acts like a particle known as a photon, which is also a demonstrable, experimentally proven fact. It sounds nonsensical, but in some cases light acts like a wave and in some cases it acts like a particle. This is known as wave–particle duality.

Even more astonishingly, it's not just light that behaves like this, but also electrons, protons, atoms and even molecules. At times, they act like a wave and at other times like particles. This helps to explain another troubling aspect of the quantum world: that, unlike in the normal world, we can't know both the position and the momentum (or speed) of a quantum entity like an electron. In fact, the more we know about the momentum of an electron, the less we know about its position and vice-versa. It actually turns out that we can know the momentum of an electron when it's behaving like a wave and know the position when it's behaving like a particle.

Furthermore, this propensity to behave like both a wave and a particle extends to other properties, such that a single subatomic particle can possess two conflicting properties at the same time. For instance, an electron possesses a property known as spin, which can be either up or down. But it is only up or down when the property is actually measured, before that the spin of the electron is both up and down at the same time. This ability to exist in what is known as a 'superposition' of states is fundamental to the development of quantum computers (see Chapter 27).

It also means that scientists can't be objective and independent when studying the quantum world. In their undisturbed state, subatomic particles exist in a superposition of states. It's only when scientists actually probe these particles that they adopt a defined state, such as a specific position or spin. Thus, scientists can't study the quantum world without affecting it, meaning that the classic scientific method by necessity falls short.

Because of this, there is still much about the quantum world that scientists don't understand. This includes how the indeterminacy of the quantum world transforms into the certainty of our normal world, where objects can't possess conflicting properties and where we can know both their position and momentum. It may be that the quantum world is just too different for us ever to understand it fully (see Box).

Nevertheless, scientists will never stop trying to understand it or to explore the many other questions that remain unanswered, even if this requires going far beyond the classic scientific method. For science, the future holds a myriad of exciting possibilities, even though in many cases science fiction got there first.

How much can we understand?

The bizarre and confusing nature of the quantum world raises the possibility that there are some things humans will just never understand. Our large brains evolved to help us survive in groups on the African plains, not to uncover the intricacies of the universe. It may be that we just don't have the mental capacities to probe to the very depths of reality; after all, we don't expect fish to understand algebra.

Alternatively, it may be that there are various different ways to understand the universe and that our brains are only capable of perceiving one of those ways. Alien life forms with different brains may perceive the universe in completely different, but still consistent, ways. Or perhaps we are imposing structure on to the universe; protons and electrons may exist solely in our scientific instruments and theories. In that case, we are not discovering scientific knowledge but inventing it.

Further reading

Barrow, John D., *Impossibility: Limits of science and the science of limits* (London: Vintage, 1999).

Part six

Science of the future

26

Back to the future

In this chapter you will learn:
- *how difficult it can be to make accurate predictions*
- *why some predicted technologies have not come to pass and why some were never predicted*
- *how science fiction plays a major role in influencing our scientific future*.

By now, we should have flying cars, moon bases and mental telepathy. Instead, we've got rain-sensitive window wipers, satellite television and mobile phones; all impressive technologies, but very different from what was predicted.

'Prediction is very difficult, especially about the future' is an aphorism that has been attributed to various different people, from Nobel Prize-winning physicist Niels Bohr to the US baseball player and coach Yogi Berra. But it's true enough, and never more so than for predictions of future technologies.

One of the reasons why it's so difficult to make accurate technological predictions is that just because a technology seems theoretically possible doesn't mean it will ever be developed or become widely adopted.

Incorrect predictions

VIDEOPHONES

Videophones have been on the cards ever since the development of the telephone over 100 years ago, with the US communications company AT&T developing a working videophone in the 1960s.

But only now, with the rise of the internet and services such as Skype, are we able to see who we are talking to.

AT&T's videophone didn't catch on because the system was fairly expensive and most people don't need to see the person on the other end of the line. The modern, internet version of the videophone doesn't cost any more than a standard phone call (indeed, it often costs less) and so people are much more inclined to use it.

Economics is perhaps the single most important factor in whether or not a new technology becomes a success, with an expensive new technology having to offer substantial benefits over and above existing technologies. If intriguing but not essential, most people will simply wait for the technology to become cheaper, which may of course never happen.

ELECTRIC CARS

This is the current position with electric cars, whether powered by a rechargeable battery or a fuel cell (see Chapter 19). Despite being heralded for many years, electric cars are not yet ready to challenge the internal combustion engine. Although the necessary technology exists, electric cars are too expensive and don't yet match the performance of conventional cars.

The fuelling infrastructure for electric cars is also not in place, whether in the form of electric charging points or pumps that supply the fuel for fuel cells (probably methane or hydrogen). This is a perennial catch-22 problem for new technologies that require an associated infrastructure. Companies are loath to establish the infrastructure until there is a strong demand for the main technology and consumers won't buy the technology until the infrastructure is in place.

At some point, however, the balance of pluses and minuses will tip in electric cars' favour and then they will probably take over quite rapidly. This will be driven by further improvements in the technology of electric cars, reducing their cost and enhancing their performance, and by rising oil prices. Government legislation may also play a role in encouraging the switchover, as well as in establishing the necessary infrastructure.

SPACE EXPLORATION

It's not just consumer technologies that can fall foul of economic reality. In 1967, *The Futurist*, a US magazine devoted to thinking about the future, asked a selection of the great and good to offer predictions for what would happen in the following decades. Reviewing the accuracy of 34 of these predictions in 1997, the editor of *The Futurist* concluded that 23 were 'hits' and 11 were 'misses'. Most of the misses could be blamed on a single factor: the slowdown in manned space exploration.

Following the first Moon landings on 21 July 1969, it was assumed that by the end of the 20th century the first permanent bases would be established on the Moon and maybe even Mars. That this didn't happen was mainly down to the huge cost of sending men to the Moon. This cost was deemed worth paying if it meant getting there before the Soviets, but there really wasn't any other rational basis for doing it.

If huge quantities of oil or (more realistically) valuable minerals had been found on the Moon, things might have been different. But as it stands, there is no compelling reason to send a man to the Moon or to establish a base there. As many commentators have pointed out, there are far more important things for governments to spend their money on.

FLYING CARS

Other predicted technologies have proved simply unfeasible or impractical. At the end of the 19th century, flying cars seemed to be everywhere, especially in France for some reason. They could be found on French cigarette cards displaying visions of the future, surrounding the Eiffel Tower in a sketch of what life would be like in 1940 and in a print showing people leaving the Parisian opera in 2000.

Once the internal combustion engine had been invented in the late 19th century, it seemed only a matter of time before motor cars took to the air. But obviously there's no easy mechanism for doing that. The production of the first modern helicopters in the 1920s led to a slightly more realistic vision of personal helicopters, but that never really happened either. The sad truth is that it's simply much easier, cheaper, safer and more convenient for large numbers of vehicles to travel on the ground.

Why do we have rockets?

It's also not just that many predicted technologies never arrive; other important technologies arrive with no warning at all. In 1937, the US

National Academy of Sciences organized a study aimed at predicting future technological breakthroughs. Although the study scored some successes, it completely failed to predict some of the most ground-breaking future technologies, including computers, jet aircraft, antibiotics, rockets and nuclear energy.

Where did all these computers come from?

One technology that seemed to catch everyone by surprise was the computer. As we saw, a 1937 study of future breakthroughs by the US National Academy of Sciences entirely failed to predict them. Although science fiction stories of the 1930s were full of robots, spaceships and ray guns, there was hardly any mention of computers. Edward Cornish, editor of *The Futurist*, has described the computer as 'history's greatest stealth invention'.

Even after computers became reality in the late 1940s, no one foresaw how small or ubiquitous they would become, even those developing them. In 1949, the US magazine *Popular Mechanics* would only go so far as to predict that 'Computers in the future may weigh no more than 1.5 tons'.

In the 1940s, the founder of IBM, Thomas J. Watson, allegedly stated that he didn't see the need for any more than a handful of computers in the whole of the US. Even in the 1970s, the chairman of the Digital Equipment Corporation was declaring that 'there is no reason for any individual to have a computer in their home'.

THE EFFECT OF THE SECOND WORLD WAR

But this shouldn't come as too much of a surprise, as it illustrates another major difficulty with making technological predictions: sometimes a single, unforeseen event transforms the entire technological landscape. This was definitely the case with the Second World War, which started a few years after the study and provided the impetus for the development of all these unpredicted technologies.

Computers partly emerged from code-breaking activities; nuclear energy emerged from the atom bomb; and the development of rockets and jet planes were boosted by the war. Although the first antibiotic, penicillin, was discovered in the 1920s, it was in treating casualties during the war that antibiotics really demonstrated their worth. The disruption and altered priorities caused by the war set scientific and technological research off in completely new and unpredicted directions, ultimately leading to our modern world.

Predictions in science fiction

Of course, many proposed future technologies are not offered as specific predictions, but simply as elements in a story. Even before science fiction was a recognized genre, authors have been imagining futuristic technologies, versions of which have subsequently turned up in the real world.

For example, in his utopian book *New Atlantis*, published in 1627, the early British scientist Francis Bacon imagined a rational society guided by science, technology and trade, whose inhabitants benefited from refrigerators, airplanes and submarines. In his 1655 book *The States and Empires of the Moon and Sun*, the French writer Cyrano de Bergerac sent his hero to the Moon using a system of rockets lit in sequence, similar in concept to the multi-stage rockets used today.

It would take the dawn of the industrial revolution, however, for authors to start basing their futuristic speculations on the latest scientific knowledge. Jules Verne and H.G. Wells are the best-known 19th century proponents of this approach, although neither would go so far as to let scientific reality get in the way of a good story.

In *From the Earth to the Moon*, Verne used a 300 m-long cannon to fire his characters to the Moon, even though he knew in reality that the sudden acceleration would kill them. In Wells' *The First Men in the Moon*, one of the characters invents a substance that cancels the effects of gravity and uses it to travel to the Moon.

Despite these occasional flights of fancy, both authors did accurately predict future technologies. Verne famously prefigured modern submarines in *Twenty Thousand Leagues Under the Sea*, while Wells predicted nuclear energy and the atomic bomb in *The World Set Free*.

Since then, science fiction authors have correctly predicted a whole range of future technologies, including solar power, robots, television, nanotechnology and waterbeds. In fact, so detailed was the US author Robert Heinlein's description of waterbeds in several of his science fiction stories that the inventor of the first practical waterbed couldn't get a patent on it.

FROM SCIENCE FICTION TO FACT

In predicting the future, science fiction writers have some important advantages over other technological forecasters. For a start, they come up with so much futuristic technology it's not surprising that some of it eventually becomes reality. They also don't have to specify a timescale for when the technology will appear. Another important advantage is that they can actually stimulate the development of their fictional technology.

Sometimes this is deliberate. In 1945, the British science fiction writer Arthur C. Clarke published a serious proposal for a system of orbiting communication satellites. Although other scientists were thinking along the same lines, this proposal foreshadowed the current blanket of commercial and military satellites around the Earth.

Russian rocket pioneer Konstantin Tsiolkovsky's novel *Beyond the Planet Earth*, published in 1920, outlined many of the technologies subsequently adopted for space flight, including rocket fuel comprising a mixture of liquid hydrogen and oxygen. His ideas were influential on many future space scientists, especially in the Soviet Union.

But often it's not deliberate; it's just that many practising scientists and engineers are science fiction fans and are inspired by what they have read about or seen. The television programme *Star Trek* has been particularly influential in this respect: not only did it apparently give rise to automatic sliding doors, but flip-up mobile phones look an awful lot like Star Trek communicators.

William Thomson (Lord Kelvin), 1824–1907

Lord Kelvin is a giant of 19th century British science. He helped to formulate the laws of thermodynamics; he did important work on the mathematical analysis of electricity; and he played an important role in the effort to lay the first transatlantic telegraph cable. He also introduced the concept of 'absolute zero' (−273°C), which is

(Contd)

the coldest possible temperature where all molecular movement effectively ceases. But he wasn't very good at making predictions.

In 1900, he gave an infamous speech at the Royal Institution in London in which he said that classical physics was more or less complete, with only two black clouds on the horizon. Unfortunately, resolving these two black clouds ultimately led to the formation of quantum theory and Albert Einstein's theories of relativity, which revolutionized physics and showed that it was very far from being complete.

Furthermore, in 1896 he stated that 'heavier than air flying machines are impossible' and asserted that the newly-discovered X-rays were a hoax, although he did subsequently change his mind on that front.

Further reading

Wilson, Daniel H., *Where's My Jetpack?* (London: Bloomsbury, 2007).

27

A.I.

In this chapter you will learn:
- *what artificial intelligence is*
- *why silicon chips may be nearing retirement*
- *about parallel processing with qubits*
- *how near we are to developing conscious robots.*

In science fiction films, robots and intelligent machines tend to get a bit of a bad press. Either they're going mad and trying to kill us, like the computer HAL in the film *2001: A Space Odyssey*; or they've been programmed to kill us as part of some nefarious plot, like the android Ash in the film *Alien*; or they're trying to kill all of humanity because they think we're inferior, as happens in *The Terminator* films. If we're lucky, though, they may merely enslave us, as in *The Matrix* films.

There are obviously less hostile exceptions, like R2-D2 and C-3PO in *Star Wars* and Data in *Star Trek: The Next Generation*. But even machines that are meant to serve humanity can be pretty deadly when required, such as the 'replicants' in the film *Blade Runner*, and so aren't to be trusted. Science fiction tells us that as soon as machines become more intelligent and powerful than humans, they quickly turn on us.

Despite these stark warnings, however, scientists and engineers are hard at work developing ever more sophisticated computers and robots, which can act, think and learn for themselves. This branch of computer science is known as artificial intelligence (A.I.).

Robots and intelligent machines

The aim is to produce machines that are just as intelligent, autonomous and dextrous as their fictional counterparts, but hopefully without the hostility. Such machines could help us do everything from solving currently intractable problems to dusting the furniture. Eventually, we may even develop machines that are, for all intents and purposes, conscious, although this would obviously raise a whole host of moral and ethical questions.

The spotter's guide to robots

In science fiction films and books, a whole host of terms are used to refer to autonomous machines: from robots to androids to cyborgs. So what is the difference between them?

Robots are essentially machines that move without direct human control; androids are robots that look like humans; and cyborgs are machines with both mechanical and biological parts. So R2-D2 is a robot; Ash and Bishop from the *Alien* films are androids; and the original Terminator is a cyborg.

THE LIMITATIONS OF SILICON CHIPS

To create such futuristic machines, scientists are not only producing more powerful versions of existing computers, but developing entirely new computing technologies.

As we saw in Chapter 18, modern computers are built around the semiconducting properties of silicon (and germanium), in the form of the ubiquitous silicon chip. By squeezing ever greater numbers of transistors onto silicon chips, scientists and engineers have produced increasingly powerful computers, able to conduct ever more complex operations in less and less time. But scientists are now starting to come up against physical limitations that will make it difficult for this to continue.

Indeed, even though transistors are still shrinking, the speed of silicon chips has levelled off since around 2005. The reason for this is that the speed of a silicon chip depends on how fast the transistors can be switched on and off, which depends on the size of the voltage applied to the transistor. We have now reached a point where this voltage cannot get any smaller and still reliably switch transistors on and off.

What is more, transistors may not shrink for much longer. Current methods for fabricating transistors, which involve carving them into silicon chips using beams of light, appear to be reaching their fundamental limits. Even if these limits can be overcome, as transistors shrink down to the molecular level, they will increasingly be exposed to the weird and wonderful world of quantum effects.

One of these quantum effects is electron tunnelling, whereby the probabilistic nature of electrons causes them to tunnel through physical barriers. As a consequence, electric current will start to leak across transistors even when they're supposedly switched off. So before scientists have got anywhere near making a highly intelligent, conscious computer, silicon may be nearing its retirement.

New types of computer chips

Scientists are therefore working on new types of computer chips that would be less prone to these kinds of limitations. For example, they are looking at replacing silicon with nanomaterials like carbon nanotubes, which could theoretically assemble themselves into transistors and circuits, and replacing electric currents with beams of light, which are faster (as they travel at the speed of light) but harder to manipulate and control.

Others are exploring even more radical approaches. If silicon transistors have problems operating at molecular scales, perhaps the answer is to replace them with actual molecules. This is the idea behind molecular computing and scientists have already produced molecular systems that can replicate various different logic gates, including AND, OR and NOT (see Chapter 18).

The basic approach is to design a molecule that only performs a certain action, such as conducting electricity or emitting light (output), if it binds with one or more other molecules (inputs). As with silicon-based logic gates, these molecular logic gates can be joined together to conduct more complex operations, such as addition and subtraction.

Logic gates have also been created from biological molecules such as DNA and RNA, which have the added advantage that they can act as a form of data storage. Here, the inputs tend to be biological molecules like enzymes and the output is a DNA or RNA strand that is modified in some way, such as being cleaved in two.

PARALLEL PROCESSING

But molecules don't just offer a new way to conduct conventional computing; they also offer the possibility of a totally new kind of computing. Current silicon-based computers can conduct simple operations very quickly, but only one at a time. This is mitigated by the fact that modern computer processors are compartmentalized, so that different sections conduct different operations at the same time. Nevertheless, conventional computers are inherently serial: each section needs to complete an operation before it moves on to the next.

This means that computers are very good at performing complex mathematical calculations, but are less good at solving other kinds of problems, especially those that require parallel processing.

A good example is the 'travelling salesman' problem, which involves determining the shortest route between several cities. Courier firms face this kind of problem every day, but conventional computers can only solve it by painstakingly comparing every possible option. If there are a lot of cities, then even powerful computers struggle to come up with a solution.

On the other hand, a molecular computer could be designed to consider all possible options at the same time. This can be done by creating molecules or DNA strands that represent each solution and then getting them to react together in such a way that at the end of the process only the correct solution is left. It sounds too good to be true, but molecular computers working in this way have already solved simple logical problems that silicon computers find tricky.

PROCESSING WITH QUBITS

For truly parallel processing, however, scientists are turning to the quantum world and replacing bits with qubits. As we saw in Chapter 18, a single bit can be either 1 or 0. By taking advantage of the fact that a quantum entity can exist in a 'superposition' of states (see Chapter 25), a single qubit can be both 1 and 0.

The implications of this are staggering: 10 bits can exist in over 1,000 different states (210), but only one at a time, whereas 10 qubits can exist in over 1,000 different states at the same time. Just 300 qubits could simultaneously exist in more states than there are atoms in the universe (2^{300} or 10^{90}).

Taking advantage of this massive parallel processing ability will be difficult, but by no means impossible. Scientists have already investigated various particles as possible qubits, including photons, electrons and individual ions. All you need is for the particles to possess a property that can exist in two states, representing 1 and 0; electrons, for example, have a property known as spin, which can be either up or down.

Scientists also have the technology to manipulate individual qubits, allowing them to be set up to conduct a calculation. For instance, individual atoms and ions can be manipulated by lasers and instruments known optical frequency combs, which produce light at specific frequencies.

USING QUANTUM CALCULATIONS

A more challenging problem is how to read out the answer of any quantum calculation, because a string of qubits can only exist in a superposition if it is not disturbed in any way. As soon as a scientist probes these qubits, the superposition collapses and each qubit adopts a fixed value of either 0 or 1, just like a bit. In a similar manner to molecular computing, this problem can be overcome by setting up the conditions in such a way that the superposition automatically collapses to the string of 0s and 1s that represent the correct answer.

A related problem is that any disturbance to the qubits, even being hit by a stray photon, will cause the superposition to collapse to a random mix of 0s and 1s. One solution to this problem is for a qubit to be represented by a collection of particles that all have the same quantum state, rather than by an individual particle.

Such collections can contain trillions and trillions of individual atoms. Because they all possess the same quantum state, they can still act as a single qubit and because there are trillions of them, they are much more resistant to disturbances. For example, a technique known as nuclear magnetic resonance can be used to put all the hydrogen nuclei (otherwise known as protons) in a flask of water into the same quantum state.

Using these kinds of techniques, scientists have already developed functioning quantum computers, which are proving particularly adept at factoring numbers (breaking a number down to a string of smaller numbers that produce the original number when multiplied together). This is something that silicon-based computers find difficult to do for large numbers, which is why factoring forms the basis for the encryption systems that allow us to conduct secure financial transactions over the internet.

Computers that are able to learn

Saying all this, scientists looking to develop intelligent machines are not quite yet ready to abandon silicon. Current computers may actually be more than complex and powerful enough to demonstrate high levels of intelligence, creativity and learning; we just need to find an effective way to program them with these kinds of abilities.

Already, scientists have produced computers that are able to learn. One way to do this is via neural networks, which aim to replicate the structure of the human brain. They consist of numerous nodes with specific values connected together in a huge network that transforms inputs into specific outputs. Because the values of the nodes and the strength of the connections between them can be altered, the network changes as a result of experience, allowing the host computer to learn.

These neural networks are already being used to create robots that can learn to perform specific tasks, such as finding and distinguishing between small blocks with different patterns on them. In this case, the inputs to the neural network are visual and auditory information provided by a video camera and a microphone and the output is the correct behaviour.

Such an approach could even one day lead to conscious machines. One of the possible reasons why humans are conscious while even the most powerful supercomputers aren't is our immersion from birth in a rich sensory environment that we can interact with. If machines had this kind of rich sensory experience, they too might naturally develop consciousness.

At which point, perhaps, we should become seriously concerned for our welfare.

Flexible friends

Some scientists aren't looking to develop more powerful computers, but instead want to take electronics to totally new places. One way of doing this is to replace silicon with plastic.

Most plastics are insulators, meaning they don't conduct electricity, which is why electric cables are coated with plastic to stop current leakage. But scientists have discovered that plastics with a certain molecular structure can act as semiconductors and have developed numerous different examples. They have also shown that these semiconducting polymers can be used to produce transistors, as well as solar cells and small light sources known as organic light emitting diodes.

One of the great advantages that semiconducting plastics have over silicon is that they are flexible, whereas silicon chips will snap if bent too much. Added to this is the fact that many of these semiconducting plastics can be dispersed in a liquid, which means they can be printed onto surfaces with an inkjet printer. This offers the possibility of extending electronics into places where silicon just can't go, such as on to paper and fabrics, and producing devices such as roll-up displays and pressure-sensitive skins.

Further reading

Wilson, Daniel H., *How to Survive a Robot Uprising: Tips on defending yourself against the coming rebellion* (London: Bloomsbury, 2005).

28

....

Innerspace

In this chapter you will learn:
- *how nanoparticles are used to treat cancer*
- *how silicon can help nanoparticles reach cancer cells*
- *about ways of releasing drugs to treat other diseases.*

Even if we manage to avoid being hunted to extinction or enslaved by super-intelligent computers, we could still be wiped out by swarms of mindless, nanoscale robots, or nanobots. This is the 'grey goo' scenario, as first postulated by the US nanotechnology pioneer Eric Drexler and then popularized in various works of fiction, including Michael Crichton's novel *Prey*.

The concern is that autonomous, self-replicating nanobots developed for some benign purpose, such as clearing up an oil spill, start to replicate out of control, consuming everything in their path. According to Drexler, if these nanobots replicate every 1,000 seconds, then within ten hours they would number almost 70 billion, within a day they would weigh 1 tonne and within two days they would weigh more than the Earth.

Now this is obviously rather far-fetched, especially as organic versions of these kinds of autonomous, self-replicating nanobots already exist, So far, however, bacteria and viruses have not yet consumed the entire planet in an orgy of replication, although they are pretty ubiquitous.

However less destructive, non-reproducing versions of these nanobots are a more realistic prospect, especially if used in confined spaces such as within our bodies. Here, they would constantly monitor our health, looking out for signs of disease, cellular damage or things running out of control, like the abnormal cell division that leads to the growth of cancerous tumours. Working with the body's immune system, they would stop these processes in their tracks, banishing sickness and greatly extending our lives.

Treating cancer with gold nanoparticles

Although tiny robot surgeons and doctors are still a long way off, much simpler versions, designed to treat specific diseases and disorders, are already being developed. For example, scientists are taking advantage of the impressive abilities of gold nanoparticles (see Chapter 19) to treat cancer.

The idea is to encourage gold nanoparticles to congregate around a tumour and then shine infrared light at them; infrared light is used because it is better at passing through human tissue than visible light (otherwise we would be translucent). Absorbing this infrared light causes the gold nanoparticles to fluoresce at infrared frequencies, allowing doctors to identify the precise location and extent of the tumour.

But that's not all, because absorbing infrared light also causes the gold nanoparticles to heat up, until they become hot enough to kill the cancer cells. A quick blast with infrared light produces an image of the tumour and a longer blast cooks it.

Obviously, the trick is to get the gold nanoparticles to congregate only around the tumour, thereby ensuring no damage to healthy cells. There are two ways this can be done. The easiest way is to take advantage of the fact that the blood vessels feeding tumours tend to have larger pores in their walls than normal blood vessels. Thus, all you need do is create gold nanoparticles that are too large to escape from normal blood vessels but small enough to escape from the blood vessels around tumours. A more targeted approach is to coat the gold nanoparticles with antibodies to proteins only found on the surface of cancer cells or found in much greater concentrations.

An alternative form of treatment is to develop hollow nanoparticles and fill them with an anti-cancer drug, which the nanoparticles release when they get to the tumour. This offers a much safer way to deliver anti-cancer drugs, many of which are highly toxic to both healthy and cancer cells; hence, the intense physical suffering experienced by cancer patients undergoing chemotherapy. Early versions of this approach, in which the anti-cancer drug is enclosed within fatty bubbles called liposomes or natural blood proteins, are already being employed in clinics.

Using nanoparticles in this way allows tumours to be destroyed with far smaller quantities of these highly toxic drugs and without exposing healthy cells. Again the nanoparticles can be directed to the tumour by taking advantage of 'leaky' blood vessels or by attaching cancer cell-targeting antibodies. Still, that leaves a number of other challenges to be overcome and scientists are exploring a whole range of options for doing that.

GETTING PAST THE BODY'S OWN IMMUNE SYSTEM

For a start, it's by no means certain that the nanoparticles will actually get to the tumour. Ironically, the reason for this is the body's own immune system, which as we saw in Chapter 9 is pretty quick to jump on any foreign particles. So to reach the tumour, the nanoparticles first have to avoid being engulfed by macrophages or attacked by enzymes.

One way to do this is to house the nanoparticles within a material that the human immune system doesn't consider to be a threat and doesn't attack. Rather strangely, silicon is just such a material and scientists in the US have shown that housing nanoparticles within a microscopic silicon particle allows them to travel through the body unhindered. The silicon particle is designed to degrade after a certain period of time, releasing the nanoparticles.

But that raises another question: how to release the anti-cancer drug when the nanoparticle finally gets to the tumour. If the nanoparticle is permeable, then the drug can simply diffuse out, but that's no good if you only want to release the drug at the tumour. Or, as with the silicon particles, you could design the nanoparticles to degrade after a set period of time, ensuring this is long enough for the nanoparticles to reach the tumour, but that's a bit haphazard.

Alternatively, you design a nanoparticle that actively releases the drug only in response to a specific cue. This could be provided externally by a doctor; for instance, by shining infrared light at the nanoparticles. Or it could be provided internally by the environment around the tumour cells, which differs in certain ways from the environment around healthy cells, such as by being more acidic.

Just such a nanoparticle has been developed by another group of US scientists. It comprises a silica nanoparticle covered in tiny pores, each of which is filled with an anti-cancer drug. Attached to the walls of each of the pores are light-responsive, paddle-shaped molecules that ordinarily block the pore, preventing the drug from escaping. But when exposed to light, the paddle-shaped molecules waggle about, actively wafting the drug out of the pores.

Smart implants for other diseases

For other long-term diseases and disorders, the challenge is not so much releasing a drug at a specific time and place, but repeatedly releasing a drug when it's needed. To do this, scientists are developing the next generation of smart implants, able to activate appropriate treatments in response to some disease-specific cue.

The fact that the body considers silicon harmless is immensely useful in developing these kinds of smart implants, which can take advantage of the computing power of silicon chips. For example, scientists are looking to develop chips that release life-saving drugs at the first physiological signs of an oncoming heart attack, which could be abnormal behaviour of the heart or the presence of certain characteristic proteins in the blood. Alternatively, smart implants could be made from flexible semiconducting plastics (see Chapter 27), which unlike rigid silicon chips would be able to mould to the interior of the body.

The behaviour of the heart is already being monitored by the latest implanted pacemakers and defibrillators, both of which stimulate the heart with electricity to prevent it beating abnormally. These pacemakers and defibrillators regularly communicate wirelessly with a base station about both their activity and the heart's behaviour. The base station then sends this information over the internet to a doctor, allowing early intervention if the heart starts to fail.

Eventually, our bodies could contain whole suites of clever implants, constantly monitoring our vital functions, wirelessly communicating with each other and the outside world, and automatically triggering the appropriate treatment, from electrical stimulation to the release of drugs. This system will probably then evolve into the suite of constantly circulating medical nanobots mentioned earlier.

Stimulating tissue growth

Until that time, however, we will continue to suffer from disease and disorders, some of which can result in the loss of large amounts of tissue and even whole organs. At the moment, the only option is to replace the lost tissue and organs with transplanted material, either from the patient's own body or from others, usually after death. But obviously the amount of spare material that can be harvested from a person's own body is limited and the supply of donated organs is inherently unreliable.

So scientists are working on ways to grow spare tissues and organs in the laboratory. For instance, scientists are now able to stimulate the growth of excess bone on a patient's normal bone; this excess bone can then be harvested and used to replace bone lost as a result of disease or accidents.

An alternative approach is to implant some kind of scaffold into a patient's body to give the tissue cells something to grow on. This can already be done to fix small holes in the heart: a fabric is placed over the hole and heart cells then grow over the fabric, which eventually degrades. But scientists are now working on doing this at much larger scales and in three dimensions.

USING HYDROGEL TO GROW NEW CELLS

Instead of flat fabrics, scientists are building scaffolds from a material known as a hydrogel. This is a highly absorbent gel consisting of an interlinked network of long molecules, either synthetic or biological, in which water can account for up to 99 per cent of the weight.

The idea is to introduce the hydrogel into a patient's body as a liquid and turn it into a gel by exposing it to infrared light. The hydrogel then provides a three dimensional scaffold for the growth of new cells, with this process perhaps encouraged by incorporating some of the patients own cells and various growth-promoting chemicals into the hydrogel.

Already, scientists have used hydrogels as scaffolds for growing new cartilage, a bone-like tissue that is a common component in many joints. Eventually, scientists would like to grow whole organs in the laboratory, using the patient's own cells, and then transplant these organs into the patient.

Enhancing our bodies

But perhaps all this new implant technology could do more than simply keep us healthy, perhaps it could actually improve us. The fictional counterpart here is the 1970s television programme *The Six Million Dollar Man*, in which a former astronaut is given bionic limbs and eyes that provide him with enhanced strength, speed and vision.

Scientists are now developing such bionic limbs, but are currently finding it difficult enough to replicate our existing physical abilities. Nevertheless, certain technologies being developed would give us enhanced abilities, such as contact lenses with built-in displays. In addition, scientists have developed versions of biological material that are tougher than the real thing, such as bone grown on carbon nanotubes. There is even talk of implanting electronic devices into the brain to enhance intelligence and memory.

Improving our bodies in this way may be essential if we are to undertake the next great technological leap: travel into the depths of space.

Further reading

Jones, Richard A.L., *Soft Machines: Nanotechnology and life* (Oxford: OUP, 2007).

29

A space odyssey

In this chapter you will learn:
- *how rockets travel into space*
- *about fission rockets and the development of ion propulsion*
- *about travelling in space with a solar sail, a ramjet or a generation ship.*

In films, traversing the vast expanse of interstellar space presents no problem at all. You just leap into the USS Enterprise or Millennium Falcon, turn on your warp drive or make the jump into hyperspace and, hey presto, you've soon arrived at another star system. In reality, not only are we obviously far from developing this kind of spacecraft technology, but it may actually be impossible for us to do so.

That does not mean, however, that mankind will not at some point travel across the whole galaxy. It just may take a bit of time.

Even to colonize the galaxy at a leisurely pace, we'll need to develop novel kinds of spacecraft and propulsion systems. At the moment, getting into space requires rockets, which work on the same principle as a firework. A chemical propellant is transformed into a hot gas, comprising lots of fast-moving molecules that are directed out the back of the rocket, moving it in the opposite direction.

Getting a rocket into space

This movement is all down to the principle of action and reaction, as first formulated by the British scientific genius Isaac Newton in the 17th century. According to Newton's third law of motion, for every action there is always an equal, opposing reaction. This means that if you shoot hot gas out the back of a rocket, it moves forward.

The hot gas doesn't need to press against anything to provide this movement; if it did, then rockets wouldn't be able to move in the emptiness of space. Simply applying a force in one direction produces an equal force in the opposite direction.

Numerous different kinds of propellant can be used in rockets, but the one employed in many space-bound rockets is a mixture of liquid hydrogen and liquid oxygen. Reacting liquid hydrogen and oxygen together at high temperatures and pressures produces a hot blast of water vapour, which is directed out the back of the rocket at speeds of up to 4.5 kilometres a second (km/s).

Keeping a rocket travelling in space

This is sufficient to accelerate a spacecraft to the speed needed to escape from the Earth's gravitational pull, which is 11.2 km/s (over 40,000 kilometres an hour). But once in space, the rockets generally stop firing, often detaching and falling back to Earth, and the spacecraft simply coasts along at the same speed. It doesn't slow down because it is travelling through an almost empty vacuum, meaning no friction. Although most current spacecraft also have their own small rocket engines, these are mainly used for manoeuvring.

A spacecraft can still accelerate once in space, however, by performing gravitational slingshots, in which it picks up speed by skirting around a planet. In this way, the spacecraft essentially captures some of the planet's momentum as it orbits the sun. Performing several gravitational slingshots around Venus and Earth allowed NASA's Cassini spacecraft to travel to Jupiter at a cruising speed of almost 32 km/s.

TRAVELLING BETWEEN THE PLANETS

Even at these speeds, travelling between the planets takes a long time. It may only have taken three days for astronauts to travel the 384,400 km to the Moon, but it takes at least 180 days for current spacecraft to travel to Mars. Travelling the 4.3 light years (40 trillion kilometres) to our nearest star, Proxima Centauri, at these speeds would take 40,000 years.

These journeys would be much quicker if a spacecraft could continue firing its rocket engines once it entered space. This would allow it to accelerate for longer and thus reach higher speeds, but simply requires too much propellant. To accelerate a single atom to a speed of 10,000 km/s (3 per cent the speed of light), taking us to Proxima Centauri in 130 years, using current chemical rockets would require 10^{434} atoms of propellant, which are many more atoms than exist in the observable universe.

Getting there faster

FISSION ROCKETS

So if we want faster travel to the planets in our solar system, and especially if we ever want to travel to the stars, then we need other means of propulsion. One alternative is to replace chemical rockets with nuclear rockets. As we saw in Chapter 24, nuclear reactions are a million times more efficient at generating energy than chemical reactions.

The simplest approach would be a variation of existing rockets. A fission reactor would be used to heat hydrogen to a temperature of several thousand degrees, producing fast moving hydrogen molecules that are fired out the back of the rocket. Tests on prototype fission rockets performed in the 1960s and 1970s indicated that hot hydrogen molecules could be expelled at speeds of up to 70 km/s. Even faster ejection speeds (perhaps up to several thousand kilometres a second) could theoretically be generated by replacing the fission reactor with a fusion reactor, but as we discovered in Chapter 21 scientists are still unable to produce a sustainable fusion reaction.

ION PROPULSION

Various practical problems, together with the high expense, explain why US scientists abandoned the development of fission rockets in the 1970s. But the recent successful deployment of a new kind of propulsion system, known as ion propulsion, could open the door to a new kind of nuclear-powered spacecraft.

In ion propulsion, an electrical generator strips electrons from the atoms of a gas such as xenon, transforming the atoms into positively charged cations. By attracting them towards a negative electrode, these cations are fired out the back of the spacecraft, providing thrust.

Even though the cations can be expelled at speeds of up to 100 km/s, the thrust they generate is minuscule: equal to keeping a piece of paper in the air by blowing on it. Current ion propulsion engines take four days to accelerate a small spacecraft from a standstill to 100 kilometres an hour. This means that spacecraft with ion propulsion engines still need to be launched into space using conventional rockets.

The reason for the lack of thrust is that although the cations are expelled at great speed, there aren't that many of them. But that means that not only can the amount of xenon gas used as the propellant be quite small – less than 30 kg would take a spacecraft to Mars – but the engines can be fired all the time, providing constant – if gentle – acceleration. Over time, this gentle acceleration can produce impressive speed increases.

NASA's Deep Space 1 craft, which travelled to a nearby asteroid, and the European Space Agency's Smart-1 craft, which travelled to the Moon, both had ion propulsion engines. More recently, NASA's Dawn spacecraft, which is travelling to the asteroid belt, is being powered by an ion propulsion engine that is expected to increase the spacecraft's speed by more than 10 km/s over the course of its eight-year mission.

Replacing the electrical generator with a fission reactor could theoretically increase ejection speeds to 1,000 km/s, sufficient to take a spacecraft to Proxima Centauri in 100 years. But this would require huge amounts of uranium to fuel the fission reactor: a 10 tonne spacecraft (about four times the size of Cassini) would require 50 million tonnes of uranium, many times greater than the Earth's known uranium resources.

The depressing reality is that in order to reach our nearest star in less than a human lifetime, we need a spacecraft that could reach speeds of at least 30,000 km/s (10 per cent the speed of light) and this is well beyond our current technological capabilities. That has not stopped scientists thinking up possible ways to achieve this goal, however.

USING ANTIMATTER TO GENERATE ENERGY

One idea is to take advantage of antimatter, which is exactly the same as normal matter but with opposite physical properties. So a positron is exactly the same as an electron, but with a positive rather than negative charge. When a particle meets its antimatter equivalent, they annihilate each other, transforming all their mass into energy in accordance with Albert Einstein's famous equation $E = mc^2$ (see Chapter 16).

The annihilation of antimatter thus represents the most efficient way possible to generate energy, being thousands of times more efficient than nuclear fission. If antimatter annihilation is used to convert a liquid propellant into a hot gas, then accelerating a one tonne spaceship to 30,000 km/s would require only four tonnes of propellant and around 12 kg of antimatter.

Unfortunately, we are far from being able to produce even that small amount of antimatter. At the moment, antimatter is only produced in particle accelerators, at a rate of just a billionth of a gram a year.

THE SOLAR SAIL AND THE RAMJET

If the perennial problem is the amount of propellant, perhaps the best option is to do away with the propellant. This is the reasoning behind both the solar sail and the ramjet.

A solar sail takes advantage of the fact that photons of light exert a small force when they bounce off a reflective surface. A solar sail consists of a thin, reflective surface tethered to a spacecraft. The idea is that photons emitted by the sun reflect off the solar sail, exerting a combined force large enough to generate forward momentum, just like wind on a conventional sail.

Obviously the solar sail would need to be massive – several hundred metres across – to reflect sufficient photons to accelerate itself and an attached spacecraft. But it does conjure up an attractive retro-future image of astronauts majestically sailing around the solar system. By taking advantage of the sun's gravity, these astro-sailors could use the solar sail to travel in any direction, even towards the sun. Although this sounds like science fiction, the first prototype solar sail, just 20 m across diagonally, was deployed in space in June 2010.

The solar sail could also theoretically take a spacecraft to another star, but in this case the sail would need to be 30 km wide and it would need to be driven by a more intense source of photons than can be provided by the sun. The idea would be to build a giant solar-powered laser in space. This would fire an immensely powerful laser beam at the solar sail, accelerating it to 60,000 km/s (20 per cent the speed of light) over the course of 30 years, allowing it to reach Proxima Centauri in 50 years.

With an even larger, multi-component solar sail (around the size of France), the spacecraft could even be slowed down as it reached its destination and then returned to Earth. If a central section of the solar sail popped out behind the main sail and light was reflected from the main sail onto this smaller sail, then the force of the laser would slow the craft down. This larger sail could also accelerate the spacecraft to 50 per cent the speed of light (150,000 km/s).

In essence, a ramjet would simply be a fusion-powered rocket, but one that collected all its fuel from space. As we saw in Chapter 1, hydrogen is by far the most common element in the universe, forming dense molecular clouds and also widely dispersed throughout interstellar space.

By extending a magnetic field as big as the Earth in front of it, a ramjet would funnel all the available hydrogen into its fusion reactor, using the energy generated to expel the fusion products out the back. The really clever bit is that as the ramjet speeds up it collects more hydrogen, allowing it to accelerate even more. The faster it goes, the faster it will be able to go. Calculations show that after a year of travelling, a ramjet could accelerate to 270,000 km/s (90 per cent the speed of light).

As the ramjet accelerates, it will get closer and closer to the speed of light, but it will never be able to exceed it. Because, as Albert Einstein proved, nothing can travel faster than the speed of light: 300,000 km/s is the universe's ultimate speed limit. This means that the idea of hopping in your spaceship and quickly zooming over to another star system will probably remain a fiction (although see Box).

Taking the shortcut

We may not be able to travel faster than the speed of light if taking the usual route through the universe, but what about a shortcut?

Wormholes could possibly provide just such a shortcut. They are breaks in the fabric of space joining two regions that might be separated by thousands of light years. It's as if you're standing in a first-floor bedroom and want to get to the kitchen directly beneath you. You could walk down the stairs to the kitchen, but it would be faster if you could jump through a hole in the bedroom floor.

(Contd)

Although wormholes have never been detected, their existence does not contravene our current physical theories. Unfortunately, if they do exist, they're probably highly unstable, only lasting for a fraction of a second. Scientists have suggested, however, that something called 'exotic matter', which quantum theory suggests is constantly being created and annihilated at tiny scales, could stabilize wormholes, potentially allowing a spacecraft to pass through.

GENERATION SHIPS

Even at light speed, a trip to Proxima Centauri will take over 4 years, while getting to the centre of our galaxy, the Milky Way, would take 27,000 years (although see Box). But that doesn't mean that mankind won't eventually colonize the galaxy, even at much slower speeds. Using massive spaceships containing hundreds or thousands of people and entire ecosystems, multiple generations could travel between the stars, even if a single journey took thousands of years. This is the idea behind so-called generation ships.

Not so fast

Although it would take a spacecraft travelling at the speed of light 27,000 years to reach the centre of our galaxy, it wouldn't seem that long to those on board. This is because, as Albert Einstein again proved, the faster you move, the more time slows down.

This ensures that nothing can travel faster than the speed of light. Otherwise, if you were travelling in a spacecraft at half the speed of light and turned on the headlights, the subsequent beam of light would be travelling at one and a half times the speed of light. But it doesn't, because time slows down.

At low speeds, this slowing is barely perceptible, although it has been experimentally proven by flying highly accurate atomic clocks in airplanes. At close to the speed of light, though, the effects become dramatic.

At 86 per cent of the speed of light, time elapses at half its normal rate and at 99.5 per cent of the speed of light it elapses at only one-tenth its normal rate. Indeed, to those on board a spaceship travelling close to the speed of light, it would appear to take just 20 years to reach the centre of the galaxy.

Interstellar travellers could travel to a star system and colonize it. A thousand years later, some of their descendants could then start the journey to a new star system. In this way, it has been estimated that even if it took several thousand years to travel between stars, mankind would spread over the whole galaxy in 100 million years. This may sound like a long time, but the dinosaurs bestrode the Earth for longer.

Further reading

Rogers, Lucy, *It's Only Rocket Science: An introduction in plain English* (New York: Springer, 2008).

30

Things to come

In this chapter you will learn:
- *what will happen in the future*
- *how we can make use of the asteroid belt*
- *how we might live on Mars*
- *where it will all end.*

'In the past century, there were more changes than in the previous thousand years. The new century will see changes that will dwarf those of the last.' So said the British science fiction writer H.G. Wells (who also wrote the screenplay of the 1936 film that gives this chapter its title) in a lecture he gave in 1902.

His prediction was correct and will probably continue to be correct for the foreseeable future, as our rate of technological development keeps on increasing. The 19th century brought railways, electricity, photography and the first motor cars, but the 20th century brought airplanes, nuclear power, genetic modification and the internet. Imagine what we'll achieve in the next 100 years or the next 1,000 years or the next 10,000 years. Providing, that is, we don't destroy ourselves in the meantime (see Chapter 24).

Imagining what we'll achieve in the future is not just the domain of science fiction writers. Several scientists have also made predictions for how mankind might progress and of the advanced technologies we might develop. Unfortunately, the spectre of that other major British science fiction writer, Arthur C. Clarke, hangs over these predictions. Specifically, his famous dictum: 'Any sufficiently advanced technology is indistinguishable from magic.'

The temptation when making these predictions is to assume that within a few thousand years mankind will be so technologically advanced as to be able to do almost anything, no matter how inconceivable it seems at the moment. Unlike many science fiction writers, scientists try to resist this temptation by ensuring their predictions don't contradict any of our current physical theories. Their predictions may be practically impossible with our current technology, but they shouldn't be theoretically impossible.

That's not to say, however, that in a few thousand years our science and technology won't have developed to a stage where we are able to achieve the currently inconceivable, such as travel faster than the speed of light. But when making predictions, it's often useful to have a few self-imposed restrictions. So, based on our current understanding of science, all the advanced technologies detailed in this chapter are theoretically possible.

Colonizing space

What almost everyone looking into the future of mankind agrees on, whether science fiction writers or scientists, is that at some point we'll make a major push into space, probably using some of the novel propulsion technologies detailed in Chapter 29. Now this may be a risky prediction to make, seeing as in the 1960s many believed that we would have bases on the Moon and perhaps even Mars by the beginning of the 21st century. At some point, however, the advantages of colonizing space will start to outweigh the disadvantages.

THE ASTEROID BELT

Although it may take a few hundred years, we will reach that point when mankind starts to need more living space or natural resources than can be provided by the Earth. The simplest way to resolve both of these shortages may be to turn to the large rocks making up the asteroid belt, which orbits between Mars and Jupiter.

Because these asteroids formed from the same disk of dust and gas as the Earth, they are rich in many of the same materials as found on Earth, including iron, silicon, nickel, copper, lead and zinc, as well as carbon, water, hydrogen and nitrogen. So when we've used up all the deposits of these materials that are easily extractable from the Earth's crust, we could start obtaining them from asteroids.

This would either involve establishing mining colonies on the asteroids while they're still in the belt, several thousand of which are known to have diameters greater than 1 km, or transporting the asteroids back to the Earth and dismantling them in orbit. This could be achieved by simply firing bits of the asteroid into space. According to the principle of action and reaction (see Chapter 29), this would accelerate the asteroid in the opposite direction, potentially taking it all the way to Earth.

Furthermore, in an extreme form of recycling, after an asteroid was hollowed out by mining it could subsequently be used as a habitat. The idea would be for colonists to live on the inside walls of the asteroid, which would be set spinning to simulate the force of gravity. Taken together, the thousands of asteroids in the belt with diameters greater than 1 km have a surface area greater than that of all the continents on Earth.

SPACE HABITATS

Alternatively, the resources derived from asteroids could be used to construct tailor-made space habitats. Scientists have already come up with potential designs for such habitats. In the 1970s, an American physicist called Gerard O'Neil designed a cylindrical space habitat, in which people would live in three equally spaced strips running down the length of the cylinder. These habitable strips would be separated by three equally sized strips of transparent wall.

On the outside, three aluminium mirrors would run the length of the cylinder, reflecting sunlight through the transparent walls onto the habitable strips. In addition, these mirrors could be moved to cover the transparent walls, blocking off all incoming light and simulating night. As with the asteroids, the habitat would spin about its axis, with one full rotation every minute, to simulate gravity, while all its energy requirements would be supplied by an array of solar panels deployed at one end of the cylinder.

O'Neil envisaged these space habitats coming in several different sizes. The smallest would be 1 km long and 200 m wide, housing 10,000 people; the largest would be 32 km long and 6.4 km wide, housing 1 million people. Attaching engines to these habitats would turn them into the kind of star-travelling generation ships mentioned in Chapter 29.

LIFE ON MARS

If we became really short of land, either because the human population had grown too large or because we had made large areas of the Earth uninhabitable, then our only option would be to move to Mars. Before we did this, however, we would have to make Mars habitable, because it currently lacks liquid water or a breathable atmosphere and has an average surface temperature of $-65°C$. Such terraforming, as it is known, does seem to be feasible, although it would be a massive undertaking.

According to a study conducted by NASA scientists in the early 1990s, tens of billions of tonnes of a greenhouse gas such as the ozone-destroying chlorofluorocarbons (CFCs) would need to be pumped into the thin atmosphere of Mars. This would thicken up the atmosphere and instigate global warming, increasing the planet's average temperature by around $20°C$. As a consequence, both the polar ice caps and the permafrost that covers the surface of Mars would start to melt, releasing trapped carbon dioxide and thereby enhancing global warming. More greenhouse gases could be supplied by seeding the planet with genetically modified or synthetic bacteria designed to thrive in these harsh conditions.

Focusing solar energy onto the polar ice caps would transform the melting ice into water vapour, further enhancing global warming. This water vapour would condense to form clouds and then torrential rain, eventually producing rivers, seas and oceans on the surface of Mars. Finally, plants would be introduced to release oxygen into the atmosphere. In total, this terraforming effort would probably take over 1,000 years.

Capturing more of the sun's energy

By then, it won't just be land and resources that mankind could be running short of, but also energy. All our current energy sources are ultimately derived from the sun, but the Earth receives less than one billionth of the energy produced by the sun. In the future, we should be able to capture more of the sun's energy by constructing huge solar panels in space, but eventually that would not be enough.

Between 1973 and 2007, mankind's consumption of energy grew by an average of just over 0.01 per cent a year. If that rate of increase continues, we will be using the equivalent of all the energy released by the sun within 300,000 years.

To capture all of the sun's energy, our only option would be to build a huge sphere around it, with a radius equal to the distance from the sun to the Earth. Mankind could then live on the inner surface of this sphere, which would have room for hundreds of billions or even trillions of people. This is known as a Dyson sphere, after the US physicist Freeman Dyson, who first came up with the idea.

In actual fact, a solid sphere of that size would not be stable, so Dyson suggested a system of rings that together would fully encircle the sun. Obtaining the material needed to construct these giant rings would unfortunately require taking apart several of the planets in the solar system.

The death of the sun

In the very long term, however, even Dyson spheres won't be enough to safeguard the future of humanity. For start, in about 6 billion years time, our sun will expire, turning first into a huge red giant and then into a tiny spent star known as a white dwarf. Hopefully by then, mankind will have colonized the whole galaxy, making the death of the sun and the destruction of our home planet less of a trauma than it otherwise might have been. Mankind may well have also split into numerous different species, driven by both natural evolution and genetic engineering, with each species adapted to the conditions in their particular star system.

So long as there are stars in the galaxy, mankind will probably have a plentiful supply of energy. Unfortunately, however, that won't always be the case. As we learned in Chapter 16, entropy within the universe is steadily increasing: usable energy is being transformed into unusable, diffuse heat. In practical terms, this means that the huge molecular dust clouds that are the birthing grounds of new stars are gradually being used up. According to calculations, the era of star formation will come to an end in around one hundred trillion years.

At that point, the Milky Way will consist of white dwarfs, brown dwarfs (small stars that are unable to ignite nuclear fusion in their cores), planets, asteroids and massive black holes (see Chapter 24) swallowing up everything else. For quite a long time, around 10^{27} years, we could conceivably derive energy from these massive black holes, but they too will eventually evaporate away.

It's not even as though we could escape to other galaxies. Not only because the same processes would probably be occurring there, but because those other galaxies would by then be too far away. Recent astronomical observations have indicated that the expansion of the universe is actually speeding up, perhaps due to the action of a mysterious force dubbed 'dark energy'. If that is the case, then at some point in the distant future all the other galaxies that we now see would have disappeared over the horizon (apart from our nearest galaxy neighbour Andromeda, which may well collide with the Milky Way in around 6 billion years). We would be utterly alone in the universe.

So is there no way for mankind to survive as the universe gradually winds down? Well, there might be. Some scientists theorize that when a massive star collapses to produce a black hole it may trigger the formation of a new universe, completely separate from our existing universe. If mankind could somehow travel through a black hole, perhaps one that we have created, then it might end up at the very dawn of a new universe.

And that, I believe, is where we came in.

Further reading

Impey, Chris, *How it Ends: From you to the universe* (New York: W.W. Norton & Co., 2010).

Index